P9-BZV-377

EXPLOSIVE PRAISE FOR *NEW YORK TIMES* BESTSELLING AUTHOR ROBERT LUDLUM

"Ludlum stuffs more surprises into his novels than any other six-pack of thriller writers combined."
—*The New York Times*

"Reading a Ludlum novel is like watching a James Bond film . . . slickly paced . . .all-consuming."
—*Entertainment Weekly*

"Ludlum is light-years beyond his literary competition in piling plot twist upon plot twist, until the mesmerized reader is held captive . . . Ludlum pulls out all the stops and dazzles his readers." —*Chicago Tribune*

"Welcome to Robert Ludlum's world . . . fast pacing, tight plotting, international intrigue." —*The Plain Dealer*

"Robert Ludlum continues to jolt his readers with fresh juice." —*The New York Post*

"Don't ever begin a Ludlum novel if you have to go to work the next day." —*Chicago Sun-Times*

"Robert Ludlum is the master of gripping, fast-moving intrigue. He is unsurpassed at weaving a tapestry of stunningly diverse figures, then assembling them in a sequence so gripping that the reader's attention never wavers."
—*The Daily Oklahoman*

"If a Pulitzer prize were awarded for escapist fiction, Robert Ludlum undoubtedly would have won it. Ten times over." —*Mobile Register*

THE
SIGMA
PROTOCOL

Also by Robert Ludlum

THE
SIGMA
PROTOCOL

ROBERT LUDLUM

St. Martin's Paperbacks

THE SIGMA PROTOCOL

Copyright © 2001 by Myn Pyn LLC.
Excerpt from *The Janson Directive* copyright © 2002 by Myn Pyn LLC.

ISBN: 0-312-98251-8

Printed in the United States of America

St. Martin's Press hardcover edition / October 2001
St. Martin's Paperbacks edition / October 2002

St. Martin's Paperbacks are published by St. Martin's Press, 175 Fifth Avenue, New York, NY 10010.

10 9 8 7 6 5 4 3

CHAPTER ONE

Zurich

"May I get you something to drink while you wait?"

The *Hotelpage* was a compact man who spoke English with only a trace of an accent. His brass nameplate gleamed against his loden-green uniform.

"No, thank you," Ben Hartman said, smiling wanly.

"Are you sure? Perhaps some tea? Coffee? Mineral water?" The bellhop peered up at him with the bright-eyed eagerness of someone who has only a few minutes left to enhance his parting tip. "I'm terribly sorry your car is delayed."

"I'm fine, really."

Ben stood in the lobby of the Hotel St. Gotthard, an elegant nineteenth-century establishment that specialized in catering to the well-heeled international businessman—*and, face it, that's me*, Ben thought sardonically. Now that he had checked out, he wondered idly whether he could tip the bellhop *not* to carry his bags, *not* to follow his every move a few feet behind, like a Bengali bride, *not* to offer unceasing apologies for the fact that the car that was to take Ben to the airport had not yet arrived. Luxury hotels the world over prided themselves on such coddling, but Ben, who traveled quite a bit, inevitably found it intrusive, deeply irritating. He'd spent so much time trying to break out of the cocoon, hadn't he? But the cocoon—the stale rituals of privilege—had won out in the end. The *Hotelpage* had his number, all right: just another rich, spoiled American.

Ben Hartman was thirty-six, but today he felt much older. It wasn't just the jet lag, though he had arrived from New York yesterday and still felt that sense of dislocation. It was something about being in Switzerland again: in happier days, he'd spent a lot of time here, skiing too fast, driving too fast, feeling like a wild spirit among its stone-faced, rule-bound burghers. He wished he could regain that spirit, but he couldn't. He hadn't been to Switzerland since his brother, Peter—his identical twin, his closest friend in all the world—had been killed here four years ago. Ben had expected the trip to stir up memories, but nothing like this. Now he realized what a mistake he'd made coming back here. From the moment he'd arrived at Kloten Airport, he'd been distracted, swollen with emotion—anger, grief, loneliness.

But he knew better than to let it show. He'd done a little business yesterday afternoon, and this morning had a cordial meeting with Dr. Rolf Grendelmeier of the Union Bank of Switzerland. Pointless, of course, but you had to keep the clients happy; glad-handing was part of the job. If he was honest with himself, it *was* the job, and Ben sometimes felt a pang at how easily he slipped into the role, that of the legendary Max Hartman's only surviving son, the heir presumptive to the family fortune, and to the CEO's office at Hartman Capital Management, the multibillion-dollar firm founded by his father.

Now Ben possessed the whole trick bag of international finance—the closet full of Brioni and Kiton suits, the easy smile, the firm handshake, and, most of all, the gaze: steady, level, concerned. It was a gaze that conveyed responsibility, dependability, and sagacity, and that, often as not, concealed desperate boredom.

Still, he hadn't really come to Switzerland to do business. At Kloten, a small plane would take him to St. Moritz for a ski vacation with an extremely wealthy, elderly client, the old man's wife, and his allegedly beautiful granddaughter. The client's arm-twisting was jovial but persistent. Ben was being fixed up, and he knew it. This was one of the hazards of being a presentable, well-off, "eligible" single man in Manhattan: his clients were forever trying to set him up with their daughters, their nieces, their cousins. It was hard to say no politely. And once in a while he actually met a woman whose company he enjoyed. You never knew. Anyway, Max wanted grandchildren.

Max Hartman, the philanthropist and holy terror, the founder of Hartman Capital Management. The self-made immigrant who'd arrived in America, a refugee from Nazi Germany, with the proverbial ten bucks in his pocket, had founded an investment company right after the war, and relentlessly built it up into the multibillion-dollar firm it was now. Old Max, in his eighties and living in solitary splendor in Bedford, New York, still ran the company and made sure no one ever forgot it.

It wasn't easy working for your father, but it was even harder when you had precious little interest in investment banking, in "asset allocation" and "risk management," and in all the other mind-numbing buzzwords.

Or when you had just about zero interest in money. Which was, he realized, a luxury enjoyed mainly by those who had too much of it. Like the Hartmans, with their trust funds and private schools and the immense Westchester County estate. Not to mention the twenty-thousand-acre spread near the Greenbrier, and all the rest of it.

Until Peter's plane fell out of the sky, Ben had been able to do what he really loved: teaching, especially teaching kids whom most people had given up on. He'd taught fifth grade in a tough school in an area of Brooklyn known as East New York. A lot of the kids were trouble, and yes, there were gangs and sullen ten-year-olds as well armed as Colombian drug lords. But they needed a teacher who actually gave a damn about them. Ben did give a damn, and every once in a while he actually made a difference to somebody's life.

When Peter died, however, Ben had been all but forced to join the family business. He'd told friends it was a death-bed promise exacted by his mother, and he supposed it was. But cancer or no cancer, he could never refuse her anyway. He remembered her drawn face, the skin ashen from another bout of chemotherapy, the reddish smudges beneath her eyes like bruises. She'd been almost twenty years younger than Dad, and he had never imagined that she might be the first to go. *Work, for the night cometh*, she'd said, smiling bravely. Most of the rest she left unspoken. Max had survived Dachau only to lose a son, and now he was about to lose his wife. How much could any man, however powerful, stand?

"Has he lost you, too?" she had whispered. At the time, Ben was living a few blocks from the school, in a sixth-floor walk-up in a decrepit tenement building where the corridors stank of cat urine and the linoleum curled up from the floors. As a matter of principle, he refused to accept any money from his parents.

"Do you hear what I'm asking you, Ben?"

"My kids," Ben had said, though there was already defeat in his voice. "They need me."

"*He* needs you," she'd replied, very quietly, and that was the end of the discussion.

So now he took the big private clients out to lunch, made them feel important and well cared for and flattered to be cosseted by the founder's son. A little furtive volunteer work at a center for "troubled kids" who made his fifth-graders look like altar boys. And as much time as he could grab traveling, skiing, parasailing, snowboarding, or rock-climbing, and going out with a series of women while fastidiously avoiding settling down with any of them.

Old Max would have to wait.

Suddenly the St. Gotthard lobby, all rose damask and heavy dark Viennese furniture, felt oppressive. "You know, I think I'd prefer to wait outside," Ben told the *Hotelpage*. The man in the loden-green uniform simpered, "Of course, sir, whatever you prefer."

Ben stepped blinking into the bright noontime sun, and took in the pedestrian traffic on the Bahnhofstrasse, the stately avenue lined with linden trees, expensive shops, and cafés, and a procession of financial institutions housed in small limestone mansions. The bellhop scurried behind him with his baggage, hovering until Ben disbursed a fifty-franc note and gestured for him to leave.

"Ah, thank you so *much*, sir," the *Hotelpage* exclaimed with feigned surprise.

The doormen would let him know when his car appeared in the cobbled drive to the left of the hotel, but Ben was in no hurry. The breeze from Lake Zurich was refreshing, after time spent in stuffy, overheated rooms where the air was always suffused with the smell of coffee and, fainter but unmistakable, cigar smoke.

Ben propped his brand-new skis, Volant Ti Supers, against one of the hotel's Corinthian pillars, near his other bags, and watched the busy street scene, the spectacle of anonymous passersby. An obnoxious young businessman braying into a cell phone. An obese woman in a red parka pushing a baby carriage. A crowd of Japanese tourists chattering excitedly. A tall middle-aged man in a business suit with his graying hair pulled back in a ponytail. A delivery-man with a box of lilies, attired in the distinctive orange and black uniform of Blümchengallerie, the upscale flower chain. And a striking, expensively dressed young blonde, clutching a Festiner's shopping bag, who glanced generally in Ben's direction, and then glanced at him again—quickly, but with a flicker of interest before averting her eyes. *Had we but world enough and time*, thought Ben. His gaze wandered again. The sounds of traffic were continuous but muted, drifting in from the Löwenstrasse, a few hundred feet away. Somewhere nearby a high-strung dog was yipping. A middle-aged man wearing a blazer with an odd purple hue, a tad too stylish for Zurich. And then he saw a man about his age, walking with a purposeful stride past the Koss Konditerei. He looked vaguely familiar—

Very familiar.

Ben did a double-take, peered more closely. Was that— could that really be—his old college buddy Jimmy Cavanaugh? A quizzical smile spread over Ben's face.

Jimmy Cavanaugh, whom he'd known since his sophomore year at Princeton. Jimmy, who'd glamorously lived off-campus, smoked unfiltered cigarettes that would have choked an ordinary mortal, and could drink *anybody* under the table, even Ben, who had something of a reputation in that regard. Jimmy had come from a small town in western upstate New York called Homer, which supplied him with a storehouse of tales. One night, after he taught Ben the finer points of downing Tequila shots with beer chasers, Jimmy had him gasping for breath with his stories about the town sport of "cow tipping." Jimmy was rangy, sly, and worldly, had an immense repertory of pranks, a quick wit, and the gift of gab. Most of all, he just seemed more *alive* than most of the kids Ben knew: the clammy-palmed pre-professionals trading tips about the entrance exams for law school or B-school, the pretentious French majors with their clove cigarettes and black scarves, the sullen burn-out cases for whom rebellion was found in a bottle of green hair dye. Jimmy seemed to stand apart from all that, and Ben, envying him his simple ease with himself, was pleased, even flattered by the friendship. As so often happens, they'd lost touch after college; Jimmy had gone off to do something at the Georgetown School of Foreign Service, and Ben had stayed in New York. Neither of them was big on college nostalgia, and then distance and time had done their usual job. Still, Ben reflected, Jimmy Cavanaugh was probably one of the few people he actually felt like talking to just now.

Jimmy Cavanaugh—it was *definitely* Jimmy—was now near enough that Ben could see that he was wearing an expensive-looking suit, under a tan trench coat, and smoking a cigarette. His build had changed: he was broader-shouldered now. But it was Cavanaugh for sure.

"Jesus," Ben said aloud. He started down the Bahnhofstrasse toward Jimmy, then remembered his Volants, which he didn't want to leave unattended, doormen or no doormen. He picked the skis up, hefted them over one shoulder, and walked toward Cavanaugh. The red hair had faded and receded a bit, the once-freckled face was a little lined, he was wearing a two-thousand-dollar Armani suit, and what the hell was he doing in Zurich of all places? Suddenly they made eye contact.

Jimmy broke out in a wide grin, and he strode toward Ben, an arm outstretched, the other in the pocket of his trench coat.

"Hartman, you old dog," Jimmy crowed from a few yards away. "Hey, pal, great to see you!"

"My God, it really *is* you!" Ben exclaimed. At the same time, Ben was puzzled to see a metal tube protruding from his old friend's trench coat, a *silencer*, he now realized, the muzzle pointing directly up at him from waist level.

It had to be some bizarre prank, good old Jimmy was always doing that kind of thing. Yet just as Ben jokingly threw his hands up in the air and dodged an imaginary bullet, he saw Jimmy Cavanaugh shift his right hand ever so slightly, the unmistakable motions of someone squeezing a trigger.

What happened next took a fraction of a second, yet time seemed to telescope, slowing almost to a halt. Reflexively, abruptly, Ben swung his skis down from his right shoulder in a sharp arc, trying to scuttle the weapon but in the process slamming his old friend hard in the neck.

An instant later—or was it the same instant?—he heard the explosion, felt a sharp spray on the back of his neck as a very real bullet shattered a glass storefront just a few feet away.

This couldn't be happening!

Caught by surprise, Jimmy lost his balance and bellowed in pain. As he stumbled to the ground, he flung out a hand to grab the skis. *One hand.* The left. Ben felt as if he'd swallowed ice. The instinct to brace yourself when you stumble is strong: you reach out with both hands, and you drop your suitcase, your pen, your newspaper. There were few things you wouldn't drop—few things you'd still clutch as you fell.

The gun was real.

Ben heard the skis clatter to the sidewalk, saw a thin streak of blood on the side of Jimmy's face, saw Jimmy scrambling to regain his orientation. Then Ben lurched forward and, in a great burst of speed, took off down the street.

The gun was real. And Jimmy had fired it at him.

Ben's path was obstructed by crowds of shoppers and businessmen hurrying to lunch appointments, and as he wove through the crowd he collided with several people, who shouted protests. Still he vaulted ahead, running as he'd never run before, zigzagging, hoping that the irregular pattern would make him an elusive target.

What the hell was going on? This was madness, absolute madness!

He made the mistake of glancing behind him as he ran, inadvertently slowing his pace, his face now a flashing beacon to a once-friend who for some unfathomable reason seemed bent on killing him. Suddenly, barely two feet away, a young woman's forehead exploded in a mist of red.

Ben gasped in terror.

Jesus Christ!

No, it couldn't be happening, this wasn't reality, this was some bizarre nightmare—

He saw a small scattering of stone fragments, as a bullet pitted the marble facade of the narrow office building he was racing past. Cavanaugh was on his feet and running, now just fifty feet or so away from Ben, and though he had to fire in mid-stride, Cavanaugh's aim was still unnervingly good.

He's trying to kill me, no, he's going *to kill me—*

Ben feinted suddenly to the right, then jerked to the left, leaping forward as he did. Now he ran flat out. On the Princeton track team, he was an eight-hundred-meter man, and, fifteen years later, he knew his only chance for survival was to find a surge of speed inside him. His sneakers weren't made for running, but they'd have to do. He needed a destination, a clear goal, an endpoint: that was always the key. *Think, dammit!* Something clicked in his head: he was a block away from the largest underground shopping arcade in Europe, a garish, subterranean temple of consumption known as Shopville, beneath and adjacent to the main train station, the Hauptbahnhof. In his mind's eye, he saw the entrance, the bank of escalators at the Bahnhofplatz; it was always quicker to enter there and walk underneath the square than to fight through the crowds that typically thronged the streets above. He could seek refuge underground in the arcade. Only a madman would dare chase him down there. Ben sprinted now, keeping his knees high, his feet ghosting along with great soft strides, falling back into the discipline of the speed laps he used to devour, conscious only of the breeze at his face. Had he lost Cavanaugh? He didn't hear his footsteps anymore, but he couldn't afford to make any assumptions. Single-mindedly, desperately, he *ran.*

The blond woman with the Festiner's bag folded up her tiny cellular phone and placed it in a pocket of her azure Chanel suit, her pale glossy lips compressed in a small moue of annoyance. At first everything had gone like— well, like clockwork. It had taken her a few seconds to decide that the man standing in front of St. Gotthard was a probable match. He was clearly in his mid-thirties, with an angular face and strong jaw, curly brown hair flecked with gray, and hazel-green eyes. A pleasant-looking fellow,

she supposed, handsome, even; but not so distinctive that
she had been able to ensure a definite identification from
this distance. That was of no consequence. The shooter
they'd chosen could make the identification; they'd made
sure of that.

Now, however, matters seemed less than perfectly controlled. The target was an amateur; there was little chance
he would survive an encounter with a professional. Still,
amateurs made her uneasy. They made mistakes, but er-
ratic, unpredictable ones, their very naïveté defying rational
prediction, as the subject's evasive actions had demonstrated. His wild, protracted escape attempt would merely
postpone the inevitable. And yet it was all going to take
time—the one thing that was in short supply. Sigma One
would not be pleased. She glanced at her small, bejeweled
wristwatch, retrieved the phone, and made one more call.

Winded, his starved muscles screaming for oxygen, Ben
Hartman paused at the escalators to the arcade, knowing he
had to make a split-second decision. 1. UNTERGESCHOSS
SHOPVILLE read the blue overhead sign. The down escalator
was crowded with shoppers laden with bags and strollers;
he'd have to use the up escalator, which had relatively few
riders. Ben charged down it, elbowing aside a young couple
who were holding hands and blocking his path. He saw the
startled looks his actions had provoked, looks that mingled
dismay and derision.

Now he raced through the underground arcade's central
atrium, his feet scudding along the black rubberized floor,
and he allowed himself a glimmer of hope before he realized the error he'd made. From all around him arose
screams, frenzied shouting. Cavanaugh had followed him
here, into this enclosed, contained space. In the mirrored
facade of a jewelry store, he caught a glimpse of muzzle
fire, a burst of yellow-white. Instantly, a bullet tore through
the burnished mahogany panels of a travel bookstore, exposing the cheap fiberboard beneath. Everywhere was pan-

demonium. An old man in a baggy suit a few feet away clutched his throat and toppled like a bowling pin, blood drenching his shirtfront.

Ben dove behind the information station, an oblong concrete-and-glass structure perhaps five feet wide, on which was mounted a list of stores, elegant white lettering on black, a shoppers' guide in three languages. A hollow explosion of glass told him that the information box had been hit. Half a second later, there was a sharp crack, and a piece of concrete fell heavily from the structure, landing near his feet.

Inches away!

Another man, tall and stout in a camel-hair topcoat and a jaunty gray cap, staggered a few feet past him before collapsing to the floor, dead. He'd been shot in the chest.

Amid the chaos, Ben found it impossible to distinguish Cavanaugh's footsteps, but, gauging his position from the reflected muzzle flash, he knew no more than a minute remained before he would be overtaken. Remaining in position behind the concrete island, he stood, to his full six feet, and peered around wildly, looking for new refuge.

Meanwhile, the screams crescendoed. Ahead, the arcade was crowded with people, shrieking, crying out hysterically, crouching and cowering, many of them trying to hide their heads beneath folded arms.

Twenty feet away there were escalators marked 2. UN-TERGESCHOSS. If he could close the distance without being shot, he could get to the level below. His luck might change there. It couldn't get any worse, he thought—then he changed his mind as he saw a widening pool of blood flowing from the man in the camel-hair coat a few feet away. Dammit, he had to *think!* There was no way he could close the distance in time. Unless . . .

He reached for the dead man's arm and dragged him over. Seconds remained. He yanked off the dead man's tawny coat and grabbed the gray cap, conscious of baleful eyes upon him from shoppers cowering near the Western Union. This was no time for delicacy. Now he shrugged into the roomy overcoat, pulled the cap down hard on his head. If he was to remain alive, he would have to resist the urge to dart toward the second-level escalators like a jack-rabbit: he had gone hunting enough to know that anything that moved too abruptly was likely to be shot by an itchy-fingered gunman. Instead, he clambered slowly to his feet, hunched, staggering, weaving like an old man who had lost blood. He was now visible and supremely vulnerable: the ruse had to last just long enough to get him to the escalator. Maybe ten seconds. So long as Cavanaugh thought he was a wounded bystander, he wouldn't waste another bullet on him.

Ben's heart was hammering in his chest, his every instinct screaming at him to break into a sprint. *Not yet.* Hunched over, shoulders rounded, he staggered on with an unsteady gait, his strides as long as he could make them without exciting suspicion. Five seconds. Four seconds. Three seconds.

At the escalator, which had emptied out, abandoned by the terrified pedestrians, the man in the bloodied camel-hair overcoat seemed to crumple face forward, before the movement of the stairs took him out of view.

Now!

Inaction had been as strenuous as exertion, and, every nerve in his body twitching, Ben had broken his fall with his hands. As quietly as he could, he raced down the remaining stairs.

He heard a bellow of frustration from upstairs: Cavanaugh would now be after him. Every second had to count.

Ben put on another burst of speed, but the second below-ground level of the arcade was a virtual maze. There was no straight route of egress to the other side of the Bahnhofplatz, just a succession of byways, the wider walkways punctuated with kiosks of wood and glass that sold cellular phones, cigars, watches, posters. To a dilatory shopper, they were islands of interest—to him, an obstacle course.

Still, they reduced the number of sight lines. They lessened the chance of the long-distance kill. And so they bought him time. Perhaps enough time for Ben to secure the one thing he had on his mind: a shield.

He ran past a blur of boutiques: Foto Video Ganz, Rest-seller Buchhandlung, Presensende Stickler, Microspot. Kin-derboutique, with its window crammed with furry stuffed animals, the display framed by green-and-gold-painted wood with an incised ivy pattern. There was the chrome and plastic of a Swisscom outlet . . . All of them festively plying their goods and services, all utterly worthless to him. Then, straight ahead, to his right, next to a Credit Suisse/ Volksbank branch office, he spotted a luggage store. He looked through the window, heaped high with soft-sided leather suitcases —no good. The item he was after was in-side: a large, brushed-steel briefcase. No doubt the gleam-ing steel cladding was as much cosmetic as functional, but it would serve. It would have to. As Ben darted in the store, grabbed the article, and ran out, he noticed that the propri-etor, pale and sweating, was jabbering hysterically in *Schweitzerdeutsch* on the telephone. No one bothered to run after Ben; word of the insanity had already spread.

Ben had gained a shield; he had also lost precious time. Even as he sprang out of the luggage store, he saw its display window transformed into an oddly beautiful spi-derweb in the instant before it disintegrated into shards. Cavanaugh was close, so close Ben didn't dare look around to try to locate his position. Instead, Ben charged forward into a crowd of shoppers emerging from Franscati, a large department store at one end of the cruciform plaza. Holding up the briefcase, Ben lunged forward, tripping on some-one's leg, regaining his footing with difficulty, losing a few precious moments.

An explosion inches from his head: the sound of a lead bullet slamming into the steel briefcase. It jolted in his hands, partly from the impact of the bullet, partly from his own muscular reflex, and Ben noticed a bulge on the steel casing facing him, as if it had been struck by a small ham-mer. The bullet had penetrated the first layer, had almost penetrated the second. His shield had saved his life, but only just.

Everything around him had gone blurry, but he knew he was entering the teeming Halle Landesmuseum. He also knew that carnage was still trailing him.

Throngs of people were screaming—huddled, cringing, running—as the horror, the gunfire, the bloodshed came closer.

Ben plunged into the frenzied crowd, was swallowed up by it. For a moment the gunfire seemed to have stopped. He tossed the briefcase to the floor: it had served its purpose, and its gleaming metal would now make him too easy to pick out of the crowd.

Was it over? Was Cavanaugh out of ammunition? Reloading?

Jostled one way, then another, Ben scanned the labyrinthine arcade for an exit, an *Ausgang*, through which he could disappear unseen. *Maybe I've lost him*, Ben thought. Yet he didn't dare look back again. No going back. Only forward.

Along the walkway that led to the Franscati department store, he spotted a fake-rustic sign of dark wood and gilt lettering in script: KATZKELLER-BIERHALLE. It hung above an alcove, an entrance to a deserted restaurant. GESCHLOSSEN, a smaller sign read. Closed.

He raced toward it, his movement camouflaged by a frenzied rush of people in that general direction. Through a faux-medieval archway beneath the sign, he ran into a spacious, empty dining room. Cast-iron chains from the ceiling supported enormous wooden chandeliers; medieval halberds and engravings of medieval nobility adorned the walls. The motif continued with the heavy round tables, which were crudely carved in keeping with someone's fantasy of a fifteenth-century arsenal.

On the right side of the room was a long bar, and Ben ducked behind it, gasping loudly for breath, as desperately as he tried to remain silent. His clothes were soaked with sweat. He couldn't believe how fast his heart was thudding, and he actually winced from the chest pain.

He tapped the cabinetry in front of him; it made a hollow sound. Obviously fashioned from veneer and plaster, it was nothing that could be relied upon to stop a bullet. Crouching, he made his way around a corner and to a protected stone alcove, where he could stand and catch his breath. As he leaned back to rest against the pillar, his head cracked into a wrought-iron lantern mounted on the stone. He groaned involuntarily. Then he examined the light fixture that had just lacerated the back of his head, and he saw that the whole thing, the heavy black iron arm attached to the ornamental housing that held the bulb, could be lifted right out of the mounting bracket.

It came out with a rusty screech. He managed to get a firm grip and held it against his chest.

And he waited, trying to slow the beating of his heart. He knew something about waiting. He remembered all those Thanksgivings spent at the Greenbrier; Max Hartman was insistent that his sons learn how to hunt, and Hank McGee, a grizzled local from White Sulfur Springs, was given the job of teaching them. *How hard could it be?* he remembered thinking; he was an ace at skeet shooting, had reason to be proud of his hand-eye coordination. He let this slip to McGee, whose eyes darkened: *You think the hunt's really about shootin'? It's about waitin'.* And he fixed him with a glare. McGee was right, of course: the waiting was the hardest part of all, and the part he was temperamentally least suited for.

Hunting with Hank McGee, he had lain in wait for his quarry.

Now he *was* the quarry.

Unless . . . somehow . . . he could change that.

In a few moments, Ben heard approaching footsteps. Jimmy Cavanaugh entered stealthily, tentatively, glancing from side to side. His shirt collar was grimy and torn and bloodied from a gash on the right side of his neck. His

trench coat was soiled. His flushed face was set in a determined grimace, his eyes wild.

Could this really be his friend? What had Cavanaugh
become in the decade and a half since Ben had last seen
him? What had turned him into a killer?

Why was this happening?

In his right hand Cavanaugh gripped his blue-black pistol, the ten-inch-long tube of a sound suppressor threaded
to its barrel. Ben, flashing back on target-practice memories
from twenty years ago, saw that it was a Walther PPK, a
.32.

Ben held his breath, terrified that his gasping would give
him away. He drew back into the alcove, clutching the iron
light fixture he had just torn from the wall, flattening himself out of sight as Cavanaugh made a sweep of the restaurant. With a sudden but sure movement of his arm Ben
flung the iron lantern fixture, smashing it into Cavanaugh's
skull with an audible thud.

Jimmy Cavanaugh screamed in pain, his cry high-
pitched like an animal's. His knees buckled, and he
squeezed the trigger.

Ben could feel a flare of heat, a fraction of an inch away
from his ear. But now, instead of drawing back farther, or
attempting to run, Ben lunged forward, slamming himself
into his enemy's body, pummeling him to the ground, Cavanaugh's skull cracking against the stone floor.

Even badly wounded, the man was a powerhouse. A
rancid miasma of sweat arose from him as he reared up and
vised a massive arm around Ben's neck, compressing his
carotid artery. Desperately, Ben reached for the gun, trying
to grab it but succeeding only in wrenching the long silencer up and back toward Cavanaugh. With a sudden ear-
shattering explosion the gun went off. Ben's ears rang with
a sustained squeal; his face stung from the blowback.

The grip on Ben's throat loosened. He twisted his body
around, free of the chokehold. Cavanaugh was slumped on

the ground. With a jolt Ben saw the dark red hole just above his old friend's eyebrows, a horrific third eye. He was suffused with a mixture of relief and revulsion, and the sense that nothing would ever be the same.

CHAPTER TWO

Halifax, Nova Scotia, Canada

It was still early in the evening, but already it was dark, and an icy wind roared along the narrow street, down the steep hill toward the roiling waters of the Atlantic. Fog had settled over the gray streets of this port town, blanketing it, closing it in. A miserable drizzling rain had begun to fall. The air had a salty tang.

A sulfurous yellow light illuminated the ramshackle porch, the worn front steps of a large, gray clapboard house. A dark figure in a yellow hooded oilcloth slicker stood under the yellow light, jamming his finger against the front door buzzer insistently, over and over and over. Finally there came the clicks of the safety bolts, and the weathered front door came slowly open.

The face of a very old man appeared, peering out angrily. He was wearing a stained pale blue dressing gown over rumpled white pajamas. His mouth was caved in, the baggy skin of the face pallid, the eyes gray and watery.

"Yes?" the elderly man demanded in a high, raspy voice. "What do you want?" He spoke with a Breton accent, a legacy of his French Acadian forebears who fished the seas beyond Nova Scotia.

"You've got to *help* me!" cried the person in the yellow slicker. He shifted his weight anxiously from one foot to the other. "Please! Oh, God, please, you've got to *help!*"

The old man's expression became clouded with confusion. The visitor, though tall, looked to be in his late teens. "What are you talking about?" he said. "Who are you?"

"There's been a horrible accident. Oh, *God!* Oh, Jesus! My dad! My dad! I think he's *dead!*"

The old man pressed his narrow lips together. "What do you want from me?"

The stranger flung a gloved hand toward the handle of the storm door, then dropped it. "Please just let me make a call. Let me call an ambulance. We had an accident, a terrible accident. The car is totaled. My sister—badly hurt. My dad was driving. God, my *parents!*" The boy's voice broke. Now he seemed more a child than a teenager. "Oh, Lord, I think he's dead."

Now the old man's glare seemed to soften, and he slowly pushed open the storm door to let the stranger in. "All right," he said. "Come in."

"Thank you," the boy exclaimed as he entered. "Just for a moment. Thank you so much."

The old man turned around and led the way into a dingy front room, flicking on a wall switch as he entered. He turned to say something just as the boy in the hooded rain slicker came closer and with both hands, clasped the man's own hand, seemingly a gesture of awkward gratitude. Water ran down from the sleeve of his yellow slicker onto the old man's dressing gown. The boy made a sudden, jerking movement. "Hey," the old man protested, confused. He pulled away, then slumped to the floor.

The boy stared down at the crumpled body for a moment. He slipped off his wrist the small device that held a tiny retractable hypodermic needle and put it in an inside pocket of his slicker.

Quickly he surveyed the room, spotted the ancient television, and turned it on. An old black-and-white movie was playing. Now he set about his task with the confidence of someone much older.

He went back to the body, set it carefully on a shabby orange lounge chair, arranging the arms and head so that it looked as if the old man had fallen asleep in front of the TV.

Pulling a roll of paper towels from inside his slicker, he swiftly mopped up the water that had pooled on the wide pine boards of the entrance hall. Then he returned to the front door, which was still open, glanced around outside, and when he was satisfied, stepped out onto the porch and closed the door behind him.

The Austrian Alps

The silver Mercedes S430 wound up the steep mountain road until it arrived at the clinic gates. A security guard in the booth by the gate came out, saw who the passenger was, and said with great deference, "Welcome, sir." He did not bother to ask for identification. The chief of the clinic was to be admitted with dispatch. The car turned onto the ring drive through a sloping campus where the vibrant green of well-tended grass and sculpted pines contrasted with drifting patches of powdery snow. Towering in the distance overhead were the magnificent white crags and planes of the Schneeberg peak. The car drove around a dense stand of tall yews, and over to a second, hidden security booth. The guard, who had already been alerted to the director's arrival, pressed the button that raised the steel bar and, at the same time, touched the switch that lowered the steel spikes set into the pavement, which would ruin the tires of any vehicle that entered without being cleared through.

The Mercedes drove up a long narrow road that led only to one place: an old clock factory, formerly a *Schloss* that had been built two centuries ago. A coded remote signal was sent, an electronic door opened, and the car pulled into the reserved parking space. The driver got out and opened the door for his passenger, who strode quickly into the entrance. There another security guard, this one behind bulletproof glass, nodded and smiled a welcome.

The director entered the elevator, an anachronism in this ancient Alpine structure, inserted his digitally encoded identification card to unlock it, and made his way to the third, and top, floor. There he passed through three sets of doors, each unlocked by means of an electronic card reader, until he came to the conference room, where the others were already seated around the long burnished mahogany table. He took his place at the head of the table and looked around at the others.

"Gentlemen," he began, "only days remain before the fulfillment of our dream so long deferred. The long gestation period is nearly over. Which is to say, your patience is about to be rewarded, and beyond the wildest dreams of our founders."

The sounds of approval around the table were gratifying, and he waited for them to subside before continuing. "As for security, I have been assured that very few of the *angeli rebelli* remain. Soon there will be none. There is, however, one small problem."

Zurich

Ben tried to stand, but his legs would not support him. He sank to the ground, on the verge of becoming violently ill, feeling at once cold and prickly-hot. Blood roared in his ears. An icicle of fear was lodged in his stomach.

What had just happened? he asked himself. Why in the hell was Jimmy Cavanaugh trying to kill him? What kind of madness was this? Had the man's mind snapped? Had Ben's sudden reappearance after a decade and a half triggered something in a disturbed brain, a rush of twisted memory that for some reason had propelled him to murder?

He could taste liquid, brackish and metallic, and he

touched his lips. Blood was seeping from his nose. It must have happened in the struggle. He'd gotten a bloody nose, Jimmy Cavanaugh a bullet in the brain.

The noise from the shopping arcade outside was subsiding. There were still shouts, the occasional anguished cry, but the chaos was diminishing. Steadying himself with his hands on the floor, he pushed himself up, managed to get to his feet. He felt dizzy, vertiginous, and knew it was not from any loss of blood; he was in shock.

He forced himself to look at Cavanaugh's body. By now he'd calmed down enough to think.

Somebody I haven't seen since the age of twenty-one turns up in Zurich, goes insane, and tries to kill me. And now he lies here dead, in a tacky medieval-themed restaurant. No explanation to offer. Maybe there'd never be an explanation.

Carefully avoiding the pool of blood around the head, he went through Cavanaugh's pockets, first the suit jacket, then the pants, then the pockets of the trench coat. There was absolutely nothing there. No ID cards, no credit cards. Bizarre. Cavanaugh seemed to have emptied his pockets, as if in preparation for what happened.

It had been premeditated. *Planned.*

He noticed the blue-black Walther PPK still clutched in Cavanaugh's hand and considered checking the magazine to see how many rounds were left. He pondered taking it, just slipping the slim pistol into his pocket. What if Cavanaugh wasn't alone?

What if there were others?

He hesitated. This was a crime scene of sorts. Best not to alter it in any way, in case there was legal trouble down the line.

Slowly, he got up and made his way, dazed, into the main hall. Now it was mostly deserted, apart from a few clusters of emergency medical technicians tending to the wounded. Someone was being carried on a stretcher.

Ben had to find a policeman.

*   *   *

The two cops, one clearly a rookie and one middle-aged, looked at him dubiously. He'd found them standing by the Bijoux Suisse kiosk, near the Marktplatz food court. They wore navy-blue sweaters with red shoulder patches that read *Zürichpolizei*; each had a walkie-talkie and a pistol holstered to the belt.

"May I see your passport, please?" the young one asked after Ben had spoken for a few minutes. Evidently the older one either didn't speak English or preferred not to.

"For God's sake," Ben snapped in frustration, "people have been killed. A guy's lying dead in a restaurant down there, a man who tried—"

"*Ihren Pass, bitte*," the rookie persisted sternly. "Do you have identification?"

"Of course I do," Ben said, reaching for his billfold. He pulled it out and handed it over.

The rookie examined it suspiciously, then gave it to the senior man, who glanced at it without interest and thrust it back at Ben.

"Where were you when this happened?" the rookie asked.

"Waiting in front of the Hotel St. Gotthard. A car was supposed to take me to the airport."

The rookie took a step forward, uncomfortably close to him, and his neutral gaze became frankly mistrustful: "You are going to the airport?"

"I was on my way to St. Moritz."

"And suddenly this man fired a gun at you?"

"He's an old friend. *Was* an old friend."

The rookie lifted an eyebrow.

"I hadn't seen him in fifteen years," Ben continued. "He recognized me, sort of came toward me as if he was happy to see me, then suddenly he pulls out a gun."

"You had a quarrel?"

"We didn't exchange two words!"

The younger cop's eyes narrowed. "You had arranged to meet?"

"No. It was pure coincidence."

"Yet he had a gun, a loaded gun." The rookie looked at the older cop, then turned back to Ben. "And it was outfitted with a silencer, you say. He must have known you would be there."

Ben shook his head, exasperated. "I hadn't talked to him in years! He couldn't possibly have known I'd be here."

"Surely you must agree that people do not just carry around guns with silencers unless they mean to use them."

Ben hesitated. "I suppose that's right."

The older policeman cleared his throat. "And what kind of gun did you have?" he asked in surprisingly fluent English.

"What are you talking about?" Ben asked, his voice rising in indignation. "I didn't have a gun."

"Then forgive me, I must be confused. You say your friend had a gun, and that you did not. In which case, why is he dead, and not you?"

It was a good question. Ben just shook his head as he thought back to the moment when Jimmy Cavanaugh leveled the steel tube at him. Part of him—the rational part—had assumed it was a prank. But obviously part of him had not: he'd been primed to react swiftly. Why? He replayed in his mind Jimmy's easy lope, his wide welcoming grin . . . and his cold eyes. Watchful eyes that didn't quite match the grin. A small discordant element that his subconscious mind must have registered.

"Come, let us go to see the body of this assassin," the older policeman said, and he placed a hand on Ben's shoulder in a way that was not at all affectionate but instead conveyed that Ben was no longer a free man.

Ben led the way across the arcade, which now swarmed with policemen, reporters snapping pictures, and made his way down to the second level. The two *Polizei* followed close behind. At the KATZKELLER sign Ben entered the dining room, went to the alcove, and pointed.

"Well?" demanded the rookie angrily.

Astonished, Ben stared, wide-eyed, at the spot where Cavanaugh's body had been. He felt light-headed, his mind frozen in shock. There was nothing there.

No pool of blood. No body, no gun. The lantern arm had been replaced in its fixture as if it had never been removed. The floor was clean and bare.

It was as if nothing had ever happened there.

"My God," Ben breathed. Had he snapped, lost touch with reality? But he could feel the solidity of the floor, the bar, the tables. *If this was some elaborate stunt . . .* but it wasn't. He had somehow stumbled into something intricate and terrifying.

The policemen stared at him with rekindled suspicion.

"Listen," Ben said, his voice reduced to a hoarse whisper, "I can't explain this. I was here. *He* was here."

The older policeman spoke rapidly on the walkie-talkie, and soon they were joined by another officer, stolid and barrel-chested. "Perhaps I am easily confused, so let me try to understand. You race through a busy street, and then through the underground shopping arcade. All around you, people are shot. You claim that you are being chased by a maniac. You promise to show us this man, this American. And yet there is no maniac. There is only you. A strange American spinning fairy tales."

"*Goddammit,* I've told you the *truth!*"

"You say a madman from your past was responsible for the bloodshed," the rookie said in a quiet, steely voice. "I see only one madman here."

The older policeman conferred in *Schweitzerdeutsch* with his barrel-chested colleague. "You were staying at the Hotel St. Gotthard, yes?" he finally asked Ben. "Why don't you take us there?"

Accompanied by three policemen—the barrel-chested one walking behind him, the rookie ahead of him, and the older policeman close by his side—Ben made his way through the underground arcade, up the escalator, and down the Bahnhofstrasse toward his hotel. Though he was not yet cuffed, he knew that this was merely a formality.

In front of the hotel, a policewoman, whom the others had clearly sent ahead, was keeping a custodial watch over his luggage. Her brown hair was short, almost mannish, and her expression was stony.

Through the lobby windows, Ben caught a glimpse of the unctuous *Hotelpage* who'd attended to him earlier. Their eyes met, and the man turned away with stricken look, as if he'd just learned he'd toted bags for Lee Harvey Oswald.

"Your luggage, yes?" the rookie asked Ben.

"Yes, yes," Ben said. "What of it?" Now what? What more could there be?

The policewoman opened the tan leather hand luggage. The others looked inside, then turned to face Ben. "This is yours?" the rookie asked.

"I already said it was," Ben replied.

The middle-aged cop took a handkerchief from his pants pocket and used it to lift an object out of the satchel. It was Cavanaugh's Walther PPK pistol.

CHAPTER THREE

Washington, D.C.

A serious-looking young woman strode briskly down the long central corridor of the fifth floor of the United States Department of Justice Building, the mammoth Classical Revival structure that occupied the entire block between Ninth and Tenth Streets. She had glossy dark brown hair, caramel-brown eyes, a sharp nose. At first glance she looked part-Asian, or perhaps Hispanic. She wore a tan trench coat, carried a leather briefcase, and might have been taken for a lawyer, a lobbyist, maybe a government official on the fast track.

Her name was Anna Navarro. She was thirty-three and worked in the Office of Special Investigations, a little-known unit of the Justice Department.

When she arrived at the stuffy conference room, she realized that the weekly unit meeting was already well under way. Arliss Dupree, standing by a whiteboard on an easel, turned as she entered and stopped in mid-sentence. She felt the stares, couldn't help blushing a little, which was no doubt what Dupree wanted. She took the first empty seat. A shaft of sunlight blinded her.

"There she is. Nice of you to join us," Dupree said. Even his insults were predictable. She merely nodded, determined not to let him provoke her. He'd told her the meeting would be at eight-fifteen. Obviously it had been scheduled to start at eight, and he would deny ever having told her otherwise. A petty, bureaucratic way of giving her a hard time. They both knew why she was late, even if nobody else here did.

Before Dupree was brought in to head the Office of Special Investigations, meetings were a rarity. Now he held them weekly, as a chance to parade his authority. Dupree was short and wide, mid-forties, the body of a weight lifter in a too-tight light gray suit, one of three shopping-mall suits he rotated. Even across the room she could smell his drugstore aftershave. He had a ruddy moon face the texture of lumpy porridge.

There was a time when she actually cared what men like Arliss Dupree thought about her and tried to win them over. Now she didn't give a damn. She had her friends, and Dupree was simply not among them. Across the table, David Denneen, a square-jawed, sandy-haired man, gave her a sympathetic glance.

"As some of you may have heard, Internal Compliance has asked for our colleague here to be temporarily assigned to them." Dupree turned to her, his eyes hard. "Given the amount of unfinished work you've got here, I'd consider it less than responsible, Agent Navarro, if you accepted an assignment from another division. Is this something you've been angling for? You can tell us, you know."

"This is the first I've heard of it," she told him truthfully.

"That right? Well, maybe I've been leaping to conclusions here," he said, his tone softening a bit.

"Quite possibly," she replied, dryly.

"I was making the assumption that you were wanted for an assignment. Maybe you *are* the assignment."

"Come again?"

"Maybe you're the one under investigation," Dupree said in a mellower tone, evidently pleased by the idea. "It

wouldn't surprise me. You're a deep one, Agent Navarro."
There were laughs from some of his drinking buddies.

She shifted her chair to get the light out of her eyes.

Ever since Detroit, when the two of them were staying
on the same floor of the Westin and she turned down (politely, she thought) Dupree's drunken, highly explicit proposal, he'd been leaving condescending little remarks, like
rat droppings, in her performance evaluation folder: ... *as
best she can given her obviously limited interest ... errors
a result of inattention, not incompetence ...*

He described her to a male colleague, she'd heard, as "a
sexual harassment suit waiting to happen." He tarred her
with the most vicious insult you can give someone in the
Bureau: *not a team player.* Not a team player meant she
didn't go out drinking with the boys, including Dupree,
kept her social life separate. He also made a point of pa-
pering her files with mentions of mistakes she'd made—a
few minor procedural omissions, nothing at all serious.
Once, on the trail of a rogue DEA agent who'd been turned
by a drug lord and was implicated in several homicides,
she'd neglected to submit an FD-460 within the required
seven days.

The best agents make mistakes. She was convinced that
the best ones in fact made more minor gaffes than average,
because they were focused more on following the trail than
on following every single procedure in the manual of rules
and regs. You could slavishly observe every last ridiculous
procedural requirement and never crack a case.

She felt his stare on her. She looked up, and their eyes
locked.

"We've got an unusually heavy caseload to deal with,"
Dupree went on. "When somebody doesn't do their share,
it means more work for everyone else. We've got a mid-
level IRS manager suspected of organizing some pretty
complicated tax scams. We've got a rogue FBI guy who
seems to be using his shield to pursue a personal vendetta.
We've got some ATF shit-heel selling munitions from the
evidence vaults." That was a typical array of cases for the

OSI: investigating ("auditing" was the term of art) misconduct involving members of other government agencies—in
essence, the federal version of internal affairs.

"Maybe the workload here is a little much for you,"
Dupree said, pressing. "Is that it?"

She pretended to jot down a note and didn't reply. Her
face was prickly warm. She inhaled slowly, struggling to
tamp down her anger. She refused to give in to his baiting.
Finally she spoke. "Look, if it's inconvenient, why don't
you refuse the request for interdepartmental transfer?" Anna
asked it in a reasonable tone of voice, but it wasn't an
innocent question: Dupree lacked the authority to challenge
the highly secretive, all-powerful Internal Compliance Unit,
and any reference to the limits of his authority was bound
to infuriate him.

Dupree's little ears reddened. "I'm expecting a brief consult. If the spook hunters at ICU knew as much as they
pretend, they might realize that you aren't exactly cut out
for that line of work."

His eyes shone with what she imagined was contempt.

Anna loved her work, knew she was good at it. She
didn't require praise. All she wanted was not to have to
spend her time and energy trying to hang on to her job,
clinging by her fingernails. Again she kept her face a mask
of neutrality. She felt the tension localize itself in her stomach. "I'm sure you did your best to make them understand."

A beat of silence. Anna could see he was debating how
to reply. Dupree glanced at his beloved whiteboard, at the
next item on his agenda. "We'll miss you," he said.

Shortly after the meeting broke up, David Denneen sought
her out in her tiny cubbyhole of an office. "The ICU wants
you because you're the best," he said. "You know that,
don't you?"

Anna shook her head wearily. "I was surprised to see
you at the meeting. You're in operations oversight now.

Doing great, by all accounts." Word was he was on the fast track for a position in the AG's office.

"Thanks to you," Denneen said. "I was there today as divisional representative. We take turns. Got to keep an eye on the budget numbers. And on you." Gently, he placed a hand on hers. Anna noticed that the warmth in his eyes was mixed with concern.

"It was good to see you there," Anna said. "And send my best to Ramon."

"I'll do that," he said. "We'll have to have you over for paella again."

"But there's something else on your mind, isn't there?"

Denneen's eyes didn't leave hers. "Listen, Anna, your new assignment, whatever it is, isn't going to be like getting a new call sheet. What people say around here is true—the ways of the Ghost are mysterious to man." He repeated the old jest with little humor. The Ghost was an in-house nickname for the longtime director of the Internal Compliance Unit, Alan Bartlett. During closed hearings before the Senate subcommittee on intelligence, back in the seventies, a deputy attorney general had referred to him, archly, as "the ghost in the machine," and the honorific had stuck. If Bartlett wasn't ghostly, he was a legendarily elusive figure. Seldom seen, reputedly brilliant, he ruled over a rarefied dominion of highly classified audits, and his own reclusive habits made him emblematic of its clandestine ways.

Anna shrugged. "I wouldn't know. I've never met him, and I don't think I know anyone who has. Rumors thrive on ignorance, Dave. You of all people know that."

"Then take a word of advice from an ignoramus who cares about you," he said. "I don't know what this ICU thing is about. But be careful, O.K.?"

"Careful how?"

Denneen just shook his head, uneasily. "It's a different world over there," he said.

*   *   *

Later that morning, Anna found herself in the immense marble lobby of an office building on M Street, on her way to her appointment at the Internal Compliance Unit. The unit's workings were obscure even within the department, and its operational purview was—or so certain senators had occasionally charged—dangerously undefined. *It's a different world over there*, Denneen had said, and so it seemed.

The ICU was located on the tenth floor of this modern office complex in Washington, isolated from a bureaucracy it was sometimes obliged to scrutinize, and she tried not to gawk at the splashing indoor fountain, the green marble floors and walls. She thought: *What kind of government agency gets fitted out like this?* She got on the elevator. Even that was trimmed with marble.

The only other passenger on the elevator was a too-handsome guy around her age in a too-expensive suit. A lawyer, she decided. Like just about everyone else in this city.

In the mirrored elevator walls she saw him giving her The Look. If she caught his eye, she knew he'd smile and say good morning and strike up a banal Elevator Conversation. Even though he was no doubt well intentioned and probably just wanted to flirt politely, Anna found it mildly annoying. Nor did she respond well when men asked her why a woman as beautiful as she was had become a government investigator. As if what she did for a living were the special province of the homely.

Normally, she pretended not to notice. Now, however, she threw him a scowl. He looked away hastily.

Whatever it was that the ICU wanted from her, it had come at a damn inconvenient time; Dupree was right about that. *Maybe you* are *the assignment*, he'd said, and though Anna had shrugged off the suggestion, it nagged at her, absurdly. What the hell was that supposed to mean? No doubt Arliss Dupree was in his office right now, gleefully sharing his speculation with some of his drinking buddies on the staff.

The elevator opened onto a lavishly appointed, marble-lined hall that could have been the executive floor of a high-priced law firm. Off to the right she spotted the seal of the Department of Justice mounted on one wall. Visitors were instructed to buzz for admittance. She did so. It was 11:25 A.M., five minutes before her scheduled appointment. Anna prided herself on her punctuality.

A female voice demanded her name, and then she was buzzed in by a handsome dark-skinned woman with a squared-off haircut—almost too chic for government work, Anna thought to herself.

The receptionist assessed her coolly and directed her to take a seat. Anna detected a very faint Jamaican accent.

Within the office suite, the trappings of the swanky building gave way to a setting of utter sterility. The pearl-gray carpet was immaculate, like no government carpet she'd ever seen. The waiting area was brightly lighted with an array of halogen bulbs that left virtually no shadows. Photos of the President and the Attorney General were framed in lacquered steel. The chairs and the coffee table were of hard blond wood. Everything looked brand new, as if it had been freshly uncrated, unsoiled by human habitation.

She noticed the foil hologram stickers on both the fax machine and the telephone on the receptionist's desk, government labels indicating that these were secure lines, employing officially certified telephony encryption.

At frequent intervals, the phone purred quietly, and the woman spoke in a low voice using a headset. The first two calls were in English; the third must have been in French, because the receptionist responded in that language. Two more in English, gently eliciting contact information. And then another in which she spoke in a language, sibilant and clicky, that Anna had a hard time identifying. Anna glanced at her watch again, fidgeted in the hard-backed chair, and then looked at the receptionist. "That was Basque, wasn't it?" she said. It was something more than a guess, but less than a certainty.

The woman responded with a fractional nod and a demure smile. "It won't be much longer, Ms. Navarro," she said.

Now Anna's eye was drawn to the tall wooden island behind the receptionist's station, which extended all the way to the wall; from the legally required exit sign, she realized that the wooden structure concealed the entrance to a staircase. It was artfully done, and it allowed ICU agents or their guests to arrive and depart unnoticed by anyone in the official waiting room. What kind of outfit was this?

Another five minutes went by.

"Does Mr. Bartlett know I'm here?" Anna asked.

The receptionist returned her gaze levelly. "He's just finishing up with someone."

Anna returned to her chair, wishing she'd brought something to read. She didn't even have the *Post*, and clearly no reading material would be allowed to soil the pristine waiting area. She took out an automatic-teller-machine slip and a pen and started making a list of things to do.

The receptionist placed a finger on her ear and nodded. "Mr. Bartlett says he'll see you now." She emerged from her station and guided Anna down a series of doors. No names were posted; only numbers. Finally, at the end of a hallway, she opened a door marked DIRECTOR and took her into the tidiest office she had ever seen. On a far table, stacks of paper were perfectly arrayed in equidistant piles.

A small, white-haired man in a crisp navy suit came out from behind a vast walnut desk and extended a small, delicate hand. Anna noticed the pale pink moons of his perfectly manicured nails and was surprised by the strength of his grip. She noticed that the desk was barren, save for a handful of green file folders, and a sleek, black telephone; mounted on the wall just behind it was a velvet-lined glass display case containing two antique-looking pocket watches. It was the one eccentric touch in the room.

"I'm so terribly sorry to keep you waiting," he said. His age was indeterminate, but he was probably in his early sixties, Anna decided. His eyes were owlish through his glasses, large round lenses in flesh-colored frames. "I know how busy you are, and you were so very kind to have come by." He spoke softly, so softly that Anna found herself straining to hear him over the white noise of the ventilation system. "We're very grateful for your making the time."

"If I may speak candidly, I didn't know we had a choice when ICU called," she said tartly.

He smiled as if she had said something amusing. "Please do sit down."

Anna settled into the high-backed chair opposite his desk. "To tell you the truth, Mr. Bartlett, I'm curious about why I'm here."

"You weren't inconvenienced, I hope," Bartlett said, interlacing his small fingers in a prayerful tent.

"It's not a matter of inconvenience," Anna replied. In a strong voice, she added, "I'm happy to answer whatever questions you may have."

Bartlett nodded encouragingly. "That's rather what I'm hoping. But I'm afraid these answers won't be easy to come by. In fact, if we could even frame the questions, we'd be halfway home. Am I making any sense to you?"

"I return to my own question," Anna said with banked impatience. "What am I doing here?"

"Forgive me. You're thinking that I'm being maddeningly elliptical. Of course you're right, and I apologize for it. Occupational hazard. Too much time shut away with paper and more paper. Deprived of the bracing air of experience. But that must be your contribution. Now let me ask you a question, Ms. Navarro. Do you know what it is that we do here?"

"The ICU? Vaguely. Intragovernmental inquiries—only, the classified kind." Anna decided that the query called for reticence; she knew a little more than what she volunteered. She was aware that behind its bland title was an extremely secretive, powerful, and far-reaching investigative agency charged with highly classified audits and examinations of other U.S. government agencies that couldn't be done in-house, and which involved highly sensitive matters. ICU officials were deeply involved, it was said, in scrutinizing the CIA's Aldrich Ames fiasco; in investigating the Reagan White House's Iran-Contra affair; in examining numerous Defense Department acquisitions scandals. It was the ICU, people whispered, that had first uncovered the suspicious activities of the FBI's counterintelligence agent Robert Philip Hanssen. There were even rumors that the ICU was behind the "Deep Throat" leaks that led to Richard Nixon's downfall.

Bartlett looked off into the middle distance. "The techniques of investigation are, in their essentials, everywhere the same," he said, finally. "What changes is the bailiwick, the ambit of operations. Ours has to do with matters touching on national security."

"I don't have that kind of clearance," Anna put in quickly.

"Actually"—Bartlett allowed himself a small smile—"you do now."

Had she been cleared without her knowledge? "Regardless. It's not my terrain."

"That's not strictly the case, is it?" Bartlett said. "Why don't we talk about the NSC member you did a Code 33 on last year?"

"How the *hell* do you know about that?" Anna blurted. She gripped the arm of her chair. "*Sorry.* But how? That one was strictly off the books. By the direct request of the AG."

"Off *your* books," Bartlett said. "We have our own way of keeping tabs. Joseph Nesbett, wasn't it? Used to be at the Harvard Center for Economic Development. Got a high-level appointment at State, then on to the National Security Council. Not *born* bad, shall we say? Left to his own devices, I suspect he'd be all right, but the young wife was a bit of a spendthrift, a rather grasping creature, wasn't she? Expensive tastes for a government employee. Which led to that lamentable business with the offshore accounts, the diversion of funds, all of it."

"It would have been devastating had it come out," Anna

said. "Damaging to foreign relations at a particularly sensitive moment."

"Not to mention the embarrassment to the Administration."

"That wasn't a primary consideration," Anna retorted sharply. "I'm not political that way. If you think otherwise, you don't know me."

"You and your colleagues did precisely the right thing, Ms. Navarro. We admired your work, in fact. Very deft. Very deft."

"Thank you," Anna said. "But if you know so much, you'll know that it was far from my usual turf."

"My point remains. You've done work of genuine sensitivity and displayed the utmost discretion. But of course I know what your daily fare consists of. The IRS man guilty of peculation. The rogue FBI officer. The unpleasantness involving Witness Protection—now, that was quite an interesting little exercise. Your background in homicide forensics was indispensable there. A mob witness is killed, and you single-handedly proved the involvement of the DOJ case officer."

"A lucky break," Anna said stolidly.

"People make their own luck, Ms. Navarro," he said, and his eyes were unsmiling. "We know quite a bit about you, Ms. Navarro. More than you might imagine. We know the account balances on that ATM slip you were writing on. We know who your friends are, and when you last called home. We know you've never padded a travel-and-expense report in your life, which is more than most of us can say." He paused, peering at her closely. "I'm sorry if any of this causes you disquiet, but you realize that you relinquished any civil rights to privacy when you joined the OSI, signed the disclaimers and the memoranda of agreement. No matter. The fact is that your work has invariably been of a very high caliber. And quite often extraordinary."

She raised an eyebrow, but said nothing.

"Ah. You look surprised. I told you, we have our own way of keeping tabs. And we have our own fitness reports,

Ms. Navarro. Of course, what immediately distinguishes you, given our concerns, is your particular combination of skills. You have a background in the standard 'audit' and investigative protocols, but you also have an expertise in homicide. This makes you, may I say, unique. But to the matter at hand. It's only fair to let you know that we've done the most thorough background check on you imaginable. Everything I'm going to tell you—anything I state, assert, conjecture, suggest, or imply—must be regarded as classified at the topmost level. Do we understand each other?"

Anna nodded. "I'm listening."

"Excellent, Ms. Navarro." Bartlett handed her a sheet of paper with a list of names on it, followed by dates of birth and countries of residence.

"I'm not following. Am I supposed to contact these men?"

"Not unless you've got a Ouija board. All eleven of these men are deceased. All passed from this vale of tears within the past two months. Several, you'll see, in the United States, others in Switzerland, in England, Italy, Spain, Sweden, Greece . . . All apparently of natural causes."

Anna glanced at the sheet. Of the eleven, there were two names she recognized—one a member of the Lancaster family, a family that once owned most of the steel mills in the country, but was now better known for its foundation grants and other forms of philanthropy. Philip Lancaster was, in fact, somebody she'd assumed had died long ago. The other, Nico Xenakis, was presumably from the Greek shipping family. To be honest, she knew the name mainly in connection to another scion of the family—a man who had made a tabloid name for himself as a roué back in the sixties, when he'd dated a series of Hollywood starlets. None of the other names rang any bells. Looking at their dates of birth, she saw that all of them were old men—in their late seventies to late eighties.

"Maybe the news hasn't reached the ICU whiz kids,"

she said, "but when you've had your three score and ten . . . well, no one gets out alive."

"In none of these cases is exhumation possible, I'm afraid," Bartlett continued implacably. "Perhaps it's as you say. Old men doing what old men will do. In those instances, we cannot prove otherwise. But in the last few days, we've had a stroke of luck. In a pro forma way, we put a roster of names on the 'sentinel list'—one of those international conventions that nobody seems to take any notice of. The most recent death was of a retiree in Nova Scotia, Canada. Our Canadian friends are sticklers about procedures, and that's how the alarm was sounded in time. In this instance, we have a body to work with. More precisely, *you* do."

"You're leaving something out, of course. What is it that connects these men?"

"To every question, there's a surface answer and a deeper one. I'll give you the surface answer, because it's the only one I have. A few years ago, an internal audit was conducted of the CIA's deep-storage records. Was a tip received? Let's say it was. These were nonoperational files, mind you. They weren't agents or direct contacts. They were, in fact, clearance files. Each was marked 'Sigma,' presumably a reference to a codeword operation—of which there seems to be no trace in the Agency's records. We have no information as to its nature."

"Clearance files?" Anna repeated.

"Meaning that some time long ago each man had been vetted and cleared—for something, we don't know what."

"And the source of origin was a CIA archivist."

He didn't reply directly. "Each file has been authenticated by our top forensic document experts. They're old, these files. They date as far back as the mid-forties, before there even *was* a CIA."

"You're saying they were started by OSS?"

"Exactly," Bartlett said. "The CIA's precursor. Many of the files were opened right around the time the war was ending, the Cold War beginning. The latest ones date from the mid-fifties. But I digress. As I say, we have this curious pattern of deaths. Of course, it would have gone nowhere, a question mark in a field full of question marks, except that we began to see a pattern, cross-checked and correlated with the Sigma files. I don't believe in coincidences, do you, Ms. Navarro? Eleven of the men named in these files have died in a very short interval. The actuarial odds of this happening by chance are . . . remote at best."

Anna nodded impatiently. As far as she could see, the Ghost was seeing ghosts. "How long is this assignment for? I've got a real job, you know."

"This *is* your 'real' job now. You've already been reassigned. We've made the arrangements. You understand your task, then?" His gaze softened. "This doesn't seem to quicken your pulse, Ms. Navarro."

Anna shrugged. "I keep coming back to the fact that these guys are all in the graduating class, if you know what I mean. Old guys tend to pop off, O.K.? These were old guys."

"And in nineteenth-century Paris, getting trampled by a carriage was pretty commonplace," Bartlett said.

Anna furrowed her brow. "Excuse me?"

Bartlett leaned back in his chair. "Have you ever heard of the Frenchman Claude Rochat? No? He's someone I think about quite a bit. A dull, unimaginative, plodding, dogged fellow, who, in the 1860s and 1870s, worked as an accountant in the employ of the *Directoire*, France's own bureau of intelligence. In 1867, it came to his attention that two low-level clerks at the *Directoire*, apparently unacquainted, had both been killed in the course of a fortnight— one the victim of an apparent street robbery, the other trampled to death by a mail coach. It was the sort of thing that happened all the time. Quite unremarkable. But still he wondered, especially after he learned that at the time of death, both of these humble clerks had on their persons costly gold pocket watches—in fact, as he confirmed, the two watches were *identical*, both with a fine cloisonné landscape on the inside of the watchcase. A small oddity, but it arrested his attention, and, to the exasperation of his superiors, he spent the next four years trying to figure out why, and how, this small oddity had come about. In the end, he uncovered a spy ring of extraordinary intricacy: the *Directoire* had been penetrated and manipulated by its Prussian counterparts." He registered her darting glance and smiled: "Yes, those pocket watches in the case are the very ones. Exquisite craftsmanship. I acquired them a couple of decades ago at an auction. I like having them nearby. It helps me to remember."

Bartlett closed his eyes for a contemplative moment. "Of course, by the time Rochat completed his investigations, it was too late," he went on. "Bismarck's agents, through a cunning diet of misinformation, had already tricked France into declaring war. '*À Berlin*' was the great cry. The result was disastrous for France: the military dominance it had enjoyed since the Battle of Rocroi in 1643 was completely destroyed, in just a couple of months. Can you imagine? The French army, with the Emperor at its head, was led straight into an ingenious ambush near Sedan. And that was the end, needless to say, for Napoleon III. The country lost Alsace-Lorraine, it had to pay staggering reparations, and it had to submit to two years of occupation. An extraordinary blow, it was—one that shifted the whole course of European history irreversibly. And just a few years earlier, Claude Rochat was tugging at a little thread, not knowing where it would lead, not knowing whether it would lead anywhere. It was just those two lowly clerks and their matching pocket watches." Bartlett made a sound that wasn't quite a laugh. "Most of the time, something that looks trivial really *is* trivial. *Most* of the time. My job is to worry about such matters. The tiny threads. The boring little discrepancies. The trivial little patterns that just might lead to larger patterns. The most important thing I do is the least glamorous thing imaginable." An arched eyebrow. "I look for matching pocket watches."

Anna was silent for a few moments. The Ghost was living fully up to his reputation: cryptic, hopelessly obscure. "I appreciate the history lesson," she said slowly, "but my frame of reference has always been the here and now. If you really think these deep-storage files have on-going relevance, why not simply have the CIA investigate?"

Bartlett withdrew a crisp silk pocket square from his suit jacket and began to polish his eyeglasses. "Things get rather awkward around here," he said. "The ICU tends to get involved only in cases where there's a real possibility of internal interference or anything else that might preclude a thorough inquiry. Let's leave it at that." There was a hint of condescension in his voice.

"Let's not," Anna said sharply. It wasn't a tone to take with the head of a division, especially one as powerful as the ICU, but subservience wasn't in her skill set, and Bartlett might as well know at the outset whose services he had engaged. "With respect, you're talking about the possibility that someone in, or retired from, the Agency may be behind the deaths."

The director of the Internal Compliance Unit blanched slightly. "I didn't say that."

"You didn't deny it."

Bartlett sighed. "Of the crooked timber of humanity, nothing straight was ever made." A tight smile.

"If you think Central Intelligence might be compromised, why not bring in the FBI?"

Bartlett snorted delicately. "Why not bring in the Associated Press? The Federal Bureau of Investigation has many strengths, but discretion isn't among them. I'm not sure you appreciate the sensitivity of this matter. The fewer people who know about it, the better. That's why I'm not involving a team—just an individual. The right individual, I dearly hope, Agent Navarro."

"Even if these deaths really are murders," she said, "it's highly unlikely you'll ever find the killer, I hope you know that."

"That's the standard bureaucratic response," Bartlett said, "but you don't strike me as a bureaucrat. Mr. Dupree says you're stubborn and 'not exactly a team player.' Well, that's precisely what I wanted."

Anna forged ahead. "You're basically asking me to investigate the CIA. You want me to examine a series of deaths to establish that they are murders, and then—"

"And then to amass any evidence that would allow us to conduct an audit." Bartlett's gray eyes shone through his plastic-rimmed glasses. "No matter who's implicated. Is that clear?"

"As mud," Anna said. A seasoned investigator, she was used to conducting interviews with witnesses and suspects alike. Sometimes you simply needed to listen. Sometimes, however, you needed to goad, to provoke a response. Art and experience came in knowing when. Bartlett's story was perforated with elisions and omissions. She appreciated the need-to-know reflexes of a wily old bureaucrat, but in her experience, it helped to know more than you strictly needed to. "I'm not going to play blindman's bluff," she said.

Bartlett blinked. "I beg your pardon?"

"You must have copies of these Sigma files. You must have scrutinized them closely. And yet you claim you have no idea what Sigma was about."

"Where are you going with this?" His voice was cool.

"Will you show me these files?"

A rictuslike smile: "No. No, that won't be possible."

"Why not?"

Bartlett put his glasses on again. "I'm not under investigation here. As much as I admire your tactics of interrogation. Anyway, I believe I've been clear on the relevant points."

"No, dammit, that's not good enough! You're fully acquainted with these files. If you don't know what they add up to, then at least you've got to have your suspicions. An educated hypothesis. Anything at all. Save your poker face for your Tuesday-night card game. I'm not playing."

Bartlett finally erupted. "For Christ's sake, you've seen enough to know that we're talking about the reputation of some of the major figures of the postwar era. These are *clearance* files. By themselves, they prove nothing. I had you vetted before our conversation—did that implicate you in my affairs? I trust your discretion. Of course I do. But we're talking about prominent individuals as well as obscure ones. You can't simply go stomping around in your sensible shoes."

Anna listened carefully, listened to the undertone of tension in his voice. "You talk about reputations, yet that's not what you're really concerned about, is it?" she pressed. "I need more to go on!"

He shook his head. "It's like trying to fashion a rope ladder out of gossamer. Nothing that we've ever been able to pin down. Half a century ago, something was hatched. *Something*. Something that involved vital interests. The Sigma list encompasses a curious collection of individuals—some were industrialists, we know, and there are others whose identity we haven't been able to figure out at all. What they have in common is that a founder of the CIA, someone with enormous power in the forties and fifties, took a direct interest in them. Was he enlisting them? *Targeting* them? We're *all* playing blindman's bluff. But it would seem that an undertaking of enormous secrecy was launched. You asked what connects these men. In a real sense, we simply don't know." He adjusted his cuffs, the nervous tic of a fastidious man. "You might say we're at the pocket-watch stage."

"No offense, but the Sigma list—that goes back half a *century!*"

"Ever been to the Somme, in France?" Bartlett asked abruptly, his eyes a little too bright. "You ought to go—just to look at the poppies growing among the wheat. Every once in a while, a farmer in the Somme cuts down an oak tree, sits down on the trunk, and then sickens and dies. Do you know why? Because during the First World War, a battle had taken place on that field, a canister of mustard gas deployed. The poison gets absorbed by the tree as a sapling, and decades later it's still potent enough to kill a man."

"And that's Sigma, do you think?"

Bartlett's gaze grew in intensity. "They say the more you know, the more you know you don't know. I find the more you know, the more unsettling it is to come across things you don't know about. Call it vanity, or call it caution. I worry about what becomes of unseen little saplings." A wan smile. "The crooked timber of humanity—it always comes down to the crooked timber. Yes, I appreciate that all this sounds like ancient history to you, and perhaps it is, Agent Navarro. You'll come back and set me straight."

"I wonder," she said.

"Now, you'll be making contact with various law-enforcement officials, and as far as anyone knows, you'll be conducting a completely open homicide investigation. Why the involvement of an OSI agent? Your explanation will be terse: because these names have cropped up in the course of an ongoing investigation into the fraudulent transfer of funds, the details of which nobody will press you to disclose. A simple cover, nothing elaborate required."

"I'll pursue the sort of investigation I've been trained to do," Anna said warily. "That's all I can promise."

"That's all I'm asking for," Bartlett replied smoothly. "Your skepticism may be well founded. But one way or the other, I'd like to be sure. Go to Nova Scotia. Assure me that Robert Mailhot really did die of natural causes. Or—confirm that he *didn't*."

CHAPTER FOUR

Ben was driven to the headquarters of the *Kantonspolizei*, the police of the canton of Zurich, a grimy yet elegant old stone building on Zeughausstrasse. He was led in through an underground parking garage by two silent young policemen and up several long flights of stairs into a relatively modern building that adjoined the older one. The interior looked like it belonged in a suburban American high school, circa 1975. To any of his questions, his two escorts answered only with shrugs.

His thoughts raced. It was no accident that Cavanaugh was there on Bahnhofstrasse. Cavanaugh had been in Zurich with the deliberate intent to murder him. Somehow the body had disappeared, had been removed swiftly and expertly, and the gun planted in his bag. It was clear that others were involved with Cavanaugh, professionals. But who—and, again, *why?*

Ben was taken first to a small fluorescent-lit room and seated in front of a stainless-steel table. As his police escorts remained standing, a man in a short white coat emerged and, without making eye contact, said, "*Ihre*

Hände, bitte." Ben extended his hands. It was pointless to argue, he knew. The technician pumped a mist from a plastic spray bottle on both sides of his hands, then rubbed a cotton-tipped plastic swab lightly but thoroughly over the back of his right hand. Then he placed the swab in a plastic tube. He repeated the exercise for the palm, and then did the same with Ben's other hand. Four swabs now reposed in four carefully labeled plastic tubes, and the technician took them with him as he left the room.

A few minutes later, Ben arrived at a pleasant, sparely furnished office on the third floor, where a broad-shouldered, stocky man in plainclothes introduced himself as Thomas Schmid, a homicide detective. He had a wide, pockmarked face and a very short haircut with short bangs. For some reason Ben remembered a Swiss woman he'd once met at Gstaad telling him that cops in Switzerland were called *bullen*, "bulls," and this man demonstrated why.

Schmid began asking Ben a series of questions—name, date of birth, passport number, hotel in Zurich, and so on. He sat at a computer terminal, typing out the answers with one finger. A pair of reading glasses hung from his neck.

Ben was angry, tired, and frustrated, his patience worn thin. It took great effort to keep his tone light. "Detective," he said, "am I under arrest or not?"

"No, sir."

"Well, this has been fun and all, but if you're not going to arrest me, I'd like to head on back to my hotel."

"We would be happy to arrest you if you'd like," the detective replied blandly, the barest glint of menace in his smile. "We have a very nice cell waiting for you. But if we can keep this friendly, it will all be much simpler."

"Aren't I allowed to make a phone call?"

Schmid extended both hands, palms up, at the beige phone at the edge of his crowded desk. "You may call the American consulate here, or your attorney. As you wish."

"Thank you," Ben said, picking up the phone and glancing at his watch. It was early afternoon in New York. Hart-

man Capital Management's in-house attorneys all practiced
tax or securities law, so he decided to call a friend who
practiced international law.

Howie Rubin and he had been on the Deerfield ski racing team together and had become close friends. Howie had
come to Bedford several times for Thanksgiving and, like
all of Ben's friends, had particularly taken to Ben's mother.

The attorney was at lunch, but Ben's call was patched
through to Howie's cell phone. Restaurant noise in the
background made Howie's end of the conversation hard to
make out.

"*Christ*, Ben," Howie said, interrupting Ben's summary.
Someone next to him was talking loudly. "All right, I'll tell
you what I tell all my clients who get arrested while on ski
vacations in Switzerland. Grin and bear it. Don't get all
high and mighty. Don't play the indignant American. No
one can grind you down with rules and regulations and
everything-by-the-book like the Swiss."

Ben glanced at Schmid, who was tapping at his keyboard
and no doubt listening. "I'm beginning to see that. So what
am I supposed to do?"

"The way it works in Switzerland, they can hold you for
up to twenty-four hours without actually arresting you."

"You're kidding me."

"And if you piss them off, they can throw you in a dirty
little holding cell overnight. So don't."

"Then what do you recommend?"

"Hartman, you can charm a dog off a meat truck, buddy
boy, so just be your usual self. Any problems, call me and
I'll get on the phone and threaten an international incident.
One of my partners does a lot of corporate espionage work,
point being we've got access to some pretty high-powered
databases. I'll pull Cavanaugh's records, see what we can
find. Give me the phone number where you are right now."

When Ben had hung up, Schmid led him into an adjoining room and sat him at a desk near another terminal. "Have
you been to Switzerland before?" Schmid asked pleasantly,
as if he were a tour guide.

"A number of times," Ben said. "Mostly to ski."

Schmid nodded distractedly. "A popular recreation. Very good for relieving stress, I think. Very good for letting off tension." His gaze narrowed. "You must have a lot of stress from your work."

"I wouldn't say that."

"Stress can make people do remarkable things. Day after day they bottle it up, and then, one day, *boom!* They explode. When this happens, they surprise themselves, I think, as much as other people."

"As I told you, the gun was planted. I never used it." Ben was livid, but he spoke as coolly as he could. It would do no good to provoke the detective.

"And yet by your own account, you killed a man, bludgeoned him with your bare hands. Is this something you do in your normal line of work?"

"These were hardly normal circumstances."

"If I were to talk to your friends, Mr. Hartman, what would they tell me about you? Would they say you had a temper?" He gave Ben an oddly contemplative look. "Would they say you were . . . a violent man?"

"They'd tell you I'm as law abiding as they come," Ben said. "Where are you going with these questions?" Ben looked down at his own hands, hands that had slammed a lamp fixture against Cavanaugh's skull. *Was* he violent? The detective's imputations were preposterous—he'd acted purely in self-defense—and yet his mind drifted back a few years.

He could see Darnell's face even now. One of his fifth-graders at East New York, Darnell had been a good kid, an A student, bright and curious, the best in his class. Then something happened to him. His grades dropped, and before long he stopped handing in homework altogether. Darnell never got in fights with the other kids, and yet from time to time welts would be visible on his face. Ben talked to him after class one day. Darnell couldn't look him in the eye. His expression was cloudy with fear. Finally he told him that Orlando, his mother's new boyfriend, didn't want him to waste time on schoolwork; he needed him to help bring in money. "Bring in money how?" Ben had asked, but Darnell wouldn't answer. When he telephoned Darnell's mother, Joyce Stuart, her responses were skittish, evasive. She wouldn't come into the school, refused to discuss the situation, refused to admit anything might be wrong. She, too, sounded scared. A few days later, he found Darnell's address from student records and paid a visit.

Darnell lived on the second floor of a building with a ruined facade, a stairwell festooned with graffiti. The buzzer was broken, but the apartment door was unlocked, and so he traipsed up the stairs and knocked on 2B. After a long wait, Darnell's mother appeared, visibly battered— her cheeks bruised, her lips swollen. He introduced himself and asked to come in. Joyce paused, then led him toward the small kitchen, with its deeply gouged countertops of beige Formica and yellow cotton drapes flapping in the breeze.

Ben heard yelling in the background before the mother's boyfriend strode over. "Who the fuck are you?" demanded Orlando, a tall, powerfully built man in a red tank top and loose jeans. Ben recognized a convict's physique: an upper body so overdeveloped that the muscles looked draped over his chest and shoulders like a lifejacket.

"He's Darnell's schoolteacher," Darnell's mother said, the words cottony from her bruised lips.

"And you—are you Darnell's guardian?" Ben asked Orlando.

"Hell, you could say I'm his teacher now. Only, I'm teaching him shit he needs to know. Unlike you."

Now Ben saw Darnell, fear making him look even younger than his ten years, padding into the kitchen to join them. "Go away, Darnell," his mother said in a half-whisper.

"Darnell don't need you filling his head with bullshit. Darnell needs to learn how to move rocks." Orlando smiled, revealing a gleaming gold front.

Ben felt a jolt. *Moving rocks:* selling crack. "He's a fifth-grader. He's ten years old."

"That's right. A juvenile. Cops know he ain't worth arresting." He laughed. "I gave him the choice, though: he could either peddle rocks or peddle his ass."

The words, the man's casual brutality, sickened Ben, but he forced himself to speak calmly. "Darnell has more potential than anyone in his class. You have a duty to let him excel."

Orlando snorted. "He can make his living on the street, same as me."

Then he heard Darnell's treble voice, shaky but resolute. "I don't want to do it anymore," he told Orlando. "Mr. Hartman knows what's right." Then, louder, bravely: "I don't want to be like you."

Joyce Stuart's features froze in a preemptive cringe: "Don't, Darnell."

It was too late. Orlando lashed out, cracking the ten-year-old in the jaw, the blow propelling him out of the room. He turned to Ben: "Now get your ass out of here. In fact, let me help you."

Ben felt himself stiffen as rage coursed through his body. Orlando slammed his open hand against Ben's chest, but instead of staggering backward, Ben lunged toward him, pounding a fist into the man's temple, then another, pummeling his head like a speedbag. Stunned, Orlando froze for a crucial few moments, and then his powerful arms banged uselessly against Ben's sides—Ben was too close for him to land a punch. And the frenzy of rage was an anaesthetic, anyway: Ben didn't even feel the body blows until Orlando slid limply to the floor. He was down, not out.

Orlando's eyes flicked at him, the leering defiance replaced by fear. "You crazy," he murmured.

Was he? What had come over him? "If you ever touch Darnell again," Ben said, with a deliberate calm he did not feel, "I will kill you." He paused between each word for emphasis. "Do we understand each other?"

Later, from his friend Carmen in social services, he'd find out that Orlando left Joyce and Darnell later that day, never to return. If Ben hadn't been told, though, he soon would have guessed from the dramatic improvement in Darnell's grades and general demeanor.

"All right, man," Orlando had said at the time, in a subdued tone, gazing up at him from the kitchen floor. "See, we just had a misunderstanding." He coughed. "I ain't looking for more trouble." He coughed again and murmured, "You crazy. You crazy."

"Mr. Hartman, can you please put your right thumb here?" Schmid indicated a small white oblong marked IDENTIX TOUCHVIEW, on top of which a small oval glass panel glowed ruby red.

Ben placed his right thumb on the glass oval, then did the same with his left. His prints appeared immediately, much enlarged, on a computer monitor angled partly toward him.

Schmid tapped in a few numbers and hit the return key, setting off the high-pitched screech of a modem. He turned toward Ben and said apologetically, "This goes right to Bern. We will know in five or ten minutes."

"Know what?"

The detective rose and gestured for Ben to follow him back to the first room. "Whether there is already a warrant for your arrest in Switzerland."

"I think I might remember if there was one."

Schmid stared at him a long time before he started to speak. "I know your type, Mr. Hartman. For rich Americans like you, Switzerland is a country of chocolates, banks, cuckoo clocks, and ski resorts. You'd like to imagine that each of us is your *Hausdiener*, your manservant, yes? But you do know Switzerland. For centuries, every European power wished to make us its duchy. None ever succeeded. Now maybe your country, with its power and wealth, thinks it can do the same. But you are not—what is your expression—'calling the shots' here. There is no chocolate for you in this office. And it is not up to you to decide when, or whether, you are released." He leaned back in his chair, smiling gravely. "Welcome to Switzerland, Herr Hartman."

Another man, tall and thin, in a heavily starched white lab coat, came into the room as if on cue. He wore rimless glasses and had a small bristle mustache. Without introducing himself, he pointed to a white-tiled section of the wall marked with metric gradations. "You will please to stand there," he ordered.

Trying not to show his exasperation, Ben stood with his back flat against the tiles. The technician measured his height, then led him to a white lab sink, where he turned a lever that extruded a white paste and instructed Ben to wash his hands. The soap was creamy yet gritty and smelled of lavender. At another station, the tech rolled sticky black ink onto a glass plate and had Ben place each hand flat onto it. With long, delicate, manicured fingers, he rolled each of Ben's fingers first on blotter paper, then carefully onto separate squares on a form.

While the technician worked, Schmid got up and went into the adjoining room, then returned a few moments later. "Well, Mr. Hartman, we did not get a hit. There is no warrant outstanding."

"What a surprise," Ben muttered. He felt oddly relieved.

"Still, there are questions. The ballistics will come back in a few days from the *Wissenschaftlicher Dienst der Stadtpolizei Zürich*—the ballistics lab—but we already know that the bullets recovered from the platform are .765 Browning."

"Is that a kind of bullet?" Ben asked innocently.

"It is the sort of ammunition used in the gun that was found during the search of your luggage."

"Well, what do you know," Ben said, forcing a smile, then tried another tack: bluntness. "Look, there's no question the bullets were fired by the gun in question. Which was planted in my luggage. So why don't you just do whatever that test is on my hands that tells you whether I fired a gun?"

"The gunshot residue analysis. We've already done it."
Schmid mimed a swabbing motion.

"And the results?"

"We'll have them soon. After you are photographed."

"You won't find my fingerprints on the gun either."
Thank God I didn't handle it, Ben thought.

The detective shrugged theatrically. "Fingerprints can be
removed."

"Well, the witnesses—"

"The eyewitnesses describe a well-dressed man of about
your age. There was much confusion. But five people are
dead, seven seriously injured. Again, you tell us you killed
the perpetrator. Yet when we look there is no body."

"I—I can't explain that," Ben admitted, aware of how
bizarre his account sounded. "Obviously the body was removed and the area cleaned. That just tells me that Cavanaugh was working with others."

"To kill you." Schmid regarded him with dark amusement.

"So it appears."

"But you offer no motive. You say there was no grudge
between the two of you."

"You don't seem to understand," Ben said quietly. "I
hadn't seen the guy in fifteen years."

The phone on Schmid's desk rang. He picked it up.
"Schmid." He listened. In English, he said, "Yes, one minute, please," and handed the receiver to Ben.

It was Howie. "Ben, old buddy," he said, his voice now
as clear as if he were calling from the next room. "You did
say Jimmy Cavanaugh was from Homer, New York, right?"

"Small town midway between Syracuse and Bingham-
ton," Ben said.

"Right," Howie said. "And he was in your class at
Princeton?"

"That's the guy."

"Well, here's the thing. Your Jimmy Cavanaugh doesn't
exist."

"Tell me something I don't know," Ben said. *He's dead as a doornail.*

"No, Ben, listen to me. I'm saying your Jimmy Cavanaugh *never existed*. I'm saying there *is* no Jimmy Cavanaugh. I checked with alumni records at Princeton. No Cavanaugh, first or middle initial J, ever enrolled in the school, at least not in the decade you attended. And there have never been any Cavanaughs in Homer. Not anywhere in that county. Not at Georgetown, either. Oh, and we checked with all sorts of hifalutin databases, too. If there were a James Cavanaugh that came close to matching your description, we'd have found him. Tried every spelling variant, too. You have no idea how powerful the databases are they've got these days. A person leaves tracks like a slug, we all do. Credit, Social Security, military, you name it. This guy's totally off the grid. Weird, huh?"

"There's got to be some mistake. I *know* he was enrolled at Princeton."

"You *think* you know that. Doesn't seem possible, does it?"

Ben felt sick to his stomach. "If this is true, it doesn't help us."

"No," Howie agreed. "But I'll keep trying. Meantime, you got my cellular, right?"

Ben replaced the receiver, stunned. Schmid continued: "Mr. Hartman, were you here on business or holiday?"

He forced himself to focus, and spoke as civilly as he could. "Ski vacation, as I said. I had a couple of bank meetings, but only because I was passing through Zurich." *Jimmy Cavanaugh never existed.*

Schmid clasped his hands. "The last time you were in Switzerland was four years ago, yes? To claim the body of your brother?"

Ben paused a moment, unable to stop the sudden flood of memories. *The phone call in the middle of the night: never good news. He'd been asleep next to Karen, a fellow teacher, in his grubby apartment in East New York. He grumbled, rolled over to answer the call that changed everything.*

A small rented plane Peter was flying solo had crashed a few days earlier in a gorge near Lake Lucerne. Ben's name was listed on the rental papers as next-of-kin. It had taken time to identify the deceased, but dental records made a definitive identification possible. The Swiss authorities were ruling it an accident. Ben flew to Lake Lucerne to claim the body and brought his brother home—what was left of him after the fuselage had exploded—in a little cardboard carton not much bigger than a cake box.

The entire plane flight home he didn't cry. That would only come later, when the numbness began to wear off. His father had collapsed, weeping, upon hearing the news; his mother, already confined to bed because of the cancer, had screamed with all of her strength.

"Yes," Ben said quietly. "That was the last time I was here."

"A striking fact. When you come to our country, death seems to accompany you."

"What are you getting at?"

"Mr. Hartman," Schmid said, in a more neutral tone of voice, "do you think there is any connection between your brother's death and what happened today?"

At the headquarters of the Swiss national police, the *Stadtpolizei*, in Bern, a plump middle-aged woman with heavy black horn-rimmed glasses glanced up at her computer screen and was surprised to see a line of text begin to flash. After staring at it for a few seconds, she remembered what she had long ago been instructed to do, and she jotted down the name and the long series of numbers after the name. Then she knocked at the glass-paned door of her immediate supervisor.

"Sir," she said. "A name on the RIPOL watch list was just activated." RIPOL was an acronym for *Recherche Informations Policier*, the national criminal and police database that contained names, fingerprints, license plate numbers—a vast range of law-enforcement data used by the federal, canton, and local police.

Her boss, a priggish man in his mid-forties who was known to be on the fast track at the *Stadtpolizei*, took the slip of paper, thanked his loyal secretary, and dismissed her. Once she had closed his office door, he picked up a secure phone that was not routed through the main switchboard, and dialed a number he rarely ever called.

A battered old gray sedan of indeterminate make idled down the block from *Kantonspolizei* headquarters on Zeughausstrasse. Inside, two men smoked and said nothing, weary from the long wait. The sudden ringing of the cellular phone mounted on the center console startled them. The passenger picked it up, listened, said, "*Ja, danke*," and hung up.

"The American is leaving the building," he said.

A few minutes later they saw the American emerge from the side entrance and get into a taxi. When it was halfway down the block, the driver pulled the car into the early-evening traffic.

CHAPTER FIVE

Halifax, Nova Scotia

When the Air Canada pilot announced they were about to land, Anna Navarro removed her files from the tray table, lifted it closed, and tried to focus her mind on the case ahead of her. Flying terrified her, and the only thing worse than landing was taking off. Her stomach flip-flopped. As usual she fought an irrational conviction that the plane would crash and she would end her life in a fiery inferno.

Her favorite uncle, Manuel, had been killed when the clattering old cropduster he worked in dropped an engine and plummeted. But that was so long ago, she'd been ten or eleven, and a deathtrap cropduster had no resemblance to the sleek 747 she was in now.

She'd never told any of her OSI colleagues about her anxiety, on the general principle that you should never let them see your vulnerabilities. But she was convinced that somehow Arliss Dupree knew, the way a dog smells fear. In the last six months he'd forced her to practically live on planes, flying from one lousy assignment to another.

The only thing that allowed her to keep her composure was to spend the flight immersed in her case files. They always absorbed her, fascinated her. The dry-as-dust au-topsy and pathology reports beckoned to her to solve their mysteries.

As a child she'd loved doing the intricate five-hundred-piece puzzles her mother brought home, the gifts from a woman whose house her mother cleaned and whose kids had no patience for puzzles. Far more than seeing the glossy image emerge, she loved the sound and feel of the puzzle pieces snapping into place. Often the old puzzles were missing pieces, lost by their careless original owners, and that had always irritated her. Even as a kid she'd been a perfectionist.

On some level, this case was a thousand-piece puzzle spilled on the carpet before her.

During this Washington-Halifax flight she had pored over a folder of documents faxed from the RCMP in Ot-tawa. The Royal Canadian Mounted Police, Canada's equivalent of the FBI, was, despite its archaic name, a top-notch investigative agency. The working relationship be-tween DOJ and RCMP was good.

Who are you? she wondered, staring at a photograph of the old man. Robert Mailhot of Halifax, Nova Scotia, the kindly retiree, devout member of the Church of Our Lady of Mercy. Not the sort of person you'd expect to have a CIA clearance file, deep-storage or no.

What could have connected him to the vaporous mach-inations of long-dead spymasters and businessmen that Bartlett had stumbled on? She was certain that Bartlett had a file on him, but had chosen not to give her access to it. She was certain, too, that he wanted her to find out the relevant details for herself.

A provincial judge in Nova Scotia agreed to issue a search warrant. The documents she wanted—telephone and credit-card records—had been faxed to her in D.C. in a matter of hours. She was OSI; nobody thought to question her vague cover story about an ongoing investigation into fraudulent international transfer of funds.

Still, the file told her nothing. The cause of death, recorded on the certificate in the crabbed and almost illegible handwriting of a physician, presumably the old man's doctor, was "natural causes," with "coronary thrombosis" added in brackets. And maybe it was only that.

The deceased had made no unusual purchases; his only long-distance calls were to Newfoundland and Toronto. So far, no traction. Maybe she'd find the answer in Halifax.

Or maybe not.

She was intoxicated by the same strange brew of hope and despair she always felt at the beginning of a case. One minute she knew for sure she'd crack it, the next it seemed impossible. This much she knew for sure: the first homicide in a series she investigated was always the most important. It was the benchmark. Only if you were thorough, if you turned over every rock, did you have any hope of making connections. You'd never connect the dots unless you saw where all the dots were.

Anna was wearing her travel suit, a navy-blue Donna Karan (though the cheaper line), and a white Ralph Lauren blouse (not couture, of course). She was known around the office for dressing impeccably. On her salary she could scarcely afford designer labels, but she bought them anyway, living in a dark one-bedroom apartment in a lousy part of Washington, taking no vacations, because all her money went to clothes.

Everyone assumed she dressed so nicely to make herself attractive to men, because that was what young single women did. They were wrong. Her clothes were body armor. The finer the outfits, the safer and more secure she felt. She used designer cosmetics and wore designer clothes because then she was no longer the daughter of the dirt-poor Mexican immigrants who cleaned the houses and tended the yards of rich people. Then she could be anyone. She was self-aware enough to know how ridiculous this was in rational terms. But she did it anyway.

She wondered what it was about her that rankled Arliss Dupree more—that she was an attractive woman who'd turned him down, or that she was a Mexican. Maybe both.

Maybe in the world according to Dupree, a Mexican-American was inferior and therefore had no right to reject him.

She had grown up in a small town in Southern California. Both her parents were Mexicans who'd escaped the desolation, the disease, the hopelessness south of the border. Her mother, soft-spoken and gentle, cleaned houses; her father, quiet and introverted, did yardwork.

When she was in grade school she wore dresses sewn by her mother, who also braided her brown hair and put it up. She was aware that she dressed differently, that she didn't quite fit in, but it didn't bother her until she was ten or eleven, when the girls started forming iron cliques that excluded her. They'd never associate with the daughter of the woman who cleaned their houses.

She was uncool, an outsider, an embarrassment. She was invisible.

Not that she was in a minority—the high school was half-Latino, half-white, the lines rarely crossed. She got used to being called "wetback" and "spic" by some of the white girls and guys. But among the Latinos there were castes, too, and she was at the bottom. The Latino girls always dressed well, and they mocked her clothes even more viciously than the white girls did.

The solution, she decided, was to dress like all the other girls. She began to complain to her mother, who didn't take her seriously at first, then explained that they couldn't afford to buy the kind of clothes the other girls had, and anyway, what was the difference, really? Didn't she like her mother's homemade clothes? Anna would snap, "No! I hate them!" knowing full well how much the words hurt. Even today, twenty years later, Anna could barely think about those days without feeling guilt.

Her mother was beloved by all her employers. One of them, a genuinely rich woman, began donating all of her children's castoffs. Anna wore them happily—she couldn't imagine why anyone would throw away such fine clothes!—until she gradually came to realize that her clothes were all last year's fashions, and then her ardor cooled. One day she was walking down the hall at school and one of the girls in a clique she very much wanted to join called her over. "Hey," the girl said, "that's my skirt!" Blushing, Anna denied it. The girl stuck a probing finger under the hem and turned it over to reveal her initials inked on the tag.

The RCMP officer who picked her up at the airport, Anna knew, had spent a year at the FBI Academy learning homicide investigation techniques. He was not the sharpest knife in the drawer, she'd heard, but a good sort.

He stood outside the security gate, a tall, handsome thirtyish man in a blue blazer and red tie. He flashed a pearly smile, seemingly genuinely happy to see her. "Welcome to Nova Scotia," he said. "I'm Ron Arsenault." Dark-haired, brown-eyed, lantern jaw, high forehead. Dudley Do-Right, she thought to herself.

"Anna Navarro," she said, shaking his hand firmly. Men always expect women to shake like a dead fish, so she always gave them her firmest handshake; it set the tone, let them know she was one of the guys. "Nice to meet you."

He reached out for her carry-on garment bag, but she shook her head, smiled. "I'm O.K., thanks."

"This your first time in Halifax?" He was obviously checking her out.

"Yeah. It looks beautiful from above."

He chuckled politely as he guided her through the terminal. "I'll be liaising with the Halifax locals for you. You got the records O.K.?"

"Thanks. Everything but the bank records."

"Those should be in by now. If I find them I'll drop them by your hotel."

"Thanks."

"Sure thing." He squinted at something: contact lenses, Anna knew. "Tell you the truth, Miss Navarro—Anna?— some folks back in Ottawa can't quite figure why you're taking such an interest in the old geezer. Eighty-seven-year-old man dies in his home, natural causes, you gotta expect that, you know?"

They had reached the parking lot.

"The body's in the police morgue?" she asked.

"Actually, in the morgue of the local hospital. Waiting in the fridge for you. You got to us before the old guy was planted, that's the good news."

"And the bad news?"

"Body had already been embalmed for burial."

She winced. "That might screw up the tox screen."

They got to a dark blue, late-model Chevrolet sedan that screamed "unmarked police vehicle." He opened the trunk and put her bag in.

They drove for a while in silence.

"Who's the widow?" she asked. It wasn't in the file. "French-Canadian, too?"

"A local. Haligonian. Former schoolteacher. Tough old biddy, too. I mean, I feel bad for the lady, she's just lost her husband, and the funeral was supposed to be tomorrow. We had to ask her to put it off. She had relatives coming in from Newfoundland, too. When we mentioned autopsy she wigged out." He glanced over at her, then back to the road. "Given how it's evening, I thought you could settle in, and we can get started bright and early tomorrow morning. ME's going to meet us at seven."

She felt a pang of disappointment. She wanted to go right to work. "Sounds good," she said.

More silence. It was good to have a liaison officer who didn't seem to resent an emissary from the U.S. government. Arsenault was as friendly as could be. Maybe too much so.

"Here's your inn. Your government doesn't exactly spend the big bucks, hey?"

It was an unlovely Victorian house on Barrington Street, a large wooden building painted white with green shutters. The white paint had been soiled to a dirty gray.

"Hey, so let me take you out to dinner, unless you've got other plans. Maybe Clipper Cay, if you like seafood.

Maybe catch some jazz at the Middle Deck . . . ?" He parked the car.

"Thanks, but I've had a long day," she said.

He shrugged, his disappointment obvious.

The inn had a faintly musty smell, as from a baseboard dampness that never quite went away. An old-fashioned carbon was made of her credit card and a brass key provided; she was prepared to tell the beefy guy at the front desk that she didn't need help with her bags, but none was volunteered. The same slight mustiness pervaded her room, on the second floor, which was decorated in floral patterns. Everything in it looked worn, but not objectionably so. She hung her clothes in the closet, drew the curtains, and changed into gray sweats. A nice run would do her good, she decided.

She jogged along the Grand Parade, the square on the west side of Barrington Street, then up George Street to the star-shaped fortress called The Citadel. She stopped, panting, at a newsstand and picked up a map of the city. She found the address; it wasn't far at all from where she was staying. She could reach it in her run.

Robert Mailhot's house was unremarkable but comfortable-looking, a two-story gray clapboard with a gabled roof, practically hidden in a wooded patch of land behind a chain-link fence.

The blue light of a television flickered behind lace curtains in a front room. The widow, presumably, was watching TV. Anna stopped for a moment across the street, watching intently.

She decided to cross the narrow street to take a closer look. She wanted to see if it was indeed the widow, and if so, how she was behaving. Did she appear to be in mourning or not? Such things couldn't always be intuited simply by observing at a distance, but you never knew what you might pick up. And if Anna positioned herself in the shadows outside the house, she might not be seen by suspicious neighbors.

The street was deserted, though music played from one house, a TV from another, and a foghorn sounded in the distance. She crossed toward the house—

Suddenly, a pair of high-intensity headlights appeared out of nowhere. They blinded her, growing larger and brighter as a vehicle roared toward her. With a scream, Anna lunged toward the curb, unseeing, desperately trying to jump out of the way of the insane, out-of-control car. It must have been gliding down the street, lights off, its quiet engine noise masked by the ambient street noise, until it was but a few feet away, then suddenly switched on its lights.

And now it was barreling toward her! There was no mistaking it, the car wasn't slowing, wasn't moving straight down the road like an automobile simply going far too fast. It veered toward the shoulder of the road, toward the curb, heading right at her. Anna recognized the vertical chrome grill of a Lincoln Town Car, its flattened rectangular headlights somehow giving it a predatory, sharklike appearance.

Move!

The car's wheels squealed, the engine at full throttle, as the maniacal car bore down on her.

She turned around to see it hurtling at her just ten or twenty feet away, the headlights dazzling. Terrified, screaming, a split-second away from death, she leaped into the boxwood hedge that surrounded the house next to the widow's, the stiff, prickly branches scraping at her sweatpants-covered legs, and rolled over and over on the small lawn.

She heard the crunch of the car hitting the boxwood, then the loud squeal of tires as she looked up to see the car veer away from her, spraying mud everywhere, the powerful engine racing down the narrow dark road, and then the headlights vanished just as abruptly as they had appeared.

The car was gone.

What had just happened?

She jumped to her feet, her heart thudding, adrenaline flooding throughout her body, the terror weakening her knees so that she could barely stand up.

What the hell was that all about?

The car had headed right for her, quite deliberately targeting her, as if trying to run her down.

And then . . . it had unaccountably disappeared!

She noticed several faces looking through windows on either side of the street, some of them closing drapes as soon as she noticed them.

If the car had for some reason been aiming for her, trying to kill her, why hadn't it finished the job?

It was entirely illogical, maddeningly so.

She walked, panting deeply, coughing painfully, drenched with sweat. She tried to clear her head, but the fear would not leave her, and she remained unable to make sense of the bizarre incident.

Had someone just tried to kill her, or not?

And if so—why?

Could it have been a drunk, a joyrider? The car's motions had seemed far too deliberate, too elaborately choreographed for that.

The only logical answers required a paranoid mind-set, and she adamantly refused to allow her thoughts to go in that direction. *That way madness lies.* She thought of Bartlett's ominous words about decades-old plans hatched in utmost secrecy, old men with secrets to hide, powerful people desperate to protect reputations. But Bartlett was a man who, by his own admission, sat in an office surrounded by yellowed paper, far removed from reality, a setting all too conducive to the weaving of conspiracy theories.

Still, was it not possible that the incident with the car had been an attempt to frighten her off the case?

If so, they had picked the wrong person to try such a technique on. For it served only to stiffen her determination to find out what the real story was.

London

The pub, called the Albion, was located on Garrick Street, at the edge of Covent Garden. It had low ceilings, rough-hewn wooden tables, and sawdust floors, the sort of place that had twenty real ales on tap and served bangers and mash, kidney pudding, and spotted dick, and was jammed at lunchtime with a stylish crowd of bankers and advertising executives.

Jean-Luc Passard, a junior security officer for the Corporation, entered the pub and saw at once why the Englishman had chosen this place to meet. It was so dense with people that the two of them would certainly go unnoticed.

The Englishman was sitting alone in a booth. He was as described: a nondescript man of about forty, with bristly, prematurely gray hair. On closer inspection, his face was smooth, almost tight, as if from surgery. He wore a blue blazer and white turtleneck. His shoulders were broad, his waist narrow; he looked, even at a distance, physically imposing. Yet you would not pick him out in a lineup.

Passard sat down at the booth, put out his hand. "I'm Jean-Luc."

"Trevor Griffiths," the Englishman said. He shook hands with barely any pressure at all, the greeting of a man who did not care what you thought of him. His hand was large, smooth, and dry.

"It's an honor to meet you," Passard said. "Your services to the Corporation over the years are the stuff of legend."

Trevor's dead gray eyes showed nothing.

"We wouldn't have brought you out of your . . . retirement if it weren't absolutely necessary."

"You screwed up."

"We had bad luck."

"You want a backup."

"An insurance policy, so to say. An added safeguard. We really can't afford to fail."

"I work alone. You know this."

"Of course. Your record puts your methods beyond

second-guessing. You will handle the matter as you see best."

"Good. Now, do we know the target's whereabouts?"

"He was last spotted in Zurich. We're not certain where he's headed next."

Trevor cocked an eyebrow.

Passard flushed. "He is an amateur. He surfaces periodically. We will pick up his trail again soon."

"I will require a good set of photographs of the target from as many angles as you have."

Passard slid a large manila envelope across the table. "Done. Also, here are the encoded instructions. As you'll understand, we want the job to be done quickly and untraceably."

Trevor Griffiths's stare reminded Passard of a boa constrictor. "You have already brought in several second-raters. Not only have you thereby lost both money and time, but you have alerted the target. He is now fearful, cautious, and no doubt has been frightened into depositing documents with attorneys to be mailed in the event of his demise, that sort of thing. He will therefore be considerably more difficult to take out. Neither you nor your superiors need to advise me on how to do my job."

"But you're confident you can do it, yes?"

"I assume that was why you came to me?"

"Yes."

"Then please don't ask foolish questions. Are we done here? Because I have a busy afternoon ahead of me."

Anna returned to her room at the inn, poured a tiny screw-top bottle of white wine from the minibar into a plastic cup, downed it, and then ran a bath, making the water as hot as she could stand. For fifteen minutes, she soaked herself, trying to think calming thoughts, but the image of the Town Car's vertical chrome grill kept intruding on her consciousness. And she remembered the Ghost's soft-spoken remark: *"I don't believe in coincidences, do you, Ms. Navarro?"*

Slowly, her sense of self-possession returned to her. These things happened, didn't they? Part of her job was to know where significance might lie, but it was an occupational hazard to impute significance where there was none.

Presently, she slipped into a terry-cloth robe, feeling much calmer and now ravenously hungry. Slipped beneath the door of her room was a manila envelope. She picked it up and sank into a floral-upholstered armchair. Copies of Mailhot's bank statements going back four years.

The phone rang.

It was Sergeant Arsenault.

"So is half past ten going to be all right for our visit with the widow?" Around him she could hear the bustle of a police station in the evening.

"I'll meet you there at ten-thirty," Anna replied crisply. "Thanks for the confirmation." She debated whether to tell him about the Town Car, her brush with death, but held back. Somehow she was afraid that it would diminish her authority—that she would sound vulnerable, fearful, easily spooked.

"Right, then," Arsenault said, and there was a hesitation in his voice. "Well, I guess I'll be heading home. I don't suppose—I'll be driving by your way, so if you have any second thoughts about grabbing a bite . . ." He spoke haltingly. "Or having a nightcap." He was obviously trying to keep it light. "Or whatever."

Anna didn't reply immediately. In truth, she wouldn't have minded company just then. "That's nice of you to offer," she said finally. "But I'm really tired."

"Me, too," he said quickly. "Long day. All right, then. See you in the morning." His voice had subtly shifted: no longer a man talking to a woman, but one professional talking to another.

She hung up with a slight sense of emptiness. Then she closed the curtains to the room and started sorting through her documents. There was still plenty of stuff to work through.

She was convinced that the real reason she hadn't yet

gotten married, had veered away from any relationship that seemed to be getting too serious, was that she wanted to control her own surroundings. You get married, you're accountable to someone else. You want to buy something, you have to justify it. You can no longer work late without feeling guilty, having to apologize, to negotiate. Your time is under new management.

At the office people who didn't know her well called her the "Ice Maiden" and probably a lot worse, mostly because she dated infrequently. It wasn't just Dupree. People didn't like to see attractive women unattached. It offended their sense of the natural order of things. What they failed to realize was that she was a genuine workaholic and seldom socialized, hardly had time to meet men anyway. The only pool of men she could draw from were in the OSI, and dating a colleague could only mean trouble.

Or so she told herself. She preferred not to dwell on the incident in high school that still shadowed her, but she thought of Brad Reedy almost daily, and with ferocious hatred. On the Metro she'd catch a whiff of the citrus cologne Brad used to wear and her heart would spasm with fear, then reflexive anger. Or she'd see on the street a tall blond teenage boy in a red-and-white-striped rugby shirt, and she'd see Brad.

She had been sixteen, physically a woman and, she was told, a beauty, though she didn't yet know it or believe it. She still had few friends, but she no longer felt like an outcast. She quarreled with her parents almost daily because she could no longer stand to live in their tiny house; she felt claustrophobic, she couldn't breathe.

Brad Reedy was a senior and a hockey player, and therefore a member of the school's aristocracy. She was a junior and couldn't believe it when Brad Reedy, *the* Brad Reedy, had stopped by her locker and asked if she wanted to go out sometime. She thought it was a joke, that he'd been put up to it or something, and she scoffed, turning away. Already she'd begun to develop a protective layer of sarcasm.

But he persisted. She flushed, went numb, said I guess, maybe, sometime.

Brad offered to pick her up at her house, but she couldn't bear the thought of his seeing how humble it was, so she pretended she had errands to do downtown anyway and insisted on meeting at the movie theater. For days before, she pored over *Mademoiselle* and *Glamour*. In a *Seventeen* magazine feature on "How to Catch His Eye" she found the perfect outfit, the sort of thing a rich, classy girl might wear, the kind of girl Brad's parents would approve of.

She wore a Laura Ashley tiny floral-print dress with a high ruffled collar she'd bought at Goodwill, which she realized only after she bought it didn't fit quite right. In her matching lime-green espadrilles and lime-green Pappagallo Bermuda bag and lime-green headband, she suddenly felt ridiculous, a little girl dressing up for Halloween. When she met Brad, who was wearing a ripped pair of jeans and a striped rugby shirt, she realized how overdressed she was. She *looked* like she was trying too hard.

She felt as if the entire theater were watching her enter, this overdressed fake preppy with this golden boy.

He wanted to go out to the Ship's Pub for pizza and a beer afterward. She had a Tab and tried to play mysterious and hard to get, but she already had a wild crush on this teenage Adonis and still couldn't believe she was on a date with him.

After three, four beers, he began to get coarse. He drew close to her in the booth and put his hands on her. She pleaded a headache—it was the only thing she could think of on the spur of the moment—and asked him to drive her home. He took her out to the Porsche, drove crazily, and then made a "wrong turn" into the park.

He was a two-hundred-pound man, incredibly strong, fueled by just enough alcohol to make him dangerous, and he forcibly removed her clothes, put his hand over her mouth to muffle her screams, and kept chanting, "*Aw, you want it, you wetback bitch.*"

This was her first time.

For a year afterward she went to church regularly. The guilt burned inside her. If her mother ever found out, she was sure, it would destroy her.

It haunted her for years.

And her mother continued to clean the Reedys' house.

Now she remembered the bank records, tented on the armchair. Couldn't ask for more compelling reading material during a room-service dinner.

After a few minutes, she noticed a line of figures, then looked at it again. How could this be right? Four months ago, one million dollars had been wired into Robert Mailhot's savings account.

She sat down in the chair, looked more closely at the page. She felt a rush of adrenaline. She studied the column of numbers for a long time, her excitement growing. An image of Mailhot's modest clapboard house popped into her head.

A million dollars.

This was becoming interesting.

Zurich

The streetlights flashed by, illuminating the backseat of the taxi like the jittery flashes of a strobe light. Ben stared straight ahead, looking at nothing, thinking.

The homicide detective had seemed disappointed when the lab results showed that Ben hadn't fired the weapon, and processed his release papers with a show of reluctance. Obviously, Howie had managed to pull some strings to get his passport returned.

"I'm releasing you on one condition, Mr. Hartman—that you get out of my canton," Schmid had told him. "Leave Zurich at once. If I ever find out you've returned here, it will not go well for you. The inquiry concerning the Bahnhofplatz shootings remains open, and there are enough un-

answered questions that I would have reason to swear out
a warrant for your arrest at any moment. And if our im-
migrations office, the *Einwanderungsbehörde*, gets involved, you should remember that you can be held in
administrative detention for one year before your case
reaches a magistrate. You have friends and connections,
very impressive ones, but they will not be able to help you
next time."

But more than the threats, it was the question the detective had put so casually that haunted Ben. *Did* the Bahnhofplatz nightmare have anything to do with Peter's death?

Ask it another way: What were the odds it *didn't* have
anything to do with Peter's death? Ben always remembered
what his college mentor, the Princeton historian John
Barnes Godwin, used to say: Calculate the odds, and recalculate, and recalculate again. And then just go with your
gut instinct.

His gut told him this was no coincidence.

Then there was the mystery surrounding Jimmy Cavanaugh. It wasn't just the body that had disappeared. It was
his identity, his entire existence. How could such a thing
happen? And how had the shooter known where Ben was
staying? It made no sense, none of it did.

The disappearance of the body, the planting of the handgun—that confirmed that the man he knew as Cavanaugh
had been working with others. But with *whom?* Working
on *what?* What possible interest, what possible *threat*,
could Ben Hartman be to anyone?

Of course it had to do with Peter. That *had* to be it.

You see enough movies, you learn that bodies are
"burned beyond recognition" only when something's being
covered up. One of Ben's first, desperate thoughts upon
hearing the unbearable news had been that maybe there'd
been a mix-up, that it wasn't really Peter Hartman who'd
died in that plane. The authorities had made a mistake.
Peter was still alive, and he'd call, and they'd laugh over
the bungle in a grim sort of way. Ben had never dared
suggest this to his father, not wanting to raise false hopes.

And then the medical evidence arrived, and it was irrefutable.

Now, however, Ben began to focus on the real question: Not *was* it Peter, but *how* had he died? A plane crash could be an efficient way to conceal evidence of murder.

And then again, maybe it had been a genuine accident.

After all, who could have wanted Peter dead? Murdering someone and then crashing a plane—wasn't that a ludicrously elaborate cover-up?

But this afternoon had redefined what was within the realm of plausibility. Because if Cavanaugh, *whoever* he was, had tried to kill him, for whatever unfathomable reason, wasn't it likely he—or others connected with Cavanaugh—had also killed Peter four years ago?

Howie had mentioned databases accessed by a colleague of his who did corporate espionage work. It struck Ben that Frederic McCallan, the aged client he was supposed to meet at St. Moritz, might be helpful in this regard. McCallan, in addition to being a serious Wall Street player, had served in more than one administration in Washington; he'd have no shortage of contacts and connections. Ben took out his multistandard Nokia phone and called the Hotel Carlton in St. Moritz. The Carlton was a quietly elegant place, opulent without being ostentatious, with a remarkable glassed-in pool overlooking the lake.

His call was put right through to Frederic McCallan's room.

"You're not standing us up, I hope," old Frederic said jovially. "Louise will be devastated." Louise was his allegedly beautiful granddaughter.

"Not at all. Things got a little hectic here, and I missed the last flight to Chur." Strictly speaking this was true.

"Well, we had them set a place for you at dinner, figuring you'd show up eventually. When can we expect you?"

"I'm going to rent a car and drive up tonight."

"Drive? But that'll take you *hours!*"

"It's a pleasant drive," he said. And a long drive was

precisely what he needed to clear his head right now.

"Surely you can charter a flight if you have to."

"Can't," he said without elaborating. The fact was, he wanted to avoid the airport, where others—if there *were* others—might be expecting him. "I'll see you at breakfast, Freddie."

The taxicab took Ben to an Avis on Gartenhofstrasse, where he rented an Opel Omega, got directions, and set off without incident on the A3 highway, heading southeast out of Zurich. It took a while to get the feel of the road, the great speed at which Swiss drivers raced along their main highways, the aggressive way they signaled that they wanted to pass by pulling up right behind you and flashing their high beams.

Once or twice he had a flash of paranoia—a green Audi seemed to be following him but then disappeared. After a while he began to feel as if he'd left all that madness behind in Zurich. Soon he'd be at the Carlton in St. Moritz, and that was inviolable.

He thought about Peter, as he'd done so often in the last four years, and he felt the old guilt, felt his stomach tighten, then flip over. Guilt that he'd let his brother die alone, because in the last few years of Peter's life he'd barely even talked to him.

But he knew Peter wasn't alone at the end. He'd been living with a Swiss woman, a medical student he'd fallen in love with. Peter had told him about it on the phone a couple of months before he was killed.

Ben had seen Peter exactly twice since college. Twice.

As kids, before Max had sent them off to different prep schools, they'd been inseparable. They fought constantly, they wrestled each other until one could claim, *You're good, but I'm better*. They hated each other and loved each other, and they were never apart.

But after college Peter had joined the Peace Corps and gone to Kenya. He had no interest in Hartman Capital Management either. Nor would he take anything out of his trust fund. What the hell do I need it for in Africa? he'd said.

The fact was that Peter wasn't just doing something meaningful with his life. He was escaping Dad. Max and he had never gotten along. "Christ!" Ben had exploded at him once. "You want to avoid Dad, you can live in Manhattan and simply not call him. Have lunch with Mom once a week or something. You don't need to live in some goddamned mud hut, for God's sake!"

But no. Peter had returned to the States twice: once when their mother had her mastectomy, and once after Ben had called to tell him that Mom's cancer had spread and she didn't have long to live.

By that time Peter had moved to Switzerland. He'd met a Swiss woman in Kenya. "She's beautiful, she's brilliant, and she still hasn't seen through me," Peter had told him over the phone. "File that one under 'strange but true.' " That was a favorite boyhood expression of Peter's.

The girl was returning to medical school and he was going with her to Zurich. Which was what had first got the two of them talking. You're tagging along with some chick you met? Ben had said scornfully. He was jealous—jealous that Peter had fallen in love, and jealous, on some crazy brotherly level, that he'd been replaced at the center of Peter's life.

No, Peter had said, it wasn't just that. He'd read an article in an international edition of *Time* magazine about an old woman, a Holocaust survivor, living in France, desperately poor, who'd tried without success to get one of the big Swiss banks to give back the modest sum her father had left for her before he'd perished in the camps.

The bank had demanded her father's death certificate.

She'd told them that the Nazis hadn't issued death certificates for the six million Jews they'd murdered.

Peter was going to get the old woman what was due her. Dammit, he said, if a Hartman can't wrest this lady's money from the greedy paws of some Swiss banker, who can?

No one was as stubborn as Peter. No one except Old Max, maybe.

Ben had little doubt Peter had won the battle.

He began to feel weary. The highway had become monotonous, lulling. His driving had fallen naturally into the rhythm of the road, and other cars no longer seemed to be trying to pass him quite so often. His eyelids began to droop.

There came a blaring car horn, and he was dazzled by headlights. With a jolt he realized that he'd momentarily fallen asleep behind the wheel. He reacted quickly, spinning the car to the right, swerving out of the oncoming lane of traffic, just barely missing a collision.

He pulled over to the side of the road, his heart pounding. He let out a long, relieved sigh. It was the jet lag, his body still on New York time, the length of the day, the madness at the Bahnhofplatz finally catching up with him.

It was time to get off the highway. St. Moritz was maybe a couple of hours away, but he didn't dare risk driving any longer. He had to find a place to spend the night.

Two cars passed by, though Ben did not see them.

One was a green Audi, battered and rusty, almost ten years old. Its driver and sole occupant, a tall man of around fifty with long gray hair pulled back in a ponytail, turned to inspect Ben's car, parked on the side of the road.

When the Audi had traveled about a hundred meters beyond Ben's car, it, too, pulled over to the shoulder.

Then a second car passed Ben's Opel: a gray sedan with two men inside. *"Glaubst Du, er hat uns entdeckt?"* the driver asked the passenger in Swiss-German. You think he's spotted us?

"It's possible," the passenger replied. "Why else would he have stopped?"

"He could be lost. He is looking at a map."

"That could be a ruse. I'm going to pull over."

The driver noticed the green Audi at the side of the road. "Are we expecting company?" he asked.

CHAPTER SIX

Halifax, Nova Scotia

The next morning Anna and Sergeant Arsenault drove up to the house belonging to Robert Mailhot's widow and rang the bell.

The widow opened the front door a suspicious few inches and stared out at them from the dark of her front hall. She was a small woman of seventy-nine with snow-white hair in a neat bouffant, a large, round head, an open face but wary brown eyes. Her wide flat nose was red, evidence either of weeping or booze.

"Yes?" She was, unsurprisingly, hostile.

"Mrs. Mailhot, I'm Ron Arsenault from the RCMP, and this is Anna Navarro from the United States Department of Justice." Arsenault spoke with a surprising tenderness. "We wanted to ask you some questions. Could we come in?"

"Why?"

"We have some questions, that's all."

The widow's small brown eyes shone fiercely. "I'm not talking to any police. My husband's dead. Why don't you just leave me *alone*?"

Anna sensed the desperation in the old woman's voice.

Her maiden name, according to the documents, was Marie LeBlanc, and she was just about eight years younger than her husband. She didn't have to talk with them, though she probably didn't know that. Everything now turned on the dance of persuasion.

Anna hated dealing with the families of murder victims. Pestering them with questions at such a terrible time, days or even hours after the death of a loved one, was unbearable.

"Mrs. Mailhot," Arsenault said in an official voice, "we have reason to believe someone may have killed your husband."

The widow stared at them for a moment. "That's ridiculous," she said. The space between front door and jamb narrowed.

"You may be right," Anna said softly. "But if anyone did anything to him, we want to know about it."

The widow hesitated. After a moment, she scoffed, "He was old. He had a bad heart. Leave me alone."

She felt sorry for the old woman, having to undergo interrogation at such a terrible time. But the widow could kick them out any minute, and she couldn't allow that to happen. In a gentle voice she said, "Your husband could have lived longer than he did. You two could have had more time together. We think someone may have taken that away from you. Something no one had the right to take. If anyone did that to you, we want to find out who it was."

The widow's stare seemed to relent.

"Without your help, we'll never know who took your husband from you."

Slowly the space widened and the screen door came open.

The front parlor was dark. Mrs. Mailhot switched on a lamp, which cast a sulfurous light. She was wide-hipped and even shorter than she had first appeared to be. She wore a neat gray pleated skirt and an ivory fisherman's sweater.

The room was gloomy but immaculate, and it smelled of lemon oil. Recently cleaned—perhaps because Mrs.

Mailhot expected relatives at her husband's funeral. Hair and fiber would be a problem. The "crime scene," such as it was, was not exactly preserved.

The room, Anna noticed, was furnished with great attention to detail. Lace doilies adorned the arms of the tweedy sofa and armchairs. All the white fringed silk lampshades matched. On little end tables silver-framed photographs were placed just so. One of them was a black-and-white wedding picture: a plain, vulnerable-looking bride, the groom dark-haired, sharp-featured, proud.

Atop the walnut television cabinet was a line of identical little ivory elephant figurines. Tacky, yet touching.

"Oh, aren't those *exquisite*," Anna said, pointing the elephants out to Arsenault.

"Sure are," Arsenault said unconvincingly.

"Are they Lenox?" Anna asked.

The widow looked surprised, then gave a proud little smile. "You collect them?"

"My mother did." Her mother had neither the time nor the money to collect anything except her meager paychecks.

The old woman gestured. "Please sit down."

Anna took a seat on the couch, Arsenault in the adjoining armchair. She remembered this was the room in which Mailhot had been found dead.

Mrs. Mailhot sat in an uncomfortable-looking ladder-back chair all the way across the room. "I wasn't here when my husband died," she said sadly. "I was visiting my sister like I do every Tuesday night. I just feel so terrible he died without me here."

Anna nodded sympathetically. "Maybe we can talk a little about the way he passed . . ."

"He died from heart failure," she said. "The doctor told me that."

"And he may have," Anna said. "But sometimes a person can be killed in such a way that it doesn't look like murder."

"Why would anyone want to kill Robert?"

Arsenault gave Anna a quick, almost undetectable glance. There was something about the woman's intonation: it wasn't a rhetorical question. She sounded as if she really wanted to know. The approach they took now would be crucial. The two had been married since 1951—half a century together. She surely had some inkling of whatever it was, if anything, that her husband might have been involved in.

"You two retired here a few years ago, is that right?"

"Yes," the old woman said. "What does this have to do with his death?"

"You lived on your husband's pension?"

Mrs. Mailhot raised her chin defiantly. "Robert took care of the money. He told me never to worry about those things."

"But did he ever tell you where the money was coming from?"

"I told you, Robert took care of everything."

"Did your husband tell you that he had one point five million dollars in the bank?"

"We can show you the bank records if you'd like," Arsenault put in.

The old widow's eyes betrayed nothing. "I told you, I know very little about our finances."

"He never talked to you about receiving money from anyone?" Arsenault asked.

"Mr. Highsmith was a generous man," she said slowly. "He never forgot the little people. The people who had helped him."

"These were payments from Charles Highsmith?" Arsenault prompted. Charles Highsmith was a famous, some would say notorious, media baron. With holdings even more extensive than his competitor Conrad Black's, he owned newspapers, radio stations, and cable companies across North America. Three years ago, Highsmith had died, evidently having fallen overboard from his yacht, although the precise circumstances of the incident remained a matter of some controversy.

The widow nodded. "My husband was in his employ for most of his life."

"But Charles Highsmith died three years ago," Arsenault said.

"He must have left instructions for his estate. My husband didn't explain such things to me. Mr. Highsmith made sure we always had enough. That's the kind of man he was."

"And what did your husband do to inspire such loyalty?" Anna asked.

"There's no secret about that," the widow replied.

"Until he retired fifteen years ago, he worked for him as a bodyguard," Arsenault said. "And factotum. Someone who did special errands."

"He was a man Mr. Highsmith could trust implicitly," the old woman said, as if echoing an overheard accolade.

"You moved here from Toronto right after Charles Highsmith's death," Anna said, glancing at her file.

"My husband . . . had certain ideas."

"About Highsmith's death?"

The old woman spoke with obvious reluctance. "Like many people, he wondered about it. About whether it was an accident. Of course, Robert was retired by that point, but he still consulted on security. Sometimes he blamed himself for what happened. I think that's why he was a little . . . funny about it. He convinced himself that if it wasn't an accident, then maybe Highsmith's enemies would come after him one day. It sounds crazy. But you understand, he was my husband. I never questioned his decisions."

"That's why you moved here," Anna said, half to herself. After decades in major cities like London and Toronto, her husband had rusticated himself—had, in fact, gone into hiding. He moved to the place his ancestors and hers had once made a home, a place where they knew all the neighbors, a place that seemed safe, where they could keep a low profile.

Mrs. Mailhot was silent. "I never really believed it. My husband had his suspicions, that was all. As he aged, he became more anxious. Some men are like that."

"You thought it was an eccentricity of his."

"We all have our eccentricities."

"And what do you think now?" Anna said gently.

"Now I don't know what to think." The old woman's eyes grew moist.

"Do you know where he kept his financial records?"

"There are checkbooks and all that sort of thing in a box upstairs." She shrugged. "You can look if you want."

"Thank you," Anna said. "We need to go through with you the last week or so of your husband's life," Anna said. "In detail. His habits, where he went, any place he traveled. Any calls he might have placed or received. Any letters he got. Any restaurants you went to. Any repairmen or workers who might have come to the house—plumbers, telephone repairmen, carpet cleaners, meter readers. Anything you can think of."

They interviewed her for the next two hours, stopping only to use the toilet. Even when it was clear the widow was becoming weary, they forged ahead, determined to push her as hard as she'd let them. Anna knew that if they were to stop and ask to come back in the morning, she might change her mind in the meantime about speaking to them. She might speak to a friend, a lawyer. She might tell them to go to hell.

But two hours later they knew little more than when they began. The widow gave them permission to inspect the house, but they found no signs of forced entry at the front door or any of the windows. Likely the killer—if indeed the old man *had* been murdered—got into the house by means of subterfuge, or was an acquaintance.

Anna found an old Electrolux vacuum cleaner in a closet and removed the bag. It was full, which meant it probably hadn't been changed since Mailhot died. Good. She'd have the crime-scene people do a fresh-bag vacuum when they arrived. Maybe there would be some trace evidence after all.

Maybe they'd even turn up footprints, tire tracks. She would order elimination prints from the widow and anyone else who visited regularly, and have all the usual surfaces printed.

When they returned to the front parlor, Anna waited for the widow to sit and then chose a chair near her. "Mrs. Mailhot," she began delicately, "did your husband ever tell you *why* he thought Charles Highsmith might have been the victim of foul play?"

The widow looked at her a long time, as if deciding what to reveal. "*Les grands hommes ont leurs ennemis*," she said at last, ominously. "Great men have great enemies."

"What do you mean by that?"

Mrs. Mailhot did not meet her gaze. "It's just something my husband used to say," she replied.

Switzerland

Ben took the first exit he came to.

The road went straight for a while, cutting through flat farmland, and then, after crossing over a set of train tracks, it began to twist through hilly terrain. Every twenty minutes or so, he'd pull over to consult his road map.

He was approaching Chur on the A3 highway, south of Bad Ragaz, when he began to focus on the dark blue Saab behind him. He didn't have the road to himself and he didn't expect to. Perhaps the Saab was carrying another lot of ski-happy vacationers. But there was something about the car, something about the way its pace seemed to synchronize with his. Ben pulled over to the side of the road, and the Saab drove right past him. There—he had been imagining things.

Now he resumed his drive. He was being paranoid, and after what he'd been through, who could blame him? He thought once more about Jimmy Cavanaugh, and then abruptly reeled his thoughts in: it filled him with vertigo, like staring into an abyss—a mystery piled upon a mystery. For his own sanity, he could not allow himself to dwell on it. There would be time to sort things out later. Right now, he needed *motion*.

Ten minutes later, images of carnage in the Shopville started to crowd his mind once more, and he reached for the radio dial to distract himself. Speed would help, too, he figured, and he stepped on the accelerator hard, felt the gears mesh smoothly and the car push faster up the sloping highway. He glanced at his rearview mirror and saw a blue Saab—the same blue Saab, he was certain. And as he accelerated, the Saab accelerated, too.

A knot formed in his stomach. At higher speeds, drivers intuitively leave greater distances between themselves and the next car, but the Saab had maintained precisely the same distance behind him as before. If it had wanted to pass him, it would have turned into the passing lane, which meant that its passengers had something else in mind. Ben peered in the rearview again, tried see through the other car's windshield, but it was hard to make out anything more than shadows. He could see only that there were two people in the front. *What the hell were they up to?* Now Ben fixed his attention on this road ahead of him. He wasn't going to let on that he was even aware of them.

But he had to lose them.

There would be plenty of opportunities in the tangle of roads around Chur; God knows he'd gotten lost there himself the last time he'd visited. Now he made a last-minute hairpin turn, veered onto the exit to the narrower Highway Number 3 going south toward St. Moritz. A few minutes later, the familiar blue Saab returned, perfectly centered in his rearview mirror. Driving too fast, Ben hurtled past Malix and Churwalden, making sharp ascents and sudden descents that made his stomach plunge. He turned onto poorly paved byways, taking them at speeds they weren't meant for, and the combination of the rough surfaces and the

Opel's overstrained suspension system caused the car to shudder and jolt. Once, he could hear the car's chassis scrape loudly against a bulge in the pavement, and he saw sparks in the rearview mirror.

Had he shaken his pursuers? The Saab would disappear for long intervals, but never long enough. Time and again, it reappeared, as if linked to him by a strong invisible coil. Ben sped through a series of tunnels cut into gorge faces, past limestone cliffs and old stone bridges spanning deep ravines. He was driving recklessly, his mounting terror overcoming anything like caution; he had to count on his pursuer's prudence and sense of self-preservation. That was his only chance.

As he headed toward the narrow mouth of a tunnel, the Saab suddenly shot ahead of him and into the tunnel. Ben was puzzled: Had it been following another car all along? Only when Ben tried to emerge from the short tunnel did he see, in the yellowish mercury lights, what was happening.

Fifty feet ahead, the Saab was now parked laterally across the narrow road, blocking the egress.

Its driver, in a dark overcoat and hat, was holding up a hand, signaling him to halt. It was a barricade, a roadblock.

Then Ben became aware that another car was following from the rear. A gray Renault sedan. A car he'd caught glimpses of before without focusing on. One of *them*, whoever they were.

Think, dammit! They were trying to wedge him in, trap him inside the tunnel. *Oh, Christ!* He couldn't allow that to happen! Ordinary caution told him to slam on the brakes before hitting the barrier ahead, but these weren't ordinary circumstances. Instead, following some mad impulse, Ben barreled ahead, flooring the gas pedal, his Opel sedan ramming into the left side of the stationary two-door Saab. The Saab was a sports car, built for speed, he knew, but it was probably eight hundred pounds lighter, too. He saw the driver jump out of the way just before the collision propelled the Saab to one side. The sudden deceleration caused

Ben to lurch forward against his straining seat belt and shoulder strap, the taut fabric cutting into his flesh like bands of steel, but the impact had cleared just enough room for him to scrape through, with a horrifying scrape of metal against metal. The car he was driving—its front end partly crumpled, viciously banged up—no longer resembled the gleaming model he'd rented, but the wheels still turned, and he roared ahead down the road, not daring to look back.

From behind him, he heard an explosion of gunfire. *Oh, dear Christ! It wasn't over. It would never be over!*

Galvanized by a fresh surge of adrenaline, Ben found his every sense gaining laser-like focus. The old gray Renault, the one that had come up from behind him in the tunnel, had somehow made its way through the wreckage, too. In his rearview, Ben could see a weapon thrust through the passenger's side window, *aiming* at him. It was a submachine gun, and, seconds later, it began firing off a nonstop fusillade of automatic fire.

Move!

Ben sped down an old stone bridge spanning a gorge so narrow there was barely room for traffic in either direction. Suddenly there came a hollow pop, an explosion of glass a few feet away. His rearview mirror had been shot out; bullets spiderwebbed the rear windshield. They knew exactly what they were doing, and soon he would be dead.

There was a muted explosion, like a dull popping noise, and the car suddenly lurched to the left: one of his tires had blown out.

They were firing at his tires. Trying to disable him. Ben remembered the security expert who'd lectured the senior executives at Hartman Capital Management about kidnapping risks in third-world countries, drilling them on a list of recommended countermeasures. They seemed laughably inadequate to the reality, then as now. *Don't get out of the car* was one of the pointers, he remembered. It wasn't clear he was going to have much of a choice.

Just then, he heard the unmistakable wail of a police siren. Through a jagged hole in the opaque rear windshield, he saw that a third vehicle was coming up fast from behind the gray sedan, this one a civilian unmarked car with a flashing blue light on its roof. That was all he could see: it was too far away to make out the model. Confusion filled Ben's mind again, but abruptly the gunfire ceased.

He watched as the gray sedan made a sudden 180-degree turn over the shoulder of the road, zooming back on the narrow embankment and taking off past the police car. The Renault, his pursuers inside, had gotten away!

Ben brought his car to a halt just after the stone bridge, lolling his head back in his shock and exhaustion, waiting for the *Polizei* to arrive. A minute went by, and then another. He craned his neck back to the lethal stretch of road.

But the police car was gone now, too. The crumpled Saab had been abandoned.

He was alone, the only sound the ticking of his car's engines, and the hammering of his own heart. He pulled his Nokia from his pocket, remembered his conversation with Schmid, and made a decision. *They can lock you up for twenty-four hours without any cause*, Howie had told him. Schmid had made it clear that he was looking for an excuse to do just that. He would put off calling the *Polizei*. He couldn't think straight anymore.

As the adrenaline ebbed, panic gave way to a sense of profound depletion. He badly needed to rest. He needed to refuel, to take stock.

He drove his ruined Opel, the engine straining, the shredded tires making for a bone-jarring ride, a few miles up a hilly road to the nearest town, although really it was a village, a *Dorf*. Its narrow streets were lined with ancient stone buildings, progressing from tiny dilapidated structures to larger, half-timbered houses. A few lights were on, but most of the windows were dark. The street was unevenly paved, and the car's undercarriage, now low to the ground, regularly bumped and scraped against the cobblestone.

The narrow road became a main street soon enough, lined now with great gabled stone houses and rows of slate-shingled buildings. Now he came to a large cobblestoned

square, marked RATHAUSPLATZ, dominated by an ancient
Gothic cathedral. At the center of the square was a stone
fountain. He appeared to be in a seventeenth-century village
built upon much older ruins, its buildings a peculiar hodge-
podge of architectural styles.

Across the town square from the cathedral was a
seventeenth-century manor house with crow-stepped gables, marked with a small wooden sign identifying it as the
Altes Gebäude, the Old Building, though it looked newer
than most of the other buildings in town. Lights blazed
from its small-mullioned windows. It was a tavern, a place
to get food and drink, to sit and rest and *think*. He parked
his wreck alongside an old farm truck, where it would be
largely concealed from view, and went in, his trembling,
twitching legs barely supporting his weight.

Inside, the place was warm and cozy, lit by a flickering
fire in an immense stone hearth. It smelled of wood smoke
and fried onions and roasted meats, wonderful and inviting.
It looked like a traditional Swiss *Stübli*, an old-style restaurant. One round wooden table was obviously the *Stamm-
tisch*, the place reserved for the regulars who came in every
day to drink beer and play cards for hours. Five or six men,
mostly farmers or laborers, regarded him with hostile suspicion, then went back to their cards. Sprinkled throughout
the room were others having dinner or drinking.

Ben realized only now how famished he was. He looked
around for a waiter or waitress, saw none, and sat down at
an empty table. When a waiter arrived, a small round man
of early middle age, Ben ordered something typically
Swiss, heavy and reliable: *Rösti*, roasted potatoes, with
Geschnetzeltes, or bits of veal in cream sauce, with a *Vier-
terl*, a quarter-liter carafe of local red wine. When the
waiter returned ten minutes later, balancing several plates
on his arm, Ben asked in English: "Where's a good place
to spend the night?"

The waiter frowned and set down the dinner plates in
silence. He moved aside the glass ashtray and the red *Altes
Gebäude* matchbook, poured the deep red wine into a

stemmed glass. "The Langasthof," he said, in a heavy Romansch accent. "It's the only place for twenty kilometers around."

While the waiter gave him directions, Ben tucked into his *Rösti*. They were brown and crisp, onion-tangy, delicious. He continued wolfing down his dinner, glancing through the partly fogged window at the small parking area outside. Another car was parked alongside his, obstructing his view. A green Audi.

Something twanged at the back of his mind.

Wasn't a green Audi behind him for a good stretch of A3 out of Zurich? He remembered having seen one, worrying whether he was being followed, dismissing it as a figment of an overactive imagination.

Turning his gaze, he thought he saw, in his peripheral vision, someone staring at him. Yet when his eyes swept the room, there was no one giving him so much as a casual glance. Ben set down his wineglass. *What I need is some black coffee*, he thought, *not more wine. I'm starting to see things that aren't there.*

Most of his dinner was gone, downed in record time. Now it sat heavily in his stomach, a leaden mass of greasy potatoes and cream sauce. He looked around for the waiter to order a strong coffee. Once again he got that creepy sensation of someone looking over at him, then looking away. He turned to his left, where most of the scarred wooden tables were empty, but a few people sat in dark booths, deep in shadow, next to a long, ornately carved wooden bar that was dark and unoccupied, the only object on its surface an old-fashioned white rotary-dial telephone. One man was sitting alone in a booth, drinking coffee and smoking, a middle-aged man in a worn brown leather bomber jacket with long graying hair pulled back into a ponytail. *I've seen him before*, Ben thought. *I know I've seen him before*. But where? Now the man casually brought an elbow to the table, leaned forward, and rested his head on the outstretched palm, the hand cradling the side of his face.

The gesture was too studied. The man was trying to hide his face, trying too hard to be casual about it.

Ben remembered a tall man in a business suit, sallow complexion, long gray hair worn in a ponytail. But from where? He had caught a quick glance of such a man, thinking in passing how ridiculous, how dated, a ponytail looked on a businessman. How . . . eighties.

The Bahnhofstrasse.

Ponytail man had been among the crowd milling around the pedestrian shopping district just before he spotted Jimmy Cavanaugh. Now he was certain of it. The man had been in the vicinity of the Hotel St. Gotthard; later, he'd followed Ben in a green Audi; now he was here, looking decidedly out of place.

Dear Christ, he's tailing me, too, Ben thought. *Since this afternoon, he's been watching me.* He felt his stomach tighten.

Who was he, and why was he here? If, like Jimmy Cavanaugh, he wanted to kill Ben—for whatever reason Cavanaugh had tried—why hadn't he done so already? There had been plenty of opportunities. Cavanaugh had pulled out a gun in broad daylight right on the Bahnhofstrasse. Why would Ponytail hesitate to fire at him in a mostly empty tavern?

He signaled the waiter, who bustled over with a questioning look. "Could I have a coffee?" Ben asked.

"Certainly, sir."

"And where's your rest room, your WC?"

The waiter pointed toward a dimly lit corner of the room, where a small corridor was barely visible. Ben pointed in that direction too, confirming the rest room's location in as broad a gesture as possible.

So Ponytail could see where he was going.

Ben slipped some money under his plate, pocketed one of the restaurant's matchbooks, got up slowly, and made his way toward the rest room. It was located just off the small corridor, on the other side of the dining room from the kitchen. Restaurant kitchens usually had service entrances from the outdoors, Ben knew, so they made good escape routes. And he didn't want Ponytail thinking he was trying to leave the restaurant through the kitchen. This rest room was small and windowless; he couldn't leave this way. Ponytail, presumably some sort of professional, would likely have already checked out the means of egress.

He locked the rest room door. There was an ancient toilet and equally ancient marble sink basin, and it smelled pleasantly of cleaning liquid. He pulled out his digital phone and dialed the telephone number of the *Altes Gebäude*. Ben could hear the faint sound of a telephone ringing somewhere in the restaurant. Probably the old rotary-dial phone he'd seen on the bar near Ponytail's booth, or one in the kitchen, if there was one there. Or both.

A man's voice answered, "*Altes Gebäude, guten Abend.*" Ben was fairly sure it was the waiter.

Making his voice deep and gravelly, Ben said, "I need to speak to one of your customers, please. Someone who's having dinner there tonight. It's urgent."

"*Ja?* Who is that?"

"Someone you probably don't know. Not a regular. It's a gentleman with long gray hair in a ponytail. He's probably wearing a leather jacket, he always does."

"Ah, yes, I think I know what you mean. A man of about fifty years?"

"Yes, that's the one. Can you please ask him to come to the phone? As I said, it's urgent. An emergency."

"Yes, at once, sir," the waiter said, responding to the tension Ben had put in his voice. He set the phone down.

Leaving the line open, Ben slipped his phone into the breast pocket of his sport coat, left the rest room, and returned to the dining room. Ponytail was no longer sitting at his booth. The telephone was at the bar, which was situated in such a way that it couldn't be seen from the entrance to the restaurant—Ben hadn't seen it until he was seated at his table—and no one standing or sitting at it could see either the entrance or the area of the restaurant roughly between the rest room and the entrance. Ben

moved quickly to the entrance and out the door. He had
bought himself maybe fifteen seconds during which he
could leave, unseen by Ponytail, who was at the moment
talking into the telephone's handset, hearing nothing but
silence, wondering what had happened to the caller who
had identified him so carefully.

Ben grabbed his bags from the ruined sedan and raced
to the green Audi; a key was in the ignition, as if the driver
had made preparations for a rapid getaway. Theft was probably unknown in this sleepy village, but there had to be a
first time. Besides, Ben had a strong suspicion that Ponytail
wasn't in a position to notify the police about his vehicle's
disappearance. This way, he gained a working vehicle while
depriving his pursuer of one. Ben leaped in and started it
up. There was no sense in trying to be quiet now; Ponytail
would hear the ignition of the engine. He threw the car into
reverse, then, with a squeal of rubber, barreled over the
cobblestoned expanse and, at top speed, out of the *Rathausplatz*.

Fifteen minutes later, he pulled up near a half-timbered
stone building in a remote, wooded area off the small country road. A small sign in front read LANGASTHOF.

He tucked the car away discreetly behind a dense stand
of pine trees and walked back to the front door of the guest
house, where a small sign said EMPFANG, reception.

He rang the bell, and waited a few minutes before a light
came on. It was midnight, and obviously he had awakened
the proprietor.

An old man with a deeply lined face opened the door
and, with a put-upon air, led Ben down a long, dark hall,
switching on little wall sconce lights as he went, until he
came to an oak-plank doorway marked 7. With an old skeleton key, he unlocked the door and switched on a small
bulb, illuminating a snug room dominated by a double bed
on which a white duvet was neatly folded. The diamond-
patterned wallpaper was peeling.

"This is all we have," the proprietor said gruffly.

"It'll do."

"I'll put the heat on. It will take a good ten minutes."

A few minutes later, after he'd unpacked only what he needed for the night, Ben went into the bathroom to run the shower. The setup looked so alien, so complicated—four or five knobs and dials, a telephone-style hand-shower hanging on a hook—that Ben decided it wasn't worth it. He splashed cold water on his face, unwilling to wait for hot water to find its way through the pipes, brushed his teeth, and undressed.

The duvet was luxurious and lofty with goose down. He fell asleep almost immediately.

Some time later—hours, it seemed, though he couldn't be sure, since his travel alarm clock was still in his suitcase—he heard a noise.

He sat upright, his heart racing.

He heard it again. It was a soft but audible squeak, floorboards beneath the carpet. It came from near the doorway.

He reached over to the end table and grabbed the brass lamp at its base. With the other hand, he slowly yanked the cord out of its wall socket, freeing the lamp to be swung.

He swallowed hard. His heart hammered. He quietly swung his feet free of the duvet and over to the floor.

He lifted the lamp slowly, careful not to disturb anything else on the end table. When he had a good grip on it, he quietly, quietly, hoisted it up above his head.

And sprang suddenly off the bed.

A powerful arm reached out, grabbed at the lamp, wrenched it from his hands. Ben lunged toward the dark shape, turned his shoulder, and jammed it into the intruder's chest.

But in the same instant a foot swung out, catching Ben at the ankles, knocking him down. With all his strength, Ben tried to rear up and pummel his attacker with his elbows, but a knee rammed into his chest and his solar plexus, and the wind was knocked out of him. Before he had the chance to attempt another move, the intruder's hands shot forward, slamming Ben's shoulders down, pinning him to the floor. As soon as his breath came back, Ben let out a great bellow, but then a large hand clapped his mouth shut and Ben found himself looking into the haunted face of his brother.

"You're good," Peter said, "but I'm still better."

CHAPTER SEVEN

Asunción, Paraguay

The rich Corsican was dying.

He had been dying for three or four years, however, and probably had a good two years or more left in him.

He lived in a grand Spanish Mission–style villa in a wealthy suburb of Asunción, at the end of a long drive lined with palm trees, surrounded by acres of beautifully landscaped property.

Señor Prosperi's bedroom was on the second floor, and though it was flooded with light, it was so choked with medical equipment that it looked like an emergency room. His much younger wife, Consuela, had slept in her own bedroom for years.

When he opened his eyes this morning, he did not recognize the nurse.

"You're not the regular girl," he said, his voice a phlegm-laden croak.

"Your regular nurse is ill this morning," said the pleasant-looking blond young woman. She was standing at the side of his bed, doing something to his IV drip.

"Who sent you?" Marcel Prosperi demanded.

"The nursing agency," she replied. "Please calm down. It will do you no good to be upset." She turned the valve on the drip fully open.

"You people are always pumping me full of things," Señor Prosperi grumbled, but this was all he was able to get out before his eyes closed and he lost consciousness.

A few minutes later the substitute nurse checked his pulse at the wrist and found there was none. Casually she turned the IV valve back to its usual setting.

Then, her face suddenly contorted by grief, she ran to break the terrible news to the old man's widow.

Ben sat up on the carpeted floor, felt the blood drain from his head, then fell forward onto his knees.

He was overcome by vertigo, felt as if his head were spinning while his body was frozen, as if his head were disconnected from his body.

He was overcome by memories, of the funeral, of the burial ceremony at the small cemetery in Bedford. Of the rabbi chanting the Kaddish, the prayer for the dead: *Yisgadal v'yiskadash shmay rabbo* . . . Of the small wooden casket that held the remains, his father's composure suddenly cracking as the casket was lowered into the hole, crumpling to the ground, fists clenched, his hoarse wail.

Ben squeezed his eyes shut. The memories kept flooding his overloaded mind. The call in the middle of the night. Driving out to Westchester County to break the news to his parents. He couldn't do it over the phone. *Mom, Dad, I have some bad news about Peter.* A beat of silence; do I really have to go through this, what else is there to say? His father had been asleep in the immense bed, of course: it was four o'clock in the morning, an hour or so before the old man normally awoke.

His mother in her mechanized hospital bed in the adjoining room, the night nurse dozing on the couch.

Mom first. It seemed the right thing. Her love for her boys was uncomplicated, unconditional.

She whispered simply, *"What is it?"* and stared at Ben uncomprehending. She seemed to have been yanked from deep in a dream: disoriented, still half in the dream world. *I just got a call from Switzerland, Mom,* and Ben, kneeling, put a gentle hand on her soft cheek as if to cushion the blow.

Her long hoarse scream awakened Max, who lurched in, one hand outstretched. Ben wanted to hug him, but Dad had never encouraged such intimacy. His father's breath was fetid. His few strands of gray hair were matted, in wild disarray. *There's been an accident. Peter* . . . At times like these we speak in clichés and mind it not a bit. Clichés are comforting; they're well-worn grooves through which we can move easily, unthinkingly.

Max had at first reacted not at all as Ben had expected: the old man's expression was stern, his eyes flashed with anger, not grief; his mouth came open in an O. Then he shook his head slowly, closing his eyes, and tears coursed down his pale lined cheeks as he shook his head and then collapsed to the floor. Now he seemed vulnerable, small, defenseless. Not the powerful, formidable man in the perfectly tailored suits, always composed, always in control.

Max didn't go to comfort his wife. The two wept separately, islands of grief.

Now, like his father at the funeral, Ben squeezed his eyes shut, felt his extremities give out, unequal to the task of supporting him. He toppled forward, hands outstretched, touching his brother as he crumpled into his arms, feeling him to see if this phantasm were real.

Peter said, "Hey, bro'."

"Oh, my God," Ben whispered. "Oh, my God."

It was like seeing a ghost.

Ben took in a deep gulp of air, embraced his brother, and hugged him hard. "You bastard . . . You *bastard!* . . ."

"Is that the best you can do?" Peter asked.

Ben released the hold. *"What the hell—"*

But Peter's face was stern. "You have to get out of here. Get out of the country as fast as you can. Immediately."

Ben realized that his eyes were flooded with tears, which blurred his vision. "You bastard," he said.

"You have to get out of Switzerland. They tried to get me. Now they're after you, too."

"What the hell . . . ?" Ben repeated dully. "How could you . . . ? What kind of twisted, sick joke? Mom died . . . she didn't want to . . . You *killed her*." Anger surged into his body, his veins and arteries, flushing his face. The two of them sat on the carpeted floor, staring at each other: an unconscious reenactment of their infancy, their toddler days, when they'd sit facing each other for hours, babbling in their invented language, the secret code no one else could understand. "What the hell was the *idea*?"

"You don't sound happy to see me, Benno," Peter said.

Peter was the only one who called him Benno. Ben rose to his feet, and Peter did the same.

It was always strange, looking into his twin brother's face: all he ever saw were the differences. How one of Peter's eyes was slightly larger than the other. The eyebrows that arched differently. The mouth wider than his, downwardly curved. The overall expression more serious, more dour. To Ben, Peter looked completely different. To anyone else the differences were microscopic.

He was almost bowled over by the sudden realization of how much he'd missed Peter, what a gaping wound his brother's absence had been. He couldn't help thinking of Peter's absence as a form of bodily violence, a maiming.

For years, for all of their childhood, they had been adversaries, competitors, antagonists. Their father had brought them up that way. Max, fearing that wealth would make his boys soft, had sent them to just about every "character-building" wilderness school and camp there was—the survival course where you had to subsist for three days on water and grass; camps for rock-climbing and canoeing and kayaking. Whether Max intended to or not he pushed his two sons to compete against each other.

Only when the two were separated during high school did the competitiveness wane. The distance from each other, and from their parents, finally allowed the boys to break free of the struggle.

Peter said, "Let's get out of here. If you checked into this place under your own name, we're screwed."

Peter's pickup truck, a rusty Toyota, was caked with mud. The cabin was littered with trash, the seats stained and smelling of dog. It was hidden in a copse a hundred feet or so from the inn.

Ben told him about the horrific pursuit on the roadways near Chur. "But that's not all," he went on. "I think I was followed most of the way here by another guy. All the way from Zurich."

"A guy driving an Audi?" Peter asked, gunning the old Toyota's arthritic engine as he pulled onto the dark country road.

"Right."

"Fiftyish, long hair sort of tied back, kind of an old hippie?"

"That's the one."

"That's Dieter, my spotter. My antenna." He turned to Ben, smiled. "And my brother-in-law, sort of."

"Huh?"

"Liesl's older brother and protector. Only recently has he decided I'm good enough for his sister."

"Some surveillance expert. I picked up on him. Stole his car, too. And I'm an amateur."

Peter shrugged. He looked over his shoulder as he drove. "Don't underestimate Dieter. He did thirteen years in Swiss army counterintelligence in Geneva. And he wasn't trying to stay out of *your* sight. He was doing *counter*surveillance. It was just a precaution, once we'd learned that you'd arrived in the country. His job was to see if anyone was following you. To watch you, follow you, make sure you weren't killed or abducted. It wasn't a police car that saved your ass on Highway Number 3. Dieter put on the cop siren to fake them out. It was the only way. We're dealing with highly skilled professionals."

Ben sighed. " 'Highly skilled professionals.' *'They're* after you.' *'They.'* Who's *they?* Jesus!"

"Let's just say the Corporation." Peter was looking in the rearview mirror. "Who the hell *knows* who they really are."

Ben shook his head. "And I thought *I* was imagining things. You're out of your goddamned mind." He felt his face flush with anger. "You *bastard*, that accident . . . I always thought there was something fishy about it."

When Peter spoke after a moment, he seemed distracted, his words disjointed. "I was afraid you'd come to Switzerland. I've always had to be so careful. I think they were never really convinced I was dead."

"Will you *please* tell me what the hell is going on?" Ben exploded.

Peter looked straight ahead at the road. "I know it was a terrible thing to do, but I had no choice."

"Dad's never been the same since, you bastard, and Mom . . ."

Peter drove for a moment in silence. "I know about Mom. Don't . . ." His voice turned steely. "I really don't give a damn what happens to Max."

Surprised, Ben looked at his brother's face. "Well, you proved that, all right."

"It's you and Mom I felt . . . sick about. What I knew it would do to you two. You have no idea how much I wanted to contact you, tell you the truth. Tell you I was alive."

"Now do you want to tell me why?"

"I was trying to protect you, Benno. I would never have done it otherwise. If I thought they'd just kill me and that would be the end of it, I'd have gladly let them do it. But I knew they'd go after my family, too. Meaning you and Mom. Dad—as far as I'm concerned, Dad died to me four years ago."

Ben was at once thrilled to see Peter and furious at the deception, and he was finding it hard to think logically.

"What are you talking about? Will you tell me a straight story already?"

Peter glanced over at what looked like a lodge set back from the road, a halogen light flooding its front entrance.

"What is it, five in the morning? But it looks like maybe someone's awake here." A light was on above the inn's front door.

He pulled the truck into a hidden clearing in the trees near the auberge and shut off the engine. The two men got out. The predawn morning was cold and quiet, with just the faint rustle of a small animal or bird from the woods behind the inn. Peter opened the front door, and they entered a small lobby. A reception desk was lit by a flickering fluorescent light, but no one was there. "The light's on, but nobody's home," Peter said. Ben smiled in appreciation: that was one of their father's favorite insults. He reached out to tap the small metal bell on the counter, but stopped when a door behind the counter opened, and a rotund woman emerged, cinching a bathrobe around her belly. She was scowling, blinking in the light, angry at being awakened. "*Ja?*"

Peter spoke quickly, fluidly in German. "*Es tut mir sehr leid Sie zu stören, aber wir hätten gerne Kaffee.*" He was sorry to disturb her, but they wanted some coffee.

"*Kaffee?*" the old woman scowled. "*Sie haben mich geweckt, weil Sie Kaffee wollen?*" They'd woken her because they wanted coffee?

"*Wir werden Sie für ihre Bemühungen bezahlen, Madame. Zwei Kaffee bitte. Wir werden uns einfach da, in Ihrem Esszimmer, hinsetzen.*" They would pay her for her trouble, Peter assured her. Two coffees. They'd simply like to sit in her dining room.

The disgruntled innkeeper shook her head as she hobbled over to a nook next to a small dark dining room, switched on the lights, and turned on a large red metal coffeemaker.

The dining room was small but comfortable. Several large curtainless windows, which in the daytime probably gave diners a beautiful view of the forest in which the auberge was nestled, were utterly black. Five or six round tables were covered with starched white tablecloths and already set for breakfast, with juice glasses and coffee cups and metal trays heaped with brown sugar cubes. Peter sat down at a table for two against the wall, near the window. Ben sat across from him. The innkeeper, foaming a pitcher of milk in her nook, was staring at the two of them, as people so often stared at identical twins.

Peter moved aside the plate and the silverware to make room for his elbows. "You remember when that whole thing erupted over the Swiss banks and Nazi gold?"

"I sure do." *So that's what this was about.*

"That was just before I moved here from Africa. I followed it pretty closely in the newspapers there—I guess I was particularly interested because of Dad's time in Dachau." There was a sardonic twist to his mouth now. "Anyway, a whole cottage industry suddenly sprang up. Lawyers and other shysters who got the bright idea to take advantage of elderly Holocaust survivors who were trying to track down their families' missing assets. I think I told you I read somewhere about an old woman in France, a survivor of the concentration camps. Turned out she'd been bilked of her entire life's savings by some French scumbag lawyer who said he had information about a dormant Swiss bank account belonging to her father. The lawyer needed money, though, up front, to do the investigative work, take on the Swiss bank, all that bullshit. Of course the old lady paid— an amount like twenty-five thousand dollars, her entire savings, money she needed to live on. The lawyer vanished, along with the twenty-five thousand. That got me worked up—I couldn't stand hearing about a defenseless old lady being taken advantage of that way—and I contacted her, offered to look for her father's Swiss account for free. She was understandably suspicious, having just been ripped off, but after we talked awhile she gave me permission to go ahead and look. I had to convince her I had no interest in her money."

Peter, who had been staring at the tablecloth as he spoke, now looked up directly at Ben. "Understand, these survivors weren't motivated by greed. They were seeking closure, justice, a connection to their dead parents, to the past. Money to get by on." He turned to glance at one of the windows. "Even as a legal representative of the old lady, I had all kinds of trouble dealing with the Swiss bank. They said they had no records of any such account. The usual story. These goddamned Swiss bankers—it's amazing, they're such anal-retentive record keepers, they keep every damned scrap of paper since time began, but now they're saying, Oops, they happened to lose a bank account. Uh huh, right. But then I heard about this security guard at the bank where the lady's father opened his account. The guard had gotten fired because he stumbled onto a shredding party—bank employees destroying heaps of documents from the forties in the middle of the night—and he rescued a pile of documents and ledgers from the shredder."

"I vaguely remember that," Ben said. The innkeeper came over with a tray and sullenly set down a metal pitcher of espresso and another one of steamed milk, then left the dining room.

"The Swiss authorities didn't like that. Violation of bank privacy, all kinds of sanctimonious bullshit. Never mind the shredding of documents. I tracked the guy down, outside of Geneva. He'd kept all the documents, even though the bank was trying to get them back, and he let me go through them to see if there was any record of the father's account."

"And?" Ben was tracing patterns on the white tablecloth with the tines of a fork.

"And nothing. I didn't find anything on it. Never did, by the way. But in one of the ledgers I found a piece of paper. Pretty eye-opening. It was a fully executed, legally valid, notarized and certified *Gründungsvertrag*—articles of incorporation."

Ben said nothing.

"In the waning years of the Second World War, some sort of corporation was established."

"Some sort of Nazi thing?"

"No. There were a few Nazis involved in it, but the majority of the principals weren't even German. We're talking about a board comprising some of the most powerful industrialists of the era. We're talking Italy, France, Germany, England, Spain, the U.S., Canada. Names you've heard of, even *you*, Benno. Some of the real big shots of world capitalism."

Ben tried to concentrate. "You said *before* the end of the war, right?"

"That's right. Early in 1945."

"*German* industrialists were founders of this corporation as well?"

Peter nodded. "It was a business partnership that cut clear across enemy lines. Does that surprise you?"

"But we were at war . . ."

"What do you mean 'we,' Kemosabe? The business of America is business, didn't anybody tell you?" Peter leaned back, his eyes bright. "I mean, let's just talk about what's on the public record. You had Standard Oil of New Jersey basically carving up the map with I. G. Farben, figuring out who'd get which oil and chemical monopolies, doing patent sharing, the whole thing. For God's sake, the entire war effort ran on juice from Standard Oil—it wasn't as if anyone in the military could afford to interfere. What if the company started having 'production problems'? Besides, John Foster Dulles himself had been a board member of Farben. Then there's the Ford Motor Company. All those five-ton military trucks that were the mainstay of German military transportation? Ford built those. The Hollerith machines that enabled Hitler to round up 'undesirables' with such incredible efficiency? All manufactured and serviced by Big Blue, good ol' IBM—hats off to Tom Watson. Oh, then there's ITT—a big stakeholder in Focke-Wulf, the company that made most of the German bombers. Want to hear something sweet? After the war was over, it sued the U.S. government for monetary compensation, given that Allied bombers had damaged those Focke-Wulf factories. I could go on and on. But that's just the stuff we know about, obviously a tiny fraction of what really went on. None of these characters gave a damn about Hitler. They owed their allegiance to a higher ideology: profit. To them, the war was like a Harvard-Yale football game—a momentary distraction from more serious matters, like the pursuit of the almighty dollar."

Ben shook his head slowly. "Sorry, bro'. Just listen to yourself. It all sounds like the usual counterculture rap: property is theft, never trust anyone over thirty—all that overheated, dated conspiracy crap. Next you're going to tell me they were responsible for Love Canal." He set his cup of coffee down sharply, and it clanked loudly against the saucer. "Funny, there was a time when anything having to do with business bored you stiff. I guess you really *have* changed."

"I don't expect you to take it in all at once," Peter said. "I'm just giving you the background. Context."

"Then tell me something real. Something *concrete*."

"There were twenty-three names on this list," his brother said, suddenly quiet. "For the most part, captains of industry, as they used to be called. A few blue blooded statesmen, back when people thought there was such a thing. We're talking about people who shouldn't even have known each other—people any historian would swear never even *met*. And here they are, all linked together in some sort of business partnership."

"There's a step missing," Ben said, half to himself. "Obviously something drew your attention to this document. Something made you pull it out. What are you leaving out?"

Peter smiled mordantly, and the haunted look returned. "A name jumped out at me, Ben. The name of the treasurer."

Ben's scalp began to prickle, as if ants were swarming over it. "Who was it?"

"The treasurer of the corporation was a young financial whiz kid. An *Obersturmführer* in Hitler's SS, to boot. You may be familiar with the name: Max Hartman."

"Dad." Ben had to remember to breathe.

"He was no Holocaust survivor, Ben. *Our father was a goddamned Nazi.*"

CHAPTER EIGHT

Ben closed his eyes, inhaled deeply, and shook his head. "That's preposterous. Jews weren't members of the SS. The document's obviously a forgery."

"Believe me," Peter said quietly. "I've had plenty of time to study this document. It's no forgery."

"But then . . ."

"In April of 1945, our father was supposedly in Dachau, remember? Liberated by the U.S. Seventh Army at the end of April '45?"

"I don't remember the exact timing—is that right?"

"You were never very curious about Dad's background, were you?"

"Not really, no," Ben admitted.

Peter smiled grimly. "That's probably the way he preferred it. And lucky for you that you weren't. It's nice to live in a state of innocence. Believing all the lies. The story, the legend Dad created about the Holocaust survivor who came to America with ten bucks in his pocket and built a financial empire. Became a great philanthropist." He shook his head, snorted. "What a fraud he is. What a myth he created." With a sneer he added: "The great man."

Ben's heart began to pound slowly. Dad was difficult to get along with; his enemies called him ruthless. But a *fraud?*

"Max Hartman was a member of the *Schutzstaffel*," Peter repeated. "The SS, okay? File it under 'strange but true.' " Peter was so damned earnest, so convincing, and Ben never knew him to lie to his face. But this was so patently false! He wanted to scream, *Stop it!*

"What kind of corporation was it?"

Peter shook his head. "Possibly a front, a sort of dummy corporation, established with millions and millions of dollars in assets pooled by the principals."

"For what? To what *end?*"

"That I don't know, and the document doesn't specify."

"Where is this document?"

"I've got it hidden away safely, don't worry. This corporation, headquartered in Zurich, Switzerland, in early April 1945, was called Sigma AG."

"And did you tell Dad you'd found this?"

Peter nodded and took his first sip of coffee. "I called him, read it aloud to him, asked him about it. He blew up, as I knew he would. Claimed the thing was a fake, like you did—as I knew he would. Got angry, defensive. Started shouting, screaming. How could I believe such slander? With all he'd been through, blah blah blah, how could I possibly believe such a lie? That sort of thing. I never expected to get anything out of him, but I wanted to gauge his reaction. So I started asking around. Looking into corporate records in Geneva, in Zurich. Trying to find out whatever happened to this firm. And then I was almost killed. Twice. The first time it was a 'car accident,' a near miss. A car swerving onto the pavement on the Limmatquai, where I was walking. The second time it was a 'mugging' on Niederdorfstrasse that was no mugging. I managed to escape both times, but then I was warned. If I persisted in digging around in things that were none of my business, next time I'd be killed. No more near misses. I was to hand over all pertinent documents. And if any of the details about this corporation got out, I'd be dead, along with everyone in our family. So don't think about phoning in a tip to the newspapers, they said. Dad I didn't care about, obviously. It was you and Mom I was protecting."

That sounded so much like Peter—he was no less fierce a protector of their mother than Ben had been. And he was levelheaded, not at all prone to paranoia. He *had* to be telling the truth.

"But why were they so concerned about what you knew?" Ben persisted. "Look at it objectively. A corporation was set up more than half a century ago. So *what?* Why the secrecy *now?*"

"We're talking about a joint partnership across enemy lines. We're talking about the risk of public exposure, and thus public disgrace, of some of the most powerful, revered figures of our time. But that's the least of it. Consider the nature of the enterprise. Mammoth corporations, Allied and Axis alike, establishing a joint entity in order to enrich all of them. Germany was blockaded at the time, but then, capital doesn't respect national boundaries, does it? Some people would call it trading with the enemy. Who knows what international laws might have been violated? What if there was some chance that the assets could be frozen or confiscated? There's no way of gauging the magnitude of those assets. A lot can happen in half a century. We could be talking about staggering sums of money. And even the Swiss have been known to waive the secrecy laws under international pressure. Obviously, some people came to the conclusion that I might just know enough to jeopardize their cozy arrangement."

" 'Some people'? Who was it who threatened you?"

Peter sighed. "Again, I wish I knew."

"Come on, Peter, if there's anyone else alive who was involved in setting up this corporation, they'd have to be ancient."

"Sure, most of the ones who were in high positions are gone. But some are still around, believe me. And some aren't all that old—in their seventies, even. If only two or three guys on the board of this company are still alive, they may be sitting on a fortune. And who knows who their successors might be? It's obvious they've got enough money to keep their secret buried, you know? By any means necessary."

"So you decided to disappear."

"They knew way too much about me. My daily sched-ule, the places I went, my unlisted home phone number, names and locations of family members. Financial, credit information. They were making a point, loud and clear, that they had extensive resources. So I made a decision, Benno. I had to die. They'd left me no other choice."

"No other *choice?* You could have given them their stu-pid document, agreed to their demands—moved on as if you'd never found the thing."

Peter grunted. "That's like trying to unring a bell, put the toothpaste back in the tube—can't be done. They were never going to let me live, now that I knew what I knew."

"So what was the purpose of the warning?"

"Keep me quiet while they determined how much I knew, whether I'd told anyone. Until they got rid of me."

Ben could hear the old woman moving about in the other room, the floorboards squeaking. After a while, he said, "How'd you do it, Peter? The death, I mean. It can't have been easy."

"It wasn't." Peter leaned back in his chair, resting the back of his head against the window. "I couldn't have done it without Liesl."

"Your girlfriend."

"Liesl's a wonderful, remarkable woman. My lover, my best friend. Ah, Ben, I never thought I'd be so lucky as to find someone like this. I hope someday you find someone even half as terrific as her. It was her idea, really. I'd have never been able to put the plan together. She agreed I had to disappear, and she insisted it had to be done right."

"But the dental records—I mean, Christ, Peter, they identified your body positively, beyond any doubt."

Peter shook his head. "They matched the body's teeth with the dental records back home in Westchester, the assumption being that those were really my dental X-rays in Dr. Merrill's office."

Ben shook his head, perplexed. "Whose body . . . ?"

"Liesl got the idea from the prank that the medical students at the University of Zurich pull almost every year at the end of the spring semester. Some joker always steals the cadaver from the gross anatomy class. It's sort of a morbid springtime ritual, medical-student humor—one day their cadaver just disappears. It's always reclaimed, sort of ransomed. Instead, she arranged to have an unclaimed body stolen from the hospital morgue. Then it was a simple matter to pull the dead guy's medical records, including dental records—this is Switzerland, everyone's documented."

Ben smiled in spite of himself. "But to switch the X-rays . . . ?"

"Let's just say I hired someone to do a simple, low-risk breaking-and-entering job. Dr. Merrill's office isn't exactly Fort Knox. One pair of films was substituted for another. No big deal. When the police came to him requesting my dental records, they got the substituted ones."

"And the plane crash?"

Peter explained, leaving out no significant detail.

Ben watched him as he spoke. Peter had always been soft-spoken, quiet, the deliberate, thoughtful one. But you'd never call him calculating or devious, and deviousness was what this plan had required. How frightened he must have been.

"A few weeks earlier, Liesl applied for a position at a small hospital in the canton of St. Gallen. Of course they were delighted to hire her—they needed a pediatrician. She found us a small cabin in the countryside, in the woods by a lake, and I joined her. I posed as her Canadian husband, a writer working on a book. All the while I maintained a network of contacts, my antennae."

"People who knew you were alive—that must have been risky."

"*Trusted* people who knew I was alive. Liesl's cousin is an attorney in Zurich. He was our listening post, our eyes and ears. She trusts him completely, and therefore so do I. An attorney with multiple international interests has his contacts in the police, in the banking community, among private investigators. Yesterday he learned about the blood-bath at the Bahnhofplatz, about a foreigner who was brought in for questioning. But as soon as Dieter had told me about the murder attempt on you, I realized what had happened. They, the inheritors, whoever on that list is still around, have probably always been suspicious that my death was faked. They've always been on the alert—either for my reappearance in Switzerland, or else for some sign that you were carrying on my investigations. I know for a fact that they've got a lot of Swiss policemen in their pocket, a bounty on my head. They practically *own* half the cops. I assume the bank where you had a meeting that morning, UBS, was the tripwire. So I had to come out of hiding to warn you."

Peter risked his life for me, Ben thought. He felt the sting of tears coming to his eyes. Then he remembered Jimmy Cavanaugh, the man who wasn't there. Hurriedly, he filled Peter in on the mystery.

"Incredible," Peter said, and he took on a faraway look.

"It's like they're trying to gaslight me. You do remember Jimmy Cavanaugh?"

"Of course. He spent Christmas with us at Bedford a couple of times. I liked the guy, too."

"What could he have had to do with the Corporation? Did they turn him, somehow, make every trace of his existence disappear at some point?"

"No," Peter said, "you're missing the point. Howie Rubin must have been right. There is no Jimmy Cavanaugh and there never was." He began speaking more quickly. "In a twisted way, there's a logic to this. Jimmy Cavanaugh—let's call him that, whatever his real name was—was never turned. He was working for them all along. Here's a kid who's older than the rest of the class, lives off campus, and before you know it, he's your asshole buddy. Don't you see, Benno? That was the plan. For whatever reason, they must have decided it was important to keep a close eye on you at that point. It was a matter of taking precautions."

"You're saying Cavanaugh was . . . *assigned* to me!"

"And probably somebody was assigned to me, too. Our dad was one of the principals. Did we learn something that might jeopardize the organization? Were we going to be a threat to them in some way? Did they need to worry about us? Maybe they needed to be sure. Until you went off to your ghetto and I went off to Africa—basically put ourselves out to pasture, as far as they were concerned."

Ben's mind reeled, and all this talk of *they* only made matters worse.

"Doesn't it make sense for a group of industrialists to bring in an operative, a killer, whose highly specific qualifications included knowing you by sight?"

"Hell, Peter, I suppose . . ."

"You *suppose?* Benno, if you think about it—"

The sound of shattering glass.

Ben gasped, saw the jagged hole that suddenly appeared in the windowpane. Peter seemed to bow his head, leaning forward deliberately onto the table in an oddly comic gesture, as if kowtowing exaggeratedly, genuflecting, giving a courtly salaam. In that same freeze-frame moment it was the expulsion of breath, the throaty *haaah*, that made no sense, until Ben saw the obscene crimson exit wound in the middle of Peter's forehead, the flecks of gray tissue and splinters of white bone fragments that sprayed over the table, on the plates and silverware.

"Oh, my *God!*" Ben keened. "*Oh, my God. Oh, my God.*" He toppled backward in his chair, tumbling to the floor, his head slamming against the hard oak floorboards. "*No*," he moaned, barely aware of the volley of silenced gunfire exploding everywhere in the small dining room. "Oh no. Oh, my God." He was frozen, paralyzed by terror and shock and disbelief, so unfathomable was the horror in front of him, until some primitive signal of self-preservation emerged from deep within his hindbrain, propelling him to his feet.

Now he looked out of the shattered window, saw nothing but blackness, and then, illuminated by a muzzle flash preceding another gunshot, there was a face. The image lasted no longer than a split second, but it was emblazoned indelibly in his mind. The assassin's eyes were dark and deep-set, his face pale and unlined, the skin almost tight.

Ben leaped across the small dining room as, behind him, another windowpane shattered, another bullet pitted the plaster in the wall not a foot away.

The assassin was aiming at him now, that was clear. Or was it? Was he still aiming at Peter, this shot just wildly astray? Had he seen him, too? *Did* he see him?

As if in answer to his unspoken question, a bullet splintered the doorframe just inches from his head as he vaulted through it into the dark corridor that connected the dining room to the entrance area. From ahead, in the foyer, came a female shout, presumably the innkeeper yelling in anger or in fear; suddenly she loomed directly in his path, arms flailing.

He knocked her aside as he bounded into the foyer. The innkeeper squawked in protest.

He was barely thinking now, he was moving fast and frantically, dazed and numb and robotic, not having to think about what had just happened, not thinking about anything now except survival.

His eyes adjusting to the near-darkness—a small lamp in the far corner of the room, behind the reception counter, cast a tiny circle of light—he saw there was only the front door and another hallway that led to the guests' rooms.

A narrow staircase off the hallway, visible from here, led to more rooms upstairs. There was no window in the room he was now standing in, which meant it was a safe haven from incoming bullets, at least for a few seconds.

On the other hand, the lack of a window meant he was unable to see whether the shooter had run around to the front of the building. Peter's killer would have realized he had missed one of his targets, and so he'd have run either to the front *or* the back of the inn. Front entrance or back, unless there were others Ben didn't know about. That gave Ben a fifty-fifty chance of making it out through the front door.

Fifty-fifty.

Ben didn't like the odds.

And what if there were more than one of them?

If there were several, they'd have fanned out to stake out all entrances, all exits from the building. Either way, one or several killers out there, escaping through the front *or* the back was out of the question.

A scream issued from the dining room: the innkeeper had no doubt just discovered the sickening carnage.

Welcome to my world, madame.

From the floor above Ben could hear the heavy tread of footsteps. Other guests awakening.

Other guests: How many were staying here?

He rushed toward the front door, turned the heavy steel safety lock.

Rapid footfalls thundered from the staircase on the other side of the room, then a hulking figure of a fat man appeared at the foot of the stairs. He was wearing a blue bathrobe, looking as if it had been hastily thrown on. The man's face was fearful. "*Was geht hier vor?*" he cried.

"Call the police," Ben yelled back in English. "*Polizei*—telephone!" He pointed at the phone behind the reception desk.

"The police? What—is someone hurt?"

"Telephone!" Ben repeated angrily. "Go! Someone's been killed!"

Someone's been killed.

The fat man lurched forward clumsily as if he'd been pushed. He rushed to the reception desk, picked up the telephone, listened for a brief moment, then dialed.

*   *   *

The fat man was now speaking in German, loudly and quickly.

Where was the gunman—gunmen?—now? He'd burst inside and look for him and do to him what he'd done to Peter. There were other guests here, others who would get in the way . . . but that wouldn't stop him, would it? He remembered the massacre in the Zurich arcade.

The fat Swiss hung up the phone. "*Sie sind unterwegs*," he said. "Police—is coming."

"How far away are they?"

The man looked at him for a moment, then understood. "Just down the road," he said. "Very near. What happened—who was killed?"

"No one you know."

Again Ben pointed, this time toward the dining room, but the woman innkeeper burst through the doorway, shrieking, "*Er ist tot! Sie haben ihn erschossen! Dieser Mann dort draussen—Dein Bruder, er wurde ermordet!*" Somehow she'd concluded that Ben had killed his own brother. Insanity.

Ben felt his stomach turn over. He'd been in a haze, a deadened stupor, and suddenly the reality of it, the horror, was sinking in. The guest shouted something at her. Ben ran toward the hall that he guessed led to the rear of the house.

The woman was screaming at his back, but Ben kept running. The high caterwauling of a police siren joined the innkeeper's shrill hysteria, then grew louder as the police car came closer. It sounded like a single siren, a single car. But that was enough.

Stay or go?

They own half the cops, Peter had said.

He ran down the hall, turned sharply to the right, then saw a small painted wooden door. He flung it open: wooden shelves piled with linens.

The siren grew louder, now accompanied by the crunch of a car's wheels on gravel. The police were arriving at the front of the building.

Ben ran toward another wooden doorway at the end of the hall. A small louvered window next to it told him the door led to the outside. He turned the knob and pulled at the door. It stuck; he pulled again, harder, and this time it yielded and the door came open.

The area outside had to be safe by now: the police sirens would have scared the gunmen away. No one would be lurking in the dense woods back here for fear of getting caught. He leaped forward into the underbrush, his foot snagging on a vine, knocking him painfully to the ground.

Christ! he thought. *Must hurry.* The police had to be avoided at all costs. *They own half the cops.* He scrambled to his feet, lunged forward into the pitch-black.

The siren had gone silent, but now there were shouts, both female and male, the crunch of feet on the gravel. Running forward, he pushed branches away from his face, but still one scraped him, just missing an eye. He kept going, not slowing for a second, turning this way, juking that, through the close vegetation, the narrow tunnels, under canopies formed by interlaced branches. Something tore at his pants. His hands were scraped and bloodied. But he kept plowing through the trees, machinelike, unthinking, until he came to the hidden clearing where Peter's truck was still parked.

He opened the driver's side door—unlocked, thank God—and of course there was no key in the ignition. He felt under the floor mat. Nothing. Under the seat. Nothing.

Panic overcame him. He inhaled sharply several times to try to calm himself. Of course, he thought. *I've forgotten what I know.*

He reached into the mess of wires beneath the dash, pulled them out to inspect the tangle by the weak overhead light. *Hot-wiring,* their beloved family groundskeeper, Arnie, had told him and Peter one summer morning. *This is a skill you may never have a use for. But if you do, you'll sure be glad you got it.*

In a few moments he'd paired the two wires, and the ignition turned over, roared to life. Slamming the gearshift into reverse, he backed out of the clearing onto the dark road. No headlights in either direction. He shifted into drive; the old truck balked, but then lurched ahead, surging down the deserted highway.

CHAPTER NINE

Halifax, Nova Scotia

The next morning was cold and dreary. Fog had settled gloomily over the port, visibility no more than ten feet ahead.

Robert Mailhot lay on a steel examination table, clothed in a blue suit, his face and hands rosy with the funeral home's garish makeup. The face was bronze-tinted but heavily lined, angry, the thin mouth sunken, the nose a prominent beak. He looked to be five foot ten or eleven, which meant he'd probably been six feet tall as a young man.

The medical examiner was a corpulent, ruddy-faced man in his late fifties named Higgins: a thatch of white hair, small suspicious gray eyes. He was perfectly cordial, while at the same time guarded, neutral. He wore a green surgical gown. "So you've got reason to believe this was a homicide?" he said jovially, his eyes watchful. He was dubious and made no attempt to mask it.

Anna nodded.

Sergeant Arsenault, in a bright red sweater and jeans, was subdued. Both of them were rattled by their long and difficult interview with the widow. In the end, of course, she had given permission for the autopsy, saving them the headache of having to ask for a court order.

The hospital morgue reeked of formalin, which always made Anna uneasy. Classical music played tinnily from a portable radio on the stainless-steel counter.

"You're not expecting to find any trace evidence on the body, I hope," Higgins said.

"I assume the body was pretty thoroughly washed at the funeral home," she said. Did he think she was an idiot?

"What are we looking for, then?"

"I don't know. Puncture marks, bruises, wounds, cuts, scratches."

"Poison?"

"Could be."

She and Higgins and Arsenault together removed Mailhot's clothing, and then Higgins swabbed the body's hands and face clean of makeup, which could hide marks. The eyes had been sutured shut at the funeral home; Higgins cut the stitches and inspected for petechial hemorrhages— tiny pinpoints of blood under the skin—that might indicate strangulation.

"Any bruising inside the lips?" Anna asked.

The mouth, too, had been sutured closed. The medical examiner quickly sliced through the twine with a scalpel, then poked around inside the mouth with a latex-gloved finger. When someone is smothered with a pillow with enough pressure to stop the flow of air, Anna knew, you usually find bruises where the lips were forced against the teeth.

"Uh-uh," he said. "None that I can see."

All three began inspecting the shriveled body with magnifying glasses, inch by inch. With an old person this is difficult work: the skin is covered with dings and bruises, moles and broken capillaries, the marks and accretions of age.

They looked for needle marks in all the usual places: the back of the neck, between fingers and toes, the backs of the hands, the ankles, behind the ears. Around the nose and cheeks. Injection marks could be disguised with a scratch, but nothing turned up. Higgins even checked the scrotum, which was large and loose, the penis a tiny stub nestled on top. Pathologists rarely checked the scrotum. The guy was thorough.

They spent over an hour at it, then turned Mailhot over and did the same. Higgins took photographs of the body. For a long time no one spoke; there was just the staticky crackle of a clarinet, the lush swell of strings, the hum of refrigerators and other machinery. The formalin smell was unpleasant, but at least there was no smell of decay, for which Anna was thankful. Higgins checked the fingernails for tears or rips—did the deceased fight an assailant?—and scraped under the nails, putting the scrapings into small white envelopes.

"Nothing on the epidermis out of the ordinary, far as I can see," Higgins declared at last.

She was disappointed but not surprised. "Poison could have been ingested," she suggested.

"Well, it'll turn up in the tox," Higgins said.

"Maybe not," she said. "There's no blood."

"May be some," Higgins said. If they were lucky. Usually, when the funeral home prepared the body, the blood was completely removed except for small residual pockets, and replaced with embalming fluid. Methanol, ethanol, formaldehyde, dyes. It broke down certain compounds, poisons, rendering them untraceable. Maybe there'd be some urine remaining in the bladder.

He cut the usual Y-shaped incision from the shoulder down to the pelvis, then reached inside the thoracic cavity to remove the organs and weigh them. This was one of the aspects of an autopsy Anna found particularly repellent. She worked with death regularly, but there was a reason she hadn't become a pathologist.

Arsenault, looking pale, excused himself to get a cup of coffee.

"Can you take some samples of brain, some bile, kidney, heart, and so on?" she said.

Higgins smiled tartly: don't tell me my business.

"Sorry," she said.

"I'd wager we'll find arteriosclerosis," Higgins said.

"No doubt," she said. "The man was old. Is there a phone around here I can use?"

The pay phone was down the hall next to a vending machine that dispensed coffee, tea, and hot chocolate. The front of the machine was a large oversaturated color photograph of cups of hot chocolate and coffee, intended to look appetizing, but actually greenish and awful. As she dialed she could hear the buzz of the Stryker saw as Higgins cut through the rib cage.

Arthur Hammond, she knew, normally got to work early. He ran a poison-control center in Virginia and taught toxicology courses at a university. They'd met on a case and liked each other instantly. He was shy, spoke with an intermittent hesitation that hid an old stammer, rarely looked you in the eyes. Yet he had a wicked sense of humor. He was a scholar of poisons and poisonings back to the Dark Ages. Hammond was far better than anyone in the federal labs, better than any forensic pathologist, and certainly far more willing to help. He was not only brilliant but intuitive. From time to time she had brought him in as a paid consultant.

She caught him at home, on his way out the door, and explained.

"Where are you?" he asked.

"Uh, up north."

He gave a short nasal snort of amusement at her secrecy. "I see. Well, what can you tell me about the victims?"

"Old. How do you kill someone undetectably?"

A throaty chuckle. "Just break up with him, Anna. You don't have to kill him." This was his way of flirting.

"What about the old bolus of potassium chloride?" she

said, politely ignoring his joke. "Stops the heart, right? Barely changes the body's overall potassium level, so it's undetectable?"

"Was he on an IV?" Higgins asked.

"I don't think so. We didn't find any of the usual puncture marks."

"Then I doubt it. It's far too messy. If he wasn't on an IV, you'd have to inject it right into a vein, and you'd find blood spewed all over the place. Not to mention signs of a struggle."

She took notes in her tiny leather-bound notebook.

"It was sudden, right? So we can rule out long-term heavy metal poisoning. Too gradual. Do you mind if I go get a cup of coffee?"

"Go ahead." She smiled to herself. He knew this stuff cold.

He returned in less than a minute. "Speaking of coffee," he said. "It's either something in their drink or their food, or else an injection."

"But we didn't find any puncture marks. And believe me, we went over that body carefully."

"If they used a 25-gauge needle you won't see it, probably. And there's always sux."

She knew he meant succinylcholine chloride, synthetic curare. "Think so?"

"Famous case back in '67 or '68—a doctor in Florida was convicted of murdering his wife with sux, which I'm sure you know is a skeletal muscle relaxant. You can't move, can't breathe. Looks like cardiac arrest. Famous trial, baffled forensic experts around the world."

She jotted a note.

"There's a long list of skeletal muscle relaxants, all with different properties. Of course, you know, with old folks, anything can tip 'em over the edge. A little too much nitroglycerin will do it."

"Under the tongue, right?"

"Usually . . . But there's ampules of, say, amyl nitrite that could kill you if inhaled. Poppers. Or butyl nitrite. You get a major vasodilator response, drops their blood pressure, they keel over and die."

She wrote furiously.

"There's even Spanish fly," he said with a cackle. "Too much can kill you. I think it's called cantharidin."

"The guy was eighty-seven."

"All the more reason he might need an aphrodisiac."

"I don't want to think about that."

"Was he a smoker?"

"Don't know yet. I guess we'll see from the lungs. Why do you ask?"

"There's an interesting case I just worked on. Some old folks in South Africa. They were killed with nicotine."

"Nicotine?"

"You don't have to give that much."

"How?"

"It's a liquid. Bitter taste, but it can be disguised. Can also be injected. Death comes within minutes."

"In a smoker you can't tell, is that it?"

"You gotta be clever. I figured this out. The whole issue is the amount of nicotine in the blood versus its metabolites. What nicotine turns into after a while—"

"I know."

"In a smoker, you see a lot more of the metabolites than pure nicotine. If it's acute poisoning, you'll see a whole lot more nicotine and a lot less metabolites."

"What should I expect from the tox?"

"A normal toxicology screen is set up to detect drugs of abuse. Opiates, synthetic opiates, morphine, cocaine, LSD, Darvon. PCP, amphetamine. Benzodiazepines—Valium— and barbiturates. Sometimes tricyclic antidepressants. Ask 'em to do the full tox screen plus all these others. Chloral hydrate's not on the screen, order that. Placidyl, an old sleeping drug. Screen for barbiturates, sleeping drugs. Fentanyl's extremely hard to detect. Organophosphates—insecticides. DMSO—dimethyl sulfoxide—used on horses. See what you come up with. I assume they're going to be doing G.C. Mass. Spec."

"I don't know. What's that?"

"Gas chromatography, mass spectrometry. It's the gold standard. How rural are you?"

"A city. Canada, actually."

"Oh, RCMP is good. Their crime labs are far better than ours, but don't quote me on that. Just make sure they check for anything in the local water or wells that might skew the tox. You said the body's embalmed, right? Have 'em get a sample of the embalming fluid and subtract it out. Ask 'em to do a full tox—blood, tissue, hair. Some proteins are fat soluble. Cocaine stores in the heart tissue, keep that in mind. The liver's a sponge."

"How long are all these tests going to take?"

"Weeks. Months."

"No way." Her exhilaration over talking with him suddenly waned. Now she was depressed.

"It's true. Then again, you might get lucky. Could be months, or it could be a day. But if you don't know exactly what poison you're looking for, odds are you're never going to find it."

"There's every evidence he died naturally," Higgins announced when she'd returned to the lab. "Cardiac arrhythmia, probably. Arteriosclerosis, of course. An old MI there."

Mailhot's face had been pulled down from the top of the scalp, like a latex mask. The top of his head was open, the pink ridges of brain visible. Anna thought she might be sick. She saw a lung on a hanging scale. "How heavy?" she asked, pointing.

He smiled in appreciation. "Light. Two hundred forty grams. Not congested."

"So he died quickly. We can rule out a CNS depressant."

"As I said, it looks like a heart attack." Higgins seemed to be running out of patience.

She told him what she wanted from the toxicology screen, reading off her notes. His eyes widened in disbelief.

"Do you have any idea how costly this is going to be?"

She exhaled. "The U.S. government will pick up the cost, of course. I need to do this one thoroughly. If I don't find it now, it's likely I never will. Now I need to ask a favor."

He looked at her steadily. She sensed his annoyance.

"I'm going to ask you to flay the body."

"You're kidding me, aren't you?"

"I'm not."

"May I remind you, Agent Navarro, that the widow wants an open-casket funeral?"

"All they see are the hands and face, right?" To flay the body meant to remove all the skin, in large chunks so it could be sewn back together. This enabled you to examine the subcutaneous skin. Sometimes this was the only way to discover injection marks. "Unless you object," she said. "I'm just a visiting fireman."

Higgins's face flushed. He turned to the body, jabbing in the scalpel a bit too violently, and began removing the skin.

Anna felt light-headed. Once again she was afraid she might be sick. She left the morgue and returned to the corridor in search of the rest room. Ron Arsenault approached, clutching a giant cup of take-out coffee. "Are we still slicing and dicing in there?" he asked, his good humor seemingly restored.

"Worse than ever. We're flaying the skin."

"You can't take it either?"

"I'm just using the little girl's room."

He looked skeptical. "No luck so far, I take it."

She shook her head, frowned.

He shook his head. "Don't you Yanks believe in old age?"

"I'll be right back," she said coolly.

She splashed her face with cold water from the sink, realizing too late that there were no paper towels here, only one of those hot-air hand dryers that never worked. She groaned, went to a stall, pulled a length of toilet paper off the roll, and blotted her face with the tissue, leaving white shreds here and there on her face. She looked in the mirror, noticed the dark circles under her eyes, flecked off the strings of toilet paper, reapplied her makeup and returned to Arsenault feeling refreshed.

"He's asking for you," Arsenault said, excited.

Higgins held up a leathery yellow sheet of skin about three inches square as if it were a trophy. "You're lucky I did the hands, too," he said. "I'm going to catch hell from the funeral-home director, but presumably they've got makeup they can cake on to cover the mending."

"What is it?" she asked, heartbeat accelerating.

"The back of the hand. The web of the thumb, the abductor pollucis. Take a look at this."

She came closer, as did Arsenault, but she saw nothing. Higgins pulled the magnifying glass from the examination table. "You see this little purplish-red flare, about half an inch long? Sort of flame-shaped?"

"Yeah?"

"There's your injection mark. Believe me, that's not where any nurse or doctor puts a syringe. You may have something, after all."

CHAPTER TEN

Bedford, New York

Max Hartman sat in his high-backed leather desk chair, in the book-lined library where he usually received visitors. It was strange, Ben thought, the way his father chose to sit behind the barrier of his immense leather-topped mahogany desk, even when meeting with his own son.

In the tall chair the old man, once tall and strong, looked wizened, almost gnomelike, surely not the effect he'd intended. Ben sat on a leather chair facing the desk.

"When you called, you sounded as if you had something you wanted to talk to me about," Max said.

He spoke with a refined mid-Atlantic accent, the German long submerged, barely detectable. As a young man recently arrived in America, Max Hartman had taken speech training and elocution lessons, as if he'd wanted to banish all traces of his past.

Ben peered at his father closely, trying to make sense of the man. *You were always an enigma to me. Distant, formidable, unknowable.* "I do," he said.

A stranger seeing Max Hartman for the first time would notice the large bald head, speckled with age spots, the prominent fleshy ears. The eyes, large and rheumy, grotesquely magnified behind the thick lenses of his horn-rimmed glasses. The jutting jaw, the nostrils permanently flared as if he were smelling a bad odor. Yet for all that age had wrought, it was evident that this was a man who'd once been quite handsome, even striking.

The old man was dressed, as he always was, in one of his bespoke suits, tailored for him on Savile Row, London. Today's was a splendid charcoal, with a crisp white shirt, his initials monogrammed on the breast pocket; a blue and gold rep tie, heavy gold cuff links. Ten in the morning on a Sunday, and Max was dressed for a board meeting.

It was funny how your perceptions were shaped by your history, Ben reflected. At times he could observe his father as he was now, old and fragile, yet at other moments he couldn't help seeing him through the eyes of an abashed child: powerful, intimidating.

The truth was, Ben and Peter had always been slightly afraid of their father, a little nervous around him. Max Hartman intimidated most people; why should his own sons be the exception? It took real effort to be Max's son, to love and understand him and feel tenderness toward him. It was like learning a complex foreign language, one that Peter couldn't, or wouldn't, learn.

Ben suddenly flashed on Peter's terrible, vindictive expression when he revealed what he'd discovered about Max. And then that image of Peter's face gave way to a flood of memories of his adored brother. He felt his throat constrict, his eyes fill with tears.

Don't think, he told himself. *Don't think of Peter. Here, in this house where we played hide-and-seek and pummeled each other, conspired in whispers in the middle of the night, screamed and laughed and cried.*

Peter's gone, and now you've got to hang in there for him too.

Ben had no idea how to begin, how to broach the subject. On the plane out of Basel he'd rehearsed how he was going to confront his father. Now he'd forgotten everything he'd planned to say. The one thing he'd resolved was not to tell him about Peter, about his reappearance, his murder. For what? Why torture the old man? As far as Max Hartman knew, Peter had been killed years ago. Why should he be told the truth now that Peter really was dead?

Anyway, confrontation wasn't Ben's style. He let his father talk business, ask about the accounts Ben was managing. Man, he thought, the old guy is still sharp. He tried to change the subject, but there really wasn't any easy or elegant way to say, By the way, Dad, were you a Nazi, if you don't mind my asking?

Finally, Ben took a stab at it: "I guess being in Switzerland made me realize how little I know about, about when you were in Germany . . ."

His father's eyes seemed to grow larger behind the magnifying lenses. He leaned forward. "Now, what inspires this sudden interest in family history?"

"Really, I think it was just being in Switzerland. It reminded me of Peter. This was the first time I'd been back there since his death."

His father looked down at his hands. "I don't dwell on the past, you know that. I never did. I only look ahead, not behind."

"But your time at Dachau—we've never talked about that."

"There's really nothing to say. I was brought there, I was fortunate enough to survive, I was liberated on April 29, 1945. I will never forget the date, but it's a part of my life I prefer to forget."

Ben inhaled, then launched in. He was keenly aware that his relationship with his father was about to be altered forever, the fabric about to be torn. "Your name isn't on the list of prisoners liberated by the Allies."

It was a bluff. He watched his father's reaction.

Max stared at Ben for a long moment, and then to Ben's surprise he smiled. "You must always be wary of historical documents. Lists thrown together at a time of enormous chaos. Names spelled wrong, names omitted. If my name is missing from some list compiled by some U.S. Army sergeant, so what?"

"But you weren't at Dachau, were you?" Ben asked quietly.

His father slowly swiveled his chair around, turning his back to Ben. His voice, when it came, was reedy, somehow distant. "What a strange thing to say."

Ben felt his stomach flutter. "But true, right?"

Max swiveled back around. His face was expressionless, blank, but a blush had appeared on his papery cheeks. "There are people who make a profession out of denying that the Holocaust ever happened. So-called historians, writers—they publish books and articles saying the whole thing was a fake, a conspiracy. That millions of Jews weren't murdered."

Ben found his heart thudding, his mouth dry. "You were a lieutenant in Hitler's SS. Your name is on a document—a document of incorporation listing members of a board of directors of a secret company. You were the treasurer."

When his father replied, it was in a terrible whisper. "I won't listen to this," he said.

"It's true, isn't it?"

"You have no idea what you're talking about."

"It's why you never spoke about Dachau. Because it was all a fiction. You were never there. You were a Nazi."

"How can you *say* such things?" the old man rasped. "How can you possibly believe this? How *dare* you insult me this way!"

"That document—it's in Switzerland. Articles of incorporation. The whole truth is there."

Max Hartman's eyes flashed. "Someone showed you a fraudulent document, designed to discredit me. And you, Benjamin, chose to believe it. The real question is why."

Ben could feel the room revolving around him slowly. "*Because Peter told me himself!*" he shouted. "Two days ago in Switzerland. He found a document! He found out the truth. Peter found out what you had done. He tried to protect us from it."

"Peter—?" Max gasped.

The expression of his father's face was terrible, but Ben forced himself to keep going.

"He told me about this corporation, who you really were. He was telling me everything when he was *shot dead*."

The blood had drained from Max Hartman's face, the gnarled hand that rested on his desk visibly trembling.

"Peter was killed *before my eyes*." And now Ben almost spat the words: "My brother, your son—another one of your victims."

"Lies!" his father shouted.

"No," Ben said. "The truth. Something you've kept from us all our lives."

Abruptly, Max's voice became hushed and cold, an arctic wind. "You speak of things you cannot possibly understand." He paused. "This conversation is over."

"I understand who *you* are," Ben said. "And it sickens me."

"Leave," Max Hartman shouted and he raised a quivering arm toward the door. Ben could picture that same arm raised in an SS salute, in a past that was distant but not distant enough. Never distant enough. And he recalled some writer's often quoted words: *The past isn't dead. It isn't even past.*

"Get out!" his father thundered. "Get out of this house!"

Washington, D.C.

The Air Canada flight from Nova Scotia arrived at Reagan National in the late afternoon. The taxi pulled up to Anna's Adams-Morgan apartment building just before six. It was already dark.

She loved coming home to her apartment. Her sanctuary. The only place where she felt utterly in charge. It was a small one-bedroom in a bad neighborhood, but it was her own perfectly realized world.

Now, as she got out of the elevator on her floor, she met

her neighbor, Tom Bertone, who was heading down. Tom and his wife, Danielle, were both lawyers, both a little effusive, a little *too* neighborly, but pleasant enough. "Hey, Anna, I met your kid brother today," he said. "I guess he'd just gotten into town. Really nice guy." And the elevator doors closed behind him.

Brother?

She had no brother.

At the door to her apartment, she waited a long moment, trying to calm her racing heart. She fished out her gun, a government-issue 9 mm Sig-Sauer, holding it in one hand as she turned the key with the other. Her apartment was dark, and, recalling her early training, she went into standard E&S, evasion and search, tactics. That meant flattening yourself against a wall with a pistol drawn, then shifting to an orthogonal wall, and repeating the process. They drilled it into field agents with the training sets, but she never imagined she'd be doing it in her own apartment, her home, her *sanctuary*.

She closed the door behind her. Silence.

But there was *something*. A barely detectable odor of cigarettes, that was it. Too faint to be from an actual lighted cigarette; it had to be the residue from the clothing of someone who smoked.

Someone who had been in her apartment.

In the dim light provided by the streetlights outside, she could see something else: one of the drawers of her file cabinets was slightly ajar. She always kept them neatly shut. *Someone had been searching through her belongings.*

Her blood ran cold.

There was a draft from the bathroom: the window had been left open.

And then she heard a sound, quiet but not quiet enough: the almost inaudible squeak of a rubber-soled shoe on the bathroom tile.

The intruder was still there.

She flipped on the main overhead light, wheeled around in a crouch, her 9 mm drawn, the weight of it balanced in her two hands. She was grateful that it was a Sig factory short trigger, which fit her hands better than the standard model. The intruder wasn't visible, but the apartment was small and there weren't many places he could be. She straightened up and, adhering to the perimeter rule—*hug the walls*, the E&S instructors liked to say—she made her way toward the bedroom.

She felt the movement of air an instant before the gun was dislodged from her hands by a powerful kick from seemingly out of nowhere. Where had he come from? Behind the bureau? The filing cabinets? The gun clattered as it hit the sitting room floor. *Retrieve it, whatever you do.*

Abruptly she was slammed backward by another kick, and she sprawled against the bedroom door, her back hitting it with a dull thud. She froze in place as the man took a few steps back.

Except that he was hardly a man. He had the slender frame of an adolescent. As powerful as he was—sinewy muscles flexed under a tight black T-shirt—he looked no older than seventeen. *It didn't make sense.*

Slowly, carefully, she got to her feet and began moving, with feigned casualness, toward the oatmeal-colored sofa. The blue-gray butt of her Sig-Sauer protruded from under its plaited hem, just barely visible.

"Burglary's a real serious problem in this neighborhood, isn't it?" the man-boy said in a tone of rich irony. His glossy, black hair was cut short, his skin looked as if he'd only recently started to shave, and his features were small and regular. "The statistics are *shocking*." He scarcely sounded like the typical delinquents who haunted Southeast Washington. If she had to guess, she'd say he wasn't a native of this country; she thought she detected a trace of an Irish brogue.

"There's nothing of value here." Anna tried to sound calm. "You must know that by now. Neither of us wants any trouble." She realized her hand was still numb from the blow. Keeping her gaze on him, she took another step toward the sofa. Trying for a light tone, she added, "Anyway, shouldn't you be in school or something?"

"Never send a man to do a boy's work," he replied agreeably. Suddenly he unleashed another roundhouse kick and she reeled backward against her small wooden bureau. The blow had landed squarely on her stomach, and she found herself gasping for breath.

"Did you know," the young intruder continued, "that as often as not it's the *owners* of handguns who are killed by them? Another statistic that bears thinking about. You really can't be too careful."

He wasn't a burglar, that much was obvious. He didn't *talk* like one either. But what was he after? She squeezed her eyes shut for a moment, mentally taking an inventory of her sparsely furnished apartment, her paltry belongings, the clothes, the lamps, the humidifier, the clothes... *the M26. Must try to find the M26!* No doubt he'd searched the place thoroughly, but this was an item whose function would not be obvious to those unfamiliar with it. "I'll get you money," she said loudly, and turned to the bureau, opening drawers. "I'll get you money," she repeated. Where had she kept the device? And would it still work? It had been at least two years. She found it in the large central drawer, next to several red cardboard boxes of checkbooks. "All right," she said, "here it is."

When she turned around to face him, she had the M26 Tasertron firmly in her grasp, switched it on, a high-pitched whine indicating that the device was fully charged.

"I want you to listen to me carefully," she said. "This is an M26 Taser, the most powerful one they make. Move away from me now, or I will use it. I don't care what kind of martial arts you know—twenty-five thousand volts will take the starch out of you."

The intruder's expression was blank, but he began to walk away from her, backing into the bathroom.

The instant the stun gun was activated, the cartridge would fire off the contactors, two fine conducting wires ending in quarter-inch needle points. The electricity discharged would be of a voltage sufficient to immobilize him for a spell, perhaps even knock him out.

She followed him toward the bathroom. He *was* inexperienced; by backing up into the small room, he had allowed himself to be cornered. A bad move, an amateurish slip. She switched the Taser on maximum; there was no point in taking any risks at this point. The device in her hand hummed and crackled. A blue arc of electricity played between two visible electrodes. She would aim for his midriff.

Suddenly she heard an unexpected sound, that of water running, the roar of the tap turned up full. *What the hell was he up to?* She lunged into the bathroom, aiming the Taser, and saw the man-child wheel around with something in his hands. Too late, she realized his gambit. It was the nozzle of her handheld shower, which propelled a drenching blast of water in her direction. Water that would ordinarily have been harmless. She dropped the primed M26 an instant too late. A bolt of electricity arced from it toward her drenched torso, a blue bolt of agony. As her major muscle groups spasmed, she collapsed to the floor, only the pain cutting through her dazed state.

"It's been a blast," the young man said tonelessly. "But I'm already running late. Catch you later." He winked, in a caricature of affection.

She watched, helpless, as he clambered out the bathroom window and disappeared down the fire escape.

By the time she was able to call the municipal police, she had verified that nothing was missing from the apartment. But that was the only question she'd been able to answer. The cops, when they arrived, asked the usual questions, debated whether to classify the incident as a home invasion or a burglary, and then seemed to run out of ideas. They'd do the crime-scene workup—they understood that she was some kind of fed, that she seemed to know what she was talking about. But it would take several hours. And in the meantime?

Anna glanced at her watch. Eight P.M. She called David

Denneen's home number. "I'm sorry to bother you," she said, "but is that guest room of yours free? It seems my apartment has just turned into a crime scene."

"A crime . . . *Jesus*," Denneen said. "What happened?"

"I'll explain later. Sorry to spring this on you."

"Have you eaten yet? Come on over now. We'll set an extra place."

David and Ramon lived in a prewar apartment near Dupont Circle, a fifteen-minute cab ride away. It wasn't grand, but it was nicely appointed, with high ceilings and leaded windows. From the savory aromas she inhaled when she came in—chile, anise, cumin—she guessed that Ramon was cooking one of his moles.

Three years ago, Denneen was a junior agent under her command. He was a fast learner, did good work, and was responsible for several breaks; he'd tailed a White House special assistant to the Qatar Embassy, a lead that resulted in a major corruption investigation. She'd filed glowing reports in his personnel file, but soon she learned that Arliss Dupree, as the unit director, had been appending "fitness" evaluations of his own. They were vague but damning in intent: Denneen "wasn't government material." He "lacked the fortitude" expected of an OSI investigator, was "soft," "possibly unreliable," "flighty." His "attitude was problematic." All of it was nonsense, the bureaucratic camouflage of a visceral hostility, a reflexive prejudice.

Anna had become friends with both David and Ramon, had met them as a couple when she'd stopped in Kramerbooks, on Connecticut Avenue, and saw them shopping together. Ramon was a small, open-faced man with an easy smile, his white teeth dazzling against his dark complexion. He worked as an administrator for the local Meals on Wheels program. He and Anna warmed to each other immediately; Ramon insisted that she dine with them that evening, as a spur-of-the-moment thing, and she agreed. It was a magical occasion, partly because of the excellence of Ramon's paella, partly because of the relaxed conversation and easy banter, none of which ever touched upon office matters; she envied them their easy intimacy and affection.

David, with his square jaw and sandy hair, was a tall, ruggedly handsome man, and Ramon noticed the way she looked at him. "I know what you're thinking," he confided to her at one point, when David was across the room with his back to them, fixing drinks. "You're thinking, 'What a waste.'"

Anna laughed. "It's crossed my mind," she said.

"All the girls say that." Ramon grinned. "Well, he ain't wasted on me."

A few weeks later, Anna had lunch with David and explained to him why he hadn't received a promotion from E-3 grade. On paper, he reported to Anna, but Anna reported to Dupree. "What would you like me to do?" Anna asked.

Denneen responded quietly, with less outrage than Anna felt on his behalf. "I don't want to make a big deal of this. I just want to do my work." He looked at her. "Truth? I want to get the hell out of Dupree's division. I happen to be interested in operations and strategy. I'm only E-3, so I can't arrange it. But you might be able to."

Anna pulled a few strings. It meant doing an end-run around Dupree, which didn't exactly endear her to OSI management. But it worked, and Denneen never forgot it.

Now she filled in Denneen about what had happened at her apartment, and between Ramon's chicken mole and a bottle of a velvety Rioja, she felt some of her tension ebb. Soon she found herself joking grimly about having been "trounced by a member of the Back Street Boys."

"You could have been killed," Denneen said solemnly, not for the first time.

"But I wasn't. Which proves that wasn't what he was after."

"And what might that have been?"

Anna just shook her head.

"Listen, Anna. I know you probably can't talk about it, but do you think there's any chance it has to do with your new assignment at ICU? Old Alan Bartlett has kept so many secrets over the years, there's no telling what he's got you up against."

"*El diablo sabe más por viejo que por diablo,*" Ramón muttered. It was one of his mother's proverbs: The devil knows more because he is old than because he is the devil.

"Is it a coincidence?" Denneen persisted.

Anna looked at her wineglass and shrugged, wordlessly. Were others interested in the death of the people in the Sigma files? She couldn't think about this right now, and didn't want to.

"Have some more *carnitas*," Ramón said helpfully.

The following morning at the M Street building, Anna was summoned to Bartlett's office the instant she arrived.

"What did you learn in Nova Scotia?" Bartlett asked, not wasting any time on social niceties this time.

She'd earlier decided against mentioning the intruder in her apartment; there was no reason to think it was related, and she worried, vaguely, that the episode would undermine his confidence in her. She told him about what was clearly relevant: the puncture mark in the old man's hand.

Bartlett nodded slowly. "What kind of poison did they use?"

"Haven't gotten the toxicology results back yet. It takes time. Always does. If they find something, they call you right away. If they don't, they keep testing and testing."

"But you really believe Mailhot might have been poisoned." Bartlett sounded nervous, as if uncertain whether this was good news or bad.

"I do," she said. "Then there's the money question. Four months ago the guy got a wire transfer of a million bucks."

Bartlett knit his brows. "From?"

"No idea. An account in the Cayman Islands. Then the trail disappears. Laundered."

Bartlett listened in perplexed silence.

She went on. "So I got the bank records going back ten years, and there it is, regular as clockwork. Every year

Mailhot got a chunk of money, wired into his account. Steadily increasing amounts."

"A business partnership, perhaps?"

"According to his wife, these were payouts from a grateful employer."

"A very *generous* employer."

"A very rich one. And a very *dead* one. The old man spent most of his life working as a personal assistant to a wealthy press baron. A bodyguard, a factotum, a lifelong gofer, best I can figure it."

"To whom?"

"Charles Highsmith." Anna watched Bartlett's reaction carefully. He nodded briskly; he'd already known this.

"The question, of course, is why the offshore payments," he said. "Why not a straightforward transfer from Highsmith's estate?"

Anna shrugged. "That's just one of many questions. I suppose one way to answer it is to trace the funds, see if they really did originate with Charles Highsmith's estate. I've done work before on laundered drug money. But I can't be optimistic."

Bartlett nodded. "What about the widow . . . ?"

"No help. She may be covering something up, but as far as I can tell, she didn't know much about her husband's business. Seemed to think he was in the grip of paranoia. Apparently, he was one of those who thought Highsmith's death might not have been an accident."

"Is that right?" Bartlett said, with a tincture of irony.

"And you're another one, aren't you? Obviously you knew about Highsmith's connection to Mailhot. Was there a Sigma file on him, too?"

"That's immaterial."

"Forgive me, but you'll have to let me be the judge of that. I have a sense that not much I'm reporting comes as news to you."

Bartlett nodded. "Highsmith was Sigma, yes. Both master and servant were, in this case. Highsmith seems to have placed great trust in Mailhot."

"And now the two are inseparable," Anna said grimly.

"You did superb work in Halifax," Bartlett said. "I hope you know that. I also hope you didn't unpack. It appears that we've got a fresh one."

"Where?"

"Paraguay. Asunción."

A fresh one. The words were, she had to admit, intriguing as well as chilling. At the same time, the Ghost's high-handed way with information filled her with frustration and a deep sense of unease. She studied the man's face, half-admiring its complete opacity. What precisely did he know? What wasn't he telling her?

And why?

CHAPTER ELEVEN

St. Gallen, Switzerland

Ben Hartman had spent the last two days traveling. From New York to Paris. From Paris to Strasbourg. At Strasbourg he had taken a short commuter flight to Mulhouse, France, near the borders of Germany and Switzerland. There he had hired a car to drive him to the regional Aéroport Basel-Mulhouse, very close to Basel.

But instead of crossing into Switzerland, which was the logical point of entry, he instead chartered a small plane to take him to Liechtenstein. Neither the charter operator nor the pilot had asked him any questions. Why would an apparently prosperous-looking international businessman be seeking to enter the duchy of Liechtenstein, one of the world's centers of money-laundering, in a manner that was undetectable, and frankly irregular, avoiding official border crossings? The code among them was understood: *don't ask.*

By the time he had arrived in Liechtenstein, it was almost one in the morning. He spent the night in a small pension outside Vaduz, and then set off in the morning to find a pilot who would be willing to cross the Swiss border, in such a way that his name would appear on no manifests or passenger lists.

In Liechtenstein, the plumage of an international businessman—the Kiton double-breasted suit, the Hermès tie, and the Charvet shirt—was protective coloration, nothing more. The duchy distinguished sharply among insiders and outsiders, among those who had something of value to offer and those who had not, among those who belonged and those who did not. It was emblematic of its clannishness that foreigners who sought to become citizens had to be approved by both the parliament and the prince.

Ben Hartman knew his way around places like these. In the past, that fact had filled him with moral unease, his permanent, ineradicable air of privilege burning like the mark of Cain. Now it was merely a tactical advantage to be exploited. Twenty kilometers south of Vaduz was an airstrip where businessmen with private jets and helicopters sometimes disembarked. There he had a conversation with a gruff, older member of the ground maintenance crew, referring to his requirements in terms that were both vague and unmistakable. A man of few words, he looked Ben over and scrawled a phone number on the back of a manifest ledger. Ben tipped him generously for the recommendation, though when he called the number, he reached a groggy-sounding man who begged off, saying he had another job today. He *did*, however, have a friend, Gaspar . . . Another call. It was afternoon before he finally met with Gaspar, a dyspeptic middle-aged man, who sized Ben up quickly and spelled out his exorbitant terms. In truth, the pilot made a handsome living flying businessmen over the border into Switzerland without leaving a trace in the computers. There were times when certain drug lords or African potentates or Middle Eastern operators needed to do some banking in both countries without the authorities watching. The pilot, who seemed to wear a perpetual sneer, assumed that Ben was up to something similar. Half an hour later, preparing for their departure, Gaspar had learned of a storm over St. Gallen and wanted to cancel the flight, but several more hundred-dollar bills had persuaded him otherwise.

As the light twin-engine propeller plane bounced through the turbulence over the eastern Alpine ranges, the taciturn pilot became almost voluble. "There's a saying where I come from. *Es ist besser reich zu leben, als reich zu sterben.*" He chuckled. "It's better to live rich than to die rich . . ."

"Just fly," Ben said dully.

He wondered whether his precautions were overly elaborate, but the truth was that he had no idea what the reach was of the people who had murdered his brother, or who had assigned the man he'd known as Jimmy Cavanaugh to try to kill him in Zurich. And he did not intend to make things easy for them.

In St. Gallen, Ben had hitched a ride with a farmer delivering vegetables to the markets and restaurants. The farmer surveyed him with bafflement; Ben explained that his car had broken down in the middle of nowhere. Later on, he rented a car and drove to the remote farming community of Mettlenberg. If the flight had been bumpy, the drive wasn't much better. The rain poured down, sheeting the windshield of the rented car. The car's wipers flicked back and forth quickly but uselessly, for the rain was too hard. It was late afternoon, and already it was dark. Ben could barely see a few feet in front of him. It was probably fortunate that the traffic in both directions on this small rural road was heavy, inching along.

He was in a remote, sparsely populated area in the northeastern part of Switzerland, in the canton of St. Gallen, not far from Lake Constance. From time to time, when the rain momentarily abated, he was able to see the large working farms on either side of the road. Herds of cattle, flocks of sheep, acres of cultivated land. There were large primitive buildings containing stables and barns and evidently living quarters as well, all under one large double-thatched roof. Beneath the eaves were woodpiles stacked with geometric precision.

As he drove he experienced a whole range of emotions,

from fear to the deepest sadness to an almost violent anger.
Now he was approaching a cluster of buildings in what had
to be the village of Mettlenberg. The rain had slowed to a
drizzle. Ben could see the ruins of a once fortified medieval
town. There was an old granary and an early sixteenth-
century church of St. Maria. There were picturesque, well-
preserved stone houses with decorated timber faces, gables,
and half-hipped red roofs. It was barely a village at all.

Peter had said that Liesl, his lover, had applied for an
opening at a small hospital here. He had checked; there was
only one hospital for kilometers around: the *Regionalspital
Sankt Gallen Nord.*

A short distance past the "town center" was a relatively
modern building of red brick, cheaply constructed, Ben
guessed, in the 1960s. The regional hospital. He found a
Migros gasoline station where he parked the car and made
a call from the pay phone.

When the hospital switchboard operator answered, Ben
said slowly, in English, "I need to speak to the pediatrician.
My child is ill." There seemed little point in using his tourist German, since he wouldn't be able to disguise his American accent, anyway, and a Swiss operator would know
English.

Peter had said that the hospital had hired Liesl because
they "needed a pediatrician," as if they had none other.
Then again, maybe there were others, but Ben doubted it,
not in a hospital as small as this one.

"I will connect you with the, eh, the *Notfallstation*, sir.
The emergency—"

"No," Ben interrupted quickly. "Not the emergency
room. I need to speak directly with the pediatrician. Is there
more than one on staff?"

"Just one, sir, but the doctor is not in at this time."

Just one! Inwardly, Ben exulted; had he found her?

"Yes, a woman named Liesl-something, right?"

"No, sir. There is no Liesl on the staff here as far as I
know. The pediatrician is Dr. Margarethe Hubli, but I tell
you, she is not in the hospital. Let me connect—"

"I must be mistaken. That was the name I was given. Was there a doctor by the name of Liesl who left recently?"

"Not that I know of, sir."

Strike out.

He had a thought. There was a chance that Dr. Hubli would know Liesl, know who she was, where she had gone. This *had* to be the hospital where Liesl had gotten a job.

"Is there a number where I can reach Dr. Hubli?"

"I'm afraid I can't give out her home number, sir, but if you bring your child into the hospital—"

"Can you page her for me?"

"Yes, sir, I can do that."

"Thank you." He gave the number of the pay phone and a false name.

Five minutes later the phone rang.

"Mr. Peters?" a woman's voice asked in English.

"Thank you for calling, Doctor. I'm an American staying with friends here, and I'm trying to reach a doctor who I believe was on the staff of the regional hospital. I'm wondering whether you might know her—a woman named Liesl?"

There was a pause—*too* long a pause. "I don't know any Liesl," the pediatrician said.

Was she lying to protect Liesl? Or was he simply imagining it?

"Are you certain?" Ben persisted. "I was told there was a pediatrician named Liesl there, and it's urgent that I reach her. It's a family matter."

"What sort of 'family matter'?"

Bingo. She had to be protecting Liesl.

"It concerns her . . . her brother, Peter."

"Her—brother?" The pediatrician seemed confused.

"Tell her my name is Ben."

Another long silence passed.

"Where are you?" the woman asked.

*   *   *

Barely twenty minutes went by before a small red Renault pulled into the gas station.

A petite woman enrobed in a large military-green rain poncho, wearing mud-caked jeans and boots, got out tentatively before slamming the car door shut. She spotted him and approached. She was a real beauty, Ben could see. Not what he had expected, for some reason. Under the poncho hood he could see her short glossy dark brown hair. She had luminous blue eyes and a milky-white complexion. But her face was drawn, pinched: she looked scared.

"Thanks for coming," he said. "You obviously know Liesl. I'm her husband's twin brother."

She kept staring at him. "Good Lord," she breathed, "you look just like him. It's, it's like seeing a *ghost*." Her face, a mask of tension, suddenly crumpled. "Dear God," she gasped, breaking out in sobs, "he was so careful! So . . . many years . . ."

Ben looked at the doctor, confused.

"He didn't come back that night," she went on in a panicked rush. "I stayed up late, worried, terrified." She covered her face with her hands. "And then Dieter came by and told me what had happened . . ."

"Liesl," Ben breathed.

"Oh, *God!*" she wailed. "He was such a—such a good man. I loved him so much."

Ben wrapped his arms around her, sustaining her in a great hug of assurance, and he too felt his tears begin to flow.

Asunción, Paraguay

Anna was stopped at Customs by a fleshy-faced Paraguayan official in a short-sleeve blue shirt and tie. From his hair and complexion she could tell he was, like most Paraguayans, a mestizo, of mixed Spanish and Indian ancestry.

He sized her up, then tapped her carry-on bag, indicating that he wanted her to open it. He asked her a few questions in heavily accented English, then, glowering with apparent disappointment, waved her through.

She felt furtive, like a criminal casing a joint. Normal federal regulations required a visiting agent to check in with the local embassy, but she would do no such thing. The risk of a leak was too great. If trouble resulted, she'd deal with the protocol breach later.

She found a pay phone in the crowded airport lobby. It took her a minute or two to figure out how to use her calling card.

A message from Arliss Dupree, demanding to know when she would be returning to the OSI unit. And a message from Sergeant Arsenault of the RCMP. The toxicology results were in. He didn't say what they were.

When she reached RCMP headquarters in Ottawa, she was put on hold for a solid five minutes while they chased down Ron Arsenault.

"How're you doin' there, Anna?"

She could tell from his voice. "Nothing, huh?"

"I'm sorry." He didn't sound sorry. "I guess you wasted your time here."

"I don't think so." She tried to mask her disappointment. "The injection mark is significant. You mind if I talk to the toxicologist?"

He hesitated a moment. "I don't see why not, but it's not going to change anything."

"I'd just feel better about it."

"Hey, why not?" Arsenault gave her a Halifax number.

The airport was loud and chaotic. It was hard to hear the voice on the phone.

The toxicologist's name was Denis Weese. His voice was high and hoarse and ageless—he could have been in his sixties or in his twenties.

"We ran every single test you requested and then some," he said defensively.

She tried to imagine him: small and bald, she decided. "I'm grateful to you."

"They were extremely costly, you know."

"We're paying for them. But let me ask you this: Aren't there substances, toxins, that cross the blood-brain barrier, and then don't cross back?" Arthur Hammond, her poison expert, had suggested such a scenario in passing.

"I suppose there are."

"Which might be found only in the spinal fluid?"

"I wouldn't count on it, but it's possible." He was grudging: he didn't appreciate her theories.

She waited, and when he didn't go on, she asked the obvious: "How about a spinal tap?"

"Can't."

"Why not?"

"For one thing, it's just about impossible to do a spinal tap on a dead body. There's no pressure. It won't come out. For another, the body's gone."

"Buried?" She bit her lower lip. Damn.

"The funeral's this afternoon, I think. The body's been moved back to the funeral home. Burial's tomorrow morning."

"But you could go there, couldn't you?"

"Theoretically, but what for?"

"Isn't the eye—the ocular fluid—the same as the spinal fluid?"

"Yeah."

"You can draw *that*, can't you?"

A pause. "But you didn't order it."

"I just did," she said.

Mettlenberg, St. Gallen, Switzerland

Now Liesl had fallen silent. The tears, which had coursed down her cheeks, dampening her denim workshirt, were beginning to dry.

Of course it was she. How could he not have known?

They were sitting in the front seat of her car. Standing on the asphalt island of the gas station was too exposed, she said, after she'd regained her composure. Ben remembered sitting in the front seat of Peter's truck.

She looked ahead, through the windshield. There was only the sound of the occasional car roaring by, a truck's deep-throated horn.

At last she spoke. "It is not safe for you to be here."

"I took precautions."

"If anyone sees you with me—"

"They'll think it's Peter, your husband—"

"But if the people who killed him, who know he is dead, have somehow tracked me down—"

"If they'd tracked you down, you wouldn't be here," Ben said. "You'd be dead."

She was silent for a moment. Then: "How did you get here?"

He told her in detail about the private planes and cars, his circuitous route. He knew she would find his caution reassuring. She nodded appreciatively.

"I imagine those kinds of security precautions became second nature to you and Peter," he said. "Peter told me it was you who devised his fake death. That was brilliant."

"If it was so brilliant," she said mordantly, "they'd never have found him again."

"No. I blame myself for that. I should never have come to Switzerland, brought them out of the woodwork."

"But how could you have *known?* You didn't think Peter was *alive!*" She turned to face him.

Her skin was pale, almost translucent, her hair chestnut with golden highlights. She was slender, with perfect small-ish breasts under a simple white blouse. She was extravagantly beautiful.

No wonder Peter had been willing to give up everything else in his life to spend it with her. Ben felt a powerful attraction, but he knew he would never act on it.

"You don't go by your real name," he said.

"Of course not. All of my friends here know me by another name. It's legally changed. Margarethe Hubli was the name of a great-aunt, actually. All they knew about Peter was that he was a boyfriend, a Canadian writer I was supporting. They knew him under a different name, too . . ."

Her words trailed off, and she fell silent, once again staring out the window. "He kept up some of his contacts, though, the ones he trusted. He called them his 'early warning system.' And then a few days ago, when he got a call telling him about the bloodbath at the Bahnhofstrasse . . . He understood what had happened. I begged him not to do anything. But no, he insisted on it! He said he had no choice." Her face had twisted into an expression of contempt, her voice a wail. Ben's heart was squeezed.

She went on in a small, choked voice, "He had to protect you. Persuade you to get out of the country. He had to save your life even if it meant putting his own in danger. Oh, God, I warned him not to go. I begged, *pleaded* with him."

Ben took her hand. "I'm so sorry." What could he say, really? That he was anguished beyond words that Peter had to die instead of himself? That he wished it was the other way around? That he had loved Peter for far longer than she had?

She said softly, "I can't even claim his body, can I?"

"No. Neither of us can."

She swallowed. "Peter loved you so much, you know."

It was painful to hear. He winced. "We fought a lot. I guess it's like that law of physics, about how every action has an equal and opposite reaction."

"You two didn't just look alike, you *were* alike."

"Not really."

"Only a twin would say that."

"You don't know me. Temperamentally, emotionally, we were totally different."

"Maybe in the way that two snowflakes are different. They're still snowflakes."

Ben smiled appreciatively. "I'm not sure I'd call the two of us snowflakes. We were always too much trouble."

Something in that set her off again. Now she was weeping, her agony heartbreaking. "Oh, God, why did they have to kill him? For *what*? To what *end*? He would never talk, he was no fool!"

Ben waited patiently until she found some composure. "Peter told me he found a document, a list of names. Twenty-three names of high-ranking statesmen and industrialists. 'Companies you've heard of,' he said. He said it was an incorporation document, setting up some organization in Switzerland."

"Yes."

"You saw the document."

"I did."

"It seemed genuine to you?"

"From what I could tell, yes. All the markings, even the typewriting, looked like papers I've seen from the 1940s."

"Where is it now?"

She pursed her lips. "Just before we left Zurich for good, he opened a bank account. He said it was mostly for the vault the bank would rent him. He wanted to keep papers in it. I don't know for sure, but I'd guess he must have put it there."

"Is it possible he hid it at home, in your cabin?"

"No," she said quickly, "there is nothing hidden in our cabin."

Ben made a mental note of her reaction. "Did he leave a key to this vault?"

"No."

"If the account was in his name, wouldn't these, these bad guys have ways of learning about its existence?"

"That is why he didn't open it in his name. It's in the name of an attorney."

"Do you remember who?"

"Of course. My cousin, Dr. Matthias Deschner. Actually, he's my second cousin. A distant relative, distant enough that no one would connect him with us—with me. But he's a good man, a trustworthy man. His office is in Zurich, on St. Annagasse."

"You trust him."

"Totally. I trusted him with our lives, after all. He never betrayed us; he never would."

"If people today, people with influence and power and far-reaching contacts, are so desperate to get this document, it must be extremely important." Ben's mind abruptly filled with a horrific image of Peter's crumpled body gouting blood. His chest was so tight he couldn't breathe. He thought: *Peter was in the way, and they killed him.*

"They must be afraid their names will get out," she said.

"But which of them can be alive after all these years?"

"There are also the inheritors. Powerful men can have powerful successors."

"And some who aren't so powerful. There must be a weak link somewhere." Ben broke off. "It's *madness*, all of this. The idea that anyone would care about a corporation set up half a century ago—it just sounds *insane!*"

Liesl laughed, bitterly, without mirth. "It's all relative, isn't it, this question of what makes sense and what does not? How much of your own well-ordered life makes sense any longer?"

A week ago, he was spending his days in the "development" department of Hartman Capital Management, cultivating old clients and new prospects, flashing on his charm like high beams. It was no longer a world he could inhabit; so much of what he'd grown up knowing was a lie, part of a larger deception he could scarcely hope to penetrate. *Cavanaugh was assigned to you*, Peter had said. The Corporation—this Sigma group, whatever it was— seemed to have operatives everywhere. Was that why his mother had been so insistent that he return to the family firm after Peter's death? Had she believed that he would be safer there, protected from dangers, from threats, from *truths* he could only begin to fathom?

"Did Peter ever learn anything more about this Sigma Corporation? About whether it had an ongoing existence?"

She pushed her hair back nervously, her bracelets jingling. "We learned very little that was concrete. So much remained conjecture. What we believe—*believed*—is that there are shadowy corporations and private fortunes that are devoted to erasing their origins. They're ruthless, these firms, as are the men funded by these companies. They're not troubled by such details as morality. Once they learned, somehow, that Peter had a paper that could reveal their involvement in Sigma, or that of their fathers—maybe expose these complicated corporate arrangements that were made during the war—once they learned this, they didn't hesitate to kill him. They will not hesitate to kill you, or me. Or anyone else who threatens to expose them or stop them, or who simply *knows* too much about their existence. But Peter also came to believe that these individuals had gathered together for larger purposes. To . . . orchestrate matters in the world at large."

"But when Peter and I spoke, he merely speculated that some of the old board members were protecting their own fortunes."

"If he had had time, he would have told you more of his theories."

"Did he ever talk about our father?"

She grimaced. "Only that he was a hypocrite and a world-class liar, that he was no Holocaust survivor. That he was actually a member of the SS." She added sardonically: "Apart from that, of course, Peter loved him."

He wondered whether the irony didn't conceal a kernel of truth. "Listen, Liesl, I need you to tell me how to get in touch with your cousin, the lawyer. Deschner—"

"Matthias Deschner. But for what?"

"You know why. To get the document."

"I said, for *what?*" She sounded bitter. "So you can be killed too?"

"No, Liesl. I don't plan to be killed."

"Then you must have some idea of why you must have this document that I can't possibly think of."

"Maybe so. I want to expose the killers."

He braced himself for an angry barrage, but was surprised when she answered quietly, serenely: "You wish to avenge his death."

"Yes."

Tears sprang to her eyes. Her mouth was contorted, twisted downward, as if to hold back another spell of weeping. "Yes," she said. "If you'll do it—if you're careful—as careful as you were in coming here—nothing would make me happier. Expose them, Ben. Make them pay." She pinched her nose between thumb and forefinger. "Now I must go home. I must say good-bye."

She seemed outwardly serene, but Ben could still detect the underlying fear. She was a strong and remarkable woman, a rock. *I'll do it for me and for you, too*, he thought.

"Good-bye, Liesl," Ben said, kissing her on the cheek.

"Good-bye, Ben," Liesl said as he got out of the car. She looked at him for a long time. "Yes, make them pay."

CHAPTER TWELVE

Asunción, Paraguay

The taxi from the airport was a rattling old Volkswagen Beetle, not as charming as it had first appeared. It seemed to have no muffler. They passed graceful Spanish colonial mansions before entering the traffic-choked downtown, tree-lined streets crowded with pedestrians, antique yellow trolley cars. There were more Mercedes-Benzes than she'd ever seen outside of Germany, many of them, she knew, stolen. Asunción seemed frozen in the 1940s. Time had passed it by.

Her hotel downtown was a small, shabby place on Colón. Her guidebook had awarded it three stars. Evidently, the guidebook's author had been paid off. The reception clerk warmed to her considerably when she began speaking to him in fluent Spanish.

Her room had high ceilings and peeling walls, and, since its windows opened on to the street, was incredibly loud. At least she had a private bathroom. But if you wanted to keep a low profile, you didn't stay where the gringos stayed.

She drank an *agua con gas* from the "honor bar," a

minuscule refrigerator that barely cooled its contents, then called the number she'd been given for the *Comisaria Centrico*, the main police station.

This was no official contact. Captain Luis Bolgorio was a homicide investigator for the Paraguayan *policía* who had sought the American government's help by telephone on a few murder cases. Anna had obtained his name, outside channels, from a friend in the FBI. Bolgorio owed the U.S. government a few favors; that was the extent of his loyalty.

"You are in luck, Miss Navarro," Captain Bolgorio said when they spoke again. "The widow has agreed to see you, even though she's in mourning."

"Wonderful." They spoke in Spanish, the language of business; the everyday language here was Guaraní. "Thanks for your assistance."

"She's a wealthy and important lady. I hope you'll treat her with the greatest respect."

"Of course. The body . . . ?"

"This isn't my department, but I'll arrange for you to pay a visit to the police morgue."

"Excellent."

"The house is on the Avenida Mariscal López. Can you find your way there in a taxi, or do you need me to pick you up?"

"I can get a taxi."

"Very well. I'll have the records with me that you asked for. When shall we meet?"

She arranged with the concierge for a cab, then spent the next hour reading through the file on the "victim"—though she had difficulty thinking of such a criminal as a victim.

She knew that the manila file folder Alan Bartlett had provided her was probably all the information she was going to get. Captain Bolgorio was helping only because the occasional technological assistance he got from the U.S. government's NCAV bolstered his own success here, made him look good. One hundred percent quid pro quo. Bolgorio had arranged to have Prosperi's body held in the morgue.

According to Bartlett, Paraguay was notoriously uncooperative on extradition cases and had been a popular refuge for war criminals and other international fugitives for decades. Its odious and corrupt dictator, "President for life" General Alfredo Stroessner, had seen to it. There had been some hope for improvement after Stroessner was toppled in 1989. But no. Paraguay remained unreceptive to extradition requests.

So it was an ideal place of residence for an aging villain like Marcel Prosperi. A Corsican by birth, Marcel Prosperi essentially ran Marseilles during and after World War II, controlling the heroin, prostitution, and weapons dealings there. Shortly after the war ended, as the ICU file detailed, he escaped to Italy, then Spain, and later Paraguay. Here, Prosperi set up the South American distribution network for heroin out of Marseilles—the so-called "French connection" responsible for putting snow-white Marseilles heroin on the streets of the United States, in collaboration with the American Mafia drug-kingpin Santo Trafficante, Jr., who controlled much of the heroin traffic into the U.S. Prosperi's accomplices, Anna knew, included some of Paraguay's highest officials. All of this meant that he was a very dangerous man, even after death.

In Paraguay, Prosperi maintained a respectable front business—the ownership of a chain of automobile dealerships. For the last several years, however, he had been bedridden. Two days ago, he had died.

As she dressed for her meeting with the widow Prosperi, Anna mulled over the details of the Prosperi and Mailhot cases. Whatever she found out from the widow, or from the autopsy, she was willing to bet that Marcel Prosperi didn't die of natural causes, either.

But whoever was murdering these men was resourceful, well connected, clever.

The fact that each of the victims had been in Alan Bartlett's Sigma files was significant, but what did it reveal?

Were there others who had access to the names attached to those files—whether in the Justice Department, in the CIA, or in foreign countries? Had the list somehow been leaked?

A theory was beginning to emerge. The killers—for there had to be more than one—were probably well financed and had access to good intelligence. If they weren't acting on their own, then they'd been hired by someone with money and power—but with what *motivation*? And why now, why so suddenly?

Once again, she was back to the question of the list—who exactly had seen it? Bartlett had spoken of an internal CIA audit, and of the decision to bring in the ICU itself. That suggested researchers, government officials. What about the Attorney General himself—had he seen it?

And there still remained several salient questions.

Why were the murders disguised as natural deaths? Why was it so important to keep the fact of the murders secret?

And what about—

The phone rang, yanking her out of her reverie. The taxi was here.

She finished applying her makeup and went downstairs.

The taxi, a silver Mercedes—probably stolen, too—hurtled through the crowded streets of Asunción with apparent disregard for the sanctity of human life. The driver, a handsome man in his late thirties with his olive complexion nicely set off by his white linen tropical-weight shirt, brown eyes, and close-shaven hair, glanced back at her periodically as if hoping for eye contact.

She pointedly ignored him. The last thing she needed was some Latin Lothario taking an interest in her. She stared out the window at a street vendor selling fake Rolexes and Cartiers, holding up his goods for her as they stopped at a light. She shook her head. Another vendor, an old woman, was peddling herbs and roots.

She hadn't seen a single gringo face since she'd arrived here. Maybe that was to be expected. Asunción was not exactly Paris. A bus in front of them belched foul-smelling smoke. There was a burst of instrumental music.

She noticed the traffic had thinned, the streets were wider, tree-lined. They were on the outskirts of town, it appeared. She had a city map in her handbag, but didn't want to unfold it if it wasn't necessary.

She remembered Captain Bolgorio mentioning that Prosperi's house was on Avenida Mariscal López, which was in the eastern sector on the way back to the airport. She had traveled down it on the way into town, the street with all the beautiful Spanish Colonial mansions.

But the streets she saw out the window didn't look at all familiar. She certainly hadn't seen this part of town before.

She looked up at the driver and said, "Where are we going?"

He didn't reply.

She said, "Hey, listen to me," as he pulled the car over to the shoulder of a quiet, untrafficked side road.

Oh, Jesus.

She didn't have a weapon. Her pistol was locked in her drawer at the office. Her training in martial arts and self-defense would scarcely—

The driver had turned around and was pointing a large black .38 at her.

"Now we talk," the man said. "You arrive at the airport from America. You wish to visit the estate of Señor Prosperi. Do you understand why some of us might find you interesting?"

Anna focused on remaining calm. Her advantage would have to be psychological. The man's one disadvantage was the limits of his knowledge. He did not know who she was. Or did he?

"If you are a DEA whore, then I have one set of friends who would enjoy entertaining you . . . before your final, unexplained disappearance. And you won't be the first. If you are an American *político*, I have other friends who will enjoy engaging you in, let us say, conversation."

Anna composed her features into a look of boredom mixed with contempt. "You keep speaking of 'friends,' " she said, and then hissed in her fluent Spanish: "*El muerto al hoyo y le vivo al bollo.*" Dead men have no friends.

"You do not wish to choose how you will die? It is the only choice most of us ever get."

"But *you* will have to choose first. *El que mucho habla, mucho yerro.* I feel sorry for you, taking on an errand and making such a botch of it. You really don't know who I am, do you?"

"If you're smart, you'll tell me."

She curled her lips in scorn. "That is the one thing I will not do." She paused. "Pepito Salazar would not want me to."

The driver's expression froze. "*Salazar*, you said?"

Navarro had mentioned the name of one of the most powerful cocaine exporters of the region, a man whose trading enterprise outstripped even that of the Medellín kingpins.

Now the man looked suspicious. "It is easy to invoke the name of a stranger."

"When I return to the Palaquinto this evening, it is *your* name I will be invoking," Anna said provocatively. The Palaquinto was the name of Salazar's mountain retreat, a name known only to the few. "I regret we were not formally introduced."

The man spoke with a tremor in his voice. To make trouble for a personal courier of Salazar was more than his life was worth. "I have heard stories of the Palaquinto, the faucets of gold, the fountains of champagne . . ."

"That's only for parties, and if I were you, I wouldn't count on any invitations." Her hand dipped into her small purse for her hotel keys.

"You must forgive me," the man said urgently. "My instructions came from people with incomplete knowledge. None of us would dream of dishonoring any member of Salazar's entourage."

"Pepito knows that mistakes will be made." Anna watched the .38 dangling loosely in his right hand, smiled at him encouragingly, and then, in a swift movement, dug

her keys into his wrist. The jagged steel stabbed through
flesh and fascia, and the gun dropped into Anna's lap. As
the man howled in agony, she scooped it up in one deft
movement and placed the muzzle at the back of his head.

"*La mejor palabra es la que no se dice*," she said
through gritted teeth. The best word is the one that is not
said.

She ordered the man out of the car, made him walk
fifteen paces into the scrubby roadside vegetation, then got
into his seat and roared off. She could not afford the time,
she told herself, to replay the terrifying encounter; nor
could she allow panic to seize her instincts and intellect.
There was work to do.

The house that had belonged to Marcel Prosperi was set
back from the Avenida Mariscal López. It was an immense
Spanish Colonial mansion surrounded by extravagantly
landscaped property, and it reminded her of the old Spanish
missions back home in California. Instead of a simple lawn,
though, the expanse of land was terraced with rows of cacti
and lush wildflowers, protected by a high wrought-iron
fence.

She parked the silver Mercedes some distance down the
road and walked toward the entrance, where a taxicab was
idling. A short, potbellied man emerged from it and ambled
toward her. He had the dark skin of a mestizo, a drooping
black *bandito* mustache, black hair combed straight back
with too much hair goo. His face gleamed with oil or perspiration, and he looked pleased with himself. His short-
sleeved white shirt was translucent in places where sweat
had soaked through, revealing a mat of dark chest hair.

Captain Bolgorio?

Where was his police cruiser? she wondered as his cab
drove away.

He approached her, beaming, and enveloped her hand in
his two large clammy ones.

"Agent Navarro," he said. "A great pleasure to meet such a beautiful woman."

"Thanks for coming."

"Come, Señora Prosperi is not used to being kept waiting. She is very rich and very powerful, Agent Navarro, and she is accustomed to getting her way. Let's go right in."

Bolgorio rang a bell at the front gate and identified themselves. There was a buzz, and Bolgorio pushed the gate open.

Anna noticed a gardener hunched over a row of wildflowers. An elderly female servant was walking down a path between ledges of cacti holding a tray of empty glasses and open bottles of *agua gaseosa*.

"We're all set to go to the morgue after this interview?" Anna said.

"As I said, this is really not my department, Agent Navarro. A magnificent house, is it not?" They passed through an archway into cool shade. Bolgorio rang the doorbell at the side of an ornately carved blond wooden door.

"But you can help arrange it?" Anna asked, just as the door opened. Bolgorio shrugged. A young woman in a servant's uniform of white blouse and black skirt invited them in.

Inside was even cooler, the floor tiled in terra-cotta. The servant led them to a large, open room that was sparely decorated with woven primitive rugs and earthenware lamps and pottery. Only the recessed lighting in the stucco ceiling seemed out of place.

They sat on a long, low white sofa and waited. The maid offered them coffee or sparkling water, but both of them declined.

Finally a woman appeared, tall and thin and graceful. The widow Prosperi. She looked around seventy but very well taken care of. She was dressed entirely in mourning black, but it was a designer dress: maybe Sonia Rykiel, Anna thought. She wore a black turban and outsized Jackie Onassis sunglasses.

Anna and Bolgorio both rose from the low sofa.

Without shaking their hands, she said in Spanish, "I don't see how I can help you."

Bolgorio stepped forward. "I am Captain Luis Bolgorio of the *policía*," he said with a bow of his head, "and this is Special Agent Anna Navarro of the American Department of Justice."

"Consuela Prosperi," she said impatiently.

"Please accept our deepest condolences on the passing of your husband," he continued. "We simply wanted to ask you a few questions, and then we'll be on our way."

"Is there some sort of problem? My husband was sick for a long time, you know. When he finally passed away it was surely a great relief for him."

Not to mention for you, too, Anna thought. "We have information," she said, "indicating that your husband may have been killed."

Consuela Prosperi looked unimpressed. "Please sit down," she said. They did, and she sat in a white chair facing them. Consuela Prosperi had the unnaturally tight skin of a woman who has had too many face-lifts. Her makeup was too orange, her lipstick glossy brown.

"Marcel was ill for the last several years of his life. He was confined to bed. He was in extremely poor health."

"I understand," Anna said. "Did your husband have enemies?"

The widow turned to her with an imperious glance. "Why would he have enemies?"

"Señora Prosperi, we know all about your husband's past endeavors."

Her eyes flashed. "I am his third wife," she said. "And we did not speak of his business affairs. My own interests lie elsewhere."

This woman could hardly be ignorant of her husband's reputation, Anna knew. She also did not seem to be much in mourning.

"Did Señor Prosperi have any regular visitors?"

The widow hesitated but an instant. "Not while we were married."

"And no conflicts that you know about with his international 'trading' partners?"

The widow's thin lips compressed, revealing a row of vertical age lines.

"Agent Navarro means no disrespect," Bolgorio put in hastily. "What she means to say is—"

"I'm quite aware of what she means to say," Consuela Prosperi snapped.

Anna shrugged. "There must have been many people over the years who wanted your husband apprehended, arrested, even killed. Rivals. Contenders for territory. Disgruntled business partners. You know that as well as I."

The widow offered no response. Anna noticed her thick orange pancake makeup cracking over her sun-lined face.

"There are also people who sometimes provide early warnings," Anna went on. "Intelligence. Security. Do you know if anyone ever contacted him to warn him of any possible threats?"

"In the nineteen years we were married," Consuela Prosperi said, turning away, "I never heard anything of this."

"Did he ever express to you the fear that people were after him?"

"My husband was a private man. He was an absentee owner of his automobile dealerships. He never liked to go out. Whereas I enjoy going out quite a bit."

"Yes, but did he say he was afraid to go out?"

"He didn't *enjoy* going out," she corrected. "He preferred to stay in and read his biographies and histories."

For some reason, Ramon's muttered words ran through her head. *El diablo sabe más por viejo que por diablo.* The devil knows more because he is old than because he is the devil.

Anna tried a different tack. "You seem to have very good security here."

The widow smirked. "You do not know Asunción, do you?"

"There is great poverty and crime here, Agent Navarro," Captain Bolgorio said, turning to her with outspread hands. "People of the Prosperis' means must always take precautions."

"Did your husband have any visitors at all in the last few weeks of his life?" Anna went on, ignoring him.

"No, my friends came over quite a bit, but none of them ever went upstairs to see him. He really had no friends in the last years. He saw only me and his nurses."

Anna looked up suddenly. "Who supplied his nurses?"

"A nursing agency."

"Did they rotate—did the same ones come regularly?"

"There was a day nurse and an evening nurse, and yes, always the same ones. They took very good care of him."

Anna chewed at the inside of her lower lip. "I'm going to have to examine certain of your household records."

The widow turned to Bolgorio with an expression of indignation. "I don't have to put up with this, do I? This is a grotesque invasion of my privacy."

Bolgorio tented his hands as if in supplication. "Please, Señora Prosperi, her only interest is to determine whether there was any possibility of homicide."

"Homicide? My husband's heart finally gave out."

"If we must, we can obtain them at the bank," Anna said. "But it would be so much simpler if—"

Consuela Prosperi got up and suddenly stared at Anna, nostrils flared, as if the American were a rodent that had made its way into her house. Bolgorio spoke in a low voice. "People like her, they do not tolerate invasions of their privacy."

"Señora Prosperi, you say there were two nurses," Anna said, soldiering on. "Were they very reliable?"

"Very."

"But were they never sick or absent?"

"Oh, from time to time, of course. Or they would ask for a night off when there was a holiday. *Año Nuevo, Día de los Trabajadores, Carnaval,* that sort of thing. But they were very responsible, and the agency was good about bringing in replacements without my ever having to worry. And the replacements were every bit as well trained as the regular nurses. Even on Marcel's last night, the substitute nurse did everything she could to try to save him—"

Substitute nurse. She sat upright, suddenly alert. "There was a substitute nurse on the night he died?"

"Yes, but as I said, she was as well trained—"

"Had you ever seen her before?"

"No . . ."

"Can you give me the name and phone number of the nursing agency?"

"Of course, but if you're implying that this nurse killed Marcel, you're being foolish. He was ill."

Anna's pulse quickened. "Can you call this agency?" she asked Bolgorio. "And I'd like to go to the morgue right now—could you please call ahead and arrange to have the body prepared for us?"

"The *body*?" Consuela Prosperi said, alarmed, rising to her feet.

"My deepest apologies if we must delay the funeral," Anna said. "We'd like your permission to do an autopsy. We can always get a court order, but it would be simpler and faster if you'd give us permission. I can guarantee you, if you're having an open-casket service, no one will ever be able to tell—"

"What are you talking about?" the widow said, genuinely puzzled. She walked to the immense fireplace and lifted an ornate silver urn from the mantel. "I just received my husband's ashes a few hours ago."

CHAPTER THIRTEEN

Washington, D.C.

Justice Miriam Bateman of the United States Supreme Court got up with great effort from her massive mahogany partners' desk to greet her visitor. Leaning on her gold-handled cane, she made her way around the desk and, smiling warmly despite the great pain from her rheumatoid arthritis, took her visitor's hand.

"How nice to see you, Ron," she said.

Her visitor, a tall black man in his late fifties, leaned over to give the diminutive Justice a peck on the cheek. "You look wonderful as always," he said in his deep, clear baritone, his enunciation precise.

"Oh, rubbish." Justice Bateman hobbled over to a high-backed wing chair by the fireplace, and he took the matching one next to her.

Her visitor was one of Washington's most influential private citizens, a widely respected, extraordinarily well-connected attorney in private practice who had never held a government job, yet had been a confidant of every President, Democrat and Republican, since Lyndon Johnson. Ronald Evers, famous, too, for his splendid wardrobe, was wearing a beautiful charcoal pin-striped suit and a subdued maroon tie.

"Madame Justice, thank you for seeing me on such short notice."

"For God's sake, Ron, it's Miriam. How long have we known each other?"

He smiled. "I believe it's thirty-five years . . . Miriam, give or take a decade. But I still keep wanting to call you *Professor* Bateman."

Evers had been one of Miriam Bateman's star students at Yale Law School, and he had been instrumental behind the scenes in getting Justice Bateman nominated to the High Court some fifteen years earlier. He hunched forward in his chair. "You're a busy lady, and the Court's in session, so let me get right to the point. The President has asked me to sound you out on something that must not leave this room, something he's been giving a lot of thought to. Please understand, this is highly preliminary."

Justice Bateman's piercing blue eyes radiated keen intelligence behind the thick lenses of her eyeglasses. "He wants me to step down," she said somberly.

Her directness caught her visitor unprepared. "He has enormous respect for your judgment and instincts, and he'd like you to recommend your successor. The President hasn't much more than a year left in office, and wants to make sure the next Supreme Court vacancy isn't filled by the other party, which looks awfully likely at this point."

Justice Bateman replied quietly, "And what makes the President think my seat's going to be vacant any time soon?"

Ronald Evers bowed his head, his eyes closed as if in prayer or deep contemplation. "This is a delicate matter," he said gently, like a priest in a confessional, "but we've always spoken openly with one another. You're one of the finest Supreme Court Justices this nation has ever seen, and I have no doubt you'll be mentioned in the same breath as Brandeis or Frankfurter. But I know you'll want to preserve your legacy, and so you have to ask yourself a very hard question: how many more years do you have left?" He lifted his head, and looked directly into her eyes. "Remember, Brandeis and Cardozo and Holmes all outstayed their welcome. They lingered at the Court well past the time when they could do their best work."

Justice Bateman's gaze was unyielding. "Can I get you some coffee?" she asked unexpectedly. Then, lowering her voice conspiratorially, she said, "I've got a *Sachertorte* I've just brought back from Demel's in Vienna, and the doctors tell me I really shouldn't have any."

Evers patted his flat midriff. "I'm trying to be good. But thank you."

"Then let me return bluntness with bluntness. I'm familiar with the reputation of just about every judge with any stature in every circuit in the country. And I have no doubt the President will find someone highly qualified, extremely bright, a legal scholar of range and breadth. But I want to let you in on something. The Supreme Court's a place that takes years to learn. One can't simply show up and expect to exert any influence. There's simply no substitute for seniority, for length of service. If there's one lesson I've learned here, it's the power of *experience*. That's where real wisdom comes from."

Her guest was prepared for this argument. "And there's no one on the Court as wise as you are. But your health is failing. You're not getting any younger." He smiled sadly. "None of us is. It's a terrible thing to say, I know, but there's just no way around it."

"Oh, I don't plan to keel over any time soon," she said, a glint in her eye. The telephone beside her chair suddenly rang, startling both of them. She picked it up. "Yes?"

"I'm sorry to disturb you," came the voice of her longtime secretary, Pamela, "but it's a Mr. Holland. You asked me to put him right through whenever he calls."

"I'll take it in my hideaway office." She put down the phone and stood with difficulty. "Will you excuse me for a moment, Ron?"

"I can wait outside," Evers said, getting to his feet and helping her up.

"Don't be silly. Stay right here. And if you change your mind about that *Sachertorte*, Pamela's right outside."

Justice Bateman closed the door to the study and laboriously made her way to her favorite chair. "Mr. Holland."

"Madame Justice, forgive this intrusion," said the voice on the phone, "but a difficulty has arisen that I thought you might be able to help us with."

She listened for a few moments and then said, "I can make a call."

"Only if it's not too great an inconvenience," said the man. "I would certainly never disturb you if it weren't extremely important."

"Not at all. None of us wants this. Certainly not at this time."

She listened as he spoke some more, then said, "Well, we all trust you to do the right thing."

Another pause, and she added, "I'll see you very soon," and then hung up.

Zurich

An icy wind blew down the Limmatquai, the quay on the banks of the Limmat River. The Limmat cuts through the heart of Zurich before it flows into the Zurichsee, splitting the city into two distinct halves, one the Zurich of high finance and high-priced shopping, the other the *Altstadt*, the quaint medieval Old Town. The river twinkled in the soft early-morning sunlight. It wasn't even six in the morning, but already people were striding to work, armed with briefcases and umbrellas. The sky was cloudy and overcast, though rain didn't appear imminent. But the Zurichers knew better.

Ben advanced tensely along the promenade, past the thirteenth-century *Zunfthausen*, the old guildhalls, with their leaded-glass windows, that now housed elegant res-

taurants. At Marktgasse he turned left, heading into the
warren of narrow cobbled streets that was the Old Town.
After a few minutes he found Trittligasse, a street lined
with medieval stone buildings, some of which had been
converted into dwellings.

Number 73 was an ancient stone townhouse that was
now an apartment building. A small brass frame mounted
beside the front door held only six names, white letters
embossed in black plastic rectangles.

One of them was M. DESCHNER.

He kept walking without slowing down, careful to
evince no particular interest. Perhaps it was baseless paranoia, but if there was any chance that spotters for the Corporation were keeping a lookout for him, he did not want
to jeopardize Liesl's cousin by simply arriving at the door.
The appearance of a strange visitor by itself might arouse
curiosity. However remote the possibility that watchers
were in place, rudimentary precautions would have to be
taken.

An hour later, a deliveryman in the distinctive orange
and black uniform of Blümchengallerie rang the bell of
Number 73 Trittligasse. The Blümchengallerie was Zurich's most upscale florist chain, and its colorfully clad de-
liverymen were not an uncommon sight in the city's
wealthiest neighborhoods. The man held a sizable bouquet
of white roses. The roses did, in fact, come from the Blümchengallerie; the uniform from the charity bazaar of a Catholic parish across town.

After a few minutes, the man rang again. This time a
voice crackled out of the speaker: "Yes?"

"It's Peter Hartman."

A long pause. "Again, please?"

"Peter Hartman."

An even longer silence. "Come to the third floor, Peter."

With a buzz, the front door lock released, and he found
himself in a dark foyer. Depositing the flowers on a marble
side table, he climbed the worn stone stairs, which rose
steeply through the gloom.

Liesl had given him Matthias Deschner's home and office addresses and phone numbers. Instead of calling the lawyer at his place of work, however, Ben had decided instead to appear unannounced at his home, early enough so that the attorney presumably wouldn't have left for the office. The Swiss, he knew, are supremely regular in their business hours, which usually begin between nine and ten. Deschner would surely be no different.

Liesl had said she trusted him—"totally," she said—but he could not assume anything anymore. Therefore he had insisted that Liesl not call ahead to introduce him. Ben preferred to surprise the attorney, catch him off guard, observe his genuine, unrehearsed first reaction to meeting a man he believed to be Peter Hartman—or would Deschner already know of Peter's murder?

The door opened. Matthias Deschner stood before him in a green plaid bathrobe. He was small, with a pale craggy face, thick wire-rimmed glasses, reddish hair that frizzed out at the temples. Age fifty, Ben supposed.

His eyes were wide with surprise. "Good God," he exclaimed. "Why are you dressed this way? But don't stand there—come in, come in." He closed the door behind Ben and said, "May I offer you coffee?"

"Thank you."

"What are you *doing* here?" Deschner whispered. "Is Liesl—?"

"I'm not Peter. I'm his brother, Ben."

"You—*what*? His *brother*? Oh, my *God!*" he gasped. Deschner pivoted around and stared at Ben with sudden dread. "They found him, didn't they?"

"Peter was killed a few days ago."

"Oh, Lord," he breathed. "Oh, Lord. They found him! He was always so afraid it would happen someday." Deschner stopped suddenly, a look of terror striking his face. "Liesl—"

"Liesl's unharmed."

"Thank God." He turned to Ben. "I mean, what am I saying—"

"That's all right. I understand. She's your blood relative."

Deschner stood before a small breakfast table and poured Ben a china cup of coffee. "How did this happen?" he asked gravely. "*Tell* me, for God's sake!"

"Surely the bank where you had a meeting the morning of the Bahnhofstrasse incident was the tripwire," Deschner said. The two of them faced each other intently across the table. Ben had peeled off the baggy orange and black uniform to reveal his ordinary street clothes. "The Union Bank of Switzerland is a merger of several older banks. Maybe there was an old, sensitive account that was flagged, being watched. Perhaps by one of the parties you met with. An assistant, a clerk. An informer who'd been given a watch list."

"Placed there by this corporation Liesl and Peter were talking about, or one of its offshoots?"

"Quite possibly. All of the giant firms have long-standing, cozy relationships with the important Swiss banks. The complete list of founders will give us the names of suspects."

"Did Peter show you the list?"

"No. At first he didn't even tell me why he wanted to open an account. All I knew was that the account was monetarily insignificant. What he was really interested in was the vault that came with it. To keep some documents, he said. Do you mind if I smoke?"

"It's your house."

"Well, you know, you Americans are such fascists about smoking, if you'll pardon the expression."

Ben smiled. "Not everyone."

Deschner pulled a cigarette from the pack of Rothmans next to his breakfast plate, lit it with a cheap plastic lighter. "Peter insisted that the account not be in his name. He was afraid—correctly, as it turned out—that his enemies might have contacts in the banks. He wanted to open it under a false name, but that's no longer possible. The banks have tightened up here. A lot of pressure from the outside, mostly America. Back in the seventies our banks started demanding a passport when you opened an account. You used to be able to open an account by mail. No more."

"So did he have to open it under his real name?"

"No. In *my* name. I'm the account holder, but Peter was what they call the 'beneficial owner.' " He exhaled a plume of smoke. "We had to go in together to open the account, but Peter's name appeared on one form only, known only to the account adviser. The Establishment of the Beneficial Owner's Identity, it's called. This form is kept locked away in the files." In another room a telephone rang.

"Which bank?"

"I chose the Handelsbank Schwciz AG because it's small and discreet. I've had clients who've happily done business with the Handelsbank, clients whose money is, shall we say, not entirely clean."

"So does this mean you can get into Peter's vault for me?"

"I'm afraid not. You'll have to accompany me. As the specified beneficiary and heir of the beneficial owner."

"If it's at all possible," Ben said, "I'd like to go to the bank straightaway." He remembered Schmid's icy warnings that he was not to return—warnings that if he violated that agreement, he would be persona non grata, subject to immediate arrest.

The phone kept ringing. Deschner crushed out his cigarette in a saucer. "Very well. If you don't mind, I'd like to answer that phone. Then I must make a call or two, reschedule my nine-thirty appointment."

He went into an adjoining room, his study, and returned a few minutes later. "All right then, no problem. I was able to reschedule."

"Thank you."

"Certainly. The account adviser—that's the banker, a senior vice president of the bank, Bernard Suchet—has all the relevant papers. He has a photocopy of Peter's passport on file. They believe he has been dead for four years. So far as anyone knows, the recent . . . *tragedy* has not been reported. Your own identity will be easy to establish."

"My arrival in this country came through somewhat irregular means," Ben said, choosing his words carefully. "My legal presence here cannot be verified through the normal passport, customs, and immigration systems. What happens if they alert the authorities?"

"Let's not think of all that can go wrong. Now, if I may finish dressing, we're in business. Then let us go at once."

CHAPTER FOURTEEN

Anna whirled around to Captain Bolgorio. "What? The body was *cremated?* We had an *agreement*, dammit . . . !"

The Paraguayan detective shrugged, hands spread, eyes wide with apparent concern. "Agent Navarro, please, let us discuss these things later, not in front of the bereaved—"

Ignoring him, Anna turned back to the widow. "Were you told there would be an autopsy?" she demanded.

"Don't raise your voice to me," Consuela Prosperi snapped. "I'm not a criminal."

Anna looked at Bolgorio, livid. "Did *you* know her husband's body was going to be cremated?" *Of course he knew, the bastard.*

"Agent Navarro, I told you, this is not my department."

"But did you know this or *not?*"

"I have heard things. But I am a low man on the totem pole, please understand."

"Are we finished here?" Consuela Prosperi asked.

"Not yet," Anna said. "Were you pressured into a cremation?" she demanded of the widow.

The widow said to Bolgorio, "Captain, please remove her from my house."

"My apologies, madame," Bolgorio said: "Agent Navarro, we must go now."

"We're not finished here," Anna said calmly. "You were pressured, weren't you?" She addressed Señora Prosperi. "What were you told—that your assets would be frozen, locked up, made inaccessible to you, unless you went along with this? Something like that?"

"Remove her from my house, Captain!" the widow commanded, raising her voice.

"Please, Agent Navarro—"

"Señora," Anna said, "let me tell you something. I happen to know that a significant portion of your assets is invested in hedge funds and other investment partnerships and equities in the U.S. and abroad. The U.S. government has the power to seize those assets if it suspects you of being part of an international criminal conspiracy." She stood and walked toward the door. "I'm getting on the phone to Washington right now, and that's precisely what I'm going to order."

From behind her, she heard the widow cry out, "She can't do this, can she? You assured me my money was safe if I—"

"Keep quiet!" the homicide detective barked suddenly. Startled, Anna turned back, and saw Bolgorio standing face to face with the widow. His obsequiousness had vanished. "I'll handle this."

He strode toward Anna and grabbed her arm.

Outside the front gates of the Prosperi estate, Anna demanded, "What are you covering up?"

"You'd be wise to leave things alone here," Bolgorio said. There was malevolence in his voice now, a gleaming assuredness she hadn't seen before. "You're a visitor here. You are not in your own country."

"How was it done? Were morgue orders 'lost' or 'misfiled'? Did someone pay you off, is that how it happened?"

"What do you know of the way things work in Para-

guay?" Bolgorio said, moving uncomfortably close to her.
She could feel his hot breath, the spray of spittle. "There
are many things you don't understand."

"You *knew* the body had been destroyed. From the moment I called you, I had a feeling. You knew there was no
body waiting for me in the morgue. Just tell me this: were
you ordered, or were you paid? Where did the request come
from—from outside the government, or from above?"

Bolgorio, unfazed, said nothing.

"*Who ordered the body destroyed?*"

"I like you, Agent Navarro. You're an attractive woman.
I do not want anything to happen to you."

He intended to frighten her, and unfortunately it was
working. But she gave him only a blank look. "That's not
a very subtle threat."

"This is not a threat. I truly don't want anything to happen to you. You need to listen to me, and then leave the
country at once. There are people high up in our government who protect the Prosperis and others like them.
Money changes hands, a great deal of it. You'll accomplish
nothing by putting your own life in peril."

Oh, she thought, *you don't know who you're dealing
with. Threatening me that way is like waving a red flag at
a bull.*

"Did you order the cremation personally?"

"It happened, that's all I know. I told you, I'm not a
powerful man."

"Then someone must know that Prosperi's death wasn't
natural. Why else would they destroy the evidence?"

"You are asking me questions I don't know the answer
to," he said calmly. "Please, Agent Navarro. Please take
care of your own safety. There are people here who prefer
to keep things quiet."

"Do you think *they*—these 'people who prefer to keep
things quiet'—had Prosperi killed and didn't want that revealed?"

Bolgorio looked away, as if in contemplation. "I'll deny
I ever told you this. I called the nursing agency before you

got here. When I knew you were investigating Prosperi's death. That seemed to me the obvious place to ask questions."

"And?"

"The substitute nurse—the one who was with Prosperi the night he died—she has vanished."

She felt her stomach plummet. *I knew it was too easy*, she thought.

"How did this nurse come to the agency?"

"She came with excellent credentials, they said. Her references checked out. She said she lived within walking distance of here, and if they had any assignments nearby . . . She did three different assignments, all in this area, and all very well. Suddenly, the regular night nurse assigned to Prosperi fell ill, and the substitute was available, and . . ."

"They have no way to reach her?"

"As I said, she disappeared."

"But her paychecks, her bank account—"

"She was paid in cash. Not unusual in this country. Her home address was false. When we looked closely, everything about her was false. It was as if she had been created just for this occasion, like some stage set. And when the job had been accomplished, the set was struck."

"Sounds like a professional backstopping job. I want to talk to the nursing agency."

"You'll learn nothing. And I will not help you do that. I've already told you too much. Please, leave at once. There are so many ways for an overly inquisitive foreigner to be killed here. Especially when very powerful people do not want things uncovered. Please—go."

She knew he was completely serious. This wasn't just a threat. She was more stubborn than anyone she knew, and she hated giving up. *But sometimes you just have to move on*, she told herself. *Sometimes the most important thing is just to stay alive.*

Zurich

By the time Ben Hartman and Matthias Deschner were walking down the Löwenstrasse, it had begun to drizzle. The sky was steel gray. The linden trees that lined the street rustled in the wind. A steeple clock struck the hour of nine o'clock in a melodious chime. Trams passed by down the middle of the street—the 6, the 13, the 11—each stopping with a squeal. FedEx trucks seemed to be everywhere: Zurich was a world banking capital, Ben knew, and banking was a time-sensitive business. Bankers hurried to work beneath umbrellas. A couple of Japanese girls, tourists, giggled. Unpainted wooden benches sat unoccupied beneath the lindens.

It drizzled, it stopped, it drizzled again. They came to a busy crosswalk where Lagerstrasse crossed the Löwenstrasse. A building that housed the Société de Banque Suisse stood empty, undergoing construction or renovation.

A pair of stylishly unshaven Italian men in identical black leather jackets passed by, both smoking. Then a matron wafting Shalimar.

On the next block Deschner, who was wearing an ill-fitting black raincoat over an ugly checked jacket, stopped at a white stone building, resembling a townhouse, on the front of which was mounted a small brass plaque. Engraved on it in graceful script were the words HANDELSBANK SCHWEIZ AG.

Deschner pulled open the heavy glass door.

Directly across the street, someone with the slender build of an adolescent was sitting at a café, under a red Coca-Cola parasol. He was wearing khaki cargo pants, a blue nylon backpack, and an MC Solaar T-shirt, and he was drinking an Orangina from the bottle. With languid movements, he flipped through a copy of a music magazine while speaking on a cell phone. From time to time he glanced at the entrance to the bank across the street.

*   *   *

A set of glass doors slid open electronically. They stood
for a moment between thick doors, and then with a low
buzz, the next set slid open.

The lobby of the Handelsbank was a large marble-
floored chamber, completely empty except for a sleek black
desk at the far end. A woman sat behind it, wearing a tiny
wireless telephone headset, speaking quietly. She looked up
as they entered.

"Guten morgen," she said. *"Kann ich Ihnen helfen?"*

*"Ja, guten morgen. Wir haben eine Verabredung mit Dr.
Suchet."*

"Sehr gut, mein Herr. Einen Moment." She spoke softly
into her mouthpiece. *"Er wird gleich unten sein, um Sie zu
sehen."*

"You will like Bernard Suchet, I think," Deschner said.
"He's a very good sort, a banker of the old school. Not one
of these hustle-and-bustle young men in a hurry you see so
much of in Zurich these days."

At this point, Ben thought, *I don't care if he's Charles
Manson.*

A steel elevator pinged and slid open, and a round-
shouldered large man in a tweed jacket strode up to them
and shook hands first with Deschner, then with Ben. *"Es
freut mich Dich wiederzusehen, Matthias,"* he exclaimed,
and then, turning to Ben, "I am very pleased to make your
acquaintance, Mr. Hartman. Please, come with me."

They rode up together in the elevator. There was a camera lens mounted discreetly on the ceiling. Suchet wore a
permanent pleasant face. He had heavy rectangular-framed
glasses, a double chin, and a large potbelly. His shirt was
monogrammed with his initials on the pocket. A pocket
square in his jacket matched his tie. A senior officer, Ben
thought. Tweed jacket, not a banker's suit: he's above such
things as dress code.

Ben watched him closely, waiting for any signs of suspicion. But Suchet seemed all business as usual.

The elevator opened on a waiting area covered in a wall-to-wall oatmeal deep-pile rug and furnished with antiques, not reproductions. They moved through the waiting area to a door, where Suchet inserted a badge that he wore on a chain around his neck, into an electronic card-reader.

Suchet's office was just down the hall, a spacious, light-flooded room. A computer was the only object on his long glass-topped desk. He sat behind it, while Deschner and Ben sat across from him. A middle-aged woman entered with two espressos and two glasses of water on a silver tray and set them down on the desk before the two visitors. Then a young male came in and handed Dr. Suchet a file.

Suchet opened it. "You are Benjamin Hartman, of course," he asked, moving his owlish gaze from the file to Ben.

Ben nodded, his stomach tightening.

"We have been provided with ancillary documentation certifying that you are the sole heir to the 'beneficial owner' of this account. And you affirm that you are, correct?"

"That's correct."

"Legally I am satisfied with your documentation. And visually—well, it is clear you are indeed Peter Hartman's twin brother." He smiled. "So what can I do for you this morning, Mr. Hartman?"

The Handelsbank's vaults were located in the basement of the building, a fluorescent-lit, low-ceilinged area that was nowhere near as sleek and modern as the upstairs. There were several numbered doors off a narrow corridor, presumably room-sized vaults. Several larger alcoves off the hallway appeared from a distance to be lined with brass, which upon closer inspection Ben saw were safe-deposit boxes of various sizes.

At the entrance to an alcove numbered 18C, Dr. Suchet stopped and handed Ben a key. He did not indicate which of the hundreds of vaults in this area was Peter's. "I assume you would like privacy," he said. "Herr Deschner and I

shall leave you now. You can call me on this phone here"—
he indicated a white phone on a steel table in the center of
the room—"when you are finished."

Ben looked at the rows upon rows of vaults, and didn't
know what to do. Was this a test of some sort? Or did
Suchet merely assume that Ben would know the number of
his vault? Ben glanced at Deschner, who seemed to sense
his discomfort but, curiously, said nothing. Then Ben
looked again at the key and saw a number embossed on it.
Of course. The obvious place.

"Thank you," he said. "I'm all set."

The two Swiss left, chatting. Ben noticed a surveillance
camera mounted high in the room, where the ceiling met
the wall. Its red light was on.

He located vault 322, a small box at about eye level,
and turned the key to open it.

Oh, God, he thought, heart thrumming, *what could be
in here? Peter, what did you hide here that was worth your
life?*

Inside was what looked like an envelope made of stiff
wax paper. He pulled it out—the document inside was dis-
mayingly thin—and opened it.

There was only one item inside, and it was not a piece
of paper.

It was a photograph, measuring about five inches by
seven.

It took his breath away.

It showed a group of men, a few in Nazi uniforms, some
in 1940s suits with overcoats. A number of them were immediately recognizable. Giovanni Vignelli, the great Italian
industrialist out of Turin, automotive magnate, his massive
plants supplying the Italian military, diesel engines, railroad
cars, airplanes. The head of Royal Dutch Petroleum, Sir
Han Detwiler, a xenophobic Dutchman. The legendary
founder of the first, and greatest, American airline. There
were faces that he could not identify but had seen in the
history books. A few of the men wore mustaches. Including
the handsome, dark-haired young man standing next to an

arrogant Nazi official with pale eyes who looked familiar to Ben, though he knew little of German history.

No, please, not him.

The Nazi, whose face he'd seen before, he could not identify.

The handsome young man was unquestionably his father.

Max Hartman.

A typewritten caption on the white border at the bottom of the photograph read: ZURICH, 1945. SIGMA AG.

He returned the photograph to the envelope and slipped it into his breast pocket. Felt it burn against his chest.

There could no longer be any doubt that his father had lied to him, had lied all his adult life. His head reeled. Abruptly a voice penetrated Ben's stupor.

"Mr. Hartman! Mr. Benjamin Hartman. There is a warrant for your arrest! We must take you into custody."

Oh, Jesus.

It was the banker, Bernard Suchet, speaking. He must have contacted the local authorities. A swift search of the country's arrival records would reveal that he had no documented arrival. Schmid's chill, understated words returned to him: *If I ever find out you've returned here, things will not go well for you.*

Suchet was flanked by Matthias Deschner and two security guards, their weapons drawn.

"Mr. Hartman, the *Kantonspolizei* have informed me that you are in this country illegally. Which means that you are perpetrating a fraud," the banker said. Deschner's face was a mask of neutrality.

"What are you talking about?" Ben said indignantly. Had they seen him slip the photo into his jacket?

"We are to detain you until the authorities arrive, momentarily."

Ben stared at him, speechless.

"Your actions put you in violation of the Swiss Federal

Criminal Code," Suchet continued loudly. "You seem to be implicated in other offenses as well. You will not be permitted to leave except in the custody of the police."

Deschner was silent. In his eyes Ben could see what appeared to be fear. Why was he saying nothing?

"Guards, please escort Mr. Hartman to Secure Room Number 4. Mr. Hartman, you will take nothing with you. You are hereby detained awaiting official arrest."

The guards approached, weapons still pointed at him.

Ben got to his feet, his hands open at his side, and began walking down the corridor, the two guards falling in beside him. As he passed Deschner, he saw the attorney give the tiniest shrug of his shoulders.

Peter's words of caution: *They practically own half the cops.* Schmid's words of menace: *the* Einwanderungsbehörde *can hold you in administrative detention for a year before your case reaches a magistrate.*

He couldn't allow himself to be taken in. What galvanized him wasn't the chance that he would be killed or locked up, but the fact that in either case his investigations would come to an end. Peter's efforts would have been in vain. The Corporation would have won.

He couldn't let that happen. Whatever the price.

Secure Rooms, *die Stahlkammern,* were, Ben knew, where items of intrinsic value—gold, gemstones, bearer bonds—were displayed and assessed whenever an owner requested an official audit of his stored possessions. Though lacking vault-like impregnability, they were indeed secure, with reinforced steel doors and closed-circuit surveillance systems. At the entrance of *Zimmer Vier,* one of the guards waved an electronic reader by a blinking red light; when the door unlocked, he gestured Ben to enter first, and the two guards followed him. Then the door closed with a series of three audible clicks.

Ben looked around him. The room was brightly lit and sparely furnished; it would be difficult to lose, or hide, a single gemstone in this space. The slate-tiled floor was polished to a dark sheen. There was a long table of perfectly clear Plexiglas, and six folding chairs of gray painted metal.

One of the guards—burly and overweight, his red, fleshy face suggesting a steady diet of beef and beer—gestured for Ben to sit down on a chair. Ben paused before complying. The two guards had reholstered their sidearms, but made it abundantly clear that they wouldn't hesitate to use cruder physical means if he were less than cooperative.

"And so we wait, *ja?*" said the second guard, in heavily accented English. The man, his light brown hair brush cut, was leaner and, Ben judged, probably much faster than his cohort. Doubtless mentally swifter as well.

Ben turned to him. "How much do they pay you here? I'm a *very* rich man, you know. I can give you a very nice life if I choose. You do me a favor, I'll do you one." He made no effort to disguise his naked desperation; they would either respond or they would not.

The leaner guard snorted and shook his head. "You should speak your proposal louder, to be sure that the microphones pick it up."

They had no reason to believe that Ben would be good for his word, and there were no assurances he could make, while in captivity, to persuade them otherwise. Still, their amused contempt was encouraging: his best chance now was to be underestimated. Ben stood up, groaning, and clutched his midriff.

"Sit *down*," the guard commanded firmly.

"The claustrophobia . . . I can't take the . . . small, enclosed places!" Ben spoke in a tone that was increasingly frantic, verging on hysteria.

Both guards looked at each other and laughed scornfully—they would not be taken in by such an obvious ploy.

"No, no, I'm serious," Ben said with growing urgency. "My God! How explicit do I have to be? I have a . . . a nervous stomach. I have to get to a bathroom immediately or I'll . . . have an accident." He was playing the role of the flighty, flaky American to the hilt. "Stress brings it on much more quickly! I need my pills. Dammit! My Valium! A sedative. I have terrible claustrophobia—I can't be in en-

closed spaces. *Please!*" As he spoke he started to gesticu-
late wildly, as if having a panic attack.

The lean guard just regarded him with an amused con-
temptuous half-smile. "You will have to take it up with the
prison infirmary."

With a manic, stricken expression, Ben stepped closer
to him, his gaze flicking toward the holstered gun and then
back at the lean man's face. "Please, you don't understand!" He waved his hands even more wildly. "I'll have a
panic attack! I need to go to the bathroom! I need a *tranquilizer!*" With lightning speed, he thrust both hands into
the guard's hip holster and retrieved the short-barreled revolver. Then he took two steps back, holding the piece in
his hands, his performance abruptly over.

"Keep your hands at shoulder level," he told the thickly
built guard. "Or I fire, and you both die."

The two guards exchanged glances.

"Now one of you will take me out of this place. Or both
of you will die. It's a good deal. Take it before the offer
expires."

The guards conferred briefly in *Schweitzerdeutsch*. Then
the lean one spoke. "It would be extremely stupid of you
to use this gun, if you even know how, which I doubt. You
will be imprisoned for the rest of your life."

It was the wrong tone: wary, alarmed, yet without terror.
The guard was not at all unnerved. Perhaps Ben's earlier
performance of weakness had been *too* effective. Ben could
see that a measure of skepticism remained in their expressions and posture. At once, he knew what he must say.
"You think I wouldn't fire this gun?" Ben spoke in a bored
voice, only his eyes blazing. "I killed five at the Bahnhofplatz. Two more won't weigh on my mind."

The guards suddenly grew rigid, all condescension
having instantly evaporated. "*Das Monster vom Bahnhofplatz,*" the fleshy one said hoarsely to his partner as a look
of horror crossed his face. The blood drained from his florid
complexion.

"You!" Ben barked at him, seizing the advantage. "Take

me out of here." Within seconds, the thickset guard used
his electronic reader to open the door. "And if you want to
live, you'll stay behind," he told the leaner, evidently clev-
erer one. The door closed behind him, the three muffled
clicks verifying that the bolts had electronically slid into
place.

Frog-marching the guard in front of him, Ben traveled
swiftly down the beige-carpeted corridor. The feed from the
closed-circuit video probably went into archival storage and
examination, rather than being viewed in real time, but
there was no way to be certain.

"What's your name?" Ben demanded. "*Wie heissen
Sie?*"

"Laemmel," the guard grunted. "Christoph Laemmel."
He reached the end of the corridor and started to turn left.

"*No*," Ben hissed. "*Not* that way! We're not going out
the front. Take me out the back way. The service entrance.
Where the trash is taken out."

Laemmel paused in momentary confusion. Ben placed
the revolver near one of his beet-red ears, letting him feel
the cold metal. Moving more quickly, the guard took him
down the back stairs, the ugly, dented steel a dramatic contrast with the polished formality of the bank's public
spaces. The gloom of the stairwell was scarcely diminished
by the naked, low-wattage electric bulbs that protruded
from the wall at each landing.

The guard's heavy shoes clattered on the metal stairs.

"Quiet," Ben said, speaking to him in German. "Make
no sound, or I will make a very deafening one, and it will
be the last thing you ever hear."

"You have no chance," Laemmel said in a low, frightened voice. "No chance at all."

Finally, they reached the wide double doors that led to
the back alleyway. Ben pressed on the cross latch, made
sure that the doors opened from within. "This is the end of
our little trip together," he said.

Now Laemmel grunted. "Do you think you are any safer
outside of this building?"

Ben stepped into the shadowy alleyway, feeling the cool air against his flushed face. "What the *Polizei* do is not your personal concern," he said, keeping his gun drawn.

"*Die Polizei?*" Laemmel replied. "I do not speak of *them.*" He spat.

An eel of fear thrashed in Ben's belly. "What are you talking about?" he demanded urgently. Ben gripped the gun in both his hands and raised it to Laemmel's eyes. "*Tell me!*" he said with furious concentration. "Tell me what you know!"

There was a sudden exhalation of breath from Laemmel's throat, and a warm mist of crimson spattered Ben's face. A bullet had torn through the man's neck. Had Ben somehow lost his grip, squeezed the trigger without realizing it? A second explosion, inches away from his head, answered the question. There was a shooter in position.

Oh, Christ! Not again!

As the guard crumpled face forward, Ben lunged down the dank alley. He heard a popping noise, as if from a toy gun, then a metallic reverberation, and a pockmark suddenly appeared on the large Dumpster to his left. The shooter had to be firing from his right.

As he felt something hot crease his shoulder, he dove behind the Dumpster: temporary refuge, but any port in a storm. Out of the corner of his eye, he saw the movement of something small and dark—a rat, displaced by his arrival. *Move!* The ledge of the cement wall that separated the bank's back lot from that of its neighbor was at shoulder height; Ben stuck the gun in the waistband of his trousers and, with both hands, lifted himself up and over. A short pathway now separated him from Usteristrasse. Grasping the revolver, he fired wildly, in three different areas. He wanted the shooter to take cover, believing he was under fire. He needed the time. Every second now was precious.

There was return fire, and he could hear the slugs hitting the concrete retainer, but Ben was safely on the other side.

Now he charged, pumping his feet down the alley to Usteristrasse, fast. Faster. Faster still! "Run like your life depends on it," his track coach would tell him before competitions. Now it did.

And what if there were more than one shooter? But surely they wouldn't have had enough warning to put a whole team into position. The thoughts jostled and collided in Ben's mind. *Focus, dammit.*

A brackish smell cued him to his next move: it was a breeze from the Sihl River, the charmless narrow waterway that branched off from the Limmat at the Platz-promenade. Now he crossed the Gessner Allee, scarcely looking at the traffic, hurtling in front of a taxicab whose bearded driver honked and cursed at him before stepping on the brakes. But he'd made it across. The Sihl, banked with a declivity of blackened cinder blocks, stretched before him. His eyes scanned the water frantically until he fixed on a small motorboat. They were a common sight on the Sihl; this one had a single passenger, a plump, beer-swilling man with sunglasses and a fishing pole, though he was not yet fishing. His life jacket made his already bulky proportions look even bulkier. The river would take him to the Sihlwald, a nature preserve ten kilometers south of Zurich, where the riverbanks flattened out in the woodlands and became furrowed with brooks. It was a popular destination among the city's inhabitants.

The plump man peeled plastic wrap from a white-bread sandwich, then tossed the plastic into the waters. A notably antisocial act by Swiss standards. Ben threw himself into the water, fully clothed, and started to swim toward the boat, his clothing impeding his powerful crawl stroke.

The water was frigid, carrying the bone-chilling cold of the glacier from which it originated, and Ben felt a stiffness seep through his body even as he propelled himself through the slow-moving current.

The man in the motorboat, pushing the sandwich into his face, slurping from his bottle of Kronenberg, was aware of nothing until the small motorboat tilted abruptly leeward.

First two hands were visible, the fingers faintly bluish from
the cold, and then he saw the man, fully dressed, pull himself up and into the boat, river water sluicing down an
expensive-looking suit.

"*Was ist das!*" he shouted. He dropped his beer in alarm.
"Wer sind Sie?"

"I need to borrow your boat," Ben told him in German,
trying to stop his teeth from chattering from the cold.

"*Nie! Raus!*" Get out! The man picked up his sturdy
fishing pole and brandished it with intended menace.

"Your choice," Ben said, and then sprang toward the
man, tipping him over into the water, where he bobbed
comically, buoyed by his life jacket but sputtering with indignation.

"Save your breath." Ben pointed toward the nearby
Zollstrasse bridge. "The tramline will take you wherever
you need to go." He reached over to the engine throttle and
turned it way up. The engine coughed, and then roared, the
boat gaining speed as it headed south. He would not be
taking it all the way to the Sihlwald, the forest preserve.
Half a mile down the river bend would do it. Lying flat
against the grip-textured fiberglass floor of the boat, he was
still able to see the taller buildings and storefronts along
the Sihl, the immense Migros department store, a bland,
boxy structure; the sooty spires of the Schwarzenkirche; the
intricately frescoed walls of the Klathaus. Ben knew that
he'd be vulnerable to any marksmen in position, but also
that the chances of their having anticipated his movements
were slim. He felt for the envelope in his jacket pocket,
and the waxy enclosure crackled reassuringly. He assumed
it was waterproof, but this wasn't the time to make sure.

The motorboat moved faster, taking him beneath the al-
gaed masonry of the Stauffacherstrasse bridge. Another
fifth of a kilometer remained. Then came the unmistakable
sounds of a major expressway, the whizzing noise of tires
spinning along smooth-worn asphalt, of air against the car-
riages and contours of trucks and automobiles, the occasional bleat, treble and basso, of horns, the meshing gears

of a hundred vehicles moving like the wind. It all fused into a white noise that rose and fell in intensity, the aural vibrations of industrial transportation blended into a mechanical surf.

Ben veered the thrumming motorboat toward the gently sloped retaining wall, heard the scrape of its fiberglass hull against brick as he brought it jerking to a halt. Then he sprang from the boat and toward the roadside gas station where he'd left his rented Range Rover, only minutes from the Nationalstrasse 3, the concrete river where he would merge into the swiftly coursing traffic.

Turning the steering wheel to change lanes, Ben felt a twinge in his left shoulder. He reached over with his right hand and rubbed it gently. Another twinge, sharper this time. He took his hand away. His fingers were sticky, maroon with congealing blood.

Matthias Deschner was in the same seat in front of Suchet's desk that he had occupied just an hour before. Suchet, behind the desk, was hunched forward, his face tense.

"You should have warned me in advance," the banker said angrily. "We could have stopped him from accessing the vault!"

"I had no advance notice myself!" Deschner objected. "They only contacted me yesterday. They demanded to know whether I was sheltering him. *Preposterous!*"

"You know full well the penalty for noncompliance in such matters." Suchet's face was mottled with rage and fear.

"They made it very clear," Deschner said tonelessly.

"Only just now? Then they only just learned of your possible connection to the subject?"

"Certainly. Do you think I had any idea what these brothers were involved in? I knew nothing. *Nothing!*"

"That excuse has not always been successful in sparing the Teutonic neck, if I may speak historically."

"A distant relative asked me for a favor," Deschner protested. "I wasn't apprised of its larger significance."

"And you didn't inquire?"

"Members of our profession are trained *not* to ask too many questions. I'd think you'd agree with that."

"And now you expose us *both* to danger!" Suchet snapped.

"As soon as he showed up, I was called. I could only presume they *wanted* him to access the vault!"

There was a knock at the door. Suchet's secretary entered, holding aloft a small videocassette. "This just came for you from Security, sir."

"Thank you, Inge," Suchet said sweetly. "A messenger will be arriving momentarily. I'd like you to seal the tape in an envelope and give it to him."

"Very good, sir," the secretary said, and she left the office as quietly as she had come.

CHAPTER FIFTEEN

In a modern eight-story building on Schaffhausserstrasse, not far from the University of Zurich, three men sat in a room filled with high-powered computers and high-resolution video monitors. It was a studio rented from a multimedia production company that did duplication, restoration, and editing of video for surveillance firms and corporations.

One of the group, a white-haired, scrawny man in shirtsleeves who looked a great deal older than his forty-six years, took a videocassette from a D-2 composite digital-format videotape recorder and placed it in one of the video slots in a Quantel Sapphire video-imaging computer. He had just finished making a digital copy of the surveillance tape he'd been given. Now, using this British-made video-imaging computer that had originally been developed for the Home Office, Britain's MI-5, he was going to magnify the image.

The white-haired man, who worked in silence, had been one of the top video-enhancement specialists in the Home Office until he was lured away by a private London security firm at double his old salary. These two gentlemen in the room with him had hired him, through the security firm, to do a quick job in Zurich. He had no idea who they were. All he knew was that they were paying him a generous bonus. They had flown him from London to Zurich business class.

Now the two mysterious men sat off by themselves, talking. They could have been international businessmen from any country in the world, although in fact they were speaking Dutch, which the video expert understood reasonably well.

On the other side of the room, the white-haired technician stared at the computer screen. At the bottom it said CAM 2, along with the date and the time, which flashed by in fractions of a second. He called out to his clients: "All right, now tell me what you'd like done. You want the bloke electronically compared against a photo you've got?"

"No," replied the first Dutchman. "We know who it is. We want to see what he's reading."

"I should have figured," the technician groaned. "Good God, that piece of paper he's holding is in shadow."

"How's the quality of the tape?" the second man asked.

"Not bad," the tech said. "Two frames a second, which is standard. A lot of these banks use the most god-awful equipment, but fortunately this bank used a high-performance, high-res camera. I mean, I can't say the camera was positioned terribly well, but that's not uncommon either."

The second businessman asked, "So you can zoom in on whatever he's holding?"

"Sure. The software on this Quantel compensates for all the usual problems you get from digital enlargement—the blockiness and all that. That's not the problem. The damned thing's in shadow."

"Well, you're supposed to be the best," the first man said sourly. "You're certainly the most expensive."

"I know, I know," the tech said. "All true. Well, I can bring up the contrast." He clicked on a pull-down menu that listed "Crisp," "Zoom," "Colouring," and "Contrast." By clicking on the "+" key he lightened the shadow until the paper the man in the bank vault was looking at was almost readable, then enhanced the resolution by clicking another number. He tinkered with the contrast some more, then clicked "crisp" to sharpen the image further.

"Good," he said at last.

"Can you see what he's reading?" the second man asked.

"Actually, it's a photograph."

"A *photograph?*"

"Right. An old one. A group shot. Lots of conservatively dressed men. Looks like a bunch of businessmen. A couple of German officers, too. Yes, a group shot. Mountains in the background—"

"Can you make out their faces?"

"If you give me . . . just . . . ah, here we are." He zoomed in on the photograph until it took up the entire screen. " 'Zurich, 1945,' it says here. The 'Sig' something . . . ?"

The second man glanced at the first. "Good heavens." He approached the computer monitor.

The tech said, "Sigma AG?"

The second man muttered to the first, "He's on to it."

"As I thought," the first said.

"All right," said the second man to the technician. "I want you to print out a copy of that. I also want the best head shot of this fellow you can get."

"Make fifty copies," put in the first man, rising from his chair.

The second man crossed the room to talk to his colleague. "Put out the word," he said quietly. "Our precautions have been inadequate. The American has become a serious threat."

Washington, D.C.

Anna Navarro hunched forward in her chair. Alan Bartlett's office was as immaculate as ever, the man's expression every bit as opaque.

"I've tracked Robert Mailhot's money transfers from the Nova Scotia National Bank back to an account in the Caymans, and there, I'm afraid, I've hit a dead end," Anna said. "The one source we've got there confirms that the account shows recent activity involving one of Prosperi's funds, too. But there, as I say, the money trail goes cold. It's one thing to learn where the money ends up. It's another to learn who put the money there in the first place. Should we start working through regular channels?"

"Out of the question," Bartlett said, a little peevish. "It would compromise the security of the entire operation. That means anyone with an interest in stopping the investigation can do so easily. It also means endangering the lives of others, people who may still be targets."

"I understand," Anna said. "But I don't want a repeat of Asunción, either. That's the price you pay for going through back-channels. Whoever's behind this, this—for want of a better word, this conspiracy—obviously had enough influence to stop us."

"Granted. But once we raise this thing to an A-II level, a sanctioned investigation, it's like taking out an ad in *The New York Times*, telling the subjects of our inquiries what we're up to. We can't assume there aren't people in the intelligence community working both sides on this matter."

"An A-II is still highly privileged. I don't agree—"

"No, you wouldn't," he said freezingly. "Perhaps I was wrong—perhaps you really are a loyal bureaucrat at heart."

She ignored his barb. "I've been involved in many international investigations, including homicide investigations, that have been kept quiet. Particularly when we think someone in the government might be implicated. In El Salvador, when government officials had Americans killed to cover up—"

"As you know, I'm *intimately* acquainted with your previous exploits, Agent Navarro," Bartlett said impatiently. "You're speaking of one foreign government. I'm speaking of half a dozen or more. There's a difference."

"You say there's been a victim in Oslo now?"

"That's our latest intelligence, yes."

"Then we have the Attorney General's office make a high-level, confidential appeal to the Office of the Norwegian State Prosecutor, requesting absolute secrecy."

"*No*. The risks of a direct appeal to the Norwegian authorities are far too great."

"Then I want the list. Not the list of corpses. I want the names of people with Sigma clearance files. Your 'hot list.' "

"That's impossible."

"*I see*—I only get 'em when they're dead. Well, in that case, I want off this job."

He hesitated. "Don't play games, Ms. Navarro. You've been assigned." Bartlett's carefully cultivated air of solicitude and noblesse had evaporated. Now Anna caught a glimpse of the steel that had placed Bartlett at the helm of one of the government's most powerful investigative units. "It's really not up to you."

"I can get sick, suddenly become unable to perform my job. Be unable to travel."

"You wouldn't do that."

"No, not if you gave me the hot list."

"I told you. It's impossible. This operation must abide by certain rules. If those rules sometimes amount to constraints, you must accept them as the parameters of your inquiry."

"Look," she said, "thirteen of the old men on your Sigma list are now dead under 'questionable circumstances,' let's just say. Three remain alive, right?"

"To the best of our knowledge."

"Then let me put it to you this way. Once one of these guys dies, is killed, whatever—we can't pay the body a visit without some kind of official government cooperation, on whatever level. Right? But if we get to one of them *before* he's killed . . . Listen, I realize I'm supposed to be investigating dead people, not live ones. But if we consider them potential witnesses, put them under twenty-four-hour surveillance—*discreetly*, of course. . . ."

Bartlett stared at her, conflicting imperatives evidently playing across his face. Now he walked to a floor safe taller than he was, opened it, and pulled out a folder. He handed her a sheet of paper stamped SECRET, NOFORN, and NO-CONTRACT. Those classifications stipulated that, in addition to high-level secrecy constraints, it was under no circumstances releasable to foreign nationals or contract employees. "The list," he said quietly.

She quickly read down the columns of information—aliases, real names, names of any living relatives, and the numbers of the corresponding files. Three old men remained alive. Countries of origin: Portugal, Italy, Switzerland.

"No addresses?" she said.

"Just old ones. None current that we've been able to procure through the normal means. All of them have relocated in the past year."

"The past *year?* They could be anywhere in the world."

"That's a logical possibility. The probability is that they're in the same country, likely in the same general locale—at a certain point of life, one becomes subject to a sort of field of gravitation. It's difficult for old men to completely uproot themselves. Even when their safety is at risk, there is a level of personal tumult to which they will refuse to subject themselves. All the same, they haven't exactly left forwarding addresses. Evidently, they're keeping a low profile."

"Hiding," Anna said. "They're afraid."

"It would seem they have reason to be."

"It's like there's some geriatric grudge match going on. How could something that started even before the CIA was founded still have such power?"

Bartlett craned his neck, resting his gaze on the velvet-lined display case before he turned back. "Certain things grow more powerful with age. And, of course, it's a grave mistake to confuse size with influence. Today, the CIA is a vast, solid government institution with endless layers of bureaucracy. At the beginning, personal networks were where true power resided. It was true of Bill Donovan, the founder of the OSS, and even more so of Allen Dulles. Yes, Dulles is known for his role in creating the CIA, but that wasn't the most impressive of his accomplishments. For him, there was one battle, the battle against the revolutionary left."

"The 'gentleman spy,' they called him, didn't they?"

"The 'gentleman' part made him as dangerous as the 'spy' part. He was never more formidable than when he was a private citizen, back in the days when he and his brother Foster ran the international finance division of a certain law firm."

"The law firm? What did they do, double bill their clients?"

Bartlett gave her a slightly pitying look. "It's an amateur's error to underestimate the reach and range of private concerns. Theirs was more than just a white-shoe law firm. It had genuinely international reach. Dulles, traveling around the world, was able to weave a sort of spider's web across Europe. He enlisted confederates in all the major cities, finding them among the Allies, the Axis, *and* the neutrals."

"Confederates?" Anna interrupted. "How do you mean?"

"Highly placed individuals—contacts, friends, 'assets,' call them what you will—whom Allen Dulles effectively had on retainer. They served as sources of information and advice, but also as agents of influence. Dulles knew how to appeal to people's self-interest. After all, he facilitated an extraordinary number of deals involving governments and multinational corporations, and that made him an invaluable man to know. If you were a businessman, he could ensure that a large government contract was steered in your direction. If you were a government official, he might provide you with a crucial morsel of information that would further your career. Money and intelligence—Dulles understood that one could be readily converted to the other, like two currencies, albeit with constantly shifting exchange rates. And, of course, Dulles's own role as a go-between, an intermediary, depended upon him knowing just a little bit more than everyone else."

"A go-between?"

"Maybe you've heard of the Bank for International Settlement of Basel?"

"Maybe I haven't."

"It was essentially a counting house where businessmen on both sides of the war could settle down and parse the distribution of dividends. A very useful institution to have— if you were a businessman. After all, business didn't cease simply because the cannons began to fire. But the hostilities did interfere with the conduct of corporate partnerships and alliances, giving rise to all sorts of impediments. Dulles figured out ways to circumvent those impediments."

"That's not an attractive picture."

"It's the reality. Dulles, you see, believed in the 'network.' It's the key to understanding his life's mission. A network was an array of individuals—a whole, a complex configuration, that could have an influence vastly greater than the sum of its parts. It's a striking thing to contemplate. As I say, it always comes down to the crooked timber of humanity."

Anna raised an eyebrow. "It sounds a little frightening."

A vein pulsed on Bartlett's temple. "It is a little frightening, and perhaps more than a little. The nature of these networks, after all, is that they are invisible to those who are not part of them—invisible even to some who are. And they also have a tendency to survive the individuals they initially comprise. You could say they take on a life of their own. And they can have powerful effects on the organizations that they invade." He adjusted his French cuffs again. "I talked of spiders' webs. There's a curious parasitic wasp, very tiny, of the genus *Hymenoepimecis*—a clever little creature that stings a spider into temporary paralysis, and lays its eggs in the spider's abdomen. Soon the spider goes back to work, as if nothing had happened, even as the larvae grow inside him, nourished on its fluids. Then, on the night that the larvae will molt and kill the spider, they chemically induce it to change its behavior. On this night, the spider is induced to spin a cocoon web, useless to the spider but necessary for the larva. As soon as the spider has finished its work, the larvae consume the spider and hang the pupal cocoon in the special web. It's quite extraordinary, really, the parasite's fine-grained manipulation of the host's behavior. But it's nothing compared to what we humans can devise. That's the sort of thing I think about, Ms. Navarro. Who's inside of *us*? What forces might be manipulating the apparatus of civic governance into building a web that will serve their own purposes? When will the parasite decide to consume the host?"

"O.K., I'll play along," Anna said. "Let's say half a century ago, some dark conspiracy stings us, in effect—implants something that's going to grow and cause damage. Even if all that's so, how would we ever know?"

"That is an excellent question, Ms. Navarro," Bartlett replied. "Webs are hard to see, aren't they, even when they're big? Have you ever walked into an old basement or storage area in a dim light, seeing nothing in the gloom? Then you switch on a flashlight, and suddenly you realize that the empty space over your head isn't exactly empty—it's filled with layers of cobwebs, a vast canopy of glassy filaments. You direct the beam in another direction, and that canopy disappears—as if it were never there. Had you imagined it? You look straight up. Nothing. Then, directing the beam at just the right off-angle, focusing your eyes on some intermediate point, it all becomes visible once more." Bartlett's gaze searched her face for comprehension. "People like me spend our days looking for that one odd angle that brings the old webs into view. Often we look *too* hard, and we imagine things. Sometimes we see what's really there. You, Ms. Navarro, strike me as someone not prone to imagine things."

"I'll accept that at face value," Anna replied.

"I don't mean to imply that you lack imagination—only that you keep it under tight control. No matter. The point is simply that there were alliances forged among some individuals with considerable resources. That much is part of public history. And as for what became of this? I only wish we knew. All we have are these names."

"Three names," Anna said. "Three old men."

"I'd direct your particular attention to Gaston Rossignol. He'd been quite a powerful Swiss banker in his heyday. The most prominent person on the list, and the oldest."

"All right," she said, looking up. "The Zuricher. I assume you've prepared a background file on him."

Bartlett opened a desk drawer, withdrew a file festooned with classificatory warning stamps, and slid it to her across the desk. "It's fairly extensive, aside from the obvious lacunae."

"Good," Anna said. "I want to see him before they get to him, too."

"Assuming you can locate him."

"He's lived his entire life in Zurich. As you say, there's a field of gravitation there. Even if he's moved, he would have left behind friends, family members. Tributaries leading to the source."

"Or moats, protecting a fortress. A man like Rossignol has powerful friends, highly placed ones, who will do whatever they can to protect him. Friends who are, as the French say, *branché*. Powerful and plugged-in. They have the ability to remove him from the grid of visibility, the bureaucratic files and computer records. Do you have some clever subterfuge in mind?"

"Nothing like that. Subterfuge is what they'll be on guard against. Rossignol has nothing to fear from me. If his friends and confederates are as well informed as you suggest, they'll realize that and spread the word."

"So you're envisaging a simple 'I come in peace'?" The words were wry, but he looked intrigued.

Anna shrugged. "Some version of that. I suspect the best route will be the most direct one. But I'll find out soon enough." She glanced at her watch. "I'm taking the next flight I can catch to Zurich."

Mettlenberg, St. Gallen, Switzerland

A little over five hours later, Ben Hartman sat in his rented Range Rover in the staff parking lot of the Regionalspital Sankt Gallen Nord, watching people coming and going: doctors, nurses, hospital workers. The powerful engine idled softly. Fortunately, there weren't many people, even at a few minutes after five o'clock, the end of the workday for the office workers. Twilight was beginning to fall, and the outside lights were starting to come on.

From Zurich he had called the hospital and asked for Dr. Margarethe Hubli. He was put right through to Pediatrics, where he asked, in English, whether she was in.

Yes, he was told; would you like to make an appointment to see the doctor? The nurse's English was halting but comprehensible.

"No," he'd said, "I really just wanted to make sure the doctor was in the hospital. My child is ill, and I want to know whether you had a pediatrician on call in case we need one." He thanked the nurse and, after finding out how late Dr. Hubli worked, hung up.

Liesl was scheduled to be in the hospital only until four in the afternoon. He'd been waiting here over two hours; already she was more than an hour late in leaving. Ben was certain she had not yet emerged from the hospital. Moreover, he had spotted her Renault parked in the lot. He figured she was the sort of dedicated doctor who worked long hours and paid little attention to schedules.

He might be sitting here for quite some time, he realized.

The document of incorporation that Peter had referred to wasn't in the vault, so where else might it be? He had said he'd hidden it away safely. Was it possible that Liesl was telling the truth, that she really didn't know where it was? In that case was it possible that Peter had concealed it somewhere among his possessions in the cabin without Liesl knowing?

She'd answered too quickly when he'd asked her

whether Peter might have hidden something there. She
knew something she wasn't telling.

He had to go to the cabin.

Forty minutes later, Liesl came out of the Emergency
entrance.

She was talking to someone, bantering. She gave a wave
good-bye and zipped up her leather jacket. Then she half-
walked, half-ran to her car, got in, and started it up.

Ben waited until she'd gone some distance down the
road before he pulled out of the lot. She wouldn't recognize
the Range Rover and would have no cause for suspicion,
apart from her normal cautiousness. Still, it was better not
to alarm her.

At a travel bookstore in Zurich he'd bought a map of
the canton of St. Gallen and studied the roads in the area.
Both Peter and Liesl had mentioned living in a "cabin,"
which likely meant that it was situated in a forest or woods.
There was one wooded area about eight kilometers from
the hospital, roughly north-northwest. The only other one
within a two-hour drive was forty kilometers away. That
was quite a distance, on back roads, for someone who had
to go to work every day—sometimes even had to return to
the hospital quickly in emergencies. More likely the cabin
was located in the closer woods.

Having committed the roads in the area to memory, he
knew that the next turnoff wasn't for two kilometers. But
if she stopped somewhere along the road and turned off,
he stood a chance of losing her. All he could do was hope
she didn't.

Soon the road rose steeply, following the hilly topog-
raphy of this part of Switzerland. It enabled him to look
far ahead, and he was able to spot what he determined was
her Renault, stopped at a traffic light. At the next intersection was a highway marked 10. If she took a left onto 10,
she was heading toward the forest he had scoped out. If
she took a right, or went beyond 10, he'd have no idea
where she was going.

The Renault turned left.

He accelerated and reached the intersection with 10 just a few minutes after she had. There were enough other cars on the road that he wasn't too obvious. He felt sure she still had no idea he was tailing her.

The four-lane highway went parallel to a set of railroad tracks, past several immense farms, great fields that went on as far as he could see. Suddenly she turned off, a few kilometers before he expected she would.

Once he turned onto the narrow, winding road, he realized that his was the only car behind her. Not good. It had gotten dark, and the road was barely trafficked, and she would soon realize he was following her. How could she not? If she did, she would either slow down to see who it was behind her or, more likely, try to lose him. If she began driving strangely, he would have no choice but to show himself.

Luckily, the twisty road helped to conceal him, as long as he stayed at least one bend behind her. Now they passed a sparsely wooded area that gradually became denser. From time to time he would see the flash of her headlights, appearing and then disappearing around the bends. This enabled him to follow her at some remove, to let her gain considerable distance on him, just in case she had noticed the Rover.

But a few minutes later he could no longer see her headlights.

Where had she gone? Had she pulled off the road? He accelerated, to see whether she had herself sped up, but after a kilometer he saw no trace of her.

She had to have turned off into the woods, though he didn't seem to have passed by any roads or paths that led into the forest. He stopped, made a U-turn—no cars were coming in either direction—and reversed course, slowing down to look for any turnoffs.

It wasn't easy; it had gotten quite dark.

Soon he spotted what could barely be called a road. It was a dirt trail that looked like a footpath, but upon closer examination he saw tire ruts.

He turned onto it, and saw at once that he would have to drive slowly. It was just wide enough for the Renault, but there was not quite enough clearance for the Range Rover. Twigs and branches scraped the sides of the car. He slowed down even more: the noise might attract her attention.

The St. Gallen map had told him that the forest he had entered was not large. It surrounded a small lake—a pond, actually—and there appeared to be no other road that led into or out of the woods.

Good.

Assuming the map was accurate.

The path came to a fork, and he stopped, got out of the car, and saw that one branch of the road dead-ended a hundred feet ahead. The other branch, deeply rutted, continued. He turned down that path and navigated with some difficulty, wondering how Liesl's Renault could make it if the Range Rover was having such trouble.

It was not long before this path, too, came to an end.

And then he saw the Renault.

He parked his vehicle beside it, and got out. By now it was fully dark, and he could see nothing. Once the car's engine was shut off there was mostly silence. Rustlings now and again that sounded like small animals. The chirp and twitter of birds.

His eyes became accustomed to the dark, and he could make out another path, even narrower, canopied with branches. Ducking down under one, he entered, losing his footing a few times, his hands held out before his face to shield his eyes from the twigs.

He saw a glow, and came upon a clearing. In it was a small cabin built of split logs and rough white plaster. There were several glass windows; it clearly wasn't as rustic as it appeared. A light shone from inside. This was the back of the cabin; the entrance had to be on the other side. Treading softly, he approached the cabin and made his way around to the front, where he expected the entrance to be.

Suddenly there was a metallic click. He looked up with a jolt.

Liesl was standing before him, pointing a gun.

"*Stop right there!*" she shouted.

"Wait!" Ben called back. God, she was fearless, coming right out to confront the interloper. A split-second was all it would take for her to kill him.

"It's *you!*" she spat out with sudden realization. "What the hell are you doing here?" She lowered the gun.

"I need your help, Liesl," he said.

In the oblique moonlight her shadowed face seemed contorted with rage. "You must have followed me from the hospital! How dare you!"

"You've got to help me find something, Liesl, please." He had to make her *listen.*

She whipped her head from side to side, frantic. "You have—compromised my security! Goddamn you to hell!"

"Liesl, I wasn't followed."

"How can you possibly know? Did you rent this car?"

"In Zurich."

"Of course. *Idiot!* If they were watching you in Zurich, they'll know you rented the car!"

"But no one followed me here."

"What do you know?" she snapped. "You're an amateur!"

"So are you."

"Yes, but I am an amateur who has lived with the threat of death for four years. Now please, get out. *Go!*"

"No, Liesl," he said with quiet finality. "We need to talk."

CHAPTER SIXTEEN

The cabin was simple yet cozy, low-ceilinged, book-lined. Peter had built the bookshelves himself, Liesl said proudly. The floor was wideboard pine. There was a stone fireplace, a neat stack of split logs piled next to it, a wood stove, a small kitchen. The whole place smelled of smoke.

It was cold; she lit the wood stove for some heat. Ben took off his coat.

"You're hurt," Liesl said. "You've been hit."

Ben looked at himself, saw that the left shoulder of his shirt was stiff with dried blood. Oddly, it hadn't been painful—stress and exhaustion had somehow rendered him insensate to the injury, and he'd put it out of his mind during the long drive through the mountains.

"I'm sure it looks a lot worse than it is," Ben said.

"That depends," she said, "on what it looks like. Remove the shirt." She spoke like the doctor she was.

Ben undid the buttons of his white pinpoint Oxford cloth shirt. The fabric adhered to the top of his left shoulder, and when he tugged, there was a warning twinge of pain.

Liesl took a clean sponge, soaked it with warm water,

and wet the area. Then she carefully peeled the shirt from his wounded shoulder. "You've been incredibly lucky: a bullet creased you, no more. Tell me what happened."

As Liesl tended to his wound, Ben recounted the events that happened only hours before.

"There's debris here. It must be cleansed carefully, or there will be the risk of infection." She sat him next to the sink, poured some boiling water from a kettle, and left it to cool in a porcelain bowl. She went away for a few minutes and reappeared with a quantity of gauze and a yellow plastic bottle of antiseptic.

Ben found himself wincing as she carefully washed the area, then wincing again as she daubed it with cotton saturated with the brown-colored antiseptic. "Cleaning it hurts worse than getting it did," Ben said.

Liesl applied four strips of medical adhesive tape to secure the sterile wound dressing in place. "You won't be so lucky next time," she said dryly.

"What I most need right now isn't luck," Ben said. "It's knowledge. I need to understand what the hell is going on. I need to get a fix on Sigma. They sure seem to have a fix on me."

"Luck, knowledge—trust me, you'll need both." Now she handed him a shirt. A heavy shirt of knitted cotton. One of Peter's.

Suddenly the reality of the past few days, the reality he'd tried to hold at bay, reared up and he felt a surge of vertigo, panic, sorrow, despair.

"I'll help you put it on," she said, alert to the anguish that played across his face.

He had to regain his composure, he knew, if only for her sake. He could merely guess at her own wrenching pain. When the shirt was on him, Liesl stared at him for a few moments. "You're so alike. Peter never told me. I think he never realized how alike you are."

"Twins never recognize themselves in each other."

"It was more than that. And I don't mean physically. Some people would have said that Peter was aimless. I knew better. He was like a sail, something that's slack only until it captures the wind. And then it possesses the force of the wind." She shook her head, as if frustrated by her fumbling attempts to communicate. "I mean that Peter had a larger sense of purpose."

"I knew what you meant. It's what I admired most about him, the life he came to create for himself."

"It was a passion," Liesl said, her eyes sad, gleaming, "a passion for justice, and it infused every aspect of his being."

" 'A passion for justice.' Those aren't words that mean much in the world of asset management," Ben said bitterly.

"A world you found stifling," Liesl said. "It was suffocating you by degrees, wasn't it, just as Peter said it would?"

"There are quicker ways to die," Ben said. "As I've had reason to learn of late."

"Tell me about the school where you taught. In New York, Peter said. I've been to New York a couple of times, as an adolescent, and once, later, to a medical conference."

"It was in New York, yes. But not a New York any tourist ever sees. I taught in a place called East New York. About five square miles of some of the worst-off people in the whole city. You've got some auto shops, and bodegas, places that'll sell you cigarettes and booze, and places that'll cash your checks. The Seventy-fifth Precinct—what the cops call the Seven-Five, those unfortunate enough to be assigned to it. When I was teaching, there were more than a hundred homicides in the Seven-Five. Some nights, it sounded like Beirut. You'd go to sleep to the sound of Saturday Night Specials. A desperate place. Pretty much written off by the rest of society."

"And that's where you taught."

"I thought it was obscene that in America, the wealthiest nation in the world, this sort of desolation was still tolerable. Here was a place that made Soweto look like Scarsdale. Sure, there were the usual ineffectual poverty programs, but there was also the unspoken conviction of futility. 'The poor will always be with us'—nobody used those words anymore, but that's what they meant. They used other code words, talked about 'structural' this and 'behavioral' that, and, hey, the middle class was doing just fine, wasn't it? So I stuck it out. I wasn't going to save the world, I wasn't naïve. But I told myself that if I could save one kid, maybe two, maybe three, my efforts wouldn't have been wasted."

"And did you?"

"Possibly," Ben said, suddenly tired. "Possibly. I wasn't around any longer to find out, was I?" He spat out the words with distaste: "I was ordering truffled timbales at Aureole, quaffing Cristal with clients."

"Sounds like a terrible shock to the system, that kind of change," Liesl said gently. She attended to his words carefully, perhaps in need of distraction from her own pain.

"It was deadening, I think. The hell of it was, I was actually good at it. I had a knack for the game, the rituals of client courtship. If you wanted someone who could order at the city's most expensive restaurants without glancing at the menu, I was your man. And then, as often as I could, I'd go risk my neck—recreationally, of course. I was an extreme-sport junkie. I'd go climb the Vermillion Cliffs, in Arizona. Sail solo to Bermuda. Go para-skiing in Cameron Pass. Courtney—an old girlfriend of mine—used to insist I had a death wish, but that wasn't it at all. I did those things to feel alive." He shook his head. "It sounds silly now, doesn't it? The idle diversions of a pampered rich kid, someone who hadn't figured out a reason for getting dressed in the morning."

"Maybe it was because you'd been taken from your natural element," Liesl said.

"And what was that? I'm not sure that saving souls in East New York was going to be a lifelong calling, either. Anyway, I never got the chance to find out."

"I think you were a sail, like Peter. You just needed to find your wind." She smiled sadly.

"The wind found me, it would seem. And it's a goddamn

monsoon. Some conspiracy that was launched half a century ago and is still claiming lives. Specializing in the people I love. Maybe you've never been in a small boat during a storm, Liesl, but I have. And the first thing you do is drop the sail."

"Is that really an option now?" She poured him a small quantity of brandy in a water glass.

"I don't even know what the options are. You and Peter have spent a lot more time thinking about it than I have. What conclusions did you come to?"

"Just the ones I told you. A great deal of conjecture for the most part. Peter did a lot of research into the period. He was disheartened by what he found out. The Second World War was a conflict that had clear rights and wrongs, and yet many of those involved were utterly indifferent to what was at stake. There were numerous corporations whose only concern was to maintain their operating margin. Some, alas, even viewed the war as an opportunity to be exploited—an opportunity to increase their profits. The victors never adequately came to grips with this legacy of corporate double-dealing. It was never convenient to do so." Her sardonic half-smile reminded Ben of his brother's banked sense of outrage, his smoldering anger.

"Why not?"

"Too many American and British industries might have had to be seized for trading with the enemy, for collaboration. Better to sweep the problem under the carpet. The Dulles brothers, you know, made sure of it. Tracking down the real collaborators—it wouldn't have looked good. It would have blurred the lines between good and evil, interfered with the myth of Allied innocence. Forgive me if I don't explain myself very well—these are stories I have heard many times. There was a young attorney in the Justice Department who dared make a speech about collaborations between American businessmen and the Nazis. He was immediately fired. After the war, German officials were called to task, some of them. And yet the citadel of Axis industrialists was never probed, never disturbed. Why prosecute German industrialists who had done business with Hitler—who had, really, made Hitler possible—given that they were just as happy now to do business with America? When overzealous officials at Nuremberg had a few of them convicted, your John J. McCloy, the American High Commissioner, had their sentences commuted. The 'excesses' of fascism were regrettable, but industrialists had to look after each other, right?"

Once again, he could almost detect Peter's passionate voice in her recountings. Dully, he said, "I still have a hard time getting my mind around it—financial partnerships when the two sides were at war?"

"Things aren't always as they seem. Hitler's senior-most intelligence officer, Reinhard Gehlen, had already begun planning his own surrender in 1944. The high command knew which way the wind was blowing, they knew Hitler was mad, irrational. So they bartered. They microfilmed their files on the U.S.S.R., buried them in watertight drums in the mountain meadows of the Alps, not a hundred miles from here, and presented themselves to the American Counterintelligence Corps to make a deal. After the war, you Americans put Gehlen in charge of the 'South German Industrial Development Organization.' "

Ben shook his head blearily. "It sounds like you both got pretty immersed in this stuff. And it sounds like I'm way out of my depths." He knocked back the rest of the brandy.

"Yes, I suppose we did get rather deep into all of this. We had to. I remember something Peter told me. He said the real question isn't where they are. It's where they aren't. That the real question isn't who can't be trusted, but who can be. Once it sounded like paranoia."

"But no longer."

"No," Liesl agreed, her voice trembling slightly. "And now they have arrayed their forces against you, through both official and unofficial channels." She hesitated. "There is something else I must give you."

Once more, she disappeared into the bedroom, and then

came back with a plain cardboard box, the sort a dry cleaner might package a shirt in. She opened it on the rough-hewn table in front of them. Papers. Laminated ID cards. Passports. The folding currency of modern bureaucracy.

"They were Peter's," Liesl said. "The fruits of four years in hiding."

Ben's fingers quickly sorted through the identity papers as if they were playing cards. Three different names, all appended to the same face. Peter's face. And, for all practical intents, his own. " 'Robert Simon.' Smart. There must be thousands of people with that name in North America. 'Michael Johnson.' Likewise. 'John Freedman.' These look like good work, professional work, if I'm any judge."

"Peter was a perfectionist," Liesl said. "I'm sure they are flawless."

Ben continued to go through the documents and saw that the passports came with matching credit cards. In addition, there were documents for "Paula Simon" and other spousal identities: if Robert Simon needed to travel with his "wife," he'd be prepared. Ben marveled, but his admiration was shadowed by a deep sadness. Peter's precautions were meticulous, obsessive, exhaustive—and yet they could not save him.

"I've got to ask, Liesl: Can we be sure that Peter's pursuers—the Sigma group or whoever they are—aren't on to them? Any of these could be flagged."

"Possibilities are not likelihoods."

"When was the last time he used 'Robert Simon'? And under what circumstances?"

Liesl closed her eyes in concentration, retrieving the details with remarkable precision. After twenty minutes, Ben had satisfied himself that at least two of Peter's aliases, unused in the last twenty-four months, were unlikely to have been detected. He tucked the papers into the capacious inside pockets of his leather coat.

He placed a hand on Liesl's and looked into her clear blue eyes. "Thank you, Liesl," he said. What an astonishing woman she was, he thought once more, and how lucky his brother was to have found her.

"The shoulder wound will scab over and heal in a matter of days," she said. "You will find it considerably harder to shed your identity, though these documents will help."

Liesl opened a bottle of red wine and poured each of them a glass. The wine was excellent, deep and rich and tannic, and Ben soon began to relax.

For a few moments the two of them silently watched the fire. Ben thought: *If Peter had hidden the document here, where could it be? And if not here, where?* He'd said it was hidden away safely. Had he left it with Matthias Deschner? But that made no sense: Why would he go to such lengths to open a bank account because of the vault that came with it, and then not put the incorporation document in the vault?

Why hadn't any document been in the vault?

He wondered about Deschner. What was his role, if any, in what had happened at the bank? Had he secretly alerted the banker that Ben was in the country illegally? If so, the timing didn't track: Deschner could have done so before Ben had been admitted to the vault. Was it possible that Deschner had gotten into the vault—as he easily could have despite his claim that he could not—months or years before, taken the document, then given it to his brother's pursuers? Yet Liesl had said she trusted her cousin . . . Contradictory thoughts swirled around in his brain, warring with one another until Ben couldn't think clearly anymore.

Liesl spoke at last, interrupting his troubled ruminations. "The fact that you could so easily follow me here worries me," she said. "No offense, please, but again, you're an amateur. Think of how much easier it would have been for a professional."

Whether or not she was right, it was crucial to reassure her, Ben sensed. "But keep in mind, Liesl, that Peter had told me you two lived in a cabin in the woods, near a lake. Once I figured out which hospital it was, that narrowed things down considerably. If I didn't know as much, I'd probably have lost you pretty early on."

She said nothing, just stared with unease at the fire.

"You know how to use that thing?" Ben asked, glancing toward the revolver she'd left on a table by the door.

"My brother was in the army. Every Swiss boy knows how to fire a gun. There's even a national holiday where Swiss boys go off to shoot. My father just happened to believe that a girl is every bit the equal of a boy and should learn to use a gun too. So I'm prepared for this life." She rose. "Well, I'm famished, and I'm going to make some dinner." Ben followed her to the kitchen.

She lit the gas oven, then took a whole chicken from the tiny refrigerator, buttered it and sprinkled it with dried herbs, and put it in the oven to roast. While she boiled some potatoes and sautéed some greens, they made idle conversation about her work and his, about Peter.

After a while, Ben retrieved the photograph from his jacket pocket. He'd verified, en route, that the wax envelope had protected it from water damage. Now he showed it to her. "Do you have any idea who these men might be?" he asked.

Her eyes suddenly registered alarm. "Oh, my God, that has to be your father! He looks so much like you two. What a handsome man he was!"

"And these others?"

She hesitated, shook her head, clearly troubled. "They look like important men, but then they all did in those heavy business suits. I'm sorry, I don't know. Peter never showed this to me. He just told me about it."

"And the document I mentioned—the articles of incorporation—did he ever mention hiding it somewhere here?"

She stopped stirring the greens. "Never." She said it with absolute certainty.

"You're sure? It wasn't in the vault."

"He would have told me if he'd hidden it here."

"Not necessarily. He didn't show you this photograph.

He may have wanted to protect you, or maybe keep you from worrying."

"Well, then your guess is as good as mine."

"Would you mind if I looked around?"

"Be my guest."

While she finished making dinner, he searched the cabin methodically, trying to put himself into his brother's head. Where would Peter have hidden it? He ruled out any place that Liesl would have regularly cleaned or had any reason to look. Liesl and Peter's bedroom was one of two small rooms off the living room area, the other being Peter's study. But both rooms were spartanly furnished and yielded nothing.

He checked the floor all over for any loose planks, then inspected the log-and-plaster walls, but nothing.

"Do you have a flashlight?" Ben asked, returning to the kitchen area. "I want to look outside."

"Of course. There's a flashlight in every room—the lights go out often. There's one on the table by the door. But we'll be ready to eat in just a few minutes."

"I'll make it quick." He took the flashlight and stepped outside, where it was cold and completely dark. He made a cursory tour of the grassy area surrounding the cabin. There was a scorched place where they obviously cooked outdoors, and a large log pile covered with a tarpaulin. The document might have been hidden in a container beneath a rock, but that would have to wait until the light of morning. He beamed the flashlight on the exterior of the cabin, made his way slowly around the walls, poking around a propane tank, but again turned up nothing.

When he went back inside, Liesl had already set out two plates and silverware on a red-and-white-checked tablecloth over a small round table against a window.

"Smells delicious," Ben said.

"Please, sit."

She poured two more glasses of wine and served both of them. The food was wonderfully flavored, and Ben devoured it. They both concentrated on eating, and only began to talk after they'd satisfied their hunger. The second glass of wine made Liesl melancholy. As she spoke about Peter and how they met, she cried. She recalled how Peter had taken such pride in furnishing their cabin, their home, building the bookcases and much of the furniture himself.

The bookcases, Ben thought. Peter had built the book-cases . . .

He got up suddenly. "Would you mind if I looked a little closer at the shelves?"

"Why not?" she said with a tired wave.

The bookcases appeared to have been built as several separate units and assembled in place. They weren't open shelves; you could not see the log-and-plaster walls behind them. Instead, Peter had built a backing of wood.

Shelf by shelf, Ben removed all of the books and looked behind them.

"What are you doing?" Liesl called out in vexation.

"I'll put them all back, don't worry," Ben said.

Half an hour later, he hadn't found anything. Liesl had finished doing the dishes and announced that she was ex-hausted. But Ben kept at it, removing each shelf of books, looking behind them, becoming more and more frustrated. When he came to the row of novels by F. Scott Fitzgerald, he smiled sadly. *The Great Gatsby* had been Peter's favor-ite.

Then, behind the Fitzgeralds, he found a small com-partment that had been flush-mounted, almost invisibly, into the wooden shelf backing.

Peter had done an impeccable job of carpentry: even with all the books off the shelf, you could barely see the faint rectangular outline of the compartment. He pried at it with his fingernails, but it didn't yield. He poked at it, pressed in, and then it popped open. A neat piece of crafts-manship. Peter the perfectionist.

The document was carefully rolled up. A rubber band held the roll together. Ben pulled it out, removed the rubber band, unrolled it.

It was a fragile, yellowed sheet of paper covered with

mimeographed lettering. Just one page. Merely the front page of a corporate filing.

It was headed SIGMA AG. There was a date: April 6, 1945.

Then a list of what had to be the company's officers and directors.

Dear God, he thought, thunderstruck. Peter had been right: there were names he recognized. Names of corporations that still existed, that made automobiles and weapons and consumer goods. Names of moguls and corporate chairmen. In addition to the figures he'd recognized from the photograph, there was the fabled magnate Cyrus Weston, whose steel empire had exceeded even that of Andrew Carnegie's, and Avery Henderson, who was regarded by business historians as the twentieth century's most important financier after John Pierpont Morgan. There were the chief executive officers of the major automotive companies; of early-generation technology firms that had taken the lead in developing radar, microwave, and refrigeration technologies—technologies whose full potential wouldn't be realized for years, decades, to come. The heads of the three largest petroleum companies, based in America, Britain, and the Netherlands. Telecommunication giants, before they were called that. The mammoth corporations of the time, some as intact and as vast as ever, some of them now subsumed into corporate entities even greater than themselves. Industrialists from America, Western Europe, and, yes, even a few from wartime Germany. And toward the very top of the list was the name of the treasurer: MAX HARTMAN (OBERSTURMFÜHRER, SS).

His heart was hammering away crazily. Max Hartman, a lieutenant in Hitler's SS. If this was a forgery . . . it was certainly well done. He had seen documents of incorporation many times before, and this looked very much like a page from such a document.

Liesl emerged from the kitchen. "You have found something?"

* * *

The fire was dying, and the room was beginning to get cold.

"Do you know any of those names?" Ben asked.

"The famous ones. The mighty 'captains of industry,' as Peter called them."

"But almost of all them are dead now."

"They would have heirs, successors."

"Yes. Well-protected ones," Ben said. "There are other names here, too, names that I don't recognize. I'm not a historian." He pointed to a few of those names, those that were not from the English-speaking world. "Are any of these names familiar to you? And any of them alive?"

She sighed. "Gaston Rossignol, I know, must still live in Zurich, everyone's heard of him. A pillar of the Swiss banking establishment for much of the postwar era. Gerhard Lenz was an associate of Josef Mengele, who did all those terrible medical experiments on prisoners. A monster. He died somewhere in South America many years ago. And, of course . . ." Her voice trailed off.

"Peter was right," Ben said.

"About your father?"

"Yes."

"It's strange. *Der Apfel fällt nicht weit vom Stamm*, my people say—the apple doesn't fall far from the tree. You and Peter are really so alike. And when I look at Max Hartman as a young man, I see you in him. Yet you're both so utterly different from your father. Appearance is an uncertain guide."

"He is an evil man."

"I'm sorry." She looked at him for a long while. Whether it was out of sorrow, or pity, or something more, Ben couldn't decide. "Just now you look more like your brother than ever before."

"How do you mean?"

"You look . . . haunted. As he came to look in the last— the last months." She closed her eyes, blinking back tears. After a moment, she said, "The couch in Peter's study pulls out into a bed. Let me get it ready for you."

"That's all right," he said. "I can do it."

"Let me at least get you some linens. And then I'll say good night. I'm about to drop from exhaustion and too much wine. I was never a drinker."

"You've been through some hard times recently," he said. "We both have."

He said good night, undressed, then carefully folded the document and tucked it into the pocket of his leather jacket, next to Peter's identity papers. Within moments he had fallen into a deep, almost drugged sleep.

He and his brother were packed into a sealed boxcar, jammed with other people, unbearably hot, foul-smelling, because none of the prisoners had bathed in days. He was unable to move his limbs. Soon he passed out, and the next thing he knew they were somewhere else, again in a crowd of prisoners, walking skeletons with shaved heads. But Peter looked relieved, because at last he would be allowed to take a shower, and so what if it was a communal shower? Ben was overcome with panic, because he knew. Somehow he knew. He tried to shout: "Peter! No! This is not a shower—it's a gas chamber! Get out! It's a gas chamber!" Yet his words would not come out. The others stood there like zombies, and Peter just glared at him, not understanding. A baby was crying, and then a few young women. He tried to shout again, but nothing came out. He was wild with terror. He felt suffocated, claustrophobic. He saw his brother's upturned head, welcoming the water he expected to come from the nozzles. At the same time, he could hear the knobs being turned, the rusty squeak-squeak-squeak of the valves opening, the hiss of the gas. He shouted, "No!" opened his eyes, and looked around at the pitch-dark study.

Slowly he sat up, listening. There was no rusty squeak; he had dreamed it. He was in his late brother's cabin in the woods, and he had been sleeping.

But had he heard a noise, or had he dreamed that, too?

Then he heard the thunk of a car door closing.

It was unmistakable; there is no other sound like that. And it was a big car, perhaps a truck. His Range Rover?

He bolted out of bed, grabbed the flashlight, slipped quickly into his jeans and sneakers, and threw on his leather jacket. He thought: Could it be Liesl who'd gotten into, or out of, the Range Rover for some reason? He passed by her bedroom and pushed open the door.

She was in bed, eyes closed, asleep.

Oh, God. It was someone else. Someone was out there!

He rushed to the front door, grabbed the revolver from the table, opened the door silently. He looked around the clearing, illuminated by the pale light of a crescent moon. He didn't want to switch on the flashlight, didn't want to call attention to himself or alert whoever was out there.

Then he heard an ignition turn and the roar of an engine coming to life. He raced outside, saw the Range Rover still parked there, caught the red taillights of a truck.

"Hey!" he shouted, running after it.

The truck was barreling down the narrow dirt path at maximum speed, constrained only by the closeness of the trees. Ben ran faster, gun in one hand, clutching the Mag-Lite flashlight in the other like a baton at one of his college track meets. The taillights grew farther away even as he put on a burst of speed, the branches whipping his face, though he barely noticed. He was a machine, a running machine, a track star once again, and he would not let that truck get away, and as he tore down the dirt road that connected with the path from the cabin he thought, Did they hear a noise in the cabin? Were they planning a break-and-enter but were frightened away? and he kept on going, faster and faster, and the red lights grew smaller and smaller, the truck getting away from him, and then he knew that he'd never catch it. The truck was gone. He turned around, headed back toward the cabin, suddenly remembering the Range Rover. He could try to chase them down in the Rover! There were only two directions the truck could have gone; he could race after them in his vehicle. He ran back down the path toward the cabin, and was suddenly jolted by a tremendous, ear-splitting explosion in front of him, coming from the cabin, an explosion that turned the night sky orange and red like a giant Roman candle, and then he saw with terror that the cabin was ablaze, a ball of fire.

CHAPTER SEVENTEEN

Washington, D.C.

The zipper on Anna's garment bag snagged on one of her dresses just as the taxi arrived and honked impatiently.

"All right, all right," she groaned. "Cool it."

She yanked at the zipper again, with no luck. Then the telephone rang. "Good God!"

She was late, trying to get to Reagan National Airport to catch the evening flight to Zurich. No time to get the phone. She decided to let the voice mail answer it; then she changed her mind.

"Agent Navarro, forgive me for calling you at home." She recognized the high, hoarse voice at once, though she'd only spoken to him once before. "I got your home number from Sergeant Arsenault. It's Denis Weese from the Chemistry Section of the Nova Scotia Forensic Laboratory."

He spoke excruciatingly slowly. "Yes," she said impatiently, "the toxicologist. What's up?"

"Well, the ocular fluid you asked me to look at?"

She finally worked the fabric of her dress loose from the zipper's teeth. She tried not to think of how much the dress had cost. Damage had been done, but maybe it wouldn't be too noticeable. "You find anything?"

"It's most interesting." The taxi's honking grew more insistent.

"Can you hold on a second?" she said, then dropped the phone to the carpet and ran to the window. "I'll be down in a few minutes," she shouted.

The driver yelled up, "Navarro? You called for a taxi?"

"You can put the meter on. I'll be down in a few." She ran back to pick up the phone. "Sorry. The ocular fluid, you said."

"The band showed up on electrofluoresis," the toxicologist went on. "It's not a naturally occurring protein. It's a peptide, a sort of folded chain of amino acids—"

She dropped the garment bag to the floor. "Some synthetic compound, is that what you're saying?" Not a naturally occurring protein. Something that was created in a laboratory. What could this mean?

"One that selectively binds to neuroreceptors. That explains why we didn't find any traces of it in the bloodstream. It can only be detected, in trace quantities, in the spinal and ocular fluid."

"Meaning it goes right to the brain, basically."

"Well, yes."

"What kind of compound are we talking here?"

"It's an exotic. I guess the closest thing to it found in nature is a venom peptide, like snake venom. But the molecule's clearly synthetic."

"It's a poison, then."

"An entirely new molecule, one of the new toxins that scientists are now able to synthesize. I'm guessing that what it does is induce cardiac arrest. It goes right to the brain, crossing the blood-brain barrier, but leaves no traces in the blood serum. Really quite something."

An entirely new molecule.

"Let me ask you something. What do you think this toxin is intended to be used for? Biological warfare?"

He laughed uneasily. "No, no, no, nothing of the sort. One does see such synthetic peptides created, sort of modeled, on naturally occurring poisons found in toads or snails or snakes or whatever, in basic biotech research. You see, the fact that they selectively bind to certain proteins makes them useful for tagging them. It's the same property that makes them toxic, but that's not why people concoct them."

"So this—this substance—might have been made by a biotechnology company."

"Or any company with a research arm in molecular biochemistry. Could be any of the big agricultural firms, too. Monsanto, Archer Daniels Midland, you name it. I don't know where this was created, of course."

"I'm going to ask you a favor," she said. "I'm going to ask you to fax whatever you got on this to this number, O.K.?" She gave him a fax number, thanked him, hung up, and called the ICU. If she missed the plane, so be it. Right now nothing was more important than this.

"Can you patch me in to whoever has liaison with the U.S. Patent Office?" she said. When she'd been put through, she said, "Agent Stanley, this is Agent Anna Navarro. I need you to check something for me real quick and get back to me. In a couple of minutes you're going to get a fax from the Nova Scotia Forensic Laboratory. It's a description of a synthetic molecule. I need you to do a search for me at the U.S. Patent Office. I want to know if any company has filed a patent for this thing."

Find out who makes it, and you'll find the killer. One will lead to the other.

She hoped it would be that simple.

The taxi driver was honking again, and she went to the window to tell him to cool his jets.

Switzerland

Virtually catatonic, Ben drove to Zurich. Back into the lion's den, he thought ruefully to himself. Yes, he was persona non grata there, but it was a city of nearly four hundred thousand; he'd make out so long as he kept a low profile and avoided any tripwires. And where would those be? It was a risk, a definite, calculated risk, but there was no reason to believe that safe refuge lay elsewhere. Liesl had quoted Peter's warning words: the question isn't where they are, it's where they aren't.

Oh, God. Liesl! The odor of wood smoke that permeated his clothes was a wrenching, steady reminder of her, of the once-comfortable cabin, of the explosion he had witnessed but could scarcely comprehend.

The one thing he clung to, the one thing that allowed him to keep his sanity, was that Liesl had probably been dead when the cabin had burst into flames.

Oh, Christ!

By now he had put together how it had happened; it all made a chilling kind of sense. The squeaking he had heard in the middle of the night, which had incorporated itself into his terrible dream, had come from the valve of the propane tank being turned all the way open. The cabin had quickly filled with the odorless propane—he had already stepped outside by then—which was intended to over-whelm, put to sleep, then kill the occupants of the cabin. To cover up the evidence, a timed fuse had somehow gone off. Certainly it hadn't taken much to ignite the highly flam-mable gas. The accident would be ascribed by the local authorities to a faulty propane tank, not an uncommon haz-ard in rural areas.

And then whoever had done it had gotten into his truck and stolen away.

By the time Ben returned to the Range Rover—a matter of seconds, really, after the explosion—the cabin was pretty much gone.

She had not suffered. She had surely been either asleep or dead before her little cabin became an inferno.

He couldn't stand to think of it!

For four years Liesl and Peter had lived there, lived their lives in hiding, surely always fearful, but fundamentally undisturbed. Probably they could have gone on living there for years.

Until Ben had shown up in Zurich.

And brought out these zealots, in effect luring Peter to his death.

And led these faceless, anonymous zealots to Liesl, the woman who had once saved Peter's life.

Ben was beyond grief. He no longer felt the sharp stab of guilt, because he was numb. He felt nothing anymore. The shock had turned him into a cadaver, driving through the night, staring straight ahead, a machine without emotions.

But as he approached the darkened city, he began to feel one single emotion: a slowly growing, burning anger. A fury at those who had targeted innocent and good people who'd done nothing wrong but come across a bit of information by accident.

These killers, and those who directed them, remained faceless in his mind. He could not picture them, but he was determined to unmask them. They wanted him dead; they intended to frighten him into silence. But instead of running away, instead of hiding, he had made up his mind to run *toward* them, though from a direction they could not anticipate. They wanted to operate from the shadows; he would shine light on them. They wanted to conceal; he would expose.

And if his father was one of them . . .

He needed to dig into the past now, to excavate, to learn who these murderers were, and where they came from, and above all what they were hiding. Ben knew the rational response was to be frightened, and though that he certainly was, his fear was now subordinate to his rage.

He knew he had crossed some line into an obsession beyond any rationality.

But who were these faceless attackers?

Men who had been mobilized by the board of the corporation Max Hartman had helped set up. Madmen? Fanatics? Or simply mercenaries, hired by a corporation that had been founded, decades ago, by a group of prominent industrialists and high-ranking Nazis—among them his own father—who were now trying to conceal the unlawful origins of their original wealth? Cold-blooded mercenaries without any ideology except the profit motive, the almighty dollar, the Deutschmark, the Swiss franc . . .

There were layers upon layers of interlocking possibilities.

He needed cold hard information.

Ben vaguely remembered being told that one of Switzerland's great research libraries was at the University of Zurich, in the hills overlooking the city, and that was where he now headed, the logical place to begin digging up the past.

Washington, D.C.

Anna watched queasily as the flight attendant demonstrated the flimsy thing you put over your nose and mouth to help you breathe if the plane goes down. She'd once read an article in one of those on-line magazines that said that nobody had ever survived an emergency water landing of an airplane. Never. She took a pharmacy bottle of Ativan from her purse. It was beyond the expiration date, but she didn't particularly care. This was the only way she was going to make it across the Atlantic.

She was startled to hear her ICU-issue StarTac trilling from deep in the recesses of her purse. Government-standard cryptotelephony, and hardly bulkier than the usual consumer model. She'd forgot to turn it off.

She pulled it out. "Navarro."

"Please hold for Alan Bartlett," she heard in a lightly accented Jamaican voice.

She felt a tap on her shoulder. It was a flight attendant. "I'm sorry, ma'am," he said. "You're not allowed to have any cellular phones turned on during the flight."

"We're not flying yet," Anna pointed out.

"Agent Navarro," Bartlett said. "I'm glad I caught you."

"Ma'am," the flight attendant persisted, "airline regulations forbid you from using cell phones once the aircraft has left the gate."

"Sorry, this'll just be a minute." To Bartlett she said, "What have you got for me? I'm on a plane to Zurich."

"Ma'am," the flight attendant said loudly, exasperated.

Without looking at him she took out her Justice Department ID with her free hand and flashed it at him.

"We lost another one," Bartlett said.

Another one? So soon? The murders were accelerating. The flight attendant drew back. "My apologies, ma'am."

"You're kidding me," Anna groaned.

"In Holland. A town called Tilburg, a couple of hours south of Amsterdam. You might want to change planes in Zurich and go there."

"No," she said. "I'm going to Zurich. It's a simple matter for me to have the FBI legat in Amsterdam request an immediate autopsy. This time at least we can tell them exactly what poisons to screen for."

"Is that right?"

"I'm on my way to Zurich, Director. I'm going to catch myself a live one. Dead men don't talk. Now, what was the name of the Tilburg victim?"

Bartlett paused. "A certain Hendrik Korsgaard."

"Wait a minute!" Anna said sharply. "That name wasn't on my list."

There was silence on the other end.

"Talk to me, Bartlett, dammit!"

"There are other lists, Agent Navarro," Bartlett said slowly. "I was hoping they wouldn't prove . . . relevant."

"Unless I'm greatly mistaken, this is a violation of our understanding, Director Bartlett," Anna said quietly, her eyes darting around to verify that she wasn't being overheard.

"Not at all, Ms. Navarro. My office works like any other, by a division of labor. Information is edited accordingly. Your responsibility was to find the killers. We had reason to believe that the names on the list I gave you, from the clearance files, were being targeted. We had no reason to believe that . . . the others were in jeopardy as well."

"And did you know where the Tilburg victim resided?"

"We didn't even know he was still living. Certainly, all efforts to locate him were in vain."

"Then we can rule out the possibility that the killers have simply gained access to your files."

"It's gone far beyond that," Bartlett said crisply. "Whoever's killing these old men, they've got better sources than we do."

It was not much past four in the morning by the time Ben located the *Universitätsbibliothek* on Zähringerplatz. The library wouldn't open for another five hours.

In New York, he calculated, it was ten at night. His father would probably still be awake—he usually went to bed late and arose early, always had—and even if he were asleep, Ben wasn't much concerned about waking him. Not anymore.

Wandering down the Universitätstrasse to stretch his legs, he made sure his cell phone was switched to the GSM standard used in Europe and placed a call to Bedford.

The housekeeper, Mrs. Walsh, answered.

Mrs. Walsh, an Irish version of Mrs. Danvers from *Rebecca*, Ben had always thought, had worked for the family for over twenty years, and Ben had never got past her haughty reserve.

"Benjamin," she said. Her tone was strange.

"Good evening, Mrs. Walsh," Ben said wearily. "I need to talk to my father." He readied himself to do battle with his father's gatekeeper.

"Benjamin, your father's gone."

He went cold. "Gone where?"

"Well, that's just it, I don't know."

"Who does?"

"No one. A car came for Mr. Hartman this morning, and he wouldn't say where he was going. Not a word. He said it would be 'a while.' "

"A car? Was it Gianni?" Gianni was his father's regular driver, a happy-go-lucky sort whom the old man regarded with a certain distanced affection.

"Not Gianni. Not a company car. He's just gone. No explanation."

"I don't understand. He's never done that before, has he?"

"Never. I know he packed his passport, because it's gone."

"His passport? Well, that tells us something, doesn't it?"

"But I called his office, talked to his secretary, and she knew nothing about any international trip. I was hoping he might have said something to you."

"Not a word. Did he get any phone calls . . . ?"

"No, I don't . . . Let me look at the message book." She came back to the phone a minute later. "Just a Mr. Godwin."

"Godwin?"

"Well, actually, it says Professor Godwin."

The name took him by surprise. That had to be Ben's college mentor, the Princeton historian John Barnes Godwin. Then again, he realized, it wasn't particularly bizarre for Godwin to be calling Max: a few years ago, impressed by what Ben had told him about the famous historian, Max had given money to Princeton to set up a Center for the Study of Human Values, of which Godwin became the director. Yet his father hadn't mentioned Godwin. Why were the two of them talking on the morning before Max disappeared?

"Let me have the number," he said.

He thanked her and clicked off.

Strange, he thought. For a brief moment he imagined that his father was fleeing somewhere, because he knew his past had been uncovered or was about to be uncovered. But that made no sense—fleeing what? Fleeing where?

Ben was exhausted and emotionally depleted, and he knew he was not thinking clearly. He badly needed sleep. He was making connections now that weren't quite logical.

He thought: Peter knew things, things about their father's past, about a company Max had helped set up, and then Peter was killed.

And then . . .

And then I found a photograph of the founders of this corporation, my father among them. And I followed to Liesl and Peter's cabin, and I found a page from the incorporation document setting this company up. And then they'd tried to kill both me and Liesl and cover up the evidence by blowing up the cabin.

So is it possible that they . . . again, the faceless, anonymous They . . . had gotten to my father, informed him that the secret was out, the secret of his past, or maybe the secret of this strange corporation? Or both?

Yes, of course it was possible. Since They seem to be trying to eliminate anyone who knows about this company . . .

Why else had Max disappeared so suddenly, so mysteriously?

Might he have been compelled to go somewhere, to meet with certain people . . .

There was only one thing Ben felt sure of: that his father's sudden disappearance was in some way connected with the murders of Peter and Liesl, and with the uncovering of this document.

He returned to the Range Rover, noticed in the light of the rising sun the deep scratches that defaced its sides, and drove back to Zähringerplatz.

Then he settled back in the Rover and placed a call to Princeton, New Jersey.

"Professor Godwin?"

The old professor sounded as if he'd been asleep.

"It's Ben Hartman."

John Barnes Godwin, historian of Europe in the twentieth century and once Princeton's most popular lecturer, had been retired for years. He was eighty-two but still came into his office every day to work.

An image of Godwin came into Ben's mind—tall and

gaunt, white-haired, the deeply wrinkled face.

Godwin had been not just Ben's faculty adviser but a sort of father figure as well. Ben remembered once sitting in Godwin's book-choked office in Dickinson Hall. The amber light, the vanilla-mildew smell of old books.

They'd been talking about how FDR managed to maneuver the isolationist United States into the Second World War. Ben was writing his senior thesis about FDR and had told Godwin that he was offended by Roosevelt's trickery.

"Ah, Mr. Hartman," Godwin replied. That was what he called Ben in those days. "How is your Latin? *Honesta turpitudo est pro causa bona.*"

Ben looked at the professor blankly.

" 'For a good cause,' " Godwin translated with a slow, sly smile, " 'wrongdoing is virtuous.' Publilius Syrus, who lived in Rome a century before Christ, and said a lot of smart things."

"I don't think I agree," Ben said, the morally indignant undergraduate. "To me that sounds like a rationalization for screwing people over. I hope I never catch myself saying that."

Godwin regarded him with what seemed to be puzzlement. "I suppose that's why you refuse to join your father's business," he said pointedly. "You'd rather be pure."

"I'd rather teach."

"But why are you so sure you want to teach?" Godwin had asked, sipping tawny port.

"Because I love it."

"You're certain?"

"No," Ben admitted. "How can a twenty-year-old be certain of anything?"

"Oh, I find that twenty-year-olds are certain of most things."

"But why should I go into something I have no interest in, working in a company my father built, to make even more money that I don't need? I mean, what good does our money do for society? Why should I have great wealth while others have no food on the table?"

Godwin closed his eyes. "It's a luxury to thumb your nose at money. I've had some extremely rich students, even a Rockefeller, in my class. And they all struggle with this same dilemma—not to let the money rule your life or define you, but, instead, to do something meaningful with your life. Now, your father is one of our nation's great philanthropists—"

"Yeah, wasn't it Reinhold Niebuhr who said that philanthropy is a form of paternalism? The privileged class tries to preserve its status by doling out funds to the needy?"

Godwin glanced up, impressed. Ben tried not to smile. He'd just read this in his theology class, and the line had stuck in his mind.

"A question, Ben. Is becoming a grade school teacher actually your way of rebelling against your father?"

"Maybe so," Ben said, unwilling to lie. He wanted to add that it was Godwin who had inspired him to teach, but that might sound too . . . something.

He was surprised when Godwin replied, "Bully for you. That takes guts. And you'll be a great teacher, I have no doubt of it."

Now, Ben said, "I'm sorry to be calling you so late—"

"Not at all, Ben. Where are you? The connection—"

"Switzerland. Listen, my father's disappeared "

"What do you mean, 'disappeared'?"

"He left home this morning, went somewhere, we don't know where, and I was wondering because you called him this morning, just before that . . ."

"I was returning his call, really. He wanted to talk about another gift to the center he was planning to make."

"That's it?"

"I'm afraid so. Nothing out of the ordinary, as far as I can recall. But if he happens to call me again, is there a way I can get in touch with you?"

Ben gave Godwin his digital number. "Another question. Do you know anyone on the faculty of the University of

Zurich? Someone who does what you do—modern European history."

Godwin paused for a moment. "At the University of Zurich? You can't do any better than Carl Mercandetti. A first-class researcher. Economic history's his specialty, but he's very wide-ranging in the best European tradition. The fellow also has an astounding collection of grappa, though I suppose that's neither here nor there. Regardless, Mercandetti's your man."

"I appreciate it," Ben said, and he hung up.

Then he put the car seat back and tried to doze for a few hours.

He slept fitfully, his sleep disturbed by unceasing nightmares in which he was forced to see the cabin explode time and again.

When he awoke at a few minutes after nine, he saw in the rearview mirror how unshaven and dirty he looked, saw the deep circles under his eyes, but he didn't have what it took to find a place to shave and wash.

There wasn't any time in any case.

It was time to begin excavating a past that was no longer the past.

CHAPTER EIGHTEEN

Paris

Only a small brass plaque marked the office of Groupe TransEuroTech SA, on the third floor of a limestone building on the avenue Marceau in the eighth arrondissement. The plaque, mounted on the stone to the left of the front door, was but one of seven brass plaques bearing the names of law firms and other small companies, and as such it attracted little attention.

The office of TransEuroTech never received unscheduled visitors, but anyone who happened to pass by the third floor would see nothing out of the ordinary: a young male receptionist sitting behind a glass teller's window made of a bullet-resistant polycarbonate material that looked like plain glass. Behind him, a small, bare room furnished with a few molded-plastic chairs, and a single door to the interior offices.

No one would, of course, realize that the receptionist was actually an armed and experienced ex-commando, or see the concealed surveillance cameras, the passive infrared motion detectors, the balanced magnetic switches embedded in every door.

The conference room deep inside the offices was actually a room within a room: a module separated from the surrounding concrete walls by foot-thick rubber blocks that kept all vibrations (specifically human speech) from transferring out. Immediately adjacent to the conference module was a permanent installation of antennae constantly searching for HF, UHF, VHF, and microwave transmissions—any attempt, that is, to listen in on the discussions held within the room. Attached to the antennae was a spectrum analyzer programmed to check across the spectrum for any anomalies.

At one end of a coffin-shaped mahogany conference table sat two men. Their conversation was protected against interception by both white-noise generators and a "babble tape," which sounded like the yammer of a crowded bar at happy hour. Anyone somehow able to bypass the elaborate security and listen in would be unable to separate the words of the two men at the table from the background noise.

The older of the two was speaking on a sterile telephone, a flat black box of Swiss manufacture. He was a pasty-faced, worried-looking man in his mid-fifties with gold-framed glasses, a soft jowly face, oily skin, and receding hair dyed an unnatural russet. His name was Paul Marquand, and he was a vice president of security for the Corporation. Marquand had come to the Corporation by a route common to corporate-security directors of international businesses: he had spent time in the French infantry, was forced out for wild behavior and joined the French Foreign Legion, later moving to the U.S., where he'd worked as a strikebreaker for a mining company before he was hired to do corporate security for a multinational firm.

Marquand spoke rapidly, quietly, and then hung up the phone.

"Vienna Sector is disturbed," Marquand told the man beside him, a dark-haired, olive-skinned Frenchman some twenty years younger named Jean-Luc Passard. "The American survived the propane accident in St. Gallen." He added darkly, "There can be no more errors. Not after the Bahn-hofplatz debacle."

"It was not your decision to assign the American soldier," Jean-Luc said softly.

"Of course not, but neither did I object. The logic was persuasive: he'd spent time in proximity to the subject and could pick the face out of a crowd in a matter of seconds. No matter how often a stranger is shown a photograph, he could never move as quickly or as reliably as someone who has known the target personally."

"We've now mobilized the very best," Passard said. "With the Architect on the case, it will not be long before the mess is eliminated completely."

"His perfectionism leads to persistence," Marquand observed. "Still the pampered American is not to be under-estimated."

"The marvel is that he is still alive, the amateur," Passard agreed. "Being a fitness freak does not give one survival skills." He snorted and spoke mockingly in heavily accented English: "He doesn't know the jungle. He knows the jungle gym."

"All the same," Marquand said, "there is such a thing as beginner's luck."

"He is no longer a beginner," Passard observed.

Vienna

The elderly, well-dressed American emerged from the gate, walking stiffly and slowly, clutching a carry-on bag. He searched the crowd until he saw a uniformed limousine driver holding up a little sign with his name on it.

The old man gave a wave of acknowledgment, and the driver, accompanied by a woman in a white nurse's uniform, hurried up to him. The driver took the American's bag, and the nurse said, "How was your flight, sir?" She spoke in English with an Austrian-German accent.

The man grumbled, "I despise traveling. I can't tolerate it anymore."

The nurse escorted him through the crowds and to the street immediately outside, where a black Daimler limousine was parked. She helped him into the interior, which was equipped with the standard appurtenances—phone, TV, and bar. Tucked unobtrusively into one corner was an array of emergency medical equipment, including a small oxygen tank, hoses and face mask, defibrillator paddles, and IV tubes.

"Well, sir," the nurse said once he was settled in the deeply cushioned leather seat, "the ride is not long at all, sir."

The old man grunted, reclined the seat back, and closed his eyes.

"Please let me know if there's anything I can do to make you more comfortable," the nurse said.

CHAPTER NINETEEN

Zurich

Anna was met at her hotel by a liaison officer from the office of the Public Prosecutor of the canton of Zurich. He was Bernard Kesting, a small, powerfully built, dark-haired young man with a heavy beard and eyebrows that joined in the middle. Kesting was unsmiling, all business, very professional: the quintessential Swiss bureaucrat.

After a few minutes of stilted introductory chat, Kesting led her to his car, a BMW 728, parked in the semicircular drive in front of the hotel.

"Rossignol is of course well known to us," Kesting said, holding the car door open for her. "A revered figure in the banking community, for many, many years. Certainly my office has never had reason to question him." She got into the car, but he stood there with the car door still open. "I'm afraid the nature of your inquiry was not made clear to us. The gentleman has never been accused of any crime, you know."

"I understand." She reached for the handle and closed the door herself. He made her nervous.

Behind the wheel, Kesting continued as he pulled out of

the drive and headed down Steinwiesstrasse, a quiet residential street near the Kunsthaus. "He was, or is, a brilliant financier."

"I can't disclose the nature of our investigation," Anna said, "but I can tell you that he's not the target of it."

He was silent for a while, then said with some embarrassment, "You asked about protective surveillance. As you know, we haven't been able to locate him precisely."

"And this is customary for prominent Swiss bankers? To simply . . . disappear?"

"Customary? No. But then he is retired, after all. He is entitled to his eccentricities."

"And how are his official communications handled?"

"Received by a trust, domestic representatives of an offshore entity that remains, even to them, completely opaque."

"Transparency not being a notable Swiss value."

Kesting glanced at her quickly, apparently unsure whether she was being snide. "It seems that at some point in the past year or so, he decided he wanted to, well, keep a lower profile. Perhaps he had the delusion that he was being stalked, pursued—he's in his early nineties, after all, and mental deterioration can sometimes lead to paranoid fantasies."

"And perhaps it wasn't a delusion."

Kesting gave her a sharp look but said nothing.

Herr Professor Doktor Carl Mercandetti had warmed immeasurably when Ben mentioned that he was a friend of Professor John Barnes Godwin. "There is no inconvenience, and nothing to apologize for. I have an office in the library. Why don't you meet me there midmorning? I'll be there anyway. I hope Godwin didn't tell you—I'm supposed to be publishing a monograph as part of a Cambridge University Press series that he's editing, and already I'm two years late with it! He tells me my sense of timing is a

touch Mediterranean." Mercandetti's laugh was booming
·:ven over the phone line.

Ben had been vague about what he'd wanted from Mercandetti, and Mercandetti, judging from his high jollity, had
probably assumed it was as much by way of a social call
as anything.

Ben spent the first part of the morning searching through
every directory of corporations in Switzerland he could
find, even running a computer search of all telephone list-
ings. But he could find no record of such a corporation as
Sigma AG. So far as he could see, there was no public
record that it ever did exist.

Carl Mercandetti was more austere-looking in person
than Ben had imagined when they spoke on the telephone.
He was around fifty, slight, with a gray crew cut and oval
wire-rimmed glasses. When Ben introduced himself, however, the eyes became lively, and his handclasp was welcoming.

"Any friend of God's . . ." Mercandetti said.

"And I thought it was only Princeton undergraduates
who called him that."

Mercandetti shook his head, smiling. "In the years I've
known him, I'd say he's only grown into his nickname. I'm
quite terrified he'll be there at the pearly gates, saying,
'Now, a small query about footnote forty-three in your last
article . . .' "

After a few minutes, Ben mentioned his efforts to track
down a corporation named Sigma AG, one founded in Zurich toward the end of the Second World War. He didn't
explain further: the scholar would doubtless assume it was
the sort of thing that an international banker might well
pursue, perhaps in the course of corporate due diligence. In
any case, Ben knew he would not be ill-served by reticence.

When he learned of Ben's immediate concerns, Mercandetti was polite but unengaged. The name Sigma clearly
meant little to him.

"You say it was established in 1945?" the historian
asked.

"That's right."

"A magnificent year for Bordeaux, did you know that?" He shrugged. "Of course, we're talking well over half a century ago. Many companies that were founded during the war, or right after, failed. Our economy was not so good as it is now."

"I have reason to believe it still exists," Ben said.

Mercandetti cocked his head good-naturedly. "What sort of information do you have?"

"It's not solid information, really. It's more along the lines of—of, well, people talking. People in a position to know."

Mercandetti seemed amused and skeptical. "Do these people have any more information? The name could easily have been changed."

"But isn't there some record somewhere of corporate name changes?"

The historian's eyes scanned the vaulted ceiling of the library. "There's a place you might check. It's called the *Handelsregisteramt des Kantons Zürich*—the registry of all corporations founded in Zurich. All companies established here must file papers with the registry."

"All right. And let me ask you something else. This list here." He slid the list of directors of Sigma AG, which he had recopied in his own hand, across the sturdy oak table. "Do you recognize any of these names?"

Mercandetti put on a pair of reading glasses. "Most of these names—they are names of well-known industrialists, you know. Prosperi, here, is a sort of underworld figure—I think he just died, just recently. In Brazil or Paraguay, I forget which. These men are mostly dead or very ancient by now. Oh, and Gaston Rossignol, the banker—he must live in Zurich."

"Is he still alive?"

"I haven't heard otherwise. But if he's alive he must be in his eighties or nineties."

"Is there a way to find out?"

"Have you tried the telephone book?" An amused look.

"There were a handful of Rossignols. None of them with the right first initial."

Mercandetti shrugged. "Rossignol was a major financier. Helped restore the solidity of our banking system after the Second World War. He had many friends here. But perhaps has retired to the Cap d'Antibes, and is slathering coconut oil on his liver-spotted shoulders even as we speak. Or perhaps he now seeks to avoid any sort of attention, for some reason of his own. With the recent controversies over Swiss gold and the Second World War, there have been agitators, some of them vigilantes. Even a Swiss banker cannot live in a vault, of course. So one takes precautions."

One takes precautions. "Thanks," he said. "This is extremely helpful." Now he pulled out the black-and-white photograph he'd taken from the Handelsbank and handed it to the academic. "Do any of these men look familiar?"

"I don't know if you are a banker, at heart, or a history buff," Mercandetti said merrily. "Or a dealer in old photographs—quite a trade these days. Collectors pay fortunes for nineteenth-century tintypes. Not my sort of thing at all. Give me color any day."

"This isn't exactly a vacation snap," Ben said mildly.

Mercandetti smiled and picked up the photo. "That must be Cyrus Weston—yes, with his trademark hat," he said. He pointed with a stubby finger. "That looks like Avery Henderson, dead many years. This is Émil Ménard, who built Trianon, really the first modern conglomerate. This may be Rossignol, but I'm not sure. One always imagines him with his great bald dome, not this thatch of dark hair, but he was a much younger man here. And over here . . ." A minute passed in silence before Mercandetti dropped the photo. His smile had vanished. "What sort of prank is this?" he asked Ben, looking at him over his reading glasses. A bemused expression crossed his face.

"How do you mean?"

"This must be some sort of montage, something involving trick photography." The academic spoke with a trace of annoyance.

"Why do you say that? Surely Weston and Henderson were acquainted."

"Weston and Henderson? Surely they were. And surely they were never in the same place as Sven Norquist, the Norwegian shipping magnate, and Cecil Benson, the British automotive magnate, and Drake Parker, the head of the petrochemical giant, and Wolfgang Siebing, the German industrialist, whose family company once made military equipment and now is best known for its coffeemakers. And a dozen more of their ilk. Some of these men were archrivals, some in completely different lines of enterprise. To posit that all these people had met—now that would involve rewriting twentieth-century business history, for a start."

"Couldn't this have been a sort of mid-century economic conference, like Davos?" Ben ventured. "A precursor to the Bilderberg conferences, maybe? Some meeting of the corporate titans?"

The historian pointed to another figure. "This can only be someone's idea of a joke. A very cleverly doctored image."

"Who's that you're pointing at?"

"That, of course, is Gerhard Lenz, the Viennese scientist." Mercandetti's tone was hard.

The name sounded vaguely familiar, but Ben wasn't sure in what context he knew it. "Who is he again?"

"Was. He died in South America. Dr. Gerhard Lenz, a brilliant mind, by all accounts, was not to mention the product of Vienna's finest medical training, the epitome of Viennese civilization. Sorry, I'm being sarcastic, and that doesn't suit a historian. The fact is that Lenz, like his friend Josef Mengele, was infamous in his own right for his experiments on concentration camp prisoners, on crippled children. He was already in his late forties when the war ended. His son still lives in Vienna."

My God. Gerhard Lenz was one of the twentieth century's great monsters. Ben felt lightheaded. Gerhard Lenz, a light-eyed Nazi officer, was standing immediately next to Max Hartman.

Mercandetti fished an 8x loupe from a jacket pocket—he regularly had to resort to magnification in his archival research, Ben guessed—and scrutinized the image. Then he examined the yellowed card stock on which the emulsion was fixed. After a few minutes, he shook his head. "Indeed, it looks real. And yet it is not possible. It cannot be real." Mercandetti spoke with quiet vehemence, and Ben wondered whether he was mostly trying to persuade himself. For even as he denied the evidence of his eyes, the historian looked ashen. "Tell me," he said, and now his tone was brittle, all traces of bonhomie having evaporated. "Where did you get this?"

One takes precautions. Gaston Rossignol was alive: the death of so august a figure would not have passed without notice. And yet after another hour of research, Mercandetti and he came up empty-handed. "I apologize for a fruitless search," Mercandetti said resignedly. "But then I am a historian, not a private detective. Besides, I would have imagined that this sort of thing would be down your alley, given your familiarity with financial stratagems."

The academic was right; it should have occurred to Ben already. What Mercandetti was alluding to—financial stratagems, he called it—went by the name of asset protection, and it was something Ben had some familiarity with. Now it was his turn to sit back and think. Prominent men do not simply disappear; they create legal edifices behind which to shelter. The task of hiding one's place of residence from pursuers was not so unlike the task of hiding it from creditors or from the taxation powers of the state. Rossignol would want to retain control of his possessions while seeming to have been divested of them. It would not be easy to keep tabs on a man without property.

Ben Hartman recalled a particularly miserly client of Hartman Capital Management, who had an obsession with asset protection schemes. Ben came to dislike the man with a passion, but as much as he begrudged the time he'd spent working on the miser's account, Ben realized that what he'd learned about the subterfuges of "asset protection" would now come in handy. "Gaston Rossignol must have blood relatives in the area," Ben said to Carl Mercandetti. "I'm thinking of someone both reliable and compliant. Someone close enough to do his bidding, but decidedly younger than he is." In any variant of a gift-leaseback scheme, Ben knew, it was an undesirable complication to be predeceased by the pseudo-beneficiary. And the clandestinity of any scheme depended upon the discretion of the enlisted partner.

"You're talking about Yves-Alain, of course," the professor said.

"Am I?"

"You've just described him. Yves-Alain Taillé, the banker's nephew. A civic leader here of some distinction, thanks to his family's prominence, and a banker of no distinction at all, thanks to his intellectual mediocrity. Weak but well-meaning is the general consensus on him. Used to chair the Zurich Arts Council or some such. He has a sinecure at one of the private banks, a vice president of something or other. Easy enough to find out."

"And if I wanted to find out whether Taillé had title to property in the canton besides his primary residence? Aren't there public tax documents in connection to estate transfers?"

"There are municipal records in the Rathaus, just off the Limmat. But if it's a recent title transfer, from the past five years, you can do an on-line search. The same with the tax documents you seek. They're supposedly public documents, but they're kept on a secure server, honoring one of the two great Swiss passions—those being for chocolate and for secrecy. I myself have a user ID and password that will provide access. Not so long ago, you see, the town fathers hired me to write something for a brochure to mark the six hundred and fiftieth anniversary of Zurich's joining the Swiss Confederation. A bit more local than my usual research, but they were openhanded with the francs."

An hour later, Ben had an address, a residence decidedly more modest than Rossignol had formerly inhabited. Two hours later, after immersing himself in a series of tax documents of astounding intricacy, he had satisfied himself that it was Gaston Rossignol's. For one thing, the title was in Taillé's name, and yet it was not his primary residence. A country house? No one would have one in Zurich proper. A pied-à-terre for a mistress? But it was too grand for that. And what of the real-estate investment trust that maintained co-management privileges? Taillé did not enjoy unilateral control over the property's disposition; he could not sell it or transfer the title without permission of the trust. And where was the trust headquartered? In one of the Channel Islands, Jersey. Ben smiled. Nicely done—a tax haven but not one of the truly infamous ones. It wasn't as notorious as Nauru, but its banking establishment was even more tightly knit, more difficult to penetrate.

Ben glanced again at the address he had jotted down. It was incredible to think that a brief car ride would take him to one of Sigma's founders. Peter had tried to hide from Sigma, and it had destroyed him. Ben took a deep breath, and felt his stores of anger burn within him. *Well, there's been a change of plans*, he thought. *Now let Sigma try to hide from me.*

CHAPTER TWENTY

Ben found Gaston Rossignol's house in the area of Zurich called Hottingen, a steep, hilly area overlooking the city. The houses here were situated on large lots and hidden by trees: very private, very secluded.

Rossignol's house was on Hauserstrasse, close to the Dolder Grand Hotel, the grande dame of Zurich hotels, generally considered the finest in all of Europe. The house was wide and low-slung, built of brownish stone apparently in the early part of the century.

It didn't look like any kind of safe house, Ben reflected, but perhaps that was what made it so effective. Rossignol had grown up in Zurich, but spent much of his career in Bern. He knew certain Zurichers of power and influence, of course, but it was not a place where he had casual acquaintances. Besides, the residents of the Hauserstrasse were the sort who kept to themselves; this was a neighborhood without neighborliness. An old man who cultivated his own garden would never attract notice. It would be a comfortable life, but an effectively obscure one, too.

Ben parked the Range Rover on an incline down the

block and set the emergency brake to keep it from rolling. He opened the glove compartment and took out Liesl's revolver. There were four shells remaining in the chamber. He would have to buy more ammunition somewhere if he wanted to use the weapon for protection. Making sure the safety was engaged, he slipped it into his jacket pocket.

He rang the doorbell. There was no answer, and after a few minutes, he rang again.

Still no answer.

He tried the knob, but the door was locked.

He noticed a late-model Mercedes parked in the carport at one side of the house. Rossignol's car or someone else's, he couldn't know.

He turned to leave when it occurred to him to try all the doors, and he went around the side of the house. The lawn was newly mown, flower gardens well tended. Someone took good care of the property. The back of the house was grander than the front, a large sweep of land bordered by more flower gardens, bathed by the morning sun. A cupola sat in the middle of a large terrace at the back of the house, near an arrangement of deck chairs.

Ben approached the back entrance. He pulled open a glass storm door and then tried the knob.

The knob turned.

He opened the door, his heart hammering, and braced for an alarm to go off, but heard none.

Was Rossignol here? Or anyone else, a servant, a housekeeper, family?

He entered the house, into a dark, tiled mud room. A few coats hung on hooks, along with an assortment of wooden canes with ornamental handles. Passing through the mud room, he entered what looked like a study, a small room furnished with a large desk, a few bookcases. Gaston Rossignol, once the pillar of Switzerland's banking establishment, seemed to be a man of relatively modest tastes.

On the desk was a green blotter pad, next to it a sleek black Panasonic telephone with modern gimmicks built in:

conference, caller ID, intercom, speakerphone, digital answering machine.

As he was staring at the phone, it rang. It was ear-splittingly loud, the ringer turned up to maximum volume. He froze, expecting Rossignol to enter, wondering how he would explain himself. It rang again, three times, four, then stopped.

He waited.

No one had picked up. Did that mean no one was home? He glanced at the caller ID screen, saw that the number was a long series of digits, obviously long distance.

He decided to move on farther into the house. As he walked down a corridor, he heard faint music playing—Bach, it sounded like—but where was it coming from?

Was someone in fact home?

From the far end of the hall he saw the glow of light coming from a room. He approached, and the music grew louder.

Now he entered what he immediately recognized as a formal dining room, a long table in the center of the room covered with a crisp white linen tablecloth and set with a silver coffeepot on a silver tray, a single place setting at which was a plate of eggs and sausage. Breakfast appeared to have been served by a housekeeper, but where was he or she? A portable tape player on a buffet against one wall was playing a Bach cello suite.

And sitting at the table, his back to Ben, was an old man in a wheelchair. A tanned bald head, fringed with gray, a bull neck, round shoulders.

The old man didn't seem to have heard Ben entering. He was probably hard of hearing, Ben decided, a guess confirmed by the hearing aid in the old man's right ear.

Still, taking no chances, he slid his hand into the front pocket of his leather jacket, felt the bulk of the revolver, pulled it out, and cocked the hammer. The old man didn't move. He had to be seriously deaf, or his hearing aid was turned off.

Suddenly Ben was jolted by the ring of the telephone,

just as loud in here as it had been in the study a minute ago.

Yet the old man didn't move.

It rang again, a third time, a fourth, and stopped.

Then he heard a man's voice coming from down the hall, the tone frantic. After a moment, Ben realized that the voice was coming from the answering machine, but he couldn't make out what it was saying.

He took a few steps closer, then placed the barrel of the revolver against the old man's head. "Don't move."

The old man's head fell forward, lolling on his chest.

Ben grabbed the arm of the wheelchair with his free hand and spun it around.

The old man's chin was on his chest, the eyes wide and staring at the floor. Lifeless.

Ben's body flooded with panic.

He felt the food on the plate. The eggs and sausage were still warm.

Apparently Rossignol had died just moments ago. Had he been *killed*?

If so, the killer could be in the house right now!

He raced down the corridor from which he had come, and the telephone rang again. In the study, he looked at the caller ID screen: the same long series of digits, beginning with 431. Where was the call from? The numbers were familiar. A country in Europe, he felt sure.

The answering machine came on.

"Gaston? Gaston?" a man's voice shouted.

The words were in French, but spoken by a foreigner, and Ben could make out few of the heavily accented words.

Who was calling Rossignol, and why?

Another ring: the doorbell!

He raced to the back entrance, which he'd left partially open. No one was there.

Move it!

He stepped outside and ran around the side of the house, slowing when he got near the front. From behind some tall shrubbery, he could see a white police cruiser passing slowly by, patrolling the neighborhood, he guessed.

A low wrought-iron fence separated Rossignol's yard from the neighbor's. He raced to the low fence, and leaped over it into the neighbor's yard, which was roughly the same size as Rossignol's, though not as ornately landscaped. He was taking an enormous chance of being spotted by anyone in the neighbor's house, but no one called out to him, there were no shouts, and he kept running, around the far side of the house and out to Hauserstrasse. A hundred feet or so down the street was the Rover. He ran to it, leaped in, and keyed the ignition. It roared to life.

He made a quick U-turn and then drove down the steep street, deliberately slowing his pace to that of a local driving to work.

Someone had just tried to call Rossignol. Someone calling from a place whose telephone number began with 431.

The digits tumbled around in his brain until something clicked.

Vienna, Austria.

The call had come from Vienna. These men have successors, heirs, Liesl had said. One of them, Mercandetti had told him, resided in Vienna: the son of the monster Gerhard Lenz. With Rossignol dead, it was as logical a lead to follow as any. Not a certainty—far from a certainty—but at least a possibility. A possible lead when there was a paucity of leads.

In a few minutes he had arrived in the heart of the city, near the Bahnhofplatz, where Jimmy Cavanaugh had tried to kill him. Where it had all begun.

He had to get on the next train to Vienna.

The Austrian Alps

There was a soft knock on the door, and the old man called out irritably, "Yes?"

A physician in a white coat entered, a short, rotund man with round shoulders and a potbelly.

"How is everything, sir?" the physician asked. "How is your suite?"

"You call this a suite?" Patient Eighteen asked. He lay atop the narrow single bed, fully dressed in his rumpled three-piece suit. "It's a goddamned monk's cell."

Indeed, the room was simply furnished, with only a chair, a desk, a reading lamp, and a television set. The stone floor was bare.

The physician smiled wanly. "I am Dr. Löfquist," he said, sitting in the chair beside the bed. "I would like to welcome you, but I must also warn you. This will be a very rigorous and difficult ten days. You will be put through the most extensive physical and mental tests you have ever had."

Patient Eighteen did not bother to sit up. "Why the hell the mental?"

"Because, you see, not everyone is eligible."

"What happens if you think I'm crazy?"

"Anyone not invited to join is sent home with our regrets."

The patient said nothing.

"Perhaps you should take a rest, sir. This afternoon will be tiring. There will be a CAT scan, a chest X-ray, then a series of cognitive tests. And, of course, a standard test for depression.

"I'm not depressed," the patient snapped.

The doctor ignored him. "Tonight you will be required to fast, so that we may accurately measure plasma cholesterol, triglycerides, lipoproteins, and so on."

"Fast? You mean starve? I'm not starving myself!"

"Sir," the doctor said, rising, "you are free to go any time you wish. If you stay, and if you are invited to join us, you will find the procedure to be lengthy and quite painful, I must be honest. But it will be like nothing you have ever experienced in your long life. Ever. This I promise you."

*   *   *

Kesting did not conceal his surprise when Anna returned several hours later with an address; and in truth Anna shared a measure of that surprise. She had done what she'd determined to do, and it had worked. After a few readings of the Rossignol file, she had come up with one name that could be of help: that of a Zurich civil servant named Daniel Taine. The name recurred in several different contexts, and further inquiries had confirmed her intuition. Gaston Rossignol had been Taine's first employer, and, it appeared, something of a mentor. In the seventies, Taine and Rossignol were partners in a limited liability venture involving high-yield Eurobonds. Rossignol had sponsored Taine's application to the Kifkintler Society, a men's club whose membership included many of Zurich's most powerful citizens. Now Taine, having made his small fortune, served in various honorific capacities in the canton. He was someone with precisely the sort of access and resources to ensure that his old mentor's plans ran smoothly.

Anna had dropped in on Taine at his home unannounced, identified herself, and laid her cards on the table. Her message was simple. Gaston Rossignol was in serious, imminent danger.

Taine was visibly rattled, but closemouthed, as she expected. "I cannot help you. He has moved. No one can say where, and it is no one's concern."

"Except the killers'?"

"Even if there are such assassins," Taine spoke with a display of skepticism, but he acceded too readily to her stipulation, "who's to say they can find him if you cannot? Your own resources are obviously considerable."

"I have reason to believe they've already made headway."

A sharp glance: "Really? And why is that?"

Anna shook her head. "There are certain matters I can only discuss with Gaston Rossignol himself."

"And why do you suppose anyone would want to kill

him? He is among the most admired of Zurichers."

"Which explains why he's living in hiding."

"What nonsense you speak," Taine said, after a beat.

Anna stared at him levelly for few moments. Then she handed him a card with her name on it, and her numbers at the Office of Special Investigations. "I will return in an hour. I have reason to think your own resources are pretty considerable. Check me out. Satisfy yourself as to my bona fides. Do whatever will help you to see that I am who I say I am, and that I'm representing myself accurately."

"How can I, a mere Swiss citizen . . ."

"You have ways, Mr. Taine. And if you don't, your friend does. I'm quite sure you'll want to help your friend. I think we understand each other."

Two hours later, Anna Navarro paid a call to Taine at his place of work. The ministry of economic affairs was located in a marble building constructed in the familiar late-nineteenth-century Beaux Arts style. Taine's own office was large, sunny, and book-lined. She was ushered in to him immediately upon her arrival; the dark-paneled door closed discreetly behind her.

Taine sat quietly behind his burled walnut desk. "This was not my decision," he stressed. "This is Monsieur Rossignol's decision. I do not support it."

"You checked me out."

"You have been checked out," Taine replied carefully, hewing to the passive voice. He returned her card to her. "Good-bye, Ms. Navarro."

The address was penciled in small print, in a blank space to the left of her name.

Her first call was to Bartlett, updating him as to her progress. "You never cease to amaze me, Ms. Navarro," he'd replied, a surprising note of genuine warmth in his voice.

As she and Kesting drove to the Hottingen address, he said, "Your request for surveillance was approved this morning.

Several unmarked police cars shall be engaged for the purpose."

"And his telephone."

"Yes, we can have a tap in place within hours. An officer at the *Kantonspolizei* will be assigned to listen in at the *Mutterhaus*."

"The *Mutterhaus?*"

"Police headquarters. The Mother House, we call it."

They headed steadily uphill on Hottingerstrasse. The houses became larger and nicer, the trees denser. Finally they came to Hauserstrasse, and pulled into the driveway of a low-slung brownstone house set in the middle of a nicely landscaped yard. She noticed there were no unmarked police cruisers anywhere nearby.

"This is the correct address," Kesting said.

She nodded. Another Swiss banker, she thought, with a big house and a nice yard.

They got out and walked to the front door. Kesting rang the bell. "You do not mind, I hope, if I lead the interview."

"Not at all," Anna replied. Whatever "international cooperation" meant on paper, that was the protocol and they both knew it.

After waiting a few minutes, Kesting rang again. "He is an old man, and for some years he has been wheelchair-bound. It must take him time to move around his house."

After a few minutes more, Kesting said, "I cannot imagine he goes out very much at his age." He rang again.

I knew this was too easy, Anna thought. *What a botch.*

"He may be ill," Kesting said. Uneasily he turned the doorknob but the door was locked. Together, they walked around to the back door; it opened readily. He called into the house, "Dr. Rossignol, it is Kesting from the Public Prosecutor's office." The "Dr." seemed purely an honorific.

Silence.

"Dr. Rossignol?"

Kesting stepped into the house, Anna following. The lights were on, and she could hear classical music.

"Dr. Rossignol?" Kesting said more loudly. He ventured

forward into the house. Soon they found themselves in the dining room, where the lights were on, and a tape deck played music. Anna could smell coffee, eggs, some kind of fried meat.

"Dr.—Oh, dear God!"

Horrified, Anna saw what Kesting had seen.

An old man sat in a wheelchair at the table, before a plate of breakfast. His head was on his chest, the eyes fixed and dilated. He was dead.

They'd gotten to him too! That in itself didn't surprise her. What stunned her was the timing—so soon before their arrival, it had to be. As if they knew the authorities were coming.

She tasted fear.

"Dammit," she said. "Call an ambulance. And the homicide squad. And please, don't let them touch anything."

CHAPTER TWENTY-ONE

A squad of crime-scene officers from the homicide squad of the Zurich *Kantonspolizei* arrived within the hour and took video and still photographs. The victim's house was dusted carefully for fingerprints, particularly the front and back doors and the three windows that could be accessed from the ground level. Anna asked the specialist to print both Rossignol's wheelchair and all exposed skin on the deceased's body. Elimination prints were taken from Rossignol himself before the body was removed.

Had the Americans not taken such an interest in Rossignol prior to his murder, even requesting surveillance, the old man's death would certainly have been treated as a natural occurrence. Gaston Rossignol had been ninety-one, after all.

But instead an autopsy was ordered, with special attention paid to the ocular fluid. The postmortem would be done in the facilities of the University of Zurich Institute of Legal Medicine, as was standard, since Zurich had no medical examiner.

Anna returned to her hotel. Exhausted—she hadn't slept

on the plane, had decided against taking an Ativan—she drew the curtains, got into an oversize T-shirt, and climbed into the bed.

She was jarred awake by the telephone. Momentarily disoriented, she thought she was back in Washington, that it was the middle of the night. She glanced at the phosphorescent dial of her watch and saw that it was two-thirty in the afternoon, Zurich time. She picked up the phone.

"Is this Miss Navarro?" a man's voice asked.

"That's me," she croaked, then cleared her throat. "Who's this?"

"I'm Sergeant Major Schmid from the *Kantonspolizei*. I'm a homicide detective. I'm sorry, did I wake you?"

"No, no, I was just dozing. What's up?"

"The fingerprints have come back with some interesting results. Can you find your way to police headquarters?"

Schmid was an affable man with a wide face, short hair, and ridiculous little bangs. He wore a navy blue shirt and had a gold chain around his neck.

His office was pleasant, light-filled, sparsely furnished. Two blond-wood desks faced one another; she sat at one, he at the other.

Schmid toyed with a paper clip. "The fingerprints were run at the *Kriminaltechnik*. Rossignol's prints were eliminated, leaving a number of other prints, most of them unidentified. He was a widower, so we assume they belong to his housekeeper and a few others who worked at his house. The housekeeper was on duty overnight, until this morning, when she made his breakfast and then left. They must have been watching the house and saw her depart."

"He didn't have a nurse?"

"No," Schmid said, bending the wire paper clip back and forth. "You know, we now have a computerized database of fingerprints just like yours." He was referring to the Automated Fingerprint Identification Service, which stored a bank of millions of prints. "The prints were scanned in, digitized, and sent by modem to the central registry in Bern, where they were run against all available databases. The search did not take long. We got a match very quickly."

She sat up. "Oh?"

"Yes, this is why the case was assigned to me. The prints belong to an American who was detained here just a few days ago in connection with a shooting in the vicinity of the Bahnhofplatz."

"Who is he?"

"An American named Benjamin Hartman."

The name meant nothing to her. "What do you know about him?"

"A fair amount. You see, I questioned him myself." He handed her a file folder containing photocopies of Hartman's U.S. passport, driver's license, credit cards, and his Swiss police records with mug shots.

She examined the copies closely, fascinated. Could this be her man, the killer? An American? Mid-thirties, an investment banker for a financial firm called Hartman Capital Management. A family business, she assumed. That probably meant he had money. Lives in New York City. Here on a Swiss ski vacation, he had told Schmid.

But that could be a lie.

Three of the remaining Sigma victims had been killed during the time he was here in Zurich. One victim had lived in Germany, which was a train ride away, so that was a possibility. Another was in Austria; also possible.

But Paraguay? That was a long plane flight from here.

Yet the possibility could not be ruled out. Neither could the possibility that he was not working alone.

"What happened on the Bahnhofstrasse?" she asked. "He shoot someone?"

The paper clip Schmid was worrying snapped in the middle. "There was gunfire along the street and in the shopping arcade beneath the Bahnhofplatz. He was questioned in connection with that. Personally, I don't think he was the shooter. He insists someone tried to shoot him."

"Anyone killed?"

"Several bystanders. And, in his account, the guy he insists tried to shoot him."

"Hmm," she said, puzzled. A bizarre tale: How much of it was true? Who was this guy? "You let him go?"

"We had no basis on which to hold him. And there was some string-pulling from his firm. He was instructed to leave the canton."

Not in my backyard: Was that the Zurich approach to law enforcement? Anna wondered sourly. "Any idea where he is now?"

"At the time, he claimed he was planning to go to St. Moritz. The Hotel Carlton. But we've since learned that he never checked in. Then, yesterday, we received a report that he'd reappeared in Zurich, at the Handelsbank Schweiz. We tried to bring him in for further questioning, but he escaped. Another misadventure, accompanied by shooting. It follows him around."

"Surprise, surprise," Anna said. "Do you have a way of finding out whether Hartman is staying at some other hotel in Zurich, or anywhere else in the country?"

Schmid nodded. "I can contact the Hotel Control in each of the cantons. Copies of all hotel registration forms go to the local police."

"How current are they?"

"Sometimes not so current," Schmid admitted. "At least we can tell where he was."

"If he checked in under his own name."

"All legitimate hotels require foreigners to show their passports."

"Maybe he has more than one passport. Maybe he's not staying at a 'legitimate' hotel. Maybe he has friends here."

Schmid looked mildly annoyed. "But you see, I've met him, and he didn't look to me like someone who carries false passports."

"Some of these international businessmen, you know, have second passports from places like Panama or Ireland or Israel. They come in handy sometimes."

"Yes, but such passports would still have their true names on them, right?"

"Maybe yes, maybe no. Is there a way to tell if he left the country?"

"There are many different ways to leave the country—plane, automobile, train, even on foot."

"Don't the border police keep records?"

"Well, the border police are supposed to look at passports," Schmid admitted, "but often they don't. Our best bet would be the airlines. They keep records of all passengers."

"What if he left by train?"

"Then we may find no trace, unless he made a seat reservation on an international train. But I wouldn't be hopeful."

"No," Anna said, ruminating. "Can you start the search?"

"Of course," Schmid said indignantly. "It is standard."

"When can I expect the autopsy results back? I'm particularly interested in the toxicology." She knew she was probably pushing the man a little too hard. But there was no choice.

Schmid shrugged. "It could be a week. I could put in a request to speed things up."

"I have one specific neurotoxin I'd like them to search for," she said. "That shouldn't take so long."

"I can call for you."

"Would you? And bank records. I need Rossignol's bank records going back two years. Will Swiss banks cooperate, or are they going to give us that whole secrecy song-and-dance?"

"They will cooperate with the police on a homicide," Schmid said huffily.

"That's a nice surprise. Oh, and one more thing. The photocopies you took of his credit cards—think I could have those?"

"I don't see why not."

"Wonderful," she said. She was actually starting to like the fellow.

São Paulo, Brazil

The wedding reception was being held at the most ultra-exclusive private club in all of Brazil, the Hipica Jardins.

The club's members were mainly drawn from the quatrocentões, Brazil's aristocracy, descendants of the original Portuguese settlers who had been in the country for at least four hundred years. They were the land barons, the owners of paper mills and newspapers and publishing houses and playing-card factories, the hotel magnates—the richest of the rich, as the long line of Bentleys and Rolls-Royces parked in front of the clubhouse attested.

Tonight many of them had turned out, resplendent in white tie and tails, to celebrate the wedding of the daughter of one of Brazil's plutocrats, Doutor Otavio Carvalho Pinto. His daughter, Fernanda, was marrying into an equally illustrious family, the Alcantara Machados.

One of the guests was a dignified, white-haired man of almost ninety. Although he was not one of the quatrocentões—he was in fact a native of Lisbon who had immigrated to São Paulo in the fifties—he was an enormously wealthy banker and landowner, and he had been for decades a business partner and friend of the bride's father.

The old man's name was Jorge Ramago, and he sat watching the couples dance, his noisettes de veau Périgourdine untouched. One of the waitresses, a dark-haired young woman, tentatively approached the old man and said in Portuguese, "Señor Ramago, there is a telephone call for you."

Ramago turned slowly to look at her. "Telephone?"

"Yes, señor, they say it is urgent. From your home. Your wife."

Ramago at once looked worried. "Where?—where?—" he faltered.

"This way, sir," the waitress said, and she gently helped him to his feet. They walked slowly across the banquet room, for the old Lisboner was afflicted with rheumatism, though he was otherwise in excellent health.

Outside the banquet room, the waitress guided Ramago to an antique wooden telephone booth and assisted him into it, solicitously smoothing his rumpled dinner jacket.

Just as Ramago reached for the telephone, he felt a sharp pinprick in his upper thigh. He gasped, looked around, but the waitress was gone. The pain quickly subsided, though, and he put the handset up to his ear and listened. But all he could hear was the dial tone.

"There is no one on the line," Ramago managed to say to no one just before he lost consciousness.

A minute or so later, one of the waiters noticed the old man passed out in the telephone booth. Alarmed, he called out for help.

The Austrian Alps

Patient Eighteen was awakened at midnight.

One of the nurses gently applied a tourniquet to his upper arm and began to draw blood.

"What the hell is this?" he groaned.

"I'm sorry, sir," the nurse said. Her English was heavily accented. "We are required to take venous blood samples every four hours from midnight on, throughout the day."

"Good God, for what?"

"It is to measure the levels of your serum Epo—erythropoietin."

"I didn't know I had any." All this medical stuff was unsettling, but he knew there was much more to come.

"Please, go back to sleep, sir. You have a long day ahead of you."

*   *   *

Breakfast was served in a lavish banquet room with the others. There was a buffet overflowing with fresh fruits, freshly baked biscuits and rolls, breakfast sausages, eggs, bacon, and ham.

When Patient Eighteen finished, he was escorted to an examination room in another wing.

There, another nurse gingerly cut into the skin of the inner part of his upper arm with a small scalpel.

He moaned.

"I'm sorry if I caused you pain," the nurse said.

"My entire damned body's one big pain. What's this for?"

"A skin biopsy to examine the elastic fibers in the reticular dermis," she replied, applying a bandage.

In the background, two white-coated physicians were quietly conferring in German. Patient Eighteen understood every word.

"His brain function is somewhat impaired," the short, rotund one said, "but nothing you wouldn't expect in a man of his age. No sign of senile dementia or Alzheimer's."

A tall, thin, gray-faced man said, "What about cardiac muscle mass?"

"Acceptable. But we measured the blood pressure at the posterior tibial artery, this time using Doppler ultrasonography, and we did find some peripheral arterial disease."

"So his blood pressure is elevated."

"Somewhat, but we expected that."

"Have you counted the number of pitted blood cells?"

"I believe that's being done in the lab right now."

"Good. I think this one is a good candidate. I suggest we accelerate the tests."

A good candidate, Patient Eighteen thought. So it would happen after all. He turned to the conferring doctors behind and smiled widely at them, feigning gratitude.

CHAPTER TWENTY-TWO

Vienna

The private investigator was almost half an hour late. Ben sat in the spacious lobby of his hotel just off the Kärntner Strasse, his mélange untouched, waiting for the detective whose name he had plucked from the yellow pages.

He knew there were far better ways to find the name of a PI than the Vienna telephone book—such as calling one of his several business contacts here and asking for a recommendation. But his instincts told him to avoid anyone he knew right now if he could possibly help it.

He'd gotten on the first train, showed up unannounced at a small hotel, and been lucky enough to get a room, registering under the name Robert Simon, one of his brother's aliases. He was asked for his passport, and held his breath as it was inspected, but it obviously looked in order, plausibly battered and stamped, as if from a few years' use.

The first thing he'd done was to look through the Vienna phone book for an investigator who seemed, from his advertisement anyway, reputable. Several were located in the first district, the heart of the city where Ben's hotel was;

one in particular advertised his services in locating long-lost relatives. Ben had hired him over the phone, asking him to run a background check on an Austrian citizen.

Now he was beginning to wonder whether the PI was going to show at all.

Then a portly man of about forty plopped himself into the chair across the low table from Ben. "You are Mr. Simon?" He set down a battered leather portfolio on the table.

"That's me."

"Hans Hoffman," the PI said. "You have the money?"

"Nice to meet you too," Ben said sardonically. He took out his wallet, counted out four hundred dollars, and slid it across the table.

Hoffman stared at it for a moment.

"Something wrong?" Ben asked. "You prefer Austrian shillings? Sorry, I haven't gone to a bank yet."

"There was an additional expense involved," the detective said.

"Oh really?"

"A courtesy payment to an old buddy of mine in the HNA, the *Heeres Nachrichtenamt*—Austrian military intelligence."

"Translation, a bribe," Ben said.

Hoffman shrugged.

"I don't imagine this buddy of yours gave you a receipt?"

Hoffman sighed. "This is how we do things here. You can't get the sort of information you're looking for without exploring various channels. This friend will have to use his military intelligence ID card to get information. It will be another two hundred dollars. The number—it was unlisted, by the way—and address I can get you now."

Ben counted it out; it was the end of his cash.

The detective counted the bills. "I don't know why you wanted this person's number and address, but you must be involved in some interesting business."

"Why do you say that?"

"Your man is a very important figure in Vienna." He signaled for the waitress; when she came, he ordered a mélange and a Maximilian torte.

From his briefcase he removed a laptop computer, snapped it open, and turned it on. "The very latest in biometrics," he said proudly. "Fingertip sensor. Uses my fingerprint as a password. Without it, the computer's locked. No one does these things like the Germans."

The detective tapped at the keys for a few seconds, then turned it around to face Ben. The screen was blank except for the name and address of Jürgen Lenz.

"You know him?" Hoffman said, turning the laptop back toward himself. "He is an acquaintance of yours?"

"Not exactly. Tell me about him."

"Ah, well, Dr. Lenz is one of the wealthiest men in Vienna, a leading philanthropist and patron of the arts. His family foundation builds medical clinics for the poor. He's also on the board of the Vienna Philharmonic."

The waitress set down a coffee and pastry in front of Hoffman. The detective lunged for them before the waitress had even turned to leave.

"What kind of doctor is Dr. Lenz?"

"A medical doctor, but he gave up his practice years ago."

"How old?"

"In his fifties, I would say."

"Medicine must be something of a family tradition."

Hoffman laughed. "You're remembering his father, Gerhard Lenz. An interesting case. Our country is perhaps not the most progressive, in some ways. My compatriots would prefer to forget any such unpleasantness. It's the Austrian way: as the saying goes, we've convinced ourselves that Beethoven was an Austrian, and Hitler was a German. But Jürgen is cut from a different cloth. This is a son who seeks to make up for the crimes of the father."

"Really?"

"Oh, very much. Jürgen Lenz is resented in some circles for being so outspoken about these crimes. Even denouncing his own father. He is known to feel deep shame about what his father did." He looked at his torte impatiently. "But unlike many children of the famous Nazis, he does something about it. The Lenz Foundation is Austria's leading supporter of Holocaust studies, historical scholarship, libraries in Israel . . . they fund anything that seeks to fight hate crimes, racism, that sort of thing." He returned to his pastry, wolfing it down as if fearing it would be snatched away.

Lenz's son was a leading anti-Nazi? Perhaps they had more in common than he had supposed. "All right," Ben said, gesturing to the waitress for the check with the universal air-scrawl. "Thank you."

"Anything else I can do for you?" the detective asked, brushing crumbs off the lapels of his jacket.

Trevor Griffiths left his hotel, the Imperial, on the Kärntner Ring a few blocks from the Opera. Not only was the Imperial the finest hotel in Vienna, Trevor reflected, but it was famous as the headquarters of the Nazis during the war, the location from which they governed the city. He liked the hotel anyway.

It was a short stroll down Mariahilfer Strasse to a small bar on Neubaugasse. The garish red neon sign flashed the bar's name: BROADWAY CLUB. He sat in a booth at the back of the ill-lit basement room and waited. In his bespoke gray worsted double-breasted suit, he looked somewhat out of place here, like a businessman, a high-level executive perhaps, or a prosperous attorney.

The bar was choked with foul cigarette smoke. Trevor could not tolerate it, hated the way his hair and clothes would stink afterward. He glanced at his watch, an Audemars Piguet, top of the line, one of the few indulgences he allowed himself. Expensive suits and watches and good rough sex. What else was there, really, if you had no interest in food, art, or music?

He was impatient. The Austrian contact was late, and
Trevor could not abide. tardiness.

Finally, after almost half an hour, the Austrian showed
up, a square, hulking troglodyte named Otto. Otto slid into
the booth and placed a worn red felt bag in front of Trevor.

"You're English, yes?"

Trevor nodded, zipped open the bag. It contained two
large metal pieces, a 9 mm Makarov, the barrel threaded
for a silencer, and the long, perforated sound-suppressor
itself. "Ammo?" Trevor asked.

"Is in there," Otto said. "Nine by eighteen. Lots."

The Makarov was a good choice. Unlike the 9 mm Par-
abellum, it was subsonic. "What's the make?" Trevor
asked. "Hungarian? Chinese?"

"Russian. But it's good one."

"How much?"

"Three thousand shillings."

Trevor grimaced. He didn't mind spending money, but
he resented highway robbery. He switched to German, so
Otto, whose English was poor, would miss nothing. "*Der
Markt ist mit Makarovs überschwemmt.*" The market's
flooded with Makarovs.

Otto became suddenly alert.

"These things are a dime a dozen," Trevor continued in
German. "Everyone makes them, they're all over the place.
I'll give you a thousand shillings, and you should count
yourself lucky to get that."

Respect entered Otto's expression. "You're German?"
he asked, amazed. Actually, if Otto were a perceptive lis-
tener, he'd have placed Trevor's German as coming from
the Dresden region.

Trevor had not spoken German in quite a while; he'd
had no opportunity to do so. But it came back easily.

It was, after all, his native tongue.

Anna had dinner alone at a Mövenpick restaurant a few
blocks from her hotel. There was nothing on the menu that

interested her, and she decided she was no connoisseur of Swiss cuisine.

Normally, she found dining alone in a foreign city depressing, but tonight she was too absorbed in her thoughts to feel lonely. She was seated by the window, in a long row of lone diners, most of them reading newspapers or books.

At the American consulate, she used a secure fax line to transmit everything she had on Hartman, including his credit cards, to the ICU and had asked that the ID unit contact each of the credit-card companies and activate an instant trace, so that they would be informed within minutes whenever he used one of the cards.

She had also asked them to dig up whatever they could on Hartman himself, and someone had called her back on the encrypted cell phone less than an hour later.

They had struck gold.

According to Hartman's office, he was on vacation in Switzerland, but hadn't checked in with the office in several days. They didn't have his travel itinerary; he hadn't provided one. They had no way to contact him.

But then the ID tech had learned something interesting: Hartman's only sibling, a twin brother, had died in a plane crash in Switzerland four years earlier. Apparently he'd been on some Swiss-gold crusade before his death. She didn't know what to make of that except that it raised all sorts of questions.

And Benjamin Hartman, the tech told her, was loaded. The company he worked for, Hartman Capital Management, managed investment funds and had been founded by Hartman's father.

Who was a well-known philanthropist and a Holocaust survivor.

Possibilities suggested themselves. Poor little rich boy, son of a survivor, gets it in his head that the Swiss bankers haven't been doing right by the Holocaust victims. Now his twin takes up the same crusade, trying for some sort of misguided revenge on a Swiss banking bigwig. A rich boy's half-cocked vendetta.

Or maybe he was in it deeper—working for whatever this Sigma outfit had morphed into. For some unexplained reason.

Then the question was, where did he get the names and addresses of all these old men in hiding?

And how was his brother's death connected—if at all?

At a little after nine o'clock in the evening she returned to the hotel and was handed a message slip by the night manager. Thomas Schmid, the homicide detective, had called.

She called him back immediately from the room. He was still in his office.

"We have some of the autopsy results back," he said. "On that poison you asked the toxicology people to screen for?"

"Yes?"

"They found that neurotoxin in the ocular fluid, a positive match. Rossignol was indeed poisoned."

Anna sat down in the chair beside the phone. Progress. She felt the pleasant tingle she always had when there was a breakthrough. "Did they find an injection mark on the body?"

"Not as yet, but they say it's very difficult to find tiny marks like that. They say they will keep looking."

"When was he killed?"

"Apparently this morning, shortly before we got there."

"That means Hartman may still be in Zurich. Are you on top of that?"

A pause, then Schmid said coldly, "I am on top of that."

"Any news on the bank records?"

"The banks will cooperate, but they take their time. They also have their procedures."

"Of course."

"We should have Rossignol's bank records by tomorrow—"

On her end of the line a beep interrupted Schmid. "One

second, I think I've got another call coming in." She pressed the "flash" button. The hotel operator told her it was a call from her office in Washington.

"Miss Navarro, this is Robert Polozzi in ID."

"Thanks for calling. Turn up anything?"

"MasterCard security just called. Hartman used his card a few minutes ago. He made a charge at a restaurant in Vienna."

Kent, England

At his country estate in Westerham, Kent, Sir Edward Downey, the retired Prime Minister of England, was in the middle of a game of chess in the rose garden with his grandson when the telephone rang.

"Not again," eight-year-old Christopher groaned.

"Hold your horses, young man," Sir Edward snapped good-naturedly.

"Sir Edward, it's Mr. Holland," the voice said.

"Mr. Holland, is everything all right?" Sir Edward asked, suddenly concerned. "Our meeting is still going ahead as scheduled?"

"Oh, without a doubt. But a minor matter has come up and I wondered whether you might be able to help."

As he listened, Sir Edward gave his grandson a menacing scowl, at which Christopher giggled, as he always did. "Well, Mr. Holland, let me make a few calls and see what I can do."

Vienna

Jürgen Lenz's house was in an exclusive, densely wooded district in the southwest part of Vienna called Hietzing: an enclave of some of Vienna's wealthiest residents. Lenz's house, or, more properly, his villa, was large, modern, an intriguing and handsome mix of Tyrolean architecture and Frank Lloyd Wright.

The element of surprise, Ben thought. *I need it when I confront Lenz*. In part, it was a question of survival. He didn't want Peter's murderers to discover he was in Vienna, and, despite the seed of doubt that Hoffman had planted, the likeliest assumption was that Lenz was one of them.

Of course, he couldn't just show up on Lenz's doorstep and hope to gain admittance. The approach had to be more sophisticated. Ben ran through a mental list of the most prominent and influential people he knew personally who would vouch for him, even lie for him.

He remembered the head of a major American charity who had come to see him several times to ask for money. Each time the Hartman family, and the firm, had given generously.

Payback time, Ben thought.

The charity head, Winston Rockwell, was seriously ill with hepatitis, laid up in the hospital, last Ben had heard, and impossible to reach. This was terribly unfortunate for Rockwell—but convenient for Ben.

He called Lenz's home, asked for Jürgen Lenz, told the woman who answered the phone—Mrs. Lenz?—that he was a friend of Winston Rockwell's and was interested in the Lenz Foundation. Code language for: I have money to give you. Even rich foundations don't turn away contributions.

Mrs. Lenz replied in fluent English that her husband should be home by five, and would Mr. Robert Simon like to come by for a drink? Jürgen would be delighted to meet any friend of Winston Rockwell's.

The woman who opened the door was an elegant, fine-boned woman in her early fifties, wearing a gray sweater-dress, a pearl choker, and matching pearl earrings.

"Please come in," she said. "Mr. Simon, is it? I'm Ilse Lenz. How nice to meet you!"

"Nice to meet you, too," Ben said. "Thanks for seeing me, particularly on such short notice."

"Oh, don't be silly, we're thrilled to meet anyone Winston recommends. You're from—where, did you say?"

"Los Angeles," he replied.

"We were there years ago for some beastly technology conference. Jürgen should be right down—ah, here he is!"

A whippet-thin, athletic-looking man was bounding down the stairs. "Hallo, there!" Jürgen Lenz called out. In his blue blazer, gray flannel slacks, and rep tie he could have been an American chief executive, maybe an Ivy League college president. His smooth face glowed with health; his smile was sunny.

This was not at all what Ben had expected. Liesl's gun, holstered to his shoulder inside his sport coat and loaded with ammunition—he'd stopped at a sporting-goods shop on the Kärntner Strasse—suddenly felt bulky.

Lenz shook Ben's hand firmly. "Any friend of Winston Rockwell's is a friend of mine!" Then his voice became soft, tender. "How's he doing these days?"

"Not well," Ben said. "He's been in the George Washington University Medical Center for weeks now, and the doctors are telling him he's not likely to go home for at least two weeks more."

"I'm so sorry to hear that," Lenz said, putting his arm around his wife's slender waist. "What a nice fellow he is. Well, let's not stand here. A drink, shall we? What's the American expression—somewhere it's got to be six o'clock, hmm?"

Trevor parked his stolen Peugeot across the street from Lenz's house in Hietzing, switched off the engine, and sat back to wait. When the target emerged from the house, he would get out of the car, cross the street, and come close to him. He did not plan to miss.

CHAPTER TWENTY-THREE

There was no time.

Certainly no time to go through channels, Anna realized.

Hartman had just made a charge at a hotel in the first district of Vienna. It was for a small amount, the equivalent of about fifteen dollars. Did that mean he had only stopped at the hotel for a drink, a coffee, a late lunch? If so, he'd be long gone. But if he was staying there, she had him.

She could go through the FBI legat in Vienna, but by the time the office had made contact with the local police through the Austrian Justice Ministry, Benjamin Hartman could well have gone on to another city.

So she had rushed to Zurich-Kloten Airport, bought a ticket on the next Austrian Airlines flight to Vienna, and then located a pay phone.

The first call she made was to a contact of hers in the Vienna police, the *Bundespolizeidirektion*. He was Dr. Fritz Weber, chief of the *Sicherheitsbüro*, the security unit of the Vienna police specializing in violent crimes. This wasn't exactly the section of the police she needed to reach, but she knew Weber would be happy to help.

She'd met Weber a few years earlier when she'd been sent to Vienna on a case involving a cultural attaché at the American embassy there who had become involved in a sex ring purveying somewhat underaged *Mädchen*.

Weber, an affable man and a smooth politician, had been grateful for her help, and her discretion, in rooting out a problem that presented potential embarrassment for both countries—and had taken her out to a festive dinner before she left. Now he seemed delighted to hear from Agent Navarro and promised to get someone on the case immediately.

Her second call was to the FBI's legat in Vienna, a man named Tom Murphy, whom she didn't know but had heard good things about. She gave Murphy an abbreviated, sanitized rundown on why she was coming to Vienna. He asked her whether she wanted him to arrange liaison with the Vienna police, but she said no, she had her own contact there. Murphy, a real by-the-book man, did not sound happy about it but made no objection.

As soon as she arrived at Vienna's Schwechat Airport, she placed another call to Fritz Weber, who gave her the name and phone number of the District Inspector on the surveillance squad who was now working the case.

Sergeant Walter Heisler wasn't fluent in English, but they managed to muddle through.

"We went to the hotel where Hartman made the credit-card charge," Heisler explained. "He is a guest at the hotel."

The sergeant worked fast. This was promising. "Great work," she said. "Any chance of finding the car?"

The compliment seemed to warm him up. Given that the target of investigation was an American, he also realized that the involvement of a representative of the U.S. government would eliminate most of the complicated paperwork and jurisdictional issues that an apprehension of a foreign national would normally present.

"We have already the, how you say, the tail on him," Heisler said with some enthusiasm.

"You're kidding. How'd you do that?"

"Well, once we found out that he is at the hotel, we put two men in newsstand in front of the place. They saw he goes in rented car, an Opel Vectra, and they follow him to part of Vienna called Hietzing."

"What's he doing there?"

"Visiting someone, maybe. A private home. We're trying to know who it is."

"Amazing. Fantastic work." She meant it.

"Thank you," he said exuberantly. "You would like me to pick you up at airport?"

There was some small talk for a few minutes, which was stressful, since Ben's cover was only half thought out. The mythical Robert Simon ran a successful financial management firm based in L.A.—Ben figured that if he kept it close to the truth, there'd be less chance of a serious gaffe—and handled the assets of movie stars, real estate tycoons, Silicon Valley IPO paper billionaires. Ben apologized that his client list had to remain confidential, though he didn't mind mentioning a name or two they'd no doubt heard of.

And all the while he wondered: Who is this man? The sole heir of Gerhard Lenz—the notorious scientist and a principal in something called Sigma.

As he and the Lenzes chatted, all three of them drinking Armagnac, Ben furtively inspected the sitting room. It was furnished comfortably, with English and French antiques. Paintings of the Old Master school were framed in gilt, each one perfectly lighted. On a table beside the couch he noticed silver-framed photographs of what he assumed were family. Conspicuously absent was any picture of Lenz's father.

"But enough about my work," Ben said. "I wanted to ask you about the Lenz Foundation. I understand its main purpose is to promote study of the Holocaust."

"We fund historical scholarship, yes, and we give to Israeli libraries," Jürgen Lenz explained. "We give a lot of money to combat hatred. We think it's extremely important that Austrian schoolchildren study the crimes of the Nazis. Don't forget, many of the Austrians welcomed the Nazis. When Hitler came here in the thirties and gave a speech from the balcony of the Imperial, he attracted enormous crowds, women weeping at the sight of such a great man." Lenz sighed. "An abomination."

"But your father . . . if you don't mind my saying . . ." Ben began.

"History knows that my father was inhuman," Lenz said. "Yes, he certainly was. He performed the most gruesome, the most unspeakable experiments on prisoners in Auschwitz, on children—"

"Will you excuse me, please?" Ilse Lenz said, rising to her feet. "I can't hear about his father," she murmured. She walked from the room.

"Darling, I'm sorry," Lenz called after her. He turned to Ben, anguished. "I can't blame her. She didn't have to live with this legacy. Her father was killed in the war when she was a child."

"I'm sorry to have brought it up," Ben said.

"Please, not at all. It is a perfectly natural question. I'm sure it strikes Americans as strange that the son of the notorious Gerhard Lenz devotes his life to giving away money to study the crimes of his father. But you must understand, those of us who, by the accident of birth, have had to struggle with this—we, the children of the most important Nazis—we each react in very different ways. There are those, like Rudolph Hess's son Wolf, who spend their lives trying to clear their fathers' names. And there are those who grow up confused, struggling to make some sense of it all. I was born too late to have retained any personal memories of my father, but there are many who knew their fathers only as they were at home, not as Hitler's men."

Jürgen Lenz grew steadily more impassioned as he spoke. "We grew up in privileged homes. We drove through the Warsaw ghetto in the back of a limousine, not understanding why the children out there looked so sad.

We watched our fathers' eyes light up when the Führer himself called to wish the family a merry Christmas. And some of us, as soon as we were old enough to think, learned to loathe our fathers and everything they stood for. To despise them with every fiber of our being."

Lenz's surprisingly youthful face was flushed. "I don't think of my father as my father, you see. He's like someone else to me, a stranger. Shortly after the war ended, he escaped to Argentina, I'm sure you know, smuggled out of Germany with false papers. He left my mother and me penniless, living in a military detention camp." He paused. "So you see, I've never had any doubts or conflicts about the Nazis. Creating this foundation was the very least I could do."

The room was silent for a moment.

"I came to Austria to study medicine," Lenz continued. "In some ways it was a relief to leave Germany. I loved it here—I was born here—and I stayed, practicing medicine, keeping as anonymous as I could. After I met Ilse, the love of my life, we discussed what we could do with the family money she'd inherited—her father had made a fortune publishing religious books and hymnals—and we decided I'd give up medicine and devote my life to fighting against what my father fought for. Nothing can ever efface the darkness that was the Third Reich, but I've devoted myself to trying, in my own small way, to be a force of human betterment." Lenz's speech seemed a little too polished, too rehearsed, as if he'd delivered it a thousand times before. No doubt he had. Yet there didn't seem to be a false note. Beneath the calm assuredness, Lenz was clearly a tormented man.

"You never saw your father again?"

"No. I saw him two or three times before his death. He came to Germany from Argentina to visit. He had a new name, a new identity. But my mother wouldn't see him. I saw him, but I felt nothing for him. He was a stranger to me."

"Your mother simply cut him off?"

"The next time was when she traveled to Argentina for his funeral. She did do that, as if she needed to see that he was dead. The funny thing was, she found she loved the country. It's where she finally retired to."

There was another silence, and then Ben said quietly but firmly, "I must say I'm impressed by all the resources you've devoted to shedding light on your paternal legacy. I wonder, in this connection, if you can tell me about an organization known as Sigma." He studied Lenz's face closely as he spoke the name.

Lenz looked at him for a good long while. Ben could hear his own heart thudding in the silence.

At last Lenz spoke. "You mention Sigma casually, but I think this may be the entire reason you have come here," Lenz said. "Why are you here, Mr. Simon?"

Ben felt a chill. He had let himself be cornered. Now the roads diverged: now he could try to hold on to his false identity, or come out with the truth.

It was time to be direct. To draw out the quarry.

"Mr. Lenz, I'm inviting you to clarify the nature of your involvement with Sigma."

Lenz frowned. "Why are you here, Mr. Simon? Why do you sneak into my house and lie to me?" Lenz smiled strangely, his voice quiet. "You're CIA, Mr. 'Simon,' is that right?"

"What are you talking about?" Ben said, baffled and frightened.

"Who are you really, Mr. 'Simon'?" Lenz whispered.

"Nice house," Anna said. "Whose is it?"

She sat in the front seat of a smoke-filled blue BMW, an unmarked police vehicle. Sergeant Walter Heisler was at the wheel, a beefy, hearty-looking man in his late thirties, smoking Casablancas. He was cordial enough.

"One of our more, eh, prominent citizens," Heisler said, taking a drag on his cigarette. "Jürgen Lenz."

"Who is he?"

They were both looking out at a handsome villa a hundred yards or so down Adolfstorgasse. Anna saw that most of the parked cars had black license plates with white letters. Heisler explained that you had to pay to maintain such plates; it was the old, aristocratic style.

He blew out a cloud of smoke. "Lenz and his wife are active in the social circles here, the Opera Ball and so on. I guess you'd call them, how you say, philo—philanthropists? Lenz runs the family foundation. Moved here twenty-some years ago from Germany."

"Hmmm." Her eyes were smarting from the smoke, but she didn't want to complain. Heisler was doing her a major favor. She rather liked sitting here in the smoke-filled cop car, one of the fellas.

"How old?"

"Fifty-seven, I believe."

"And prominent."

"Very."

There were three other unmarked vehicles idling on the street, one near them, the other two a few hundred yards down the block, on the other side of Lenz's villa. The cars were arranged in a classic box formation, so that no matter how Hartman chose to leave the neighborhood, they would have him trapped. The officers waiting in the cars were all highly trained members of the surveillance squad. Each of them was equipped with weapons and walkie-talkies.

Anna had no weapon. It was highly unlikely, she thought, that Hartman would put up any resistance. His records showed that he'd never owned a gun or applied for a license to carry. The murders of the old men had all been done by means of poison, by syringe. He probably had no weapon with him.

In fact, there wasn't much she knew about Hartman. But her Viennese comrades knew even less. She had told her friend Fritz Weber only that the American had left prints at the crime scene in Zurich, nothing more. Heisler, too, knew only that Hartman was wanted in Rossignol's murder. But that was enough for the *Bundespolizei* to agree to apprehend Hartman and, at the formal request of the FBI legat in Vienna, to place him under arrest.

She wondered how much she could trust the local police.

This was no theoretical question. Hartman was in there meeting with a man who . . .

A thought occurred to her. "This guy, Lenz," she said, her eyes burning from the smoke. "This may be a strange question, but does he have anything to do with the Nazis?"

Heisler stubbed out his cigarette in the car's overflowing ashtray. "Well, this is a strange question," he said. "His father—do you know the name Dr. Gerhard Lenz?"

"No, should I?"

He shrugged: naïve Americans. "One of the worst. A colleague of Josef Mengele's who did all kinds of horrifying experiments in the camps."

"Ah." Another idea suggested itself. Hartman, a survivor's son with an avenging spirit, was going after the next generation.

"His son is a good man, very different from his father. He devotes his life to undoing his father's evil."

She stared at Heisler, then out the windshield at Lenz's magnificent villa. The son was anti-Nazi? Amazing. She wondered whether Hartman knew that. He might not know anything about the younger Lenz except that he was the son of Gerhard, son of a Nazi. If he were really a fanatic, he wouldn't care if Lenz Junior could turn water into wine.

Which meant that Hartman might already have given Jürgen Lenz a lethal injection.

Jesus, she thought, as Heisler lit another Casablanca. *Why are we just sitting here?*

"Is that yours?" Heisler suddenly asked.

"Is what mine?"

"That car." He pointed at a Peugeot that was parked across the street from Lenz's villa. "It's been in the area since we get here."

"No. It's not one of yours?"

"Absolutely not. I can tell from plates."

"Maybe it's a neighbor, or a friend?"

"I wonder could your American colleagues be involving in this, maybe checking on you?" Heisler said heatedly. "Because if that's the case, I'm calling this operation off right now!"

Unsettled and defensive, she said, "It can't be. Tom Murphy would have let me know before sending someone in." Wouldn't he? "Anyway, he barely seemed interested when I first told him."

But if he were checking up on her? Was that possible?

"Well, then who is it?" Heisler demanded.

"Who are you?" Jürgen Lenz repeated, fear now showing on his face. "You are not a friend of Winston Rockwell's."

"Sort of," Ben admitted. "I mean, I know him from some work I've done. I'm Benjamin Hartman. My father is Max Hartman." Once more, he watched Lenz to gauge his reaction.

Lenz blenched, and then his expression softened. "Dear God," he whispered. "I can see the resemblance. What happened to your brother was a terrible thing."

Ben felt as if he'd been punched in the stomach. "What do you know?" he shouted.

The police radio crackled to life.

"*Korporal, wer ist das?*"

"*Keine Ahnung.*"

"*Keiner von uns, oder?*"

"*Richtig.*"

Now the other team wanted to know whether the Peugeot was one of theirs; Heisler confirmed he had no idea who it was. He took a night-vision monocular from the backseat and held it up to one eye. It was dark on the street now, and the unidentified car had switched off its lights. There was no street lamp nearby, so it was impossible to see the driver's face. The night-vision scope was a good idea, Anna thought.

"He has a newspaper up before his face," Heisler said. "A tabloid. *Die Kronen Zeitung*—I can just make it out."

"Can't be easy for the guy to read the paper in the dark, huh?" She thought: *Lenz Junior could be dead already, and we're sitting here waiting.*

"I do not think he's getting much reading done." Heisler seemed to share her sense of humor.

"Mind if I take a look?"

He handed her the scope. All she saw was newsprint. "He's obviously trying not to be identified," she said. What if he really was Bureau? "Which tells us something. O.K. if I use your cell phone?"

"Not at all." He gave her his clunky Ericsson, and she punched out the local number of the U.S. embassy.

"Tom," she said when Murphy came on the line. "It's Anna Navarro. You didn't send anyone out to Hietzing, did you?"

"Hietzing? Here in Vienna?"

"My case."

A pause. "No, you didn't ask me to, did you?"

"Well, someone's screwing up my stakeout. No one in your office would have taken it upon himself to check up on me without clearing it with you first?"

"They better not. Anyway, everyone's accounted for here, far as I know."

"Thanks." She disconnected, handed the phone back to Heisler. "Strange."

"Then who is in that car?" Heisler asked.

"If I may ask, why did you think I was CIA?"

"There are some old-timers in that community who have rather taken against me," Lenz said, shrugging. "Do you know about Project Paper Clip?" They had graduated to vodka. Ilse Lenz had still not returned to the sitting room, more than an hour after she had so abruptly left. "Perhaps not by that name. You're aware that immediately after the war, the U.S. government—the OSS, as the CIA's predecessor was called—smuggled some of Nazi Germany's leading scientists to America, yes? Paper Clip was the code name for this plan. The Americans sanitized the Germans' records, falsified their backgrounds. Covered up the fact that these were mass-murderers. You see, because as soon as the war was over, America turned its attention to a new war—the Cold War. Suddenly all that counted was fighting the Soviet Union. America had spent four years and countless lives battling the Nazis and suddenly the Nazis were their friends—so long as they could help in the struggle against the Communists. Help build weapons and such for America. These scientists were brilliant men, the brains behind the Third Reich's enormous scientific accomplishments."

"And war criminals."

"Precisely. Some of them responsible for the torture and murder of thousands upon thousands of concentration-camp inmates. Some, like Wernher von Braun and Dr. Hubertus Strughold, had invented many of the Nazis' weapons of war. Arthur Rudolph, who helped murder twenty thousand innocent people at Nordhausen, was awarded NASA's highest civilian honor!"

Twilight settled. Lenz got up and switched on lamps around the sitting room. "The Americans brought in the man who was in charge of death camps in Poland. One Nazi scientist they gave asylum to had conducted the freezing experiments at Dachau—he ended up at Randolph Air Force Base in San Antonio, a distinguished professor of space medicine. The CIA people who arranged all this, those few who survive, have been less than appreciative of my efforts to shed light on this episode."

"Your efforts?"

"Yes, and those of my foundation. It is not an insignificant part of the research that we sponsor."

"But what threat could the CIA pose?"

"The CIA, I understand, did not exist until a few years after the war, but they inherited operational control of these agents. There are aspects of history that some old-guard types in the CIA prefer to have left undisturbed. Some of them will go to quite extraordinary lengths to ensure this."

"I'm sorry, I can't believe that. The CIA doesn't go around killing people."

"No, not anymore," Lenz conceded, a note of sarcasm in his voice. "Not since they killed Allende in Chile, Lumumba in the Belgian Congo, tried to assassinate Castro. No, they're prohibited by law from doing such things. So now they 'outsource,' as you American businessmen like to say. They hire freelancers, mercenaries, through chains of front organizations, so the hit men can never be connected with the U.S. government." He broke off. "The world is more complicated than you seem to think."

"But that's all ancient, irrelevant history!"

"Scarcely irrelevant if you're one of the ancient men who may be implicated," Lenz pressed on inexorably. "I speak of elder statesmen, retired diplomats, former dignitaries who did a stint with the Office of Strategic Services in their youth. As they putter around their libraries and write their memoirs, they cannot avoid a certain unease." He gazed into the clear fluid in his glass as if seeing something there. "These are men accustomed to power, and deference. They would not look forward to revelations that would darken their golden years. Oh, of course, they'll tell themselves that what they do is for the good of the country, sparing the good name of the United States. So much of the wickedness men do is in the name of the commonweal. This, Mr. Hartman, I know. Frail old dogs can be the most dangerous. Calls can be made, favors called in. Mentors drawing on the loyalty of protégés. Frightened old men determined to die with at least their good names intact. I wish I could discount this scenario. But I know what these men are like. I have seen too much of human nature."

Ilse reappeared, carrying a small leather-bound book; on its spine Ben made out the name Hölderlin, lettered in gilt. "I see you gentlemen are still at it," she said.

"You understand, don't you, why we can be slightly on edge?" Lenz told Ben smoothly. "We have many enemies."

"There have been many threats against my husband," Ilse said. "There are fanatics on the right who view him, somehow, as a turncoat, as the man who betrayed his father's legacy." She smiled without warmth and repaired to the adjoining room.

"They worry me less, to be frank, than the self-interested, ostensibly rational souls who simply don't understand why we can't let sleeping dogs lie." Lenz's eyes were alert. "And whose friends, as I say, may be tempted to take rather extreme measures to ensure that their golden years remain golden. But I go on. You had certain questions about the postwar period, questions you hoped I might be able to answer."

Jürgen Lenz examined the photograph, gripping it in both hands. His face was tense. "That's my father," he said. "Yes."

"You look just like him," Ben said.

"Quite the legacy, hmm?" Lenz said ruefully. No longer was he the charming, affable host. Now he peered intently at the rest of the photograph. "Dear God, no. It can't be." He sank into his chair, his face ashen.

"What can't?" Ben was unrelenting. "Tell me what you know."

"Is this genuine?" The same reaction that Carl Mercandetti, the historian, had had.

"Yes." Ben took a deep breath, and replied with the utmost intensity. "Yes." The lives of Peter, Liesl, and who knew how many others had been its guarantors of authenticity.

"But Sigma was a myth! An old wives' tale! We'd all satisfied ourselves that it was."

"Then you do know of it?"

Lenz leaned forward. "You have to remember that in the tumult following the war, there were all sorts of wild tales. One of those was the legend of Sigma, vague and shrouded as it was. That some sort of alliance was forged among the major industrialists of the world." He pointed at two faces. "That men like Sir Alford Kittredge and Wolfgang Siebing, one revered and one reviled, made common cause. That they met in secrecy, and forged a clandestine pact."

"And what was the nature of that pact?"

Lenz shook his head hopelessly. "I wish I knew, Mr. Hartman—may I call you Ben? I'm sorry. I'd never taken the stories seriously until now."

"And your own father's involvement?"

Lenz shook his head slowly. "You're exceeding my own knowledge. Perhaps Jakob Sonnenfeld would know of these things."

Sonnenfeld—Sonnenfeld was the most prominent Nazi hunter alive. "Would he help me?"

"Speaking as a major benefactor of his institute," Lenz replied, "I am certain he'll do his best." He poured himself a fortifying quantity of spirits. "We've been dancing around one issue, haven't we? You still haven't explained how you came to be involved in all of this."

"Do you recognize the man next to your father?"

"No," Lenz said. He squinted. "He looks a little like . . . but that's not possible either."

"Yes. That's my father next to yours." Ben's voice was flatly declarative.

"That makes no sense," Lenz protested. "Everyone in my world knows about your father. He's a major philanthropist. A force for good. And a Holocaust survivor, of course. Yes, it looks like him—like you, in fact. But I repeat: that makes no sense."

Ben laughed bitterly. "I'm sorry. But things stopped making sense for me when my old college buddy tried to murder me on the Bahnhofstrasse."

Lenz's eyes looked sorrowful. "Tell me how you found this."

Ben told Lenz about the events of the past several days, trying to stay as dispassionate as he could.

"Then you, too, know danger," Lenz said solemnly.

"There are filaments, invisible filaments, that link this photograph to those deaths."

Frustration welled up in Ben as he struggled to make some sense of everything Lenz was telling him, tried to rearrange the pieces of information to make a coherent picture. Instead of becoming clearer, things were even more bewildering, more maddening.

Ben was first conscious of Ilse's return to the room from the scent of her perfume.

"This young man brings danger," she said to her husband, and her voice was like sandpaper. She turned to Ben. "Forgive me, but I cannot keep silent any longer. You bring death to this house. My husband has been menaced by extremists for so many years because of his fight for justice. I am sorry for what you have undergone. But you are careless, the way you Americans always are. You come to see my husband under false pretenses, pursuing some private vendetta of your own."

"Please, Ilse," Lenz interjected.

"And now you have brought death here with you, like an unannounced guest. I would be grateful to you if you would leave my house. My husband has done enough for the cause. Must he give his life for it, too?"

"Ilse is upset," Lenz said apologetically. "There are aspects of my life that she has never grown accustomed to."

"No," Ben said. "She's probably right. I've already put too many lives in jeopardy." His voice was hollow.

Ilse's face was a mask, the muscles immobilized by fear. "*Gute Nacht*," she said with quiet finality.

Walking Ben to the foyer, Lenz spoke with murmured urgency. "If you want, I'll be glad to help you. To do what I can. Pull strings where I am able to, provide contacts. But Ilse is right about one thing. You can't know what you're up against. I'd advise you to be cautious, my friend." There was something familiar about the harrowed look on Lenz's face, and after a moment Ben realized that it reminded him of what he'd seen on Peter's. Within both men, it seemed, a passion for justice had been worn down by vast forces, and yet it could be mistaken for nothing else.

Ben left Lenz's house, dazed. He was far over his head: why couldn't he just admit that he was powerless, hopelessly unequipped for a task that had defeated his own brother? And the very facts he had already established now ground deeper into his psyche, like glass shards under his feet. Max Hartman, philanthropist, Holocaust survivor, humanitarian—was he, in fact, a man like Gerhard Lenz, a confederate in barbarity? It was sickening to contemplate. Might Max have been complicit in Peter's murder? Was the man behind his own son's death?

Was this why he'd suddenly disappeared? So he wouldn't have to face his own exposure? And what about the complicity of the CIA? How the hell did an *Obersturm-führer* in Hitler's SS come to emigrate and settle in the States, if not with help from the U.S. government? Were allies of his, very old friends indeed, behind the horrific events? Was there some chance they were doing it on his father's behalf—to protect him and themselves as well—without the old man's knowledge?

You talk of things you cannot understand, his father had said, speaking past him as much as to him.

Ben was seized with conflicting emotions. Part of him, the devoted, loyal son, wanted to believe that there was some other explanation, had wanted to since Peter's revelations. Some reason to believe his own father was not a . . . a what? A monster. He heard his mother's voice, whispering as she died, pleading with him to understand, to try to heal the breach, to get along. To love this complicated, difficult man who was Max Hartman.

While another part of Ben felt a welcome clarity.

I've worked hard to understand you, you bastard! Ben found himself shouting inwardly. *I've tried to love you. But a deception like this, the ugliness of your real life—how can I feel anything but hatred?*

He had parked, once again, a good distance from Lenz's house. He did not want his license plates to be traced back to him; at least, that had been his thinking before, when he had assumed Lenz was one of the conspirators.

He walked down the path in front of Lenz's house. Just before he reached the street, he saw, in his peripheral vision, a light come on.

It was the interior dome light of a car, just a few yards away.

Someone was getting out of the car and walking toward him.

Trevor saw a light come on across the street and turned his head to look. The front door was open. The target was chatting with an older gentleman, whom he assumed was Lenz. Trevor waited until the two men had shaken hands and the target was strolling down the front path before he got out of the car.

CHAPTER TWENTY-FOUR

"I want you to run the plates," Heisler said on the police radio. He turned to Anna. "If is not you, and not us, then who is it? You must have some idea."

"Someone who's also staking out the house," she said. "I don't like this."

She thought: *Something else is going on here. Should I tell Heisler my suspicions about Hartman?* Yet it was such a half-baked bit of speculation—after all, what if Hartman was there simply to get information out of Lenz, information about where some of his father's old friends might be living—and not to kill him?

Still . . . they had all the legal justification they needed to storm the villa. And what if it turned out that, while they were all sitting here watching the house, one of the city's leading citizens was inside being murdered? The outcry would be enormous; it would be an international incident, and it would all be on her shoulders.

Heisler interrupted her thoughts. "I want you to walk by that car and look at the man's face," he said. It seemed an order, not a request. "Make absolute certain you don't recognize."

She agreed, wanting to see for herself.

"I need a weapon," she said.

Heisler handed her his gun. "You took this from floor of car. I must have left it. I did not give it to you."

She got out of the car and started walking toward Lenz's villa.

The front door of Lenz's house came open.

Two men were standing there, talking. One older, one younger.

Lenz and Hartman.

Lenz was alive, she saw with relief.

The two men shook hands cordially. Then Hartman started down the path toward the street.

And suddenly a light inside the Peugeot went on, and the man got out of the driver's seat, a trench coat draped over his right arm.

That was when she saw the man's face for the first time.

The face!

She knew the face. She had seen it before.

But where?

The man with the trench coat over his arm closed his car door as Hartman reached the street, not five yards away.

Just for an instant she saw the man in profile.

It stirred an old memory.

A profile shot. She had seen a profile shot of this man. Front and side views. The association was unpleasant, one of danger.

Mug shots. At work. Fairly poor-quality photos of this man, front and profile. A bad guy.

Yes, she had seen the photos once or twice in the Weekly Intelligence Briefing.

But they weren't mug shots, strictly speaking; they had been surveillance photographs taken at a distance, magnified to the point of graininess.

Yes.

Not an ordinary criminal, of course.

An assassin.

The man was an international assassin, and an extraordinarily accomplished one. Little was known about him—only fragmentary bits of evidence had ever been gathered; as to his employers, assuming he wasn't a freelancer, they had nothing at all. But the evidence they had suggested someone of uncommon resourcefulness and range. She flashed on another photograph: the body of a labor leader in Barcelona, whom he was believed to have slain. The image had lodged in her memory, perhaps because of the way blood ran down the victim's shirtfront like a neck tie. Another image: a popular political candidate in southern Italy, a man who had been leading a national reform movement. His death was originally attributed to the Mafia, but had been reclassified after snippets of information implicated a man they knew only as the Architect. The candidate, already under threats from organized crime, had been well protected, she recalled. And the assassination had been brilliantly engineered, from the perspective not merely of ballistics but of politics as well. The politician was shot dead while in a brothel staffed by illegal immigrants from Somalia, and the awkward circumstances ensured that his supporters could not transfigure his death into martyrdom.

The Architect. An international assassin of the first order.

Targeting Hartman.

She tried to make sense of it: *Hartman's on a vendetta,* she thought. *And the other man?*

Oh, my God. Now what do I do? Try to apprehend the killer?

She held the transmitter to her lips, depressed the Talk button.

"I know this guy," she told Heisler. "He's a professional assassin. I'm going to try to take him out. You cover Hartman."

*   *   *

"Pardon me," the man called out to Ben, striding quickly toward him.

Something seems wrong with this guy, Ben thought. *Something's off.*

The coat folded over his right arm.

The rapid pace at which he was approaching.

The face—a face he had seen before. A face he would never forget.

Ben slipped his right hand under his left jacket lapel, reached for the cold hard steel of the gun and was afraid.

She needed Hartman alive; Hartman dead did her no good.

The assassin was about to take out Hartman, she was certain. Everything was suddenly one complex calculation. As far as she was concerned, it was better for Hartman, her suspect, to flee than to be killed. In any case, she'd have to leave the pursuit of Hartman to the others.

She raised Heisler's Glock.

The assassin seemed unaware of her. He was focused only on Hartman. She knew from her training that he had fallen victim to the professional's greatest weakness: target fixation. He'd lost a sense of situational awareness. Big cats are most vulnerable to hunters precisely when they're tensing to pounce.

Maybe that would give her the advantage she needed.

Now she had to suddenly break his concentration, distract his attention.

"Freeze!" she shouted. "Halt, goddammit!"

She saw Hartman turn and look at her.

The assassin jerked his head slightly to the left but didn't turn to see where the shout had come from, didn't shift his catlike gaze away from Hartman.

Anna aimed directly at the middle of the assassin's chest, at the center of his mass. It was a reflexive gesture for her; she had been trained to shoot to kill, not to wound.

But what was he doing now? The hit man had turned back toward Hartman, who, she suddenly saw, had his own gun out.

The Architect had his target in his sights; he assumed that whoever had just shouted wasn't an immediate threat, but in any case he had made his own calculation. To turn around and engage her—whoever she was—was to lose his target, and he was unwilling to do that.

Suddenly the assassin began to turn—

She'd figured him wrong.

His movements were as preternaturally smooth as a ballet dancer's. Pivoting on the balls of his feet, he turned one hundred and eighty degrees, his gun extended and firing all the while, in precise intervals of a fraction of a second. The gun scarcely bucked in his powerful grip. Only when she turned to look did she realize what he had accomplished. Good God! A moment before, there were four armed Vienna policemen who had drawn a bead on him. Every one of them had now been shot! Each one of his shots had hit its target. The four policemen were down!

It was a breathtaking execution, displaying a level of skill she had never encountered in her life. She was filled with sheer terror.

Now she heard panicked noises, the gasping and lowing of the incapacitated gunshot victims.

The man was a professional; he had determined to eliminate all impediments before turning back to his target— and she was his final impediment.

But as he spun toward her, Anna had already aimed. She heard Hartman shout. Now it was her turn to focus singlemindedly, and she squeezed the trigger.

Bull's-eye!

The hit man tumbled to the ground, his gun clattering off to one side.

She'd dropped him.

Was he dead?

Everything was chaos. The suspect, Hartman, was tearing away down the street.

But she knew the street was blockaded in both directions by the police. She ran toward the downed man, scooped up his gun, and continued running after Hartman.

Amid the screams of the surviving gunshot victims, she heard shouts in German, but they meant nothing to her.

"Er steht auf!"

"Er lebt, er steht!"

"Nein, nimm den Verdächtigen!"

Down the block, Hartman had run directly into the clustered team of surveillance experts, all of whom had their weapons out and aimed at him, and she heard more shouting—

"Halt! Keinen Schritt weiter!"

"Polizei! Sie sind verhaftet!"

But a noise coming from behind her, from where the assassin lay, attracted her attention, and she turned around just in time to see the assassin stagger into his Peugeot and yank the door behind him.

He was wounded, but he had survived, and now he was getting away!

"Hey," she shouted to anyone, everyone, "stop him! The Peugeot! Don't let him escape!"

They had Hartman; he was surrounded by five *Polizei*. For now she could safely ignore him. Instead, she lunged toward the Peugeot just as it roared to life and barreled straight toward her.

On the few occasions when she'd permitted herself to replay in her mind her close encounter with the Lincoln Town Car in Halifax, she'd fantasized that she'd a gun in her hands and could fire at the driver. Now she did, and she squeezed off shot after shot at the man. But the windshield only pitted and spider-webbed in small areas, and the car kept bearing down on her. She threw herself to one side, out of the way, just as the Peugeot thundered by, tires squealing, down the block past two empty surveillance cars—their drivers and passengers all on the street now—and out of sight.

He'd gotten away!

"Shit!" she shouted, turning back to see Hartman with his hands up.

Shaken, she ran down the block toward her newly apprehended suspect.

CHAPTER TWENTY-FIVE

Patient Eighteen was slowly jogging on a treadmill.

A snorkel-like device came out of his mouth, connected to two long hoses. His nose had been clamped shut.

Taped to his crepey, concave bare chest were twelve wires that fed into an EKG monitor. Another wire sprouted from a small device clamped onto the end of a forefinger. He was sweating and looked pale.

"How are you doing?" said the doctor, a tall gray-faced man.

The patient could not talk, but he gave a trembling thumbs-up.

"Remember, there's a panic button right in front of you," the doctor said. "Use it if you need to."

Patient Eighteen kept jogging.

The doctor said to his short, rotund colleague, "I think we're at maximal exercise capacity. He seems to have crossed the respiratory exchange ratio—he's over one. No signs of ischemia. He's strong, this one. All right, let's give him the rest of the day off. Tomorrow he'll begin the treatment."

For the first time all day, the gray-faced doctor allowed
himself a smile.

Princeton, New Jersey

The grand old Princeton historian was working in his study
at Dickinson Hall when the telephone rang.

Everything in Professor John Barnes Godwin's office
dated from the forties or fifties, whether it was the black
rotary-dial phone or the oak card-catalog drawers or the
Royal manual typewriter (he had no use for computers). He
liked it that way, liked the way the old things looked, the
solidity of objects from the time they made things out of
Bakelite and wood and steel and not plastic, plastic, and
plastic.

He was not, however, one of those old men who lived
in the past. He loved the world today. Often he wished his
darling Sarah, his wife of fifty-seven years, were here to
share it with him. They had always planned to do a lot of
traveling when he retired.

Godwin was a historian of twentieth-century Europe, a
winner of the Pulitzer Prize whose lectures had always been
immensely popular on the Princeton campus. Many of his
former students now occupied positions of great prominence in their fields. The chairman of the Federal Reserve
had been one of his brightest, as were the chairman of
WorldCom, both the Secretary of Defense and the Deputy
Secretary of Defense, the United States ambassador to the
UN, countless members of the Council on Economic Advisers, even the current chairman of the Republican National Committee.

Professor Godwin cleared his throat before answering
the phone. "Hello."

The voice was immediately familiar.

"Oh yes, Mr. Holland, good to hear your voice. We're
still on, I hope?"

He listened for a moment. "Of course I know him, he

was a student of mine . . . Well, if you're asking for my opinion, I remember him as charming if a bit strong-headed, very bright though not really an intellectual, or at least not interested in ideas for their own sake. A very strong sense of moral purpose, I always thought. But Ben Hartman always struck me as quite reasonable and level-headed."

He listened again. "No, he's not a crusader. He just doesn't have that temperament. And he's certainly no martyr. I think he can be reasoned with."

Another pause.

"Well, none of us wants the project disrupted. But I do wish you'd give the fellow a chance. I'd really hate to see anything happen to him."

Vienna

The interrogation room was cold and bare, with the standard furnishings of police interrogation rooms everywhere. *I'm becoming an expert*, Ben thought grimly. The one-way observation mirror, unsubtle, and as big as a bedroom window in a suburban house. The wire mesh over the window overlooking a bleak inner courtyard.

The American woman sat across the small room, in a gray suit, coiled on the metal folding chair like a clock spring. She had identified herself as Special Agent Anna Navarro of the U.S. Department of Justice, Office of Special Investigations, and flashed an ID card to prove it. She was also a serious beauty, a real stunner: wavy dark brown hair, eyes the color of caramel, olive skin; tall and slim and long-legged. Nicely dressed, too—a sense of style, which had to be rare in the Department of Justice. Yet she was all business, not a hint of a smile. No ring, which probably meant divorced, because women this gorgeous were usually snatched up early, no doubt by some gallant fellow government investigator with a square chin who'd wooed her with tales of his bravery in apprehending miscreants . . .

until the stress of two high-powered government careers had taken its toll on the marriage . . .

In the folding chair next to her sat a bruiser of a cop, a beefy guy who sat silent and brooding and chain-smoking Casablanca cigarettes. Ben had no idea whether the cop understood English. He'd only said his name: Sergeant Walter Heisler of the *Sicherheitsbüro*, the major-crimes squad of the Viennese police.

Half an hour into the questioning, Ben became impatient. He'd tried being reasonable, tried to talk sense, but his interrogators were implacable. "Am I under arrest?" he asked finally.

"Do you want to be?" Agent Navarro snapped back.

Oh, good God, not this again.

"Does she have the right to do this?" Ben asked of the hulking Viennese cop, who just smoked and stared at him bovinely.

Silence.

"Well?" Ben demanded. "Who's in charge here?"

"As long as you answer my questions, there's no reason to arrest you," Agent Navarro said. "Yet."

"So I'm free to go."

"You're being held for questioning. Why were you visiting Jürgen Lenz? You still haven't explained properly."

"As I said, it was a social visit. Ask Lenz."

"Are you in Vienna for business or pleasure?"

"Both."

"You don't have any business meetings lined up. Is that the way you normally travel on business?"

"I like to be spontaneous."

"You were booked for five days at a ski resort in the Swiss Alps, but you never showed up there."

"I changed my mind."

"Why do I doubt that?"

"I have no idea. I felt like seeing Vienna."

"So you just showed up in Vienna with no hotel reservations."

"As I said, I like to be spontaneous."

"I see," said Agent Navarro, clearly frustrated. "And your visit to Gaston Rossignol, in Zurich—was that business as well?"

My God, so they knew about that, too! But how? He felt a wave of panic.

"He was a friend of a friend."

"And that's how you treat a friend of a friend—you kill him?"

Oh, Christ. "He was dead when I got there!"

"Really," Navarro said, clearly unconvinced. "Was he expecting you?"

"No. I just showed up."

"Because you like to be spontaneous."

"I wanted to surprise him."

"Instead he surprised you, huh?"

"It was a shock, yes."

"How did you get to Rossignol? Who put you in touch with him?"

Ben hesitated, a beat too long. "I'd rather not say."

She picked up on it. "Because he was no mutual acquaintance or anything like that, was he? What was Rossignol's connection to your father?"

What the hell did that mean? How much did she know? Ben looked at her sharply.

"Let me tell you something," Anna Navarro said dryly. "I know your type. Rich boy, always gets whatever he wants. Whenever you get yourself in deep doodoo, your daddy saves you, or maybe the family lawyer bails you out. You're used to doing whatever the hell you want and you think you'll never have to pay the bill. Well, not this time, my friend."

Ben smiled involuntarily, but he refused to give her the satisfaction of putting up an argument.

"Your father is a Holocaust survivor, is that right?" she persisted.

So she doesn't know everything.

Ben shrugged. "That's what I'm told." She certainly wasn't entitled to the truth.

"And Rossignol was a big-deal Swiss banker, right?" She was watching him closely now.

What was she driving at? "That's why you and all those Austrian cops were staked out in front of Lenz's house," he said. "You were there to arrest me."

"No, actually," the American woman said coolly. "To talk to you."

"You could have just asked to talk to me. You didn't need half the Vienna police force. I'll bet you'd love to pin the Rossignol murder on me. Gets the CIA off the hook, right? Or do you Justice Department guys hate the CIA? I get confused."

Agent Navarro leaned forward, her soft brown eyes gone hard. "Why were you carrying a gun?"

Ben hesitated, but just for a second or two. "For protection."

"Is that right." A statement of skepticism, not a question. "Are you registered to carry a gun in Austria?"

"I believe that's a matter between me and the Austrian authorities."

"The Austrian authorities are sitting in this chair next to me. If he decides to prosecute you for illegally carrying a gun, I won't stand in his way. The Austrians strongly disapprove of foreign visitors carrying unregistered weapons."

Ben shrugged. She had a point, of course. Though it seemed the least of his worries right now.

"So let me tell you this, Mr. Hartman," Agent Navarro said. "I find it a little hard to believe that you carried a gun to visit a 'friend of a friend.' Particularly when your fingerprints were found all over Rossignol's house. Understand?"

"No, not really. Are you accusing me of murdering him? If so, why don't you come right out and say it?" He was finding it hard to breathe, his tension steadily rising.

"The Swiss think your brother had a vendetta against the banking establishment. Maybe something in you got twisted when he died, something that made you take his pursuit of them to a more lethal level. It wouldn't be hard

to show motive. And then there are your fingerprints. I
think a Swiss court would have no problem convicting
you."

Did she genuinely believe he'd murdered Rossignol—
and if so, why was this special investigator from the Department of Justice so interested? He had no idea how much
power she really had here, what kind of trouble he was
really in, and the uncertainty alone made him anxious.
Don't be defensive, he thought. Fight back.

Ben sat back. "You have no authority here."

"Absolutely right. But I don't need authority."

What the hell did she mean? "So what do you want from
me?"

"I want information. I want to know why you were really visiting Rossignol. Why you were really visiting Jürgen
Lenz. What you're really up to, Mr. Hartman."

"And if I don't care to share?" He tried to project an
image of confidence.

She cocked her head. "Would you like to find out what'll
happen? Why don't you spin the wheel and take a chance?"

Jesus, she was good, Ben thought. He breathed deeply.
The room's walls seemed to be closing in. He kept his face
blank, unreadable.

She continued: "Do you know that there's a warrant for
your arrest in Zurich?"

Ben shrugged. "That's a laugh." He decided that it was
time for him to be aggressive, aggrieved, undefensive—as
a wrongfully arrested American would be. "Maybe I know
the ways of the Swiss a little better than you do. For one
thing, they'll swear out a warrant if you spit out your gum
on the sidewalk. For another, there's no goddamn possibility of extradition." He'd established this much from his
conversations with Howie. "The canton of Zurich has a
hard enough time getting cooperation from the *Polizei* of
the other Swiss cantons. And the fact that the Swiss have
made a name for themselves in harboring tax fugitives
means that other countries ignore Swiss extradition requests
as a matter of policy." These were Howie's words, and he

recited them stolidly, facing her down. She might as well know that she couldn't game him. "The Zurich bulls claim they want me for 'questioning.' They don't even pretend to have a case. So why don't we cut the crap here?"

She leaned closer. "It's a matter of public record that your brother had been trying to build a case against the Swiss banking establishment. Gaston Rossignol was a pre-eminent Swiss banker. You visit him, and he turns up dead. Let's get back to that. Then suddenly you're in Vienna meeting with the son of an infamous Nazi. And your father was in a concentration camp. It looks an awful lot like some kind of vengeance trip you're on."

So that was it. Maybe it would look like that to someone who didn't know the truth. But I can't tell her the truth!

"That's preposterous," Ben snapped. "I don't even want to dignify your fantasies about vendettas and violence. You talk about Swiss bankers. I do deals with these people, Agent Navarro. It's my job. International finance doesn't really lend itself to murderous rampages, O.K.? In my world, the main injuries you inflict are paper cuts."

"Then explain what happened on the Bahnhofplatz."

"I can't. I've been through that with the Swiss bulls over and over again."

"And explain how you tracked down Rossignol."

Ben shook his head.

"And the others. Come on. I want to know where you got their names and their whereabouts."

Ben just looked at her.

"Where were you on Wednesday?"

"I don't recall."

"Nova Scotia, by any chance?"

"Come to think of it, I was being arrested in Zurich," he shot back. "You can check with your friends at the Zurich police. See, I like to get arrested in every country I visit. It's really the best way to appreciate the local customs."

She ignored his barb. "Tell me what got you arrested."

"You know as well as I do."

Navarro turned to her brooding sidekick, who exhaled a plume of smoke, then looked back at Ben. "Several times in the last couple of days you yourself were almost killed. Including today—"

In his dull, dazed anxiety, he was surprised to feel a warm rush of gratitude. "You saved my life. I guess I should thank you."

"Damn right you should," she replied. "Now tell me, why do you think someone was trying to kill you? Who might have known what you were up to?"

Nice try, lady. "I have no idea."

"I'll bet you have some idea."

"Sorry. Maybe you can ask your friends over at the CIA what they're trying to cover up. Or is your office involved in the cover-up, too?"

"Mr. Hartman, your twin brother was killed in Switzerland, in a suspicious plane crash. More recently, you've had some unexplained connection to shootings in that country. Death seems to follow you around like a cheap cologne. What am I supposed to think?"

"Think whatever you like. I didn't commit any crime."

"I'm going to ask you this one more time: Where did you get their names and addresses?"

"Whose?"

"Rossignol and Lenz."

"I told you, mutual acquaintances."

"I don't believe that."

"Believe what you like."

"What are you hiding? Why don't you level with me, Mr. Hartman?"

"Sorry. I've got nothing to hide."

Agent Navarro folded, then unfolded, her long shapely legs. "Mr. Hartman," she said with utmost exasperation. "I'm going to offer you a deal. You cooperate with me, and I'll do my best to get the Swiss and the Austrians to back off."

Was she sincere? His distrust had become almost a reflex. "Given that you seem to be the one pushing them to come after me, that strikes me as a hollow promise. I don't have to stay here any longer, do I?"

She watched him silently, nibbling at the inside of a cheek. "No." She took out a business card and jotted something down on the back of it, then handed it to him. "If you change your mind, here's my hotel in Vienna."

It was over. Thank God. He inhaled, felt the air reach the very bottom of his lungs, the anxiety suddenly lift.

"Nice to meet you, Agent Navarro," Ben said, rising. "And thanks again for saving my life."

CHAPTER TWENTY-SIX

The pain was intense and overwhelming; another man would have passed out. Gathering his powers of mental concentration, Trevor assigned the pain to another body— a vividly imagined doppelgänger, someone who was convulsed with agony but who was not he. By sheer force of will, he managed to find his way through the streets of Vienna to a building on Taborstrasse.

Then he remembered that the car was stolen—his thinking was sluggish, that was what alarmed him most of all— and he drove five blocks away and abandoned it, the keys dangling from the ignition. Maybe some idiot would steal it and get caught in the citywide dragnet that was sure to follow.

He limped down the street, ignoring the many glances of the passersby. He knew his suit jacket was drenched with his own blood; he had put the trench coat on over it, but even that, too, had gotten soaked through. He had lost a great deal of blood. He felt lightheaded.

He was able to get back to Taborstrasse, to the street-level office marked with a brass plaque that said DR. THEO-

DOR SCHREIBER, INTERNIST & GENERAL SURGEON.

The office was dark, and there was no answer when he buzzed. Trevor didn't find this surprising, since it was after eight o'clock in the evening, and Dr. Schreiber kept regular hours. But he kept ringing the bell anyway. Schreiber lived in the flat behind his small office, and the bell rang in his living quarters as well, Trevor knew.

After five minutes, the light went on in the office, and then a voice came through the speaker, loud and annoyed: "*Ja?*"

"*Dr. Schreiber, es is Christoph. Es ist ein Notfall.*"

The front door of the building unlocked electronically. Then the door off the lobby, marked with the doctor's name on another brass plaque, unlocked as well.

Dr. Schreiber was disgruntled. "You have interrupted my dinner," he said gravely. "I trust it is important—" He noticed the blood-soaked trench coat. "All right, all right, follow me." The physician turned and walked back toward the examination room.

Dr. Schreiber had a sister who lived in Dresden, in East Germany, for decades. Until the Wall came down, this simple accident of geography—he had escaped from East Berlin in 1961, while his sister had been forced to stay behind—had been enough to give East German intelligence leverage over the doctor.

But Stasi did not seek to blackmail him or to turn him into some sort of spy, as if a physician could ever be useful as a spy. No, Stasi had a far more mundane use for him: simply to serve as a doctor on call for its agents in Austria in cases of emergency. Physicians in Austria, as in many countries in the world, are required by law to report gunshot wounds to the police. Dr. Schreiber would be more discreet than that when the occasional wounded Stasi agent appeared at his office, usually in the middle of the night.

Trevor, who had lived as a Stasi illegal in London for many years before he was recruited to Sigma, had from time to time been dispatched to Vienna, under the cover of business travel, and twice he had needed to visit the good doctor.

Even now that the Cold War was long over, and Schreiber's days of covert assistance to East Germany were pretty much finished, Trevor had little doubt that the physician would cooperate. Schreiber could still be prosecuted for his covert assistance to Stasi. That he would not want.

But his vulnerability did not keep Dr. Schreiber from bristling with resentment. "You are a most fortunate man," the doctor said brusquely. "The bullet, you see, entered just over your heart. A slightly more direct angle and you would have died immediately. Instead, it appears to have entered at an oblique angle, digging a sort of trench in the skin and the fatty tissue beneath. It even tore away some of the surface fibers of the pectoralis major, your breast muscle. And exited right here, at the axilla. You must have turned just in time."

Dr. Schreiber glanced over his half-glasses at Trevor, who did not reply.

He poked with a pair of forceps, and Trevor winced. The pain was overwhelming. His body was suffused with an unpleasant prickly heat.

"It also came close to causing great damage to the nerves and blood vessels in the area of the brachial plexus. Had it done so, you'd have lost the use of your right arm permanently. Maybe even lost the arm itself."

"I'm left-handed," Trevor said. "Anyway, I don't need to know the gory details."

"Yes," the doctor said absently. "Well, you really should go to the hospital, the Allgemeines Krankenhaus, if we're going to do this right."

"That's out of the question, and you know it." A lightning bolt of pain shot down his arm.

The doctor changed into his scrubs, and injected several syringes of a local anesthetic around the wound. With a small pair of scissors and forceps he excised some blackened tissue, irrigated the wound, and then set about suturing it.

Trevor could feel a deep, tugging discomfort, but no real pain. He gritted his teeth. "I want you to make sure the wound doesn't open up if I move around," he said.

"You should take it easy for a little while."

"I'm a fast healer."

"That's right," the doctor said. "I remember now." The man was a fast healer—freakishly so.

"Time is the one luxury I don't have," Trevor said. "I want you to sew it up tight."

"Then I can use heavier suture materials—3-0 nylon, say—but it may leave a rather ugly scar."

"It doesn't concern me."

"Fine," the doctor said, turning back to his steel cart of equipment.

When he had finished, he said, "For the pain, I can give you some Demerol." He added dryly, "Or would you prefer to go without anything?"

"Some ibuprofen should be enough," Trevor said.

"As you wish."

Trevor stood, wincing. "All right then, I appreciate your help." He handed the doctor a few thousand-shilling notes.

The physician looked at him and said, quite insincerely, "Any time."

Anna splashed her face with hot water. Thirty times, her mother had trained her: her mother's only vanity. Keeps the skin vital and glowing.

Over the running water she heard the phone ringing. Grabbing a towel to dry her face, she ran to catch it.

"Anna, it's Robert Polozzi. Am I calling you too late?"

Robert Polozzi from ID Section.

"No, not at all, Robert. What is it?"

"Listen: about the patent search."

She'd forgotten about the patent search. She patted her dripping face.

He said: "The neurotoxin—"

"Oh, right. You found something?"

"So get this. May 16 of this year, patent number—well, it's a long number—anyway, a patent for this exact synthetic compound was applied for by a small Philadelphia-based biotech company called Vortex. It's a, it says, 'a synthetic analog of the venom of the conus sea snail for proposed in-vitro applications.' And then some mumbo jumbo about 'localizing ion channels' and 'tagging chemochyme receptors.' " He paused, then resumed, his voice tentative. "I called the place. Vortex, I mean. On a pretext, of course."

A little unorthodox, but she didn't mind. "Learn anything?"

"Well, not exactly. They say their stocks of this toxin are minimal and under tight control. It's hard to produce, so they don't have much, and anyway the stuff is used in ridiculously tiny quantities, and it's still experimental. I asked them whether it could be used as a poison, and the guy I talked to, the scientific director of the firm, said of course it could—the conus sea snail's venom, as found in nature, is highly deadly. He said a tiny amount could induce immediate heart failure."

She felt a growing excitement. "He told you the stuff is under tight control—that means it's under lock and key?"

"Right."

"And this guy strikes you as on the level?"

"I think so, but who knows?"

"Great work, thanks. Can you find out from them whether any of their supply of this stuff has been found missing or otherwise unaccounted for?"

"Already did," the researcher said proudly. "The answer's no."

A pang of disappointment. "Can you find out for me everything you can about Vortex? Owners, principals, employees, and so on?"

"Will do."

She hung up, sat on the edge of the bed, pondered. It was possible that tugging at this thread would unravel the conspiracy behind the murders. Or unravel nothing.

The whole investigation was proving increasingly frustrating. Nor had the Vienna police had any luck chasing down the shooter. The shooter's Peugeot had previously been reported stolen—surprise, surprise. Another dead end.

This Hartman she found baffling. Against her will she also found him appealing, even attractive. But he was a type. A golden boy, born to money, graced with good looks, overconfident. He was Brad, the football player who'd raped her. The world cut men like that a break. Men like that, a blunt-speaking girlfriend of hers in college used to say, thought their shit didn't stink. They thought they could get away with anything.

But was he a killer? Somehow it seemed unlikely. She believed his version of what had happened at Rossignol's in Zurich; it jibed with the fingerprint patterns and with her own sense of him. Yet he was carrying a gun, passport control had no record of him arriving in Austria, and he'd offered no explanation for that. . . . On the other hand, a thorough search of his car hadn't revealed anything. No syringe, no poisons, nothing.

Whether he was a part of this conspiracy was hard to say. He'd thought his brother had been killed four years ago; maybe that murder had been the catalyst for those murders that came later. But why so many, and in such a short span of time?

The fact remained: Benjamin Hartman knew more. Yet she didn't have the authority, or the grounds, to hold him. It was deeply frustrating. She wondered whether her desire—all right, obsession—to get him had to do with the rich-boy thing, the old wounds, Brad . . .

She took her address book from the end table, looked up a phone number, and dialed.

It rang several times before a gravelly male voice answered, "Donahue." Donahue was a money-laundering guru at DOJ, and she'd quietly enlisted his help before she'd left for Switzerland. No context; just some account information. Donahue didn't mind being kept in the dark about the nature of her investigation; he seemed to regard it as a challenge.

"It's Anna Navarro," she said.

"Oh yeah, right, how ya doin' there, Anna?"

She found herself switching into her regular-guy voice. This she did easily; it was how her father's buddies talked, her neighbors back home. "Doin' good, thanks. How're we doin' on the money trace?"

"Na-a-ah, nothin'. We're buttin' our heads against a big brick wall. It's lookin' like each of the dead guys got regular contributions booted into their accounts from some haven country. Cayman Islands, British Virgins, Curaçao. That's where we keep hittin' the wall."

"What happens when you go to these offshore banks with an official request?"

A short bark of derision from Donahue. "They give us the finger. We give 'em an MLAT request for their financial records, they say they'll get around to it some time next few years." MLAT, she knew, was the mutual assistance treaty, which in principle obtained between the United States and many of these offshore havens. "BVI and Caymans are the worst, they tell us maybe two, three years it'll take 'em."

"Huh."

"But even if they should just open up the magic doors and show us everything, all we're going to get is where they got the money from, and you can bet your paycheck it's some other offshore. Isle of Man, Bahamas, Bermuda, Lux, San Marino, Anguilla. Probably a whole chain of offshores and shell companies. These days money can zip around the world, movin' between a dozen accounts in, like, seconds."

"Mind if I ask you something?" she said.

"Go 'head."

"How do you guys ever get anything on money-laundering?"

"Oh, we get stuff," he said, a little defensively. "It just takes years."

"Great," she said. "Thanks."

In a small room on the fifth floor of the *Sicherheitsbüro*, at Vienna police headquarters on Rossauer Lände, a young man sat before a computer screen, wearing headphones. From time to time he snubbed out a cigarette in a large gold ashtray that sat on the gray Formica table next to a No Smoking sign.

In a small box on the top left of the screen was the telephone number he was monitoring, along with the date, the start time, duration of call measured in a tenth of a second, the telephone number called. Elsewhere on the screen was a list of telephone numbers, representing each call made from this number. All you had to do was to move the cursor to any of the numbers and double-click, and the digitally recorded conversation would start playing, either on the headphones or through the external speakers. Little red bars would dance as the volume fluctuated. You could adjust not only the volume but even the speed of playback.

Every telephone call the woman had made from her hotel room was recorded onto this computer's hard disk. The technology was most impressive; it had been provided to the Vienna police by the Israelis.

The door to the little room opened and in came Detective Sergeant Walter Heisler across the institutional green linoleum floor. He, too, was smoking. He gave a little jerk of his head by way of greeting. The tech removed his headphones, put out his cigarette, looked up.

"Anything interesting?" the detective asked.

"Most of the calls have been to Washington."

"Strictly speaking, we're supposed to inform Interpol when we record any international calls." There was a twinkle in the detective's eye.

The tech raised his eyebrows in silent complicity. Heisler pulled up a chair. "Mind if I join you?"

California

The young billionaire computer mogul Arnold Carr took the call on his cellular phone while he was strolling through a redwood forest in Northern California with his old friend and mentor the investment whiz Ross Cameron.

The two were spending a weekend in the company of some of America's richest and most powerful men at the exclusive retreat known as the Bohemian Grove. There was some sort of idiotic game called paintball going on back at the encampment, presided over by the chief executive of BankAmerica and the U.S. ambassador to the Court of St. James.

But Carr, the founder of a vastly successful software company, rarely had the chance to hang out with his billionaire buddy Ross Cameron, the so-called sage of Sante Fe. So they had spent a lot of time hiking through the woods talking about money and business, philanthropy and art collecting, their kids, and the extraordinary, highly secret project they had both been invited to join.

Carr pulled the tiny, burring phone out of the pocket of his Pendleton plaid shirt with visible annoyance. Hardly anyone had this number, and the few employees who'd dare call had been instructed not to bother him for any reason during his retreat weekend.

"Yeah," Carr said.

"Mr. Carr, I'm so sorry to bother you on a Sunday morning," the voice purred. "This is Mr. Holland. I hope I didn't wake you."

Carr recognized the voice instantly. "Oh, no way," he said, suddenly cordial. "I've been up for hours. What's up?"

When "Mr. Holland" had finished, Carr said, "Let me see what I can do."

CHAPTER TWENTY-SEVEN

Ben arrived at his hotel around nine o'clock at night, hungry but unable to eat, jittery from too much caffeine. He'd taken a cab from police headquarters, since driving the Opel Vectra was out of the question. Two of its windows had been shattered in the shootout, the leather seats covered with rounded shards of glass.

The lobby was quiet, the hotel guests either out at dinner or returned to their rooms. Several Oriental rugs overlapped one another; here and there patches of highly polished marble floor gleamed.

The concierge, a too-slick middle-aged man with alert eyes behind steel-rimmed glasses, handed him the room key before Ben said a word.

"Thanks," Ben said. "Any messages for me?" Perhaps the private detective.

The concierge tapped at his computer keyboard. "No, sir, just the one you already retrieved."

"Which one was that?" *What?* he thought, alarmed. *I haven't gotten a single message since I got to Vienna.*

"I don't know, sir. You called in a few hours ago." More

tapping. "At six-twenty this evening you got a message from the hotel operator."

"Could you give it to me again?" This was either a mistake or . . .

"I'm sorry, sir, once the guest retrieves a message, it's deleted from the system." He gave Ben a feral smile. "We can't keep all messages forever, you know."

Ben took the small brass-cage elevator to the fourth floor, nervously fingering the large brass sphere that dangled from the room key. He couldn't put it past Agent Navarro to have had some male colleague call the hotel to get his messages, see whom he was in touch with.

But who had left a message? Besides Agent Navarro, only the private detective knew his whereabouts. It was surely too late to call the detective, Hans Hoffman; he wouldn't be in his office this late at night.

Navarro was suspicious about his motives, yet she couldn't seriously think he had killed Rossignol. Could she? She had to know she wasn't dealing with a serial murderer. After all, she'd mentioned she had expertise in homicide; she had to know who fit the profile and who didn't.

So what was she really after?

Was it possible she was actually working for the CIA or some gray-haired contingent thereof, mopping up, helping cover up their involvement by shifting suspicion to him?

And the fact remained: Gaston Rossignol, a founder of this mysterious corporation that might or might not have had CIA involvement, had just been murdered. As had Peter, whose single error, it seemed, was to have dug up a list of directors of this very same corporation. Had the same people killed both of them? It certainly seemed likely.

But American killers? CIA?

It was difficult to fathom. Jimmy Cavanaugh was an American . . . Yet couldn't he have been working for foreigners?

And then there was Max's baffling disappearance.

Why had he vanished? Godwin had shed no light on that

mystery. Why had Max called Godwin just before leaving?

Was his father dead now, too?

It was time to place another call to Bedford.

He walked down the long corridor, struggled with the room key for a moment, and then the door came open. He froze.

The lights were off.

Yet he had left all the lights in the room on when he'd left. Had someone turned them off?

Oh, come on, he told himself. Surely the chambermaid had turned them off. The Austrians prided themselves on being environmentally conscientious.

Was he overthinking this? Was he being ridiculously paranoid? Was this what the last few days had done to him?

Still . . .

Quietly, without entering, he closed the door, turned the key to lock it again, and went back down the hall in search of a porter or bell captain. None was anywhere to be seen. He circled back and took the stairs down to the third floor. There, at the end of another long hall, he spotted a porter coming out of a room.

"Excuse me," Ben said, accelerating his stride. "Can you help me?"

The young porter turned. "Sir?"

"Listen," Ben said, "I locked myself out of my room. Can you let me in?" He palmed the porter a fifty-shilling note, about eight dollars, and added sheepishly, "This is the second time I've done it. I don't want to have to go back to the concierge. It's up one flight. Four-sixteen."

"Oh yes, certainly, sir. Ah, moment please." He searched through a ring of keys on his belt. "Yes, sir, please."

They took the elevator up to the fourth floor. The porter opened the door to 416. Feeling a little foolish, Ben stood behind him and off to one side, so that he could see into the room at an oblique angle, without being seen.

He noticed a shape, a silhouette! The figure of a man outlined against backlight from the open bathroom door.

The man was crouching down, pointing a long-barreled gun toward the door!

The man turned, and his face became visible. It was the assassin who'd tried to kill him a few hours ago in front of Jürgen Lenz's villa! The assassin in the Swiss auberge.

The man who killed his brother.

The porter screamed, "No!" and ran away down the hall.

For a moment the killer was confused—he'd expected Ben, not a uniformed hotel employee. The hesitation was long enough for Ben to take off. Behind him came a series of muted spits, then the much louder explosions of bullets pocking the walls. The porter's screams became even louder, more frantic, and the gunfire came closer, and then came the racing footsteps of the gunman, and Ben put on a burst of speed. Straight ahead was the door to the stairway, and he quickly rejected it—he didn't want to be a prisoner in a stairwell with an armed killer after him. Instead he whipped around the corridor to the right, saw an open room door, a housekeeping cart in front of it, and he leaped into the room, swinging the door shut behind him. His back pressed against the door, he gasped for breath, wondering whether the killer had seen him enter the room. He heard muffled footsteps racing by: the killer had passed. He heard the porter shout, calling someone; he didn't sound as if he'd been wounded, which was a relief.

A cry from inside the room! He saw a small, dark-skinned maid in a light blue uniform cowering in the corner of the room.

"Quiet!" Ben hissed.

"Who are you?" the maid gasped, terrified. She spoke in heavily accented English. "Please don't hurt me!"

"Quiet," Ben repeated. "Get down. If you keep quiet, you won't get hurt!"

The maid flattened herself against the carpeting, whimpering in abject terror.

"Matches!" Ben said. "I need matches!"

"The ashtray! Please—the desk, next to the television!"

Ben found them and located the smoke/heat detector

mounted on the ceiling above him. He stood on a chair, lit a match, held it to the coil. In a few seconds he could hear the Klaxon of a fire alarm sounding in the room and in the corridor outside—a rasping metallic shriek caterwauling at regular, rapid intervals. The sound was everywhere! Shouts and screams came from the hall as hotel guests ran from their rooms. In another few seconds, water began spraying from the sprinkler system in the ceiling, drenching the carpet and bed. The maid screamed again as Ben turned and opened the door, quickly looking out in either direction. The hall was chaos: people running about, some huddled in bafflement, gesturing this way and that, yelling to one another as water spewed from the sprinklers all along the ceiling the length of the corridor. Ben ran out of the room, joining the frenzied crowd in a rush to the stairwell. He knew, from the height of the main staircase that led into the hotel's front entrance, that the stairwell had to have its own exit onto the street or back alley.

The stairwell door opened onto a dark corridor, illuminated only by a flickering, buzzing fluorescent ceiling fixture, but it was enough light to make out the double doors of the hotel kitchen. He raced toward it, pushed the doors open without stopping, and saw the inevitable service entrance. He reached the door, felt the flow of cold air from the outside, slid open the heavy steel bolt, and pulled the massive door open. A ramp led down into a narrow alley crowded with trashcans. He propelled himself down, and, with fire engine sirens sounding in the distance, disappeared into the dark alley.

Twenty minutes later he came to the tall modern building overlooking the Danube canal, on the far side of the Stadtpark, a characterless American hotel that was part of an international chain. He strode purposefully through the lobby to the elevators, a hotel guest who obviously belonged.

He knocked on the door of Room 1423.

Special Agent Anna Navarro cracked open the door. She

was in a flannel nightgown, her makeup was off, and yet she was luminous.

"I think I'm ready to cooperate," Ben said.

Anna Navarro fixed Hartman a drink from the honor bar: a toy bottle of Scotch, a little green bottle of mineral water, a few miniature cubes of ice from the tiny freezer. She was, if possible, even more businesslike than she'd been at the police station. Over her flannel nightgown she'd cinched a white terry-cloth robe. Probably it didn't help, Ben reflected, having a strange man in the close quarters of her hotel room when she was dressed for bed.

Ben took the drink gratefully. It was watery. She was not a drinker. But shaken as he was, he needed a drink badly, and it did the job.

Despite the sofa on which he sat, the room was not set up for visitors. She started to sit facing him, on the edge of the bed, then rejected it in favor of a big wing chair, which she pulled out at an angle to the sofa.

The plate-glass window was a black pointillist canvas. From up here, Vienna was neon-lit, its lights twinkling under the starry sky.

Navarro leaned forward, crossed her legs. She was barefoot, her feet slender and high-arched, delicate, the toenails painted.

"It was the same guy, you think?" Her abrasive edge was gone.

Ben took another sip. "Definitely. I'll never forget his face."

She sighed. "And I thought at least I'd seriously wounded him. From everything I've heard, this guy's incredibly dangerous. And what he did to those four policemen—astonishing. Like an execution machine. You were lucky. Or maybe I should say you were smart—sensing something wasn't right, using the porter to confuse him, putting our friend off balance, buying yourself time to escape. Well done."

He shrugged in self-deprecation, secretly pleased by the unexpected compliment. "You know something about this guy?"

"I've read a dossier, but it's incomplete. He's believed to live in England, probably London."

"He's British?"

"Formerly East German intelligence—Stasi. Their field agents were among the most highly trained. Certainly some of the most ruthless. Seems to have left the organization a long time ago."

"What's he doing living in England?"

"Who knows? Maybe avoiding the German authorities, like most of his ex-colleagues. What we don't know is whether he's an assassin for hire, or whether he's in the employ of some organization with diverse interests."

"His name?"

"Vogler, I think. Hans Vogler. Obviously here on some sort of job."

Some sort of job. *I am next.* Ben felt numb.

"You said he might be in some organization's employ."

"That's what we say when we haven't figured out the pattern yet." She pursed her lips. "You might be in some organization's employ, and I don't mean Hartman Capital Management."

"You still don't believe me, do you?"

"Well, who are you? What are you really up to?"

"Oh, come on," he said heatedly. "Don't tell me you guys don't have a goddamned file on me!"

She glared. "All I know about you are isolated facts without a logical explanation tying them all together. You say you were in Zurich when suddenly someone from your past pops up and tries to kill you and instead gets killed himself. And then his body disappears. Next thing I know, you've entered Switzerland illegally. Then your fingerprints turn up all over the house of a banker named Rossignol, who you claim was dead when you got there. You carry a gun, though where you got it—and why—you won't say."

Ben listened in silence, letting her go on.

"Why were you meeting with this Lenz, this son of a famous Nazi?"

Ben blinked, unsure how much to divulge. But before he could formulate a reply, she spoke again. "Here's what I want to know. What does Lenz have in common with Rossignol?"

Ben drained his Scotch. "My brother . . ." he began.

"The one who died four years ago."

"So I thought. He turned out to be hiding from some dangerous people. He didn't know who they were, exactly; I still don't know. Some conclave of industrialists, or their descendants, or maybe CIA hirelings, maybe something else entirely—who knows? But apparently he'd uncovered a list of names—"

Agent Navarro's caramel eyes grew wide. "What kind of list?"

"A very old one."

Her face flushed. "Where did he get this list?"

"He came across it in the archives of a Swiss bank."

"A Swiss bank?"

"It's a list of board members of a corporation that was founded in the last days of the Second World War."

"Jesus Christ," she breathed. "So that's it."

Ben drew a folded, grimy square of paper from his breast pocket and handed it to her. "Sorry, it's a bit soiled. I've been keeping it in my shoe. To keep it out of the hands of people like you."

She perused it, frowning. "Max Hartman. Your father?"

"Alas."

"Did he tell you about this corporation?"

"No way. My brother came across it."

"But wasn't your father a Holocaust survivor—?"

"And now we come to the sixty-four-thousand-dollar question."

"Wasn't there some physical mark—a tattoo or something?"

"A tattoo? At Auschwitz, yes. At Dachau, no."

She didn't seem to be listening. "My God," she said.

"The string of mysterious homicides—every single name is here." She seemed to be speaking to herself, not to him. "Rossignol . . . Prosperi . . . Ramago . . . they're all here. No, they're not all on my list. Some overlap, but . . ." She looked up. "What did you hope to learn from Rossignol?"

What was she getting at? "I thought he might know why my brother was killed, and who did it."

"But he was himself killed before you got to him."

"So it seems."

"Did you look into this Sigma company, try to locate it, trace its history?"

Ben nodded. "But I turned up nothing. Then again, maybe it never existed, if you know what I mean." Seeing her frown, he went on. "A notional entity, like a shell company."

"What kind of shell company?"

Ben shook his head. "I don't know. Something involving American military intelligence, maybe." He told her of Lenz's worries.

"I don't think I buy it."

"Why not?"

"I work for the government, don't forget. The bureaucracy leaks like a sieve. They'd never be able to coordinate a series of murders without the world finding out."

"Then what do you figure the link is? Apart from the obvious, I mean."

"I'm not sure how much I can tell you."

"Look," Ben said fiercely, "if we're going to share information—if we're going to help each other—you can't hold back. You have to trust me."

She nodded, then seemed to come to a decision. "For one thing, they aren't, or weren't, janitors, believe me, none of them. They all had great, visible wealth, or most of them, anyway. The only one who lived modestly, at least that I saw, still had tons of money in the bank." She told him about her investigation in general terms.

"You said one of them worked for Charles Highsmith, right? So it's as if you've got your titans here, and then the

guys who work for them, their trusted lieutenants and what-
not. And back in 1945 or so, Allen Dulles is running clearances on them, because they're all playing together, and
Dulles doesn't like to be surprised by his playmates."

"Which still leaves the larger question unanswered.
What's the game? Why was Sigma formed in the first
place? For what?"

"Maybe the explanation is simple," Ben said. "Bunch of
moguls got together in 1944, '45, to siphon off a huge
amount of money from the Third Reich. They divided up
the spoils and got even richer. The way guys like that think,
they probably told themselves they were reclaiming what
was properly theirs."

She seemed perplexed. "O.K., but here's what doesn't
fit. You've got people who, right up until their deaths just
days ago, were receiving regular, large payments. Wire
transfers into their bank accounts, in amounts ranging from
a quarter-million to a half-million bucks."

"Wired from where?"

"Laundered. We don't know where the money originated; we only know the very last links in the chains—
places like the Cayman Islands, Turks and Caicos."

"Haven countries," Ben said.

"Exactly. Beyond that, it's impossible to get any information."

"Not necessarily," Ben said. "Depends on who you
know. And whether you're willing to bend the law a little.
Grease some palms."

"We don't bend the law." Agent Navarro said this with
an almost haughty pride.

"That's why you don't know shit about where the money
came from."

She looked startled, as if he'd slapped her face. Then
she laughed. "What do you know about laundering
money?"

"I don't do it myself, if that's what you're thinking, but
my company does have an offshore division that manages
funds—to avoid taxes, government regulations, all that

good stuff. Also, I've had clients who are very good at hiding their assets from people like you. I know people who can get information out of offshore banks. They specialize in it. Charge a fortune. They can dig up financial information anywhere in the world, all through their personal contacts, knowing who to pay off."

After a few seconds, she said, "How would you feel about working with me on this? Informally, of course."

Surprised, Ben asked, "What does that mean, exactly?"

"Share information. We have an overlap of motivations. You want to know who killed your brother and why. I want to know who's been killing the old men."

Is she on the level? he wondered. Was this some kind of trick? What did she really want?

"You think the murderers are one and the same? My brother and these men on that list of yours?"

"I'm convinced of it now. All part of the same pattern, the same mosaic."

"What's in it for me?" He looked at her boldly but softened it with a grin.

"Nothing official, let me tell you that right up front. Maybe a little protection. Put it this way—they've already tried to kill you more than once. How long is your luck going to hold?"

"And if I stick close to you, I'm safe?"

"Safer, maybe. You got a better idea? You did come to my hotel, after all. Anyway, the cops took your gun, right?"

True. "I'm sure you understand my reluctance—after all, until very recently you wanted me in prison."

"Look, feel free to go back to your hotel. Have a good night's sleep."

"Point taken. You're making a generous offer. Maybe one I'd be foolish to turn down. I—I don't know."

"Well, sleep on it."

"Speaking of sleep—"

Her eyes searched the room. "I—"

"I'll call down to the front desk and get myself a room."

"I doubt you'll get one. There's some conference here,

and they're booked to capacity. I got one of the last rooms available. Why don't you sleep on the couch?"

He gave her a quick look. Did the uptight Special Agent Navarro just invite him to spend the night in her room? No. He was deluding himself. Her body language, the unspoken signals, made it clear: she'd invited him here to hide out, not to slip into her bed.

"Thanks," he said.

"Just one thing: the couch is a little small, maybe a bit too short."

"I've slept on worse, believe me."

She got up, went to a closet, and found a blanket, handed it to him. "I can ask room service to bring up a toothbrush. In the morning we're going to have to retrieve your clothes, your luggage, from your hotel."

"I don't plan to go back."

"Definitely not a good idea. I'll make arrangements." She seemed to realize that she was standing a little too close, and she took a step backward, the gesture awkward. "Well, I'm going to turn in," she said.

He thought of something suddenly, an idea that had been teasing at the back of his mind since leaving Lenz's villa. "The old Nazi hunter Jakob Sonnenfeld lives in this town, doesn't he?"

She turned toward him. "That sounds right."

"I read somewhere recently he may be ancient but he's as sharp as ever. Plus, he's supposed to have extensive files. I wonder . . ."

"You think he'll see you?"

"I think it's worth a try."

"Well, be careful if you do go. Take some security precautions. Don't let anyone follow you there. For his sake."

"Hey, I'll take any advice on that you want to give me."

While she got ready for bed, he called Bedford on his digital phone.

Mrs. Walsh answered. She sounded agitated. "No, Benjamin, I haven't heard a word. Not a word! He seems to have vanished without a trace. I've—well, I've brought the police in on this. I'm at my wits' end!"

Ben felt a dull headache starting: the tension, which for a while had abated, had returned. Rattled, he mumbled a few empty words of reassurance, disconnected the call, took off his jacket, and hung it on the back of the desk chair. Then, still dressed in his slacks and shirt, he settled onto the sofa and pulled the blanket over him.

What did this mean, his father's disappearing without leaving a word? He had voluntarily gotten into a limousine; it wasn't a kidnapping. Presumably he knew where he was going.

Which was where?

He struggled to get comfortable on the couch, but Navarro was right, it was just an inch or two too short for comfort. He saw her sitting up in bed reading a file by the light of the bed lamp. Her soft brown eyes were caught by the pool of light.

"Was that about your father?" she asked. "I'm sorry, I know I shouldn't have been eavesdropping, but—"

"It's O.K. Yeah, my father vanished a few days ago. Got in a limousine to the airport and was never heard from again."

She put down the file, sat up straight. "That's a possible kidnapping. Which makes it federal business."

He swallowed, his mouth dry. Could he really have been abducted?

"Tell me what you know," she said.

The phone jangled some hours later, awakening them both.

Anna picked it up. "Yes?"

"Anna Navarro?"

"Yes, who's this?"

"Anna, I'm Phil Ostrow, from the American embassy here. I hope I'm not calling you too late." A flat Midwestern American accent with Chicagoan vowels.

"I had to get up to answer the phone anyway," she said

dryly. "What can I do for you?" What State Department hack called at midnight?

"I—well, Jack Hampton suggested I call." He paused significantly.

Hampton was an operations manager for the CIA, and someone who had done Anna more than one assist on a previous assignment. A good man, as straightforward as you could be in an oblique business. She recalled Bartlett's words about the "crooked timber of humanity." But Hampton wasn't built that way.

"I have some information about the case you're working."

"What's your—Who are you, if you don't mind my asking?"

"I'd rather not get into all that over the phone. I'm a colleague of Jack's."

She knew what that meant: CIA. Hence the Hampton connection. "What's your information, or would you rather not get into that either?"

"Let's just say it's important. Can you come by the office tomorrow morning, first thing? Seven too early for you?" What could it be that was so urgent? she wondered.

"You guys do start early, don't you? Yeah, I guess I can."

"All right—tomorrow morning, then. You been to the office before?"

"Embassy?"

"Across the street from the consular section."

He gave her directions. She hung up, puzzled. From across the room Ben said, "Everything O.K.?"

"Yeah," she said unconvincingly. "Everything's fine."

"We can't stay here, you know."

"Correct. Tomorrow we should both move."

"You seem worried, Agent Navarro."

"I'm always worried," she said. "I live my life worried. And call me Anna."

"I never used to worry much," he said. "Good night, Anna."

CHAPTER TWENTY-EIGHT

It was the sound of a blow-dryer that awakened Ben; after a few groggy moments, he realized that he was in a hotel room in Vienna, and that his back ached from a night on the couch.

He craned his neck forward, heard the satisfying crack of vertebrae, felt some welcome relief from the stiffness.

The bathroom door opened and light flooded half the room. Anna Navarro was dressed in a tweedy brown suit, a little dowdy but not unbecoming, and her face was made up.

"I'll be back in an hour or so," she said crisply. "Go back to sleep."

Directly across the street from the consular section of the U.S. embassy, just as Ostrow had described, was a drab modern office building. The placard in the lobby listed a number of U.S. and Austrian business offices, and on the eleventh floor, sure enough, the Office of the United States Trade Representative—the cover for the Vienna office of the CIA. Such feelers from agencies she was investigating were far from unusual; they'd sometimes resulted in her best leads.

Anna entered an unremarkable reception area, where a young woman sat at a government-issue desk, beneath the Great Seal of the United States, answering the phone and typing at a computer keyboard. She didn't look up. Anna introduced herself, and the receptionist pressed a button and announced her.

In less than a minute a man with the pallor of a bureau-cratic lifer bustled out. His cheeks were acne-scarred and sunken, his hair graying auburn. His eyes were small and gray behind large wire-rimmed glasses.

"Miss Navarro?" he said, thrusting out a hand. "I'm Phil Ostrow."

The receptionist buzzed them through the door from which he had appeared, and Ostrow guided her to a small conference room where a slender, darkly handsome man was sitting at a fake-wood-grain Formica-topped table. He had bristling, brush cut black hair salted with gray, brown eyes, long black lashes. Late thirties, maybe, Middle East-ern. Ostrow and Anna sat on either side of him.

"Yossi, this is Anna Navarro. Anna, Yossi."

Yossi's face was tanned, the lines around his eyes deeply etched, whether from squinting in the sun or from a life of great stress. His chin was square and cleft. There was some-thing almost pretty about his face, though it was masculin-ized by his weathered skin and a day-old growth of beard.

"Good to meet you, Yossi," she said.

She nodded warily, unsmiling; he did the same. He did not offer his hand.

"Yossi's a case officer—you don't mind my telling her that much, do you, Yossi?" said Ostrow. "He works under deep commercial cover here in Vienna. A good setup. He emigrated to the States from Israel when he was in his late teens. Now everyone assumes he's an Israeli—which means every time he gets into trouble, someone else gets the blame." Ostrow chuckled.

"Ostrow, enough—no more," Yossi said. He spoke in a gruff baritone, his English accented with guttural Hebrew R's. "Now, we should understand each other: a number of men all around the world have been found dead in the last few weeks. You are investigating these deaths. You know these are murders, but you do not know who is behind them."

Anna gazed at him dully.

"You interrogated Benjamin Hartman at the *Sicherheitsbüro*. And you've been in close contact with him since. Yes?"

"Where are you going with this?"

Ostrow spoke. "We're making an official interagency request that you remand Hartman to our custody."

"What the hell . . . ?"

"You're over your head here, Officer." Ostrow returned her gaze levelly.

"I'm not following you."

"Hartman's a security risk. A two-woman man, O.K.?"

Anna recognized the agency slang—it referred to double agents, American assets who had been recruited by hostile parties. "I don't understand. Are you saying that Hartman's one of yours?" That was madness. Or was it? It would explain how he was able to travel through European countries without alerting passport control, among other things that had puzzled her. And wouldn't his cover as an international financier lend itself to all sorts of agency work? The named scion of a well-known financial outfit—no concocted legend could ever be as versatile and as persuasive.

Yossi and Ostrow exchanged glances. "Not one of ours, exactly."

"No? Then whose?"

"Our theory is that he's been on retainer from someone in our outfit who's been freelancing, let's say. We could be talking false-flag recruitment."

"You bring me here and talk to me about theories?"

"We need him back on American soil. Please, Agent

Navarro. You really don't know who you're dealing with here."

"I'm dealing with someone who's confused about a number of things. And who's still in shock from the death of his twin brother—killed, he believes."

"We know all about it. Hasn't it occurred to you that he may have killed him, too?"

"You're joking." The imputation was incredible, and terrible; could it be true?

"What do you really know about Benjamin Hartman?" Ostrow demanded testily. "I'll ask another question. What do you know about how your list of targets started to make the rounds? Information doesn't want to be free, Agent Navarro. Information wants to command top dollar, and someone like Benjamin Hartman has the wherewithal to pay it."

Grease some palms: Hartman's words.

"But why? What's his agenda?"

"We're never going to find out so long as he's cavorting around Europe, are we?" Ostrow paused. "Yossi hears things from his former compatriots. Mossad has caseworkers in this town, too. There's a possible connection with your victims."

"A splinter group?" she asked. "Or are you talking about the Kidon?" She meant the assassination unit of Mossad.

"No. It is nothing official. It is private business."

"Involving Mossad agents?"

"And some freelancers they hire."

"But these murders aren't Mossad signature killings."

"Please," Yossi said, his face creasing with distaste. "Don't be naïve. You think my brethren all the time are leaving their business cards? When they want to be credited, sure. Come on!"

"So then they don't want to be credited."

"Of course not. Is too sensitive. Potentially can be explosive in the current climate. Israel doesn't want to be connected."

"So who are they working for?"

Yossi glanced at Ostrow, then back at Anna. He shrugged.

"Not for Mossad, is that what you're saying?"

"For Mossad to order assassinations, this is very formalized thing. There is whole internal system, 'execution list,' that the Prime Minister must sign off on. He must initial each name on the list, or it must not be carried out. People in Mossad and Shin Bet have been forced out for ordering killings without approval from top. That is why I tell you this is not authorized sanctions."

"So I ask you again: Who are they working for?"

Again Yossi looked at Ostrow, but this time his glance seemed to be a prompt, a nudge.

"You didn't hear this from me," Ostrow said.

She felt gooseflesh. Thunderstruck, she whispered, "You're kidding me."

"See, the Agency would never dirty its own hands," Ostrow said. "Not anymore. In the good old days, we wouldn't hesitate to rub out some tin-pot dictator if he looked at us the wrong way. Now we got presidential directives and congressional oversight committees and CIA directors whose balls have been lopped off. Christ, we're afraid to give a foreign citizen a head cold."

There was a knock on the door. A young man stuck his head in. "Langley on three, Phil," he said.

"Tell 'em I didn't get in yet." The door closed, and Ostrow rolled his eyes.

"Let me get this straight," Anna said, addressing Ostrow. "You guys passed intelligence on to some Mossad freelancers?"

"Someone did. That's all I know. The rumor is that Ben Hartman served as a go-between."

"You got hard evidence?"

"Yossi's come up with some suggestive details," Ostrow said quietly. "He described enough of the 'watermarks,' the 'sanitation' procedures, the interoffice markings, to tell me this came directly from CIA. I'm talking about shit that can't be made up, marks and glyphs that are rotated daily."

Anna could put two and two together: Yossi himself had to have been an American penetration agent, a deep-cover asset, spying on Mossad for the CIA. She considered asking about it directly, but decided it would be a breach of professional etiquette. "Who at Langley?" she asked.

"I told you, I don't know."

"You don't know, or you won't tell me?"

Yossi, a spectator at a bullfight, smiled for the first time. His smile was dazzling.

"You don't know me," Ostrow said, "but anyone who does knows I'm an avid enough bureaucratic gameplayer to want to screw someone there I don't like. If I had the name, I'd hand it to you just to burn the guy."

That she believed: that would be the natural response of an Agency infighter. But she was determined not to let him see that she was persuaded. "What's the motivation here? Are you talking about fanatics in the CIA?"

He shook his head. "I'm afraid I don't know anyone there who has strong feelings about anything except vacation policy."

"Then why? What possible motivation?"

"My guess? Let me tell you something." Ostrow took off his glasses, cleaned the lenses on his shirt. "You've got a list of crooks and capitalists, small fry working for big fry. When it comes to CIA and the Nazis, right after the war, that's where some serious skeletons are buried. My theory? Someone highly placed, and I do mean highly placed, saw that some names from a long time ago were about to get out."

"What does that mean?"

He put the glasses back on. "Names of old guys we used, paid off. Guys who'd mostly disappeared into the mists of history, O.K.? Suddenly a list comes out, and guess what? The names of some of the old-timers in the Agency who aided and abetted this shit are gonna come out, too. Maybe some financial shenanigans, some double-dipping into the old well. The old geezers sure as hell are gonna squeal like pigs, rat out their handlers. So who're you gonna call? Who else but some fanatical Israelis. Neat and clean. Talk about ghosts left over from the Second World War, do some hand-waving about inexplicable vengeance killings, save Old Boy asses—everybody's happy."

Yeah, she thought grimly. Everybody's happy.

"Listen to me. There's a convergence of interests here. You're trying to figure out a string of homicides. We're trying to figure out a string of security breaches. But we can't chase this thing down without Ben Hartman. I'm not going to dump a load of supposition on you. There's a good chance that he's being hunted by the same people he works for. Mop-ups never end—that's the problem with them."

Mopping up: Was that what she herself was doing?

Ostrow seemed to respond to the hesitant look on her face. "We just need to know what's true and what isn't."

"You've got paperwork?" Anna asked.

Ostrow tapped a stapled document with a blunt finger. A capitalized section heading stood out: CUSTODIAL CONVEYANCE OF AN AMERICAN CITIZEN. "Yes, I've got the paperwork. Now all I need's the body. Jack Hampton said you'd understand about these things."

"What do you have in mind for the delivery?"

"Look, there are delicate issues of extraterritoriality here . . ."

"Meaning you don't want me to bring him here."

"You got that right. We will make house calls, though. You can cuff him, give us the signal, and we'll show up with bells on. If you want to keep your hands completely clean, that's fine, too. Give us a time and location, preferably someplace semi-secluded, and . . ."

"And we'll handle the rest." Yossi was somber once more.

"Christ, you guys really are cowboys, aren't you?" Anna said.

"Cowboys who ride Aeron chairs, for the most part," Ostrow replied wryly. "But, sure, we can still manage an exfiltration when we have to. Nobody gets hurt. It's a clean snatch-and-grab—surgical."

"Surgery hurts."

"Don't overthink it. It's the right thing to do. And it means we all get our jobs done."

"I'll take it under advisement," Anna said, grimacing.

"Then take this under advisement, too." Ostrow took out a sheet of paper with departure times of nonstop flights from Vienna to Dulles International Airport in Washington, and to Kennedy Airport in New York. "Time is of the essence."

In a dark second-floor office on Wallnerstrasse, the portly *Berufsdetektiv* Hans Hoffman slammed down the telephone and cursed aloud. It was ten in the morning and he had already called the American four times at his hotel, with no luck. The message he'd left the night before had gone unanswered, too. The hotel had no other telephone number for Hartman and would not divulge whether or not he'd even spent the night at the hotel.

The private investigator needed to reach Hartman at once.

It was urgent. He had steered the American wrong, given him a dangerous lead, and whatever else people might say about Hans Hoffman, no one denied that he was a scrupulous man. It was vitally important that he reach Hartman before he went to see Jürgen Lenz.

For what the detective had discovered late yesterday afternoon was nothing less than sensational. The routine inquiries he had put out concerning Jürgen Lenz had come back with the most unexpected, the most astonishing answers.

Hoffman knew that Dr. Lenz no longer practiced medicine, but he wanted to know why. To that end he had requested a copy of Lenz's medical license from the *Arztekammer*, the archives where the licenses of all doctors in Austria are kept.

There was no medical license for a Jürgen Lenz.

There had never been one.

Hoffman had wondered: How can this possibly be? Was Lenz lying? Had he never practiced medicine?

Lenz's official biography, freely handed out at the Lenz Foundation offices, had him graduating from medical school at Innsbruck, so Hoffman checked there.

Jürgen Lenz had never gone to medical school at Innsbruck.

Driven now by an insatiable curiosity, Hoffman had gone to the Universität Wien, where the records of medical licensing examinations for all physicians in Austria are kept.

Nothing.

Hans Hoffman had furnished his client with the name and address of a man whose biography was faked. Something was very, very wrong.

Hoffman had pored over his notes, stored in his laptop computer, trying to make sense of it, attempting to assemble the facts in some other way.

Now he stared at the screen again, scrolling down the list of records he had checked, trying to think of some omission that might explain this strange situation.

A loud flat buzz jolted him. Someone was calling up to his office from the street. He got up and went over to the intercom mounted on the wall.

"Yes?"

"I'm looking for Mr. Hoffman."

"Yes?"

"My name is Leitner. I don't have an appointment, but I have some important business to discuss."

"What sort of business?" Hoffman asked. Not a salesman, he hoped.

"Some confidential work. I need his help."

"Come on up. Second floor." Hoffman pressed the button that electronically unlocked the building's front door.

He saved the Lenz file, shut off his laptop, and opened his office door.

A man in a black leather jacket, with steel-gray hair, a

goatee, and a stud earring in his left ear, said, "Mr. Hoffman?"

"Yes?" Hoffman sized him up, as he did all potential clients, attempting to assess how much money the fellow might have to spend. The man's face was smooth, unlined, almost tight around his high cheekbones. Despite the steel-gray hair, he was probably no older than forty. Physically an impressive specimen, but the features were unremarkable, undistinguishable, except for the dead gray eyes. A serious man.

"Come on in," Hoffman said cordially. "Tell me, what can I do for you?"

It was only nine in the morning when Anna returned to the hotel.

As she inserted the electronic key-card into the slot above the doorknob, she could hear the sound of water running. She entered swiftly, hanging up her coat in the closet by the door, and made her way into the bedroom. An important decision lay ahead of her: she would have to rely upon her intuitions, she knew.

Presently, there was the sound of the shower being turned off, and Ben appeared in the doorway of the bathroom, evidently unaware that she had returned.

He was still dripping water, a towel draped loosely around his midriff. His body was chiseled, heavily muscled in a way that once suggested manual labor and now, she knew, suggested privilege—a personal trainer, an active sports life. With a clinical eye, she surveyed the evidence of his physical regimen—the washboard stomach, the pectorals like twin shields, the swelling biceps. Water beaded on his tan skin. He'd removed the dressing from his shoulder, where a small, angry red patch was visible.

"You're back," he said, finally taking in her presence. "What's new?"

"Here, let me take a look at the shoulder," she said, and he walked toward her. Was her interest in him purely professional? Something in the pit of her stomach made her wonder.

"It's pretty much healed," she pronounced. She ran a finger around the perimeter of the reddened area. "You don't really need the dressing anymore. A thin layer of Bacitracin, maybe. I've got a first-aid kit in my luggage."

She went to retrieve it. When she returned, he was wearing boxer shorts, and had toweled himself off, but was still shirtless.

"Yesterday you were saying something about the CIA," she said as she fumbled with the tube of ointment.

"Maybe I'm wrong about them, I don't know anymore," he said. "Lenz had his suspicions. But I can't really bring myself to believe it."

Could he be lying? Had he been deceiving her last night? It seemed incredible. It defied every instinct, every intuition she possessed. She could detect no bravado, no tension in his voice—none of the usual signals of deception.

As she rubbed the antiseptic ointment on his shoulder, their faces were close. She smelled the soap, and the green-apple fragrance of the hotel shampoo, and something more, something faintly loamy, which was the man himself. She inhaled quietly, deeply. And then, abruptly beset by a storm of emotions, she moved away.

Was her radar, her assessment of his honesty, being distorted by other feelings? That wasn't something she could afford in her position, especially under the current circumstances.

On the other hand, what if the CIA officers had been misinformed? Who were their sources, anyway? A caseworker was only as good as his assets. She knew as well as anyone how fallible the system could be. And if there were CIA involvement, would it be safe to remand him to that agency? There was too much uncertainty in her world: she had to trust her instincts, or she was lost.

Now she dialed Walter Heisler. "I need to ask you a favor," she said. "I called Hartman's hotel. He seems to have left without checking out. There was some sort of shootout. Evidently he's left his luggage there. I want to go through it, really take my time with it."

"Well, you know, that's actually our property, once an investigation is started."

"Have you started one?"

"No, not yet, but—"

"Then could you please do me a huge favor and have the luggage shipped over to me, at my hotel?"

"Well, I suppose this can be arranged," Heisler said sullenly. "Though it is . . . rather unorthodox."

"Thanks, Walter," she said warmly, and hung up.

Ben wandered over to her, still wearing nothing but boxer shorts. "Now, that's what I call full service," he said, grinning.

She tossed him an undershirt. "It's a little chilly outside," she said, her throat dry.

Ben Hartman walked out of the hotel, glancing around nervously. Showered and shaved, even though he was wearing the same now-rumpled clothes he'd slept in, he felt decently crisp. He took in the broad, heavily trafficked avenue and beyond, the green of the Stadtpark, feeling exposed, vulnerable, then he turned right and headed toward the first district.

He had spent the last half hour making telephone calls, one after another. First he had awakened a contact, a friend of a friend, in the Cayman Islands, who operated a two-man "investigative" service that supposedly did background checks for multinational corporations on potential hires. In reality, the firm was most often engaged by wealthy individuals or multinationals who once in a while had a reason to penetrate the secrecy of the banks down there.

O'Connor Security Investigations was the highly secretive enterprise of an Irish expatriate and former constabulary officer named Fergus O'Connor, who had first come to the Caymans as a security guard for a British bank there and stayed. He'd become a security officer, then chief of security. When he realized that his web of contacts and his expertise were marketable—he knew all the other chiefs of security, knew who could be paid off and who couldn't, knew how the system really operated—he'd gone into business for himself.

"This better be bloody important," Fergus had growled into the phone.

"I don't know about that," Ben replied. "But it will be awfully lucrative."

"Now we're talkin'," Fergus said, mollified.

Ben read a list of routing codes and wire-transfer numbers to him, and said he'd call back at the end of the day.

"It'll take me a hell of a lot longer than that," Fergus objected.

"Even if we double your usual fee? Does that speed things up?"

"Bloody well right it does." There was a pause. "By the way, you do know that they're saying the most appalling things about you, don't you?"

"What do you mean?"

"A whole load of bollocks. You know how the rumor mill goes. They say you've gone off on some murderous rampage."

"You're kidding."

"They say you killed your own brother."

Ben didn't respond, but felt sick. Was there not a sense in which it was true?

"Just crazy stuff like that. Not my specialty, but I know a thing or two about how people spread rumors in the financial world, just to stir things up. A load of bollocks, as I say. Still, it's interesting that someone's decided to put it out."

Jesus. "Thanks for the heads-up, Fergus," Ben said, sounding wobblier than he would have liked.

He took a few deep breaths to steady himself, and placed a second call, to a young woman in the New York office of a different sort of investigative firm. This company was large, international, legitimate, staffed with ex–FBI agents and even a few ex–CIA officers. Knapp Incorporated specialized in helping corporations conduct "due diligence" on potential business partners and solving white-collar crime, embezzlements, inside thefts—a gumshoe agency on a global scale. From time to time it was hired by Hartman Capital Management.

One of Knapp's star investigators was Megan Crosby, a Harvard Law grad who did corporate background checks like no one else. She had an uncanny knack for rooting out and then untangling Byzantine, heavily cloaked corporate structures designed to escape the scrutiny of regulators, wary investors, or competitors, and was as good as anyone at flushing out who really owned whom, who was behind what shell company. How she did it she never divulged to her clients. A magician must not divulge his tricks. Ben had taken Megan out to lunch a number of times and, since he sometimes had occasion to call her from Europe, she had given him her home phone number.

"It's three in the morning, who's calling?" was how she answered the phone.

"Ben Hartman, Megan. Forgive me, it's important."

Megan was instantly alert for her lucrative client. "No problem. What can I do for you?"

"I'm in the middle of a big-deal meeting in Amsterdam," he explained, lowering his voice. "There's a small biotech firm in Philadelphia called Vortex Laboratories I'm intrigued by." Anna, wanting his help, had mentioned Vortex to him. "I want to know who owns them, who they might have quiet partnerships with, that kind of thing."

"I'll do what I can," she said, "but no promises."

"End of the day possible?"

"Jesus." She paused. "End of which day are we talking? Yours or mine? That extra six hours will make a difference."

"Then make it the end of your day. Do what you can."

"Got it," she said.

"One more thing. There's a guy named Oscar Peyaud, based in Paris, that HCM has used for French due-diligence. Knapp has him on retainer. I need direct contact info for him."

By ten o'clock the Graben, one of Vienna's great pedestrian thoroughfares, was bustling with window-shoppers, businesspeople, tourists. He turned onto Kohlmarkt and passed Café Demel, the renowned pastry shop, where he turned to look at the lavish display windows. In its reflection, he noticed someone glancing at him and then quickly looking away.

A tall, thuggish-looking man in an ill-fitting dark blue raincoat. He had a thatch of unruly salt-and-pepper black hair, a ruddy face, and the heaviest eyebrows Ben had ever seen, a veritable wheat field of brow almost an inch thick, mostly black but salted with a little gray. The man's cheeks were covered with gin blossoms, the spiderwebs of broken capillaries that come from heavy drinking.

Ben knew he had seen the man before. He was convinced of it.

Somewhere, some time in the last day or two he had seen this same ruddy-cheeked man with the wheat-field eyebrows. In a crowd somewhere, but where?

Or had he?

Was paranoia overcoming him? Was he seeing faces, imagining that his enemies were everywhere?

Ben turned to look again, but the man had disappeared.

"My dear Ms. Navarro," Alan Bartlett said. "I wonder if we have different conceptions of what the fulfillment of your brief consists of. I must say I'm disappointed. You created high expectations."

Anna had placed a call to Robert Polozzi, of ID Section, only to be switched over, with no warning, to Bartlett.

"Listen," she protested, phone handset vised between her neck and left shoulder, "I think I'm on the verge—"

Bartlett talked over her words. "You are supposed to

check in on a regular basis, Agent Navarro. And not disappear like a college student on spring break."

"If you'll listen to what I've turned up—" Anna began, exasperated.

"No, you listen to me, Agent Navarro. Your instructions are to wrap this matter up, and that's what you are going to do. We've learned that Ramago has already been taken out. Rossignol was our last, best chance. I can't speak to what means you used to reach him, but it quite clearly resulted in his death. Apparently I was misled as to your sense of discretion." Bartlett's voice was an icicle.

"But the Sigma list—"

"You spoke to me of surveillance and preemption with respect to this subject. You did not alert me that you meant to draw a large bull's-eye on him. How many times did I emphasize the delicacy of your charge? How many times?"

Anna felt as if she'd been punched in the stomach. "I apologize if anything that I did had the effect of—"

"No, Agent Navarro, I blame myself. It was I who made the assignment. I cannot say I wasn't counseled against it. It was my own mulishness, you see. Trusting you with this assignment was my mistake. I take full responsibility."

"Cut the crap," Anna said, suddenly fed up. "You don't have the data to support your accusations."

"You're already facing administrative charges. I expect you in my office no later than five o'clock tomorrow afternoon, and I don't care if you have to charter a private jet to get here."

It was a few seconds before Anna realized he had hung up. Her heart pounded, her face was flushed. Had he not ended the call when he did, she'd have gone off on him, and no doubt finished her career once and for all.

No, she told herself, you've already done that. It's over. Dupree, when he got wind that she'd run afoul of the Internal Compliance Unit, would revoke her privileges within five minutes.

Well, at least go out with a bang.

She felt a delicious sense of inevitability. It was like being on a speeding train you couldn't get off. Enjoy the rush.

CHAPTER TWENTY-NINE

The office of the legendary and world-famous Jakob Sonnenfeld—the Nazi hunter extraordinaire who had been on the cover of countless newsmagazines, the subject of innumerable profiles and documentaries, had even made cameo appearances in movies—was located in a small, gloomy, relatively modern building on Salztorgasse, an inelegant street of discount stores and glum cafés. Sonnenfeld's phone number had simply been listed in the Vienna telephone directory without an address; Ben had called the number at around eight-thirty that morning and was surprised when it was answered. A brusque woman asked what his business was, why he wanted to see the great man.

Ben told her that he was the son of a Holocaust survivor and was in Vienna doing some personal research into the Nazi regime. Stick to what you know was his principle here. He was further surprised when the woman agreed to his request to meet the legend that morning.

The night before, Anna Navarro had suggested a few of what she called "evasive measures," to lose anyone who might be following. On his circuitous way here, after seeing the ruddy-faced man with the wheat-field eyebrows, he had doubled back a few times, abruptly crossed the street, suddenly turned into a bookstore, and browsed and waited. He seemed to have lost the tail, or perhaps, for some reason, the man hadn't wanted to be spotted again.

Now, having reached Sonnenfeld's office building on Salztorgasse, he was buzzed in and took the elevator to the fourth floor, where a solitary guard waved him along. The door was opened by a young woman who pointed him to an uncomfortable chair in a hallway lined with plaques and awards and testaments in Sonnenfeld's honor.

While he waited, he took out his digital phone and left a message for Oscar Peyaud, the Paris-based investigator. Then he called the hotel he had so unceremoniously abandoned the night before.

"Yes, Mr. Simon," the hotel operator answered with what struck him as undue familiarity. "Yes, sir, there is a message for you—it is, if you will wait, yes, from a Mr. Hans Hoffman. He says it is urgent."

"Thank you," Ben said.

"Please, Mr. Simon, can you hold on, please? The manager has just signaled me that he would like to speak with you."

The hotel manager got on the line. Ben ignored his first instinct, which was to disconnect immediately; more important by far was to determine how much the hotel management knew, how complicit they might be.

"Mr. Simon," the manager said in a loud and authoritative basso profundo, "one of our chambermaids tells me that you threatened her, and moreover, there was an incident here last night involving gunfire, and the police wish you to return here immediately for questioning."

Ben pressed the *End* button.

It was not surprising that the manager would want to talk to him. Damage had been done to the hotel; the manager was duty-bound to call the police. But there was something about the man's voice, the suddenly bullying self-assurance of a man who is backed by the full weight of the authorities, that alarmed Ben.

And what did Hoffman, the private investigator, want so urgently?

The door to Sonnenfeld's office opened and a small, stoop-shouldered old man emerged and gestured feebly for Ben to enter. He gave Ben a tremorous handshake and sat behind a cluttered desk. Jakob Sonnenfeld had a bristly gray mustache, a jowly face, large ears, and red-rimmed, hooded, watery eyes. He wore an unfashionably wide, clumsily knotted tie, a moth-eaten brown sweater-vest under a checked jacket.

"Many people want to look at my archives," Sonnenfeld said abruptly. "Some for good reasons, some for not so good. Why you?"

Ben cleared his throat, but Sonnenfeld rumbled on. "You say your father is a Holocaust survivor. So? There are thousands of them alive. Why are you so interested in my work?"

Do I dare level with the man? he wondered. "You've been hunting Nazis for decades now," he began suddenly. "You must hate them with all your heart, as I do."

Sonnenfeld waved dismissively. "No. I'm not a hater. I couldn't work at this job for over fifty years fueled by hate. It would eat away at my insides."

Ben was at once skeptical and annoyed at Sonnenfeld's piety.

"Well, I happen to believe that war criminals should not go free."

"Ah, but they are not war criminals really, are they? A war criminal commits his crimes to further his war aims, yes? He murders and tortures in order to help win the war. But tell me: Did the Nazis need to massacre and gas to death millions of innocents in order to win? Of course not. They did it purely for ideological reasons. To cleanse the planet, they believed. It was wholly unnecessary. It was something they did on the side. It diverted precious wartime resources. I'd say their campaign of genocide hindered their war effort. No, these were most certainly not war criminals."

"What do you call them, then?" Ben asked, understanding at last.

Sonnenfeld smiled. Several gold teeth glinted. "Monsters."

Ben took in a long breath. He'd have to trust the old Nazi hunter; that was the only way, he realized, to secure his cooperation. Sonnenfeld was too smart. "Then let me be very direct with you, Mr. Sonnenfeld. My brother—my twin brother, my closest friend in all the world—was murdered by people I believe are in some way connected with some of these monsters."

Sonnenfeld leaned forward. "Now you have me very confused," he said very intently. "Surely you and your brother are much, much too young to have been through the war."

"This happened not much over a week ago," Ben said.

Sonnenfeld's brow furrowed, eyes narrowing in disbelief. "What can you be saying? You are making no sense."

Quickly Ben explained about Peter's discovery. "This document drew my brother's attention because one of the board members was our own father." He paused. "Max Hartman."

Stunned silence. Then: "I know the name. He has given much money to good causes."

"In the year 1945, one of his causes was something called Sigma," Ben continued stonily. "The other incorporators included many Western industrialists, and a small handful of Nazi officials. Those included the treasurer, who is identified by the title *Obersturmführer*, and by the name Max Hartman."

Sonnenfeld's rheumy eyes did not blink. "Extraordinary. You did say 'Sigma,' yes? Dear God in heaven."

"I'm afraid it's an old story," said the visitor in the black leather jacket.

"The wife," suggested the private detective, Hoffman, with a wink.

The man smiled sheepishly.

"She is young and very pretty, yes?"

A sigh. "Yes."

"They are the worst of all, the pretty young ones," Hoffman said, man to man. "I'd advise you to simply forget her. You'll never be able to trust her anyway."

The visitor's eye seemed to be caught by Hoffman's fancy new laptop computer. "Nice," the man said.

"I don't know how I ever used anything else," Hoffman said. "I am not so good with technical things, but this is easy. Who needs filing cabinets anymore? Everything is here."

"Mind if I take a look at it?"

Hoffman hesitated. A man come in off the street—he could easily be a thief after all. He glanced at him again, took in the man's broad shoulders, narrow waist, not a gram of body fat. Quietly he nudged open the long metal desk drawer next to his lap an inch or two and checked for the Glock.

"Maybe another time," Hoffman said. "All of my confidential files are there. So, please give me the details about your pretty young wife and the bastard she's fucking."

"Why don't you turn it on?" the visitor said. Hoffman looked up sharply. This was not a request but a demand.

"Why are you here?" Hoffman snarled, and then realized he was staring into the barrel of a Makarov attached to a silencer.

"Put the computer on," the man said softly. "Open your files."

"I will tell you one thing. This document was never meant to see the light of day," Sonnenfeld said. "It was a legalism intended for internal Swiss bank use only. For the gnomes of Zurich alone."

"I don't understand."

"Sigma has long been the stuff of legend. Not a scintilla of evidence has ever emerged to give body to the shadow of supposition. I would know. Believe me."

"Until now, correct?"

"So it would seem," he said softly. "Clearly, it is a fictional enterprise. A front, a ruse—a means for industrialists on both sides to secure a separate peace, whatever the terms of armistice might be. The paper your brother uncovered may be the only material reality that it has."

"You say it was the stuff of legend—what was the nature of that legend?"

"Powerful businessmen and powerful politicians, meeting secretly to transfer immense, stolen state assets out of the Fatherland. Not everyone who opposed Hitler was a hero, you might as well know that. Many were cold-eyed pragmatists. They knew the war effort was doomed, and they knew who was to blame. What concerned them more was the prospect of repatriation, nationalization. They had their own empires to look after. Empires of industry. There is abundant evidence of such plans. But we've always believed that the plan remained just a plan. And almost everyone involved has since gone to their graves."

"You said 'almost everyone,' " Ben repeated sharply. "Let me ask about the few board members who fall under your professional purview. The Nazis. Gerhard Lenz. Josef Strasser." He paused before pronouncing the final name. "Max Hartman."

Sonnenfeld fell silent. He cradled his head in his large craggy hands. "Who are these people?" he said to himself, the question purely rhetorical. "That is your question. And here, always, is mine: who is asking? Why do you want to know?"

"Put your gun down," Hoffman said. "Don't be foolish."

"Close the desk drawer," the intruder said. "I am watching you very closely. One wrong move and I will not hesitate to kill you."

"Then you'll never access my files," Hoffman said triumphantly. "The computer is equipped with a biometric authentication device—a fingerprint scanner. Without my fingerprint, no one can log on. So you see, you would be very foolish to kill me."

"Oh, I don't need to go quite that far yet," said the visitor serenely.

"But do you know the truth about my father?" Ben asked. "It strikes me that you might have assembled a file on such a high-profile survivor and—forgive me—potential benefactor to your efforts. You, more than anyone, would have been in a position to see through his lies. You have all the lists of concentration-camp victims, a more exhaustive storehouse of records than anyone else. That's why I have to ask: Did you know the truth about my father?"

"Do you?" Sonnenfeld returned sharply.

"I've seen the truth in black and white."

"You have seen in black and white, yes, but you have not seen the truth. An amateur's error. Forgive me, Mr. Hartman, but these are never black-and-white matters. You're dealing with a situation whose ambiguities are very familiar to me. Your father's case, I can tell you only a little about it, but it is a sadly familiar story. You must be prepared to enter a realm of moral chiaroscuro, however. Of shadow, of ethical vagueness. Begin with the simple fact that if a Jew had money, the Nazis were willing to deal with him. This was one of the ugly secrets of the war that people seldom talk about. Often enough, the rich ones bought safe passage. The Nazis would take gold, jewels, securities, whatever. It was outright extortion, plain and simple. They even had a price schedule—three hundred thousand Swiss francs for a life! One of the Rothschilds traded his steel mills for his freedom—gave them to the Hermann Goering Works. But you won't read about any of this. No one ever talks about it. There was a very rich Hungarian-Jewish family, Weiss—they had businesses in twenty-three countries around the world. They gave their entire fortune to the SS, and in return they were escorted safely to Switzerland."

Ben was flustered. "But an *Obersturmführer* . . ."

"A Jewish *Obersturmführer?* Can that possibly be? Bear with me for a moment." Sonnenfeld paused before resuming. "I can tell you about an SS colonel, Kurt Becher, who was in charge of making deals like this for Eichmann and Himmler. Becher made a deal with a Hungarian, Dr. Rudolf Kastner—seventeen hundred Jews at a thousand dollars each. A whole train full. Jews in Budapest fought to get on that train. You know your family had money before the war, didn't you? The way it worked was very simple, if you were Max Hartman. One day *Obergruppenführer* Becher comes to see you. You make a deal. What good was your fortune if you were all going to die anyway? So you ransom your family out. Your sisters and you. This was hardly a moral conundrum. You did whatever you could to stay alive."

Ben had never thought of his father as a young man, frightened and desperate. His mind reeled. His aunt Sarah had died before he was born, but he remembered his aunt Leah, who passed away when he was in high school: a small, quiet, gentle soul, who had lived quietly as a librarian in Philadelphia. The affection she had for her brother was real, but so, too, was her recognition of his strength of character; she deferred to him in all things. If there were secrets to be kept, she would have kept them.

But his father—what else was he keeping inside?

"If what you're saying is true, why did he never tell us?" Ben asked.

"You think he wanted you to hear this?" There was a hint of scorn in Sonnenfeld's voice. "You think you would really have understood? Millions incinerated, while Max Hartman comes to America simply because he was fortunate enough to have money? People in his situation never told anyone, my friend. They often did their best to try to forget it themselves. I know these things because it is my business to know, but they are best left unexposed."

Ben didn't know how to reply, said nothing.

"Even Churchill and Roosevelt—Himmler made them an offer, you know. In May of '44. He was prepared to sell the Allies every single Jew the Nazis had, if the Allies would give them one truck for every hundred Jews. The Nazis would dismantle the gas chambers, stop murdering the Jews at once—all for some trucks they could use against the Russians. The Jews were for sale—but there were no buyers! Roosevelt and Churchill said no—they wouldn't sell their souls to the devil. Easy for them to say, no? They could have saved a million European Jews, but no. There were Jewish leaders who desperately wanted to make this deal. You see, you want to talk about morality, this wasn't so simple, was it?" Sonnenfeld's tone was bitter. "Now it's so easy to talk about clean hands. But the result is that you're here today. You exist because your father made an unsavory deal to save his own life."

Ben's mind flashed back to the image of his father, old and frail in Bedford, and the image of him, crisp and chiseled in the old photograph. What he had to go through to get here, Ben couldn't begin to imagine. Yet would he really feel compelled to hide this? How much else had he been hiding? "But still, this all leaves unanswered the matter of his name on that document," Ben prompted, "identifying him as SS. . . ."

"In name only, I'm sure."

"Meaning what?"

"How much do you know about your father?"

Good question, Ben thought. He said, "Less and less, it seems." Max Hartman, powerful and intimidating, conducting a board meeting with gladiatorial self-confidence. Hoisting Ben, age six, way up in the air. Reading *The Financial Times* at breakfast, distant and elusive.

How I tried to earn his love, his respect! And what a warm glow his approval gave me when he so rarely granted it.

What an enigma the man has always been.

"I can tell you this much," Sonnenfeld said impassively. "When your father was still a young man, he was already a legend in German financial circles. A genius, it was said. But he was a Jew. Early in the war, when the Jews were being sent away, he was given the opportunity to work for the *Reichsbank* instead, designing intricate financial schemes that would allow the Nazis to circumvent the Allied blockades. He was given this SS title as a sort of cover."

"So in a sense he helped finance the Nazi regime," Ben said in a monotone. This was somehow no surprise, but still he felt his stomach plummet at hearing it confirmed.

"Unfortunately, yes. I'm sure he had his reasons—he was pressured, he had no choice. He would have been enlisted in this Sigma project as a matter of course." He paused again, watching Ben steadily. "I think you are not very good at seeing shades of gray."

"Odd talk for a Nazi hunter."

"Again with that journalist's tag," Sonnenfeld said. "I fight for justice, and in the fight for justice you must be able to distinguish between the venial and the venal, between ordinary and outsized wrongdoing. Make no mistake: hardship brings out the best in no one."

The room seemed to revolve slowly around him. Ben clasped his arms around himself, and breathed deeply, trying for a moment of calm, a moment of clarity.

He had a sudden mental picture of his father in his study, listening to Mozart's *Don Giovanni* as he sat in his favorite overstuffed chair in darkness. Often in the evenings after dinner Max would sit alone with the lights off, *Don Giovanni* on the stereo. How lonely the man must have been, how frightened that his ugly past would someday emerge. Ben was surprised at the tenderness he suddenly felt. *The old man loved me as much as he was able to love anyone. How can I despise him?* It occurred to Ben that the real reason Lenz grew to hate his own father was not so much the repugnance of Nazism as the fact that he had abandoned them.

"Tell me about Strasser," Ben said, realizing that only a change of subject could diminish the vertigo he was undergoing.

Sonnenfeld closed his eyes. "Strasser was a scientific adviser to Hitler. *Gevalt*, he was not a human being. Strasser was a brilliant scientist. He helped run I. G. Farben, you know this famous I. G. Farben, the big industrial firm that was controlled by the Nazis? There, he helped to invent a new gas in pellet form called Zyklon-B. You would shake the pellets and they would turn into gas. Like magic! They first tried it in the showers at Auschwitz. A fantastic invention. The poison gas would rise in the gas chambers, and as the level rose the taller victims would step on the others to try to breathe. But everyone would die in four minutes."

Sonnenfeld paused, gazed into some middle distance. In the long silence Ben could hear the ticking of a mechanical clock.

"Very efficient," Sonnenfeld at last resumed. "For this we must thank Dr. Strasser. And do you know that Allen Dulles, your CIA director in the fifties, was I. G. Farben's American lawyer and loyal defender? Yes, it is true."

Somewhere Ben had heard this before, but it still amazed him. Slowly, he said, "So both Strasser and Lenz were partners, in a sense."

"Yes. Two of the most brilliant, most terrible Nazi scientists. Lenz with his experiments on children, on twins. A brilliant scientist, far ahead of his time. Lenz took a particular interest in the metabolism of children. Some he would starve to death in order to observe how their growth slowed and stopped. Some he would actually freeze, to see how that affected their growth. He saw to it that all the children who suffered from progeria, a horrible form of premature aging, were sent to him for study." He went on bitterly: "A lovely man, Dr. Lenz. Very close to the high command, of course. As a scientist, he was better trusted than most politicians. He was thought to have 'purity of purpose.' And of course our Dr. Strasser. Lenz went to Buenos Aires too, as so many of them did after the war. Have you been there? It is a lovely city. Truly. The Paris of South America. No wonder all the Nazis wanted to live there. And then Lenz died there."

"And Strasser?"

"Perhaps Lenz's widow knows the whereabouts of Strasser, but don't even think of asking her. She'll never reveal it."

"Lenz's widow?" Ben asked, sitting upright. "Yes, Jürgen Lenz mentioned his mother had retired there."

"You spoke with Jürgen Lenz?"

"Yes. You know him, I gather?"

"Ah, this is a complicated story, Jürgen Lenz. I must admit to you, at first I found it extremely difficult to accept money from this man. Of course, without contributions we would have to close down. In this country, where they have always protected the Nazis, even protect them to this day, I get no donations. Not a cent! Here they haven't prosecuted a single Nazi case in over twenty years! Here I was for years Public Enemy Number One. They used to spit at me on the street. And Lenz, well, from Lenz this so clearly seemed to be guilt money. But then I met the man, and I quickly changed my mind. He's sincerely committed to doing good. For example, he's the sole underwriter of the progeria foundation in Vienna. No doubt he wants to undo his father's work. We mustn't hold against him his father's crimes."

Sonnenfeld's words resounded. His father's crimes. How bizarre that Lenz and I should be in a similar situation.

"The prophet Jeremiah, you know, he tells us, 'They shall say no more, the fathers have eaten a sour grape, and the children's teeth are set on edge.' And Ezekiel says, 'The son shall not bear the iniquity of the father.' It is very clear."

Ben was silent. "You say Strasser may be alive."

"Or he may be dead," Sonnenfeld replied quickly. "Who knows about these old men? I've never been able to make certain."

"You must have a file on him."

"Don't speak to me of such things. Are you in the grip of the fantasy that you will find this creature and he will tell you what you want, like some genie?" Sonnenfeld sounded evasive. "For years I have been dogged with young fanatics seeking vengeance, to slake some sense of disquiet with the blood of a certified villain. It is a puerile pursuit, which ends badly for everyone. You had persuaded me you were not one of them. But Argentina is another country, and surely the wretch is dead."

The young woman who had answered the door when Ben arrived now reappeared, and a murmured conversation ensued. "An important telephone call which I must take," Sonnenfeld said apologetically, and he withdrew to a back room.

Ben looked around him, at the huge slate-colored filing cabinets. Sonnenfeld had been distinctly evasive when the subject came to Strasser's current whereabouts. Was he holding out on him? And if so, why?

From Sonnenfeld's manner, he inferred that the telephone call was expected to be a long one. Perhaps long enough to allow a quick search of the files. Impulsively, Ben moved to an immense, five-drawer filing cabinet marked R–S. The drawers were locked but the key was on top of the cabinet: not exactly high security, Ben noted. He opened the bottom drawer, found it densely packed with yellowed file folders and crumbling papers. Stefans. Stern-geld. Streitfeld.

STRASSER. The name penned in brown faded ink. He plucked it out, and then had a sudden thought. He went to the K–M file. There was a thick file for Gerhard Lenz, but that wasn't the one he was interested in. It was the thin file next to it—the file for his widow—that he wanted.

This one was tightly wedged in. He heard footsteps: Sonnenfeld was returning, more quickly than Ben had expected! He tugged on the folder, worried it from side to side until it was slowly released from the others. Taking the trench coat he'd draped on an adjoining chair, he quickly shoved the yellowed folders under it and returned to his seat just as Sonnenfeld entered.

"It's a dangerous thing to disturb the peace of old men," Sonnenfeld announced as he rejoined him. "Maybe you think they're toothless, wizened creatures. Indeed they are. But they have a powerful support network, even now. Especially in South America, where they have extensive loyalists. Thugs, like the *Kamaradenwerk*. They are protected the way wild animals protect their enfeebled elders. They kill whenever they must—they never hesitate."

"In Buenos Aires?"

"There more than anywhere else. Nowhere are they so powerful." He looked weary. "This is why you must never go there and ask about the old Germans."

Sonnenfeld got up unsteadily, and Ben rose, too. "Even today, you see, I must have a security guard at all times. It is not much, but it is what we can afford to pay for."

"Yet you insist on living in a city where they don't like questions about the past," Ben said.

Sonnenfeld put his hand on Ben's shoulder. "Ah, well, you see, if you are studying malaria, Mr. Hartman, you must live in the swamp, no?"

Julian Bennett, assistant deputy of operations at the National Security Agency, sat facing Joel Skolnik, the deputy director of the Department of Justice in the small executive dining room in the NSA's Fort Mead headquarters. Though Skolnik, lanky and balding, held a higher bureaucratic rank, Bennett's manner was peremptory. The National Security Agency was structured in such a way as to insulate people like Bennett from bureaucratic oversight outside of the agency. The effect was to encourage a certain arrogance, and Bennett was not one to disguise it.

An overdone lamb chop and a lump of steamed spinach, mostly uneaten, sat on the plate in front of Skolnik. His appetite had long since disappeared. Past a thin veneer of amiability, Bennett's manner was subtly hectoring, and his message frankly alarming.

"This doesn't look good for you," Bennett was telling him, not for the first time. His small, wide-spaced eyes and light-colored eyebrows gave him a vaguely porcine look.

"I realize this."

"You're supposed to be running a tight ship here," Bennett said. His own plate was clean; he had devoured his porterhouse in several swift bites: plainly a man who ate simply for fuel. "And the stuff we've been coming across is pretty damn disquieting."

"You've been clear about that," Skolnik said, hating the way it came out—deferential, even cowed. He knew it was always a mistake to show fear to a man like Bennett. It was like blood in the water to a shark.

"The recklessness about matters of national security your people have shown—it compromises us all. I look at the way your staffers have conducted themselves, and I don't know whether to laugh or cry. What's the use of bolting the front door when the back door is swinging in the wind?"

"Let's not exaggerate the possible exposure at issue," Skolnik said. Even to himself, the starchy words sounded defensive.

"I want you to assure me that the rot is contained with the Navarro woman." Bennett leaned over and patted Skolnik's forearm in a gesture that was half intimate and half menacing. "And that you'll use all means at your disposal to bring the woman in."

"That much goes without saying," the DOJ man said, swallowing hard.

"Now stand up," the goateed man said, waving the Makarov in his left hand.

"It'll do you no good. I won't put my finger on the sensor," said the detective, Hans Hoffman. "Now get out of here, before something happens that you'll regret."

"I never have regrets," the man said blandly. "Stand up."

Hoffman stood up reluctantly. "I tell you—"

The intruder rose too and approached him.

"I tell you again," Hoffman said, "it will do you no good to kill me."

"I don't need to kill you," the man said blandly. In one lightning-swift movement he lunged.

Hoffman saw the glint of something metallic even before he felt the unbelievable pain explode in his hand. He looked down. There was a stump where his index finger had been. The cut had been perfect. At the base of where his finger had been, right next to the fatty part of the thumb, he could see a white circle of bone within a larger circle of flesh. In the millisecond before he screamed, he saw the razor-sharp hunting knife in the man's hand, and then he noticed with dazed fascination the dismembered finger lying on the carpet like a useless discarded chicken part flung there by some careless butcher.

He bellowed, a high-pitched scream of disbelief and terror and excruciating, incomprehensible pain. "Oh, my God! Oh, my God! Oh, my God!"

Trevor picked up the dismembered finger and held it aloft. At the severed end, blood still wept.

CHAPTER THIRTY

Anna put in a call to David Denneen.

"Is that you, Anna?" he said tersely, his customary warmth crimped by uncustomary wariness. "The shit's flying."

"Talk to me, David. Tell me what the hell's going on."

"Crazy stuff. They're saying you're..." His voice trailed off.

"What?"

"Crazy stuff. You on a sterile line?"

"Of course."

There was a pause. "Listen, Anna. The department's been ordered to place a P-47 on you, Anna—full-out mail, wire, phone intercepts."

"Jesus Christ!" Anna said. "I don't believe it."

"It gets worse. Since this morning, you've been a 12-44: apprehend on sight. Bring in by any means necessary. Jesus, I don't know what you've been up to, but you're being called a national security risk. They're saying you've been accepting money from hostiles for years. I shouldn't even be talking to you."

"What?"

"Word is the FBI's discovered all sorts of cash and jewelry in your apartment. Expensive clothes. Offshore bank accounts."

"Lies!" Anna exploded. "All goddamn lies."

There was a long pause. "I knew they had to be, Anna. But I'm glad to hear you say it, all the same. Someone's messing with you in a very serious way. Why?"

"Why?" Anna closed her eyes briefly. "So I don't get in a position to discover why. That's my guess." She rang off hurriedly.

What the hell was going on? Had "Yossi" or Phil Ostrow put poison in Bartlett's ear? She'd never called them; maybe Bartlett was angry that they'd found out about her investigation in the first place, even though she wasn't the responsible party. Or maybe Bartlett was angry that she hadn't gone along with their request to bring Hartman in.

She suddenly realized that neither agency official had mentioned Hans Vogler, the ex-Stasi assassin. Did that mean "Yossi" knew nothing about it? If so, did that mean that the Mossad freelancers had nothing to do with hiring Vogler? She retrieved Phil Ostrow's card and dialed the number. It went to automated voice mail; and she decided against leaving a message.

Maybe Jack Hampton would know something about it. She phoned him at home, in Chevy Chase. "Jack," she began. "It's—"

"Jesus Christ, tell me you're not calling me," Hampton said in a rush. "Tell me you're not jeopardizing the security clearance of your friends by a misjudged phone call."

"Is there an intercept on your end?"

"My end?" Hampton paused. "No. Never. I make sure of it myself."

"Then you're not in danger. I'm on a secure line on this end. I don't see any way by which a connection could be traced."

"Let's say you're right, Anna," he said dubiously. "You're still presenting me with a moral conundrum. Word has it you're some primo villainness—the way I've heard you described, it's like you're a combination of Ma Barker and Mata Hari. With the wardrobe of Imelda Marcos."

"It's bullshit. You know that."

"Maybe I do, Anna, and maybe I don't. The kind of sums I've heard bandied about would be awfully tempting. Buy yourself a nice spit of land in Virgin Gorda. All that pink sand, blue sky. Go snorkeling every day . . ."

"Goddamn it, Jack!"

"A word of advice. Don't take any woolen kopeks and don't whack any more Swiss bankers."

"Is that what they're saying about me?"

"One of the things. One of the many things. Let's just say it's the biggest pile-on I've heard of since Wen Ho Lee. It's a bit overdone, to tell you the truth. I keep asking myself, Who's got that kind of money to throw around? Russia's so strapped for cash that most of its nuclear scientists have left to drive taxicabs in New York. And what kind of hard currency does China have—the place is Zambia with nukes. I mean, let's get real." Hampton's voice seemed to soften. "So what are you calling me for? Want our current missile codes to sell to the Red Chinese? Just let me jot down your fax number."

"Give me a break."

"That's my hot tamale," Hampton teased, relaxing further.

"Screw you. Listen, before all this shit fell from the sky, I had a meeting with your friend Phil Ostrow . . ."

"Ostrow?" Hampton said, guardedly. "Where?"

"In Vienna."

There was a flare of anger: "What are you trying to pull, Navarro?"

"Wait a minute. I don't know what you're talking about."

Something in her voice gave him pause. "Are you shitting me, or was somebody shitting you?"

"Ostrow's not attached to Vienna station?" she asked hesitantly.

"He's on O-15."

"Help me out here."

"That means he's kept officially on the lists, but he's really on leave. Sow confusion among the bad guys that way. Diabolical, what?"

"On leave how?"

"He's been stateside for a few months now. Depression, if you want to know. He had episodes in the past, but it got real bad. He's actually been hospitalized at Walter Reed."

"And that's where he is now." Anna's scalp became tight; she tried to quell a rising sense of anxiety.

"That's where he is now. Sad but true. One of those wards where all the nurses have security clearances."

"If I said Ostrow was a short guy, grayish-brownish hair, pale complexion, wire-rim glasses . . . ?"

"I'd tell you to get your prescription checked. Ostrow looks like an aging surfer bum—tall, slim, blond hair, the works."

Several seconds of silence ensued.

"Anna, what the hell is going on with you?"

CHAPTER THIRTY-ONE

Stunned, she sat back on the bed.

"What's wrong?" Ben asked.

"I really can't get into it."

"If it concerns the business we're both working on—"

"It doesn't. Not this. Those *bastards!*"

"What happened?"

"*Please*," she exclaimed. "Let me *think!*"

"Fine." Looking irritated, Ben took his digital phone from the pocket of his jacket.

She thought: No wonder "Phil Ostrow" had called her late at night—when it was too late to call the American embassy and check out his bona fides. But then who was it she'd met with at CIA station?

Was it in fact CIA station?

Who were "Ostrow" and "Yossi"?

She heard Ben speaking quickly in French. Then he fell silent, listening for a while. "Oscar, you're a genius," he finally said.

A few minutes later, he was talking on his phone again. "Megan Crosby, please."

If "Phil Ostrow" was some kind of impostor, he had to be an enormously skilled actor. And what was he doing? "Yossi" could indeed have been Israeli, or of some other Middle Eastern nationality; it was hard to tell.

"Megan, it's Ben," he said.

Who *were* they? she wondered.

She picked up the phone and called Jack Hampton again. "Jack, I need the number of CIA station."

"What am I, directory assistance?"

"It's in the building across the street from the consular office, right?"

"CIA station is in the main embassy building, Anna."

"No, the annex. A commercial building across the street. Under the cover of the Office of the United States Trade Representative."

"I don't know what you're talking about. CIA doesn't have any cover sites outside of the one right in the embassy. That *I* know of anyway."

She hung up, panic suffusing her body. If that hadn't been a CIA site where she'd met Ostrow, what was it? The setting, the surroundings—every detail had been right. *Too* right, *too* convincing?

"You've got to be kidding," she heard Ben say. "*Jesus*, you're fast."

So who was trying to manipulate her? And to what end? Obviously someone, or some group, who knew she was in Vienna, knew what she was investigating, and knew which hotel she was staying in.

If Ostrow was some kind of impostor, then his story about the Mossad had to be false. And she had been the unwitting victim of an elaborate scam. They'd planned to kidnap Hartman—and have her deliver the "package" right into their clutches.

She felt dazed and lost.

In her mind she ran through everything, from "Ostrow's" phone call, to the place she'd met him and "Yossi." Was it really possible the whole thing had been an elaborate ruse?

She heard Hartman say: "All right, let me write this down. Great work, kid. Terrific."

So the Mossad story, with all its rumors and undocumented whispers, was nothing but a tale spun by liars out of plausible fragments? My God, then how much of what she knew was wrong?

And who was trying to mislead her—and to what end? *What was the truth?* Good God, *where* was the truth?

"Ben," she said.

He held up an index finger to signal her to wait, said something quickly into his phone, then flipped it closed.

But then she quickly changed her mind, decided not to reveal to Ben anything of what she'd just found out. Not yet. Instead, she asked, "Did you learn anything from Sonnenfeld?"

Hartman told her about what Sonnenfeld had said, Anna interrupting every once in a while to clarify a point or ask for a fuller explanation.

"So are you saying your father wasn't a Nazi, after all?"

"Not according to Sonnenfeld, at least."

"Did he have some inkling as to the meaning of Sigma?"

"Beyond what I said, he was vague about it. And downright evasive when it came to Strasser."

"And as to why your brother was killed?"

"Obviously he was killed because of the *threat of exposure*. Someone, maybe some group, feared the revelation of those names."

"Or of the fact this corporation *existed*. Clearly someone with a major financial stake. Which tells us that these old guys were—" Suddenly she stopped. "Of course! The laundered money! These old guys were being paid off. Maybe by someone controlling the corporation they'd all helped form."

"Either paid off, as in *bribed*," Ben added, "or else they were receiving an agreed-upon distribution, a share of the profits."

Anna stood. "Eliminate the payees, then there's no more wire transfers. No more big paydays for a bunch of doddering old men. Which tells us that whoever's ordering the murders stands to gain *financially* from them. *Has* to be. Someone like Strasser, or even your father." She looked at him. She couldn't automatically rule it out. Even if he didn't want to hear it. His father might have been a murderer himself—might have blood on his hands, might have been *behind* the murders at least.

But how to explain the intricate deception of Ostrow, the false CIA man? Might he have been somehow connected to the heirs to some vast hidden fortune?

"Theoretically, I suppose, my father could be one of the bad guys." Ben said. "But I really don't believe it."

"Why not?" She didn't know how far to push him on this.

"Because my father already has more money than he knows what to do with. Because he may be a ruthless businessman, and he may be a liar, but after talking with Sonnenfeld, I'm coming to think that he wasn't fundamentally an evil man."

She doubted Hartman was holding anything back, but surely he was hampered by filial loyalty. Ben seemed to be a loyal person—an admirable quality, but sometimes loyalty could blind you to the truth.

"What I don't get is this: these guys are old and failing," Hartman continued. "So why bother hiring someone to eliminate them? It's hardly worth the risk."

"Unless you're afraid one of them will talk, reveal the financial arrangement, whatever it is."

"But if they haven't talked for half a century, what's going to make them start now?"

"Maybe some sort of pressure by legal authorities, triggered by the surfacing of this list. Faced with the threat of legal action, any one of them might easily have talked. Or maybe the Corporation is moving to a new phase, a transition, and sees itself as peculiarly vulnerable while it's happening."

"I'm hearing a lot of conjecture," he said. "We need facts."

She paused. "Who were you talking to on the phone just now?"

"A corporate researcher I've used before. She found some intriguing background on Vortex Laboratories."

Anna was suddenly alert. "Yes?"

"It's wholly owned by the European chemicals and technology giant Armakon AG. An Austrian company."

"Austrian . . ." she murmured. "That *is* interesting."

"Those mammoth technology firms are always buying up tiny tech startups, hoping to snag the rights to stuff their own in-house research scientists haven't invented." He paused. "And one more thing. My friend in the Caymans was able to trace a few of the wire transfers."

Jesus. And her guy at the DOJ had turned up nothing. She tried to conceal her excitement. "Tell me."

"The money was sent from a shell company registered in the Channel Islands, a few seconds after it came in from Liechtenstein, from an *Anstalt*, a bearer-share company. Sort of a blind entity."

"If it came from a company, does that mean the names of the true owners are on file somewhere?"

"That's the tricky part. *Anstalts* are usually managed by an agent, often an attorney. They're essentially dummy corporations that exist only on paper. An agent in Liechtenstein might manage thousands of them."

"Was your friend able to get the name of the *Anstalt*'s agent?"

"I believe so, yes. Trouble is, barring torture, no agent will release information on any of the *Anstalts* he manages. They can't afford to sabotage their reputation for discretion. But my friend's working on it."

She grinned. The guy was growing on her.

The phone rang.

She picked it up. "Navarro."

"Anna, this is Walter Heisler. I have results for you."

"Results?"

"On the gun that was dropped by the shooter in Hietzing. The prints you asked me to run. It matched a print, a digitized print, on file at Interpol. A Hans Vogler, ex-Stasi. Maybe he doesn't expect to miss, or doesn't expect us to be there, because he wears no gloves."

Heisler's information was nothing new, but the fingerprints would be a valuable piece of evidence.

"Fantastic. Walter, listen, I need to ask you another favor."

"You don't sound surprised," Heisler said, miffed. "I said he was ex-*Stasi*, you understand? Former East German secret intelligence service."

"Yes, Walter, I do understand, and I thank you. Very impressive." She was being too brusque again, too businesslike, and she tried to soften her approach. "Thank you so much, Walter. And just one more thing . . ."

Wearily: "Yes?"

"One second." She covered the phone's mouthpiece and said to Ben, "You still haven't reached Hoffman?"

"Not a word. No answer there—it's bizarre."

She removed her hand from the mouthpiece. "Walter, can you find out for me whatever you can about a private investigator in Vienna named Hans Hoffman?"

There was silence.

"Hello?"

"Yes, Anna, I am here. Why do you ask about this Hans Hoffman?"

"I need some outside help here," she replied, thinking quickly, "and his name was given to me—"

"Well, I think you may have to find someone else."

"Why is that?"

"About an hour ago a call came in to the *Sicherheitsbüro* from an employee of a *Berufsdetektiv* named Hans Hoffman. The woman, an investigator in Hoffman's office, came to work and discovered her boss dead. Shot at point-blank range in the forehead. And, curious—his right forefinger was cut off. Can this be the Hoffman you're talking about?"

*   *   *

Ben had stared in disbelief when Anna told him what she'd learned. "Christ, it's as if they're always just one behind us, whatever we do," he murmured.

"Maybe 'ahead of us' is the more accurate term."

Ben massaged his temples with the fingertips of both hands, and at last he spoke in a quiet voice. "The enemy of my enemy is my friend."

"How do you mean?"

"Sigma has obviously been killing its own. Those victims you're trying to find—they all have something in common with me, a shared enemy. We've observed the pattern—frightened old men going into hiding in the twilight of their lives, living under aliases. It's a virtual certainty that they have some idea what the hell's going on. That means our only hope is to establish contact with someone on the list who's still alive, who can talk. Someone with whom I can establish common ground, a conduit of sympathy, enlist his help for reasons of his own self-protection."

Anna stood, paced the room. "That's if there is anyone alive, Ben."

He stared at her a long while, saying nothing, the resolve in his eyes wavering. She could tell that he longed to trust her every bit as fervently as she hoped she could trust him. Softly, hesitantly, he replied: "I have a feeling—it's just a feeling, an educated guess—that there may be at least one still alive."

"Who's that?"

"A Frenchman named Georges Chardin."

She nodded slowly. "Georges Chardin . . . I've seen the name on the Sigma list—but he's actually been dead for four years."

"But the fact that his name was in the Sigma files means Allen Dulles had him vetted for some reason."

"Back in the fifties, yeah. But remember, most of these people have been dead for a long while. My focus was on the ones who had fallen victim to the recent spate of killings—or who were about to. Chardin isn't in either category. And he's not a *founder*, so he's not on your incorporation document." The Sigma list contains more names than just the original incorporators. She looked at Ben hard. "My question is, how did you know to ask about him? Are you holding out on me?"

Ben shook his head.

"We don't have time to play games," Anna said. "Georges Chardin—I know him as a name on paper. But he's no one famous, no one I'd ever heard of. So what's his significance?"

"The significance is his boss, a legendary French industrialist—a man who *was* one of the incorporators in the photo. A man named Émil Ménard. In his time, one of the greatest corporate titans. Back in 1945 he was a grand old man; he's long dead."

"Him I know. He was the founder of Trianon, generally considered the first modern corporate conglomerate, correct?"

"Right. Trianon is one of the biggest industrial empires in France. Émil Ménard built Trianon into a French petrochemical giant that made even Schlumberger look like a five-and-dime."

"And so this Georges Chardin worked for the legendary Émil Ménard?"

"Worked for him? He just about did his breathing for him. Chardin was his trusted lieutenant, aide-de-camp, factotum, whatever you want to call him. He wasn't just Ménard's right-hand man, he was practically his right hand. Chardin was hired in 1950 when he was only twenty, and in a few short years the greenhorn changed the way the cost of capital was accounted for, introduced a sophisticated new way of calculating return on investment, restructured the company accordingly. Way ahead of his time. A major figure."

"In your world, maybe."

"Granted. Point is, in very short order, the old man trusted his young protégé with everything, every detail in running his vast enterprise. After 1950, Émil Ménard didn't go anywhere without Chardin. They say Chardin had all the firm's ledgers memorized. He was a walking computer." Ben produced the yellowed photograph of the Sigma group and placed it in front of Anna, pointing out Émil Ménard's countenance. "What do you see?"

"Ménard looks pretty haggard, to tell the truth. Not well at all."

"Correct. He was pretty seriously ill at that point. Spent the last decade of his life fighting cancer, though he was an incredibly formidable man right up until the end. But he died with the supreme confidence that his corporation would remain strong, continue to grow, because he had such a brilliant young *Directeur Général du Département des Finance*—basically, his chief financial officer."

"So you're speculating that Ménard would have trusted Georges Chardin with the secret of the Sigma enterprise as well?"

"I'm virtually certain of it. No doubt Chardin was completely in the background. But he was Ménard's shadow every step of the way. It's inconceivable that Chardin wouldn't have been completely privy to the substance of Sigma, whatever its objectives and methods. And look at it from Sigma's point of view: in order to stay alive, regardless of its true purpose, Sigma had to keep bringing in new recruits to replace the original founders. So Chardin is bound to have played a significant role, likely as a member of its inner council—Ménard would have made sure of that."

"O.K., O.K., you've got me convinced," Anna put in impatiently. "But where does that get us today? We already know Chardin died four years ago. You think he might have left files, papers, or something?"

"We're told that Chardin died four years ago, sure. Right around the same time that my brother, Peter, arranged his fake death. What if he did something like what Peter did—arranged to disappear, go into hiding, escape the killers he knew were after him?"

"Come on, Ben! You're making all sorts of assumptions, jumping to unwarranted conclusions!"

Ben replied patiently, "Your list indicated that he perished in a fire, right? The old 'burned beyond recognition' ruse? Like my brother? Sorry; won't get fooled again." He seemed to recognize the skepticism in her face. "Listen to me! You said it yourself. We have a string of old men who were killed presumably because somebody viewed them as a threat. Sigma, or its heirs or controllers. So let's think this out: why might a bunch of old guys in the twilight of their lives be considered a serious enough threat to be murdered?" He stood up, began to pace. "You see, the mistake I was making all along was in viewing Sigma as merely a front organization, a false corporation—instead of a genuine one."

"How do you mean?"

"It should have been so obvious! I can give you a hundred instances from my Wall Street days. In 1992, one guy ousted another rival to become the sole CEO of Time Warner, and his first order of business was what? To purge the hostiles from the board of directors. That's what management does. You get rid of your adversaries!"

"But the Time Warner guy didn't kill his opponents, I assume," she said dryly.

"On Wall Street we have different techniques for eliminating enemies." Ben gave a twisted smile. "But he eliminated them all the same. It's what always happens when there's an abrupt change in management."

"So you're suggesting there's been a 'change in management' at Sigma."

"Exactly. A purge of what you might call dissident trustees."

"Rossignol, Mailhot, Prosperi, and the rest—you're saying they were all dissidents? On the wrong side of the new management?"

"Something like that. And Georges Chardin was known to be brilliant. No doubt he saw it coming, and so he arranged to disappear."

"Maybe yes, maybe no. But it's still all in the realm of wild speculation."

"Not quite," Ben said softly. He turned to face Anna directly. "Beginning with the time-honored principle 'Follow the money,' I hired a French investigator we've used before at Hartman Capital Management. A wizard named Oscar Peyaud. We've used him for due-diligence work in Paris, and every time he blows us away with the speed and quality of his work. And the size of his bill, but that's another matter."

"Thanks for keeping me in the loop about what you were doing," Anna said with heavy sarcasm. "So much for being partners."

"Listen to me. A man can't live without some form of financial support. So I got to thinking, what would happen if you could track down the executor to Chardin's estate—see in what form he left his assets, how he might have retained access to them?" He paused, took out a folded sheet of paper from his jacket pocket. "An hour ago this arrived from Paris, from Oscar Peyaud."

The page was blank except for a brief address:

> *Rogier Chabot*
> *1554 rue des Vignoles*
> *Paris 20*

Anna looked up, at once puzzled and excited. "Chabot?"

"Georges Chardin's alias, I would bet. I think we have our man. Now it's just a matter of our getting to him before Sigma does."

An hour later, the phone on Walter Heisler's desk rang. A cycle of two short rings: an internal line. Heisler was drawing deep on a cigarette—he was working through the third pack of Casablancas of the day—when he picked up, and there was a two-second pause before he spoke: "Heisler."

It was the tech from the small room on the fifth floor.

"Did you get the bulletin on the American, Navarro?"

"What bulletin?" Heisler slowly let the warm smoke plume through his nostrils.

"Just came in."

"Then it's probably been sitting in the message center all morning." The *Sicherheitsbüro* message center, operating with what he regarded as third-world inefficiency, was a bane of his existence. "What's up, then? Or do I need to find out by listening to the news on the radio?" This was how he had taken to formulating the complaint. Once he really did find out the whereabouts of a fugitive from a local radio station, the messengers having misplaced the morning's faxed bulletin somewhere en route to his desk.

"She's a rogue, it seems. We've been used. The U.S. government has a warrant out for her. Not my department, but I thought somebody should give you a heads-up."

"*Christ!*" Heisler said, and let his cigarette drop from his mouth into his mug of coffee, heard the quick sizzle of the quenched butt. "*Shit!* A fucking embarrassment."

"Not so embarrassing if you're the one who brings her in, eh?" the tech said carefully.

"Checking out of Room 1423," Anna said to the harried-looking clerk at the front desk. She placed her two electronic key-cards on the black granite counter.

"One moment, please. If I can just have your signature on the final bill, *ja?*" The man was weary-looking, and fortyish, with slightly concave cheeks, and dirty-blond hair—dyed?—combed forward, flat against his skull, in a seeming attempt to simulate youth. He wore a crisp uniform jacket of some sort of brown synthetic, with slightly fraying epaulets. Anna had a sudden vision of him as she imagined he became after hours—dressed in black leather, heavily spritzed with musky cologne, haunting nightclubs where the dim light might help him get lucky with a *schöne Mädchen*.

"Of course," Anna said.

"We hope you enjoyed your stay, Ms. Navarro." He typed numbers on a keyboard, and then looked up at her, showing a toothy, yellow-tinged smile. "Apologies. It's going to take a few moments to bring the records up. A problem in the system. Computers, right?" He smiled wider, as if he had said something witty. "Wonderful labor-saving devices. When they work. Let me get the manager." He picked up a red handset, and said a few words in German.

"What's going on?" asked Ben, who was standing behind her.

"A computer problem, he says," Anna murmured.

From behind the counter, a short, big-bellied man emerged in a dark suit and tie. "I'm the manager, and I'm so sorry for the delay," the man said to her. He exchanged glances with the clerk. "A glitch. It's going to take a few minutes to retrieve the records. Phone calls, all of that. We'll get it for you soon, and then you can take a look and make sure it looks right. Wouldn't want you billed for the phone calls in Room 1422. Sometimes happens with the new system. Miracle of modern technology."

Something was wrong, and it wasn't the computer system.

The manager was jovial and reassuring and effusive, and yet, despite the lobby's slight chilliness, Anna noticed the beads of sweat on his forehead. "Come and sit in my office while we get this straightened out. Take a load off your feet, yes? You're off to the airport, yes? You have transportation arranged? Why don't you let the hotel car take you?—our compliments. The least we can do for the inconvenience."

"That's very kind of you," Anna said, thinking that she recognized the type well from her years of investigations—the type of person whom tension made talkative. The man was under orders to detain them. That much was clear.

"Not at all. Not at all. You come with me, and have a nice cup of coffee. Nobody makes it like the Viennese, yes?"

Most likely, he hadn't been informed why, or whether

they were dangerous. He must have been instructed to notify security, but security must not have arrived yet, or he
wouldn't be so anxious. She was checking out of the hotel
prematurely. Which meant . . . well, there was more than
one possibility. Perhaps she—he? they?—had only recently
been targeted. In which case, preparations would not be
fully in place.

"Listen," she said. "Why don't you just figure it out on
your own time and send me the bill? No biggie, huh?"

"It will be just a few minutes," the manager said, but he
was not looking at her. Instead, he was making eye contact
with a guard across the lobby.

Anna looked at her wristwatch ostentatiously. "Your
cousins are going to be wondering what happened to us,"
she said to Ben. "We'd better get a move on."

The manager stepped around the counter, and placed a
clammy hand on her arm. "In just a few minutes," he said.
Up close, he smelled unappetizingly of grilled cheese and
hair oil.

"Get your hands off me," Anna said in a tone of low
menace. Ben was startled by the sudden steel in her voice.

"We can take you wherever you want to go," the manager protested, in a tone that was more wheedling than
threatening.

From across the lobby, the security guard was reducing
the distance between him and them with long, fast strides.

Anna hoisted her garment bag over her shoulder and
headed for the front door. "Follow me," she said to Ben.

The two made their way quickly toward the entrance.
The lobby guard, she knew, would have to confer with the
manager before pursuing them outside of the building.

On the sidewalk in front of the hotel, she looked around
carefully. At the end of the block, she saw a police officer
speaking into a walkie-talkie, presumably giving his location. Which meant that he was likely the first on the scene.

She tossed her bag to Ben, and headed straight over to
the policeman.

"*Christ*, Anna!" Ben snapped.

Anna stopped the policeman, and spoke to him in a loud, official-sounding voice. "You speak English?"

"Yes," the cop said uncertainly. "English, yes." He was crew-cut, athletic, and seemed to be in his late twenties.

"I'm with the U.S. Federal Bureau of Investigation," Anna said. "The Federal Bureau of Investigation, do you understand? The FBI. We're looking for an American fugitive from justice, and I've got to ask for your help. The woman's name is Anna Navarro." She flashed her OSI badge quickly while holding his gaze; he would see it without really looking at it.

"You say Anna Navarro," the policeman said with recognition and relief. "Yes. We've been notified. In the hotel, yes?"

"She's barricaded herself in her room," Anna said. "Fourteenth floor. Room 1423. And she's traveling with someone, right?"

The policeman shrugged. "Anna Navarro is the name we have," he said.

Anna nodded. It was an important piece of information. "I've got two agents in place, all right? But as observers. We can't act on Austrian territory. It's up to you. I'm going to ask you to take the service entrance, on the side of the building, and make your way to the fourteenth floor. Are you O.K. with that?"

"Yes, yes," the policeman said.

"And spread the word, O.K.?"

He nodded eagerly. "We'll get her for you. Austria is, how do you say, a law-and-order place, yes?"

Anna shot him her warmest smile. "We're counting on you."

A few minutes later, Ben and Anna were in a taxicab en route to the airport.

"That was pretty ballsy," Ben said quietly. "Going up to the cop that way."

"Not really. Those are my people. I figured they'd just

got word, or they would have been better prepared. Which means they had no idea what I look like. All they know is that they're looking for an American, on behalf of the Americans. No way of knowing whether I'm the one to pursue or the one in pursuit."

"When you put it that way . . ." Ben shook his head. "But why are they after you anyway?"

"I haven't exactly figured it out, yet. I do know that somebody's been spreading the word that I've gone rogue. Selling state secrets or whatever. The question is who, and how, and why."

"Sounds to me like Sigma is going through channels. Using real police through manipulation."

"Does, doesn't it?"

"This is not good," Ben said. "The idea that we're going to have every cop in Europe on our ass, on top of whatever psycho-killers Sigma has on the payroll—it's going to put a crimp in the game plan."

"That's one way to put it," Anna said.

"We're dead."

"That's a little harsh." Anna shrugged. "How about we approach this thing one step at a time?"

"How?"

"Ben Hartman and Anna Navarro are going to book a flight from Graz, about a hundred and fifty kilometers south, to Munich."

"And what are we going to do in Munich?"

"We're not going to Munich. The thing is, I already put a trace on your credit cards. That's a genie I can't put back in the bottle. You use any card under your name, and it's going to sound an immediate alarm in Washington and God knows what branch offices we've got."

"So we're screwed."

"So we *use* that. I need you to focus, Ben. Look, your brother prepared travel documents for him and Liesl, in case they needed to take off incognito. As far as we know, the IDs are still good, and the credit card ought to be functional. John and Paula Freedman are going to book tickets from Vienna on the next available flight to Paris. Replacing Liesl's photo with mine won't be a problem. A couple of generic-looking Americans, among tens of thousands who come in and out of the airport every day."

"Right," Ben said. "Right. I'm sorry, Anna. I'm not thinking clearly. But there are still risks, aren't there?"

"Of course there are. Whatever we do has risks. But if we leave now, the chances are good that they're not going to have photographs in place, and they're not looking for Mr. and Mrs. Freedman. The main thing is to stay calm and stay smart. Ready to improvise, if need be."

"Sure," Ben said, but he didn't sound it.

She looked at him. He somehow seemed young, younger than he'd been; the cockiness was gone, and he needed, she sensed, some reassurance. "After all you've been through, I know you're not going to lose your head. You haven't yet. And right now, that's probably the most important thing."

"Getting to Chardin is the most important thing."

"We'll get to him," Anna said, gritting her teeth in resolve. "We'll get to him."

Zurich

Matthias Deschner pressed both hands to his face, hoping for a moment of clarity in the darkness. One of the credit cards that Liesl's boyfriend had, through his offices, established and maintained, had finally been put to use. The call was pro forma: because the account had not been used in quite some time, it fell to a clerk in a credit-security department somewhere to place a call and ascertain that the card had not gone missing.

Peter had provided for the automatic payment of the annual fee; the name, telephone number, and mailing address involved a corporate entity that Matthias had set up for him; all communications went to Deschner, as its legal representative. Deschner had felt quite uncomfortable with the whole thing—it seemed legally dubious, to say the least—but Liesl implored him for his help, and, well, he had done what he had done. In retrospect, he should have run, *run* in the opposite direction. Deschner believed himself to be an honorable man, but he had never had illusions of heroism.

Now a dilemma had arisen for a second time in a matter of days. *Damn* that Ben Hartman. Damn *both* the Hartman boys.

Deschner wanted to keep his word to Peter and Liesl—wanted to even though they both were now dead. But they *were* dead, and with it his oath. And there were now larger considerations.

His own survival, for one.

Bernard Suchet, at the Handelsbank, was too smart to have believed him when he said he'd been completely ignorant of what Peter Hartman was involved in. In truth, it was more a case of not wanting to know, of believing that what he did not know could not hurt him.

That was no longer true.

The more he thought about it, the angrier he became.

Liesl was a lovely girl—he got a lump in his throat when he thought about the necessary past tense—but it had been wrong of her, all the same, to have involved him in her affairs. It was an abuse of familial loyalties, was it not? He imagined himself carrying on a conversation, an argument, really, with his deceased cousin. It was wrong of her, so very wrong. He never wanted any part of her crusade. Had she any idea of the position she put him in?

Her words returned to him: *We need your help. That is all. There is nobody else we can turn to.* Deschner remembered the luminous clarity of her blue eyes, like a deep reservoir of alpine water, eyes whose righteousness seemed to expect equal righteousness in everyone else.

Deschner felt the beginnings of a throbbing headache. The young woman had asked for too much, that was all. Probably of the world, and certainly of him.

She had made enemies of an organization that murdered

people with the simple indifference of a meter maid dis-
pensing parking tickets. Now Liesl was dead, and it seemed
quite possible that she would take him with her.

They would learn that the card had been activated. And
then they would learn that Dr. Matthias Deschner had himself been notified of this fact but failed to report it. Soon
there would be no more Dr. Matthias Deschner. He thought
of his daughter, Alma, who in just two months would be
getting married. Alma had talked about how much she was
looking forward to walking down the aisle with her father
by her side. He swallowed hard and imagined Alma walking down the aisle alone. No, it could not be. It would be
not just reckless but actively *selfish* of him.

The throbbing behind his eyes was undiminished. He
reached into his desk drawer, removed a bottle of Panadol,
and dry-swallowed a bitter, chalky tablet.

He looked at the clock.

He would report the credit activation call. But not immediately. He would wait for several hours to pass. Then
he would call.

The tardiness could be easily explained, and they would
be grateful for his having volunteered the information.
Surely they would.

And just maybe the delay would give the Hartman boy
a running start. A few more hours on this earth, anyway.
He owed him that much, Deschner decided, but perhaps no
more.

CHAPTER THIRTY-TWO

Paris

The twentieth arrondissement of Paris, its easternmost, and seamiest, district, slopes on a butte adjoining the highway that rings Paris and defines its limits, the *Périphérique*. In the eighteenth century, the land supported a village of wine-growers called Charonne. Over the years, the vineyards gave way to small houses, and the houses, in turn, had largely given way to charmless, unlovely structures of concrete. Today, such street names as the rue des Vignoles seem laughably out of place in the downtrodden urban milieu.

The trip to Paris had been nerve-racking; every incidental glance seemed to hold meaning, the very impassivity of *les douaniers*, the customs officials, seemed a possible subterfuge, a prelude to arrest. But Anna had experience with the balkiness of international alerts, knew how the bureaucracies of each border authority impeded the efficient execution of security directives. She wasn't surprised that they'd slipped through. She also knew that, next time, it was a good bet they wouldn't.

Only in the near anonymity of the dense-packed RER

from De Gaulle did they start to relax. Now Anna and Ben
emerged from the Gambetta métro stop, walked passed the
large *Mairie,* or courthouse, and down the rue Vitruve to
the rue des Orteaux. They turned right. Opposite them, to
either side of the rue des Vignoles, were several narrow
streets that followed the precise layout of the vineyards that
they supplanted.

The area around Charonne, just south of Belleville, was
among the least prototypically Parisian of Parisian neighborhoods, its denizens as likely to be Africans, Spaniards,
or Antilleans as French. Even before recent waves of immigration, however, it had long earned the scorn of the
city's bourgeois. It was a place where the poor and the
criminal classes were seen to have congregated, a place
where the insurrectionists of the Paris Commune, fueled by
the disarray of the Second Empire, found populist support.
A place of the disaffected, and the neglected. The twentieth
arrondissement's one claim to fame was the cemetery du
Père Lachaise, a forty-four-hectare garden of graves; starting in the nineteenth century, Parisians who would never
otherwise deign to visit this arrondissement, let alone live
there, agreed to consign their bodies there after death.

Dressed in the casual attire of American tourists, Anna
and Ben took in their surroundings as they walked: the
aroma of falafel stands, the thudding rhythm of North African pop spilling from open windows, street vendors hawk-
ing tube socks and dog-eared copies of *Paris Match.* The
people on the street came in every color, and spoke in a
variety of accents. There were the young artists with complicated body piercings who no doubt saw themselves as
the legitimate successors to Marcel Duchamp; there were
immigrants from the Mahgreb hoping to earn enough
money to send to their relatives in Tunisia or Algeria. The
smell of pot or hashish, rich and resinous, wafted from the
occasional alleyway.

"It's hard to imagine a corporate honcho retiring to this
sort of neighborhood," Anna said. "What, did they run out
of beachfront properties at Côte d'Azure?"

"Actually, it's nearly perfect," Ben said, reflective. "If you wanted to disappear, there's no better place. Nobody notices anybody else, nobody *knows* anybody else. If for some reason you wanted to stay in town, it's the most heterogeneous place you'll find, thronged with strangers, new immigrants, artists, eccentrics of every persuasion." Ben knew this city, as Anna did not, and his familiarity gave him a measure of much needed confidence.

Anna nodded. "Safety in numbers."

"Plus you're still near local mass transit, a maze of streets, a fast train out of town, and the *Périphérique*. A good setup when you're planning multiple escape routes."

Anna smiled. "You're a fast learner. Sure you don't want a job as a government investigator? We can offer you a salary of fifty-five thousand dollars and your very own parking space."

"Tempting," Ben said.

They walked past La Flèche d'Or, the red-tile-roofed restaurant that was perched over a rusted ghost track. Then Ben led the way down another block to a small Moroccan café, where the air was humid and fragrant with various couscous dishes. "I can't vouch for the food," he said. "But the view has a lot to recommend it."

Through the plate glass, they could see the stone triangle that was 1554 rue des Vignoles. Seven stories high, the building occupied a freestanding island surrounded by narrow streets on three sides. Its facade was stained dark with automotive exhaust and dappled with acidic bird droppings. Squinting, Anna could make out the anomalous remains of decorative gargoyles; erosion from the elements made them look as if they had melted in the sun. The marble ledges, ornamental revetment, and parapets seemed the folly of a long-ago builder, a throwback to an era when some still harbored upmarket dreams for the arrondissement. The building, unremarkable in most ways, breathed the gentle decrepitude of neglect and indifference.

"According to my source, Peyaud, he's known as 'L'Ermite.' The hermit. He lives on the entire top floor.

Makes noises from time to time, so they know he's there. That and the deliveries he gets—groceries and the like. But even the delivery boys have never seen him. They drop off the stuff in the dumbwaiter, and collect their francs when the dumbwaiter comes back down. The few people who pay him any mind at all pretty much dismiss him as a real eccentric. Then again, this place is populated with eccentrics." He tucked into his lamb tagine greedily.

"So he's reclusive."

"*Very* reclusive. It's not just the delivery boys he avoids—*nobody's* ever seen him. Peyaud talked to the woman who lives on the ground floor. She and everyone else in the building have decided he's an elderly, paranoid, morbidly shy *rentier*. A case study in advanced agoraphobia. They don't realize that he owns the building."

"And you think we're going to make an unannounced visit to this possibly unhinged, possibly paranoid, possibly dangerous, and certainly disturbed and frightened individual, and he's going to pour us some decaf and tell us whatever we want to know?"

"No, I'm not saying that at all." Ben gave her a reassuring grin. "It might not be decaf."

"You have boundless faith in your own charm, I'll give you that." Anna looked doubtfully at her vegetarian couscous. "He does speak English?"

"Fluently. Almost all French businessmen do, which is how you can tell them apart from French intellectuals." He wiped his mouth with a flimsy paper napkin. "My contribution is, I got us here. You're the professional; you're in charge now. What do the field manuals say? What do you do in a situation like this—what's the established modus operandi?"

"Let me think. The MO for a friendly visit with a psychotic whom the world believes to be dead and who you think holds the secret to a menacing global organization? I'm not so sure that one's in the field manual, Ben."

The lamb tagine started to weigh heavily in his stomach.

She took his hand as they stood up. "Just follow my lead."

Thérèse Broussard gazed sullenly out the window, down at the foot traffic on the rue des Vignoles seven stories below. She gazed as she might have gazed at a fire, if her chimney hadn't been plugged with concrete years back. She gazed as she might have gazed at her little television set, if it hadn't been *détraquée* for the past month. She gazed to soothe her nerves and alleviate her boredom; she gazed because she had nothing better to do. Besides, she'd just spent ten minutes ironing her large, baggy undergarments, and needed a break.

A heavy-set, doughy-faced woman of seventy-four with piggy features and lank black-dyed hair, Thérèse still told people she was a dressmaker, even though she hadn't cut a piece of fabric in ten years, and even though she was never particularly accomplished at it. She grew up in Belleville, left school at the age of fourteen, and was never pretty enough to count on attracting the sort of man who would support her. In short, she had to learn a trade. As it happened, her grandmother had a friend who was a dressmaker and who agreed to take the girl on as an assistant. The old woman's hands were stiff with arthritis, and her eyes had grown dim; Thérèse could be helpful, though the old woman—Tati Jeanne, Thérèse was encouraged to call her—always parted with the paltry few francs she paid her each week with an air of reluctance. Tati Jeanne's already small clientele was dwindling, and with it her earnings; it was painful to have to share even a tiny amount with someone else.

One day in 1945, a bomb fell near Thérèse as she was walking down the Porte de la Chapelle, and, though she was physically unharmed, the blast entered her dreams at night and stopped her from sleeping. Her nervous condition only worsened over time. She would start at the slightest noise, and she began to eat voraciously, whenever she could find the food to stuff herself with. When Tati Jeanne died, Thérèse took on her remaining clients, but it was scarcely a living.

She was alone, as she'd always feared, but she had also learned there were worse things: she owed Laurent that much. Shortly after her sixty-fifth birthday, she met Laurent at the rue Ramponeau, in front of the Soeurs de Nazareth, where she collected a weekly parcel of food. Laurent, another native of the Ménilmontant area, was a decade older than she was, and looked older still. Hunched and bald, he wore a leather jacket whose sleeves were too long for him. He was walking a small dog, a terrier, and she asked the dog's name, and they began to talk. He told her that he fed his dog, Poupée, before he fed himself, gave the dog first choice of everything. She told him about her panic attacks, and the fact that a magistrate for social services, *l'Assedic*, had once placed her under supervision. The magistrate also made sure that the state would provide her with five hundred francs a week. His interest in her perked up when he learned of the support she received. A month later, they were married. He moved into her flat near Charonne; to an impartial eye, it may have appeared small, spare, and dingy but it was still more appealing than his own place, from which he was about to be evicted. Soon after they were married, Laurent pressed her to return to her sewing: they needed the money, the food parcels from the Soeurs scarcely lasted them half the week, the checks from *l'Assedic* were woefully inadequate. She told people she was a dressmaker, didn't she? Why, then, didn't she make dresses? She demurred, quietly at first, holding out her pudgy, blunt fingers, and explaining she no longer had the manual dexterity. He remonstrated, less quietly. She countered with no little vehemence, pointing out that he had a knack for getting fired from even the lowliest jobs, and that she would never have married him if she'd known what a drunkard he was. Seven months later, in the heat of one of these increasingly frequent arguments, Laurent keeled over. His last words to her were *"T'es grasse comme une truie"*—You fat sow. Thérèse let a few minutes pass and her temper subside before she phoned for an ambulance. Later, she'd learn that her husband had been felled by a massive hemorrhagic stroke—an aneurysm deep in the brain. A harried physician told her something about how blood vessels were like inner tubes, and how a weakness in a vessel wall could suddenly give way. She wished Laurent's last words to her had been more civil.

To her few friends, she referred to her husband as a saint, but no one was fooled. Having been married was, at any rate, an education. For much of her life, she believed that a husband would have made her life complete. Laurent had showed her the untrustworthy nature of all men. As she watched various figures on the street corner near her hulking, poured-concrete apartment building, she fantasized about their private deviances. Which of these men was a junkie? Which a thief? Which beat his girlfriend?

A knock at the door, loud and authoritative, jarred her from her reveries. "*Je suis de l'Assedic, laissez-moi entrer, s'il vous plaît!*" A man from the welfare department, asking to be let in.

"Why did you not buzz?" barked Madame Broussard.

"But I did buzz. Repeatedly. The buzzer is broken. As is the gate. Do you claim you didn't know?"

"But why are you here? Nothing about my status has changed," she protested. "My support . . ."

"Is under review," the man said, officiously. "I think we can straighten this all out if we just go over a few matters. Otherwise, the payments come to an end. I do not wish that to happen."

Thérèse trudged heavily over to the door and peered through the peephole. The man had the familiar haughtiness she associated with all *fonctionnaires* of the French state— clerks who imagined themselves to be civil servants, men given a thimbleful of power, and made despotic by it. Something about his voice, his accent seemed less familiar. Perhaps he came from a Belgian family. Thérèse did not like *les Belges*.

She squinted. The man from social services was attired in the thin worsted wool jacket and cheap tie that seemed to come with the job; his hair was a thatch of salt and pepper and he seemed an unremarkable specimen except for his smooth, unlined face; the skin would be babyish, if it didn't look almost tight.

Thérèse unlocked the two deadbolts and released the chain before pressing the final latch and opening the door.

As Ben followed Anna out of the café, he kept his eye on 1554 rue des Vignoles, trying to fathom its mysteries. The building was a picture of ordinary dilapidation—too distressed to excite anyone's admiration, while not so distressed as to arrest anyone's attention. But looking at it carefully—an exercise, Ben imagined, that no one had engaged in for many years—one could see the bones of a once elegant apartment building. It was evident from the oriel windows, crested with carved limestone, now randomly chipped and fractured. It was evident from the corners of the building, the quoins, where dressed stones had been laid so that their faces were alternately large and small; and the mansard roof, edged with a low, crumbling parapet. It was evident even from the narrow ledges that had once provided a balcony, before the iron rail was removed, no doubt after it had rusted to pieces and posed a hazard to public safety. A century ago, a measure of care had gone into the building's construction, which decades of indifference could not entirely efface.

Anna's instructions to him had been clear. They would join a group of passersby as they crossed the street, falling into rhythm with their stride. They would be indistinguishable from people whose destination was the nearby shop that sold cheap liquor and cigarettes, or the *shawarma* place next to it, where a large, fatty oval loaf of meat rotated, close enough to the sidewalk that you could reach out and touch it; certainly swarms of flies did. Anyone watching from the window would see no departure from the ordinary patterns of pedestrian traffic; only when they passed in front of the main door would the two stop and enter.

"Ring the bell?" Ben asked as they reached the building's main entrance.

"If we rang the bell, we wouldn't be unannounced, would we? I thought that was the plan." Glancing around quickly, Anna inserted a narrow tongue of steel into the lock and played with it for a few moments.

Nothing.

Ben felt a sense of rising panic. So far, they had been careful to blend in, to synchronize their pace with those of other pedestrians. But now they found themselves frozen in place; any casual observer would notice that something was wrong, that they did not belong here.

"Anna," he murmured with quiet urgency.

She was bent over her work, and he could see that her forehead was damp with nervous perspiration. "Take out your wallet and start counting your bills," she whispered. "Take out a phone and check for messages. Do something. Calmly. Slowly. *Languorously.*"

The faint sound of metal rattling against metal continued as she spoke.

Then finally, there was the sound of a bolt retracting. Anna turned the lever knob and opened the door. "Sometimes these locks require a little tender loving care. Anyway, it's not exactly high security."

"Hidden in plain view, I think is the idea."

"Hidden, anyway. I thought you said nobody had ever seen him."

"That's true."

"Did you stop and reflect that if he wasn't crazy when he started out, he might have become so? Total social isolation will do that to a person." Anna led him to the disheveled elevator. She pressed the call button, and they briefly listened to a rattling chain before they decided that taking the stairwell was the safer option. They made their way up seven flights, taking care to make as little noise as possible.

The hallway of the top floor, an affair of grimy white tiles, stretched before them.

Startlingly, the doorway of the sole apartment on the floor was already swinging open.

"Monsieur Chabot," Anna called out.

There was no response.

"Monsieur *Chardin!*" she called, exchanging a look with Ben.

There was a movement from within, shrouded in the gloom.

"Georges Chardin!" Anna called again. "We come with information that may be of value to you."

A few moments of silence followed—and then a deafening blast.

What had happened?

A glance at the hallway directly facing the open door made things clear: it was cratered with a deadly spray of lead pellets.

Whoever was in there was firing a shotgun at them.

"I don't know what's *wrong* with you people," Thérèse Broussard said, color rising to her cheeks. "Nothing has changed about my circumstances since my husband died. *Nothing*, I tell you."

The man appeared with a large black suitcase, and strode past her to the window, ignoring her for the moment. A very strange man.

"A nice view," the man said.

"It gets no direct light," Thérèse contradicted him scoldingly. "For most of the day, it is dark. You could develop film in here."

"For some pursuits, that can be an advantage."

Something was wrong. His accent was slipping, his French losing the straightened cadences of the social-services bureaucracy, sounding more casual, somehow less *French*.

Thérèse took a few steps away from the man. Her pulse

quickened as she suddenly remembered the reports of a
rapist who had been brutalizing women in the vicinity of
the Place de la Réunion. Some of the women had been
older, too. This man was an impostor, she decided. Her
instincts told her so. Something about the way the man
moved, with coiled, reptilian strength, confirmed her growing suspicion that he was, in fact, the Réunion rapist. *Mon
dieu!* He'd gained the trust of his victims, she had heard—
victims who had invited the assailant into their very homes!

All her life, people had told her that she suffered from
une maladie nerveuse. She knew better: she saw things, felt
things, that others did not. Yet now, crucially, her antennae
had failed her. How could she have been so foolish! Her
eyes darted wildly around her apartment, looking for something she could use to protect herself. She picked up a
heavy clay pot that contained a slightly shriveled rubber
plant.

"I demand that you leave at once!" she said in a trembling voice.

"Madame, your demands are meaningless to me," the
smooth-faced man said quietly. He looked at her with quiet
menace, a confident predator who knew that his prey was
hopelessly outmatched.

She saw a flash of silver as he unsheathed a long, curved
blade, and then she threw the heavy pot at him with all her
might. But its weight worked against her: it arced quickly
downward, striking the man in the legs, knocking him a
few steps back but leaving him unharmed. *Jésus Christ!*
What else could she use to defend herself? Her little
broken-down TV! She yanked it from the countertop,
hoisted it with great effort above her head, and tossed it at
him as if aiming for the ceiling. The man, smiling, side-
stepped the crude projectile. It thudded against the wall,
then dropped to the floor, its plastic casing shattered along
with the picture tube.

Dear God, no! There had to be something else. *Yes*—
the iron on the ironing board! Had she even turned it off?

Thérèse dashed toward the iron, but as she grabbed it the intruder saw what she was attempting.

"Stop where you are, you revolting old cow," called the man, a look of disgust crossing his face. *"Putain de merde!"* With a lightning-fast motion, he grabbed another, smaller knife and flung it across the room. The deeply beveled steel came to a razor-sharp edge along the entire, arrow-shaped blade; the hollowed tang provided a streamlined counterweight.

Thérèse never saw it coming, but she felt its impact as the blade buried itself deep into her right breast. At first she thought whatever it was had struck her and bounced off. Then she looked down and saw the steel handle protruding from her blouse. It was odd, she thought, that she felt nothing; but then a sensation—cold, like an icicle—began to grow, and an area of red blossomed around the steel. Fear drained from her, replaced with sheer rage. This man thought she was just another victim, but he had misjudged her. She remembered the nighttime visits from her drunken father, which started when she was fourteen, his breath smelling like sour milk as he worked his stubby fingers into her, hurting her with his ragged nails. She remembered Laurent, and his last words to her. Indignation flooded her like water from an underground cistern, from every time she'd ever been taunted, cheated, bullied, abused.

Bellowing, she charged the evil intruder, all two hundred and fifty pounds of her.

And she tackled him, too, slammed him to the ground by sheer momentum.

She would have been proud of what she'd accomplished, *truie grasse* or no, if the man hadn't shot her dead a split-second before her body crashed into his.

Trevor shuddered with revulsion as he pushed the obese, lifeless body off him. The woman was only slightly less off-putting in death that she'd been in life, he reflected as he returned his silenced pistol to its holster, feeling the cylinder's heat against his thigh. The twin bullet holes in her forehead were like a second pair of eyes. He dragged her away from the window. In retrospect, he should have shot her immediately upon gaining entry, but who knew she would turn out to be such a maniac? Anyway, there was always something unexpected. That was why he liked his vocation. It was never entirely routine; there was always the possibility of surprise, new challenges. Nothing, of course, he couldn't handle. Nothing had ever turned up that the Architect couldn't handle.

"*Christ,*" Anna whispered. She had avoided the shotgun spray by a couple of feet at most. "Not exactly the welcome wagon."

But where was the shooter?

A steady succession of blasts was coming from the open apartment door, from somewhere within its darkened interior. Apparently the gunman was firing through the gap between the heavy steel door and the doorjamb.

Ben's heart was thudding. "Georges Chardin," he called out, "we haven't come to harm you. We want to *help* you— and we need your help as well! Please, *listen* to us! Hear us out!"

From the dark recesses of the apartment emanated a bizarre rasping, a shuddering moan of terror, seemingly involuntary, like the night cry of a wounded animal. Still the man remained invisible, cloaked in darkness. They heard the click of a cartridge sliding into the chamber of a shotgun, and each of them raced to opposite ends of the long hallway.

Another explosion! A fusillade of pellets came through the open door, splintering the woodwork in the hall, gouging jagged crevices in the plaster walls. The air was heavy with the pungent odor of cordite. The entire hall now looked like a war zone.

"*Listen!*" Ben called out to their unseen adversary.

"We're not firing back, can't you see that? We're not here to harm you in any way!" There was a pause: was the man hiding inside the apartment actually listening now? "We're here to protect you against Sigma!"

Silence.

The man was listening! It was the invocation of the name of Sigma, the shibboleth of a long-buried conspiracy thundering in its impact.

At that same instant, Ben could see Anna hand-signaling to him. She wanted him to stay where he was while she made her own way into Chardin's apartment. But *how*? With a glance, he saw the large double-hung window, saw her silently nudging open its heavy sash, felt a gust of cold air from outside. She was going to climb out the window, he realized with horror, walk along the narrow exterior ledge until she came to a window that opened directly into the Frenchman's apartment. It was *madness*! He was seized with dread. A stray gust of wind, and she would fall to her death. But it was too late for him to say anything to her; she already had the window open and had stepped onto the ledge. *Christ Almighty!* he wanted to shout. *Don't do it!*

Finally a strange, deep baritone voice emerged from the apartment: "So this time they send an American."

"There's no 'they,' Chardin," replied Ben. "It's just us."

"And who are you?" the voice came back, heavy with skepticism.

"We're Americans, yes, who have . . . personal reasons why we need your help. You see, Sigma killed my brother."

Another long silence ensued. Then: "I am not an idiot. You wish me to come out, and then you will trap me, take me alive. Well, you will *not* take me alive!"

"There are far easier ways, if that's what we wanted to do. Please, let us in—let us speak with you, if only for a minute. You can keep your weapon trained on us."

"For what purpose do you want to speak with me?"

"We need your help in defeating them."

A pause. Then a short, sharp bark of derisive laughter. "In defeating Sigma? You cannot! Until just now I thought one could only hide. How did you find me?"

"Through some damned clever investigative work. But you have my utmost admiration: You did a good job covering your tracks, I must say. A damned good job. It's hard to relinquish control of family property. I understand that. So you used a *fictio juris*. Remote agency. Well designed. But then you've always been a brilliant strategic thinker. It wasn't for nothing that you got to be Trianon's *Directeur Général du Département des Finance*."

Another long silence, followed by the scrape of a chair from inside the apartment. Was Chardin preparing to show his face after all? Ben glanced down the hall apprehensively, saw Anna carefully sliding one foot after another along the ledge while clinging to the parapet with both hands. Her hair blew in the wind. Then she was out of his line of sight.

He had to distract Chardin, keep him from noticing Anna's appearance at his window. *He had to keep Chardin's attention.*

"What is it you want from me?" came Chardin's voice. His tone seemed neutral now. *He was listening; that was the first step.*

"Monsieur Chardin, we have information that could be invaluable to you. We know a great deal about Sigma, about the inheritors, the new generation that has seized control. The only protection—for either of us—is in knowledge."

"There *is* no protection against them, you fool!"

Ben raised his voice. "*Goddamn it!* Your rationality was once legendary. If you've lost that, Chardin, then they've won anyway! Can't you see how unreasonable you're being?" In a gentler tone, he added, "If you send us away, you'll always wonder what you might have learned. Or perhaps you'll never have the opportunity—"

Suddenly there was the sound of glass breaking from inside the apartment, followed immediately by a loud crash and a clatter.

Had Anna made it through a window into Chardin's

apartment safely? A few seconds later he heard Anna's voice, loud and clear. "I've got his shotgun! And it's trained on him now." She obviously spoke for Chardin's benefit as well as Ben's.

Ben strode toward the open door and entered the still-darkened room. It was hard to see anything but shapes; when his eyes adjusted, after a few seconds, he made out Anna, dimly outlined against a thick curtain, holding the long-barreled gun.

And a man in a peculiar, heavy robe with a cowl rose slowly, shakily to his feet. He did not appear to be a vigorous man; he was indeed a shut-in.

It was plain what had happened. Anna, plunging through the window, had leaped onto the long, ungainly shotgun, pinioning it to the floor; the impact must have knocked him over.

For a few moments, all three of them stood in silence. Chardin's breathing was audible—heavy, nearly agonal, his face shadowed within his cowl.

Watching carefully to make sure Chardin didn't have another weapon concealed in the folds of his monklike garment, Ben fumbled for a light switch. When the lights went on, Chardin abruptly turned away from them both, facing the wall. Was Chardin reaching for another gun?

"Freeze!" Anna shouted.

"Use your vaunted powers of reason, Chardin," Ben said. "If we wanted to kill you, you'd already be dead. That's obviously *not* why we're here!"

"Turn and face us," Anna commanded.

Chardin was silent for a moment. "Be careful of what you ask for," he rasped.

"*Now*, dammit!"

Moving as if in slow motion, Chardin complied and when Ben's mind grasped the reality of what he saw, his stomach heaved and he nearly retched. Nor could Anna disguise her shocked intake of breath. It was a horror beyond imagining.

They were staring into an almost featureless mass of scar

tissue, wildly various in texture. In areas it appeared crenellated, almost scalloped; in other areas, the proud flesh was smooth and nearly shiny, as if lacquered or covered in plastic wrap. Naked capillaries made the oval that had once been his face an angry, beefy red, except where varicosities yielded coils of dark purple. The staring, filmy gray eyes looked startlingly out of place—two large marbles left on a slick blacktop by a careless child.

Ben averted his gaze, and then, wrenchingly, forced himself to look again. More details were visible. Embedded in a horribly webbed and wrinkled central concavity were two nasal openings, higher than the nostrils would once have been. Below, he made out a mouth that was little more than a gash, a wound within a wound.

"*Oh, dear God.*" Ben slowly breathed the words.

"You are surprised?" Chardin said, the words scarcely appearing to come from his wound-like mouth. It was if he were a ventriloquist's dummy, one designed by a deranged sadist. A cough-laugh. "The reports of my death were quite accurate, all except for the assertion of death itself. 'Burned beyond recognition'—yes, indeed I was. I should have perished in the blaze. Often I wish that I had. My survival was a freak accident. An enormity. The worst fate a human being can have."

"They tried to kill you," Anna whispered. "And they failed."

"Oh no. I think that in most respects they quite succeeded," Chardin said, and winced: a twitch of dark red muscle around one of his eyeballs. It was apparent that the simple act of talking was painful to him. He was enunciating with exaggerated precision, but the damage meant that certain consonants remained blurry. "A close confidant of mine had suspicions that they might try to eliminate me. Talk had already begun about dispatching the *angeli rebelli*. He came by my country estate—too late. There were ashes, and blackened timber, and charred ruins everywhere. And my body, what was left of it, was as black as any of it. He thought he could detect a pulse, my friend did. He brought me to a tiny provincial hospital, thirty kilometers away, told them a tale about an overturned kerosene lamp, gave them a false name. He was canny. He understood that if my enemies knew I had survived, they would try again. Months passed in that tiny clinic. I had burns over ninety-five percent of my body. I was not expected to live." He spoke haltingly but hypnotically: a tale never before spoken. And then he sat down in a tall-backed wooden chair, seemingly depleted.

"But you survived," Ben said.

"I did not have the strength to force myself to stop breathing," Chardin said. He paused again, the memory of pain imposing further pain. "They wanted to move me to a metropolitan hospital, but of course I would not permit it. I was beyond help anyway. Can you imagine what it is like when consciousness itself is nothing other than the consciousness of pain?"

"And yet you *survived*," Ben repeated.

"The agony was beyond anything our species was meant to endure. Wound dressings were an ordeal beyond imagining. The stench of necrotic flesh was overpowering even to me, and more than one orderly would routinely vomit upon entering my room. Then, after the granulation tissue formed, a new horror was in store for me—contracture. The scars would shrink and the agony would be rekindled all over again. Even today, the pain I live with every moment of every day is of a degree I never experienced in the whole of my preceding life. When I *had* a life. You cannot look at me, can you? No one can. But then I cannot look at myself, either."

Anna spoke, clearly knowing that human contact had to be reestablished. "The strength you must have had—it's extraordinary. No medical textbook could ever account for it. The instinct for survival. You emerged from that blaze. You were saved. Something inside you fought for life. It *had* to be for a reason!"

Chardin spoke quietly. "A poet was once asked, If his house were on fire, what would he save? And he said, 'I would save the fire. Without fire, nothing is possible.' " His laughter was a low, disconcerting rumble. "Fire is after all what made civilization possible: but it can equally be an instrument of barbarity."

Anna returned the shotgun to Chardin after removing a last shell from the chamber. "We need your help," she said urgently.

"Do I look like I am in a position to help anyone, I who cannot help myself?"

"If you want to call your enemies to account, we may be your best bet," Ben said somberly.

"There is no revenge for something like this. I did not survive by drinking the gall of rage." He withdrew a small plastic atomizer from the folds of his robes, and directed a spray of moisture toward his eyes.

"For years, you were at the helm of a major petrochemical corporation, Trianon," Ben prompted. He needed to show Chardin that they had puzzled out the basic situation, needed to *enlist* him. "An industry leader, it was and remains. You were Émil Ménard's lieutenant, the brains behind Trianon's midcentury restructuring. He was a founder of Sigma. And in time you must have become a principal as well."

"Sigma," he repeated in a quavering voice. "Where it all begins."

"And no doubt your genius in accounting helped in the great undertaking of spiriting assets out of the Third Reich."

"Eh? Do you think *that* was the great project? That was *nothing*, a negligible exercise. The grand project . . . *le grand projet* . . ." He trailed off. "That was something of an entirely different order. And nothing you are equipped to comprehend."

"Try me," Ben said.

"And divulge the secrets I have spent my life protecting?"

"You said it yourself: What life?" Ben took a step toward him, forcing down his revulsion in order to maintain eye contact. "What have you left to lose?"

"At last you speak truly," Chardin said softly, and his naked eyes seemed to swivel, peering penetratingly at Ben's own eyes.

For a long moment he was silent. And then he began to talk, slowly, mesmerizingly.

"The story begins before me. It will continue, no doubt, after me. But its origins lie in the closing months of the Second World War, when a consortium of some of the world's most powerful industrialists gathered in Zurich to determine the course of the postwar world."

Ben flashed on the steely-eyed men in the old photograph.

"They were angry men," Chardin went on, "who caught wind of what the ailing Franklin Roosevelt was planning to do—let Stalin know he would not stand in the way of a massive Soviet land grab. And, of course, it's what he did do before his death. In effect he was ceding half of Europe to the Communists! It was the grossest betrayal! These business leaders knew they would be unable to derail the disgraceful U.S.-Soviet bargain at Yalta. And so they formed a corporation that would be a beachhead, a means to channel vast sums of money into fighting communism, strengthening the will of the West. The next world war had begun."

Ben looked at Anna, then stared off into space, hypnotized and astonished by Chardin's words.

"These leaders of capitalism accurately foresaw that the people of Europe, embittered and sickened by fascism, would, in reaction, turn to the left. The soil had been scorched by the Nazis, these industrialists realized, and without the massive infusion of resources at key moments, socialism would begin to take root, first in Europe, then throughout the world. They saw their mission as preserving, fortifying, the industrial state. Which meant, as well, muffling the voices of dissent. Do these anxieties seem overstated? Not so. These industrialists knew how the pendulum of history worked. And if a fascist regime was followed by a socialist regime, Europe might be truly lost, as they saw it.

"It was seen as only prudent to enlist certain leading Nazi officials, who knew which way the wind was blowing and were also committed to combating Stalinism. And once the syndicate had established its political as well as financial foundations, it began manipulating world events, bankrolling political parties as if from behind a curtain. They were successful, astonishingly so! Their money, judiciously targeted, brought to life de Gaulle's Fourth Republic in France, preserved the rightist Franco regime in Spain. In later years, the generals were placed in power in Greece, bringing to an end the leftist regime that the people had elected. In Italy, Operation Gladio ensured that a continual campaign of low-level subversion would cripple the attempt of leftists to organize and influence national politics. Plans were drawn up for the paramilitary police, the *carabinieri*, to take over radio and television stations if necessary. We had extensive files on politicians, unionists, priests. Ultra-right-wing parties everywhere were secretly bolstered from Zurich, so as to make the conservatives seem moderate by contrast. Elections were controlled, bribes paid, leftist political leaders assassinated—and the strings were pulled by the puppet masters in Zurich, in conditions of absolute secrecy. Politicians such as Senator Joseph McCarthy in the U.S. were funded. Coups were financed throughout Europe and Africa and Asia. On the left, extremist groups were created, too, to serve as *agents provocateur* and guarantee popular revulsion toward their cause.

"This cabal of industrialists and bankers had seen to it that the world was made safe for capitalism. Your President Eisenhower, who warned about the rise of the military-industrial complex, saw only the tip of the iceberg. In truth, much of the entire history of the world in the last half-century was scripted by these men in Zurich and their successors."

"*Christ!*" Ben interrupted. "You're talking about . . ."

"Yes," Chardin said, nodding his hideous faceless head.

"Their cabal gave birth to the Cold War. They did. Or, as perhaps I should say, *we* did. Now do you begin to understand?"

Trevor's fingers moved swiftly as he opened his suitcase and assembled the .50 caliber rifle, a customized version of the BMG AR-15. It was, in his view, a thing of beauty, a precision-machined sniper weapon with relatively few moving parts, and a range of up to seventy-four hundred meters. At more proximate distances, its penetrative capacities were astonishing: it could pierce three inches of steel plate, would leave an exit hole in an automobile or hammer off a corner of a building. It could drive through crumbling mortar handily. The bullet would have a projection velocity of over three thousand feet per second. Resting on a bipod, and surmounted by a Leupold Vari-X scope with thermal imaging, the rifle would have the accuracy that he needed. He smiled as he seated the rifle into the bipod. He could hardly be considered underequipped for the job at hand.

His target, after all, was directly across the street.

CHAPTER THIRTY-THREE

"It's *incredible*," Anna said. "It's . . . it's too much to take *in!*"

"I have lived with it so long that it is to me a commonplace," Chardin said. "But I recognize the immense upheavals that would ensue if others realized that the public history of their times was, in no small part, *scripted*—and scripted by a cadre of men like me: businessmen, financiers, industrialists, working through their widely dispersed confederates. *Scripted by Sigma*. The history books would all have to be rewritten. Lives of purpose would suddenly seem like nothing more than the twitching at the end of a marionette's string. Sigma is a story of how the mighty have fallen, and the fallen become mighty. It is a story that must *never* be told. Do you understand that? *Never*."

"But who would be brazen—*mad*—enough to undertake such a venture?" Ben rested his gaze on Chardin's soft brown robes. Now he understood the physical necessity of such strange, loose clothing.

"You must first understand the visionary, triumphalist sense of mission and accomplishment that suffused the midcentury corporation," Chardin said. "We had already transformed man's destiny, remember. My God, the automobile, the airplane, soon the jet: man could move along the ground at speeds inconceivable to our ancestors—man could fly through the heavens! Radio waves and sound waves could be used to provide a sixth sense, vision where vision had never been possible. Computation itself could now be automated. And the breakthroughs in the material sciences were equally extraordinary—in metallurgy, in plastics, in production techniques yielding new forms of rubber and adhesives and textiles, and a hundred other things. The ordinary landscape of our lives was being transformed. A revolution was taking place in every aspect of modern industry."

"A second industrial revolution," Ben said.

"A second, a third, a fourth, a *fifth*," Chardin replied. "The possibilities seemed infinite. The capabilities of the modern corporation seemed to be unbounded. And after the dawn of nuclear science—my God, what *couldn't* we achieve if we set our minds to it? There was Vannevar Bush, Lawrence Marshall, and Charles Smith, at Raytheon, doing pioneering work in everything from microwave generation to missile guidance systems to radar surveillance equipment. So many of the discoveries that became ubiquitous in later decades—xerography, microwave technologies, binary computing, solid-state electronics—had already been conceived and prototyped at Bell Labs, General Electric, Westinghouse, RCA, IBM, and other corporations. The material world was succumbing to our will. Why not the political realm as well?"

"And where were *you* during all this?" Ben asked.

Chardin's eyes fixed on a point in the middle distance. From the folds of his cloak, he withdrew the atomizer, and moistened his eyes again. He pressed a white handkerchief to the area under his slash-like mouth, which was slick with saliva. And, haltingly at first, he began to speak.

*   *   *

I was a child—eight years old when the war broke out. A student at a shabby little provincial school, the Lycée Beaumont, in the city of Lyon. My father was a civil engineer with the city, my mother a schoolteacher. I was an only child, and something of a prodigy. By the time I was twelve, I was taking courses in applied mathematics at the École Normale Supérieure de Lyon, the teacher's college. I had genuine quantitative gifts, and yet the academy held no appeal for me. I wanted something else. The ozone-scented arcana of number theory held little allure. I wanted to affect the real world, the realm of the everyday. I lied about my age when I first sought employment in the accounting department of Trianon. Emil Ménard was already heralded as a prophet among CEOs, a true visionary. A man who had forged a company out of disparate parts, where no one had previously seen any potential for connection. A man who realized that by assembling once segmented operations you could create an industrial power infinitely greater than the sum of its parts. To my eyes, as an analyst of capital, Trianon was a masterpiece—the Sistine Chapel of corporate design.

Within a matter of months, word of my statistical prowess had reached the head of the department for which I worked, Monsieur Arteaux. He was an older gentleman, a man of few hobbies and a near total devotion to Ménard's vision. Some of my co-workers found me cold, but not Monsieur Arteaux. With us, conversation flowed as if between two sports fans. We could discuss the relative advantages of internal capital markets or alternate measurements of equity risk premiums, and do so for hours. Matters that would stupefy most men, but which involved the architecture of capital itself—rationalizing the decisions of where to invest and reinvest, how risk was best to be apportioned. Arteaux, who was nearing retirement, put everything on the line by arranging for me to be introduced to the great man himself, catapulting me over endless managerial layers. Ménard, amused by my obvious youth, asked me a few condescending questions. I replied with rather serious and rather provocative responses—in truth, responses that verged on rudeness. Arteaux himself was appalled. And Ménard was, so it seems, captivated. An unusual response, but it was, in capsule form, an explanation of his own greatness. He told me later that my combination of inso- lence and thoughtfulness reminded him of no one so much as himself. A magnificent egotist, he was, but it was an earned egotism. My own arrogance—for even as a child I was tagged with that attribute—was perhaps not un- founded, either. Humility was a fine thing for men of the cloth. But rationality decreed that one be sensible to one's own capabilities. I had considerable expertise in the tech- niques of valuation. Why shouldn't it logically extend to the valuation of oneself? My own father was, I believed, hand- icapped by a deferential manner; he esteemed his own gifts too little, and persuaded others to undervalue them in turn. That would not be my mistake.

I became, in a matter of weeks, Ménard's personal as- sistant. I accompanied him absolutely everywhere. No one knew whether I was an amanuensis or a counselor. And in truth I moved, smoothly, from playing the first role to play- ing the second. The great man treated me far more like an adopted son than a paid employee. I was his only protégé, the sole acolyte who seemed worthy of his example. I would make proposals, sometimes bold ones, occasionally pro- posals that reversed years of planning. I suggested, for ex- ample, that we sell off an oil-exploration division that his managers had spent years in developing. I suggested mas- sive investments in still unproven technologies. Yet when he heeded my advice, he almost invariably found himself pleased by the results. L'ombre de Ménard—the shadow of Ménard—became my nickname in the early 1950s. And even as he fought the disease, the lymphoma, that would ultimately claim his life, he and Trianon came to rely in- creasingly upon my judgment. My ideas were bold, unheard of, seemingly mad—and soon widely mimicked. Ménard studied me as much as I studied him, with both detachment and genuine affection. We were men in whom such qualities enjoyed an easy coexistence.

Yet for all the privileges he granted me, I had sensed, for a while, that there was one final sanctum to which I had not been granted entry. There were trips he made without explanation, corporate allocations I could not make sense of and about which he would brook no discussion. Then the day came when he decided that I would be inducted into a society I knew nothing about, an organization you know as Sigma.

I was still Ménard's wunderkind, still the corporate prodigy, still in my early twenties, and utterly unprepared for what I was to see at the first meeting I attended. It was at a château in rural Switzerland, a magnificent ancient castle situated on a vast and isolated tract of land owned by one of the principals. The security there was extraordinary: even the landscaping, the trees and shrubbery surrounding the property, was designed to permit the clandestine arrival and departure of various individuals. So on my first visit, I was in no position to see the others arrive. And no form of surveillance equipment could have survived the high-intensity blasts of high and low electromagnetic pulses, the latest technology in those days. All items made of metal were required to be deposited in containers made of dense osmium; otherwise, even a simple wristwatch would have been stopped dead by the pulses. Ménard and I came there in the evening, and were escorted directly to our rooms, he to a magnificent suite overlooking a small glacial lake, I to an adjoining chamber, less grand but exceedingly comfortable.

The meetings began the next morning. About what was said then, I actually remember little. Conversations continued from earlier ones of which I knew nothing—it was difficult for a newcomer to orient himself. But I knew the faces of the men around the table, and it was a genuinely surreal experience, something a fantasist might have tried to stage. Ménard was a man who had few peers, with respect to his own wealth, his corporate power, or his vision. But what peers he had were there in the room. The heads of two warring, mighty steel conglomerates. The head of America's leading electrical equipment manufacturers. Heavy industry. Petrochemicals. Technology. The men responsible for the so-called American century. Their counterparts from Europe. The most famous press baron in the world. The chief executives of wildly diversified portfolio companies. Men who, in combination, wielded control over assets that exceeded the gross domestic product of most of the countries in the world put together.

My worldview was shattered that day, then and forever.

Children, in history classes, are taught the names, the faces of political and military leaders. Here is Winston Churchill, here is Dwight Eisenhower, here is Franco and de Gaulle, Atlee and Macmillan. These men did matter. But they were, really, little more than spokesmen. They were, in an exalted sense, press secretaries, employees. And Sigma made sure of it. The men who truly had their hands on the levers of power were sitting around that long mahogany table. They were the true marionette masters.

As the hours passed, and we drank coffee and nibbled on pastries, I realized what I was witness to: a meeting of the board of directors of a massive single corporation that controlled all other corporations.

A board of directors in charge of Western history itself!

It was their attitude, their perspective, that stayed with me, far more than any actual words that were uttered. For these were professional managers who had no time for useless emotion or irrational sentiments. They believed in the development of productivity, in the promulgation of order, in the rational concentration of capital. They believed, in plain English, that history—the very destiny of the human race—was simply too important to repose in the hands of the masses. The upheavals of two world wars had taught them that. History had to be managed. *Decisions had to be made by dispassionate professionals. And the chaos threatened by communism—the turmoil, the redistribution of wealth it augured, made their project a matter of genuine and immediate urgency. It was a present danger to be averted, not some utopian scheme.*

They assured each other of the need to create a planet where the true spirit of enterprise would ever be safe from the envy and avarice of the masses. After all, was a world purulent with communism and fascism a world any of us wished to bequeath to our children? Modern capital showed us the way—but the future of the industrial state had to be protected, sheltered from the storms. That was the vision. And though the origins of this vision lay in the global depression that preceded the war, the vision became infinitely more compelling in the wake of the destruction wreaked by the war itself.

I said little that day, not because I was by nature taciturn, but because I was quite literally speechless. I was a pygmy among giants. I was a peasant supping with emperors. I was beside myself, and all the while it was the most I could do to maintain a look of dispassion, in emulation of my great mentor. Those were the first hours I spent in the company of Sigma, and my life would never be the same again. The daily fodder of the newspapers—a labor strike here, a party assembly there, an assassination somewhere else—was no longer a record of random events. Behind these events could now be discerned a pattern—the complex and intricate machinations of a complex and intricate machine.

To be sure, the founders, the principals, profited immensely. Their corporations, in every instance, thrived, while so many others, not fortunate enough to be part of Sigma, perished. But the real motivation was their larger vision: the West had to be united against a common foe, or it would soften and succumb. And the hardening of its battlements had to proceed with discretion and prudence. Too aggressive, too quick a push could trigger a backlash. Reform had to be titrated. One division focused on assassinations, removing thoughtful voices from the left. Another forged—the word is appropriate—the sorts of extremist groups, the Baader-Meinhofs and Red Brigades, that would be guaranteed to antagonize any moderate sympathizers.

The Western world, and much of the rest, would respond to its ministrations, and it would accept the cover stories that accompanied them. In Italy, we created a network of twenty thousand "civic committees," channeling money to the Christian Democrats. The Marshall Plan itself, like so much else, was hammered out by Sigma—very often Sigma had devised the very language of the acts that would be submitted to, and passed by the American Congress! All of the European recovery programs, economic cooperation agencies, eventually even NATO itself became organs of Sigma, which remained invisible—because it was ubiquitous. Wheels within wheels—that was the way we worked. In every textbook, you find boilerplate about the reconstruction of Europe accompanied by a photograph of General Marshall. Yet every detail had been outlined by us, mandated by us, long before.

It never crossed anyone's mind that the West had fallen under the administration of a hidden consortium. The notion would be inconceivable. Because if true, it would mean that over half of the planet was effectively a subsidiary of a single megacorporation.

Sigma.

Over time, older moguls died and were replaced with younger protégés. Sigma persisted, metamorphosing where necessary. We weren't ideologues. We were pragmatists. Sigma merely sought to remodel the whole of the modern world. To claim nothing less than the ownership of history itself.

And Sigma succeeded.

Trevor Griffiths squinted through the thermal imaging scope. The heavy room-darkening drapes were optically opaque, but to the thermal scope, they were a gauzy scrim. Human figures were hazy green forms, like blobs of mercury, visibly changing shape as they moved around pillars and objects of furniture. The seated figure would be his primary target. The others would move away from the windows, thinking themselves safe, and he would destroy them through the wall of brick itself. One bullet would clear the way; the second would destroy his target. The remaining shells would complete the job.

"If what you're saying is true . . ." Ben began.

"Men lie, for the most part, in order to save face. You can see I no longer have such motivation." The slit that was Chardin's mouth pulled up at the sides, in what was either a grimace or a smile. "I warned you that you were ill-equipped to understand what I had to say. Perhaps, though, you may now understand the situation somewhat more clearly than before. A great many powerful men everywhere—even today—have reason to keep the truth buried. More so than ever, indeed. For Sigma has, over the past several years, been moving in a new direction. In part, it was the result of its own successes. Communism was no longer a threat—it seemed pointless to continue to pour billions into the orchestration of civil acts and political forces. Not when there might be a more efficient way of achieving Sigma's objectives."

"Sigma's objectives," Ben echoed.

"Which is to say, stability. Tamping down dissent, 'disappearing' troublemakers and threats to the industrial state. When Gorbachev proved troublesome, we arranged his ouster. When regimes in the Pacific Rim proved balky, we arranged for an abrupt, massive flight of foreign capital, plunging their economies into a recession. When Mexico's leaders proved less than cooperative, we arranged for a change in government."

"My *God*," Ben said, his mouth dry. "Listen to what you're saying . . ."

"Oh yes. A session would be convened, a decision rendered and, shortly thereafter, executed. We were good at it, frankly—we could play the governments of the world like a pipe organ. Nor did it hurt that Sigma came to own an immense portfolio of companies, its ownership stakes hidden through various private equity firms. But a small inner circle came to believe that, in a new era, the answer wasn't merely to tack to the latest winds, cope with cyclical crises. It was to perpetuate a stable leadership for the long run. And so in recent years, one very special project of Sigma's came to the fore. The prospect of its success would revolutionize the nature of world control. No longer would it be about the allocation of funds, the directing of resources. It became, instead, a simple matter of who the 'chosen' would be. And I fought this."

"You had a falling out with Sigma," Ben said. "You became a marked man. And yet you kept its secrets."

"I say it again: if ever the truth were to get out, about how many of the major events of the postwar era were secretly manipulated, scripted by this cabal, the reaction would be violent. There would be riots in the streets."

"Why the sudden escalation of activity—you're describing something that has unfolded over a period of *decades!*" Ben said.

"Yes, but we are talking about *days*," Chardin replied.

"And you *know* this?"

"You wonder that a recluse like me should keep abreast of what is going on? You learn how to read the entrails. You *learn*, if you want to survive. And then there is precious little else to occupy a shut-in's hours. Years among their company have taught me to detect signals in what would sound to you like static, mere noise." He gestured toward the side of his head. Even through the cowl, Ben could tell that the man's external ear was completely absent, the auditory canal simply a hole within an outgrowth of proud flesh.

"And this explains the sudden flurry of killings?"

"It is as I explained: Sigma has, of late, been undergoing one final transformation. A change of management, if you will."

"Which you resisted."

"Long before most were attuned to it. Sigma always reserved the right to 'sanction' any members whose absolute loyalty came into question. In my arrogance, I did not realize that my exalted position conferred no protection. Quite the contrary. But the cleansing, the purging of the dissidents, only began in earnest in the last several weeks. Those who were perceived as hostile to the new direction— along with those who worked for us—were designated as disloyal. We were called the *angeli rebelli*: rebel angels. If you recall that the original *angeli rebelli* had revolted against God Almighty himself, you grasp the sense of power and entitlement of Sigma's current overlords. Or, shall I say, overlord, since the consortium has come under the direction of one . . . redoubtable individual. In the event, Sigma has run out the clock, so to say."

"*What* clock? *Explain* it to me," Ben began. So many questions crowded his mind.

"We're talking about days," Chardin repeated. "If *that*. What fools you are, coming to me as if knowing the truth could help you anymore. Coming to me when there is no time! Surely it is already too late."

"What are you talking about?"

"It's why I had assumed you'd been sent, at first. They know that they are never more vulnerable than shortly before the final ascendancy. As I've told you, now is a time for final mop-ups, for sterilization and autoclaving, for eliminating any evidence that might point to them."

"Again, I ask you, *why now?*"

Chardin took out the atomizer and misted his filmy gray eyes again. There came a sudden explosion, bone-jarringly loud, which propelled Chardin, in his chair, backward to the floor. Both Ben and Anna sprang at once to their feet and saw with terror the two-inch round hole that instantaneously appeared in the plaster wall opposite, as if somehow put there by a large-bore drill.

"*Move!*" Anna screamed.

Where had this projectile—it seemed far too big to be a mere gunshot—come from? Ben leaped to one side of the room as Anna jumped to the other, and then he whirled around to look at the splayed body of the legendary financier. Forcing himself to survey, once more, the horrible ravines and crevices of scar tissue, he noticed Chardin's eyes had rolled back into his head, leaving only the whites visible.

A wisp of smoke arose from a charred segment of his cowl, and Ben realized that an immense bullet had passed through Chardin's skull. The faceless man—the man whose will to survive had enabled him to endure years of indescribable agony—was dead.

What had happened? *How?* Ben knew only that if they didn't seek cover immediately they would be killed next. But where could they move, how could they escape an assault when they didn't know where it came from? He saw Anna race to the far side of the room, then swiftly lower herself to the floor, lying flat, and he did the same.

And then came a second explosion, and another round punched through the solid exterior wall and then through the plaster interior wall. Ben saw a circle of daylight in the brick wall, saw now that the shots had come from outside!

Whatever their assailant was firing, the rounds had penetrated the brick wall as if it were a bead curtain. The last round had come dangerously close to Anna.

Nowhere was safe.

"Oh, my *God!*" Anna shouted. "We've got to get out of here!"

Ben whirled and looked out the window. In a glint of reflected sunlight, he caught the face of a man in a window directly across the narrow street.

The smooth, unlined skin, the high cheekbones.

The assassin at Lenz's villa. The assassin at the auberge in Switzerland . . .

The assassin who had murdered Peter.

Stoked by a towering rage, Ben let out a loud shout, of warning, of disbelief, of anger. He and Anna simultaneously raced to the apartment's exit. Another hole exploded, deafeningly, in the outside wall; Ben and Anna made a dash to the staircase. These missiles would not lodge in the flesh, nor sear skin; they would tear through the human body like a spear through a spider's web. Clearly they were designed for use against armored tanks. The devastation they had done to the old building was incredible.

Ben ran after Anna, leaping and bounding down the dark stairs, as the volley of explosions continued, plaster and brick crumbling audibly behind them. Finally they staggered down to the small lobby. "This way!" whispered Anna, racing to an exit that would take them not to the rue des Vignoles but to a side street, making it far more difficult for the assassin to target them. Emerging from the building, they looked frantically about them.

Faces all around. At the corner of the rue des Orteaux, a blond woman, in denim and fake fur. At first glance, she looked like a hooker, or a junkie, but there was something about her that struck Ben as *off*. Again, it was a face he'd *seen* before. But where?

Suddenly he flashed back to the Bahnhofstrasse. An expensively dressed blonde, holding shopping bags from an upscale boutique. The flirtatious exchange of glances.

It was the same woman. A sentry for the Corporation? Across the street from her, a male adolescent in a ripped T-shirt and jeans: he, too, looked familiar, although Ben couldn't place him. My God! Another one?

At the opposite end of the street stood a man with ruddy, weathered cheeks and wheat-field eyebrows.

Another familiar face.

Three Corporation killers placed strategically around them? Professionals intent on making sure they'd never escape?

"We're boxed in," he said to Anna. "At least one of them's on either end of the street." They froze in place, unsure how or where to move next.

Anna's eyes searched the street, then she replied. "Listen, Ben. You said Chardin had chosen this district, this block, for good reason. We don't know what contingency plans he had, what escape routes he'd mapped out in advance, but we know that he must have had something in

mind. He was too smart *not* to have arranged for path redundancy."

"Path redundancy?"

"Follow me."

She ran straight toward the very apartment building
where the assassin had taken up his seventh-floor perch.
Ben saw where she was headed. "That's insane!" he protested, but he followed nonetheless.

"No," Anna replied. "The base of the building is one
place he *can't* reach." The alleyway was dark and fetid, the
scampering of rats evidence of the quantities of refuse that
had been allowed to accumulate there. A locked metal gate
blocked off its egress to the rue des Halles.

"Should we climb?" Ben looked doubtfully at the top of
the gate whose sharp-pointed spearlike rods loomed twelve
feet above them.

"*You* can," Anna said, and unholstered a Glock. Three
carefully aimed blasts, and the chain that locked the gate
swung free. "The guy was using a .50 caliber rifle. There
was a flood of them after Desert Storm. They were a hot
commodity, because with the right ammunition they could
put a hole right through an Iraqi tank. If you've got one of
those monsters, a city like this might as well be made out
of cardboard."

"Shit. So what do we do?" Ben asked.

"Don't get hit," Anna replied tersely, and she began running, Ben close behind.

Sixty seconds later they found themselves on the rue de
Bagnolet in front of La Flèche d'Or restaurant. Suddenly
Ben darted across the street. "Stay with me."

A heavy-set man was just getting off a Vespa, one of
those small motorized *vélocipedes* that had achieved nui-
sance status among French drivers.

"*Monsieur*," Ben said. "*J'ai besoin de votre vélo.
Pardonnez-moi, s'il vous plaît.*"

The bear-like man gave him an incredulous look.

Ben pointed his gun at him and grabbed the keys. The
owner stepped backward, cowering, as Ben leaped onto the

small vehicle and revved the motor. "Get on," Ben called out to Anna.

"You're crazy," she protested. "We'd be vulnerable to anyone in an automobile, once we get on the *Périphérique*. These things don't go any faster than fifty miles an hour. It's going to be a turkey shoot!"

"We're not going on the *Périphérique*," Ben said. "Or any other road. Climb *on*!"

Bewildered, Anna complied, taking the seat behind Ben on the motorbike.

Ben drove the Vespa around La Flèche d'Or and then, joltingly, down a concrete embankment that led to old railroad tracks. The restaurant, Anna could now see, was actually built directly over the tracks.

Now Ben steered onto the rusted tracks. They drove through a tunnel, then back into an open stretch. The Vespa kicked up dust, but the passage of time had flattened the tracks here into the earth, and the ride became smooth and swifter.

"So what happens when we meet a train?" Anna shouted, grasping onto him tightly as they rolled over the tracks.

"There hasn't been a train on these tracks for over half a century."

"Aren't we full of surprises."

"The product of a misspent youth," Ben shouted back. "I once messed around here as a teenager. We're on a ghost railroad line known as the *Petite Ceinture*, the little belt. It runs all the way around the city. Phantom tracks. La Flèche d'Or is actually an old railroad station, built in the nineteenth century. Connected twenty stations in a loop around Paris—Neuilly, Porte Maillot, Clichy, Villette, Charonne, plenty more. The automobile killed it off, but nobody ever reclaimed the belt. Now it's mostly a long stretch of nothing. I was thinking some more about why Chardin decided on this particular neighborhood, and then I remembered the phantom line. A useful piece of the past."

They passed through another spacious tunnel, then back into the open air.

"Where are we now?" Anna asked.

"Hard to gauge, since you can't see any of the landmarks from here," Ben said. "But probably Ford d'Obervillier. Maybe Simplon. Way the hell away. Central Paris isn't very big, of course. The whole thing is about forty square miles. If we can make our way into the métro and join a few hundred thousand Parisians there, we can begin to make our way to our next appointment."

The Flann O'Brien—the bar's name was displayed in coiled neon as well as painted in curlicued script in the window—was in the first arrondissement, on the rue Bailleul, near the Louvre-Rivoli stop. It was a dark, beery establishment, with lots of deeply grooved old wood and a dark wood floor that had soaked up sloshes of Guinness for years.

"We're meeting him at an Irish bar?" Anna asked. Her head swiveled around by something like reflex, as she scanned their surroundings, alert to any sign of threat.

"Oscar has a sense of humor, what can I say?"

"And remind me why you're so sure he can be trusted?"

Ben turned serious. "We've got to deal with probabilities, not possibilities, we're agreed on that. And so far he's been on the level. What makes Sigma a menace is the fact that it commands the loyalty of true believers. Oscar's too damn *greedy* to be a believer. Our checks have always cleared. I think that counts with Oscar."

"The honor of the cynic."

Ben shrugged. "I've got to go with my gut. I like Oscar, always have. I think he likes me."

The din in the Flann O'Brien, even at this hour, was overwhelming, and it took their eyes a while to adjust to the dim lighting.

Oscar was tucked away at a banquette toward the back, a diminutive gray-haired man behind an enormous tankard of viscous stout. Beside the tankard was a neatly folded newspaper, with a half-completed crossword puzzle. He had an amused expression on his face, as if he were about to wink—Anna soon realized that this was simply his habitual expression—and he greeted the two with a simple wave of the hand.

"I've been waiting for forty minutes," he said. He grabbed Ben's hand in an affectionate, wrestling clasp. "Forty *billable* minutes." He seemed to be savoring the world as it rolled off his tongue.

"A bit of a holdup at our previous engagement," Ben said tersely.

"I can imagine." Oscar nodded at Anna. "Madame," he said. "Please, sit."

Ben and Anna slid onto the banquette on either side of the small Frenchman.

"Madame," he said, turning his full attention to her. "You are even more beautiful than your photograph."

"Sorry?" Anna replied, puzzled.

"A set of photographs of you was recently wired to my colleagues in *la Sûreté*. Digital image files. I got a set of them myself. Came in handy."

"For his work," Ben explained.

"My *artisans*," Oscar said. "So very good and so *very* expensive." He tapped Ben on his forearm.

"I'd expect nothing less."

"Of course, Ben, I can't say your photograph does justice to you either. Those paparazzi, they never find the flattering angle, do they?"

Ben's smile faded. "What are you talking about?"

"I'm very proud of myself for doing the *Herald Tribune* crossword puzzle. Not every Frenchman could do it, you'll grant. I've almost finished this one. All I need now is a fifteen-letter word for an internationally wanted fugitive from justice."

He turned the newspaper over.

" 'Benjamin Hartman'—would that do it?"

Ben looked at the front page of the *Tribune* and felt as

if he had been plunged headfirst into ice water. SERIAL KILLER SOUGHT was the headline. Beside it was a low-resolution photograph of him, apparently taken from a surveillance camera. His face was shadowed, the image grainy, but it was unmistakably him.

"Who knew my friend was such a celebrity?" Oscar said, and turned the paper over again. He laughed loudly, and Ben belatedly joined him, realizing it was the only way one escaped notice in a bar filled with drink-fueled merriment.

From the next banquette over, he overheard a Frenchman trying to sing "Danny Boy," with uncertain pitch and an only rough approximation of the vowels. *Oh, Danny Boy, ze peeps ze peeps are caaalling.*

"This is a problem," Ben said, his urgent tone belying the soapy grin on his face. His eyes darted back to the newspapers. "This is an Eiffel Tower–sized problem."

"You *kill* me," Oscar said, slapping Ben on the back as if he had uttered a hilarious joke. "The only people who say there's no such thing as bad publicity," he said, "have never gotten bad publicity." Then he tugged a package from beneath the cushion of his seat. "Take this," he said.

It was a white plastic bag with gaudy lettering, from a tourist gift shop somewhere. *I love Paris in the Springtime,* it said, with a heart standing in for the word "love." It had the kind of stiff plastic handles that snapped shut when pressed together.

"For us?" Anna asked doubtfully.

"No tourist should be without," Oscar said. His eyes were playful; they were also intensely serious.

'Teez I'll be here in sunshine or in shaadow.

Oh, Danny boy, I love you sooo.

The drunken Frenchman at the next banquette was now joined, in various keys, by his three companions.

Ben sank lower in his seat, as the full weight of his predicament bore upon him.

Oscar punched him in the arm; it looked jocular, but it stung. "Don't slink down in your seat," he whispered. "Don't look furtive, don't avoid eye contact, and don't try to look inconspicuous. That's about as effective as a movie star putting on sunglasses to shop at Fred Segal, *tu comprends?*"

"*Oui*," Ben said weakly.

"Now," Oscar said, "what's that charming American expression you have? 'Get the fuck out of here.' "

After acquiring a few items at some small side-street stalls, they returned to the métro, where they were just another couple of moony-eyed tourists to the casual spectator.

"We've got to make plans—plans for what the hell to do next," Ben said.

"Next? I don't see what choice we have," Anna said. "Strasser's the one surviving link we know about—a member of Sigma's board of incorporators who's still alive. We've got to reach him somehow."

"Who says he's still alive?"

"We can't afford to assume otherwise."

"You realize they're going to be watching every airport, every terminal, every gate."

"It's occurred to me, yes," Anna replied. "You're beginning to think like a professional. A real fast learner."

"I believe they call this the immersion method."

On a long underground journey to one of the *banlieues*, the downtrodden areas that ringed Paris proper, the two conversed in low voices, making plans like lovebirds, or fugitives.

They got out at the stop at La Courneuve, an old-fashioned working-class neighborhood. It was only a few miles away, but a different world—a place of two-story houses and unpretentious shops that sold things to use, not to display. In the windows of the bistros and convenience stores, posters for Red Star, the second-division soccer team, were prominent. La Courneuve, due north of Paris, wasn't far from Charles De Gaulle airport, but that was not where they'd be heading.

Ben pointed to a bright red Audi across the street. "How about that one?"

Anna shrugged. "I think we can find something less noticeable." A few minutes later, they came across a blue Renault. The car had a light coating of grime, and on the floor inside there were yellow wrappers from fast-food meals, and a few cardboard coffee cups.

"I'll put my money on the owner being home for the night," Ben said. Anna set to work with her rocker pick, and a minute later had the car door unlocked. Disassembling the ignition cylinder on the steering column took a little more time, but soon the motor roared to life and the two took off down the street, driving at the legal speed limit.

Ten minutes later, they were on the A1 highway, en route to the Lille-Lesquin airport in Nord–Pas de Calais. The trip would take hours, and involve risks, but they were calculated ones: auto theft was commonplace in La Courneuve, and the predictable police response would be to make perfunctory inquiries among the locals known to be involved in the activity. The matter would almost certainly not be referred to the *Police Nationale*, which patrolled the major thoroughfares.

They drove in silence for half an hour, lost in their own thoughts.

Finally, Anna spoke. "The whole thing Chardin talked about—it's just impossible to absorb. Somebody tells you that everything you know about modern history is wrong, upside down. How can that be?" Her eyes remained fixed on the road in front of her, and she sounded as utterly drained as Ben felt.

"I don't know, Anna. Things stopped making sense for me that day at the Bahnhofplatz." Ben tried to stave off a profound sense of enervation. The rush of their successful escape had long since given way to a larger sense of dread, of terror.

"A few days ago, I was essentially conducting a homicide investigation, not examining the foundations of the modern age. Would you believe?"

Ben did not directly reply: what reply could there be? "The homicides," he said. He felt a vague unease. "You said it started with Mailhot in Nova Scotia, the man who worked for Charles Highsmith, one of the Sigma founders. And then there was Marcel Prosperi, who was himself one of the principals. Rossignol, likewise."

"Three points determine a plane," Anna said. "High-school geometry."

Something clicked in Ben's mind. "Rossignol was alive when you flew off to see him, but dead by the time you arrived, right?"

"Right, but—"

"What's the name of the man who gave you the assignment?"

She hesitated. "Alan Bartlett."

"And when you'd located Rossignol, in Zurich, you told him, right?"

"First thing," Anna said.

Ben's mouth became dry. "Yes. Of course you did. That's why he brought you in, in the first place."

"What are you talking about?" She craned her neck and looked at him.

"Don't you see? You were the cat's-paw, Anna. *He was using you.*"

"Using me *how?*"

The sequence of events cascaded in Ben's mind. "*Think*, dammit! It's just the way you might prepare a bloodhound. Alan Bartlett first gives you the scent. He knows the way you work. He knew the next thing you'd demand . . ."

"He knew I'd ask him for the list," Anna said, her voice hollow. "Is this possible? That damned show of reluctance on his part—a piece of theater for my benefit, knowing it would only steel my resolve? The same with the goddamn car in Halifax: maybe he knew a scare like that would make me that much keener."

"And so you get a list of names. Names of people connected with Sigma. But not just any names: these are people who are *in hiding*. People whom Sigma *cannot find*—not without alerting them. Nobody connected with Sigma could possibly reach these people. *Otherwise they would have been dead already*."

"Because . . ." Anna began slowly. "Because all of the victims were *angeli rebelli*. The apostates, the dissidents. People who could no longer be trusted."

"And Chardin told us that Sigma was approaching a delicate transitional phase—a time of maximum vulnerability. It *needed* these people eliminated. But *you* could find somebody like Rossignol precisely because *you were who you said you were*. You really *were* trying to save his life. And your bona fides could be verified in meticulous detail. Yet you had been unknowingly *programmed!*"

"Which is why Bartlett gave me the assignment in the first place," Anna said, her voice growing steadily louder, a realization dawning. "So that I would locate the remaining *angeli rebelli*." She banged a hand on the dashboard.

"Whom Bartlett would then arrange to have killed. *Because Bartlett is working for Sigma*." He hated himself for the pain that his words had to be causing her, but everything was now coming into sharp focus.

"And in effect so was I. God*damn* it to hell! *So was I*."

"*Unwittingly*," Ben emphasized. "As a *pawn*. And when you were becoming too hard to control, he tried to pull you off the case. They'd already found Rossignol, they didn't need you anymore."

"*Christ!*" Anna said.

"Of course, it's no more than a theory," Ben said, though he felt certain he was speaking the truth.

"A theory, yes. But it makes too much damned *sense*."

Ben didn't reply. The demand that reality make sense seemed now an outlandish luxury. Chardin's words filled his mind, their meaning as hideous as the face of the man who spoke them. *Wheels within wheels—that was the way we worked . . . organs of Sigma, which remained invisible . . . Every detail had been outlined by us . . . long be-*

fore . . . it never crossed anyone's mind that the West had fallen under the administration of a hidden consortium. The notion would be inconceivable. Because if true, it would mean that over half the planet was effectively a subsidiary of a single megacorporation. Sigma.

Another ten minutes of silence elapsed before Ben said flatly, "We've got to work out an itinerary."

Anna studied the article in the *Herald Tribune* again. " 'The suspect is believed to have used the names Robert Simon and John Freedman in his travels.' So those IDs are blown."

How? Ben recalled Liesl's explanation of how the credit accounts were kept current, how Peter had made the arrangements through her impeccably trustworthy second cousin. "Deschner," Ben said tightly. "They must have gotten to him." After a moment, he added, "I wonder why they didn't release my real name. They've supplied aliases, but not the name 'Benjamin Hartman.' "

"No, it's the smart thing to do. Look, they knew you weren't traveling under your real name. Bringing your true identity into it might have muddied the waters. You'd get your Deerfield English teacher opining that the Benny she knew would never do such a thing. Plus the Swiss have gunshot residue analysis that puts you in the clear—but it's all filed under Benjamin Hartman. If you're running a dragnet, it makes sense to keep it simple."

Near the town of Croisilles, they saw a sign for a motel and pulled into a modern low-slung concrete building, a style Ben thought of as International Ugly.

"Just one night," Ben said, and counted out several hundred francs.

"Passport?" the stone-faced clerk asked.

"They're in our bags," Ben said apologetically. "I'll bring them down to you later."

"Just one night?"

"If that," Ben said, giving Anna a theatrically lascivious look. "We've been touring France on our honeymoon."

Anna stepped over and put her head on Ben's shoulder.

"This is such a beautiful country," she told the clerk. "And so sophisticated. I can't get over it."

"Your honeymoon," the clerk repeated, and, for the first time, smiled.

"If you don't mind, we're in a hurry," Ben said. "We've been driving for hours. We need a rest." He winked.

The clerk handed him a key attached to a heavy rubberized weight. "Just at the end of the hall. Room 125. You need anything, just call."

The room was sparsely furnished; the floor was covered with dull, mottled green carpeting and the brashly cherry-scented air freshener did not conceal the faint, unmistakable smell of mildew.

Once the door closed behind them, they emptied the plastic bag Oscar had given them on the bed, along with their other recent purchases. Anna picked up an EU passport. The photograph was of her, although digitally altered in various ways. Anna said her newly assigned name aloud a few times, trying to get accustomed to the unfamiliar sounds.

"I still don't see how this is going to work," Ben said.

"Like your Oscar said, they categorize you before they really look at you. It's called profiling. If you don't belong to the suspect genus, you get a free pass." Anna took out a tube of lipstick and, looking into a mirror, applied it carefully. She wiped it off a few times before she was confident that she had done it correctly.

By then, Ben was already in the bathroom, his hair slick with syrupy, foamy hair dye, which gave off a tarry, ammoniac smell. The instructions said to wait twenty minutes before rinsing. It also cautioned against dyeing eyebrows, at the risk of blindness. Ben decided to take that risk. With a cotton swab, he applied the thick fluid to his brows, pressing a wad of tissue paper against his eyes to prevent it from dripping down.

The twenty minutes felt like two hours. Finally, he stepped into the shower, blasted himself with water, and opened his eyes only when he was certain the peroxide had all been washed down the drain.

He stepped out of the shower and looked at himself in the mirror. He was a plausible blond.

"Say hello to David Paine," he said to Anna.

She shook her head. "The hair's too long." She held up the multi-cut electric clippers, chrome-clad except for the clear rubberized grip. "That's what this baby is for."

In another ten minutes, his curls were flushed away, and he was ready to put on the neatly creased U.S. Army fatigues that Oscar Peyaud had provided him. Blond, crew cut, he looked like an officer, consistent with the insignia, patches, and overseas service bars on his green uniform coat. U.S. Army officers wore identifying badges when traveling by air, he knew. It wasn't an inconspicuous way to travel; but being conspicuous in the right way could amount to a life-saving distraction.

"Better make tracks," Anna said. "The faster we can get out of this country, the safer we'll be. Time's on *their* side, not ours."

Carrying their belongings with them, the two walked to the end of the hall and stepped out into the parking lot.

They tossed Anna's garment bag in the backseat of the blue Renault, along with the white plastic sack that Oscar had given them. It contained the spent bottle of hair dye, and a few other pieces of garbage they didn't want to leave behind. At this point, the smallest detail could give them away.

"As I said, we're down to our last card, our last play," Anna said, as they made their way back on the highway heading north. "Strasser was a founder. We've got to find him."

"*If* he's still alive."

"Was there any indication either way in Sonnenfeld's file?"

"I reread it this morning," Ben said. "No, to be honest. And Sonnenfeld thought it was entirely possible that Strasser died, maybe even *years* ago."

"Or maybe not."

"Maybe not. You're an incurable optimist. But what makes you think we're not going to get arrested in Buenos Aires?"

"Hell, like you've said, there were notorious Nazis living there openly for decades. The local police are going to be the least of our troubles." .

"What about Interpol?"

"That's what I was thinking—they might be able to help us locate Strasser."

"Are you crazy? Talk about going into the lion's den. They're going to have your name on some watch list, aren't they?"

"You obviously don't know anything about the way the Interpol office is run down there. Nobody checks IDs. You are who you claim you are. Not the most sophisticated operation, let's just say. You got a better idea?"

"Sonnenfeld said Gerhard Lenz's widow may be alive," Ben said broodingly. "Wouldn't she be in a position to know?"

"Anything's possible."

"I'll try to remember that," Ben said. "You really think we've got a shot at getting out of this country undetected?"

"There aren't going to be any transatlantic flights at this airport. But we can get to some of the European capitals. I suggest that we both travel separately. There's a decent chance they're looking for a man and a woman traveling together."

"Of course," he said. "I'll go via Madrid; you take Amsterdam."

They settled into another silence, less tense and more companionable. From time to time, Ben found his gaze drifted toward Anna. Despite all they had been through today, she was extravagantly beautiful. At one point, their glances met; Anna defused the faint awkwardness with a crooked grin.

"Sorry, I'm still trying to get used to your new Aryan officer look," she said.

Some time later, Anna fished her cell phone out of her handbag and punched in a number.

David Denneen's voice had the tinny, artificial clarity conferred by decrypted telephony. "Anna!" he said. "Everything O.K.?"

"David, listen. You've *got* to help me—you're the only one I can trust."

"I'm listening."

"David, I need whatever you can get me on Josef Strasser. He was like Mengele's smarter older brother."

"I'll do whatever I can," Denneen replied, his voice tentative, baffled. "Of course. But where do you want the material sent?"

"BA."

He understood the abbreviation for Buenos Aires. "But I can't exactly send the file care of the embassy, can I?"

"How about care of the American Express office?" Anna gave him a name to use.

"Right. Low profile's a good idea down there."

"So I hear. How bad is it?"

"Great country, great people. But some long memories. Watch your back down there. Please, Anna. I'll get right on to it." And with that Denneen clicked off.

The main border-control security room of the *aéroport* Lille-Lesquin was a drab, windowless interior space, with low acoustic-tiled ceilings, a white projection screen at one end of the room. Color photographs of internationally sought criminals hung beneath a black-and-white sign that read DÉFENSE DE FUMER. Nine immigration and border-control officials sat on folding chairs of tube metal and beige plastic while their boss, Bruno Pagnol, the director of security, filled them in on the new advisories of the afternoon. Marc Sully was one of them, and he tried not to look as bored as he felt. He had no love for his job, but wasn't eager to lose it, either.

Just in the past week, Pagnol reminded them, they had

arrested seven young Turkish women arriving from Berlin with illicit cargo in their bellies: having been recruited as "mules," they had swallowed condoms packed with China White. Finding the seven was partly a matter of luck, but credit had to go to Jean-Daniel Roux (Roux gave a slit-eyed nod when the boss singled him out, pleased but determined not to look it), who was alert enough to catch the first of them. The woman had looked visibly woozy to him; as they later learned, one of the knotted condoms in her colon had started to leak. In fact, the woman almost overdosed on the contraband. In the hospital, they'd retrieved fifteen small balls, double-wrapped in latex, tied off with fishing line, each containing several grams of extremely pure heroin.

"How'd they get it out of her?" one of the officers asked.

Marc Sully, sitting in the back, farted audibly. "Rear extraction," he said.

The others laughed.

The red-faced director of airport security frowned. He saw nothing funny. "The courier nearly died. These are desperate women. They'll do anything. How much money do you think she was paid? A thousand francs, nothing more, and she almost died for it. Now she's facing a very long jail sentence. These women are like walking suitcases. Hiding drugs in their own shit. And it's our job to keep that poison out of the country. You want your kids hooked on it? So some fat-ass Asian can get rich? They think they can promenade right past us. Are you going to teach them better?"

Marc Sully had been a member of the *police aux frontières* for four years, and sat through hundreds of briefings just like this one. Every year Pagnol's face got a little redder, his collar a little tighter. Not that Sully was anyone to talk. He himself had always a little weight on him, wasn't ashamed of it. Bit his nails to the quick, too, had given up trying to stop. The boss once told him he looked "sloppy," but when Marc asked him how, he just shrugged. So nobody was going to put him on a recruitment poster.

Marc knew he wasn't popular with some of his younger colleagues, the ones who bathed every single day, afraid of smelling like a human being instead of a walking bar of deodorant soap. They'd walk around with their quiffs of freshly shampooed hair, smiling nicely at the prettier female passengers, as if they were going to find dates on the job. Marc thought they were fools. It was a dead-end job. Giving strip searches might be a way to get a sniff, especially if you were into third-world *cul*, but you weren't going to bring anybody home that way.

"Now two advisories fresh from *la DCPAF*." The *Direction centrale de la police aux frontière* was the national bureau that gave them their orders. Pagnol pressed a few switches, and was able to project photographs directly from a computer. "Highest priority. This one's an American. Mexican ancestry. She's a professional. You find her, you be very careful. Treat her like a scorpion, right?"

Grunts of assent.

Sully squinted at the images. He wouldn't mind giving her a taste of his baguette.

"And here's another one," the security director said. "White male in his mid-thirties. Curly brown hair, green or hazel eyes, approximately one and three-quarters meters in height. Possible serial killer. Another American, they think. Very dangerous. There's reason to believe he's been in the country today, and that he'll be trying to make his way out. We'll be posting photographs at your stations, but I want you to take a careful look right now. If it turns out that they left through Lille-Lesquin and that the people here let them slip through, it won't just be *my* job on the line. Everybody understand?"

Sully nodded with everyone else. It annoyed Sully that Roux, that apple-cheeked hard-on, was still riding high for having lucked out with that *Gastarbeiter* whore. But who knew? Maybe it was Sully's day to get lucky. He took another look at the photographs.

*   *   *

Ben dropped off Anna by an airport shuttle bus stop, and deposited the blue Renault at the long-term parking lot at the *aéroport* Lille-Lesquin. They'd enter the airport separately, and take different flights.

They agreed to meet in Buenos Aires within ten hours. Assuming nothing went wrong.

Anna looked at the blond, crew-cut American officer, and felt confident that he'd elude detection. But despite her brave words to Ben, she felt no such confidence herself. Her hair was neither cut nor colored. It was combed out, and she had changed her garb, but otherwise she was entrusting her camouflage to something very small indeed. She felt a knot of fear in the pit of her stomach, and the fear fed on itself, for she knew nothing would betray her faster than the appearance of fear. She had to focus. Her usual hyperattentiveness to her surroundings could now be her undoing. Before she stepped into the terminal, she had to let every bit of fear and anxiety wash from her. She imagined herself traipsing through meadows filled with Bermuda grass and dandelions. She imagined holding hands with somebody constant and strong. It could be anybody—it was simply a mental exercise, as she was perfectly aware—but the person she kept imagining was Ben.

Sully kept a sharp eye out at the incoming passengers by his station, alert for signs of anxiety or agitation, for customers traveling with too few bags or too many, for customers who fit the description they'd received from *DCPAF*.

The man, third from the front of the line, caught his attention. He was the approximate height of the man they were looking for, had curly brown hair, and kept jingling the change in his pocket, a nervous tic. From his dress, he was almost certainly an American. Perhaps he had reason to be nervous.

He waited until the man showed his ticket and passport to the airline security officer, and then stepped forward.

"Just a few questions, sir," Sully said, his eyes boring in on him.

"Yeah, all right," the man said.

"Come with me," Sully said, and drew him to a station post near the ticket counter. "So what took you to France?"

"Medical conference."

"You're a doctor?"

A sigh. "I work in sales for a pharmaceutical company."

"You're a drug dealer!" Sully smiled, though his eyes remained wary.

"In a matter of speaking," the man replied wanly. He had a look on his face like he'd smelled something bad.

Americans and their obsession with hygiene. Sully scrutinized his face for a moment longer. The man had the same angular cast to his face, square chin, curly hair. But the features didn't look quite right—they were too small. And Sully didn't hear real stress in the man's voice when he answered questions. Sully was wasting his time.

"O.K.," he said. "Have a good trip."

Sully went back to scrutinizing the check-in line. A blond-haired woman with swarthy skin caught his eye. The suspect could have dyed her hair; the other specifics matched. He drifted toward her.

"Could I see your passport, madame?" he said.

The woman looked at him blankly.

"*Votre passeport, s'il vous plaît, madame.*"

"*Bien sûr. Vous me croyez être anglaise? Je suis italienne, mais tous mes amis pensent que je suis allemande ou anglaise ou n'importe quoi.*"

According to her passport, she resided in Milan, and Sully thought it unlikely that an American could speak French with such an egregious Italian accent.

No one else on line just then looked terribly promising. A dot-head with two bawling children was ahead of the blond Italian. As far as Sully was concerned, her kind couldn't leave the country fast enough. Chicken vindaloo was going to end up being the national dish at the rate the goddamn dot-heads were immigrating. The Muslims were

worse, of course, but the dot-heads with their unpronounceable names were pretty awful. Last year, when he'd dislo-
cated his arm, the Indian doctor at the clinic had flatly
refused to give him a real painkiller. Like maybe he was
supposed to do some fakir-style mind control. If his arm
wasn't half out of its socket, he would have punched the
guy.

Sully glanced at the woman's passport without interest
and waved her and her sniveling brood through. The dot-
head whore even smelled like saffron.

A young Russian with acne. Last name was German, so
probably a Jew. *Mafiya?* Not his problem just now.

An honest-to-goodness Frenchman and his wife, off to
a vacation.

Another goddamn dot-head in a sari. Gayatri was the
name, and then something unpronounceable. Curry *cul.*

None of the other men fit the profile: too old, too fat,
too young, too short.

Too bad. Maybe it wasn't going to be his lucky day after
all.

Anna settled into her coach-class seat, adjusting her sari
and mentally repeating her name: Gayatri Chandragupta. It
wouldn't do to stumble over it if anyone were to ask. She
was wearing her long black hair straight back, and when
she'd caught a glimpse of her reflection in a window, she
hardly recognized herself.

CHAPTER THIRTY-FOUR

Buenos Aires

Anna looked anxiously through the plate glass of the American Express office at sedate, tree-lined Plaza Libertador General San Martín. The park, once a bull ring, once a slave market, was now dominated by the great bronze statue of General José de San Martín astride his horse. The sun blazed fiercely. Inside it was air-conditioned, ice-cold, and quiet.

"Señorita Acampo?"

She turned to see a slender man in a close-fitting blue blazer, stylish heavy black-framed glasses. "I am very sorry, señorita, but we cannot locate this package."

"I don't understand." She switched to Spanish so there would be no mistake. *"Está registrado que lo recibió?"*

"We received it, yes, madam, but it cannot be found."

Maddening, but this at least was progress. The last employee had adamantly denied a package had ever been received in her name.

"Are you saying it's lost?"

A quick reflexive shrug like a nervous tic. "Our computers show it was sent from Washington, D.C., and received here yesterday, but after that, I cannot say. If you'll fill out this form, we'll begin a search throughout our system. If it's not located, you're entitled to full replacement value."

Damn it! It seemed unlikely to her that the envelope had been lost. More likely it had been stolen. But by whom? And why? Who knew what was inside? Who knew to look? Had Denneen given her up? She could scarcely credit it. Possibly his phone was tapped, unknown to him. In truth, there were too many potential explanations, and none of them changed the basic fact: if it *had* been stolen, whoever had done it now knew who she was—and why she was here.

The office of Interpol Argentina is located within the headquarters of the *Policía Federal Argentina* on Suipacha. Interpol's man in Buenos Aires was Miguel Antonio Peralta, the *Jefe Seccion Operaciónes*. A plaque on his door read SUBCOMISARIO DEPARTAMENTO INTERPOL. He was a round-shouldered, bulky man with a large, round head. Strands of black hair matted across the top of his pate advertised his baldness instead of disguising it.

His wood-veneered office was jammed with tributes to Interpol's work. Plaques and commemorative plates from grateful police forces around the world crowded the walls, along with crucifixes and diplomas and images of saints and a framed apostolic benediction on his family from the Pope himself. An antique silver–framed sepia photograph of his policeman father was almost as prominent.

Peralta's lizard eyes were sleepy behind his perfectly round tortoiseshell glasses. A holstered pistol sat atop his gleaming bare desk, the leather holster old but lovingly cared for. He was genial and flawlessly courteous. "You know we are always eager to help in the cause of justice," he said.

"And as my assistant explained, we at CBS find ourselves in a rather competitive situation right now," Anna said. "The people at *Dateline* are apparently on the verge of locating and exposing this man. If they reach him first, so be it. But I didn't get where I am today by being a pushover. I'm working with an Argentine field producer who thinks we can get the story, with a little assistance from you."

"In Argentina, football—soccer, I think you say—is our national sport. I gather network TV plays that role in the States."

"You could say that." Anna rewarded him with a wide smile, and crossed her legs. "And I'm not at all putting down my colleagues at *Dateline*. But we both know what sort of story they'll do, because it'll be the same old tune. Argentina as a backward country that harbors these bad, bad people. They'll do something very exploitative, very cheap. We're not like that. What we have in mind is much more sophisticated and I think much more accurate. We want to capture the *new* Argentina. A place where people like yourself have been seeing that justice is done. A place with modern law enforcement, yet respect for democracy"— she wiggled a hand vaguely—"and like that." Another wide smile. "And certainly your efforts would be handsomely compensated with a consultant's fee. So, Mr. Peralta. Can we work together?"

Peralta's smile was thin. "Certainly if you have proof that Josef Strasser is living in Buenos Aires, you must only to tell me. Produce the evidence." He jabbed the air with a silver Cross pen to emphasize how simple it all was. "That is all."

"Mr. Peralta. Someone is going to do this story, whether it's my team or the competition." Anna's smile faded. "The only question is how the story will be done. Whether it's a story of one of your successes, or one of your failures. Come on, you must have a file of leads on Strasser—some sort of indication that he's here," Anna said. "I mean, you don't *doubt* he's living in Buenos Aires, do you?"

Peralta leaned back in his chair, which squeaked. "Ms. Reyes," he said, his tone that of a man with a delicious piece of gossip to impart, "a few years ago my office received a credible tip from a woman living in Belgrano, one of our wealthiest suburbs. She had seen Alois Brunner, the SS *Hauptsturmführer*, on the street, coming out of a neighboring house. Immediately we have a round-the-clock surveillance on this man's house. Indeed she was correct, the old man's face matched our file photos of Brunner. We moved in on the gentleman. Indignant, he produced his old German passport, you know, imprinted with the eagles of the Third Reich—and a big J, for Jew. The man's name was Katz." Peralta came forward in his chair until he was upright again. "So how do you apologize to a man like this, who had been in the camps?"

"Yes," Anna agreed equably, "that must have been terribly embarrassing. But our intelligence on Strasser is solid. *Dateline* is filming their second-unit footage—background shots—even as we speak. They must be very confident."

"*Dateline, 60 Minutes, 20/20*—I am familiar with these investigative programs. If you people were so very sure Josef Strasser was, as you Americans like to say, alive and living in Argentina, you would have found him long ago, no?" His lizard eyes were fixed on her.

She could not tell him the truth—that her interest was not in his Nazi past, but in what he may have been involved in when he parted company with his Führer, and joined forces with the invisible architects of the postwar era. "Then where would you suggest I begin looking?"

"Impossible to answer! If we knew there was a war criminal living here, we would arrest him. But I must tell you, there *are* no more." He dropped his pen onto his desk definitively.

"Really." She made some meaningless marks on her yellow pad.

"Times have changed in Argentina. The bad old days, when a Josef Mengele could live openly here, under his own name, they are gone. The days of the Perón dictatorship are over. Now Argentina is a democracy. Josef Schwammberger was extradited. Erich Priebke was extradited. I cannot even recall the last time we arrested a Nazi here."

She crossed out her doodle with a slash of her pen. "What about immigration records? Records of people who entered the country in the forties and fifties?"

He frowned. "Maybe there are records of entries, arrivals. The National Registry, the Migrations Department— it is index cards, everything entered by hand. But our coastline is thousands of kilometers long. Who knows how many tugboats and rowboats and fishing trawlers landed decades ago at one of the hundreds of *estancias*—the ranches—and were never detected? Hundreds of kilometers of coastline in Patagonia, no one is there to see."

He again jabbed the air. "And then in 1949, Perón issued a blanket amnesty for anyone who had entered the country under a false name. So it is unlikely there will be any immigration record of Josef Strasser even if he really is here. Maybe you can go down to Bariloche, the ski resort, and ask around. The Germans love Bariloche. It reminds them of their beloved Bavaria. But I would not hold out much hope. I am terribly sorry to disappoint you."

Anna Navarro was not gone from Miguel Antonio Peralta's office two minutes before the Interpol man picked up his telephone. "Mauricio," he said. "I've just had a most interesting visitor."

In a modern office building in Vienna, a bland-looking middle-aged man watched without interest as the plasterboard walls that had enclosed a carpeted "reception area" and "conference room" were dismantled and wheeled away toward a freight elevator by a team of construction workers. Next came a Formica conference table, a plain metal desk, and assorted office equipment including a dummy telephone system and a working computer.

The bespectacled man was an American who for the last decade or so had been engaged to perform a variety of services around the world, the significance of which was invariably obscure to him. He had never even met the company's chief, had no idea who he was. All he knew was that the mysterious head of the firm was a business associate of this building's owner, who'd been happy to lend use of the eleventh floor.

It was like watching a stage set being struck. "Hey," called out the bespectacled American, "someone's gotta take down the sign in the lobby. And leave that U.S. seal with me, will ya? We might need it again."

New York

Dr. Walter Reisinger, the former Secretary of State, took the call in the back of his limousine as it inched through morning rush-hour traffic on Manhattan's East Side.

Dr. Reisinger disliked the telephone, which was unfortunate, since these days he spent virtually every waking moment on the phone. His international consulting firm, Reisinger Associates, was keeping him even busier than his days at State.

Secretly he had been afraid that, after retiring from the government and writing his memoirs, he'd be gradually marginalized, treated as an éminence grise, invited to appear on *Nightline* once in a while, and to write the occasional thumb-sucker for the *New York Times* Op-Ed page.

Instead, he had become more famous, and certainly far richer. He found himself globe-hopping more now than during his shuttle-diplomacy days in the Middle East.

He pressed the speaker button. "Yes?"

"Dr. Reisinger," said the voice on the other end of the phone, "this is Mr. Holland."

"Ah, good morning, Mr. Holland," Reisinger said jovially. The two men chatted for a minute or so, and then Reisinger said, "This shouldn't be a problem. I have good friends in just about every government in the world—but I think the most direct route would be to go right to Interpol.

Do you know its Secretary-General? A most interesting man. Let me give him a call."

Patient Eighteen lay on a hospital bed with his eyes closed, an IV feeding tube in his left arm. He was shaking, as he had done constantly since the treatments began. He was also nauseated, and periodically retched into a bedpan placed beside the bed. A nurse and a technician stood watch nearby.

A doctor, whose name was Löfquist, came into the examination room and went up to the nurse. "How is the fever?" he asked. They spoke in English, because his English was still better than his German, even after working here in the clinic for seven years.

"It hasn't broken," the nurse replied tensely.

"And the nausea?"

"He's been vomiting regularly."

Dr. Löfquist raised his voice to address Patient Eighteen. "How're you feeling?"

The patient moaned. "My goddamned *eyes* hurt."

"Yes, that's normal," Dr. Löfquist said. "Your body is trying to fight it off. We see this all the time."

Patient Eighteen gagged, leaned over to the bedpan, and was sick. The nurse wiped his mouth and chin with a damp washcloth.

"The first week is always the most difficult," Dr. Löfquist said cheerily. "You're doing wonderfully well."

CHAPTER THIRTY-FIVE

Our Lady of Mercy, Nuestra Señora de la Merced, was an Italianate basilica perched on the swarming Calle Defensa, across from a disconcertingly contemporary branch office of the Banco de Galicia. The church's granite facade was crumbling. A wrought-iron fence enclosed a forecourt paved with worn and cracked black-and-white harlequin stone tiles, where a Gypsy mother and her brood begged for alms.

Ben watched the mother in her jeans, black hair tied back, sitting on the steps against the ruins of a column's pedestal, kids spilling out of her lap and at her feet. Deeper into the courtyard an old man in coat and tie dozed, one arm locked in a crutch, the top of his bald pate tanned.

At one-fifteen exactly, as instructed, Ben entered the church's foyer, and walked through swinging wooden doors into the loamy darkness of the narthex, which smelled of beeswax candles and sweat. The interior, once his eyes accustomed to the dark, was immense, daunting, and shabby. The Romanesque ceilings were high and vaulted, the floor paved with ancient encaustic tiles, beautifully inlaid. A priest's singsong Latin chant, electronically amplified, echoed in the cavern, and the congregants responded dutifully. Call and response. All rise.

One o'clock weekday Mass and it was, impressively, almost half full. *But then Argentina is a Catholic country*, Ben thought. Here and there the trilling of cell phones. He oriented himself, spotted the chapel on the right.

A few rows of benches were arrayed before a glassed-in tabernacle containing the bloodied figure of Christ and bearing the words HUMILIDAD Y PACIENCIA. To its left, another statue of Jesus, this one in the open, beneath the words SAGRADO CORAZÓN EN VOS CONFIO. Ben sat on the front bench, also as instructed, and waited.

A priest in his vestments sat praying by a bottle-blond young woman in miniskirt and high heels. The swinging doors squeaked and slammed, and when they opened, the throaty blare of a motorcycle intruded. Each time Ben turned to look: Which one was it? A businessman with a cell phone entered the narthex, crossed himself, then turned into the alcove—was it him?—but then touched the figure of Jesus, closed his eyes, and prayed. More unison chanting, more electronically amplified Latin, and still Ben waited.

He was afraid but determined not to show it.

A few hours earlier he'd dialed a number he'd pilfered from Sonnenfeld's files, one that had, so it appeared, once belonged to Lenz's widow.

It still did.

The woman obviously wasn't in hiding, but she hadn't come to the phone herself. A brusque, hostile baritone answered: her son, he'd said. Lenz's brother? Half brother?

Ben had identified himself as a trusts-and-estates lawyer from New York, come to Buenos Aires to settle a huge bequest. No, he could not identify the deceased. He would only say that Vera Lenz had been left a good deal of money, but he would first have to meet with her.

A long silence ensued while the son decided what to do. Ben interjected one more piece of irrelevant-seeming information, which probably turned out to be the deciding one. "I've just come from Austria," he said. No names, no mention of her son—nothing specific to hang on to or object to. Less said the better.

"I don't know you," the son at last replied.

"Nor I you," Ben came back smoothly. "If this is inconvenient for you or for your mother . . ."

"No," he said hastily. He would meet Ben—"Mr. Johnson"—at a church, in a certain chapel, a certain bench.

Now he sat with his back to the entrance, turning with each squeak of the doors, each gust of noise from the outside.

Half an hour went by.

Was this a setup? The priest looked at him, wordlessly offered a couple of beeswax candles to light. "No, thanks," Ben said, turning back to the door.

A group of tourists with cameras and green guides. He turned back to Jesus in his display case and saw the priest move close to him. He was swarthy, tall, and strong-looking, fiftyish, balding, barrel-chested.

He spoke to Ben in a hushed baritone. "Come with me, Mr. Johnson."

Ben rose, followed him out of the chapel and down the nave, then a sharp right across an empty row to a narrow passage that ran parallel to the nave, along a stone wall, until they were almost at the apse.

A small, almost concealed wooden door. The priest opened it. The room was pitch-black, dank and musty. The priest flicked a switch and a wan yellow light illuminated what appeared to be a dressing room. A coatrack with priestly garb. A few scuffed wooden chairs.

The priest was pointing a gun.

Ben felt a jolt of fear.

"Do you have anything on you?" the priest asked with unexpected courtesy. "Weapon of any kind, any electronic devices?"

Fear gave way to anger. "Just my cell phone, if you consider that a deadly weapon."

"May I have it, please?"

Ben handed it over. The priest ran his free hand down the front and back of Ben's suit jacket, beneath the shoulders, at the waist, the legs and ankles. A swift and expert frisking. He then examined the cell phone carefully and returned it to Ben.

"I need to see your passport, some form of identification."

Ben produced his Michael Johnson passport and slipped out a business card as well. Earlier in the morning he had taken the precaution of stopping at a printing-and-copy shop on Avenue 9 de Julio and ordering fifty of them, surcharge for rush. An hour later he had plausible-looking cards for Michael Johnson, partner in a fictional Manhattan law firm.

The priest examined it.

"Look," Ben said, summoning high dudgeon, "I really don't have time for this. And put the damn gun away."

Ignoring his request, the priest indicated the exit. "This way."

He pulled the door open to the dazzling sun, a tiny courtyard, and the sliding side doors of a windowless black van.

"Please." A wave of the gun barrel. He meant: into the van.

"Sorry," Ben said. So this was the widow's son? He could scarcely credit it: he didn't look anything like Jürgen, who would have to be his half brother at least. "Nothing doing."

The priest's eyes blazed. "Then you are, of course, free to go. But if you wish to see my mother you must go my way." His tone softened. "You see, people still come to Buenos Aires to talk to her. Journalists sometimes, but sometimes also bounty hunters, crazy people with guns. Maybe agents from the Mossad. They used to threaten her to make her tell where is Lenz. For a long time people did not believe he was dead. Like with Mengele, they thought he made a trick. Now I will not let her see anyone she does not know unless I clear it."

"You say 'Lenz'—he's not your father?"

A scowl. "My father married Lenz's widow. But she has outlived both husbands. A strong woman. I take care of her. Please, get in."

Everything is a chance. He had not come this far to back out now. This man could finally lead him to the truth. After studying the enigmatic priest for a moment, he climbed into the back of the van.

The priest slid the doors closed with the rumble of thunder. Now the only illumination came from a dim roof light. Except for pull-down seats the van was entirely empty.

Everything is a chance.

Ben wondered: *What have I done?*

The engine started up, then protested all the way into first gear.

This is how they execute people, Ben thought. *I don't know this man, genuine priest or not. Maybe he's from one of those groups Sonnenfeld mentioned who defend and protect the old Nazis.*

After some twenty minutes, the van came to a halt. Its doors slid open, revealing a cobblestone street in dappled light that filtered through a canopy of trees. The length of the journey told him they were still in Buenos Aires, but the street looked entirely different from the city he had seen so far. It was serene and quiet but for birdsong. And, just barely audible, piano music.

No, I'm not about to be killed.

He wondered what Anna would think. No doubt she'd be appalled at the risk he'd taken. And she'd be right.

They were parked in front of a two-story brick house with a roof of barrel tiles, not particularly large, but graceful. Wooden shutters on all the windows were closed. The piano music seemed to be coming from within the house, a Mozart sonata. A tall, serpentine wrought-iron fence enclosed the house and its small patch of yard.

The priest took Ben by the elbow and helped him out of the van. Either his gun was now concealed or, less likely, it had been left in the van. At the front gate he keyed a code into a number pad, unlocking the gate with an electrical buzz.

Inside, the house was cool and dark. The Mozart recording was coming from a room straight ahead. A note was bungled, the passage begun again, and Ben realized that this was no recording; someone was playing the piano with great skill. The old woman?

He followed the priest into the room from which the piano music emanated. It was a small sitting room, booklined, Oriental carpets on the floor. A tiny, birdlike old woman was hunched over a Steinway grand. She did not seem to notice when they entered. They sat down on a coarse, uncomfortable couch and waited in silence.

When the piece was finished, she kept her hands frozen in the air, poised over the keys, then brought them slowly to her lap. The affectations of a concert pianist. Slowly she turned. Her face was prune-like, her eyes sunken, her neck crepey. She had to be ninety.

Ben clapped a few times.

She spoke in a quavering, hoarse small voice. "*¿Quién es éste?*"

"Mother, this is Mr. Johnson," the priest said. "Mr. Johnson, my stepmother."

Ben went over to her and took her fragile hand.

The priest continued, to Ben, "And I am Francisco."

"*Póngame en una silla cómoda,*" the old woman said.

Francisco put an arm around his stepmother and helped her into a chair. She said in decent English, "You come from Austria?"

"I was just in Vienna, yes."

"Why have you come?"

Ben began to speak, but she interrupted, fearful, "You are from the company?"

The *company?* Did she mean Sigma? If so, he had to make her talk.

"Frau . . . Frau Lenz, I'm afraid I've come here under false pretenses."

Francisco swiveled his head toward Ben, furious. "I'll kill you!"

"You see, Jürgen Lenz asked me to see you," Ben said, ignoring him. He offered no explanation. Mention Austria, suggest that he had gained the trust of Jürgen Lenz. If pressed, he would improvise. He was getting good at that. "He asked me to meet with you and warn you to be especially careful, to tell you that your life may be in danger."

"I am *not* Frau Lenz," she said haughtily. "I have not been Lenz for over thirty years. I am Señora Acosta."

"My apologies, señora."

But the old woman's hauteur had given way to fear. "Why does Lenz send you? What does he want?"

"Señora Acosta," Ben began, "I've been asked—"

"Why?" she asked, raising her quavering voice. "*Why?* You come here from Semmering? We've done nothing wrong! We've done nothing to break the agreement! Leave us alone!"

"*No! Silence*, Mother!" the priest shouted.

What was she referring to? *The agreement . . .* Was *this* what Peter had stumbled on to?

"Señor Acosta, your son specifically asked me—"

"My son?" the old woman rasped.

"That's right."

"You say my son in *Vienna?*"

"Yes. Your son Jürgen."

The priest rose. "Who are you?" he asked.

"Tell him, Francisco," the old woman said. "Francisco is my *step*son. From my second marriage. I never had any children." Her face was contorted with fear. "*I have no son.*"

The priest loomed menacingly over Ben. "You're a liar," he snapped. "You say you're a lawyer for an estate, and now you lie to us again!"

Head reeling, Ben attempted a quick recovery. "You have no son? Then I'm glad I'm here. Now I see I haven't wasted my time, or my firm's money, in coming down here to Buenos Aires."

The priest glowered. "Who sent you here?"

"He is not from the company!" his stepmother croaked.

"This is exactly the sort of fraud I need to clear up," Ben said, feigning a sense of triumph. "So this Jürgen Lenz of Vienna—he says he is your son, but he is *not* your son? *Then who is he?*"

The priest turned to his stepmother, who looked as if she were about to speak. "Say nothing!" he ordered. "Do *not* answer him!"

"I cannot talk about him!" the old woman said. To her stepson, she added, "Why does he ask me about Lenz? Why do you invite him here?"

"He is a liar, an impostor!" the priest said. "Vienna would send word ahead first before sending a messenger!" He reached behind him and produced his revolver, aiming it directly at Ben's forehead.

"What kind of a priest are you?" Ben asked in a hush. *Not a priest. A priest would not put a gun to my head.*

"I'm a man of God who protects my family. Now leave here at once."

A sudden thought occurred to Ben, the obvious explanation, and he said to the old woman, "Your husband had another family. A son with another wife."

"You're not welcome in this house," the priest said with a wave of his weapon. "Out."

"*Gerhard Lenz had no children!*" the old woman cried.

"*Silence!*" the priest thundered. "*Enough!* Say nothing more!"

"He pretends to be the son of Gerhard Lenz," Ben said, half to himself. "Why in the world would he pretend to be the son of . . . a monster?"

"Stand up!" the priest commanded.

"Gerhard Lenz didn't die here, did he?" Ben said.

"What are you *saying?*" the stepmother gasped.

"If you don't get out of here, I'll kill you," the priest said.

Ben rose obediently, but looked at the old woman, sunk deep within her easy chair. "The rumors were true, then," he said. "Gerhard Lenz wasn't buried in Chacarita cemetery in 1961, was he? He escaped from Buenos Aires, evaded his pursuers—"

"He died *here!*" the old woman said frantically. "There was a funeral! I myself flung dirt on his coffin!"

"But you never saw his body, did you?" Ben said.

"*Out!*" the priest barked.

"Why is he saying these things to me?" she cried.

She was interrupted by the ring of the telephone on a sideboard behind the priest. Without moving his revolver he reached to his right and snatched up the receiver. "*Sí?*"

He seemed to be listening intently. Ben took advantage of the priest's momentary inattention to sidle ever so subtly in the priest's direction. "I need to reach Josef Strasser," he said to the old woman.

She spat out her reply, "If you're really sent from Austria, you *know* how to reach him. You're a *liar!*"

Then Strasser *was* alive!

Ben inched closer to the priest and continued talking to the stepmother. "I myself was lied to—set up!" There was in fact no logic in what he said, not without a fuller explanation, but he wanted only to confuse the old woman, rattle her further.

"That confirms it," the priest said, hanging up the phone. "That was Vienna. This man's a fraud." He looked at Ben. "You lied to us, Mr. *Hartman!*" he said, glancing behind him for an instant, and Ben immediately lunged. He grabbed the priest's right wrist, the one holding the gun, twisting it with all his strength, and at the same time slammed his other hand into the priest's throat, forefinger and thumb in a rigid V. The old woman screamed with terror. Caught by surprise, the priest cried out in pain. The revolver fell from his hand and clattered to the floor.

With one immense movement Ben forced the priest to the floor, closing his grip around the priest's neck. He could feel the bony cartilage of the larynx shift to one side. The man's cry grew strangled as he sprawled against the tiled floor, his head at an unnatural angle, trying to rear up, trying to reach his free, left hand around, but it was vised beneath his rib cage. He struggled with great strength, gasping for breath. The old woman flung the backs of her hands against her face in a strange protective gesture.

The gun! Must get the gun!

Ben jammed his left hand more forcefully into the man's throat, and thrust a knee into his stomach, aiming for the solar plexus. The priest's sudden, involuntary exhalation of breath told Ben that he'd hit the mark. The priest's dark eyes rolled upward so that only the whites were showing. He was momentarily paralyzed by the blow. Ben snatched the revolver from the floor, swung it around, and shoved it against the man's forehead.

He cocked the trigger. "Make a move, and you're dead!"

Immediately the priest's body fell slack. "No!" he choked out.

"Answer my questions! Tell the truth if you want to live!"

"Don't, please don't! I'm a man of God."

"Right," Ben snapped disdainfully. "How do I reach Josef Strasser?"

"He is—I don't know—*please*—my *throat!*"

Ben eased the pressure a bit, enough to allow him to breathe and to speak. "*Where's Strasser?*" he thundered.

The priest gulped air. "Strasser—I don't know how to reach Strasser—he lives in Buenos Aires, that's all I know!" A small rivulet of urine appeared on the floor between the man's legs.

"Bullshit!" Ben shouted. "You give me an address or a phone number, or your stepmother will have *no one* to take care of her!"

"No, please!" the old widow said, still cowering in her chair.

"If—if you kill me," the priest gasped, "you won't get out of Buenos Aires alive! They'll track you down—they'll do things—you'll wish—*wish* you were dead!"

"Strasser's *address!*"

"I don't have it!" the priest said. "Please! I have no way to reach Strasser!"

"Don't lie," Ben said. "You all know each other. You are all tied together in a network. If you had to reach Strasser you have ways."

"I'm nothing! You kill me, I'm nothing to them! They'll find you!"

Ben wondered, who were "they"? Instead, he asked: "Who's Jürgen Lenz?" He pressed the barrel of the gun against the priest's forehead. There were a few drops of blood; he had broken the skin.

"He—please, he's powerful, he controls—he owns her house, her property, the man who calls himself Jürgen Lenz—"

"Then who is he really?"

"Put the gun down and get away from him."

The voice—low, calm, Spanish-accented—came from the doorway behind Ben. A tall man stood there holding a sawed-off shotgun. He was dressed in heavy green slacks and a denim work shirt, and he looked to be in his late twenties or early thirties, broad-chested and powerful.

"Roberto, help!" the widow cried. "Save my Francisco! Get this man out of here at once!"

"Señora, should I kill this intruder?" Roberto asked.

The man's demeanor told Ben he would fire without remorse. Ben hesitated, unsure what to do. The priest was a hostage, with the revolver to his forehead, yet Ben knew he could not bring himself to pull the trigger. And even if he did, the man with the sawed-off shotgun would kill him in the blink of an eye.

But I can still bluff, he realized.

"Roberto!" the old woman croaked. "Now!"

"Put the gun down or I'll fire," said the young man. "I don't care what happens to this scumbag." He indicated the priest.

"Yes, but the señora does," Ben said. "We will lower our weapons at the same time."

"All right," the young man agreed. "Take the weapon away from his head, stand up, and get out of here. If you want to live." He lowered the shotgun's barrel, pointing it toward the floor, as Ben pulled the revolver away from the priest's forehead. He got up slowly, the gun still lowered.

"Now move toward the door," the man said.

Ben backed away, his right hand gripping the revolver, his left patting the air behind him, feeling for obstacles as he moved. The young man moved with him into the hall, his rifle still lowered.

"I just want you out of this house," the man said calmly. "If you ever come near this house again, you'll be killed on sight." The priest had sullenly raised himself to a sitting position, looking drained and humiliated. Ben backed out of the open door—either the priest had left it open or Roberto had entered this way—and then pulled it shut.

In a few seconds he was running.

Anna paid the cabdriver and entered the small hotel, located on a quiet street in the district of Buenos Aires called La Recoleta. It was not, she thought uneasily, the sort of place where a single young woman traveling alone would easily go unnoticed.

The concierge greeted her by name, which disturbed her. Earlier in the day she and Ben had checked in, separately and several hours apart. They'd also called in their reservations separately and at different times. Staying in the same hotel made logistical sense, but it also increased certain risks.

The chambermaid's cart was parked outside her room. Inconvenient. She wanted to be alone, go over the files, make phone calls; now she'd have to wait. As she entered she saw the maid, hunched over her open suitcase.

Taking files out of Anna's leather portfolio.

Anna stopped abruptly. The maid looked up, saw Anna, and dropped the files and portfolio back into the suitcase.

"What the hell are you doing?" Anna said, advancing on her.

The maid protested indignantly in Spanish, a mix of haughty denials. Anna followed her out into the hall, demanding to know what she was doing. "*Eh, ¿qué haces? ¡Ven para acá! ¿Qué cuernos haces revisando mi valija?*"

Anna tried to read the woman's name tag, but the woman suddenly bolted, running down the corridor at top speed.

The maid hadn't been just pilfering. *She had been going through Anna's papers.* Whether she read English or not was beside the point; most likely she had been hired to steal any documents, papers, files, notes.

But hired by whom?

Who could possibly know Anna was here, or what she was investigating? She was being watched—but by whom?

Who knows I'm here? Denneen, yes, but had he told someone, some associate?

Had Peralta, the Interpol representative, figured out who she was? Was that possible?

Just as she reached for the bedside phone, it rang. The manager, calling to apologize? Or Ben?

She picked it up. "Hello?"

There was only dead air. No, not dead air: it was the familiar hiss of a surveillance tape. Then the sounds of faint, indistinct voices, becoming sharper, amplified.

A surge of adrenaline. "Who is this?"

She made out a voice: "*What about immigration records? Records of people who entered the country in the forties and fifties?*" It was her own voice. Then the voice of a male interlocutor. Peralta.

On the telephone, someone was playing back a tape recording of the conversation between Peralta and herself.

They had heard everything, and they—whoever "they" were—knew precisely where she was and what she was after.

She sat on the edge of the bed, stunned and terrified. Now there could be no question her presence was known, despite all the precautions. The pilfering maid was no isolated player.

The phone rang again.

Prickly all over with terror, she snatched up the receiver. "Yes?"

"*We want to capture the new Argentina. A place where people like yourself have been seeing that justice is done. A place with modern law enforcement, yet respect for democracy . . .*" Her own voice, tinnily but crisply rendered through whatever eavesdropping equipment had been in place.

A click.

In her haste, she had left the room door open; she ran to close it. No one was in the corridor. She shut the door, double-locked it, seated the slide bolt of the safety chain in its socket.

She ran to the window, its heavy drapes open, realizing she was exposed, a target for a shooter stationed in a window of any of the tall buildings across the street. She yanked the drapes closed to block the line of sight.

The phone rang again.

She walked to it slowly, put the handset to her ear, said nothing.

"*I didn't get to be where I am today by being a pushover . . .*"

"Keep calling," she finally forced herself to say into the phone, feigning calm. "We're tracing the calls."

But no one was listening. There was only the dull hiss of a surveillance recording.

She depressed the phone's plunger and, before it could ring again, called down to the front desk. "I've been getting obscene calls," she said in English.

"Obscene . . . ?" the switchboard operator repeated, not comprehending.

"*Amenazas*," she said. "*Palabrotas*."

"Oh, I'm very sorry, señorita, would you like me to call the police?"

"I want you to hold all calls."

"Yes, ma'am, certainly."

She brooded for a minute, then retrieved a slip of paper from her purse, torn from a notepad in the Schiphol departure lounge. On it she had scrawled the phone number of a local private investigator that Denneen had recommended. Someone reliable, highly skilled, well connected with the authorities, but entirely honest, Denneen had assured her.

She punched out the number, let it ring and ring.

An answering machine came on. Sergio Machado identified himself and his agency. After the beep, she left her name and number, mentioned Denneen's name. Then she called the hotel switchboard operator again and told her she would accept a call only from a Sergio Machado.

She needed someone knowledgeable and resourceful and most of all trustworthy. You couldn't hope to get anywhere, learn anything, without someone like that, unless you had a reliable contact in the governmental bureaucracy, and that she did not have.

She went to the bathroom, splashed her face at the sink, first cold water, then hot. The telephone rang.

Thickly, in a stupor, she walked to the bedside table.

The phone rang again, then again.

She stood over the phone, stared at it, considered what to do.

She picked it up.

Said nothing, waited.

There was silence.

"Hello?" a male voice said finally. "Is anyone there?"

Quietly, mouth dry, she said: "Yes?"

"Is this Anna Navarro?"

"Who's this?" She tried to keep her tone neutral.

"It's Sergio Machado—you just called me? I went out to get the mail, now I'm returning your call."

Relieved, she sighed, "Oh, God, I'm sorry. I've just been getting a bunch of obscene calls. I thought it might be the caller again."

"What do you mean, obscene calls—like heavy breathing, that sort of thing?"

"No. Nothing like that. It's too complicated to get into."

"You in some kind of trouble?"

"No. Yes. I don't know, probably. Anyway, listen, thanks for calling back. David Denneen thought you might be able to help me."

"Sure, you want to get a cup of coffee? Not like the shit you drink in America. Real coffee."

"Yeah, sure, I'd like that." Already the anxiety was beginning to ebb.

They agreed to meet early that evening in front of a café/restaurant not too far from his office. "I'll do what I can," he said. "I can't promise anything more than that."

"That's good enough for me," she said.

She hung up and stood over the phone for a moment, looking at it as if it were some alien life-form that had invaded the room.

Ben and she would have to change hotels. Perhaps she had been followed from her visit with Peralta. Perhaps she had been followed from the airport. But her location and her mission were known: that was the real message of those calls. She knew better than to take them as anything other than threats.

A knock at the door.

Adrenaline propelled her to a position beside it. The safety chain was securely looped from the slide bolt in the door plate to the doorjamb.

The door could not be opened with just a key.

Could it?

There was no peephole.

"Who is it?" she said.

The voice that replied was male, familiar. She never would have thought she'd be so glad to hear it.

"It's Ben," the voice said.

"Thank God," she muttered.

CHAPTER THIRTY-SIX

He was bedraggled, shirt and tie askew, hair wild.

"What's with the door chain?" he said. "You used to live in East New York, too?"

She stared. "What happened to you?"

After they'd each recounted the events of the last few hours, she said, "We have to get out of here."

"Damn right," Ben said. "There's a hotel downtown, in the *centro*—sort of a fleabag, but supposed to be kind of charming. Run by British expatriates. The Sphinx." He'd bought a South America guide at the airport. He thumbed through it, found the entry. "Here we go. We can either show up or call from the street, on my cell phone. Not from here."

She nodded. "Maybe we should stay in the same room this time. Husband and wife."

"You're the expert," he said. Was there a glint of amusement in his eyes?

She explained: "They're going to call around looking for an American man and woman traveling together but staying in separate rooms. How long do you think it'll take them to locate us?"

"You're probably right. Listen—I have something." He produced a folded sheet of paper from his inside jacket pocket.

"What's that?"

"A fax."

"From?"

"My researcher in New York. It's the names of the board of directors of Armakon AG of Vienna. Owners of that little biotech startup in Philadelphia that made the poison that killed the old men."

He handed it to her. "Jürgen Lenz," she breathed.

"One of the directors. Is that an intriguing coincidence or what?"

Once again, Arliss Dupree returned to the paperwork in front of him and once again he found it impossible to focus. It was a long report prepared by the deputy director of the Executive Officer for U.S. Trustees, which oversees bankruptcy estates; the report detailed allegations of corruption involving the federal bankruptcy courts. Dupree read the same sentence three times before he set it aside and got himself another cup of the near-rancid coffee produced by the sputtering machine down the hall.

He had other things on his mind—that was the trouble. The developments involving Agent Navarro were annoying. Worse than annoying. They spelled major aggravation. He didn't give a damn what happened to her. But if she'd been guilty of security breaches, it reflected badly on him. Which was totally unfair. And he couldn't help thinking that it all started with that goddamn liver-spotted spook at the Internal Compliance Unit, Alan Bartlett. Whatever the hell *that* was about. Several times he'd made inquiries—proper, interdepartmental inquiries—and each time he had been rebuffed. As if he had some lowly custodial capacity at the Office of Special Investigations. As if the OSI itself weren't worthy of a civil word. Whenever Dupree thought about it for too long, he had to loosen his tie. It was *galling*.

First that bitch Navarro was cherry-picked from his team to go gallivanting off God only knew where. Next thing, word came down that she was rotten, had been selling off information to traffickers and hostiles and whoever else. If so, she was Typhoid Mary, which—he kept coming back to it—was bad news for the person she'd reported to, namely, Arliss Dupree. If Dupree had any sense of which way the wind was blowing—and his career was based on his having that sense—a shit storm was coming his way.

And he was damned if his career was going to be dented by Navarro's misconduct or—since the charges mostly sounded like bullshit to him—by Bartlett's double-dealing. Dupree was, above all, a survivor.

Sometimes surviving meant that you took the bull by the goddamn horns. Dupree had friends of his own—friends who would tell him stuff he needed to know. And maybe paying a visit on the Ghost might help concentrate the old guy's mind. Bartlett looked like a goddamned vapor trail, but he was a major power in the department, a mini J. Edgar Hoover. Dupree would have to deal with him carefully. Even so, Bartlett had to learn that Dupree wasn't somebody to mess with. The Ghost spent his days directing investigations into his colleagues; when was the last time anybody looked into what *he* was up to?

Dupree tore open a couple of envelopes of sugar and dumped it into his coffee. It still tasted foul, but he slurped it down anyway. He had a lot of work ahead of him. With any luck at all, Alan Bartlett would be getting a dose of his own medicine.

The rooms at the Sphinx were large and light-filled. There was one double bed, which they each glanced at warily, deferring any decisions on sleeping arrangements until later.

"What I still don't understand," she said, "is how anyone knew I was here and *why*."

"The Interpol man—"

"Except that I saw him *after* the package was stolen from American Express." She was standing by the tall windows, fiddling with the sheer, gauzy curtains. "Once the package was stolen, the bad guys knew I was looking for Strasser. Question is, how did anyone even know to take it? You didn't tell anyone you were traveling to Buenos Aires with me, right?"

He didn't like her implication, but he ignored it. "No. But did you make any phone calls from the hotel?"

She was silent a moment. "Yeah, I did. One to Washington."

"Not hard to tap hotel phones if you have the proper contacts, right?"

She looked at him, visibly impressed. "That might also explain the fake CIA man. Yes. Did you give Jürgen Lenz any indication—"

"I never told Lenz I was even thinking of going to Buenos Aires, because at that point I *wasn't*."

"I wish there was a way to get Lenz's fingerprints, run 'em through a bunch of databases, see what we turn up. Maybe there's even a criminal record. Did he give you anything—a business card, anything?"

"Nothing, as far as I can recall—well, actually, I gave him the photograph to look at, the one I got from Peter's bank vault in Zurich."

"How many people have you shown it to?"

"You. A historian at the University of Zurich. Liesl. And Lenz. That's all."

"He handled it?"

"Oh yeah. Front and back, turned it over. His fingers were all over it."

"Great, I'll have a copy made and send the original off to AFIS."

"How? I get the impression your DOJ privileges have been revoked."

"But Denneen's haven't. If I can get it to him, he can pass it along to a friend in another agency, probably FBI. He'll figure it out."

He hesitated. "Well, if it enables us to get something on Lenz. Or to find Peter's killers . . ."

"Excellent. Thank you." She glanced at her watch. "Let's continue this over supper. We're meeting this detective, Sergio whatever, in a part of the city called La Boca. We can grab something to eat there."

The cabdriver was a middle-aged woman with flabby arms, wearing a tank top. On the dashboard was a framed color photo of a child, presumably her own. A tiny leather moccasin dangled from the rearview mirror.

"A gun-toting priest," Anna mused. "And I thought the Dominican nuns in church were scary." She'd changed into a gray pleated skirt and white blouse, a pearl choker around her swan neck, and smelled of something floral and crisp. "He told you that Jürgen Lenz actually owns her house?"

"Actually, he used the phrase, 'the man who *calls* himself Jürgen Lenz.' "

They entered a seedy working-class barrio on the southernmost tip of Buenos Aires. On their left was the Riachuelo Canal, a stagnant body of water in which rusting dredges and scows and hulks were half-submerged. Along the waterway were warehouses and meat-packing plants.

"She told you Gerhard Lenz *had* no children?" Anna's brows were knit in concentration. "Am I missing something?"

"Uh-uh. He's Lenz, yet he's *not* Lenz."

"So the man you met in Vienna, who everyone knows as Jürgen Lenz, is an impostor."

"That would be the implication."

"Yet whoever he really is, this old woman and her stepson obviously fear him."

"No question about it."

"But why in the world would Jürgen Lenz pretend to be the son of someone so infamous if he's *not?*" she said. "It makes no sense."

"We're not talking about an Elvis impersonator here,

granted. The thing is, we don't really understand much about how succession works at Sigma. Maybe it was his way of gaining a foothold there. Representing himself as the direct descendant of one of the founders—that might have been the only way he could worm his way in."

"That's assuming that Jürgen Lenz is Sigma."

"At this point, it seems safer than assuming the contrary. And, going from what Chardin said, the question with Sigma isn't what they control, but what they *don't* control."

Darkness had settled. They were entering an area that was crowded, ill-lit, dangerous-seeming. The houses here were constructed of sheet metal, with corrugated metal roofs, painted pink and ocher and turquoise.

The cab pulled up in front of a restaurant-bar bustling with rowdy patrons at creaky wooden tables or gathered at the bar, talking and laughing. Prominently displayed behind the bar was a color portrait of Eva Perón. Ceiling fans turned slowly.

They ordered *empanadas* and a San Telmo cabernet sauvignon and a bottle of *agua mineral gaseosa*. The wineglasses had the perspirant smell of old sponge. The napkins were slick squares of deli paper.

"The widow thought you were from 'Semmering,' " Anna said when they were settled. "What do you think she meant—a place? A company?"

"I don't know. A place, I suppose."

"And when she mentioned 'the company'?"

"I took that to be Sigma."

"But there's another company. Jürgen Lenz—whoever he really is—is on the Armakon board."

"How much are you going to trust this Machado guy with what we know?"

"Not at all," she replied. "I simply want him to find Strasser for us."

They finished with a couple of *humitas*, creamy sweet-corn paste in cornhusk packets, and coffee.

"I assume the Interpol guy wasn't much help," Ben said.

"He denied the possibility that Strasser might live here. Highly suspicious. Interpol was controlled by the Nazis for a time, just before the Second World War, and some people think it never really purged itself. It wouldn't surprise me at all if this guy's in the pocket of one of these Nazi protection rackets. Now, your gun-toting priest—"

"My gun-toting priest insisted he had no way to reach Strasser, but I don't believe him."

"I'll bet he got on the phone to Strasser the moment you were out the door."

Ben reflected. "If he called Strasser . . . What if we could somehow get the widow's telephone records?"

"We can ask Machado. He may be able to do it, or know who to reach out to."

"Speaking of reaching out, do you know what this guy looks like?"

"No, but we're meeting him right in front."

The street was crowded and raucous and electric—rock music blaring from speakers set out on sidewalks, an opera's aria, tango music from a nearby cantina. *Porteños* strolled down the cobblestones of the Caminito, a pedestrian thoroughfare, browsing at the stalls of an open-air market. People came in and out of the restaurant, repeatedly colliding with Ben and Anna without apology.

Ben noticed a gaggle of young boys in their late teens or early twenties, a roving gang of eight or more toughs, heading toward him and Anna, talking loudly, laughing, drunk on alcohol and testosterone. Anna muttered something to Ben out of the side of her mouth, something he couldn't quite understand. Several of the guys were staring directly at him and Anna with something more than idle curiosity, and in an instant the gang surrounded them.

"Run!" he shouted, and he was slugged in the stomach by a fist.

He protected his abdomen with both arms, as something slammed into his left kidney—a foot!—and he lunged forward to ward off the attack. He heard Anna scream, but it seemed to come from a great distance. He was blocked, hemmed in; his assailants, though evidently teenagers, seemed to be trained in combat. He couldn't move, and he was being pummeled. In his peripheral vision he could see Anna flinging one of the attackers aside with surprising strength, but then several more grabbed her. Ben tried to break free, but was overwhelmed by a barrage of fists and kicks.

He saw the glint of knife blades, and a knife slashed against his side. A hot line of sensation exploded into vast pain, and he grabbed the hand holding the knife, twisted it hard, and heard a yelp. He kicked at his attackers, slammed wildly with his fists, connecting a few times, and he felt an elbow jabbed into his rib cage, then a knee in his stomach. Breath left him, and he gasped helplessly, then a foot kicked him in the testicles and he doubled over in pain.

He heard the whoop of a siren, and he heard Anna shout, "Over here! Oh, thank God!" A foot kicked him hard on the side of his head, and he could taste blood. He flung his hands out, half protectively, half in an attempt to grab whatever he could, to stop the pummeling; he heard shouting, new voices, and he lurched to his feet to see a couple of policemen shouting at his accosters.

One of the cops grabbed him, yelled, "¡Vamos, vamos por acá, que los vamos a sacar de acá!" Come on, get over here, we'll get you out of here! Another cop pulled Anna toward the cruiser. Somehow he made it to the police car, saw the door open, felt a shove, and he was inside. The door slammed behind him, and all the shouts and screams of the crowd were muted.

"You all right?" one of the cops said from the front seat. Ben groaned.

Anna said, "Gracias!" Ben noticed that her blouse was torn, her pearl choker was gone. "We're American . . ." she began, then seemed to think for a moment. "My purse," she said. "Shit. My money was in there."

"Passport?" Ben managed to croak out.

"Back in the room." The car was moving. She turned to

him. "My God, what was that? You O.K., Ben?"

"I'm not sure." The screaming pain in his groin was beginning to subside. There was a sticky warmth where he'd been slashed by the knife. He touched his side, felt the blood.

The car swung into traffic, barreling down the road. "That was no random attack," Anna said. "That was deliberate. Planned, coordinated."

Ben looked at her dully. "Thank you," he said to the policemen in the front seat.

There was no reply. He realized that there was a Plexiglas barrier between the front and back seats, and he heard Anna say, "The partition—?"

The Plexiglas had not been there before; it had just come up. Ben did not hear a police radio, or maybe the sound wasn't coming through the Plexiglas.

Anna seemed to notice the same thing at the same moment, for she leaned forward and banged on the Plexiglas, but the two policemen didn't respond.

The back doors locked automatically.

"Oh, my God," Anna breathed. "*They're not cops.*"

They pulled at the door handles, which did not yield. They grabbed at the door lock buttons, but they would not move.

"Where's your gun?" Ben whispered.

"I don't *have* one!"

Headlights flashed by as the car accelerated down a four-lane highway. They were now clearly outside the city limits. Ben hammered at the Plexiglas partition with both fists, but neither the driver nor the passenger in the front seat seemed to notice.

The car swerved onto an exit ramp. In a few minutes they were on a dark, two-lane road, lined with tall trees, and then without warning they turned off the road into an unlit cul-de-sac within a copse of tall trees.

The engine was switched off. For a moment there was

silence, interrupted only by the sound of an occasional car passing by.

The two men in the front seat seemed to be conferring. Then the passenger got out and went around to the back of the car. The trunk popped open.

In a moment he returned to his side of the car, clutching in his left hand something that looked like a piece of cloth. In his right he held a handgun. Then the driver got out, taking a gun from a shoulder holster. The back doors unlocked.

The driver, apparently in charge, yanked open the door on Anna's side and waved the gun at her. She got out slowly, put her hands up. He stepped back and, with his free left hand, slammed the car door shut, leaving Ben alone in the backseat.

The deserted country road, the weapons . . . this was a classic execution.

The other false policeman—or perhaps they were real ones; did it make any difference?—walked to where Anna stood, her hands in the air, and began frisking her for weapons, beginning with her underarms. His hands lingered on her breasts.

He ran his hands down her side, moving them into her crotch, his fingers spending too much time there as well, then moved down the inside of her legs to her ankles. He pulled back, seemed to determine her safe. Then he took a burlap sack and placed it over her head, tightening it around her neck.

The driver barked something, and she fell to her knees and clasped her hands behind her back.

Ben saw with horror what was about to happen to her. "*No!*"

The driver shouted another order, and the younger cop opened the car door, pointing his weapon at Ben. "Step out slowly," he said in fluent English.

There was no hope of making a dash for the road, nor of grabbing Anna and taking her to safety. Not faced with two men with guns. He got out of the car, thrust his hands in the air, and the younger one began frisking him too, this time more roughly.

"*No está enfierrado*," the man said. He's clean.

To Ben, he said conversationally, "Any sudden movements and we'll kill you. Understand?"

Yes, I understand. They'll kill us both.

A burlap sack went over his head. It stank of a horse barn, and was cinched tight at his neck, too tight, choking him. Everything was dark. He croaked, "Hey, watch it!"

"Shut the hell up," one of the men said. It sounded like the older man's voice. "Or I kill you and no one find your body for days, hear me?"

He heard Anna whisper, "Go along with them for now. We don't exactly have a choice."

He felt something hard pressed against the back of his head. "Kneel," a voice said.

He knelt, and without being asked, he clasped his hands behind his back. "What do you want?" Ben said.

"Shut the hell up!" one of them shouted. Something hard cracked against the back of his head. He groaned in pain.

His abductors didn't want to talk. They were going to die in this godforsaken field off a dark road in the middle of a country he didn't know. He was thinking of how it all began, at the Bahnhofplatz in Zurich, with his near-death, or did it really begin with Peter's disappearance? He recalled the agony of Peter's murder in the country inn in rural Switzerland, but instead of demoralizing him, the memory gave him resolve. If he were killed here, at least he would have the satisfaction of knowing that he had done everything he could to find his brother's murderers, and if he had failed to bring them to justice, or to discover what their reasons were, at least he had come close. He would leave behind no wife, no child, and in time he would be mostly forgotten by his friends, but in the history of the world all our lives are as brief as the winking of a firefly on a summer night, and he would not feel sorry for himself.

He thought of his father, wherever he'd vanished to, and

regretted only that he'd never know the entire truth about the man.

Out of the darkness came a sudden voice. The older man.

"Now you answer some questions. What the hell you want with Josef Strasser?"

So they wanted to talk after all.

These goons were protecting Strasser.

He waited for Anna to speak first, and when she didn't, he said, "I'm an attorney. An American lawyer. I'm probating an estate—that means I'm trying to get him some money that's been left to him."

Something cracked hard against the side of his head.

"I want the truth, not your *bullshit!*"

"I'm *telling* you the truth." Ben's voice was shaky. "Leave this woman out of it—she's just my girlfriend. She's got nothing to do with it. I dragged her along, she'd never been to Buenos Aires—"

"Shut *up!*" one of them bellowed. Something slammed into his right kidney, and he tumbled to the ground, his face inside the burlap flat against the dirt. The pain was so acute he could not even groan. Then came a blinding pain as something cracked into the side of his face, perhaps a foot, and he smelled and tasted blood. Everything was bleached out.

He screamed, "*Stop!* What do you want? I'll tell you what you want!"

He hunched forward, brought his hands around to protect his face, gasping from the unfathomable pain, and he felt blood seeping from his mouth. He braced himself for the next blow, but for a moment nothing happened.

Then came the voice of the older one, quiet and matter-of-fact, as if making a reasonable point in a pleasant conversation. "The woman is not 'just' your girlfriend. She is Agent Anna Navarro, and she is on the payroll of the United States Justice Department. This we know. You, we want to know about."

"I'm helping her," he managed to get out, cringing, and

it came, a swift blow to the other side of his head. A lightning bolt of pain pierced his eyes. The pain was so great now, so constant and overwhelming, that he thought he could not possibly survive it.

Then a pause, a momentary intermission in the torture session, and there was silence, the men seemingly waiting for him to speak again.

But Ben's mind was sluggish. Who—where were these men from? The man called Jürgen Lenz? Sigma itself? Their methods seemed too homespun for that. The *Kamaradenwerk?* That was more plausible. What answer would satisfy them, end the beatings, forestall the execution?

Anna spoke. His ears were plugged, probably with blood, and he could barely hear what she said. "If you're protecting Strasser," she said in a voice that was surprisingly steady, "you'll want to know what I'm doing here. I've come to Buenos Aires to warn him—not to seek his extradition."

One of the men laughed, but she kept speaking. Her voice seemed so far away. "Do you know that a number of Strasser's comrades have been murdered in the last few weeks?"

There was no response. "We have information that Strasser is about to be killed. The U.S. Justice Department has no interest in trying to seize him, or we'd have done it long ago. Whatever terrible things he's done, he's not wanted for war crimes. I'm trying to keep him from being murdered, so I can talk to him."

"Liar!" one of the men screamed. There was a thud, and Anna cried out.

"Stop!" she shouted, her voice cracking. "There are ways you can check that I'm telling you the truth! We need to get to Strasser to warn him! If you kill us, you'll be harming *him!*"

"Anna!" Ben yelled. He needed to connect with her. "Anna, you O.K.? Just tell me you're O.K."

His throat felt as if it were going to burst. The exertion of yelling made his head throb excruciatingly.

Silence. Then her muffled voice: "I'm O.K."

It was the last thing he heard before everything vanished.

His horror-struck eyes fixed on Dean's face. He desperately
cried out. The floor beneath their feet began to...

Wen said in her muffled voice, "No."
It was then that Ben heard something chilling below the

CHAPTER THIRTY-SEVEN

Ben awoke in a bed in a large, unfamiliar room with high ceilings, and tall windows that looked out over a city street he didn't recognize.

Evening, traffic noise, twinkling lights.

A lanky woman with dark brown hair and brown eyes, in a T-shirt and black Lycra bicycle shorts, languidly curled in a chair, watching him.

Anna.

His head throbbed.

In a sedate voice, she said, "Hey."

"Hey," he said. "I'm alive." The nightmarish scene began to come back to him, but he couldn't remember when he lost consciousness.

She smiled. "How're you feeling?"

He thought about this for a moment. "Sort of like the guy who falls from the top of a skyscraper, and someone sticks his head out of a tenth-floor window and asks how he's doing, and the guy says, Well, so far I'm fine."

Anna chuckled.

"I have kind of a low-grade headache." He turned his

head from side to side, felt the pain sear and sparkle behind his eyeballs. "Maybe not so low-grade."

"Well, you got bashed up pretty bad. For a while I thought you might have a concussion, but I guess not. Not from what I can tell." She paused. "They kicked me around a little, but they seemed to be focusing on you."

"Real gentlemen." He thought a moment, still disoriented. "How'd I get back here?"

"I guess they got tired of beating on you, or maybe they got scared when you passed out. At any rate, they brought us back to town, dropped us off somewhere in La Boca."

The only light in the room came from a lamp beside the bed where he lay. He became aware of bandages, on his forehead and side. "Who did this?"

"What do you mean—who were they? Or who bandaged you up?"

"Who fixed me up?"

"*Moi*," she said, bowing her head modestly. "Medical supplies courtesy the Sphinx, mostly peroxide and Betadine."

"Thank you." His thinking was muzzy and slow. "So who *were* those guys?"

"Well, we're alive," she said, "so I'm guessing they're local muscle. *Pistoleros*, they're called, guns for hire."

"But the police car . . ."

"The Argentine police are famous for corruption. A lot of them moonlight as *pistoleros*. But I don't think they were connected with Sigma. *Kamaradenwerk*, or something along those lines—thugs who look out for the old Germans. The local network could have been alerted lots of ways. My Interpol friend—I gave him a fake name, but he might have seen an ID photo. Maybe it was the stolen package at American Express. Maybe it was my investigator guy, Machado. Maybe your pistol-packin' priest. But enough questions. I want you to take it easy."

He tried to sit up, felt a pain in his side, lay back down. Now he remembered being kicked in the stomach, the groin, the kidneys.

His eyelids kept drooping, the room going in and out of focus, and soon he succumbed to sleep.

When he awoke again, it was still night, and the room was mostly dark. The only light came from the street, but it was enough to see the shape in bed next to him. He could smell her faint perfume. He thought, *Now she's willing to share a bed.*

The next time he awoke, the room was bright. It hurt his eyes to look around. He heard the sound of water running in the bathroom, and struggled to sit up.

Anna emerged in a cloud of steam, wrapped in a bath towel.

"He's awake," she said. "How's it feel?"

"A little better."

"Good. You want me to order some coffee from room service?"

"They have room service here?"

"Yeah, you're feeling better," she said with a laugh. "The old sense of humor's starting to come back."

"I'm hungry."

"Understandable. We didn't have a chance to eat dinner last night." She turned back toward the bathroom.

He was in a clean T-shirt and boxer shorts. "Who changed my clothes?"

"Me."

"My shorts, too?"

"Mm-hmm. You were soaked in blood."

Well, well, he thought, amused. *Our first moment of intimacy and I slept through it.*

She began brushing her teeth and reemerged a few minutes later, makeup applied, wearing a white T-shirt and violet gym shorts.

"What do you think happened?" he asked. His head was beginning to clear. "You think your call to that private detective, what's-his-name, was intercepted?"

"Possibly."

"From now on we use my digital phone only. Let's assume even the Sphinx's switchboard is tapped."

She placed two pillows behind him. She wore no perfume now but smelled pleasantly of soap and shampoo. "Mind if I use it now to call our last hotel? My friend in Washington thinks I'm staying there, and might be trying to reach me." She tossed him a copy of the *International Herald Tribune*. "You take it easy. Read, sleep, whatever."

"Make sure it's charged. You might have to plug it in."

He leaned back and idly flipped through the pages. An earthquake in the Gujarat state in India. A California utilities company facing a shareholders' lawsuit. World leaders set to gather at the International Children's Health Forum. He put the paper aside and shut his eyes, but only to rest. He'd had enough sleep. He listened to her talk to the hotel in La Recoleta, her voice lulling. She had a lively, infectious laugh.

She appeared to have lost her sharp edge, her defensiveness. Now she seemed confident and assured, but without the brittleness. Maybe it was his weakness that allowed her to be strong. Maybe she liked to nurture. Maybe it was the shared adventure they had just been through, or his concern for her, or maybe it was pity for what had happened to him, or misplaced guilt. Maybe it was all these things.

She ended the phone conversation. "Well, this is interesting."

"Hmm?" He opened his eyes. She was standing beside the bed, her hair tousled, her breasts outlined beneath the white cotton T-shirt. He felt the tug of arousal.

"I got a message from Sergio the private eye, apologizing for being late, he was tied up on a case. Sounds entirely innocent."

"Call was intercepted at the hotel, probably."

"I'm going to meet him."

"Are you crazy? Haven't you had enough traps for one lifetime?"

"On my terms. My arrangement."

"Don't."

"I know what I'm doing. I may screw up—I *do* screw

up sometimes—but you know, I'm actually considered pretty good at what I do."

"I don't doubt it. But you don't do organized crime or drugs, you don't do shoot-'em-up stuff. I think we're *both* in over our heads."

He felt oddly protective of her, even though she was no doubt a far better shot than he, more equipped to defend herself. Yet at the same time—even more perplexing—he felt safer with her around.

She came over and sat on the bed next to him. He edged over a bit to give her room. "I appreciate your worrying about me," she said. "But I've been trained, and I *have* been a field agent."

"I'm sorry, I didn't mean to imply—"

"No apology necessary. No offense taken."

He stole a quick glance at her. He wanted to say, *My God, you're beautiful*, but he didn't know how she might take it. She still seemed pretty defensive.

She said, "Are you doing this for your brother or for your father?"

The question caught him by surprise. He hadn't expected such bluntness. And he realized the answer wasn't simple. "Maybe both," he said. "Mostly for Peter, of course."

"How well did you and Peter get along?"

"Do you know any twins?" he asked.

"Not well."

"I suspect it's the closest relationship there is, closer than many husbands and wives. Not that I know about *that* first-hand. But we protected each other. We could almost read each other's mind. Even when we fought—and we did, believe me—afterward we each felt more guilty than angry. We competed with each other in sports and such, but not really in any other way. When he was happy, I was happy. When something good happened to him, I felt like it had happened to me. And vice versa."

To his surprise he saw tears in her eyes. For some reason that brought tears to his own.

He continued, "When I say we were close, that seems

so inadequate. You don't say you're 'close' to your leg or your hand, right? He was like a part of my body."

It all came back to him suddenly, a jumble of memories, or really, images. Peter's murder. His mind-boggling reappearance. The two of them, as kids, running through the house, laughing. Peter's funeral.

He turned away in embarrassment, covered his face with his hand, unable to stanch the sob that welled up.

He heard a low keening and realized that Anna was crying too, which surprised him and, most of all, moved him. She took his hand in hers and squeezed tight. Her cheeks glistening with tears, she put an arm gently around his shoulders, then both of her arms, and she embraced him, seemingly careful of his wounds, and laid her face damply on his shoulder. It was a moment of intimacy that at once startled him and felt natural, part of the complex, passionate Anna he was slowly coming to know. He took solace from her, and she from him. He could feel her heart thudding against his chest, her warmth. She raised her head off his shoulder and slowly, tentatively at first, placed her lips against his, her eyes closed tight. They kissed slowly, tenderly at first, then deeply and with abandon. His arms encircled her lithe body, his fingers exploring her as his mouth and tongue did the same. They had crossed a line each of them had invisibly and firmly drawn some time ago, a boundary, a high wall between natural impulses, containing and isolating the powerful electrical charges that now crackled back and forth between them. And somehow, when they made love, it didn't seem as awkward as he'd imagined it might be, when he'd allowed himself to imagine it.

Finally, exhausted, they napped for half an hour or so, entwined in each other.

When he awoke, he saw that she was gone.

The gray-haired man parked his rented Mercedes and walked several cobblestone blocks down Estomba until he

located the house. He was in the heart of a barrio of Buenos
Aires called Belgrano, one of the wealthiest residential sec-
tions. A young man passed by walking six dogs at once.
The gray-haired man, in a well-tailored blue suit, gave him
a neighborly smile.

The house was a Georgian-style mansion built of red
bricks. He walked past it, seeming to admire the architecture, then he turned back, having noted the security booth
on the sidewalk in front of the house: an off-white win-
dowed sentry box in which stood a uniformed man wearing
an orange Day-Glo reflective vest. There seemed to be one
of these security booths on every block around here.

A very quiet, very safe neighborhood, Trevor Griffiths
thought. Good. The security guard looked him over. Trevor
nodded in a neighborly manner, and approached the booth
as if to ask the guard a question.

Anna carefully packaged Ben's photograph and brought it
to a DHL office, paying to get it to Denneen's home address in Dupont Circle as quickly as possible. Everything
she did now involved some degree of risk, but she hadn't
mentioned DHL on the phone or even to Ben in the room,
and she made sure that no one followed her there. She was
reasonably certain the photo would arrive safely.

Now she stood in a doorway of a shop beneath a red
Lucky Strike sign, watching the windows of a café at the
corner of Junin and Viamonte, just down the street from
the *Facultad Medecina*. The café's name, Entre Tiempo,
was painted on the plate glass in jumbled letters, presumably signifying wacky fun within. Couples strolled by absorbed in each other, gaggles of students wearing
backpacks. A slew of passing yellow-and-black taxis.

This time there would be no surprises.

She'd reconnoitered this site in advance, arranged to
meet Sergio Machado here at six-thirty precisely, arrived a
full forty-five minutes beforehand. A public place in broad
daylight. She'd asked him to take a seat at a table in the

window, if one was available, or as close to the window as possible. And to bring his cell phone. Machado seemed more amused than annoyed by her precautions.

At twenty-five after six, a silver-haired man in a blue blazer and open-neck button-down blue shirt, fitting the description he'd supplied over the phone, entered the café. A minute or so later he appeared at a table by the window and looked out onto the street. She pulled back into the shop so she couldn't be seen and continued to watch through the glass door. She'd already explained to the shopkeeper that she was waiting here for her husband.

At six thirty-five, Machado hailed a waiter.

A few minutes later the waiter set down a bottle of Coca-Cola.

If Machado had been complicit in last night's kidnapping, there would surely be others stationed nearby, but she saw no sign of anyone. No one lingering, pretending to window-shop, dawdling at a newsstand, sitting in a car idling by a curb. She knew what to look for. Machado was alone.

Were there others in place in the café awaiting her arrival?

Perhaps. But she was prepared for the possibility.

At six forty-five, she switched on Ben's phone and called Machado's cell.

It rang once. "*Sí?*"

"It's Anna Navarro."

"You get lost somewhere?"

"God, this city's so *confusing*," she said. "I guess I got the wrong place—would you mind terribly meeting me here, where I am now? I just *know* I'll get lost *again!*" She gave him directions to a café a few blocks away.

She watched as he got up, left some change, and, without appearing to signal to, or consult with, anyone inside the café, emerged. She knew what he looked like, but presumably he wouldn't recognize her.

He crossed the street and walked past her, and she got a better glimpse of him. The silver hair was premature; he was a man in his forties with soft brown eyes and a pleasant look about him. He carried no briefcase or file, just his phone.

She waited a few seconds, then followed him.

He located the café easily, and went inside. She joined him a minute or so later.

"You mind explaining what all this was about?" Machado asked.

She related what had happened to her and Ben the night before. She watched his face closely; he seemed appalled.

Machado had the saturnine look of an Italian film star of the 1960s. He was deeply and meticulously tanned. Around his neck was a thin gold chain, and another gold chain encircled his left wrist. A vertical worry line was scored deeply between his close-set fawn's eyes. He wore no wedding band.

"The police here, they are totally corrupt, you are absolutely right," he said. "They hire me to do investigative work for them, as an outside consultant, because they don't trust their own people!"

"I'm not surprised." The fear left over from the abduction had become anger.

"You know, we have no cop shows here in Argentina like you have in America, because here cops aren't heroes. They're scum. I know. I was in Federal Police for twenty-one years. Got my pension and left."

A long table nearby, some sort of student study group by the look of them, burst into laughter.

"Everyone here is afraid of the police," he went on heatedly. "Police brutality. They charge for protection. They shoot to kill whenever they want. You like their uniforms?"

"They look like New York City cops."

"That's because their uniforms were copied *exactly* from the NYPD. And that's *all* they copied." He flashed an endearing smile. "So what can I do for you?"

"I need to find a man named Josef Strasser."

His eyes widened. "Ah, well, you know, this old bastard lives under a false name. I don't know where he lives, but

I can ask some questions. Not so easy. You gonna extradite?"

"No, actually, I need to have a talk with him."

He straightened. "Really?"

"I may have a way to locate him, but I'll need your help." She related Ben's meeting with Lenz's widow. "If Vera Lenz or her stepson are in touch with Strasser, and they called to warn him, say—could you find out what number they dialed?"

"Ah," he said. "Very nice. Yes of course, but only if you can get Señora Lenz's telephone number."

She handed him a slip of paper with the number on it.

"The phone companies in Argentina, they record the beginning and end of all telephone conversations, the number called and how long the call. It is the Excalibur system, they call it. My friends in the police, for the right price, they will get for me all calls made from that number."

And as if to demonstrate how easy it was, he placed a call, spoke briefly, read off the number on the scrap of paper.

"No problem," he said. "We'll know soon. Come, I buy you a steak."

They walked a few blocks to his car, a white Ford Escort whose backseat had for some reason been removed. He took her to an old-style restaurant near the Cementerio de la Recoleta called Estilo Munich, its walls adorned with stuffed boars' and stags' heads. The floor was marble but looked like drab linoleum; the ceiling was acoustic tile. Weary waiters shuffled slowly between the tables.

"I will order for you *bife de chorizo*," Machado said. "With *chimichurri* sauce. *Jugoso*, it is O.K.?"

"Rare is how I like it, yes. Any symbolism in the fact that you brought me to a restaurant called Munich?"

"They serve one of the best steaks in Buenos Aires, and we are a city that knows steaks." He gave her a complicit glance. "Used to be a lot of restaurants in BA called Munich—very fashionable once. Not so fashionable now."

"Not so many Germans."

He took a pull of the Carrascal. His cell phone rang; he spoke briefly, put it back. "My girlfriend," he apologized. "I thought we might have some results on our search, but no."

"If Strasser has managed to live here for so long without anybody finding him, he must have some good false ID."

"People like him got excellent false papers. For a long time only Jakob Sonnenfeld was able to trace them. For years, you know, there was a rumor that Martin Bormann was still alive in Argentina, until his skull turned up in Germany. Nineteen seventy-two, in Berlin. They were building a bridge, they dug up the ground, and they found a skull. Identified it as Bormann's."

"Was it?"

"A couple of years ago they finally did the DNA test. It was Bormann's skull, yes."

"What about the rest of his body?"

"Never found. I think he was buried here, in Bariloche, and someone brought the skull to Germany. To mislead the pursuers." His eyes sparkled with amusement. "You know Bormann's son lives here. He's a Catholic priest. Really." Another swig of Carrascal. "It's true. Always rumors about Bormann. It is like with Josef Mengele. After he was buried everyone thinks he faked his own death. With Lenz the same thing. For years after his death was announced, there were rumors that he's still alive. Then they found his bones."

"Were they DNA-tested, too?"

"I don't think."

"No one found his skull anywhere."

"No skull."

"Could he still be alive somewhere?"

Machado laughed. "He'd be more than one hundred twenty."

"Well, only the good die young. He died of a stroke, didn't he?"

"This is the public line. But I think Lenz was murdered by Israeli agents. You know, when Eichmann came here, he and his wife took false names, but their three sons—

they used the name Eichmann! At school everyone knew the boys as Eichmann. But no one came to find them, you see. No one came to look for them until Sonnenfeld."

Their steaks arrived. Amazingly delicious, Anna thought. She was not much of a meat-eater, but this could convert her.

"Mind if I ask why you want to talk to Strasser?" Machado asked.

"Sorry. Can't say."

He seemed to accept it with good grace. "Strasser was one of the inventors of Zyklon-B."

"The gas used at Auschwitz."

"But it was his own idea to use it on human beings. A clever fellow, this Strasser. He came up with the way to kill Jews so much more expeditiously."

After dinner they walked a few doors down to a large café called La Biela, on Avenue Quintana, which at after eleven o'clock at night was crowded and loud.

Over coffee she asked, "Can you get me a weapon?"

He looked at her slyly. "It can be arranged."

"By tomorrow morning?"

"I'll see what I can do."

His phone rang again.

This time he jotted down notes on a little square napkin.

"His phone's listed under the name Albrecht," Machado said when he'd hung up. "The right age, too. He used his real birthdates on his application forms. I think you've found your man."

"So someone did call him from Lenz's house."

"Yes. With the phone number it was a simple thing to get the name and address. I think he must have been out of town for a long time, because no outgoing calls were made from his home for the last five weeks. Two days ago the calls started up again."

That would explain why Strasser hadn't yet been reported killed like all the others, she thought. *He was out of town.* That's how he had stayed alive. "Your contact," she said. "Whoever got this information for you—why does he think you're interested?"

"Maybe he believes I'm planning some sort of extortion."

"He wouldn't let Strasser know you've been looking?"

"My police contacts are too stupid to play those sorts of games."

"Let's hope so." But her worry was not so easily allayed. "What about the sorts of thugs who kidnapped us . . ."

He frowned. "The sons and grandsons of the fugitives, they won't mess with me. I have too many friends in the police. It is dangerous for them. Sometimes when I do this sort of job, I go home and I find Wagner on my answering machine, a veiled threat. Sometimes they walk by me on the street, take flash photographs of me. But that's all they do. I never worry." He lit another cigarette. "You have no reason to worry either."

No, no reason to worry, she thought.

Easy for you to say.

"I'm afraid Mr. Bartlett isn't able to see any visitors right now, and I don't see an appointment for you." The receptionist spoke with icy authority.

"I'm *making* an appointment—for right now," Arliss Dupree said. "Tell him he'll *want* to see me. It's about a matter of mutual concern. Interdepartmental business, O.K.?"

"I'm very sorry, Mr. Dupree, but . . ."

"Save you the trouble, I'll just mosey on down and knock on his door. You can give him a heads-up, or not. His office is down that way, right?" A grin played across Dupree's ruddy moon face. "Don't trouble yourself, girl. We're going to be fine."

The receptionist spoke hurriedly, softly, into the microphone of her headset. After a moment, she stood up. "Mr. Bartlett said he'd be pleased to see you. I'll show you to him."

Dupree looked around the director's spartan office and for the first time felt a twinge of alarm. It wasn't the comfortable burrow of the typical career officer—of the lifer who surrounded himself with photos of loved ones and stacks of unfiled paper. It barely showed signs of human habitation at all.

"And how can I help you today, Mr. Dupree?" Alan Bartlett stood behind a large desk, so uncluttered it might have been a floor model at an office-furniture store. There was something glacial, Dupree thought, about the man's polite smile, something unreadable about the gray eyes behind the aviator glasses.

"Lotsa ways, I suppose," Dupree said, and sat himself down unceremoniously on the blond-wooden chair facing Bartlett's desk. "Starting with this whole Navarro business."

"Most unfortunate, the recent revelations," Bartlett said. "Reflects poorly on all of us."

"As you know, I wasn't pleased by the TDY you arranged," he said, referring to the cross-departmental assignment of temporary duties.

"That much you made clear. Perhaps you knew something about her that you chose to be less than forthcoming about."

"Naw, that wasn't it." Dupree forced himself to meet Bartlett's steady gaze. It was like talking to an iceberg. "Frankly, it undermines my authority when a member of my staff gets shifted around like that, without my knowledge or consent. Some of the staffers will always assume it's some sort of promotion."

"I suspect you didn't come here to discuss your personnel difficulties or management style, Mr. Dupree."

"Hell, no," Dupree said. "Here's the thing. The rest of us at Justice always give you guys at ICU a wide berth. You get up to your stuff, and most of the time we're just as happy not to know about it. But this time, you started something that's leaving jelly stains on my carpet, you see what I'm saying? Putting me in a tight spot. I'm not making any accusations, I'm just saying that it got me thinking."

"An unaccustomed activity for you, no doubt. You will find it grows easier with practice." Bartlett spoke with effortless mandarin disdain.

"I may not be the sharpest tool in the shed," Dupree said. "But you'll find I can still cut."

"How reassuring."

"It's just that something about the whole thing smelled bad to me."

Bartlett sniffed. "Aqua Velva, would that be? Or Old Spice? Your aftershave arrives before you do."

Dupree just shook his head, in a show of good-natured confusion. "So I poked around a little. Learned a little more about you, about where you've been. I hadn't realized before that you owned a huge piece of property on the Eastern Shore. Not your typical federal employee, I guess."

"My mother's father was one of the founders of Holleran Industries. She was one of the heirs to the estate. That's not a secret. Nor is it something I choose to draw attention to, I'll admit. I have little interest in the high life. The life I've decided to lead is a rather plain one, and my tastes are, on the whole, modest. Anyway, what of it?"

"Right, your mother was a Holleran heiress—I found that out, too. Came as a surprise, I got to say. Way I see it, it's kind of flattering that a multimillionaire would deign to work among us."

"All of us must make decisions in our lives."

"Yup, I guess that's true. But then I'm thinking, how much else is there about Alan Bartlett that I don't know about? Probably a lot, right? Like, what's with all those trips to Switzerland? Now, Switzerland—I guess because at the OSI we're always dealing with money-laundering, that place always sets off alarm bells. So it gets me wondering about these trips of yours."

A beat. "Excuse me?"

"Well, you do head over to Switzerland a bunch, am I right?"

"What gives you that idea?"

Dupree pulled a sheet of paper from the breast pocket of his jacket. It was slightly crumpled, but he laid it flat on Bartlett's desk and smoothed it out. On it was a series of dots, in a roughly circular array. "Sorry it's so crude, I drew it myself." He pointed to the topmost dot. "Over here, we got Munich. Just under it, Innsbruck. Moving southeast, Milan. Turin. Then, a little more easterly and a little further north, Lyon. Dijon. Freiburg."

"And this would be an adult-education course in geography that you're taking?"

"Naw," Dupree said. "Took me a long time to get this stuff. I had to go through the computers at passport control and the major airlines, too. Major pain in the ass, I can tell you. But these are all airports that you traveled through at some point over the past fifteen years. A lot of them direct from Dulles, some of them with a connecting flight through Frankfurt or Paris. So here I am, and I'm looking at this scatter of points. All these dreary goddamn airports and what do they have in common?"

"I expect you're going to tell me," Bartlett said, a look of chilly amusement in his eyes.

"Well, Christ, take a look at the scatter. What would you conclude? It's obvious, isn't it? They're in a circle of points within a two-hundred-mile radius of Zurich. They're all a hop and a skip from Switzerland—that's what these places got in common. They're all places you'd go if you wanted to go to Switzerland and maybe didn't want to have 'Switzerland' stamped on your passport. *Either* of your passports, in *your* case: I was impressed to see you have two authorized passports."

"Which is not uncommon among officials in my particular line of work. You're being absurd, Mr. Dupree, but I'll play along. Let's say I have indeed visited Switzerland—so what?"

"Right, so what? No harm, no foul. Only, why'd you tell me you didn't?"

"You're really being deliberately dense, Mr. Dupree, aren't you? If I choose to discuss my vacation plans with you, you'll be the first to know. Your behavior today calls into question your fitness to discharge your official responsibilities. It also, if I may say so, verges on insubordination."

"I don't report to you, Bartlett."

"No, because seven years ago, when you sought transfer to our unit, you were turned down. Judged *not* to be of ICU caliber." Bartlett's voice remained cool, but his cheeks had colored. Dupree knew he had rattled him. "And now, I'm afraid, I'll have to call this conversation to an end."

"I'm not finished with you, Bartlett," Dupree said, standing up.

A death's-head smile: " 'Great works are never finished. Only abandoned.' So said Valéry."

"Harper?"

"Good-bye, Mr. Dupree," Bartlett said serenely. "Your commute home to Arlington is a long one at this time of day, and I know you'll want to beat the rush hour."

Ben awoke, aware first of the soft early-morning light, then of Anna's soft breathing. They had slept in the same bed. He sat up slowly, feeling the dull ache in his limbs, his neck. He could feel warmth radiating from her nightgown-clad body a few inches away.

He walked slowly to the bathroom, the pain now awakening too. He realized he'd slept through an entire day and night. Ben knew he was badly battered, but it was better to move around, stay as limber as possible, than to confine himself to bed. Either way it would take time to recover.

He returned to the bedroom, quietly picking up his phone. Fergus O'Connor in the Caymans was expecting his call. But when he tried to switch the phone on, he discovered that the battery was dead. Anna had apparently forgotten to charge it. He heard her stirring in the bed.

He slipped the phone into its charger cradle and called Fergus.

"Hartman!" Fergus exclaimed heartily, as if he'd been waiting for Ben's call.

"Give me some news," Ben said, hobbling to the window and looking out over the traffic.

"Well, I've got good news and bad news. Whaddaya want first?"

"Always the good first."

There was a beep on the line—another call coming in—but he ignored it.

"Right. There's one shady lawyer in Liechtenstein who came to his office this morning and discovered there'd been a break-in."

"Awful sorry to hear that."

"Yes. Particularly since one of his files is missing—the folder on an *Anstalt* he manages for some unnamed party or parties who reside in Vienna."

"Vienna." His stomach tightened.

"No names, unfortunately. A set of wire instructions, ID codes, and all that shit. But definitely Vienna-based. The owners were careful to keep their names secret, even from this guy. Who, by the way, probably isn't going to be calling the Liechtenstein cops about a missing file. Not with all the illegal shite he's into."

"Well done, Fergus. So what's the bad news?"

"You've run up quite a bill. The job in Liechtenstein alone cost me fifty grand. You think those guys come cheap? They're fucking *thieves*!" Even for Fergus, that was a significant charge. But given the information he'd turned up—which no law-enforcement agency could ever have gotten—it was worth it.

"I don't suppose you've got any receipts for me," Ben replied.

As soon as he disconnected the call, the phone rang. "Yes?"

"Anna Navarro, please!" a man's voice shouted. "I need to talk to her!"

"She's—who is this?"

"Just tell her it's Sergio."

"Ah, yes. Yes. Just a moment."

Anna was awake; the ringing had awakened her. "Machado?" she murmured, her voice raspy from sleep. Ben gave her the phone.

"Sergio," she said. "I'm sorry, I had the phone turned off, I think . . . All right, sure, that's . . . What? . . . *What?* . . . Sergio, hello? Are you *there?* Hello?"

She pressed the Off button. "How weird," she said.

"What is it?"

She stared at him, obviously mystified. "He said he'd been trying to reach me all night. He was calling from his car, in a part of town called San Telmo. He wants to meet at the Plaza Dorrego Bar, I think he said—he's got a gun for me."

"Why did he sound so frantic?"

"He said he didn't want any part of this investigation any longer."

"They got to him."

"He really sounded frightened, Ben. He said—he said he'd been contacted by people, threatened—that these weren't the usual locals who watch out for the fugitives." She looked up, shaken. "And the call ended in mid-sentence."

They could smell the fire even before they entered Plaza Dorrego. As their cab pulled up to the side of the Plaza Dorrego Bar, they saw a large crowd, ambulances and police cars and fire trucks.

The cabdriver spoke quickly.

"What's he saying?" Ben asked.

"He says he can't go any farther, there's been some kind of accident. Come on."

She asked the driver to wait for them, then she and Ben leaped out of the car and raced into the square. The smoke had mostly dissipated, but the air smelled of sulfur and carbon and combusted gasoline. Peddlers had temporarily abandoned their tables in the park at the center of the plaza, leaving their cheap jewelry and perfumes untended while they gathered to watch. Residents huddled in the doorways of the ancient tenements, to stare in fascinated horror.

It was immediately obvious what had happened. A car had been parked directly in front of the Plaza Dorrego Bar when it exploded, shattering the window of the bar, and blowing out windows across the street. Apparently it had burned for quite a while before the fire trucks were able to put it out. Even the white zebra stripes painted on the road near the wreck had been blackened.

A white-haired old woman in a brown print blouse was screaming, over and over, *"Madre de Dios! Madre de Dios!"*

Ben felt Anna grab his hand and squeeze it tight as they watched the emergency medical workers hacksawing at the burnt-out carcass of the once-white Ford Escort, trying without success to extricate the charred body.

He felt her shudder when one of the workers managed to wrench back a chunk of metal, revealing the black incinerated arm, the wrist encircled by the blackened gold chain, the scorched claw of a hand gripping the little cell phone.

CHAPTER THIRTY-EIGHT

They sat, stunned, in the back of the cab.

Not until they had gone several blocks did either one speak.

"Oh, my God, Ben. Dear God." Anna leaned back against the seat, eyes closed.

He put a hand on her shoulder, nothing more than a moment of comfort. There was nothing he could say to her, nothing that would mean anything.

"When Machado and I had dinner last night," she said, "he told me that in all his years of investigations, he was never afraid. That I shouldn't be afraid either."

Ben didn't know how to reply. He couldn't shake the horror of seeing Machado's incinerated body. The hand clutching the cell phone. *Some say the world will end in fire.* Shuddering, he flashed on Chardin's faceless countenance, the man's testimony that the horrors of surviving could be far greater than those of perishing. Sigma seemed to have a fondness for incendiary solutions. As gently as he could, he said, "Anna, maybe I should do this alone."

"*No*, Ben," she said sharply. Ben saw her steely resolve.

She was staring straight ahead, her face tense, her jaw clenched.

It was as if what they'd just witnessed had fueled her determination instead of deterring her. She was intent on visiting Strasser, no matter what, and getting to the bottom of the conspiracy that was Sigma. Maybe it was crazy— maybe they were *both* crazy—but he knew he wasn't going to turn back either. "Do you think either of us can just go back to our lives after what we've learned? Do you think we'd be *allowed* to?"

Another long silence elapsed.

"We'll make a circuit," she said. "Make sure no one's staking out the house, waiting for us. Maybe they assume that since they've eliminated Machado, there's no more threat." There seemed to be relief in her voice, but he couldn't be sure.

The cab barreled through the crowded streets of Buenos Aires toward the wealthy barrio of Belgrano. It occurred to Ben what a strange and terrible irony it was that a good man had just died so that they could try to save the life of an evil one. He wondered whether the same notion had occurred to her. *Now we're about to risk our lives to save the life of a world-historic villain,* he reflected.

And the true scope of his villainy? Was there any way of knowing?

The harrowing words returned to him.

Wheels within wheels—that was the way we worked. . . . It never crossed anyone's mind that the West had fallen under the administration of a hidden consortium. The notion would be inconceivable. Because if true, it would mean that over half of the planet was effectively a subsidiary of a single megacorporation—Sigma.

In recent years, one very special project of Sigma's had come to the fore. The prospect of its success would revolutionize the nature of world control. No longer would it be about the allocation of funds, the directing of resources. It became, instead, a simple matter of who the "chosen" would be.

*   *   *

Was Strasser himself one of the "chosen"? Or maybe he, too, was dead.

Ben said, "I talked to Fergus, in the Caymans. He's traced the wire transfers all the way back to Vienna."

"Vienna," she repeated without inflection.

She said nothing further. He wondered what she was thinking, but before he could ask, the cab pulled to a stop in front of a red-brick villa with white shutters. A white station wagon was parked in the small driveway.

Anna said something to the driver in Spanish, then turned to Ben. "I told him to circle the block. I want to look for parked cars, loiterers, anything suspicious."

Ben knew it was time, once again, to defer to her. He'd simply have to trust that she knew what she was doing. "What's our approach going to be?" he asked.

"All we have to do is get in the door. Warn him. Tell him his life's in danger. I've got my DOJ credentials, which should be enough to make us legitimate in his eyes."

"We've got to assume that he's been warned—by the *Kamaradenwerk* thugs, by Vera Lenz, by whatever other sort of early-warning systems he has in place. And then what if his life *isn't* in danger? What if he's the one *behind* the killings? Have you considered *that?*"

After a beat of silence, she conceded, "It's a real risk."

A real risk. That was a colossal understatement.

"You don't have a weapon," Ben reminded her.

"We only need his attention for a moment. Then if he chooses to listen further, he can."

And if he was the one behind the killings? But it was useless to argue.

When they had made a complete circuit, the cab stopped, and they got out.

Although it was a warm, sunny day, Ben felt a chill, no doubt from fear. He was sure Anna was frightened, too, but she didn't show it. He admired her strength.

Twenty-five feet before Strasser's house there was a security booth on the sidewalk. The guard was a stooped old man with wispy white hair and a drooping mustache, a blue cap perched almost comically atop his head. If ever there were a serious incident on the street, this guard would be useless, Ben thought. Still, it was best not to alert him, so the two of them continued their determined stride as if they belonged here.

They stopped before Strasser's house, which was surrounded, like most of the houses on this street, by a fence. This one was of dark-stained wood, not wrought iron, and it was no higher than Ben's chest. It was purely ornamental and seemed to send the message that the inhabitant of this house had nothing to hide. Anna unlatched the wooden gate, pulled it open, and they entered a small, well-kept garden. From behind they heard footsteps on the pavement.

Nervously, Ben turned. It was the security guard approaching, maybe twenty feet away. He wondered whether Anna had an alibi prepared; he didn't. The guard smiled. His dentures were ill-fitting and yellow. He said something in Spanish.

Anna muttered, "He wants to see our identification." To the old man she said, "*¡Cómo no, señor!*" Certainly.

The guard reached into his jacket, oddly, as if to offer identification of his own.

Ben noticed a slight movement across the street, and he turned to look.

There was a man standing across the street. A tall man who had a ruddy face, a thatch of black hair going gray, and thick wheat-field eyebrows.

Ben felt a jolt of recognition. The face was horribly familiar.

Where have I seen him before?

Paris—the rue des Vignoles.

Vienna. The Graben.

And somewhere before that.

One of the killers.

He was aiming a gun at them.

Ben shouted, "Anna, *get down!*" He flung himself onto the concrete garden path.

Anna dove to her left, out of the line of fire.

There was a spit, and the guard's chest erupted, a gusher of crimson, and he fell backward to the flagstone sidewalk. The ruddy-faced man raced toward them.

They were trapped inside Strasser's yard.

The assassin had shot the guard! Ben and Anna had ducked, and the poor guard had been caught in the line of fire.

Next time the killer would not miss.

Even if I could run, Ben thought, it would be *toward* the killer.

And both of them were unarmed!

He heard the man shout in English, "It's O.K.! It's O.K.! I'm not going to shoot!"

Ruddy-face had his gun at his side as he raced toward them.

"Hartman!" he yelled. "Benjamin Hartman!"

Ben looked up, startled.

Anna screamed, "I've got a gun! Back off!"

But the ruddy-faced man still did not raise his weapon. "It's O.K.! I'm not going to shoot!" The man flung his gun to the pavement in front of him, his hands outstretched. "He was about to kill you," the ruddy-faced man said as he ran up to the body of the old man. "Look!"

Those were the last words the ruddy-faced man spoke.

Like a mannequin twitching with incipient life, the ancient guard moved an arm, yanking a slim, silenced revolver from his trousers, and pointing it at the ruddy-faced man who stood over him. There was a *phut* and then a soft-nosed slug slammed into his forehead and blew out the back of his skull.

What the hell was going on?

The ancient guard now began to sit up, even as blood still dribbled from his shirtfront. He had been wounded, perhaps mortally, but his firing arm was absolutely steady.

An impassioned bellow came from behind them: *"No!"*

Ben turned to see another man, stationed by an oak tree, at a diagonal from them: their side of the street, but twenty yards to their left. This man was holding a large rifle with a sniper scope, a marksman's special.

The ruddy-faced killer's backup?

The barrel was directed in their general direction.

There was no time to escape its deadly aim.

Immediately, Ben heard the blast of the high-powered rifle, too paralyzed with fear even to flinch.

Two, then three bullets hit the ancient guard in the center of his chest and he slumped back to the ground.

Once again they had been spared. Why? With the scoped rifle, there was no way the sniper could have missed his intended target.

The man with the rifle—a man with glossy black hair and olive skin—raced over to the crumpled, bloodied body of the watchman, ignoring them.

It made no sense. Why were the gunmen so intent on killing the old guard? Who was their real target?

Ben stood up slowly, and saw the man reach inside the jacket of the old man's uniform, and pull out another weapon: a second slim automatic revolver, silencer screwed on to the barrel.

"Oh, dear God," Anna said.

The olive-skinned man grabbed a fistful of the guard's wispy white hair and tugged at it, and it came off in one floppy piece, like the pelt of a rabbit, revealing the steel-gray hair underneath.

He yanked at the white mustache, which came off just as easily, then grabbed at the loose skin of the old man's face, lifting off wrinkled, irregular patches of flesh-colored rubber.

"Latex prostheses," the man said. He pulled off the nose, then the wrinkled bags under the old man's eyes, and Ben recognized the smooth, unlined face of the man who had tried to kill him in front of Jürgen Lenz's house in Vienna. The man who tried to kill them all in Paris.

The man who killed his brother.

"The Architect," Anna gasped.

Ben froze.

Gaped, disbelieving, but it was true.

"He was going to kill you both when he got within point-blank range," the man said. Ben focused on his tawny skin, oddly long lashes, and square jaw. The man spoke with a vaguely Middle Eastern accent. "Which he would easily have done, since his appearance deceived you."

Ben recalled the odd gesture, the image of the frail old man reaching into his jacket, the almost apologetic expression.

"Wait a minute," Anna said. "You're 'Yossi.' From Vienna. The Israeli CIA guy. Or so you pretended."

"*Dammit*, tell me who you are!" Ben said.

"My name isn't important," he replied.

"Yeah, well it is to me. Who are you?"

"Yehuda Malkin."

The name meant nothing. "You've been following me," Ben said. "I saw your partner in Vienna and in Paris."

"Yeah, he screwed up and got spotted. He'd been following you for the entire last week. I was doing backup. You may as well know: your father hired us, Ben."

My father hired them. For what? "Hired you . . . ?"

"Max Hartman bought our parents' way out of Nazi Germany more than fifty years ago. And the man who was killed wasn't just my partner. He was my cousin." He closed his eyes for a moment. "*Goddammit* to hell. Avi wasn't meant to die. It wasn't his time. Goddammit to hell." He shook his head hard. His cousin's death evidently hadn't sunk in, and right now he wouldn't let it—it wasn't the moment. He looked hard at Ben, saw the confusion playing across his face. "Both of us owed your father everything. I guess he must've had some kind of in with the Nazis, because he did that for a bunch of other Jewish families in Germany too."

Max ransomed Jews—bought their way out of the camps? Then what Sonnenfeld said was true.

Anna broke in, "Who trained you? You're not American-trained."

The man turned to her. "I was born in Israel, on a kibbutz. My parents moved to Palestine after they escaped from Germany."

"You were in the Israeli army?"

"Paratrooper. We moved to America in '68, after the Six Day War. My parents were fed up with the fighting. After high school I joined the Israeli army."

"This whole CIA ruse in Vienna—what the hell was it about?" Anna demanded.

"For that, I brought in an American comrade of mine. Our orders were to spirit Ben away from danger. Get him back in the States, and under our direct protection. Keep him safe."

"But how did you . . ." Anna started.

"Look, we don't have time for this. If you're trying to interrogate Strasser, you'd better get in there before the cops show up."

"Right," Anna said.

"Wait," Ben interrupted. "You say my father hired you. *When?*"

The man looked around impatiently. "A week or so ago." He called Avi and me, told us you were in some kind of danger. Said you were in Switzerland. He gave us names and addresses, places he thought you might turn up. He wanted us to do what we could to protect you. He said he didn't want to lose another son." He looked around quickly. "You were almost killed on our watch in Vienna. Again in Paris. And you sure had some kind of close call here."

Ben's mind swirled with questions. "Where did my father go?"

"I don't know. He said Europe, but he didn't specify, and it's a big continent. He said he'd be out of contact with everyone for months. Left us a pile of money for travel expenses." He smiled grimly. "A whole lot more than we'd ever need, frankly."

Anna, meanwhile, was leaning over Vogler's body and had taken a weapon from a nylon shoulder holster. She unscrewed the silencer, put it in the jacket of her blazer and tucked the gun into the waistband of her skirt so it was hidden by the jacket. "But you didn't follow us *here*," she said, "did you?"

"No," he conceded. "Strasser's name was on the list Max Hartman gave me, along with his address and cover identity."

"He knows what's going on!" Ben said. "He knows who all the players are. He figured I'd eventually track Strasser down."

"But we were able to tail Vogler, who wasn't much concerned about being followed himself. So once we knew he was flying to Argentina, and we had Strasser's address . . ."

"You've been watching Strasser's house for the last couple of days," Anna said. "Waiting for Ben to show up."

He glanced around again. "You guys ought to move it."

"Right, but first tell me this," she went on. "Since you've been doing surveillance: did Strasser just recently return to Buenos Aires?"

"Apparently so. Back from some vacation, it looked like. He had a lot of luggage."

"Any visitors since his return?"

The man thought a moment. "Not that I saw, anyway. Just a nurse who got here maybe a half hour ago . . ."

"A nurse!" Anna exclaimed. She looked at the white station wagon that was parked in front of the house. The car was emblazoned with the words PERMANENCIA EN CASA. "Come *on*!" she shouted.

"Oh, man," Ben said, following her as she rushed to the front door and rang the bell repeatedly.

"Shit," she groaned. "We're too late." Yehuda Malkin stood back and to one side.

In less than a minute, the door slowly came open. Before them stood an ancient man, withered and stooped, his deeply tanned, leathery face a mass of wrinkles.

Josef Strasser.

"*¿Quién es éste?*" he said, scowling. "*Se está metiendo en mis cosas—ya llegó la enfermera que me tiene que revisar.*"

"He says his nurse is here for his checkup," Anna said. She raised her voice. "No! Herr Strasser—stay away from this nurse, I warn you!"

A white shape came into view behind the German. Ben said, "Anna! Behind him!"

The nurse approached the door, speaking quickly, chidingly it seemed, to Strasser. "*¡Vamos, Señor Albrecht, vamos para allá, que estoy apurada! ¡Tengo que ver al próximo paciente todavía!*"

"She's telling him to hurry up," Anna told Ben. "She's got another patient to see. Herr Strasser, this woman isn't a real nurse—I suggest you ask her for her credentials!"

The woman in the white uniform grasped the old man's shoulder and pulled him half toward her in one violent gesture. "*¡Ya mismo,*" she said, "*vamos!*"

With her free hand she grabbed the door to pull it closed, but Anna bent forward to block the door's arc with her knee.

Suddenly the nurse shoved Strasser aside. She reached into her uniform, and in one swift motion took out a gun.

But Anna moved even more quickly. "Freeze!"

The nurse fired.

At the same moment, Anna spun her body sideways, slamming Ben to the ground.

As Ben rolled to one side he heard a gunshot, followed by an animal-like roar.

He realized what had happened: the nurse had shot at Anna, but Anna had dodged out of the line of fire, and it was the Israeli protector who had been hit.

A red oval appeared in the middle of the man's forehead, and there was a spray of blood where the bullet exited his skull.

Anna got off two quick shots, and the fake nurse arched backward and then slumped to the floor.

And suddenly, for the briefest moment, everything was quiet. In the near-silence Ben could hear the distant singing of a bird.

Anna said, "Ben, you O.K.?"

He grunted yes.

"Oh, Jesus," she said, turning to see what had happened. Then she spun back around toward the doorway.

Strasser, crouched on the floor in his pale blue bathrobe, shielding his face with his hands, keened and keened.

"Strasser?" she repeated.

"*Gott im Himmel*," he moaned. "*Gott im Himmel. Sie haben mein Leben gerettet!*" Good God in heaven. You saved my life.

Images. Shapeless and unfocused, devoid of significance or definition, outlines blurring into plumes of gray, disintegrating into nothingness like a jet's exhaust tracks in a windy sky. At first, there was only awareness, without even any defined object of awareness. He was so cold. So very cold. Save for the spreading warmth on his chest.

And where there was warmth, he felt pain.

That was good. Pain was good.

Pain was the Architect's friend. Pain he could manage, could banish when he needed to. At the same time, it meant he was still alive.

Cold was not good. It meant that he had lost a great deal of blood. That his body had gone into shock to lessen the further loss of blood: his pulse would have slowed, his heart beating with lessened force, the vessels in his extremities constricting to minimize the flow of blood to non-vital parts of the body.

He had to do an inventory. He was on the ground, motionless. Could he hear? For a moment, nothing disturbed the profound silence within his head. Then, as if a connection had been established, he could hear voices, faintly, muffled, as if inside a building . . .

Inside a house.

Inside *whose* house?

He must have lost a great deal of blood. Now he forced himself to retrieve the memories of the past hour.

Argentina. Buenos Aires.

Strasser.

Strasser's house. Where he had expected Benjamin Hartman and Anna Navarro and where he had encountered . . . *others*. Including someone armed with a marksman's rifle.

He had taken several gunshots to the chest. Nobody could survive that. *No!* He banished the thought. It was an unproductive thought. A thought such as an amateur might have.

He had not been shot at all. He was fine. Weakened in ways he could compensate for, but not out of the running. They *thought* he was out of the running, and that would be his strength. The images wavered before his mind, but for a brief while he was able to fix them, the images, like passport photos, of his three targets. In order: Benjamin Hartman; Anna Navarro; Josef Strasser.

His mind was as thick and opaque as old crankshaft oil, but, yes, it would function. Yet again, it was a matter of mental concentration: he would *assign* the injuries to another body—a vividly conceived doppelgänger, someone who was bloodied and in shock but *who was not he*. He was fine. Once he had gathered his reserves, he would be able to move, to stalk. To kill. His sheer force of will had always triumphed over adversity, and it would again.

Had an observer been keeping a close watch on Hans Vogler's body, he might possibly have detected, amid this furious gathering of mental fortitude, the barest flicker of an eyelid, nothing more. Every physical movement would now be planned and measured out in advance, the way a man dying of thirst in a desert might ration swallows from a canteen. There would be no wasted movement.

The Architect lived to kill. It was his area of unexampled

expertise, his singular vocation. Now he would kill if only
to prove that he still lived.

"Who are you?" asked Strasser in a high-pitched, hoarse
voice.

Ben glanced from the nurse-impostor in her blood-
drenched white uniform, sprawled on the floor, to the assassin who had almost killed them both, to the mysterious
protectors his father had hired, both now lying murdered
on the red clay tiles of the patio.

"Herr Strasser," Anna said, "the police will be here any
moment. We have very little time."

Ben understood what she was saying: the Argentine police weren't to be trusted; they couldn't be here when the
police arrived.

They would have very little time to learn what they
needed from the old German.

Strasser's face was deeply creased and striated, etched
with countless crisscrossing lines. His liver-colored lips
stretched downward in a grimace, and they were wrinkled
too, like elongated prunes. Seated on either side of his crev-
iced, wide-nostriled nose were deep-sunk dark eyes like
raisins in a ball of dough. "I am not Strasser," he protested.
"You are confused."

"We know both your real name and your alias," Anna
said impatiently. "Now tell me: the nurse—was she your
regular one?"

"No. My usual nurse was sick this week. I have anemia
and I need my shots."

"Where have you been for the last month or two?"

Strasser shifted from one foot to another. "I have to sit
down," he wheezed. He moved slowly down the hallway.

They followed him down the hall, to a large, ornate,
book-lined room. It was a library, a two-story atrium with
walls and shelves of burnished mahogany.

"You live in hiding," Anna said. "Because you're a war
criminal."

"I am *no* war criminal!" Strasser hissed. "I'm as innocent as a baby."

Anna smiled. "If you aren't a war criminal," she replied,
"why are you hiding?"

He faltered, but only for a moment. "Here it has become
fashionable to expel former Nazis. And yes, I was a member of the National Socialist party. Argentina signs agree-
ments with Israel and Germany and America—they want
to change their image. Now they only care what America
thinks. They'd expel me just to make the American President smile. And you know, here in Buenos Aires, tracking
down Nazis is a business! For some journalists it's a full-
time job, how they make their living! But I was never a
Hitler loyalist. Hitler was a ruinous madman—that was
clear early in the war. He would be the destruction of all
of us. Men like me knew that other accommodations had
to be reached. My people sought to kill the man before he
could do further damage to our industrial capacities. And
our projections were correct. By the war's end, America
had three-quarters of the world's invested capital, and two-
thirds of the world's industrial capacity." He paused,
smiled. "The man was simply bad for business."

"If you'd turned against Hitler, why are you still protected by the *Kumaradenwerk?*" Ben asked.

"Illiterate thugs," Strasser scoffed. "They are as ignorant
of history as the avengers they seek to thwart."

"Why did you go out of town?" Anna interrupted.

"I was staying at an *estancia* in Patagonia owned by my
wife's family. My late wife's family. At the foot of the
Andes, in Río Negro province. A cattle and sheep ranch,
but very luxurious."

"Do you go there regularly?"

"This is the first time I go there. My wife died last year
and . . . Why do you ask these things?"

"That's why they couldn't find you to kill you," Anna
said.

"Kill me . . . But *who* is trying to kill me?"

Ben looked at Anna, urging her to continue speaking.

She replied, "The company."

"The company?"

"Sigma."

She was bluffing, Ben knew, but she did it with great conviction. Chardin's words came to his mind, unbidden. *The Western world, and much of the rest, would respond to its ministrations, and it would accept the cover stories that accompanied them.*

Now Strasser was brooding. "The new leadership. Yes, that is it. Ah, yes." His raisin eyes gleamed.

"What is the 'new leadership'?" Ben prompted.

"Yes, of course," Strasser went on as if he hadn't heard Ben. "They are afraid I know things."

"*Who?*" Ben shouted.

Strasser looked up at him, startled. "I helped them set it up. Alford Kittredge, Siebert, Aldridge, Holleran, Conover—all those crowned heads of corporate empires. They had contempt for me, but they needed me, didn't they? They needed my contacts high up in the German government. If the venture wasn't properly multinational, it had no hope of succeeding. I had the trust of the men at the very top. They knew I had done things for them that forever placed me beyond the pale of ordinary humanity. They knew I had made that ultimate sacrifice for them. I was a go-between trusted by all sides. And now that trust has been betrayed, exposed for the charade it always was. Now it has become clear that they were using me for their own ends."

"You talked about the new leaders—is Jürgen Lenz one of them?" Anna asked urgently. "Lenz's son?"

"I have never met this Jürgen Lenz. I didn't know Lenz had a son, but then I wasn't an intimate of his."

"But you were both scientists," Ben said. "In fact, you invented Zyklon-B, didn't you?"

"I was one of a *team* that invented Zyklon-B," he replied. He pulled at his shabby blue bathrobe, adjusted it at the neck. "Now all the apologists attack me for my role in this, but they do not consider how elegant was this gas."

"Elegant?" Ben repeated. For a second he thought he'd misheard. *Elegant*. The man was loathsome.

"Before Zyklon-B, the soldiers had to shoot every prisoner," Strasser said. "Terrible bloodbaths. Gas was so clean and simple and elegant. And you know, gassing the Jews actually spared them."

Ben echoed: "Spared them." Ben was sickened.

"Yes! There were so many deadly diseases that went around those camps, they would have suffered much longer, much more painfully. Gassing them was the most humanitarian option."

Humanitarian. I'm looking in the face of evil, Ben thought. *An old man in a bathrobe uttering pieties*.

"How nice," Ben said.

"This is why we called it 'special treatment.' "

"Your euphemism for extermination."

"If you wish." He shrugged. "But you know, I didn't hand-pick victims for the gas chambers like Dr. Mengele or Dr. Lenz. They call Mengele the Angel of Death, but Lenz was the real one. The real Angel of Death."

"But not you," Ben said. "You were a scientist."

Strasser sensed the sarcasm. "What do you know of science?" he spat. "Are you a scientist? Do you have any idea how far ahead of the rest of the world we Nazi scientists were? Do you have any *idea?*" He spoke in a high tremulous voice. Spittle formed at the corners of his mouth. "They criticize Mengele's twin studies, yet his findings are still cited by the world's leading geneticists! The Dachau experiments in freezing human beings—those data are still used! What they learned at Ravensbrück about what happens to the female menstrual cycle under stress—when the women learned they were about to be executed—scientifically this was a breakthrough! Or Dr. Lenz's experiments on aging. The famine experiments on Soviet prisoners of war, the limb transplants—I could go on and on. Maybe it's not polite to talk about it, but you still use our science. You'd rather not think about how the experiments were done, but don't you realize that one of the main reasons

we were so advanced was precisely *because* we were able
to experiment on live human beings?"

Strasser's creased face had gotten even paler as he
spoke, and now it was chalk-white. He had grown short of
breath. "You Americans are disgusted by how we did our
research, but you use fetal tissue from abortions for your
transplants, yes? This is acceptable?"

Anna was pacing back and forth. "Ben, don't debate
with this monster."

But Strasser would not stop. "Of course, there were
many crackpot ideas. Trying to make girls into boys and
boys into girls." He chortled. "Or trying to create Siamese
twins by connecting the vital organs of the twins, a total
failure, we lost many twins that way—"

"And after Sigma was established, did you continue to
keep in touch with Lenz?" Anna asked, cutting him off.

Strasser turned, seemingly perturbed at the interruption.
"Certainly. Lenz relied on me for my expertise and my
contacts."

"Meaning what?" Ben said.

The old man shrugged. "He said he was doing work,
doing research—*molecular* research—that would change
the world."

"Did he tell you what it was, this research?"

"No, not me. Lenz was a private, secretive man. But I
remember he said once, 'You simply cannot fathom what
I'm working on.' He asked me to procure sophisticated
electron microscopes, very hard to get in those days. They
had just been invented. Also, he wanted various chemicals.
Many things that were embargoed because of the war. He
wanted everything crated and sent to a private clinic he had
set up in an old *Schloss*, a castle, he had seized during the
invasion of Austria."

"Where in Austria?" Anna asked.

"The Austrian Alps."

"Where in the Alps? What town or village, do you remember?" Anna persisted.

"How can I possibly remember this, after all these years?

Maybe he never told me. I only remember Lenz called it 'the Clockworks'—because it had once been some kind of clock factory."

A scientific project of Lenz's. "A laboratory, then? Why?"

Strasser's lips pulled down. He sighed reproachfully. "To continue the research."

"What research?" he said.

Strasser fell silent, as if lost in thought.

"Come *on!*" Anna said. "*What* research?"

"I don't know. There was much important research that began during the Reich. Gerhard Lenz's work."

Gerhard Lenz: what was it Sonnenfeld had said about Lenz's horrific experiments in the camps? Human experimentation . . . but what?

"And you don't know the nature of this work?"

"Not today. Science and politics—it was all the same to these people. Sigma was, from the beginning, a means of funneling support to certain political organizations, subverting others. The men we're talking about—these were already men of enormous influence in the world. Sigma showed them that if they pooled their influence, the whole could be far, far greater than the sum of its parts. Collectively, there was very little they couldn't affect, direct, orchestrate. But, you know, Sigma was a living thing. And like living things, it evolved."

"Yes," Anna said. "With funds provided by the largest corporations in the world, along with funds stolen from the state *Reichsbank*. We know who the founding board members were. You're the last living member of that original board. But who are your successors?"

Strasser looked down the hall, but he seemed to be staring at nothing.

"Who controls it *now*? Give us *names!*" Ben shouted.

"I don't *know!*" Strasser's voice cracked. "They kept people like me quiet by sending us money regularly. We were lackeys, finally excluded from the inner councils of power. We should all be billionaires many, many times

over. They send us millions, but it is crumbs, table scraps."
Strasser's lips curled up in a repellent smile. "They give
me table scraps, and now they wish to cut me off. They
want to kill me because they don't want to pay me anymore. They're greedy, and they're ashamed. After all I did
for them, they regard me as an embarrassment. And a danger, because even though the doors have been shut to me
for years, they still think I know too much. For making
possible everything they do, how am I repaid? With *contempt!*" A growing sense of rage—the pent-up grievance of
years—made his words hard, metallic. "They act as if I am
a poor relation, a black sheep, a foul-smelling derelict. The
swells gather in their fancy-dress forum, and their biggest
fear is that I will crash their party, like a skunk at a kaf-
feeklatsch. I know where they gather. I am not such a fool,
such an ignoramus. I would not join them in Austria had
they *asked* me to."

Austria.

"What are you talking about?" Ben demanded. "Where
are they gathering? Tell me."

Strasser gave him a look that combined wariness and
defiance. It was clear that he would say no more.

"Goddammit, answer me!"

"You are all the same," Strasser spat. "You would think
somebody my age would be treated with respect! I have
nothing more to say to you."

Anna was suddenly alert. "I hear sirens. This is it, Ben.
We're out of here."

Ben stood directly in front of Strasser. "Herr Strasser,
do you know who I am?"

"Who you are . . . ?" Strasser stammered.

"My father is Max Hartman. I'm sure you remember the
name."

Strasser squinted. "Max Hartman . . . the Jew, our treasurer . . . ?"

"That's right. And he was an SS officer as well, I'm
told." *But Sonnenfeld had said that would merely have been*

a cover, a ruse. His heart was pounding, he dreaded hearing Strasser's confirmation of Max's ugly past.

Strasser laughed, flashing his ruined brown teeth. "SS!" he laughed. "He was no SS. We gave him fake SS papers so ODESSA would smuggle him out of Germany into Switzerland, with no questions asked. That was the deal."

Blood roared in Ben's ears. He felt a wave of relief, a physical sensation.

"Bormann chose him personally for the German delegation," Strasser went on. "Not just because he was skilled at moving money around, but because we needed a . . . a false head—"

"A figurehead."

"Yes. The industrialists from America and elsewhere were not so comfortable with what the Nazis had done. A Jewish participant was necessary to provide legitimacy—to show that we weren't the wrong kind of Germans, to show that we were not zealots, not Hitler disciples. For his part, your father got for himself a good deal—he got his family out of the camps, and a lot of other Jewish families as well, and he was given forty million Swiss francs—almost a million dollars U.S. A lot of money." A horrible smile. "Now he calls himself 'rags to riches story.' Is a million dollars rags? I don't think."

"Ben!" Anna shouted. Quickly she flashed the leather wallet that held her Department of Justice credentials. "Now you want to know who *I* am, Herr Strasser? I'm here on behalf of the U.S. Justice Department's Office of Special Investigations. I'm sure you know who they are."

"Oh ho," Strasser said. "Well, I'm sorry to disappoint you, but I'm an Argentine citizen and I don't recognize your authority."

The sirens were louder, just a few blocks away it seemed.

Anna turned back to him. "So I guess we'll see how serious the Argentine government is about extraditing war criminals. Out the back way, Ben."

Strasser's face flashed with rage. "Hartman," he said hoarsely.

"Come *on*, Ben!"

Strasser crooked a finger at Ben, beckoning him. Ben could not resist. The old man began to whisper. Ben knelt down to listen.

"Hartman, do you know your father was a weak little man?" Strasser said. "A man without a spine. A coward and a fraud who pretends to be a victim." Strasser's lips were inches from Ben's ear. His voice was singsong. "And you are the fraud's son, that's all. That is all you are to me."

Ben closed his eyes, fought to control his anger.

The fraud's son.

Was this true? Was Strasser right?

Strasser was clearly enjoying Ben's discomfort.

"Oh, you'd like to kill me right now, isn't that right, Hartman?" Strasser said. "Yet you don't. Because you're a coward, like your father."

Ben saw Anna starting down the hall.

"No," he said. "Because I'd much rather you spend your remaining life in a stinking jail cell in Jerusalem. I'd like your last days to be as unpleasant as possible. Killing you is a waste of a bullet."

He ran down the corridor, following Anna to the back of the house, as the sirens grew louder.

Crawl, don't walk. The Architect knew that the effort to maintain orthostatic blood pressure in his head would be made much more difficult by standing erect, when there was as yet no absolute need to do so. It was a rational decision, and his ability to make it was almost as reassuring as the Glock he had retained in an ankle holster.

The front door was open, the hallway deserted. He crawled, in a standard infantry crawl, indifferent to the wide smear of blood he was leaving as his shirtfront draped against the blond flooring. Every yard seemed like a mile to him. But he would not be deterred.

You're the best. He was seventeen, and the drill instructor told him so, in front of the entire battalion. *You're the best.* He was twenty-three, and his commanding officer at Stasi had said so in an official report that he showed young Hans before forwarding it to his superior. *You're the best.* These words from the head of his Stasi directorate: he had just returned from a "hunting trip" in West Berlin, having dispatched four physicists—members of an internationally distinguished team from the University of Leipzig—who had defected the day before. *You're the best*: a top-level Sigma official, a white-haired American in flesh-toned glasses, had spoken those words to him. It was after he had stage-managed the death of a prominent Italian leftist, shooting him from across the street while the man was in the throes of passion with a fifteen-year-old Somali whore. But he would hear those words again. And again. Because they were true.

And because they were true, he would not give up. He would not succumb to the nearly overpowering urge to surrender, to sleep, to stop.

With robotic precision, he moved hand and knee and propelled himself down the hallway.

Finally, he found himself in a spacious, double-height room, its walls lined with books. Lizardlike eyes surveyed the area. His primary target was not present. A disappointment, not a surprise.

Instead, there was the wheezing, sweating weakling Strasser, a traitor who, too, was deserving of death.

How many more minutes of consciousness did the Architect have left? He eyed Strasser avidly, as if extinguishing his light might help to restore his own.

Shakily, he rose from the floor into a marksman's crouch. He felt muscles in his body trying to spasm, but he held his arms completely still. The small Glock in his arms had now acquired the weight of a cannon, yet somehow he

managed to raise the firearm until it was at the precisely
correct angle.

It was at that moment that Strasser, perhaps alerted by
the old-penny odor of blood, finally became aware of his
presence.

The Architect watched the raisin-like eyes widen momentarily, then fall closed. Squeezing the trigger was like
lifting a desk with one finger, but he would do so. *Did so.
Or did he?*

When he failed to hear the gun's report, he first worried
that he had not executed his mission. Then he realized that
it was his sensory awareness that was beginning to shut
down.

The room was swiftly darkening: he knew that brain
cells starved of oxygen ceased to function—that the aural
and optical functions shut down first, but that sentience itself would soon follow.

He waited until he saw Strasser hit the ground before he
allowed his own eyes to close. As they did so, there was a
fleeting awareness that his eyes would never open again;
and then there was no awareness of anything at all.

Back in the hotel room, Ben and Anna rifled through a
stack of papers that they'd hurriedly purchased at a newsstand on the way. Chardin had referred to an imminent
development. And the "fancy-dress forum" in Austria that
Strasser had mentioned chimed with an item they'd recently
come across: but what was it?

The answer was within their grasp.

It was Anna who came across the item in *El País*, Argentina's leading newspaper. It was another brief article
about the International Children's Health Forum—a con-
vocation of world leaders to discuss matters of pressing
mutual concern, especially with respect to the developing
world. But what caught her eye this time was the city where
the meeting was to be held: Vienna, Austria.

She read on. There was a list of sponsors—among them,

the Lenz Foundation. Translating from the Spanish, she read the article out loud to Ben.

A shiver ran down his spine. "My God," he said. "This is it! It has to be. Chardin said only *days* remained. What he was talking about has to be related to this conference. Read me the list of sponsors again."

Anna did so.

And Ben started to make a few phone calls. These were calls to foundation professionals, people who were delighted to hear from one of their contributors. Slipping into a familiar role, Ben sounded hale and hearty when he spoke to them, but what he learned was profoundly dismaying.

"They're great people, the folks from the Lenz Foundation," Geoffrey Baskin, programs director for the Robinson Foundation, told him in his dulcet New Orleans accent. "It's really their baby, but they just wanted to keep a low profile. They put it together, footed most of the bill—it's hardly fair that we're getting any of the glory. But I guess they wanted to make sure it had an international feeling. Like I say, they're really selfless."

"That's nice to hear," Ben said. His kept his tone upbeat even as he felt a rising sense of dread. "We may be partnering with them on a special project, so I just wanted to get your sense of them. Really nice to hear."

Dignitaries and leaders from around the world would be gathering in Vienna, under the auspices of the Lenz Foundation . . .

They had to get to Vienna.

It was the one place in the world they shouldn't be showing their faces, and the one place where they had no choice but to go.

Anna and he paced the hotel room. They could take precautions—precautions that now came as second nature: disguise, falsified identities, separate flights.

But the risks seemed much greater now.

"If we're not just chasing a will-o'-the-wisp, we've got to assume that every commercial flight into Vienna is going

to be scrutinized very carefully," Anna said. "They're going
to be on full alert."

Ben felt the flicker of an idea. "What did you say
again?"

"They're going to be on full alert. Border control isn't
going to be a cakewalk. More like a gauntlet."

"Before that."

"I said we've got to assume that every commercial flight
into Vienna . . ."

"That's *it*," Ben said.

"What's it?"

"Anna, I'm going to take a risk here. And the calculation
is that it's a smaller risk than we'd otherwise be facing."

"I'm listening."

"I'm going to call a guy named Fred McCallan. He was
the codger I was supposed to go skiing with in St. Moritz."

"You were going to St. Moritz to go skiing with a
'codger.' "

Ben blushed. "Well, there was a granddaughter in the
picture."

"Go on."

"More to the point, though, there's a private *jet* in the
picture. A Gulfstream. I've been in it once. Very red. Red
seats, red carpeting, red TV set. Fred will still be at the
Hotel Carlton there, and the plane will probably be at the
little airport in Chur."

"So you're going to call him up and ask for the keys.
Kind of like borrowing someone's station wagon to pick
up groceries, right?"

"Well . . ."

Anna shook her head. "It's true what they say—the rich
really are different from you and me." She shot him a look.
"I mean, of course, just me."

"Anna . . ."

"I'm scared as shit, Ben. Bad jokes come with the territory. Listen, I don't know this guy from Adam. If you
think you can trust him—if that's what your gut is telling
you—then I can live with it."

"Because you're right, it's the *commercial* flights they'll be watching . . ."

Anna nodded vigorously. "So long as they're not coming from places like Colombia, private flights get pretty much a free pass. If this guy's pilot can move the Gulfstream to Brussels, let's say . . ."

"We go directly to Brussels, assuming nobody's onto the IDs Oscar made for us. Then transfer to Fred's private jet and fly to Vienna that way. That's the way the Sigma principals travel. Chances are, they're not going to be expecting a Gulfstream with two fugitives on board."

"O.K., Ben," Anna said. "I call this the beginning of a plan."

Ben dialed the number of the Hotel Carlton and waited a minute for the front desk to connect him.

Fred McCallan's voice boomed even through the international phone lines. "My God, Benjamin, do you have any idea of the hour? Never mind, I suppose you're calling to apologize. Though I'm not the one you should apologize to. Louise has been devastasted. *Devastated*. And you two have *so* much in common."

"I understand, Fred, and I . . ."

"But actually I'm glad you finally called. Do you realize they're saying the most *preposterous* things about you? A guy called me up and gave me an earful. They're saying that . . ."

"You've got to believe me, Fred," Ben said urgently, cutting him off, "there's no truth to those reports whatever—I mean, whatever they're accusing me of, you've got to believe me when I say that . . ."

"And I *laughed* in his face!" Fred was saying, having talked over Ben's interjection. "I told him, maybe that's what you get from your creepy English boarding schools, but I'm a Deerfield man myself, and there's no way on God's green earth that . . ."

"I appreciate the vote of confidence, Fred. The thing is . . ."

"Top-seeded in tennis, I told him. You were, weren't you?"

"Well, actually . . ."

"Track and field? I was a track and field man myself—did I ever show you my trophies? Louise thinks it's ridiculous that I'm still boasting about them fifty years later, and she's right. But I'm *incorrigible*."

"Fred, I've got a really, really, really big favor to ask."

"For you, Benny? You're practically family, you know that. One day you might actually *be* family. Just say the word, my boy. Just say the word."

As Anna said, it was the beginning of a plan, no more. But foolproof would take more time than they had. Because the one thing that was certain was that they had to make their way to Vienna as fast as possible, or it would be too late.

Unless it was, as Chardin had suggested, already too late.

CHAPTER THIRTY-NINE

The hotel was in Vienna's seventh district, and they had selected it because it appeared to be suitably anonymous, catering mostly to German and Austrian tourists. Traveling to Brussels in uniform as David Paine, Ben arrived first, by several hours; Anna, using the Gayatri Chandragupta alias for one last time, had traveled on a separate flight, connecting through Amsterdam. McCallan's pilot, a genial Irishman named Harry Hogan, was perplexed by the odd garb of his guests, and further perplexed that they'd refused to tell him in advance where they planned on going, but the old man had been vehement in his instructions: whatever Ben wanted, Ben would get. No questions asked.

Compared to the luxury of the Gulfstream, and the open-faced companionability of Harry Hogan, the hotel seemed drab and depressing. All the more so because Anna hadn't arrived yet: they agreed that traveling together from the airport was a risk best avoided. They'd travel separately, and by different routes.

Alone in the room, Ben felt caged and anxious. It was noontime but the weather was foul; rain spattered against the room's small windows, deepening his sense of gloom.

He thought about Chardin's life, about the incredible ways in which the governance of the Western world had been molded and directed by these corporate managers. And he thought about his father. A victim? A victimizer? Both?

Max had hired people to watch out for him—minders, *baby-sitters*, for God's sake. In a way, that was typical of the man: if Ben wouldn't let old secrets stay buried, then Max would try to control him his own way. It was both infuriating and touching.

When Anna arrived—they were sharing the room as Mr. and Mrs. David Paine—he embraced her, placing his face next to hers and feeling some of his sense of anxiety ebb.

Feeling grimy from the long flight, they each showered. Anna took a long time, emerging from the bathroom in a terry-cloth robe, her dark brown hair combed straight back, her skin glowing.

As she went to her suitcase to pick out clothes, Ben said, "I don't want you to see Lenz alone."

She didn't look up. "Oh, is that right?"

"Anna," he said, exasperated, "we don't even know who Jürgen Lenz really *is*."

Holding a blouse in one hand and a navy skirt in the other, she turned to face him. Her eyes flashed. "At this point, it doesn't matter. I *have* to talk to him."

"Look, whoever he is, we can assume that he was at least involved in the murder of eight old men around the world. My brother, too. And it's a plausible assumption that he's become a principal in a conspiracy that, if Chardin is right, has no real outer bounds. Lenz knows my face, and now he no doubt knows where I've been. So it's a fair assumption that he knows I've been traveling with you, which means he may well have seen a photograph of you. It isn't *safe* for you to go see this man."

"I'm not disputing that, Ben. We don't have the luxury of choosing between the safe thing and the dangerous thing: whatever we do at this point will involve danger. Even doing nothing. Besides, if I'm killed shortly after asking him questions about a series of murders around the world, he'd immediately be the focus of suspicion—and I seriously doubt he wants that."

"What even makes you think he'll see you?"

She set the clothes down on the edge of the bed.

"The best way to play him is not to play him."

"I don't like the sound of this."

"This is a man who's used to being in control, used to manipulating people and events. Call it arrogance or call it curiosity, but he'll *want* to see me."

"Listen to me, Anna . . ."

"Ben, I can take care of myself. I really can."

"Obviously," he protested. "It's just that—" He stopped. She was looking at him strangely. "What?"

"You're the protective type, aren't you?"

"I don't know about protective, exactly. I'm just—"

She approached him, examining him as if he were an exhibit in a museum. "When we met, I just assumed you were another rich, spoiled, self-centered preppy."

"You were probably right."

"No, I don't think so. So was that your role in the family—the caretaker?"

Embarrassed, Ben didn't know how to reply. Maybe she was right, but for some reason he didn't want to say it. Instead, he drew her close. "I don't want to lose you, Anna," he said quietly. "I've lost too many people in my life."

She closed her eyes and hugged him tight; both of them were agitated, nervous, exhausted, and yet as they embraced a moment of calm passed between them. He inhaled her delicate floral scent, and something in him melted.

Then, gently, she withdrew. "We have a plan, and we've got to follow it, Ben," she said, her voice soft but resolute and she dressed quickly. "I have to make a pickup at the DHL office, and then make a business call."

"Anna," Ben said.

"I've got to go. We can talk later."

*   *   *

"*Oh, sweet Jesus*," said Officer Burt Connelly. He had been on the I66 Virginia highway patrol for only six months, and he still wasn't accustomed to the sight of roadside carnage. He felt his stomach heaving, scurried to the side of the road, and vomited. A splash got on his crisp blue uniform, and he wiped it off with a tissue. Then he tossed the tissue out, too.

Even in the low light of the early evening, he could see only too clearly the blood spattered across the windscreen and the man's head on the dashboard. It had been severed from the body and horribly flattened by the impact—the "second collision," as they called it, which was the collision of the passenger inside the crashed vehicle itself.

Connelly's partner, Officer Lamar Graydon, had been on highway patrol for more than a year. He'd seen a few gruesome accidents before, and he knew how to keep his lunch down.

"It's a bad one, Burt," Graydon said, walking over and patting his partner's back. A sort of weary bravado played in his brown eyes. "But I've come across worse."

"Did you see the guy's head!"

"At least there's no little kids involved. Let me tell you, last year, I was at an accident scene where a baby got ejected through the open window of an Impala, thrown thirty feet in the air. Like a goddamn rag doll. Now, *that* was horrible."

Connelly coughed a few times, and straightened up. "Sorry," he said. "It's just that guy's face . . . I'm O.K. now. Ambulance on the way?"

"Should be here in ten minutes. Not that *he's* feeling any pain." Graydon nodded toward the decapitated accident victim.

"So what's the situation here? SVF?" Statistically, a single-vehicle fatality was the most common sort.

"Not a chance," Graydon said. "No guardrail does that. This is what happens when you slam into one of those

Kenworth car haulers, and there are plenty of 'em on this highway. With monsters like that, the back hangs low, and it's one flat steel edge—like a blade. If you're behind one of those things and it stops short, either you duck or it takes your head off. I'll betcha that's what you're looking at."

"Then what happened to the other guy? Where's the goddamn truck?" Connelly was starting to regain a sense of self-possession. Oddly, he even felt a little hungry again.

"Looks like he decided not to stick around," Graydon said.

"Well, are we going to find it?"

"I've radioed it in. Dispatcher's got the info. Between you and me, though, I wouldn't bet money on it. Thing to do right now is try to ID the guy. Search the pockets."

Though the top of the red Taurus was smashed in, the door on the driver's side opened easily. Connelly put on latex gloves before rummaging through the headless man's pockets; that was procedure when clothing was blood-soaked.

"Give me a name, and I'll radio that in, too," Graydon called out.

"Driver's license says Dupree, Arliss Dupree," Connelly said. "Lives on Glebe Road, in Arlington."

"That's all we need to know," Graydon said. "And you don't have to freeze your ass off, Burt. We can wait in the patrol car now."

The building that housed the Lenz Foundation was, Bauhaus style, all glass and marble. The lobby was flooded with light, furnished simply with white leather chairs and sofas.

Anna asked the receptionist to call the office of the director. That he was at the foundation she'd already verified with an earlier phone call.

"Who shall I say wishes to see Dr. Lenz?" she inquired.

"My name is Anna Navarro. I'm an agent with the U.S. Department of Justice."

She'd earlier considered and rejected the idea of approaching him under some false alias. But as she'd told Ben, she'd decided that the best way to play him was not to play him. If Lenz did even a cursory background check, he'd learn of her outlaw status. But would that make him less likely to see him, or more? If their theories about Alan Bartlett were correct, Jürgen Lenz might already know a fair amount about her. But he wouldn't know—couldn't know—precisely what she had learned, and might have conveyed to others. She had to rely upon his curiosity, his arrogance, and, most of all, his desire to control the situation. He would want to know whether she posed a threat to him, and he would want to assess that himself.

The receptionist picked up her desk phone and spoke quietly, then handed Anna the handset. "Please."

The woman on the phone was courteous but firm. "I'm afraid Dr. Lenz has a full schedule today. Perhaps you'd like to make an appointment for another day? I'm afraid that with the International Children's Health Forum, all the people here have their hands full."

He had to be evading her, but was that because he'd heard her institutional affiliation, or because he already knew her name? Maybe the woman hadn't even bothered to convey the message.

"It really can't wait," Anna said. "I need to see him as soon as possible on an extremely urgent matter."

"Can you tell me what you wish to speak with Dr. Lenz about?"

She hesitated. "Please tell him it's a personal matter."

She put the phone down and paced nervously around the lobby.

Here I am in the lair of the beast, she thought. *The heart of darkness, airy and full of light.*

The white Carrara marble walls were bare except for a line of large blowups of photographs depicting the wide range of humanitarian causes supported by the Lenz Foundation.

There was a picture of several generations of a refugee

family—a toothless, hunched old woman, a weathered and beaten-down husband and wife, their ragged children. This was entitled simply KOSOVO.

Meaning what? What did the Lenz Foundation have to do with refugees?

There was a portrait of a peculiarly wizened girl with a beaked nose, parchment skin, prominent eyes, long hair that was obviously a wig. She was smiling with crowded, irregular teeth, at once a young girl and an old woman. This photograph was labeled HUTCHINSON-GILFORD PROGERIA SYNDROME.

There was the famous stark and shocking photograph of emaciated concentration-camp inmates looking curiously at the camera from their bunk beds. THE HOLOCAUST.

A strange array of causes. What connected them?

Anna sensed a presence and looked up. A matronly woman had appeared in the lobby, a pair of reading glasses hanging from a chain around her neck. "Ms. Navarro," she said. "You're quite fortunate. Dr. Lenz has managed to free up a few minutes to see you."

At a security station on the floor above, a technician hunched over a control panel. Manipulating a joystick, he swiveled and zoomed in one of the wall-mounted cameras. The visitor's light brown face now filled the flat screen plasma display. The press of a button froze the image. By means of a thirty-seven point physiognomic metric, the face could be digitally compared with a set of image files in the system's extensive database. Somehow the technician suspected that it would not take long to come up with a match.

He was right. A quiet electronic chirp alerted him that the image matched a file from the watch list. As a column of information scrolled down the monitor, he picked up the phone and called Lenz, dialing a number that rang directly on his desk.

*   *   *

Jürgen Lenz was just as Ben had described him: whippet-thin, silver-haired, elegant, and charming. He wore a perfectly cut suit of dark gray flannel, a neatly pressed white shirt, a foulard tie. He sat in a Chippendale-style chair facing her, his hands folded in his lap.

"Well, you've got me," he said as he handed her her credentials back to her.

"Excuse me?"

"You've piqued my curiosity. I'm told a woman is here to see me from the American government in connection with a 'personal matter'—how could I possibly resist such a lure?"

She wondered how much he knew about her. She could see already that he was as smooth and hard as polished stone.

"Thank you for seeing me," Anna returned courtesy with courtesy. "I've been on special assignment, investigating a series of murders around the world—"

"*Murders?*" he said. "What in heaven's name can I tell you about murders?"

She knew she had one chance, and she'd have to hit him hard. Any weakness, any hesitation, any uncertainty, and the game was over. She would stick to one issue of narrow concern: the Sigma homicides.

"The murder victims were all involved in a corporation known as Sigma, of which Gerhard Lenz was a founder. We've established a direct connection between the deaths and a subsidiary of the chemical giant Armakon, on whose board you sit . . ."

Lenz seemed to relax. He laughed deeply, mellifluously. "Ms. Navarro, in all my years of crusading against the evil that my father did, I've been accused of many terrible things—disloyalty to family, disloyalty to my country, opportunism, insincerity, you name it—but no one has *ever* accused me of murder!"

Anna had known what to expect. He would be poised, nonconfrontational, evasive. So she had tried to anticipate his every response, and she was ready with a reply. "Dr.

Lenz," she said, "I hope you're not denying that you're on the board of Armakon."

"It's purely honorary."

She hesitated, then said, "I don't want to waste your time. As you know, Armakon is the secret owner of a biotech start-up in Philadelphia called Vortex."

She watched his face. His eyes were neutral, guarded. "I'm sure Armakon owns many inconsequential start-ups around the world. So?"

"Vortex," she went on, "is the inventor and manufacturer of a synthetic substance that's used in basic research, for molecular tagging. It's also a deadly poison that, once injected into a person's bloodstream, induces immediate death by heart failure, and is then undetectable in the blood."

He replied in a flat voice, "How interesting."

"That particular toxin was found in the ocular fluid of several of these murder victims."

"Do you have a point?"

"I do," she said quietly, eyes locked on his. She was momentarily startled by what she saw there: absolute searing contempt. "I have evidence linking you directly to those murders."

For a moment there was only the ticking of a clock. Somberly, Lenz clasped his hands. He looked like a Lutheran minister. "Agent Navarro, all these terrible charges you hurl at me. These terrible things you say I've done. I took time out of an extremely busy day—time I can scarcely afford to squander—because I thought we could help each other in some way. Perhaps a friend of mine was in trouble. Perhaps someone needed my help, or vice versa. Instead, you come here on what I believe is called a 'fishing expedition.'" He rose from his chair. "I'm afraid you'll have to leave."

Heart hammering, she thought: *Not so fast, you bastard.* "I'm not done yet," she said with a firmness that she could see surprised him.

"Agent Navarro, I really don't have to talk to you. Correct me if I'm wrong, but anyone who visits me as an agent of American law enforcement is here as a guest of my country. If you wish to interrogate me because of who my father was, you must ask permission of the Austrian government, yes? Have you done that?"

"No," she admitted, flushing. "But let me be clear—"

"*No*, madame," he said, raising his voice. "Let *me* be clear. You haven't done that because you are no longer in the employ of your country. In fact, you are yourself a fugitive from justice. Let us *both* put our cards on the table. Your investigations have taken you outside the boundaries of lawful conduct. My secretary conveys the insistent requests of an American agent to see me. At my behest, she makes a few phone calls to verify your identity." His eyes didn't leave her face. "She discovers that you are a wanted woman. But then you must have expected we would take such precautions. And yet you came to see me all the same. Which piqued my curiosity further."

"Anything to alleviate the dull tedium of your days," Anna said.

"Put yourself in my position, Ms. Navarro. A rogue U.S. agent takes a very peculiar interest in me—this isn't something that happens every day. Naturally I wonder: Have you come across someone or something that is a threat to me? Have you broken ranks and come to tell me about some hostile intrigue within American intelligence? I know our investigations of Operation Paper Clip have earned me enemies in some American circles. Have you come to warn me of some imminent menace? The imagination whirls. The mind boggles. So how could I resist meeting with you? You knew I could not."

"We're getting off the subject," Anna broke in. "None of this—"

Lenz talked over her. "So you'll appreciate how sorely disappointed I was when I learned that you're here only to hurl absurd, unfounded, and easily discredited accusations. From all indications, you're not only off the reservation, as your countrymen like to say—you're out of your mind."

He pointed to his desk. "I need only pick up this phone and call a friend of mine in the Justice Ministry and you would be remanded to the tender mercies of the U.S. authorities."

You want a fight, she thought, *you got it*. He was not going to intimidate her. Not with what she knew about him.

"You're perfectly right," she said calmly. "You could pick up that phone and do that. But I wonder whether it would best serve your interests."

Lenz had turned his back on her and was heading toward the exit. "Miss Navarro, your silly games really don't interest me. Now would you please leave my office this moment, or shall I be forced to—"

"Just before I came here I stopped at the local DHL office, where a document was waiting for me. It contained the results of a search I requested. I had submitted a set of your fingerprints and asked the lab to identify them. It took a long time. Our Latent Fingerprints Section had to dig deep to find a match. But they did." She took a breath. "Dr. Lenz, I know who you are. I don't understand it. I really can't fathom it, to be quite honest. But I know who you really are."

She was terrified, more frightened than she'd ever been before. Her heart was hammering; blood rushed in her ears. She knew she had no backup.

Lenz stopped short, a few feet from the exit, and closed the door. When he turned around, his face had gone dark with rage.

CHAPTER FORTY

Ben joined the modest crowd of journalists and cameramen assembled outside the Wiener Stadthalle Civic Center, the large, beige stone structure where the International Children's Health Forum was to be hosted. He made eye contact with a cold and miserable-looking man—paunchy, middle-aged, dressed in a fraying tan trench coat. Ben extended a hand. "I'm Ron Adams," he said. "With *American Philanthropy* magazine. Been standing out here long?"

"Too damn long," the rumpled man said. He spoke with a cockney accent. "Jim Bowen, *Financial Times*. European correspondent and pathetic wretch." He shot Ben a comic, mock-baleful glance. "My editor sweet-talked me into going with promises of schnitzel and strudel and *Sachertorte*, and I thought to myself, 'Well, that's a bit of all right then.' Higgins will *never* hear the end of it: there's a solemn vow. Two days of standing around in this lovely frigid rain, my little piggies turning into popsicles, down to practically my last fag, and all we get are the same damn press releases they're faxing all the bureaus."

"But you must be seeing some pretty grand poobahs

sauntering in and out. I've looked at the guest list."

"Well, that's the thing—wherever they are, they're not here. Maybe they're just as bored with the program as everybody else. Probably all decided to nip out and take a quick skiing vacation. Strictly B-list, the only people I've caught sight of. Our photographer's taken to drink, he has. I think he's got the right idea, too. I've got half a mind to pop down the corner for a pint, except they serve the ale too damn cold in this country. Ever notice that? Plus which, the stuff they make tastes like piss."

The big names weren't here? Did that mean that the Sigma conclave was taking place elsewhere? Ben's stomach plummeted: Had he been misled? Perhaps Strasser had been mistaken. Or perhaps he and Anna had made a false assumption somewhere along the line.

"Any rumors about where the muckety-mucks are hanging out?" Ben kept his tone light.

The cockney scribe snorted. "Bloody hell. Know what it is? It's like one of those sodding nightclubs where all the really hip people get shown to a special room, and the squares get stuck in a pen with hay on the floor." He rummaged through a badly squashed and nearly empty pack of Silk Cuts. "Bloody hell."

Ben's mind raced. Jürgen Lenz was clearly calling the shots here. Just as clearly, the real action wasn't taking place at the conference at all. The answer was no doubt to be found in the Lenz Foundation's activities. And here, an indirect approach would probably yield the quickest results. Back at the hotel, he worked the phones, keeping one eye on his watch. He wanted to collect as much information as possible before he and Anna compared notes at the end of the day.

"Cancer Foundation of Austria."

"I'd like to speak with the administrator in charge of fund-raising, please," Ben said. There was a click, several seconds of hold music—"Tales from the Vienna Woods," naturally—and then another woman's voice: "Schimmel."

"Frau Schimmel, my name's Ron Adams, and I'm an American journalist in Vienna, working on a profile of Jürgen Lenz for *American Philanthropy* magazine."

The administrator's voice changed instantly from wary to exuberant: "Yes, certainly! How may I help you?"

"I guess I'm really interested—especially in light of the International Children's Health Forum—in documenting his generosity, the extent of his support for your foundation, his involvement, that sort of thing."

The vague question elicited an even vaguer reply. She went on at length, then he hung up, frustrated. He had called the Lenz Foundation and asked a low-level staffer for a list of all charities they funded. No questions were asked: as a tax-exempt institution, the Lenz Foundation was obligated to divulge all of its gifts.

But what he was looking for specifically, he had no idea. He was probing mindlessly. There had to be a way to penetrate the facade of Jürgen Lenz, philanthropist. Yet there seemed to be no logic to the type of grants Lenz made, no commonality, no organizing principle. Cancer—Kosovo—Progeria—The German-Jewish Dialogue? Those were the main ones. But if there was a connection, he had yet to find it, even after calling three different charities.

One more try, he told himself, and then move on. He got up from the desk in the hotel room, got a Pepsi from the little refrigerator, returned to the desk, and dialed another number from the list.

"Hello, Progeria Institute."

"May I speak to the administrator in charge of fundraising, please?"

A few seconds went by.

"Meitner."

"Yes, Frau Meitner. My name is Ron Adams . . ."

Without much hope he went through his now-standard interview. The woman was, like all the administrators he talked to, a great fan of Jürgen Lenz and delighted to sing his praises.

"Mr. Lenz is really our chief benefactor," she said. "Without him, I think we could not exist. You know, this is a tragic and exceedingly rare disorder."

"I really don't know anything about it," he said politely. He realized he was wasting time when there was none to spare.

"To put it simply, it's premature aging. The full name is Hutchinson-Gilford Progeria Syndrome. It causes a child to age‑ seven or eight times faster than he should. A ten-year-old child with progeria will look like an eighty-year-old man, with arthritis and heart problems and all the rest. Most of them die by the age of thirteen. Seldom do they grow taller than the height of the average five-year-old."

"My God," Ben said, genuinely appalled.

"Because it's so rare, it is what is called an 'orphan disease,' which means it gets very little funding for research, and the drug companies have no financial incentive to find a cure. That's why his help is so terribly important."

Biotech companies . . . Vortex.

"Why do you think Mr. Lenz takes such a personal interest?"

A hesitation. "I think perhaps you should ask Mr. Lenz."

He sensed the sudden chill in her voice. "If there's anything you'd like to tell me off the record . . ."

A pause. "Do you know who Jürgen Lenz's father was?" the woman said carefully.

Did anyone? "Gerhard Lenz, the Nazi doctor," Ben replied.

"Correct. Off the record, Mr. Adams, I'm told that Gerhard Lenz did some ghastly experiments on children with progeria. No doubt Jürgen Lenz simply wishes to undo what his father did. But please don't print that."

"I won't," Ben promised. *But if Jürgen Lenz was not Gerhard's son, why the interest in the same causes? What sort of bizarre masquerade was this?*

"You know, Mr. Lenz even sends a few of these poor children to a private sanatorium in the Austrian Alps that his foundation runs."

"Sanatorium?"

"Yes, I think it's known as the Clockworks."

Ben bolted upright. The Clockworks: the place where Strasser had sent the senior Lenz electron microscopes. If Jürgen *was* Gerhard's son, he would have inherited it. But was he really using it as a sanatorium?

He attempted a breezy tone. "Oh, where's that?"

"The Alps. I don't know exactly where. I've never been there. It's exclusive, private, very luxurious. A real escape from the bustle of the city."

"I'd love to talk to a child who's been there." *And find out what's really going on.*

"Mr. Adams," she said somberly, "the children who are invited are usually at the very end of their brief lives. Frankly, I don't know of any who might still be living. But I'm sure one of the parents wouldn't mind talking to you about Mr. Lenz's generosity."

The man's apartment was a fourth-floor walk-up in a dismal apartment building in Vienna's twelfth district, a small and dark place that smelled of stale cigarette smoke and cooking grease.

After the death of their beloved son at the age of eleven, the man explained, he and his wife had divorced. Their marriage had not survived the stress of their son's illness and death. Prominently displayed next to the sofa was a large color photograph of their boy, Christoph. It was hard to tell his age; he could have been eight or eighty. He was completely bald, with a receding chin, a large head with a small face, bulging eyes, the wizened countenance of a very old man.

"My son died at the sanatorium," the man said. He had a full gray beard, bifocal glasses, a scraggly fringe around a bald pate. His eyes were filled with tears. "But at least he was happy at the end of his life. Dr. Lenz is a most generous man. I'm glad Christoph could die happy."

"Did you ever visit Christoph there, at the Clockworks?" Ben asked.

"No, parents are not permitted. It's a place only for children. All of the children's medical problems are taken care of by an expert medical staff. But he sent me postcards." He got up and returned a few minutes later with a picture postcard. The handwriting was a large, childish scrawl. Ben turned the card over and saw the color photograph of an alpine mountain. The caption beneath the photograph said SEMMERING.

Lenz's widow had mentioned Semmering.

Strasser had talked about Gerhard Lenz's research clinic in the Austrian Alps.

Could it be the same place?

Semmering.

He had to find Anna immediately, get this information to her.

He looked up from the card and saw the father weeping silently. In a minute the man was able to speak. "This is what I always tell myself. My Christoph died happy."

They had arranged to meet back at the hotel no later than seven o'clock that evening.

If she was unable to return by then, Anna said, she'd call. If for some reason she was unable to call, or thought it was unsafe to do so, she had specified a fallback meeting place: nine o'clock at the Schweizerhaus in the Prater.

By eight o'clock she hadn't returned to the hotel, and there was no message.

She'd been gone for almost the entire day. Even if Lenz had agreed to see her, Ben couldn't figure out how she could spend more than an hour or two at the foundation. But she'd been gone almost twelve hours.

Twelve hours.

He was beginning to worry.

At eight-thirty, when she still hadn't called, he left for the Schweizerhaus, on Strasse des Ersten Mai 2. By now he was beyond nervous; he was fearful that something had happened to her. He asked himself, *Am I overreacting?* She doesn't have to account for her whereabouts at all times.

Still . . .

It was a lively place, renowned for its roasted pork hocks served with mustard and horseradish sauce. Ben sat alone at a table for two, waiting, nursing a Czech Budweiser beer.

Waiting.

The beer didn't calm his nerves. All he could think about was Anna, and what might have become of her.

By ten o'clock there was still no sign of her. He called the hotel, but she had neither arrived nor left a message. He repeatedly checked his phone to make sure it was on so she could reach him if she tried.

He ordered dinner for two, but by the time the food arrived he'd lost his appetite.

Around midnight he returned to the empty hotel room. He tried to read for a while but was unable to concentrate.

The sandpaper of Chardin's voice: *Wheels within wheels—that was the way we worked. . . .* Strasser: *a cabal within a cabal . . . Lenz said he was doing work that would change the world.*

He fell asleep on top of the bed, in his clothes, with all the room lights on, and slept fitfully.

He and Peter were strapped to two gurneys, side by side; above them was Dr. Gerhard Lenz, gowned and masked in full surgical garb. His light eyes, however, unmistakable. "We will make the two of them one," he was saying to a hatchet-faced assistant. "We will connect their organs so that neither will be viable without the other. Together, both will survive—or together, both will die." A gloved hand wielded a scalpel like a violin bow, pressing it against flesh in bold, confident strokes. The pain was beyond endurance.

Struggling against the restraints, he turned to see his brother's face, staring, frozen in horror.

"Peter!" he called out.

His brother's mouth gaped open, and under the harsh overhead lights, Ben could see that Peter's tongue had been removed. The heavy smell of ether filled the air, and a black mask was forcibly placed over Ben's face. But it didn't produce unconsciousness; if anything, he grew more alert, more aware of the horrors being done to him.

He awoke at three in the morning.

And still Anna hadn't returned.

A long, sleepless night followed.

He tried to doze but was unable to. He hated not having anyone to call, or anything he could do to locate her.

He sat, tried to read, couldn't focus. He could think only of Anna.

Oh, God, he loved her so.

At seven, groggy and disoriented, he called down to the front desk, for the fifth time, to see whether Anna might have called from somewhere in the middle of the night.

No message.

He took a shower, shaved, ordered a room service breakfast.

He knew something had happened to Anna; he was certain of it. There was no way in the world she would have voluntarily gone off someplace without calling in.

Something had happened to her.

He drank several cups of the strong black coffee, then forced himself to eat a hard roll.

He was terrified.

In Währinger Strasse, there is an "Internet café," one of several such places listed in the Vienna telephone book. This one called itself an Internet Bar/Kaffehaus and turned out to be a garishly fluorescent-lit room with a few iMacs on little round Formica tables, and an espresso machine. The floor was sticky and the place smelled of beer. It charged fifty Austrian shillings for thirty minutes of Internet access time.

He typed the word *Semmering* in several different search engines and came up with the same entries each time: home pages for ski resorts, hotels, and general chamber-of-commerce-type descriptions of a village and ski resort in the Austrian Alps about ninety kilometers from Vienna.

Desperate, knowing he could be making a terrible mistake, he found a public telephone and called the Lenz Foundation. This was the last place he knew she'd gone. It was crazy, almost pointless, to ask there, but what else was there to do?

He asked for Jürgen Lenz's office, and then asked Lenz's executive assistant whether a woman named Anna Navarro had been in.

She seemed to know Anna's name immediately, without hesitation. But instead of answering his question, she demanded to know his name.

Ben identified himself as being an "attaché" from the U.S. embassy.

"Who is this calling?" the woman demanded to know.

He supplied a false name.

"Dr. Lenz has asked me to take a number, and he'll call you back."

"Actually, I'm going to be out of the office the whole day. Let me talk to Dr. Lenz, if I could," he said.

"Dr. Lenz is not available."

"Well, do you have any idea when he'll be free to talk? It's important that we speak."

"Dr. Lenz is out of the office," she said coldly.

"All right, I've got his home phone number, I'll try him there."

The secretary hesitated. "Dr. Lenz is not in Vienna," she offered.

Not in Vienna. Smoothly: "It's just that the ambassador himself asked me to speak to him. A matter of great urgency."

"Dr. Lenz is with a special delegation from the International Children's Health Forum—he's taken them on a private tour of some of our facilities. That's no secret. Did the ambassador want to join them? If so, I'm afraid it's too late."

Too late.

After a pause, the secretary said, "You must be reachable at the U.S. embassy general telephone number, yes?"

He hung up.

CHAPTER FORTY-ONE

The train to Semmering left Vienna's Südbahnhof at a few minutes after nine. Ben had left Vienna without checking out of the hotel.

He was wearing jeans and sneakers and his warmest ski parka. The ninety-kilometer journey would be brief, much faster than renting a car and driving along the twisting alpine roads.

The train cut through the dense terrain, plunged into long tunnels and skirted high above steep mountain passes. It passed gently rolling green farmland, whitewashed stone buildings with red roofs, the iron-gray mountains rising up behind; then it climbed slowly, over narrow viaducts, and sliced through breathtaking limestone gorges.

The train compartment was mostly empty, its interior amber-lit, the high-backed seats upholstered in ugly orange twill. He thought about Anna Navarro. She was in some kind of peril. He was sure of it.

He felt he knew her well enough to be certain that she'd never simply vanish of her own accord. Either she'd abruptly gone somewhere from which she couldn't call, or she'd been forcibly *taken* somewhere.

But where?

After they'd rejoined each other in the Vienna hotel, they had spent a long time discussing Lenz. Ben recalled what Gerhard Lenz's widow had blurted out—*why does Lenz send you? You come here from Semmering?* And Strasser had told them of having electron microscopes shipped to an old clinic in the Austrian Alps known as the Clockworks.

But what was in Semmering now that the old woman was so afraid of? Obviously something ongoing, perhaps connected to the string of murders.

Anna was determined to locate that clinic in the Alps. She was convinced she'd find answers there.

Which suggested that she might have gone looking for the Clockworks. And if he were wrong—if she wasn't there—then at least maybe he'd be a step closer to finding her.

He studied the Freytag & Berndt map of the Semmering-Rax-Schneeberg region he'd picked up in Vienna before he left, and tried to devise a plan. Without knowing where the clinic or research facility was, though, he had no idea how to get inside.

The Semmering station was a modest two-story structure in front of which stood only a green bench and a Coke machine. As soon as he stepped off the train he was hit by an icy wind; the climate difference between Vienna and the Austrian Alps to the south was striking. Here it was bracingly cold. After a few minutes of hiking up the steep, winding road into the town, his ears and cheeks stung from the chill.

And as he walked he began to feel misgivings. *What am I doing?* he asked himself. *What if Anna's not here, then what?*

The village of Semmering was tiny. It was one street, Hochstrasse, lined with *Gasthauses* and inns, set into the south face of a mountain, above it a couple of sprawling luxury resort hotels and sanatoriums. To the north was Höllental, Hell's Valley, a deep gorge carved out by the Schwarza River.

Above the bank on Hochstrasse was a small tourist office presided over by a plain young woman.

Ben explained that he was interested in hiking around the Semmering region and asked for a more detailed *Wanderkarte*. The woman, who clearly had nothing else to do, provided one and spent a good deal of time pointing out particularly scenic trails. "You can go, if you want, along the historic Semmering Railway—there is a panoramic vista where you can watch the train go through the Weinzettlwand Tunnel. There is also a wonderful place to stop where they took the picture for the old twenty-shilling banknote. And a magnificent view of the ruins of the castle of Klamm."

"Really," Ben said, feigning interest, and then added casually, "I'm told there is some sort of famous private clinic around here in an old *Schloss*. The Clockworks, I think it's called."

"The Clockworks?" she said blankly. "*Uhrwerken?*"

"A private clinic—maybe more of a research facility, a scientific institute, a sanatorium for sick children."

There seemed to be a quick flash of recognition in the woman's eyes—or did he imagine it?—but she shook her head. "I don't know what you're talking about, sir, I'm sorry."

"I think someone said this clinic was owned by Dr. Jürgen Lenz . . . ?"

"I am sorry," she repeated, too quickly. She had suddenly turned sullen. "There is no such clinic."

He continued down Hochstrasse until he came to what appeared to be a combination *Gasthaus* and pub. In front was a tall black chalkboard topped with a green placard for Wieninger Bier and an invitation on a painted scroll beneath it: "*Herzlich Willkommen*"—A Hearty Welcome. The day's specials were advertised in bold white chalk letters.

It was dark inside and smelled of beer. Although it was

not yet noon, three portly men were sitting at a small wooden table drinking from glass steins of beer. Ben approached them.

"I'm looking for an old *Schloss* around here that houses a research clinic owned by a man named Jürgen Lenz. The old Clockworks."

The men gazed up at him suspiciously. One of them muttered something to the others, who murmured back. Ben heard "Lenz" and "*Klinik*." "No, nothing here."

Again, Ben sensed unmistakable antagonism. He was certain that these men were concealing something, and slipped several thousand-shilling notes on the table, toying with them idly. No time for subtlety. "All right, thank you," he said, turning halfway to leave. Then, as if he'd forgotten something, he turned back. "Listen, if any of you guys have any friends who might know something about this clinic, tell them I'll pay for the information. I'm an American entrepreneur looking for some investment opportunities."

He left the pub and stood for a moment in front of the building. A cluster of men in jeans and leather jackets strolled by, hands in pockets, speaking Russian. No sense in asking them.

A few seconds later he felt a tap on his shoulder. It was one of the men from the pub. "Em, how much will you pay for this information?"

"I'd say if the information is accurate, it's worth a couple thousand shillings to me."

The man glanced around furtively. "The money first, please."

Ben regarded him for a moment, then handed him two banknotes. The man led him down the road a few meters and then pointed up toward the steep mountain. Set into the side of the snow-covered peak and surrounded by tightly packed, snow-frosted fir trees as dense as crabgrass, was an ancient medieval castle with a baroque facade and a gilded clock tower.

Semmering.

The clinic where Hitler's science adviser, Josef Strasser,

had shipped sophisticated scientific equipment decades ago.

Where Jürgen Lenz invited a few lucky children afflicted with a terrible disease.

Where—piecing together what he'd learned with what Lenz's secretary had said—a delegation of world leaders and dignitaries had come to visit.

And where Anna might have gone. Was it possible?

Certainly it was possible; in any case, it was all he had.

The Clockworks had been there all along, hidden in plain sight, and he had seen it walking up from the train station. It was by far the biggest property visible anywhere around.

"Magnificent," Ben said softly. "Do you know anyone who's ever been inside?"

"No. No one is allowed. There is much security there. It is very private, you can never go in."

"Well, they must hire local workers."

"No. All workers are flown in by helicopter from Vienna, and they have living quarters there. There is a helipad, you can see it if you look closely."

"What do they do there, do you know?"

"I only hear things."

"Like what?"

"They do strange things there, people say. You see strange-looking children arriving in buses . . ."

"Do you know who owns it?"

"Like you say, this Lenz. His father was a Nazi."

"How long has he owned it?"

"A long time. I think maybe his father owned it after the war. During the war the *Schloss* was used by the Nazis as a command center. It used to be called the Schloss Zerwald—this is the old name for Semmering from the Middle Ages. It was built by one of the Esterházy princes in the seventeenth century. For a while at the end of last century it was, how you say, abandoned, then it was used for about twenty years as a clock factory. The old-timers around here still call it the *Uhrwerken*. How do you say—?"

"Clockworks." Ben took out another thousand-shilling note. "Now, just a few more questions."

A man was looming over her, a man in a white coat whose face kept going in and out of focus. He had gray hair and was speaking softly, even smiling. He seemed friendly, and she wished she could understand what he was saying.

She wondered what was wrong with her that she couldn't sit up: had she been in an accident? Had a stroke? She was overtaken by a sudden panic.

She heard ". . . *to have to do that to you, but we really had no choice.*"

An accent, perhaps German or Swiss.

Where am I?

Then: "*dissociative tranquilizer . . .*"

Someone speaking English to her with some sort of Middle European accent.

And ". . . *as comfortable as possible while we wait for the ketamine to leave your system.*"

She began to recall things now. The place she was in was a bad place, a place she had been very curious about once but now wished she wasn't in.

She had vague memories of a struggle, of being grabbed by several strong men, of being jabbed with something sharp. After that, nothing.

The gray-haired man, who she now felt was a very bad man, was gone, and she closed her eyes.

When she opened them again, she was alone. Her head had cleared. She felt bruised all over, and she realized that she was tied down to a bed.

She lifted her head as much as she could, which was not very far because there was a belt around her chest.

But it was enough to see the cuffs and belts in which she was locked and fastened to a hospital gurney. They were polyurethane medical restraints, the kind that also came in leather and were used in mental hospitals for their most violent and dangerous patients. They were called "humane restraints," and she had used them herself back in her training days.

Her wrists were cuffed and locked and attached by a long chain to a waist belt that was also locked. The same for her ankles. Her arms were chafed and painful, indicating that she had struggled mightily.

The restraints were color-coded: red for the wrists, blue for the ankles. These were of more recent vintage than the leather ones she had used, but surely the lock hadn't changed. The key, she remembered, was small and flat with no teeth on it, straight on one side, tapered on the other to a wedge-shaped point.

She remembered that hospital restraints were actually quite easy to pick if you knew how, but she would need a paper clip or something like it, a straight and rigid piece of metal wire.

She craned her head to one side and examined the bulky anesthesia machine on one side of her bed, and, on the other side, the metal cart just a few tantalizing feet away.

It had eight drawers. On top of it were scattered medical supplies, bandages and forceps, scissors, and a sterile package of safety pins.

But there was no way to reach it.

She tried to shift her body to the left, toward the gleaming cart, hoping for slack in the restraints, but there was almost none. She shifted to the left, this time violently, a sudden hard jerk that did nothing; the only thing that moved at all was the bed itself, which had to be on wheels.

Wheels.

She was silent for a moment, listening for approaching footsteps. Then she lurched against the restraints again and felt the wheels give what she imagined was another inch or two.

Encouraged by the movement, tiny as it was, she lurched again. The wheels moved another minuscule distance.

But the cart still looked as distant and unreachable as the mirage of a lake to a thirsty man in a desert.

She rested a moment, her neck spasming in pain.

Then she summoned her strength again and, trying to ignore how far away the cart was, she *jerked* at the restraints and gained maybe an inch.

An inch, out of several feet, felt like a single step in the New York Marathon.

She heard footsteps in the hallway and voices that grew louder, and she froze, resting her strained neck while she waited, and the voices passed.

A *lunge* to the left and the gurney gave up another couple of inches.

She did not want to think about what she would do once she reached the cart; that was another challenge entirely. She would have to take this a step at a time.

An inch at a time.

Another inch or so. Another. The cart was not much more than a foot away. She jerked again and gained another inch and the silver-haired man entered the room.

Jürgen Lenz, as he called himself. But now she knew the astonishing truth.

Jürgen-Lenz-who-was-not-Jürgen-Lenz.

CHAPTER FORTY-TWO

At the end of Hochstrasse Ben found a sporting goods store that featured a wide variety of equipment for the tourist and sportsman. He rented a pair of cross-country skis and asked where he could rent a car.

No place for miles.

Parked at the side of the shop was a BMW motorcycle that looked old and decrepit but still functional. He struck a deal with the young man who managed the place, and owned the bike.

With the skis strapped to his back he set off across the ridge of the Semmering pass until he came to a narrow unmarked dirt road that wound steeply uphill through a ravine to the *Schloss*. The road was rutted and icy; it had evidently been used recently by trucks and other heavy vehicles.

When he had managed to climb perhaps a quarter of a mile, he came to a red sign that said BETRETEN VERBOTEN—PRIVATBESITZ: No Trespassing—Private Property.

Just ahead of the sign was a barrier gate whose arm was striped in yellow-and-black reflective paint. It appeared to be electronically controlled, but Ben was easily able to hop over it and then wheel the bike underneath, tipped at an angle.

Nothing happened: no Klaxon, no alarm bells.

He continued up the road, through dense snow-covered woods, and in a few minutes reached a high, crenellated stone wall. It looked centuries old, though recently restored.

From atop the wall rose several feet of thin, horizontally strung wire. At a distance, this addition was not visible, but Ben saw it clearly now. It was probably electrified, but he did not want to scale the wall and find out the hard way.

Instead, he followed the wall for a few hundred feet until it came to what appeared to be the main gate, about six feet wide and ten feet high, constructed of ornately scrolled wrought iron. Upon closer examination, Ben realized that the fence was in fact steel painted to look like iron, entirely backed with a screen of woven wire fabric. This was certainly high-security, designed to foil intruders.

He wondered whether it was made to keep people out—or in.

Had Anna somehow gotten inside? he wondered. Was it possible? Or was she being held prisoner?

The dirt road came to an end another few hundred meters from the gate. Beyond it was glistening virgin snow. He parked the motorcycle, put on his skis, and set off across the snow, staying close to the wall.

His idea was to survey the entire perimeter of the property, or at least as much as was possible to examine, in hopes of discovering any holes in the security, any possible points of entry. But it did not look promising.

The snow was soft and deep, so he sank into the powder, and the even deeper drifts and dunes made maneuvering difficult. It was no easier once he got the hang of it, because the terrain became steeper, the skiing ever more arduous.

The ground next to the wall became higher, and pretty soon Ben could see over it.

Glare coming off the snow forced him to squint, but he could now make out the *Schloss*, a great rambling stone structure, more horizontal than vertical. At first glance this could have been a tourist attraction, but then he saw a couple of guards in military-style tunics, carrying submachine guns, patrolling the property.

Whatever was happening inside these walls was not simple research.

What he saw next was a profound shock. He didn't understand it, but within the enclosed area were children, dozens and dozens of ragged-looking children, milling outside, in the cold. He peered again, squinting against the snow glare.

Who were they?

And why were they there?

This was no sanatorium, that was for sure; he wondered whether they were prisoners.

He skied uphill a short distance, close enough to get a better look, but not so close that he lost his line of sight behind the high stone wall.

Inside, next to the wall, was a fenced-in area the size of a city block. Within it were several large military-style tents jammed with children. It seemed to be a makeshift shantytown, a tent city, its inhabitants youth from some Eastern European country. The steel fence that enclosed it was topped with coils of razor wire.

It was a strange vision. Ben shook his head as if to clear it of an optical illusion, then looked again. Yes. They were children, some toddlers, some teenagers, unshaven and rough-looking, smoking and shouting to one another; girls in headscarves, shabby peasant dresses, and tattered coats, children swarming all around.

He had seen news footage of people like this. Whoever they were, wherever they were from, they had that unmistakable look of impoverished youth driven out of their homes by war—Bosnian refugees, escapees from the conflicts in Kosovo and Macedonia, ethnic Albanians, perhaps.

Was Lenz sheltering war refugees here, on the grounds of his clinic?

Jürgen Lenz, humanitarian, giving shelter to refugees and ailing children?

Unlikely.

For this was hardly a shelter. These peasant children were packed into their tent city, inadequately dressed, freezing in the cold. And there were the armed guards. This looked like some kind of internment camp.

Then he heard a shout from the encampment, an adolescent boy's voice. Someone within had spotted him. The shout was soon joined by others, the wretched inmates suddenly waving at him, beckoning to him, calling to him. He understood at once what they wanted.

They wanted to be released.

They wanted his help. They saw him as a savior, someone outside who could help them escape. His stomach turned, he shivered, and not from the cold.

What was being done to them?

Suddenly a shout arose from another direction, and one of the guards pointed his weapon toward Ben. Now several of the guards were shouting at him, waving him away.

The threat was clear: get off the private property or we'll shoot.

He heard a blast of gunfire and turned to see a fusillade of bullets pock the snow a few feet to his left.

They weren't kidding, and they weren't patient.

The refugee children were prisoners here. And Anna? Was Anna inside there too?

Please, God, I hope she's all right. I hope she's alive.

He didn't know whether to wish she was inside—or to pray she wasn't.

Ben turned around and headed back down the mountainside.

"Well, I see you're more aware now," Lenz said, smiling brightly. He stopped at the foot of her bed and clasped his hands in front of him. "Perhaps now you'd like to say to whom you've told my real identity."

"Screw you," she said.

"I thought not," he said equably. "Once the ketamine has worn off"—he glanced at his gold watch—"which will be in no more than another half an hour, certainly, you'll be infused intravenously with about five milligrams of a powerful opioid called Versed. You have had this before? During surgery, perhaps?"

Anna gazed at him blankly.

He continued, unruffled. "Five milligrams is about the proper dose to make you relaxed but still responsive. You'll feel a little rush, but this passes in ten seconds or so, and then you'll feel calmer than you've ever felt before in your life. All your anxiety will seep out of you. It's a wonderful feeling."

He cocked his head to one side like a bird. "If we were to inject you with one single bolus of this drug, you'd stop breathing and very probably die. So we must titrate it slowly over eight to ten minutes. We certainly don't want anything to happen to you."

Anna gave a grunt that communicated, she hoped, both skepticism and sarcasm at once. Despite her chemically induced calm, she was at the same time deeply frightened.

"Rather, you'll be found dead in your wrecked rental car, another victim of drunk driving—"

"I didn't rent a car," she slurred.

"Oh, in fact you did. Or rather, it was done for you, using your credit card. You were arrested last night in a neighboring town. Your blood-alcohol level was measured at two-point-five, which is surely why you got into an accident. You were kept overnight in a holding cell and then released. But you know how it is with problem drinkers—they never learn."

She displayed no reaction. But her mind raced, desperate to find a way out of the maze. There *had* to be flaws in his plan, but where?

Lenz continued, "Versed, you see, is the most effective truth serum ever invented, even though it was not intended for this use. All the drugs the CIA has tried, like sodium pentothol or scopolamine, they never worked. But with the correct dose of Versed you'll become so free of inhibitions that you'll tell me anything I want to know. And here's the magical thing: afterward you'll remember nothing. You'll talk and talk quite lucidly and yet, from the moment you're put on the IV, you'll have no memory of what happened. It's really quite remarkable."

A nurse entered the room, wide-hipped and squat and middle-aged. She rolled in a cart of equipment—tubes, blood-pressure cuffs, syringes—and began setting up. She watched Anna suspiciously as she filled a few of the syringes from little vials and then applied preprinted labels to them.

"This is Gerta, your nurse-anesthetist. She is one of our best. You are in good hands." Lenz gave Anna a little wave as he left the room.

"How are you feeling?" Gerta asked perfunctorily, in a stern contralto, as she hung a bag of clear liquid on the IV stand to the left of Anna's bed.

"Pretty . . . groggy . . ." Anna said, her voice trailing off, her eyes fluttering closed. But she was hyper-vigilant; now she had a tentative plan.

Gerta did something with what sounded like plastic tubing. After a few moments she said, "All right, I'll come back. Doctor wants to wait until the ketamine is mostly out of your system. If we start the Versed now you may stop breathing. Anyway, I have to go to the anesthesia workroom. This sat probe is no good." She closed the door behind her.

Anna opened her eyes and flung her body hard to the left, as hard as she could, augmenting the push by throwing her manacled arms into it. It was a movement she was beginning to master. The bed seemed to jump several inches toward the supply cart. There was no time to rest. One more try, and she was there.

She lifted her shoulders as far as the restraining belt would allow and pressed her face against the cold top edge of the cart. Out of the corner of her left eye she could see the safety pins, used to secure bandages, in their little square blister-wrap sterile packaging, just an inch or two away.

Yet still out of reach.

If she turned her neck to the left as far as it would go, she could almost look at the pack of safety pins straight on. The tendons on her neck and along her upper back were so strained they began to tremble. The ache quickly became excruciating.

Then, like a jeering child, she stuck her tongue all the way out. Tiny pinpoints of pain jabbed the underside of her tongue at its root.

Finally she lowered her distended tongue to the surface of the cart as if it were a steam shovel. It touched the plastic of the package, and she slowly pulled her head backward, edging the pack along as she did, right to the edge of the cart. Just before it could teeter off the edge she clenched it between her teeth.

A footfall, and the door to her room came open.

Quick as a rattlesnake she lay back on the bed, the little blister-pack concealed under her tongue, its sharp edges poking at its base. *How much had she seen?* The nurse was coming toward her. Anna gagged but kept the packet in her closed mouth in a pool of saliva.

"Yes," Gerta said, "ketamine can make you nauseated sometimes, it will do that. You're awake, I see."

Anna made a complaining *mmmmph* through her shut mouth and shut her eyes. Saliva pooled behind her front teeth. She forced herself to swallow.

Gerta came around to Anna's right and began fumbling at the head of the bed. Anna shut her eyes and tried to make her breathing sound regular.

A few minutes later Gerta left the room again and closed the door quietly behind her.

She would be back much sooner this time, Anna knew.

There was blood in her mouth from where the packet had cut into soft tissue, and Anna moved it to her lips with her tongue and then spit it out, forward. It landed squarely on the back of her left hand. She moved her hands together and reached her right index finger over, pulling the safety-pin packet into her fist.

Now she moved quickly. She knew what she was doing, because she had picked these locks on more than one occasion when she had misplaced the key and was too embarrassed to ask for a replacement.

The wrapping came off with some difficulty, but then it was an easy thing to bend the safety pin's point away from its clasp.

The left cuff first. She inserted the pinpoint into the lock, pushed the inner pins to the left, then to the right, and the lock clicked open.

Her left hand was free!

She felt exhilarated. Even more quickly now she freed her right hand, then the restraining belt, and then the door came open again with a low squeak. Gerta had returned.

Anna drew her hands back into the polyurethane cuffs so that they appeared still to be fastened and closed her eyes.

Gerta approached the bed. "I could hear you moving in here."

Heart pounding so loud it had to be audible.

Anna opened her eyes slowly and made them look unfocused.

"I say enough is enough," Gerta said menacingly. "I think you are making pretend." Under her breath she added, "So we will have to take our chances."

God, no.

She applied a rubber tourniquet to Anna's left arm until the vein popped out, and inserted the intravenous needle, then turned her back to adjust the flow clamp on the IV tubing. In one snapping-turtle motion Anna pulled her hands free of the unlocked cuffs and tried silently to undo the tourniquet, *quiet, must be quiet*, but Gerta heard the snap of the rubber and turned around, and as she did Anna raised herself up off the bed as far as the chest belt would allow and caught the nurse's neck with the crook of her right elbow, a strange gesture of affection. Pulled back hard on the rubber tube, *hard* against Gerta's fleshy neck.

A yelp.

Gerta flailed her hands, reached for her neck, tried to claw her fingers under the garrote, could not get a purchase, her fingernails scratching at her own neck, wriggling madly. Her face purpled. Her mouth gasped and sucked for breath. Gerta's fluttering hands slowed; she was probably losing consciousness.

Within a few minutes Anna, almost numb from exertion, had the nurse gagged and cuffed to the bed rail. Springing open the ankle cuffs, she slipped off the bed, her body feeling buoyant, and cuffed Gerta to the anesthesia machine as well, which would not easily move.

She removed Gerta's key ring from her belt, and glanced at the anesthesia cart.

It was full of weapons. She scooped up a handful of packaged hypodermic needles and several small glass ampules of various drugs, then remembered she was wearing a hospital johnny with no pockets.

In the supply closet hung two white cotton doctor's jackets. She put one on, stuffed the pilfered supplies in both slash pockets, and ran from the room.

CHAPTER FORTY-THREE

The records office for the Semmering area occupied a small basement room in a Bavarian-style building housing a scattering of municipal workers. There were rows of green filing cabinets, arranged by the number of the parcel of land.

"The Schloss Zerwald is not accessible to the public," the white-haired woman who ran the office said flatly. "It is part of the Semmering Clinic. Strictly private."

"I understand that," Ben said. "It's actually the old maps themselves that I'm interested in." When Ben went on to explain that he was a historian researching the castles of Germany and Austria, she looked vaguely disapproving, as if she'd just smelled something fetid, but ordered her trembling teenage assistant to snap-to and pull out the property map from one of the drawers along the side wall of the room. It was a complicated-looking system, but the white-haired woman knew exactly where to find the documents Ben wanted.

The map had been printed in the early nineteenth century. The owner of the parcel of land, which in those days took up much of the mountainside, was identified as J. Esterházy. A cryptic series of markings ran through the parcel.

"What does this mean?" Ben asked, pointing.

The old woman scowled. "The caves," she said. "The limestone caves in the mountain."

Caves. It was a possibility.

"The caves run through the *Schloss*'s property?"

"Yes, of course," she said impatiently.

Under the *Schloss*, that meant.

Trying to contain his excitement, he asked, "Can you make a copy of this map for me?"

A hostile look. "For twenty shillings."

"Fine," he said. "And tell me something: is there a floor plan of the *Schloss* anywhere?"

The young clerk at the sporting goods shop examined the property map as if it were an insoluble algebra problem. When Ben explained that the markings indicated a network of caves, he quickly agreed.

"Yes, the old caves run right underneath the *Schloss*," he said. "I think there even used to be an entrance into the *Schloss* from the caves, but that was a long time ago and it must be blocked off."

"Have you been in the caves?"

The young clerk looked up, appalled. "No, of course not."

"Do you know anyone who has?"

He thought a moment. "*Ja*, I think so."

"Do you think he might be willing to take me there, be my guide?"

"I doubt it."

"Can you ask?"

"I'll ask, but I don't value your chances."

Ben hadn't expected a man in his late sixties, but that was who entered the shop half an hour later. He was small and wiry, with cauliflower ears, a long misshapen nose, a pi-

geon chest, ropy arms. He spoke rapidly and irritably in
German to the clerk as he entered, then fell silent when he
met Ben.

Ben said hello; the man nodded.

"He's a little old, frankly," Ben told the salesman. "Isn't
there someone younger and stronger?"

"There is younger but not stronger," the older man said.
"And no one who knows the caves better. Anyway, I am
not so sure I want to do this."

"Oh, you speak English," Ben said, surprised.

"Most of us learned English during the war."

"Do the caves still have an entrance into the *Schloss*?"

"There used to be. But why should I help you?"

"I need to get inside the *Schloss*."

"You can't. It is now a private clinic."

"Still, I must get inside."

"Why?"

"Let's just say it's for personal reasons that are worth a
great deal of money to me." He told the old Austrian what
he was willing to pay for his services.

"We'll need equipment," the man said. "You can
climb?"

His name was Fritz Neumann, and he had been caving
around Semmering for longer than Ben had been alive. He
was also immensely strong, yet nimble and graceful.

Toward the end of the war, he said, when he was a boy
of eight, his parents had joined a Catholic workers' Resistance cell that was secretly fighting the Nazis, who had
invaded their part of Austria. The old Clockworks had been
seized by the Nazis and turned into a regional command
post.

Unknown to the Nazis who lived and worked in the
Schloss, there was a crawl space off the basement of the
old castle with a slot entrance to a limestone cave that ran
beneath the castle's property. The *Schloss* had in fact been
built over this mouth quite deliberately, because the original

inhabitants, concerned about attacks on their stronghold, had wanted a secret exit. Over the centuries the cave mouth had largely been forgotten.

But during the war, when the Nazis had commandeered the Clockworks, the members of the Resistance realized they were in possession of a crucial piece of knowledge that would enable them to spy on the Nazis, to commit sabotage and subversion—and, if they were quite careful about it, to do it without the Nazis even realizing how it was done.

The Resistance had spirited dozens of prisoners out of the *Schloss*, and the Nazis had never figured out how.

As an eight-year-old boy, Fritz Neumann had helped his parents and their friends, and he had committed the cave's intricate passages to memory.

Fritz Neumann was the first off the ski lift, Ben close behind. The ski area was on the north face of the mountain. The *Schloss* was on the opposite side, but Neumann had judged it easier to reach the mouth of the cave this way.

Their skis had Randonee bindings, which allow the heel to go free for cross-country skiing but can be locked in for downhill. Even more important, the bindings allowed them to wear mountaineering boots instead of ski boots. Neumann had outfitted them both: flexible twelve-point crampons favored by Austrian climbers on hard ice; Petzl headlamps; ice axes with wrist leashes; climbing harnesses; pitons; and carabiners.

All easily obtained at the shop.

The guns Ben wanted were not so easily found. But this was hunting country, and quite a few of the old man's friends had handguns as well as shotguns, and one of them was willing to make a deal.

Wearing woolen balaclavas, windproof pants and gaiters, alpine climbing packs, and thin polypropylene gloves, they cross-country skied to the summit, then locked in their bindings for the long downhill stretch on the south face.

Ben considered himself a good skier, but Neumann was a phenomenon, and Ben found it difficult to keep up as the older man negotiated the virgin snow. The air was frigid, and Ben's face, the exposed part anyway, quickly began to smart. Ben found it amazing that Neumann was able to lead the way through paths that were barely paths, until he saw the dashes of red paint on the occasional fir tree, which seemed to mark the way.

They had been skiing for twenty minutes when they came to a crevasse at the beginning of the timberline, and shortly thereafter a steep gorge. They stopped about ten feet from the edge, removed their skis, and conccaled them in a copse.

"The cave, as I tell you, it is very difficult to get to," Neumann said. "Now we rope down. But you say you know how, yes?"

Ben nodded, inspecting the cliff. He estimated the drop at about a hundred feet, maybe less. From here he could see Lenz's *Schloss*, so far down the mountain that it seemed an architect's model.

Neumann set out a neat butterfly coil of rope. Ben was relieved to see it was dynamic kernmantle rope, made of twisted nylon threads.

"It is eleven millimeters," Neumann said. "It is O.K. for you?"

Ben nodded again. For a drop like this, that was just fine. Whatever it took to reach Anna.

From this angle, he couldn't see the mouth of the cave. He assumed it was an opening on the cliff face.

Neumann knelt near the cliff edge by an outcropping of rock, and began driving the pitons in with a hammer he took from a holster. Each piton gave off a reassuring ringing sound that rose in pitch the deeper it was driven in, indicating that it was sunk in solidly.

Then, looping the rope around the largest rock, he pulled it through the pitons.

"This is not so easy to do, getting into the cave mouth," he announced. "We'll rappel down and swing a little, maneuver into the cave. Now we put on the crampons and the harnesses."

"What about the ice axes?"

"Not for here," he said. "There's very little ice here. For the cave."

"There's ice in the cave?"

But Neumann, busy unpacking, did not reply.

Ben and Peter used to go caving near the Greenbriar, but the caves there were little more than crawl holes. He'd never had to deal with ice.

For a moment he felt his stomach knot. Until this point he had been propelled by adrenaline and anger and fear, focusing on one thing only: getting Anna out of Lenz's clinic, where he was convinced she'd been taken.

Now he wondered whether this was the best way. Climbing wasn't particularly risky if you did it right, and he was confident of his climbing skills. But even very experienced cavers had been killed.

He had weighed storming the main gate, counting on the guards to seize him, and thereby attracting Lenz's attention.

But it was just as likely that the guards would shoot to kill.

Hard as it was to accept, this cave was the only alternative.

The two of them lashed the crampons' neoprene straps over the Vibram soles of their weathered mountaineering boots. These affixed twelve sharp spikes to the bottoms and toes of their boots, giving them serious traction on the cliff side. Then they attached the nylon climbing harnesses to their waists and they were ready to go.

"We use the *dulfersitz*, yes?" Neumann said, using the Austrian argot for rappelling without a rack, using only one's body to control the descent.

"No rappel rack?"

Neumann smiled, enjoying Ben's discomfort. "Who needs it?"

Without a rappel rack the descent would be unpleasant, but it saved them having to bring racks. Also, they wouldn't be tied to the rope, making the rappel more dangerous.

"You will follow," Neumann said as he tied a double figure-eight knot at one end of the rope and then wrapped the rope around his shoulder, around his hip, and through his crotch. He walked backward toward the edge, lifting the rope a bit, his feet spread widely, and then he went over the side.

Ben watched the older man dangling free, swinging slowly back and forth, facing the cliff, until he found a foothold. From there, tensioning the rope, Neumann moved his feet down the cliff face. He descended a little farther, dangling in free space again, swaying back and forth, then there was a crunching sound, followed by a shout.

"O.K., come on, now you!"

Ben straddled the rope in the same manner, walked backward to the edge, held his breath, and dropped over the side.

The rope immediately slid against his crotch, the friction creating a painful burn even through the windproof pants. Now he remembered why he hated the *dulfersitz*. Using his right hand as a brake, he descended slowly, leaning back, his feet against the cliff, groping for footholds, maneuvering downward, playing the rope. In what seemed like seconds, he spotted his target: a small, dark ellipse. The mouth of the cave. Moving his feet down a few more meters, he came to the opening, and swung his feet inward.

This wasn't going to be as easy as he'd hoped. It wasn't a matter of simply dropping into the cave mouth; it was more complicated than that. The opening was flush with the sheer cliff face.

"Move *in* a little!" Neumann shouted. "Move *in!*"

Ben saw at once what he meant. There was a narrow inset ledge on which he would have to land.

There was very little room for error. The ledge was no more than two feet wide. Neumann was crouched on it, gripping a handhold in the rock.

As Ben moved his body forward, into the cave, he began to sway backward and forward as well. He felt unstable, and he forced himself to hang until the swaying slowed.

Finally he played out the rope, braking with his right hand, swaying into the cave and then out again. Finally, when he was both forward just enough and far enough down, he dropped to the ledge, cushioning the impact by bending his knees.

"Good!" Neumann shouted.

Still gripping the rope, Ben leaned forward into the darkness of the cave and peered down. Enough sunlight streamed in at an oblique angle to illuminate the peril just below.

The first hundred or so feet of the entrance to the cave, a steep downhill slant, was thickly coated with ice. Worse, it was watered ice, slick and treacherous. It was like nothing he had ever seen before.

"Well," Neumann called to him after a few seconds, sensing Ben's reluctance. "We can't stand here on this ledge all day, hmm?"

Experience or no, negotiating that long icy slope was unnerving to contemplate. "Let's go," Ben said with all the enthusiasm he could muster.

They donned their lightweight helmets and Velcro-strapped them into place, then their headlamps. Neumann handed Ben a couple of high-tech carbon-fiber ice axes with curved picks. One axe looped over each wrist by means of a leash. They dangled from Ben's hands like useless appendages.

With a nod, Neumann turned his back to the cave mouth, and Ben followed suit, his stomach fluttering. Each took one backward step, and they were off the narrow ledge, their crampons crunching into the ice. The first few steps were awkward. Ben tried to maintain his balance, driving his crampons deep into the ice, steadying himself until he had backed down far enough to grab the ice axes in each hand and chop into the glossy surface. He saw Neumann scrambling down the steep slope as if he were walking down a staircase. The old man was a goat.

Ben continued unsteadily, spider-crawling down, stomach to the ice, leaning his body weight on the wrist loops of the axes. The crunch of a boot, the chop of the ice axe, then again, and again, and by the time he had begun to achieve some sort of rhythm, he had reached the bottom, where the ice had given way to limestone.

Neumann turned, slipped off his ice axes and crampons, and began to negotiate the gentler downward slope. Ben followed close behind.

The descent was gradual, a spiral staircase through rock, and as they went the beam of Ben's headlamp illuminated any number of passages that diverged to either side of them, branches he might easily have taken were it not for Neumann. There were no slashes of red paint here, nothing to separate the right path from the many wrong ones. Fritz Neumann was obviously navigating from memory.

The air felt warmer than it had outside, but Ben knew this was deceptive. There was permanent ice on the walls of the cave, which indicated the temperature was below freezing, and the water that ran underfoot would soon make it feel even colder. It was also extremely humid.

The floor of the cave was strewn with rubble and coursed with running water. Here and there, Ben almost lost his footing as the debris on the cave floor shifted. Soon the passage broadened into a gallery, and Neumann stopped for a moment, turning his head slowly, his helmet lamp illuminating the breathtaking formations. Some of the stalactites were fragile soda straws, slender and delicate, tapering to points as sharp as knitting needles; too, there were the banded calcite stumps of stalagmites, the occasional column formed by the meeting of a stalactite and a stalagmite. Water oozed down the walls and seeped down the stalactites, the steady drip-drip-dripping into water on the cave floor the only noise in the eerie silence. Hardened flowstone formed terraces, and translucent sheets of calcite hung down from the ceiling like drapery, their edges serrated and sharp. Everywhere was the acrid ammonia stench of bat guano.

"Ah, look!" Neumann said, and Ben turned to see the

perfectly preserved skeleton of a bear. There arose a sudden papery thunder of hundreds of batwings; a cluster of hibernating bats had been awakened by their approach.

Now Ben began to feel the chill. Somehow, for all his precautions, water had seeped into his boots, dampening his socks.

"Come," Neumann said, "this way."

He led them into a narrow passage, one of several corridors off the gallery barely distinguishable from the others. The ground gradually rose up before them, the walls growing closer together, almost to a bottleneck. The ceiling was barely head-high; had Ben been any taller than his six feet, he would have had to stoop. The walls here were icy, the seep water at their feet frigid.

Ben's toes had begun to go numb. But lithe Neumann scrambled up the steep crevice with astonishing ease, and Ben followed more gingerly, stepping over the jagged rocks, knowing that if he lost his footing here, the tumble would be nasty.

Finally the ground seemed to level off. "We're about on the same level as the *Schloss* now," Neumann said.

Then without warning the narrow passage came to a dead end. They stopped at what appeared to be a blank wall, in front of which was a pile of rubble, evidently the remains of a long-ago cave-in.

"Jesus," Ben said. "Are we lost?"

Without a word, Neumann scraped some of the rubble aside with his boot, exposing a rusty iron rod about four feet long, which he hoisted with a flourish.

"It's undisturbed," Neumann said. "This is good for you. It has not been used for many years. They have not discovered it."

"What are you talking about?"

Neumann took the iron rod, wedged it underneath a boulder, and leaned his weight on it until the rock began to dislodge, revealing a small irregular passageway no more than two feet high and three or four feet wide.

"During the war we'd move this rock back and forth to

hide the final passage." He pointed out grooves in the rock scored, Ben assumed, decades earlier. "Now you're on your own. I'll leave you here. This is a very narrow crawlway, and very low, but you can get through it, I believe."

Ben leaned closer and examined it with horrified fascination. He felt a wave of panic.

This is a goddamned coffin. I don't think I can do it.

"You'll travel about, oh, maybe two hundred meters. It's most of the way level, but then it goes uphill at the very end. Unless it's caved in since I was here as a boy, you'll come to a keyhole slot opening."

"It opens right into the *Schloss*?"

"No, of course not. The entrance is gated. Maybe even locked. Probably so."

"*Now* you tell me."

Neumann drew a rusty-looking skeleton key from a pocket of his old green parka. "I can't tell you for sure if this will work, but the last time I tried it, it did."

"The last time being fifty years ago?"

"More than that," Neumann admitted. He extended his hand. "Now I say good bye," he said solemnly "I wish you much luck."

CHAPTER FORTY-FOUR

It was a formidably tight squeeze. It must have taken real courage and determination for the Resistance fighters to make this final approach to the *Schloss*, and do it repeatedly, Ben thought. No wonder they had made use of a boy like the young Fritz Neumann, who could slip through this space easily.

Ben had wriggled through crawl holes like this before, in the caves of White Sulphur Springs, but never for more than a few feet before they broadened out. This, however, appeared to be hundreds of yards long.

Only now did he fully understand what veteran cavers meant when they insisted that their subterranean pursuit allowed them to face down primordial terrors—the fear of darkness, of falling into the void, of being trapped in a maze, of being buried alive.

But there was no choice, certainly not now. He thought only of Anna and summoned up the will.

He entered the hole, headfirst, feeling a cold rush of air. At its opening, the passage was about two feet high, which meant that the only way to move through it was to slither on his stomach like an earthworm.

He removed his pack and pushed off with his feet, pulling with his arms, nudging his pack ahead of him. There was an inch or two of frigid water on the tunnel floor. Quickly his pants became soaked through. The tunnel angled sharply one way, then another, forcing him to contort his body.

Then, at last, the passageway began to widen, its ceiling rising to four feet, enabling him to lift his numbed belly out of the ice water, get to his feet, and stoop-walk.

It was not long, though, before his back began to ache, and rather than continue he stopped for a moment and set down the pack, resting his hands on his thighs.

When he was able to go farther, he noticed that the ceiling was lowering again, back to two, maybe three feet high. He got onto his hands and knees and began scuttling along like a crab.

But not for long. The rocky floor bruised his kneecaps. He attempted to ease the stress by putting his weight on his elbows and toes instead. When he wearied of that, he continued crawling. The ceiling became lower still, and he turned onto his side, pushing with his feet and pulling with his arms along the winding tunnel.

Now the ceiling height had diminished to no more than eighteen inches, scraping against his back, and he had to stop for a moment to suppress a wave of panic. He was back to belly-crawling again, only this time there was no end in sight. His headlamp shone a beam for twenty feet or so, but the coffin-sized, even coffin-shaped tunnel seemed to go on and on. The walls seemed to narrow.

Through the scrim of his fear, he observed that the passage appeared to be winding slowly uphill, that water no longer pooled on the floor, though it was still damp, and that, horribly, rock was now scraping against both his stomach and his back.

He continued pushing his pack ahead of him. The tunnel was now barely twelve inches high.

Ben was trapped.

No, not trapped, not yet, exactly, but it certainly felt that way. Terror overwhelmed him. He had to *squeeze* himself through. His heart raced, his body flooded with fear, and he had to stop.

The worst thing, he knew, was to panic. Panic caused you to freeze up, lose flexibility. He breathed slowly in and out a few times, then exhaled completely to reduce his chest diameter so he could fit through the passage.

Sweating and clammy, he forced himself to squirm ahead, trying to focus on where he was going and why, how crucial it was. He thought ahead, to what he would do once he got into the *Schloss*.

The uphill slope was becoming steeper. He inhaled and felt the walls press in on his chest, keeping him from filling his lungs with air. This prompted a surge of adrenaline, which made his breathing fast and shallow, made him feel as if he were about to suffocate, and he had to stop once again.

Don't think.

Relax.

No one else knew he was down here. He would be buried alive here in this pitch-black hell where there was no day or night.

Ben found himself listening to this voice with skepticism, as his braver, better self now assumed command of his brain. He began to feel his heart slow, felt the delicious cold air hit the bottom of his lungs, felt calm spread through his body like ink on a blotter.

Steadily now, with an inner serenity, he urged his body along, earthwormed, wriggled, ignoring the chafing of his back.

Suddenly the ceiling soared upward and the walls widened, and he got to his aching hands and knees and crawled up the incline. He had arrived at a sort of twilit grotto, where he was able to stand fully, blessedly, upright.

He was aware of the faintest glimmering of light.

It was a very dim and distant light, but to him it seemed almost as bright as day, as joy-inspiring as sunrise.

Directly ahead of him was the cave exit, and it was indeed shaped a little like a keyhole. He scrambled up a scree pile, then sort of half-mantled himself into the lip of the opening, pushing down with both hands until he could support his body on rigid arms.

There he saw the close-set rusted iron bars of an ancient gate that was fitted into the irregular cave mouth as tightly as a manhole cover. He could not make out what lay behind the gate but he could see an oblong shaft of light, as if from under a door.

He drew out the skeleton key Neumann had given him, inserted it into the lock, and turned it.

Tried to turn it.

But it would not turn. The key would not *move*.

The lock was rusted shut. That had to be it; the old lock hadn't been replaced, at least not for decades. The entire thing, he saw, was one solid mass of rust. He wriggled the key back and forth again, but it would not turn.

"Oh, my God," Ben said out loud.

He was done for.

This was the one thing neither he nor Neumann had anticipated.

He could see no other way in. Even if he had the tools, there was no way to dig around the gate; it was embedded in solid rock. Would he now have to somehow climb back *out?*

Or maybe . . . Maybe one of the bars was so rusted through that he could push it out. He tried that, banging his gloved fist against the iron bars until the pain was too great, but no: the gate was solid. The rust was only on the surface.

In desperation, he grabbed the bars and rattled them, like an enraged lifer in San Quentin, and suddenly there was a metallic clatter.

One of the hinges had broken off.

He rattled again, harder, until another hinge popped off.

He kept rattling, exuberantly, and finally the third and last hinge fell to the ground.

He grabbed the gate with both hands, lifted it up and pushed it forward, and gently lowered it to the ground.

He was inside.

CHAPTER FORTY-FIVE

Ben felt something hard and smooth and dusty: it was a solid iron door, secured by a heavy latch. He lifted the latch and pushed at the door, and the door gave a brief high screech. Obviously it hadn't been opened in decades. He pushed with all his weight. With a moan, the door gave way.

He found himself in a larger space of some sort, though it was still small. His eyes, used to the dark, began to discern shapes, and he followed the narrow shaft of light to another door, where he felt around on either side for a light switch.

He found the switch, and a light came on from a single bulb mounted on the ceiling.

He was, he could see, in a small storage closet. The stone walls were lined with steel shelves painted an indeterminate beige, holding old cardboard boxes, wooden crates, and cylindrical metal tanks.

He removed his helmet and woolen cap, then the pack from his back, from which he took both of the semiautomatic pistols, placing everything but the weapons on one of the shelves. He slipped one of the weapons under the waistband of his heavy pants, at the small of his back. The other he held while he studied the photocopied floor plan. No doubt the place had been restored since its clock factory days, but it was unlikely that the basic plan had been much changed, or that the massive walls had been moved.

He tried the doorknob. It turned easily, and the door opened.

He emerged into a brightly lit corridor with stone floors and vaulted ceilings. There was no one in view.

Arbitrarily, he turned right. The Vibram soles of his mountaineering boots muffled his footsteps. Except for the slight squish of wet leather, his walk was silent.

He had not gone far before someone appeared at the end of the hall, striding directly toward him.

Keep calm, he told himself. *Act as if you belong.*

This was not easy, dressed as he was in his wet, mud-crusted climbing attire and heavy boots, his face still bruised and scratched from the incident in Buenos Aires.

Quickly, now.

On his left was a door. He stopped, listened for a moment, and then opened it, hoping what lay beyond was unoccupied.

As he ducked into the room, the figure passed by, a man dressed in a white tunic or jumpsuit. A handgun was holstered at his waist. Obviously a guard.

The room was perhaps twenty feet long and fifteen feet wide. By the light from the corridor he could see that this was another storeroom, also lined with metal shelves. He located a switch and turned on the light.

What he saw was too horrific to be real, and for a moment he was sure his eyes had been deceived by some sort of nightmarish optical illusion.

But it was no illusion.

God in heaven, he thought. *This can't be.*

He could barely stand to look, yet he couldn't turn his eyes away.

On the shelves were rows of dusty glass bottles, some

as small as the Mason canning jars Mrs. Walsh used to
preserve fruit in, some two feet tall.

Each bottle held a fluid of some kind, which Ben assumed to be a preservative such as formalin, slightly cloudy
with age and impurities.

And floating in them, like pickles in brine, one to a
bottle . . .

No, this could not be.

He felt his skin erupt in gooseflesh.

In each bottle was a human baby.

The bottles were arrayed with ghastly precision.

In the smallest were tiny embryos, at the earliest stage
of gestation, little pale pink prawns, translucent insects with
grotesque large heads and tails.

Then fetuses not much longer than an inch: hunched,
stubby arms and oversized heads, suspended in the shrouds
of their amniotic sacs.

Fetuses not much bigger but looking more human, bent
legs and waving arms, eyes like black currants, floating in
perfectly round sacs surrounded by the ragged halo of the
chorionic sac.

Miniature infants, eyes closed, sucking thumbs, a tangle
of tiny perfectly formed limbs.

As the bottles increased in size so did their contents,
until in the largest bottles floated full-term babies, ready to
be born, eyes closed, arms and legs splayed, little hands
waving or clenched, severed umbilical cords floating loose,
swathed in translucent wisps of amniotic sac.

There must have been a hundred embryos and fetuses
and babies.

Each bottle was labeled in German, in neat calligraphy,
with a date (the date ripped from the womb?), prenatal age,
weight in grams, size in centimeters.

The dates ranged from 1940 to 1954.

*Gerhard Lenz had done experiments on human babies
and children.*

It was worse than he'd ever imagined. The man was

inhuman, a monster . . . *But why were these ghastly exhibits still here?*

It was all he could do not to scream.

He stumbled toward the door.

On the facing wall were glass tanks, from a foot to almost five feet tall and two feet around, and in them floated not fetuses but small children.

Small wizened children, from tiny newborns to toddlers to children seven or eight years old.

Children, he guessed, who had been afflicted with the premature-aging syndrome known as progeria.

The faces of little old men and women.

His skin prickled.

Children. Dead children.

He thought of the poor father of Christoph in his gloomy apartment.

My Christoph died happy.

A private sanatorium, the woman at the foundation had said.

Exclusive, private, very luxurious, she'd said.

He turned, lightheaded, to leave the room, and heard footsteps.

Carefully peering out of the doorway he saw another white-suited guard approaching, and he backed into the room, concealed himself behind the door.

As the guard passed, he cleared his throat loudly, and he heard the footsteps halt.

The guard, as Ben had expected, entered the room. Swift as a cobra, Ben lunged, slamming the butt of his revolver into the back of the guard's head. The man collapsed.

Ben shut the door behind him, placed his fingers on the guard's neck and felt for a pulse. Alive but unconscious, though undoubtedly for a good long while.

He removed the man's holster and pulled out the Walther PPK, then stripped off the white jumpsuit.

He removed his clammy clothes and donned the uniform. It was too large for him, but acceptable. Fortunately the shoes fit. With his thumb he flicked at the left of the

Walther's slide and removed the magazine. All eight brass cartridges were there.

Now he had three handguns, an arsenal. He checked the pockets of the guard's jumpsuit and found only a pack of cigarettes and a key-card, which he took.

Then he returned to the corridor, pausing only to make sure no one else was in sight. Farther down the hall he came on the brushed steel double-doors of a large elevator, modern for this ancient building. He pressed the call button.

A ping, and the doors opened immediately to reveal an interior lined with protective gray quilting. He entered, inspected the panel, and saw that a key-card had to be inserted before the elevator would move. He inserted the guard's card, then pressed the button for the first floor. The doors closed rapidly, the elevator jolted upward, and opened a few seconds later onto another world entirely.

It was a brightly lit, ultramodern-looking corridor that could have been in any prosperous corporate headquarters.

The floors were carpeted in neutral industrial gray, the walls not the ancient stone of the floor below but smooth white tile. A couple of men in white coats, doctors or clinicians perhaps, passed by. One was pushing a metal cart. The other glanced at Ben but seemed to look through him.

He strode purposefully down the hall. Two young Asian women, also in white jackets, stood by an open door to what appeared to be a laboratory, speaking a language Ben did not recognize. Absorbed in conversation, they paid no attention to him.

Now he entered a large atrium, well lit by a combination of soft incandescent light and amber late-afternoon sun that filtered in through cathedral windows. This looked like it was once the grand entrance hall of the *Schloss*, artfully converted to a modern lobby. A graceful stone staircase wound upstairs. There were a number of doors in the lobby. Each was marked, in black type on white placards, with a number and letter, each accessible only by inserting a card into a card-reader. Each door probably led to a corridor.

A dozen or so people were passing through, to and from

the hallways, up or down the stairs, to the bank of elevators. Most wore lab coats, loose-fitting white pants, white shoes or sneakers. Only the guards, in their jumpsuits, wore heavy-duty black shoes. A man in a white coat passed by the two Asian women and said something; the two women reversed course, back toward the laboratory. Obviously the man was someone senior, someone in charge.

Two orderlies carried a stretcher across the lobby, on which an old man in a pale blue hospital gown lay still.

Another patient in a hospital johnny came through the lobby, moving from corridor 3A to corridor 2B. This was a vigorous-looking young-middle-aged man of around fifty who hobbled as if he were in great pain.

What the hell was all this?

If Anna was indeed here, where was she?

This clinic was far larger, far busier, than he had imagined. Whatever they were doing—whatever the purpose was of those nightmarish specimens in the basement, if indeed they had any bearing on the work being done here—there were a lot of people involved, both patients and doctors or laboratory researchers.

She's in here somewhere, I know she is.

But is she safe? Alive? If she'd discovered whatever horrible thing was being done here, would they have *let* her live?

Must go. Must *move it*.

He walked through the atrium hurriedly, his face stern, a security guard dispatched to check out a disturbance. He stopped at the entrance to corridor 3B and inserted his key-card, hoping it gave him access to this area.

The door lock clicked. He entered a long white corridor that could have been in any hospital anywhere.

Among the many people passing by was a white-uniformed woman, presumably a nurse, who appeared to be walking a small child on a leash.

It was as if she were walking a large, obedient dog.

Ben looked at the child more closely and realized from the papery skin, the wrinkled and wizened face, that this was a little boy afflicted with progeria, looking very much like the child in the photographs in the father's apartment he had so recently visited. He also looked like the full-grown children, preserved in formaldehyde, in that night-marish basement room.

The boy walked like an old man, his gait wide-legged and rickety.

Ben's fascination cooled to an icy anger.

The boy stopped in front of a door and waited patiently while the woman holding the leash unlocked the door with a key on a loop around her neck. The door led into a large glassed-in area fully visible from the hall.

The long room behind the plate glass could have been a hospital nursery, except that everyone inside was a pro-geric. There were seven or eight little wizened children here. At first glance, Ben thought they were on leashes, too; on closer inspection, he saw that each was connected to some sort of clear plastic tube coming from his or her back. The tubes were connected to shiny metal columns. It ap-peared that each child was being kept on an intravenous drip through the tubing. They had no eyebrows or eye-lashes, their heads were small and shriveled, their skin cre-pey. The few who were walking shuffled like old men.

Some squatted on the floor, quietly absorbed in games or puzzles. Two of them were playing together, their tubes entangled. A little girl with a long blond wig wandered aimlessly about the floor, chanting or talking to herself, her words inaudible.

The Lenz Foundation.

A few selected progeric children were invited each year to the clinic.

No visitors were allowed.

This was no summer camp, no retreat. The children were being treated like animals. They were, they *had* to be, hu-man subjects in some sort of experiment.

Children in the basement pickled in formaldehyde. Chil-dren being treated like dogs.

A private sanatorium.

This was neither a sanatorium nor, he was sure, a clinic.

Then what was it? What kind of "science" was being done here?

Nauseated, he turned and continued down the hall until it came to an end. To his left was a red door, locked, accessible only by key-card. Unlike most of the other hallway doors he'd seen here, this door had no window.

The door was unmarked. He knew he had to find out what lay behind it.

Ben inserted the guard's key-card, but this time it did nothing. Apparently this door required a different level of access.

Just as he turned away, the door came open.

A man in a white coat emerged, clutching a clipboard, a stethoscope dangling out of one pocket. A doctor. The man glanced incuriously at Ben, nodded, and held the door open for him. Ben passed through the doorway.

He was not prepared for what he saw.

He was in a high-ceilinged room as big as a basketball court. The vaulted stone ceiling and leaded stained-glass cathedral windows appeared to be all that remained of the original architecture. The floor plan indicated that this enormous chamber had originally been a grand private chapel as big as a church. Ben wondered whether it had later been used as the main factory floor. He estimated it was more than a hundred feet long, maybe a hundred feet wide, the ceilings easily thirty feet high.

Now it was clearly an immense medical facility. Yet at the same time it looked almost like a health club, at once well equipped and spartan.

In one area of the room was a line of hospital beds, each separated from the other by a curtain. Some of the beds were empty; on others, maybe five or six of them, patients lay supine, connected to some sort of monitor and IV stand.

In another area was a long row of black treadmills, each equipped with an EKG monitor. On a few of them elderly men and women were running in place, electrodes or probes sprouting from their arms and legs, necks and heads.

Here and there were nurses' stations, respirators, anesthesia equipment. A dozen or so doctors and nurses observed, assisted, or bustled about. All the way around the enormous room ran a catwalk, roughly twenty feet above the floor and ten feet from the ceiling.

Ben realized that he had been standing at the room's entrance for too long. In a guard's uniform, he had to act as if he were on assignment. So he walked, slowly and purposefully, into the room, checking one side and then another.

Sitting in a modern black-leather-and-steel chair was an old man. A plastic tube was attached to one arm and connected to an IV stand. The man was speaking on a phone, a folder of papers in his lap. Obviously he was a patient, but he was clearly engaged in some kind of business.

In a few places the man's hair had the downy look of a newborn's. Around the sides the hair was coarser, denser, and more luxuriant, white or gray at the ends, but growing in black or dark brown.

And the man looked familiar. His face was often on the cover of *Forbes* or *Fortune*, Ben thought. A businessman or investor, someone famous.

Yes! It had to be Ross Cameron, the so-called "sage of Santa Fe." One of the richest men in the world.

Ross Cameron. There was no question about it now.

Seated next to him was a much younger man whom Ben recognized right away. This was unquestionably Arnold Carr, the fortyish software billionaire and founder of Technocorp. Cameron and Carr were known to be friends; Cameron was sort of Carr's mentor or guru, kind of a father-son relationship. Carr, too, was hooked up to an IV; he also was speaking on the phone, obviously conducting business, though without any papers.

Two legendary billionaires, sitting side by side like a couple of guys in a barbershop.

In a "clinic" in the Austrian Alps.

Being infused with some kind of fluid.

Were they being studied? Treated for something? Something bizarre was taking place here, something secret and important enough to require fully armed security, important enough to kill people over.

A third man walked over to Cameron, said a few words in greeting. Ben recognized the chairman of the Federal Reserve, now in his seventh decade and among the most revered figures in Washington.

Nearby, a nurse adjusted a blood pressure cuff on—well, it had to be Sir Edward Downey, but he looked the way he had when he was England's Prime Minister, three decades ago.

Ben kept walking until he reached the treadmills, where a man and a woman were running next to each other, talking, out of breath. They each wore gray sweatpants and sweatshirts and white running shoes, and both had electrodes taped to their foreheads, the backs of their heads and necks, their arms and legs. The threadlike wires coming out of the electrodes rose neatly behind each of them, out of the way, connected to Siemens monitors that seemed to be recording their heart rates.

Ben recognized both of them, too.

The man was Dr. Walter Reisinger, the Yale professor turned Secretary of State. In person, Reisinger looked healthier than he seemed on TV or in photographs. His skin glowed, though that might have been a result of the running, and his hair seemed darker, though it was probably dyed.

The woman he was talking to on the next treadmill resembled Supreme Court Justice Miriam Bateman. But Justice Bateman was known to be nearly crippled with arthritis. During State of the Union addresses, when the Supreme Court filed in, Justice Bateman was always the slowest, walking with a cane.

This woman—*this* Justice Bateman—was running like an Olympic athlete in training.

Were these people look-alikes of famous world figures?

Ben wondered. Doubles? Yet that wouldn't explain the infusions, the training.

Something else.

He heard the Dr. Reisinger clone voice saying something to the Justice Bateman clone about "the Court's decision."

This *was* no clone. This had to be Justice Miriam Bateman.

So then what *was* this place? Was this some sort of health spa for the rich and famous?

Ben had heard of such places, in Arizona or New Mexico or California, sometimes Switzerland or France. Places where the elite went to recover from plastic surgery, from alcoholism or drug dependency, to lose ten or twenty pounds.

But this—?

The electrodes, the IV tubes, the EKG screens . . . ?

These famous people—all, except Arnold Carr, old—were being closely monitored, but what for?

Ben came upon a row of StairMasters, on one of which an ancient man was moving up and down at top speed, just as Ben regularly did at his health club. This man, too—no one Ben recognized—was clad in gray sweats. The front of his sweatshirt was darkened with sweat.

Ben knew young athletes in their twenties who couldn't sustain such a grueling pace for more than a few minutes. How in the world was this old man, with his wrinkled face and liver-spotted hands, able to do it?

"He's ninety-six years old," a man's voice boomed. "Remarkable, isn't it?"

Ben looked around, then up. The person speaking was standing on the catwalk, just above Ben.

It was Jürgen Lenz.

CHAPTER FORTY-SIX

A soft, low chime filled the air, melodic and sedate. Jürgen Lenz, resplendent in a charcoal suit, blue shirt, and silver tie, under a neatly pressed white doctor's coat, strolled down wrought-iron stairs to the main floor. He glanced over at the treadmills and StairMasters. The Supreme Court Justice and the former Secretary of State and most of the others were beginning to finish their exercise sessions, dismount from the machines, nurses removing the wires from their bodies.

"That's the signal for the next helicopter shuttle to Vienna," he explained to Ben. "Time to return to the International Children's Health Forum they were so kind as to depart. Needless to say, they're busy people despite their age. In fact, I'd say *because* of their age. They all have much to give the world—which is why I've selected them."

He made a subtle hand gesture. Both of Ben's arms were suddenly grabbed from behind. Two guards held him while another expertly frisked him, removing all three weapons.

Lenz waited impatiently as the weapons were confiscated, like a dinner-table raconteur whose tale has been interrupted by the serving of the salad course.

"What have you done with Anna?" Ben asked, his voice steely.

"I was about to ask you the very same thing," Lenz replied. "She insisted on inspecting the clinic, and of course I couldn't refuse. But somehow, along the way, we lost her. Apparently she knows something about evading security systems."

Ben studied Lenz, trying to determine how much of this was truth. Was that his way of stalling, of refusing to bring him to her? Was he negotiating? Ben felt a surge of panic.

Is he lying? Fabricating a story he knows that I'll believe, that I'll want to believe?

Have you killed her, you lying bastard?

Then again, that Anna might have disappeared to investigate what was happening in the clinic was plausible. Ben said, "Let me warn you right now, if anything happens to her—"

"But nothing will, Benjamin. Nothing will." Lenz put his hands in his pockets, head bowed. "We are in a clinic, after all, that is devoted to life."

"I'm afraid I've already seen too much to believe that."

"How much do you really *understand* of whatever you've seen?" Lenz said. "I'm sure that once you truly grasp the work we're doing, you'll appreciate its importance." He motioned for the guards to let Ben go. "This is the culmination of a lifetime's work."

Ben said nothing. Escaping was out of the question. But in fact he wanted to remain here.

You killed my brother.

And Anna? Have you killed her, too?

He became aware that Lenz was speaking. "It was Adolf Hitler's great obsession, you know. The Thousand-Year Reich, and all that nonsense—though it lasted, what, twelve years? He had a theory that the bloodlines of the Aryans had been polluted, adulterated, because of interbreeding. Once the so-called 'master race' was purified it would be extremely long-lived. Rubbish, of course. But I'll give the old madman credit. He was determined to discover how he and the Reich's leaders could live longer, and so he gave a handful of his brightest scientists free rein. Unlimited funds. Do your experiments on concentration-camp prisoners. Whatever you like."

"Made possible by the generous sponsorship of the greatest monster of the twentieth century," Ben said, biting off his words.

"A mad despot, let us agree. And his talk of a thousand-year Reich was laughable—a deeply unstable man, promising an epoch of lasting stability. But his pairing of the two desiderata—longevity and stability—was *not* ill-founded."

"I'm not following."

"We human beings are singularly ill-designed in one respect. Of all the species on the planet, we require the longest period of gestation and childhood—of development. And really, we must think about intellectual as well as physical development. Two decades for complete physical maturation, often another decade or more to attain full professional mastery in our area of specialization. Somebody with a highly involved craft, such as a surgeon, may be well into his fourth decade before he has achieved full competence at his vocation. The process of learning and progressive mastery continues—and then, just as he reaches its height, what happens? His eyes begin to dim, his fingers to lose their precision. The depredations of time begin to rob him of what he spent half a lifetime acquiring. It's like a bad joke. We're Sisyphus, knowing as soon as we have rolled the boulder toward the top of the hill, it will start hurtling back down. I'm told you once taught schoolchildren. Think how much of human society is devoted simply to reproducing itself—transmitting its institutions, its knowledge and skills, the struts and gearings of civilization. It's an extraordinary tribute to our determination to win out over time. And yet how much farther would our species have been able to advance if only its leadership, political and intellectual, had been able to focus on advancement, rather than simply self-replacement! How much farther we'd all be if some of us were able to stay the course, mount the learning curve and stay there! How much farther we'd be if the best and the brightest of us could keep that boulder rolling uphill, rather than fending off the nursing home or the grave by the time the crest came into view!"

A doleful smile. "Gerhard Lenz, whatever we think of him, was a brilliant man," Lenz went on. Ben made a mental note: was Jürgen Lenz really Gerhard's son? "Most of his theories never amounted to anything. But he was convinced that the secret to how and why human beings age was in our cells. And this was even before Watson and Crick discovered the structure of DNA, all the way back in 1953! A remarkable man, really. So farsighted in so many ways. He knew the Nazis would lose, and Hitler would be gone, and the funds would dry up. He simply wanted to make sure his work would continue. Do you know why that was important, Benjamin? May I call you Benjamin?"

But Ben was transfixed, looking around the cavernous laboratory in stupefaction, and did not answer.

Because he was there and not there.

He was entwined with Anna, their bodies slick and warm. He was watching her cry after he'd told her about Peter.

He was sitting in a rural Swiss inn with Peter; he was standing over Peter's blood-soaked body.

"An extraordinary undertaking required extraordinary resources. Hitler prattled about stability while contributing to its destruction, and so it went with other tyrants in other parts of the world. But Sigma really could contribute to the pacification of the planet. Its founders knew what was necessary. They were devoted to a single creed: rationality. The remarkable advances we'd seen over the past century in technology had to be matched with advances in the management of our race—the *human* race. Science and politics could no longer be relegated to separate dominions."

Gradually Ben focused. "You're not making sense. Technology proved an *aid* to the madness. Totalitarianism depended on mass communication. And scientists helped make the Holocaust possible."

"All the more reason why Sigma was necessary—as a bulwark against that sort of madness. You can understand that, can't you? A single madman had driven Europe to the brink of anarchy. On the other side of a great land mass, a small band of agitators had turned an empire secured by Peter the Great into a seething cauldron. The insanity of the mob amplified the insanity of the individual. That's what the century had taught us. The future of Western civilization was too important to rest in the hands of the mobs. The aftermath of the war had left a vacuum, a powerful one. Civil society was everywhere in disarray. It fell upon a small group of powerful, well-organized men to impose order. Indirect rule. The levers of power were to be manipulated, even as that manipulation would be carefully camouflaged by the official instrumentalities of governance. Enlightened leadership was necessary—leadership behind the scenes."

"And what was to guarantee that the leadership was going to be enlightened?"

"I told you. Lenz was a farsighted man, and so were the industrialists he allied with. Again, it comes down to the marriage of science and politics: one would have to heal and strengthen the other."

Ben shook his head. "That's something else that doesn't make sense. These businessmen were folk heroes, many of them. Why would they agree to consort with the likes of Strasser or Gerhard Lenz?"

"Yes, this was an extremely inclusive group. But perhaps you forget your own father's indispensable role."

"A Jew."

"Doubly indispensable, one could say. Substantial sums were transferred out of the Third Reich, and to do so without detection was a challenge of mind-numbing complexity. Your father, who was quite a wizard in such financial matters, rose to the challenge. But, equally, the fact that he was Jewish was exceedingly helpful in reassuring our counterparts in Allied nations. It helped establish the fact that this wasn't about furthering the Führer's insanity. This was about business. And about betterment."

Ben gave him a frankly skeptical look. "You still haven't explained Gerhard Lenz's special appeal to these businessmen."

"Lenz had something to offer them. Or, at that point, I should say that he had something to *promise*. The word had spread among the moguls that Lenz had made some extremely suggestive scientific breakthroughs in an area of direct personal interest to all of them. Based on some preliminary successes, Lenz had, at the time, thought he was nearer than he in fact was. He was flush with excitement, and the excitement was infectious. As things turned out, the founders didn't survive to benefit from his researches. But all of them deserve credit for making it possible. Billions of dollars invisibly went to support the research—a level of support that made the Manhattan Project look like a high school lab class. But now we touch on matters that may lie beyond your grasp."

"Try me."

"No doubt your inquiries are purely disinterested, yes?" Lenz said dryly. "Like Ms. Navarro's."

"What have you done with her?" Ben asked again, turning toward Lenz as if coming out of a stupor. He was beyond anger now. He was in another, calmer place. He was thinking about killing Jürgen Lenz, realizing with peculiar satisfaction that he did in fact have it in him to kill another person.

And he was thinking about how he would find Anna. *I'll listen to you, you bastard. I'll be civil and obedient and I'll let you talk until you take me to her.*

And then I'll kill you.

Lenz looked at him, unblinking, and then continued his explanation. "I expect you've figured out the basic scenario. Quite simply, what his work promised was the opportunity to explore the limits of mortality. A man lives for a hundred years if he's lucky. Mice only get two years. Galápagos tortoises can live *two hundred* years. Now, why in the world is that? Has nature dictated these arbitrary limits?"

Lenz had begun pacing slowly back and forth in front of Ben, his guards standing watch. "Even though my father was forced to move to South America, he continued to direct his research institute here long-distance. Traveled back and forth several times a year. In the late fifties one of his scientists made an intriguing discovery—that every time a human cell divides, its chromosomes, those tiny spindles of DNA, become shorter! Microscopically shorter, yes, but still, measurably so. So what *was* it, exactly, that was getting shorter? It took years to discover the answer." He smiled again. "Father was right. The secret really was in our cells."

"The chromosomes," Ben said. He was beginning to understand.

Father was right.

He had an idea now where Max had gone.

"Just one tiny part of the chromosomes, really. The very tip of them—looks a little like those plastic tips at the end of shoelaces. Way back in 1938 those little caps had been discovered, named 'telomeres.' Our team found that every time a cell divides, those little caps get shorter and shorter, until the cell starts to die. Our hair falls out. Our bones get brittle. Our spines curve. Our skin wrinkles and sags. We get old."

"I saw what you're doing to those children," Ben said. "The progerics. I take it you're experimenting on them." *And who else are you experimenting on?* "The world believes you invite them in for a vacation. Some vacation." No, he chided himself, must remain calm. He struggled to control his rage, keep from showing it.

Listen to him. Lead him on.

"True, it's no vacation for them," Lenz agreed. "But these poor children do not need vacations. They need a cure! It's really fascinating, you know, these little young-old people. They're *born* old. If you took a cell from a newborn progeric child and put it side by side, under a microscope, with one from a ninety-year-old man—why, even a molecular biologist couldn't tell the difference! In a progeric, those little tips start out short. Short telomeres, short lives."

"What are you *doing* to them?" Ben asked. He realized his jaw ached from clenching it so hard so long. A mental image flashed of the progeric children in the bottles.

Dr. Reisinger and Justice Miriam Bateman, Arnold Carr, and the others were straggling out of the room, conversing.

"Those little shoelace tips, they're like tiny odometers. Or timing devices, say. We have a hundred trillion cells in our bodies, and each cell has ninety-two telomeres—that makes ten *quadrillion* little clocks telling our body when it's time to shut down. We're *preprogrammed* to die!" Lenz seemed unable to contain his excitement. "But what if we could somehow reset the clocks, hmm? Keep them from getting shorter? Ah, that was the trick. Well, it turns out that some cells—certain brain cells, for instance—make a chemical, an enzyme, that fixes up their little telomeres, rebuilds them. All of our cells have the ability to make it, but for some reason they don't—it's just switched off most of the time. So . . . what if *we* could turn that switch on? Keep those little clocks ticking? So elegant, so simple. But I'd be lying to you if I said this was easy to do. Even with all the money in the world, and some of the world's most brilliant scientists to choose from, it still took decades, and a number of scientific advances, like gene splicing."

This was what the killings were about, wasn't it?

A neat little irony, Ben thought. People die so that others can live far beyond their natural life span.

Keep him talking, explaining. Bury the rage. Keep sight of the goal.

"When did you make your breakthrough?" Ben asked.

"Around fifteen, twenty years ago."

"And why hasn't anybody else caught up with you?"

"Others are working in the field, of course. But we've got an advantage they lack."

"Unlimited funding." Credit Max Hartman, he thought.

"That helps, certainly. And the fact that we've been working on it pretty much nonstop since the forties. But that's not the whole story. The big difference is human experimentation. Every 'civilized' country in the world has outlawed it. But how much can you really learn from rats or fruit flies, for God's sake? We made our earliest advances by experimenting on children with progeria, a condition that doesn't exist elsewhere in the animal world. And we still use progerics, as we continue to refine our understanding of the molecular pathways involved. One day we won't need them anymore. But we still have so much to learn."

"Human experimentation," Ben said, scarcely concealing his revulsion. There was no difference between Jürgen Lenz and Gerhard Lenz. To them, human beings—sick children, refugees, camp inmates—were nothing more than lab rats. "Like those refugee children in their tents, fenced in out there," Ben said. "Maybe you brought them in under the guise of 'humanitarianism.' But they're expendable too, aren't they?" He recalled words that Georges Chardin had spoken to him, and he said them aloud: "The slaughter of the innocents."

Lenz bristled. "That's what some of the *angeli rebelli* called it, but it's a rather inflammatory description," he said. "As such, it only impedes rational deliberation. Yes, some must die that others may live. A disquieting idea, no doubt. But put away the veil of sentimentality for one moment and face the brutal truth. These unfortunate children would otherwise be killed in war, or die from the diseases of poverty—and for what? Instead, they are *saviors*. They'll change the world. Is it more ethical to bomb their homes, let them be machine-gunned down, let them die senselessly, as the 'civilized world' permits? Or to give them the chance, instead, to alter the course of history? You see, the form of telomerase enzyme that our treatment requires is most readily isolated from the tissues of the central nervous system—the cells of the cerebrum and cerebellum. The quantities are far richer in the young. Unfortunately, it cannot be synthesized: it's a complex protein, and the shape, the conformation, of the protein is crucial. As with many such complex proteins, they cannot be produced by artificial means. And so . . . we must harvest it from human beings."

"The slaughter of the innocents," Ben repeated.

Lenz shrugged. "The sacrifice troubles you, but it has not unduly troubled the world at large."

"What do you mean?"

"You've no doubt heard the statistics—the fact that twenty thousand children disappear every year. People know, and they shrug. They've come to accept it. Perhaps it would provide a measure of consolation to know that these children haven't perished for no reason. It has taken us years to perfect our assays, techniques, dose levels. *There was no other way.* Nor will there be in the foreseeable future. We need the tissue. It must be human tissue, and it must be from juveniles. A seven-year-old's brain— a quart and a half of quivering jelly—is hardly smaller than a grown-up's, but its yield of telomerase enzymes is ten times as great. It is the greatest, most valuable natural resource on earth, yes? As your countrymen say, a terrible thing to waste."

"And so you 'disappear' them. Every year. Thousands and thousands of children."

"Typically from war-torn regions where their life expectancy would be paltry, anyway. This way, at least, they do not die in vain."

"No, they don't die in vain. They die for vanity. They die so that you and your friends can live forever, isn't that it?" *This is not a man you argue with*, Ben thought, but he was finding it increasingly difficult to contain his outrage.

Lenz scoffed, "Forever? Please, none of us will live forever. All we're doing is arresting the aging process in some cases, reversing it in others. The enzyme enables us to repair much of the damage to the skin, the integument. Reverse the damage caused by heart disease. As yet, this therapy can only occasionally restore us to the prime of our youth. And even to give someone my age his forty-year-old body back is time-consuming . . ."

"These people," Ben said, "they all come here to . . . to become younger."

"Only a few of them. Most of them are public figures who can't change their appearance drastically without attracting attention. So they come here, at my invitation, to *halt* their aging, maybe undo some of the damage that age has inflicted."

"Public figures?" Ben shot back mockingly. "They're all rich and powerful!" He was beginning to understand what Lenz was doing.

"No, Benjamin. They're the great ones. The leaders of our society, our culture. The few who advance our civilization. The founders of Sigma came to understand this. They saw that civilization was fragile, and that there was only one way to ensure the continuity that it required. The future of the industrial state had to be protected, sheltered from the storms. Our societies would only advance if we could push back the horizon of human mortality. Year by year, Sigma used whatever tools it had at its disposal, but now the original goals can be advanced by other, more effective means—good God, we're talking about something far more effective than throwing billions of dollars at coups and political action groups. We're talking about the formation of a stable, lasting elite."

"So these are the leaders of our civilizations . . ."

"Precisely."

"And you're the man who leads the leaders."

Lenz responded with a thin smile. "Please, Benjamin. I have no interest in boss-man theatrics. But in any organization, there must be a . . . coordinator."

"And there can only be one."

A pause. "Ultimately, yes."

"And what of those who oppose your 'enlightened' regime? I suppose they're purged from the body politic."

"A body *must* purge toxins if it is to survive, Benjamin." Lenz spoke with surprising gentleness.

"What you're describing isn't some utopia, Lenz. It's a slaughterhouse."

"Your reproach is as glib as it is vacuous," Lenz returned. "Life is a matter of trade-offs, Benjamin. You live in a world where vastly greater sums are spent on medications for erectile dysfunction than are spent on tropical diseases that claim the lives of millions every year. And what of your own *personal* decisions? When you buy a bottle of Dom Perignon, you have spent a sum of money that could have vaccinated a village in Bangladesh, spared lives from the ravages of disease, yes? People will *die*, Benjamin, as a result of the decisions, the priorities, entailed by your purchase. I'm quite serious: Can you deny that the ninety dollars a bottle of Dom Perignon costs could have easily saved half a dozen lives, perhaps more? Think about it. The bottle will yield seven or eight glasses of wine. Each glass, we can say, represents a life lost." His eyes were bright, a scientist having solved an equation and moved on to another one. "That is why I say that such trade-offs are inevitable. And once you understand that, you start to ask higher order questions: qualitative questions, not quantitative ones. Here we have the opportunity to vastly extend the useful life span of a great humanitarian or thinker—someone whose contribution to the commonweal is inarguable. Compared to this good, what is the life of a Serbian goatherd? Of an illiterate child who would have otherwise been destined to a life of poverty and petty criminality. Of a Gypsy girl who would otherwise spend her days picking the pockets of tourists visiting Florence, her nights picking lice out of her hair. You have been taught that lives are sacrosanct, and yet every day you make decisions signifying an awareness that some lives are more valuable than others. I *mourn* for those who have given their lives for the greater good. I truly do. I genuinely wish that the sacrifice they made was unnecessary. But I also know that every great achievement in the history of our species has come at the cost of human lives. 'There is no document of civilization that is not simultaneously a document of barbarism': a great thinker said that, a thinker who died too young."

Ben stood blinking, speechless.

"Come," Lenz said, "there's someone who wants to say hello to you. An old friend of yours."

Ben gaped. "Professor Godwin?"

"Ben."

It was his old college mentor, long since retired. But his posture seemed straighter, his once wrinkled skin was now smooth and pink. He looked younger by several *decades* than his eighty-two years. John Barnes Godwin, emeritus historian of Europe in the twentieth century, was vigorous. His handshake was firm.

"Good Lord," Ben said. If he hadn't known Godwin, he'd have put his age in the early fifties.

Godwin was one of the elect. Of course: he was a behind-the-scenes kingmaker, he was powerful and extremely well connected.

Godwin stood before him as mind-boggling proof of Lenz's achievement. They stood in a small antechamber off the great hall, which was comfortably furnished with couches and easy chairs, throw pillows and reading lamps, and racks of newspapers and magazines in a variety of languages.

Godwin seemed pleased at Ben's astonishment. Jürgen Lenz beamed.

"You must not know what to make of all this," Godwin said.

It took Ben a few seconds before he could think of a response. "That's one way of putting it."

"It's extraordinary, what Dr. Lenz has achieved. We're all deeply grateful to him. But I think we're also aware of the significance, the *gravity,* of his gift. In essence, we've been given our lives back. Not our youth so much as—as another chance. A reprieve from death." He frowned thoughtfully. "Is it against nature? Maybe. The way curing cancer is against nature. Emerson, remember, told us that old age is 'the only disease.' "

His eyes gleamed. Ben listened in stunned silence.

In college, Ben had always addressed him as Professor Godwin, but now he chose not to address him by name at all. He said simply, "Why?"

"Why? On a personal level? Do you have to ask? I've been given another lifetime. Perhaps even another *two* lifetimes."

"Will you gentlemen excuse me?" Lenz interrupted. "The first helicopter is about to leave, and I must say goodbye." He bustled, almost sprinted, out of the room.

"Ben, when you get to be my age, you don't buy green bananas," Godwin resumed. "You don't take on book projects you don't think you'll live to complete. But think of how much I can *do* now. Until Dr. Lenz called, I'd felt as if I'd struggled and worked and learned for decades to get where I am, to learn what I know, to gain the *understanding* I have—yet at any moment everything might be snatched away: 'If youth but knew, if old age but could,' right?"

"Even if all this is true—"

"You have *eyes*. You can see what's in front of you. Look at me, for God's sake! I used not to be able to climb the stairs at Firestone Library, and now I can *run*." Godwin, Ben realized, was not just a successful experiment, he was *one of them*—a conspirator with Lenz. Didn't he know about the cruelty, the murders?

"But have you *seen* what's going on here—the child refugees on the lawn? Thousands of abducted children? *That* doesn't bother you?"

Godwin looked visibly uncomfortable. "I'll admit there are aspects of all this that I prefer not to know about, and I've always made that clear."

"We're talking about the ongoing murder of thousands of children!" Ben said. "The treatment *requires* it. Lenz calls it 'harvesting,' a pretty word for systematic slaughter."

"It's . . ." Godwin faltered. "Well, it's morally complex. *'Honesta turpitudo est pro causa bona.'* "

" 'For a good cause, wrongdoing is virtuous,' " Ben translated. "Publilius Syrus. You taught me that."

Godwin, too. He'd gone over; he'd joined Lenz. "What's important is that the cause has genuine merit." He ambled over to a leather sofa. Ben sat facing him on the adjacent sofa.

"And were you involved in Sigma's cause in the old days as well?"

"Yes, for decades. And I feel so privileged to be around for this whole new phase. Under Lenz's leadership, things are going to be very different."

"I gather not all your colleagues agreed."

"Oh yes. The *angeli rebelli*, Lenz calls them. Rebel angels. There *were* a handful of people who wanted to put up a fight. Out of vanity or shortsightedness. Either they never trusted Lenz, or they felt demoted by the fact that new leadership had emerged. I guess a few of them had qualms about the . . . sacrifices that had to be made. Any time there's a shift in power, you've got to expect some forms of resistance. But a few years ago, when Lenz allowed that his project would soon be ready for actual trials, he made it clear the collective would have to recognize his leadership. He didn't do it out of any sense of self-interest, either. It's just that some difficult decisions would have to be made about who was going to be—well, admitted into the program. Inducted into the permanent elite. The risk of factionalism was too great. Lenz was the leader we needed. Most of us recognized that. A few didn't."

"Tell me, does your plan ultimately call for making this treatment available to everyone, to the masses? Or just what he calls 'the great ones'?"

"Well, you raise a serious point. I was flattered that Jürgen selected me to be a kind of recruiter, as it were, for this august group of world . . . luminaries, I suppose. The *Wiedergeborenen*, as Dr. Lenz calls us—the Reborn. We're reaching out far beyond the Sigma rump group. I brought Walter in, you know, and my old friend Miriam Bateman—Justice Miriam Bateman. I've been charged with helping choose those who seem deserving of it. From around the world—China, Russia, Europe, Africa—everywhere, without prejudice. Except for a prejudice in favor of greatness."

"But Arnold Carr's not much older than I am . . ."

"In fact, he's really at the perfect age to begin these treatments. He can stay forty-two for the rest of his very, very long life, if he chooses. Or become the biological equivalent of thirty-two again." The historian widened his eyes in wonderment. "There are forty of us by now."

"I understand," Ben interrupted, "but—"

"*Listen* to me, Ben! Good Lord, the other Supreme Court Justice we've chosen, a great jurist who's also black, he's a sharecropper's son who's lived through segregation and desegregation both. The wisdom he's accumulated in his lifetime! Who could ever replace him? A painter whose work is already transforming the art world—how many more spectacular canvases might be in him? Imagine, Ben, if history's greatest composers and writers and artists—take Shakespeare, take Mozart, take—"

Ben leaned forward. "This is insanity!" he thundered. "The rich and powerful get to live twice as long as the poor and powerless! It's a goddamned conspiracy of the elite!"

"*And what if it is?*" Godwin shot back. "Plato wrote of the philosopher-king, of the rule of the wise. He understood that our civilization advances and retreats, advances and retreats. We learn lessons only to forget them. History's tragedies repeat themselves—the Holocaust, and then the genocides that followed, as if we'd all forgotten. World wars. Dictatorships. False messiahs. Oppression of minorities. We don't seem to *evolve*. But now, for the first time, we can change all that. We can *transform* the human species!"

"How? Your numbers are tiny." Ben folded his arms on his chest. "That's another problem with elites."

Godwin stared at Ben for a moment, then chuckled. " 'We few, we happy few, we band of brothers'—yes, it all sounds hopelessly inadequate to the grand tasks, right? But humanity doesn't progress through some process of collective enlightenment. We progress because an individual or small team somewhere makes a breakthrough, and everyone else benefits. Three centuries ago, in a region with a very high rate of illiteracy, one man discovers calculus, or two men do—and the course of our species is changed forever. A century ago, one man discovers relativity, and nothing is ever the same. Tell me, Ben, do you know exactly how an internal combustion engine works—could you assemble one even if I gave you the parts? Do you know how to vulcanize rubber? Of course not, but you benefit from the existence of the automobile all the same. That's how it works. In the primitive world—I know we're not supposed to use those words anymore but indulge me—there's no great chasm between what one tribesman knows and another. Not so in the Western world. The division of labor is the very mark of civilization: the higher the degree of division of labor, the more advanced the society. And the most important division of labor is the intellectual division of labor. A minuscule number of people worked on the Manhattan Project—and yet the planet was changed by it forever. In the past decade, you had a few small teams decoding the human genome. Never mind that most of humanity can't remember the difference between Nyquil and niacin—they'll benefit all the same. People everywhere are using personal computers—people who couldn't understand a scrap of computer code, don't know the first thing about integrated circuitry. The mastery belongs to the happy few, and yet the multitudes benefit. The way our species advances isn't through vast, collective exertions—the Jews building the Pyramids. It's through individuals, through very small elites, who discover fire, the wheel, or the central processing unit, and thereby change the very landscape of our lives. And what's true in science and technology can be true of politics, as well. Except the learning curve here takes place over a far longer period of time. Which means that by the time we've learned from our errors, we've been replaced by younger upstarts who make those errors all over again. We don't learn enough, because we're not around long enough. The people who founded Sigma recognized this as an inherent limitation, one that our species would eventually have to overcome if we were to survive. Are you starting to see, Ben?"

"Keep going," Ben said, like a hesitant student.

"The efforts of Sigma—our attempt to *moderate* the politics of the postwar era—were only the beginning. Now we can change the face of the planet! Ensure universal peace, prosperity, and security, through the wise management and marketing of the planet's resources. If that's what you call a conspiracy of the elite—well, is it really such a bad thing? If a few miserable war refugees have to meet their maker ahead of schedule in order to save the world, is that really such a tragedy?"

"It's only for the ones you judge worthy, right?" Ben said. "You want to keep it from everyone else? There will be two classes of human being."

"The ruled and the rulers. But that's inevitable, Ben. There will be the Wise Men and the ruled masses. That's the only way to engineer a viable society. The world's already overpopulated. Much of Africa doesn't even have clean drinking water. If everyone lives twice or three times longer, think of what this will do! The world would collapse! That's why, in his wisdom, Lenz knows it must only be available to the few."

"And what happens to democracy? The rule of the people?"

Godwin's cheeks colored. "Spare me the sentimental rhetoric, Ben. The history of man's inhumanity to man has been history itself: *mobs* destroying what the *nobility* had painstakingly constructed. The main task in politics has always been saving the people from themselves. This wouldn't go down well with the undergraduates, but the *principle* of aristocracy was always correct: *aristos, kratos*— rule of the best. The problem was that aristocracy often didn't give you the best. But imagine if for the first time in human history, you could rationalize the system, create a hidden aristocracy based on merit—with *Wiedergebore-*

nen serving as the custodians of civilization."

Ben stood up and paced. His head spun. Goodwin, spinning his giddy justifications, had been hooked by the irresistible lure of near-immortality.

"Ben, you're what, thirty-five, thirty-six? You imagine you will live forever. I know I did at your age. But I want you to imagine being eighty-five, ninety, God willing you live so long. You have a family, you have children and grandchildren. You've had a happy life, your work is meaningful, and although you have all the normal afflictions of old age—"

"I'll want to die," Ben said curtly.

"Correct. If you're in the condition of most people at that age. But you don't ever have to *be* ninety. If you begin this therapy now, you'll always be in your prime, in your mid-thirties—God, what I'd give to be your age! Please don't tell me you have some ethical objection to it."

"I'm not sure what to think at this point," Ben said, watching Godwin closely.

Godwin seemed to believe him.

"Good. You're being open-minded. I want you to join us. Join the *Wiedergeborenen*."

Ben sank his head into his arms. "It's certainly a tempting offer." His voice was muffled. "You make some very good points—"

"Are you still here, John?" interrupted Lenz's voice, loud and enthusiastic. "The last helicopter's about to leave!"

Godwin rose swiftly. "I need to catch the shuttle," he apologized. "I want you to think about what we discussed."

Lenz entered with his arm around a stoop-shouldered old man.

Jakob Sonnenfeld.

"Did you have a good talk?" Lenz inquired.

No. Not him, too. "You—" Ben blurted out to the old Nazi hunter, revolted.

"I think we may have a new recruit," Godwin said somberly, and gave Lenz a brief but significant look.

Ben turned to face Sonnenfeld. "They knew where I was going in Buenos Aires because of you, isn't that right?"

Sonnenfeld looked pained. He averted his eyes. "There are times in life when one must choose sides," he said. "When my treatment begins—"

"Come, gentlemen," Lenz interrupted again. "We must hurry."

Ben could hear the roar of a helicopter outside, as Godwin and Sonnenfeld moved toward the exit.

"Benjamin," Lenz said without turning around. "Please stay right there. I'm so glad to hear you may be interested in our project. So now you and I must have a little talk."

Ben felt something slam him from behind, and steel clamped against his wrist.

Handcuffs.

There was no way out.

The guards dragged him through the great hall, past the exercise equipment and the medical monitoring stations.

He screamed at the top of his lungs and let himself go limp. If any of the *Wiedergeborenen* remained, they'd see him being abducted, and surely they'd object. These were not evil people.

But none of them remained, at least no one he could see.

A third guard took his upper arm and joined the others. His legs and knees slid painfully against the stone floor, the abrasions excruciating. He kicked and struggled. A fourth arrived, and now they were able to hold Ben by each limb, though he torqued himself back and forth to make it as difficult for them as possible, and he kept shouting.

They trundled him into an elevator. A guard pressed the second-floor button. In seconds the elevator opened on to a stark white corridor. As the guards carried him out—he'd ceased resisting; what was the point?—a passing nurse gaped at him, then looked away quickly.

They brought him into what looked like a modified operating room and hoisted him onto a bed. An orderly who appeared to have been expecting him—had the guards radioed ahead?—fastened colored restraints to his ankles and wrists, and then, once he was secured to the table, removed the handcuffs.

Exhausted, he lay flat, his limbs immobile. All of the guards but one filed out of the room, their work done. The remaining guard stood watch by the closed door, an Uzi across his chest.

The door opened, and Jürgen Lenz entered. "I admire your cleverness," he said. "I'd been assured that the old cave was sealed or at least impassable, so I thank you for pointing out the security risk. I've already ordered the entrance dynamited."

Ben wondered: Did Godwin really invite him to join them? Or was his old mentor simply trying to neutralize him? Lenz was far too suspicious to trust him anyway.

Or was he?

"Godwin asked me to join the project," Ben said.

Lenz wheeled a metal cart over next to the bed and busied himself with a hypodermic needle.

"Godwin trusts you," Lenz said, turning around. "I myself do not."

Ben watched his face. "Trusts me about what?"

"About respecting our need for confidentiality. About who you or your investigative friend might have already talked to."

Here was his vulnerability! "If you release her unharmed, you and I can strike a bargain," Ben said. "We each get what we want."

"And, of course, I can trust you to keep your word."

"It'd be in my own best interests," Ben said.

"People do not always act in their own self-interest. If I were ever to forget it, the *angeli rebelli* were there to remind me."

"Let's keep it simple. My interest is in having you release Anna Navarro. Yours is to keep your project secret. We have a mutual interest in striking a deal."

"Well," Lenz said dubiously. "Perhaps. But first I'll need

a little chemically inspired honesty, in case you don't come by it naturally."

Ben tried to suppress the wave of panic. "What does that mean?"

"Nothing harmful. A pleasant experience, in fact."

"I don't think you have time for this. Especially with law-enforcement agents due to arrive at any second. This is your last chance to deal."

"Ms. Navarro is here on her own," Lenz said. "She hasn't called in anyone else. She told me so herself." He held up the hypodermic. "And I assure you she was speaking the truth."

Keep conversing. Keep him diverted.

"How do you know you can trust the scientists on your team?"

"I don't. Everything, all the materials, the computers, the sequencers, the slides, the formulas for the infusions—they're all here."

Ben pressed. "You're still vulnerable. Somebody could get access to whatever offsite storage arrangements you've got for the data files. And no encryption is unbreakable."

"Which is precisely why there *is* no offsite storage," Lenz said, with evident satisfaction in demonstrating the fallacies in Ben's suppositions. "That represents a risk I cannot afford. In all honesty, I did not get where I am by placing excessive trust in my fellow man."

"As long as we're both being honest, let me ask *you* something."

"Yes?" Lenz tapped Ben's left forearm until a vein popped up.

"I'd like to know why you had my brother killed."

Lenz jabbed a needle into the vein with what seemed unnecessary force. "It should never have happened. It was done by fanatics among my security people, and it's something I deeply regret. A terrible mistake. They were concerned that his discovery of Sigma's original board would imperil our work."

Ben's heart thudded, and again he fought to control himself. "And my father? Did your 'fanatics' kill him, too?"

"Max?" Lenz looked surprised. "Max is a genius. I very much admire the man. Oh no, I wouldn't harm a hair on his head."

"Then where is he?"

"Did he go somewhere?" Lenz asked innocently.

Move on.

"Then why kill all those other old men . . . ?"

There was a slight twitch under Lenz's left eye. "House-cleaning. For the most part, we're talking about individuals with personal involvement in Sigma who sought to resist the inevitable. They complained that Sigma had fallen under my sway, felt displaced by my emerging role. Oh, all our members were treated generously . . ."

"Kept on a string, you mean. Given payments to fortify their discretion."

"As you like. But it was no longer enough, not now. What it came down to was a failure of vision. The point remains that they declined to, shall we say, get with the program. Then there were those who became importunate, possibly indiscreet, had long since ceased to have anything to offer. They were loose threads, and the time had come to snip them. Perhaps it seems harsh, but when there's this much at stake, you do not simply give people a firm talking to, or spank their wrists, or put them in 'time-out,' yes? You take more definitive measures."

Don't give up, Ben told himself. *Keep him engaged.*

"Murdering these old men in itself seems a foolish risk, don't you think? The deaths were bound to attract suspicion."

"Please. All the deaths appeared to be natural, but even if the toxin were discovered, these were men with plenty of worldly enemies—"

Lenz heard the sound at the same moment Ben did.

A burst of machine-gun fire not far away.

And then another, even closer.

A shout.

Lenz turned toward the door, hypodermic needle in one

hand. He said something to the guard standing by the door.

The door burst open in a hail of bullets.

A scream, and the guard collapsed in a pool of his own blood.

Lenz dropped to the floor.

Anna!

Ben's relief was enormous. *She's alive, somehow she's alive.*

"Ben!" she shouted, flinging the door shut behind her and turning the lock. "Ben, you all right?"

"I'm all right," he called.

"Stand up!" she screamed at Lenz. "You goddamned son of a bitch."

She advanced, machine gun leveled. She was wearing a doctor's short white coat.

Lenz stood. His face was flushed, his silver hair mussed. "My guards will be here any second." His voice quavered.

"Don't count on it," Anna replied. "I've sealed off the entire wing, and the doors are jammed from the outside."

"You've killed that guard, I think," Lenz said, bravado returning to his voice. "I thought the United States trained its agents only to kill in self-defense."

"Haven't you heard? I'm off duty," Anna said. "Hands away from your body. Where's your weapon?"

Lenz was indignant. "I have none."

Anna approached. "You don't mind if I look, do you? Hands *away* from your body, I said."

Slowly she took a step toward Lenz, slid her free hand inside his jacket. "Let's see," she said. "I sure hope I can do this without setting off the damned machine gun. I'm not too familiar with these little guys."

Lenz paled.

She produced a small handgun from inside Lenz's suit with a flourish, like a conjurer pulling a rabbit out of a top hat.

"Well, well," she said. "Pretty slick for an old man, Jürgen. Or do your friends still call you Gerhard?"

CHAPTER FORTY-SEVEN

Ben gasped, "Oh, my God."

Lenz pursed his lips, and then, oddly, he smiled.

Anna pocketed Lenz's handgun. "For the longest time it baffled me," she said. "The federal ID lab ran the prints but turned up nothing, no matter how many databases they used. They tried the army intelligence files, but still nothing. Until they went back to the old ten-print cards from the war and a few years after, which haven't yet been digitized, why should they be, right? Your SS prints were included in the Army's files, I guess because you escaped."

Lenz watched her, amused.

"The techies speculated that maybe the prints on the photo I'd sent them were old, but the strange thing was, the fingerprint oil, the perspiration residue they call it, was fresh. Made no sense to them."

Ben looked at Lenz. Yes, he resembled the Gerhard Lenz who appeared in the picture with Max Hartman. Lenz in that 1945 photo was in his mid-forties. That made him, what, over a hundred years old.

It seemed impossible.

"I was my own first successful subject," Gerhard Lenz said quietly. "Almost twenty years ago I was for the first time able to arrest, then reverse, my own aging. Only a few years ago did we devise a formulation that works reliably on everyone." He was looking off in the distance, his gaze unfocused. "It meant that everything that Sigma stood for could now be made secure."

"All right," Anna interrupted. "Give me the key to the restraints."

"I don't have the key. The orderly—"

"Forget it." She shifted the machine gun to her right hand, pulled a straightened paper clip out of a jacket pocket, and freed Ben, handing him a long plastic object, which he glanced at and understood at once.

"Don't move a muscle," Anna shouted, thrusting the Uzi in Lenz's direction. "Ben, take those restraints and lock this bastard to something immobile." She quickly looked around. "We've got to get out of here as fast as possible, and—"

"No," Ben said, steely.

She turned, startled. "What are you—?"

"He's holding prisoners here—young people in tents outside, sick kids in at least one of the wards. We've got to let them out first!"

Anna understood immediately. She nodded. "Fastest way is to shut down the security system. De-electrify the fences, unlock . . ." She turned to Lenz, adjusted the machine gun in her hands. "There's a master control panel, an override, in your office. We're taking a little walk."

Lenz looked phlegmatic. "I'm afraid I don't know what you're talking about. All security for the clinic is controlled from the central guard station on the first level."

"Sorry," Anna said. "I've already 'debriefed' one of your guards." She pointed with the Uzi toward a closed door, not the one through which they'd entered. "Let's *go*."

*   *   *

Lenz's office was immense, dark, cathedral-like.

Glimmers of pale light filtered in through slot windows cut into the stone walls high above their heads. Most of the room was in shadows, except for a small circle of light from a green-glass-shaded library lamp in the middle of Lenz's massive walnut desk.

"I assume you don't object to my putting on the lights so I can see what I'm doing," Lenz said.

"Sorry," Anna said. "We don't need it. Just go around to the other side of your desk and push the button that raises the control panel. Let's make this easy."

Lenz hesitated but a moment, then followed her directions. "This is a pointless exercise," he said with weary contempt as he walked around to his side of the desk. She followed, sidling, the weapon always leveled at him.

Ben came just behind her. A second set of eyes in case Lenz attempted something, as he was sure Lenz would do.

Lenz pushed a recessed button at the front edge of the desk. There was a mechanical rumble, and a long, flat section arose from the middle of the desktop like a horizontal tombstone: a brushed-steel instrument panel, strange-looking atop the Gothic desk.

Set into the steel was what appeared to be a flat plasma screen, on which nine small squares, glowing ice blue, were arranged in rows of three. Each square display showed a different view of the interior and exterior of the *Schloss*. Below the screen was an array of silver toggle switches.

In one display the progeric children played, tethered to their poles; in another, refugees milled about around their tents on the snow, smoking. Guards stood by various entrances. Other guards patrolled the grounds. Winking red lights every few feet along the electrified fences atop the ancient stone walls, presumably showing that the system was still operational.

"Move it," Anna commanded.

Lenz bowed his head indulgently, and began toggling each switch off in order from left to right. Nothing happened, no sign of the security system shutting down. "We will find other progerics," Lenz said as he switched them off, "and there's an endless supply of youthful war refugees, displaced children the world doesn't miss—there always seems to be a war somewhere." This thought seemed to amuse him.

The winking red lights had gone out. A cluster of refugee children was playing a game near one of the tall iron gates. One of them pointed—noticing that the red power lights had stopped blinking.

Another of them ran up to the gate, tugged at it.

The gate slowly came open.

Tentatively the child walked through the gate, looking back at the others, beckoning. Slowly another joined him, passing through the gate to freedom. They appeared to be shouting to the others, though there was no sound.

Then a few more of the children. A bedraggled-looking girl with matted curly hair. Another young boy.

More children.

Frenetic movement. The children began to scramble out, pushing and shoving.

Lenz watched, his expression inscrutable. Anna's attention was riveted on him, the Uzi still pointed.

In another screen, a door to the children's ward was now wide open. A nurse appeared to be waving the children out, looking around furtively.

"So they are escaping," Lenz said, "but for you it will not be so easy. Forty-eight security guards have been trained to shoot any intruders on sight. You will never make it outside." He reached for a large ornate brass lamp to switch it on, and Ben snapped to attention, sure that Lenz was about to pick the lamp up to hurl or swing it, but instead Lenz tugged at a protruding section of the base and pulled out a small oblong object that he instantly pointed at Ben. It was a compact, brass-plated pistol, cleverly concealed.

"Drop it!" Anna shouted.

Ben was a few feet to Anna's side, and Lenz could not cover them both. "I suggest you put down your weapon at once," Lenz said. "That way no one will be hurt."

"I don't think so," Anna said. "We're not exactly evenly matched."

Lenz, unfazed, said blandly, "But you see, if you begin to fire at me, your friend here will be killed, too. You must ask yourself how important it is to kill me—whether it's really worth it."

"Drop the goddamn toy gun," Anna said, although Ben could see it was no toy.

"Even if you succeed in killing me, you change nothing. My work will continue even without me. But your friend Benjamin will simply be dead."

"*No!*" came a hoarse shout.

An old man's voice.

Lenz spun around to look.

"*Lassen Sie ihn los! Lassen Sie meinen Sohn los!* Let him go!"

The voice came from a corner of the great room that was hidden in shadows. Lenz pointed his weapon toward the voice, then seemed to reconsider, and swung it back toward Ben.

The voice again: "Let my son go!"

In the dim light Ben could just make out the seated figure.

His father. In his hand was a gun, too.

For a moment Ben couldn't speak.

He thought it might be a trick of the strange oblique light, and he looked again, and knew that what he saw was real.

Quieter now, Max's voice: "Let them both go."

"Ah, Max, my friend," Lenz called, in a loud and hearty voice. "Perhaps you can talk reason to these two."

"Enough of the killing," Max said. "Enough bloodshed. It's over now."

Lenz stiffened. "You are a foolish old man," he replied.

"You're right," Max said. He remained seated, but his gun was still trained on Lenz. "And I was a foolish young man, too. I was beguiled by you then, just as now. All my life I've lived in fear of you and your people. Your threats. Your blackmail." His voice rose, choked with rage. "No matter what I built or what I became, you were always there."

"You can lower your gun, my friend," Lenz said mildly. His weapon was still pointed at Ben, but for a split-second he turned to Max.

I can rush him, tackle him to the floor, Ben thought. *The next time his attention is diverted.*

Max continued as if he hadn't heard, and as if there were no one in the room but Lenz. "Don't you see I'm not afraid of you any longer?" His voice reverberated against the stone walls. "I will never forgive myself for what I did, for helping you and your butcher friends. For making my deal with the devil. Once I thought it was the right thing to do, for my family, for my future, for the world's. But I was lying to myself. What you did to my son, my Peter—" His voice broke.

"But you *know* that should never have happened!" Lenz protested. "It was the work of overzealous security people who exceeded their authority."

"Enough!" Max bellowed. "No more! Enough of your goddamned lies!"

"But the *project*, Max. My God, man, I don't think you understand—"

"No, you don't understand. You think I care about your dreams of playing God? You think I ever did?"

"I invited you here as a favor to you, to make amends. What are you trying to tell me?" Lenz's voice was controlled, but only barely.

"Amends? But this is only a continuation of the horror. For you, everything and everyone were sacrificed to your dream of living forever." A labored breath. "You're about to take my only remaining child from me! After everything else you've taken from me."

"Then your overtures were merely a ploy. Yes, I'm beginning to see. When you joined us it was always with the intention of betraying us."

"It was the only way I could gain entrance to a walled city. The only way I could hope to monitor from within."

Lenz spoke as if to himself. "My mistake is always to imagine that others are as philanthropic as I am—as concerned with the greater good. How you disappoint me. And after all we've-been through together, Max."

"Ach! You pretend to be interested in human progress," Max shouted. "And you call *me* a foolish old man! You talk of others as subhuman, but you are yourself not human."

Lenz briefly turned his gaze toward Max, seated in the dim corner, and at the same instant that Ben coiled to spring forward, he heard the hollow pop, the retort of a small-caliber pistol, and Lenz looked more surprised than stricken as a small but widening red circle appeared on the breast pocket of his white lab coat near his right shoulder. Aiming in Max's general direction, Lenz squeezed the trigger three times, returning fire wildly.

Then a second blotch of red appeared on Lenz's chest. His right arm dangled uselessly at his side as his pistol clanked to the floor.

Anna lowered the Uzi slightly, watched him.

Suddenly Lenz lunged at Anna, knocking her to the floor, the Uzi clattering.

His hand was at her throat, squeezing her larynx in an iron clutch. She tried to rear up, but he slammed her head back against the floor with an audible crack.

Again he slammed her head against the stone, and then Ben, enraged, leaped on top of Lenz, gripping the plastic cylinder she'd handed him earlier. Ben roared with exertion and fury as he swung his right hand up and jabbed the hypodermic needle directly into Lenz's neck.

Lenz howled in pain. Ben had hit the internal jugular vein, he could tell, or had at least come very close to it, and he depressed the plunger.

Lenz's expression of horror seemed frozen on his face. His hands flew to his neck, found the syringe, yanked it out, and he saw the label. *"Verdammt nochmal! Scheiss Jesus Christus!"*

A bubble of saliva formed at his mouth. Suddenly he fell backward like an upended statue. His mouth opened and shut as if he were trying to scream, but instead he only gasped for air.

Then he went rigid.

Lenz's eyes stared in fury, but the pupils were fixed and dilated.

"I think he's dead," Ben gasped, short of breath.

"I *know* he's dead," Anna said. "That's the most potent opioid there is. They keep some pretty powerful stuff in their locked medicine cabinets. Now let's get *out* of here!" She glanced at Max Hartman. "*All* of us."

"Go," Ben's father whispered from his chair. "Leave me here, but you two must go *now*, the guards—"

"No," Ben said. "You're coming with us."

"Dammit," Anna said to Ben. "I heard the helicopter taking off, so that's out. How did you get in, anyway?"

"A cave—under the property—opens into the basement. But they've found it."

"Lenz was right, we're done for, there's no way out—"

"But there *is* a way," Max said, his voice faint.

Ben ran over to him, stricken by what he saw.

Max, dressed in a pale blue hospital johnny, was feebly holding his hands to the base of his throat, where, as Ben now realized, a bullet had lodged. Blood was spreading insistently beneath his trembling fingers. The thin cotton garment was stenciled with the black numeral eighteen.

"No!" Ben shouted.

The man had taken a bullet in order to kill Lenz—and protect his only surviving son.

"Lenz's private helicopter," Max whispered. "You reach the bay through the back passage on the far left . . ." He murmured instructions for a few moments longer. Finally he said, "Tell me you understand." Max's eyes were imploring. In a voice barely audible he repeated the words: "Tell me you understand."

"Yes," Ben said, hardly able to speak himself. *Tell me you understand*—his father meant the instructions to the bay, of course, but Ben couldn't help thinking that he meant something more, too. *Tell me you understand:* tell me you understand the difficult decisions I made in life, however mistaken.

Tell me you understand them. Tell me you understand who I really am.

As if in resignation, Max pulled his hands from his throat, and blood began to spurt, with the slow, regular pulse of his heartbeat.

Tell me you understand.

Yes, Ben had told him, and just then, at least, he did. *I understand.*

Within a few moments, his father slumped backward lifeless.

Lifeless, and yet the picture of health. Blinking away tears, Ben could see that his father looked decades younger, his hair beginning to grow in glossy and dark, his skin smooth, firm, toned.

In death, Max Hartman had never looked more alive.

CHAPTER FORTY-EIGHT

Ben and Anna raced down the corridor, gunfire audible all around. The bandolier swung against the barrel of her Uzi as she ran, producing a dull rattle. At any moment, they could be set upon, but the guards realized they were heavily armed, would have to approach with caution. Anna knew that no paid sentry, however loyal, would endanger his life needlessly.

Max's directions had been clear and accurate.

Another right turn brought them to a stairwell.

Ben opened the steel-plated door, and Anna directed a burst of gunfire into the landing area: anyone present would instinctively dive for cover. As they entered, there was a deafening return burst: a guard located on the level below, shooting in the narrow space between the stairs. It was not an angle that afforded any accuracy; the biggest danger was being hit by a ricochet.

"Run upstairs," Anna whispered to Ben.

"But Max said the bay level is downstairs," Ben protested in a low voice.

"Do what I say. Start running upstairs. Loudly."

He immediately understood, and did so, making sure that his shoes thundered against the stairs as he mounted them.

Anna flattened herself against the wall, just out of the sight line from the lower landing. Within a few moments, she detected the guard's movements: hearing Ben's ascent, he was scrambling to catch up with his quarry.

The seconds became hours. Anna could picture the guard bounding up to the lower landing: she'd have to work with a mental image, assembled from sounds of the man's movements. Once she was visible to the guard, she would have no advantage over him other than swiftness. She would keep out of sight until the last possible moment; and then her reflexes would have to be instantaneous.

Now she leaped into the air and fired where she pictured the guard in her mind, squeezing the trigger even as she was at last able to confirm his position visually.

The guard had a submachine gun aimed directly at her. Victory or defeat would be measured in milliseconds. Had she waited until she could see him before firing, the advantage would have been his.

Instead, she watched as his tunic erupted into blood and his weapon fired harmlessly above her, then fell noisily down the stairs.

"Anna?" Ben called out.

"Now!" she replied, and he sprinted down the two flights of stairs, joining her at the bay level, at a gate-latch door, also of gray-painted steel, which pushed out.

As they entered Bay Number 7, they felt a gust of cold, and there it was—the helicopter glinting in the waning light, a great gleaming metallic creature. It was a large, sleek, black Agusta 109, brand new. Italian-made, with wheels instead of skids.

"Can you really fly this thing?" Anna asked, after they'd both clambered into it.

Ben, seated in the cockpit, grunted assent. In truth he had flown a helicopter only once before, a training vehicle, with a licensed pilot at the twin set of controls. He had flown planes many times, but this was entirely different, counterintuitive. He scanned the dim cockpit for the controls.

For an instant, the complexities of the instrument panel dissolved into a blur. The image of his father's crumpled body seemed to hover before his eyes. He flashed on a Max Hartman just young enough that he could glimpse how he once must have looked. He could glimpse the youthful financier who found the country around him erupting into a lethal blaze of hatred. Who raced around, entering into loathsome accommodations with a loathsome regime in order to save as many families as he could. A man accustomed to mastery turned into a pawn.

He could glimpse the man—an émigré, a harrowed man, a man with secrets—whom his mother met and fell in love with. Max Hartman, his father.

Ben shook his head hard. He had to focus.

He had to focus or they would both be dead. And everything would be for nothing.

The bay was open to the elements. Outside the gunfire seemed to be coming closer.

"Anna, I want you ready with the Uzi in case any of the guards try to shoot us down," Ben said.

"They won't shoot," Anna said, a wish expressed as a declaration. "They know it's Lenz's helicopter."

A voice from the back, cultivated and precise: "Quite so. Did you suppose that Lenz had no passengers waiting for him, Ms. Navarro?"

They weren't alone.

"A friend of yours?" Ben asked Anna quietly.

They both turned around and saw the passenger crouched in the rear compartment, a white-haired but vigorous-looking man wearing large glasses with translucent flesh-toned frames. He was immaculately attired in a King Edward–style Glenn Urquhart suit, a crisp white shirt, and a tightly knotted olive silk tie.

In his hands was a short-barreled automatic weapon, the one inelegant touch.

"*Alan Bartlett,*" Anna breathed.

"Toss me the gun, Ms. Navarro. My gun is trained on you, and yours is hardly in position. I'd very much regret having to squeeze the trigger, you know. The discharge would surely blow out the windshield and possibly damage the fuselage as well. Which would be unfortunate, since we'll be needing this vehicle as a means of conveyance."

Slowly, Anna let the Uzi slide to the floor, and pushed it toward Bartlett. He did not lean over to retrieve it, but seemed satisfied that it was out of her reach.

"Thank you, Ms. Navarro," said Bartlett. "My debt of gratitude toward you only grows. I don't know that I adequately expressed my thanks for your having located Gaston Rossignol for us, and so swiftly. The wily old bird really was poised to cause us a great deal of trouble."

"You bastard," Anna said in a low voice. "You evil, manipulative son of a bitch."

"Forgive me, I realize this is hardly the time or place for a fitness report, Ms. Navarro. But I must say, it's terribly unfortunate that, having given us such excellent service, you've started to undo all the good you've achieved. Now, where is Dr. Lenz?"

Ben answered for her: "Dead."

Bartlett was silent for a moment. There was a flicker in his gray, expressionless eyes. "Dead?" His grip tightened on his automatic rifle as he digested the information. "You *idiots!*" His voice flared abruptly. "You *destructive* idiots! Vicious children seeking to ruin something whose beauty you could never comprehend. What gave you the *right* to do that? What made you think this was your decision to make?" He fell silent again, and was visibly shaking with anger when he resumed. "Damn you both to hell!"

"After you, Bartlett," Ben snapped.

"You're Benjamin Hartman, of course—I'm sorry we meet under these circumstances. But then I have only myself to blame. I should have ordered you killed at the same time as your brother: *that* shouldn't have taxed our capabilities. I must have grown sentimental in my old age. Well, my young lovers, I'm afraid the two of you have left me with some difficult decisions to make."

Faintly reflected in the windshield of the cockpit was the wide barrel of Bartlett's assault weapon. Ben kept his eyes on it.

"First things first," Bartlett went on, after a pause. "I'm going to have to rely upon your piloting skills. There's a landing strip outside Vienna. I'll direct you to it."

Ben glanced again at Bartlett's automatic weapon and toggled up the battery switch.

There was the clicking sound of the spark plugs firing, then the whine of the starter motor, which gradually deepened. It was fully automatic, Ben realized, which would make it much easier to fly.

In ten seconds there was ignition, and the engine thundered to life. The rotors began turning.

"Belt yourself in tight," Ben murmured to Anna. He pulled up on the collective's twist grip with his left hand, heard the sound of the rotors slowing.

Then some kind of horn sounded, and the engine slowed. "Damn," he said.

"Do you know what you're doing?" Bartlett asked. "Because if you don't, you're of no use to me at all. I needn't spell out what that means."

"Just a little rusty," Ben replied. He grabbed the throttles, the two sticks that came down from the top of the windshield, and pushed both of them forward.

Now the engine and both the tail and the main rotors roared again. The helicopter lurched forward, then yawed left and right.

Ben abruptly yanked back on the throttle: the helicopter came to an abrupt jarring halt. Both he and Anna pitched forward against the restraint belts; Bartlett, as Ben had hoped, was hurtled against the metal grid that backed the cockpit.

Even as he heard the clatter of the assault rifle smashing into the partition, Ben unbelted himself and sprang into action.

Bartlett, he could see, had been temporarily stunned by the impact; a rivulet of blood descended from his left nostril. Now, with the suddenness of a leopard, Ben hurled himself around his seat and pounced on Bartlett with both hands, slamming the man's shoulders to the grip-textured steel flooring. Bartlett put up no resistance.

Had the impact of the partition knocked him unconscious? Was he already dead?

It was too risky to make any assumptions.

"I've got an extra set of restraints on me," Anna said. "If you can bring his wrists together . . ."

Within moments, she had manacled both his hands and legs, leaving her old employer trundled in the back like a rolled-up carpet.

"*Jesus*," Anna said. "There's no time. We've got to get a move on. The guards—they're on their way!"

Ben pushed the two sticks forward, then twisted the collective up while maintaining his grip on the cyclic. The collective controlled the helicopter's lift; the cyclic controlled its lateral direction. The helicopter's nose moved to the right, the tail to the left, and then it started rolling out of the bay and onto the snow-covered lawn, coolly illuminated by the moonlight.

"*Shit!*" Ben shouted, pushing the collective down to reduce power, trying to stabilize the craft.

Slowly he pulled the collective up, adding power slowly, and felt the aircraft getting light.

He pushed the stick forward an inch or two, felt the nose pitch down, then added a bit more power with the collective.

They were rolling now.

The helicopter taxied forward across the snow.

The collective was now halfway up.

Suddenly, at a speed of twenty-five knots, the chopper jumped into the air.

They'd lifted off.

He pulled back on the stick to gain more power, and the nose went right. They kept rising.

Bullets clattered against the cabin.

Several guards were running, their submachine guns pointed at the helicopter, shouting.

"I thought you said they wouldn't shoot at Lenz's helicopter."

"Word must have got out about the good doctor," Anna said. "Hey, better to travel hopefully, right?" She thrust the barrel of her Uzi out the open side window and fired off a burst. One of the guards fell to the ground.

Then she fired another, more sustained burst.

The other guard was down.

"O.K.," she said, "I think we're all right for a little while."

Ben brought the collective back past center, and the nose corrected.

Higher, then higher still.

They were directly above the *Schloss* now, and the craft felt more stable. Now he could fly it like an airplane.

Ben became aware of a sudden movement, and just as he turned, he felt a jabbing, searing pain at the base of his neck and shoulders. What he felt had some resemblance to the sensation of a pinched nerve but a hundred times worse.

Anna shrieked.

From the hot moist breath near his face, Ben realized what had happened. Bartlett, his arms and legs shackled, had thrown himself at Ben, attacking him with the only thing left at his disposal—his jaws.

A guttural vocalization, like the growl of a jungle creature, rose from Bartlett's throat as he sank his teeth farther into Ben's exposed neck and shoulders.

As Ben released the collective in order to grab hold of Bartlett, the helicopter started to yaw perilously to one side.

It wasn't over! Anna knew that to fire her gun at him would be to risk killing Ben. She seized handfuls of Bartlett's lank white hair and pulled with all her might. Pulled until the hair came out, exposing bloodied pink ovals of scalp.

And still Bartlett would not let up.

It was as if he were directing all his vital force into his jaws, pushing his teeth down into Ben's flesh with the muscular strength of his entire body.

It was all he had left. A wounded animal's one chance to survive—or, at least, to ensure that his enemy did not.

Ben, obviously convulsed by agony, pounded at Bartlett's head with his fists, but to no effect.

Was it possible—to have come so far, survived so much, only to be destroyed in the midst of escape?

Bartlett was maniacal, insensible to pain—a man of elegance and supernal ambition now reduced to the most elemental posture of any vertebrate. He could have been a hyena on the Serengeti plains, sinking his incisors into another creature, hoping that only one of them would make it to another day.

Even as his mouth vised on Ben's neck and shoulders, Bartlett's body was writhing, flailing, thrashing—kicking at Anna with both feet, jolting her out of position, weakening her grasp on him. A blast of cold air suddenly filled the helicopter. Bartlett's wild, eel-like movements had kicked open the door on Anna's side.

Another violent movement of his jarred the pedals, which controlled the tail rotors, and the helicopter began to rotate left, first spinning slowly and then more swiftly. As the centrifugal force gained in power, Anna began to slide precariously toward the open door. She clawed at Bartlett's face, her nails in his flesh providing her sole purchase. What she was doing sickened her, but it was the only way: she dug deeper, harder, forcing her finger into his orbital cavity.

"Open wide, you son of a bitch!" she shouted, gouging into the yielding flesh until, at last, with a blood-curdling scream, Bartlett released his mandibular grip.

What happened next was a blur: both Anna and Bartlett were thrown toward the open door, toward the yawning drop to the earth far beneath them.

Then she felt an ironlike grip on her wrist. Ben's hand had shot out, grabbing her, holding her back as the helicopter continued to spin at a forty-five-degree incline and Bartlett, bellowing, finally succumbed to gravity and slid out of the helicopter.

His bellows became fainter as he plunged to the *Schloss* far below them.

But would the helicopter follow him down? Unlike an airplane, a helicopter that had moved beyond the limits of correct angular position would simply drop like a stone. And the rotating helicopter continued to tilt, horrifyingly, as the loss of lift became sickeningly apparent.

Regaining proper position would require both hands and feet. Ben frantically adjusted the cyclic and the collective as his feet worked the pedals, coordinating the tail rotor with the main rotor.

"Ben!" she yelled, only just managing to latch the door. "Do something!"

"*Jesus!*" he roared over the straining rotors. "I don't know if I can!"

The helicopter suddenly plunged, and Anna's stomach lurched upward, but she noticed that even as it fell, it was starting to right itself.

If it righted itself in time—found the angle required for lift—they'd stand a chance.

Ben manipulated the controls with furrowed intensity. Viscerally, they knew that the rotorcraft had only seconds remaining before the descent velocity became unrecoverable: any wrong decisions would be fatal.

She felt it before she saw it—felt the lift before she saw, from the horizon line, that the helicopter had returned to even keel.

For the first time in a long while, she experienced a small but growing abatement of panic. Deftly, she tore off a piece of her blouse and pressed it to the area of Ben's lower neck that had been attacked. The area was deeply grooved with tooth marks, but the compression wounds left very little blood, which was fortunate. No major vessels had been breached. Ben would need medical attention before too long, but it wasn't an emergency.

Now she looked down out of the window. "Look!" she called out. Directly below them she could see the toy-model castle surrounded by its serpentine fence. And at the base of the mountain a dense crowd of people was surging, streaming.

"That's them!" she shouted. "It looks like they got out!"

They heard an explosion from below, and a great crater suddenly appeared in the ground next to the *Schloss.*

A small section of the ancient stone fortress nearest the blast crumbled like a fragile confection of spun sugar.

"The dynamite," Ben said.

They were more than a thousand feet up now, cruising at 140 knots. "The idiots dynamited the mouth of the cave. Way too close to the building—look at what the explosion's done. *Jesus!*"

She saw what looked like a white cloud forming near the summit of the mountain, rolling like dense fog down the mountainside.

A white cloud of snow, a great wave, the avalanche a cruel fact of nature in the Austrian alps.

It was a strangely beautiful sight.

Apart from scores of children who managed to flee the grounds of the *Schloss,* there were no survivors.

Thirty-seven people around the world, many of them great men and women, all of them leaders in their field, were shocked to read the obituaries of the Viennese philanthropist Jürgen Lenz, in the avalanche that buried the Alpine *Schloss* he had inherited from his father.

Thirty-seven men and women, all of whom were in remarkable health.

CHAPTER FORTY-NINE

A gleaming throwback to a more elegant age, the Metropolis Club occupied the corner of a handsome block on East Sixty-eighth Street in Manhattan. It was a grand McKim, Mead & White building from the late nineteenth century, adorned with limestone balustrades, trimmed with intricate modillion courses. Inside, the curved wrought-iron railings of the double staircase led past marble pilasters and plaster medallions to the spacious Schuyler Hall. Three hundred chairs were now assembled on its black-and-white harlequinade floor. Ben had to admit, for all his misgivings, that it wasn't an inappropriate venue for his father's memorial service: Marguerite, Max Hartman's executive assistant for twenty years, had insisted on organizing the event and her efforts were, as always, beyond reproach. Now he blinked hard and looked at the faces in front of him, until the collectivity came into focus as individuals.

Seated in all those chairs was a curious community of mourners. Ben saw the careworn faces of older men from New York's banking community, grizzled, jowly, stoop-shouldered men who knew that banking, the profession to which they had devoted their lives, was now changing in ways that exalted technical competence over the cultivation of personal relationships. These were bankers who had made their biggest deals on the fairways—gentlemen of the green who glimpsed that the future of their industry belonged to callow men with bad haircuts and doctorates in electrical engineering, callow men who did not know a putter from a nine iron.

Ben saw the elegantly attired leaders of major charitable causes. He made fleeting eye contact with the executive director of the New-York Historical Society, a woman who wore her abundant hair in a tight bun; her face looked slightly stretched, in a diagonal that ran from each corner of her mouth to an area behind each ear—the familiar sign of a recent face-lift, marks of the surgeon's crude craft. In the row behind her, Ben recognized the white-haired, navy-suited head of the Grolier Society. The soigné president of the Metropolitan Museum. The neo-hippyish chairwoman of the Coalition for the Homeless. Elsewhere were provosts and deans of several major educational institutions, each keeping the others at a careful distance, each regarding Ben somberly. In the first row was the charismatic national director of the United Way charities, slightly rumpled, his brown basset-hound eyes looking genuinely moved.

So many faces, dissolving briefly and then resolving into particularity once more. Ben saw striving couples, tight-bodied wives and soft-bellied men, who had helped secure their position in New York society by enlisting Max Hartman's support in their ceaseless fund-raisers for literacy, AIDS, freedom of expression, wildlife conservation. He saw neighbors from Bedford: the softball-playing magazine mogul with his trademark bold-striped shirt; the slightly tatty-looking, long-faced scion of a distinguished old family who once directed an Egyptology program at an Ivy League university; the youngish man who had launched, and sold to a conglomerate, a company that made herbal teas with colorful New Age names and progressive box-top homilies.

Worn faces, fresh faces, familiar ones and strange ones.

There were the people who worked for Hartman Capital Management. Prized clients, like good old Fred McCallan, who'd dabbed at his eyes with a handkerchief once or twice. Former colleagues of his from his days teaching in East New York; newer colleagues of his from the job he'd just taken at an equally poor high school in Mount Vernon. There were people who had helped him and Anna in their time of need. Above all, there was Anna, his fiancée, his friend, his lover.

Before all of these people, Ben stood before a rostrum at the raised platform at the end of the hall and tried to say something about his father. In the previous hour, a very fine string quartet—one that Max Hartman had helped sponsor—had played an adagietto by Mahler, adapted from his Fifth Symphony. Erstwhile business colleagues and beneficiaries of Max had evoked the man they knew. And now Ben found himself speaking, and wondering as he spoke, whether he was really addressing the assembled or himself.

He had to speak of the Max Hartman *he* knew, even as he wondered how much he ever did know or *could* know him. His only certainty was that it was his task to do so. He swallowed hard and continued speaking: "A child imagines that his father is all-powerful. We see the pride and the broad shoulders and the sense of mastery and it's impossible to think that this strength has limits. Maybe maturity comes of recognizing our error." Ben's throat constricted, and he had to wait a few moments before resuming.

"My father was a strong man, the strongest man I've ever known. But the world is powerful, too, more powerful than any man, however bold and determined he may be. Max Hartman lived through the darkest years of the twentieth century. He lived through a time when mankind revealed how very black its heart could be. In his mind, I think, the knowledge defiled him. I know that he had to live with that knowledge, and make a life and raise a family, and pray that his knowledge would not shadow our

lives as it did his own. After such knowledge, what forgiveness?" Again Ben paused, took a deep breath, and
pressed on.

"My father was a complicated man, the most complicated man I have ever known. He lived through a history
of astonishing complexity. A poet wrote:

> *Think now*
> *History has many cunning passages, contrived*
> *corridors*
> *And issues, deceives with whispering ambitions,*
> *Guides us by vanities.*

"My father liked to say that he only looked forward,
never behind. That was a lie, a brave, defiant lie. History
was what my father was shaped by, and what he would
always struggle to overcome. A history that was anything
but black and white. The eyesight of children is very sharp.
It dims with age. And yet there is something that children
really don't see too well: the intermediate tones. Shades of
gray. Youth is pure of heart, right? Youth is uncompro-
mising, resolute, zealous. That is the privilege of inexpe-
rience. That is the privilege of a moral cleanliness untested
and untroubled by the messiness of the real world.

"What if you have no choice but to deal with evil in
order to fight evil? Do you save those you love, those you
can, or do keep yourself pure and unsullied? I know I never
had to make that call. And I know something else. A hero's
hands are chapped, scuffed, chafed and calloused, and only
rarely are they clean. My father's were not. He lived with
the sense that, in fighting the enemy, he had also done work
that served their purposes. In the end, his broad shoulders
would be bowed with a sense of guilt that none of his good
deeds could ever erase. He could never forget that he had
survived when so many he had cherished did not. Again:
After such knowledge what forgiveness? The effect was
that he redoubled his efforts to do what was right. Only
recently have I come to understand that I was never truer

to him and his own sense of mission than when I thought I was rebelling against him, and his expectations for me. A father wants, above all, to keep his children safe. But that is the one thing that no father can do."

Ben's eyes met Anna's for a long, lingering moment, and he found solace in the steady, answering gaze of her liquid brown eyes.

"One day, God willing, I will be a father, and no doubt I will forget this lesson and have to relearn it. Max Hartman was a philanthropist—in the root sense of the word, he loved people—and yet he was not an easy man to love. Every day, his children would ask themselves whether they made him proud or ashamed. Now I see that he was burdened by this question, too: would he make us, his children, proud or ashamed?

"Peter, above all else, I wish you were here with me at this very moment, to listen and to talk." Now his eyes welled. "But, Peter, this you've got to file under 'strange but true,' as you used to say. Dad lived in fear of *our* judgment."

Ben bowed his head for a moment. "I say my father lived in fear that I would judge him—and yet it seems incredible. He feared that a child bred of luxury and indolence would judge a man who had to endure the annihilation of everything he held dear."

Ben squared his shoulders, and, his voice hoarse and thickened with sadness, spoke a little louder. "He lived in fear that I would judge him. *And I do*. I judge him mortal. I judge him imperfect. I judge him a man who was mulish and complicated and hard to love and forever scarred by a history that left its mark on everything it touched.

"And I judge him a hero.

"I judge him a good man.

"And because he was hard to love, I loved him all the harder . . ."

Ben broke off, the words strangled in his throat. He could say no more, and perhaps there was nothing more that needed to be said. He looked at Anna's face, saw her cheeks glistening with tears, saw her weeping for them both, and he slowly walked away from the rostrum, and toward the back of the hall. Soon Anna joined him, standing by his side while countless guests shook his hand as they filed out through the hall and talked among themselves in an adjoining room. There were words of condolence and of affectionate reminiscence. Kindly old men squeezed his shoulder, clearly remembering him as a child, one half of the adorable Hartman twins. Ben steadily regained his composure. He'd felt wrung out, but part of what had been wrung out of him was the heaviness of grief.

Ten minutes later, when someone—the head of the tax division at HCM—told a fond, funny anecdote about his father, Ben found himself laughing out loud. Somehow he felt lighter than he had in weeks, maybe years. As the crowd thinned, a tall, square-jawed, sandy-haired man clasped his hand.

"We've never properly met," the man said, and then he glanced at Anna.

"Ben, this is someone who has been a good friend to us both," Anna said warmly. "I'd like you to meet the new director of the Internal Compliance Unit, at Justice—David Denneen."

Ben shook his hand vigorously. "I've heard a lot about you," he said. "And can I say thanks for saving our ass? Or is that just part of your job description?" Ben knew that Denneen had been chiefly responsible for clearing Anna's name; the word had been artfully "leaked" that she'd been working for a sting operation, those reports of her misdeeds faked in order to draw out some genuine malefactors. Anna had even received an official governmental letter of thanks for her "dedicated service and valor," although the letter discreetly left the circumstances of that valor unspecified. Still, it served a turn in helping her land a job as vice president in charge of risk-avoidance at Knapp Incorporated.

Now Denneen bent down and kissed Anna on the cheek. "The debt runs the other way," he said, turning back to

Ben. "As you very well know. Anyway, these days at the ICU I'm in the downsizing business. Someday, when my mother asks me what I do for a living, I'd like to be able to tell her."

"And Ben?" Anna presented the diminutive, brown-skinned man accompanying Denneen. "One more dear friend of mine I'd like you to meet: Ramon Perez."

Another vigorous handshake. Ramon smiled, showing very white teeth. "An honor," he said, bobbing his head a little.

He was still smiling when he and Anna drifted off to a corner to talk.

"You look like the cat that ate the canary," Anna said. "What is it? What's so funny?" Her moist eyes gleamed with amusement.

Ramon just shook his head. He glanced at her fiancé across the room and then at her, and still he was smiling.

"Ah," she said at last. "I know what you're thinking. 'What a waste,' right?"

Ramon shrugged but didn't deny it.

Anna looked over toward Ben until their eyes met. "Well, let me tell you something," she said. "He ain't wasted on me."

Afterward, Ben and Anna found an HCM Lincoln Town Car waiting for them in front of the Metropolis; the driver, seeing them emerge, stood stiffly in front of the car, ready to open the rear door. Ben held Anna's hand in his gently as the two walked toward the vehicle that would take them away. A faint drizzle made the streets gleam in the evening dusk.

Then Ben started, felt a twinge of adrenaline: the driver looked curiously youthful, almost adolescent, yet compactly, powerfully built. A kaleidoscope flashed before his mind, nightmarish images from a time not long in the past. Ben grasped Anna's hand fiercely.

The driver turned to face Ben, and the glow from the

arched windows of the Metropolis illuminated his face. It was Gianni, Max's driver for the last two years of his life, a gap-toothed, boyish, high-spirited fellow. Gianni took off his taupe cap, waved it.

"Mr. Hartman," he called out.

Ben and Anna entered the car, and Gianni closed the door with an efficient thunk before settling into the driver's seat.

"Where to, Mr. Hartman?" Gianni asked.

Ben glanced at his watch. The night was young, and tomorrow wasn't a school day, anyway. He turned to Anna. "Where to, Ms. Navarro?" Ben asked.

"Anywhere at all," she said. "As long as it's with you." Her hand found his again, and she rested her head on his shoulder.

Ben inhaled deeply, sensed the warmth of her face next to his, and felt at peace. It was an odd, unaccustomed feeling.

"Just drive," Ben said. "All right, Gianni? Anywhere, nowhere—just drive."

CHAPTER FIFTY

USA TODAY

INSIDERS SPECULATE ABOUT
NEXT SUPREME COURT NOMINEE

Declaring that he "deeply regretted but fully understood" Justice Miriam Bateman's decision to step
down from the U.S. Supreme Court at the conclusion
of the spring term, President Maxwell said that he
and his advisers would take their time and make a
"considered, deliberate" decision about who would be
proposed as her successor. "Living up to Justice Bateman's probity and wisdom will be a heavy burden on
any nominee, and we approach this task with humility
and with open minds," the President said in a press
conference. However, insiders have already produced

a short list of names believed to be under active consideration . . .

THE FINANCIAL TIMES

MERGER TALKS BETWEEN ARMAKON, TECHNOCORP

In what would be an unusual pairing of two New Economy powerhouses, officials at both the Vienna-based agricultural and biotechnology giant Armakon and the Seattle-based software giant Technocorp acknowledged that the corporations had entered into preliminary merger negotiations. "Biotech is increasingly about computing, and software is increasingly about applications," Arnold Carr, Technocorp's CEO, told reporters. "We've been strategic partners in the past, but a more formal consolidation would, we believe, ensure the long-term growth of both our companies." One prominent member of Technocorp's board of directors, former Secretary of State Dr. Walter Reisinger, said that the boards of both companies fully supported management in the decision. According to Reinhard Wolff, the managing director of Armakon, the merger would obviate the need for costly outsourcing of programming and potentially represent billions in savings. He credited the "truly wise and distinguished directors" of both companies with having facilitated the negotiations.

Large shareholders in both companies seemed to approve of the merger talks. "There is strength in unity," Ross Cameron, whose Sante Fe Group holds 12.5 percent of Technocorp's series A stock, said in a prepared statement, "and we believe that together these companies have a tremendous amount to offer the world."

A joint press release issued by the companies said that the combined corporation would be able to take a position of leadership in the health sciences.

"Given Armakon's record of extensive research in biotechnology, and Technocorp's enormous resources," Wolff stated, "the merged companies will be able to push back the frontiers of the life sciences in ways we cannot simply foresee."

On Wall Street, analysts had sharply divided reactions to the proposed merger . . .

Turn the page for an excerpt
from Robert Ludlum's next book

THE JANSON DIRECTIVE

On sale in hardcover
October 31, 2002
from St. Martin's Press!

Two uniformed women were standing behind a counter as he entered the Platinum Club lounge of Pacifica Airlines. The uniforms and the counter were both the same blue-gray hue. The women's jackets featured the sort of epaulets to which the major airlines were so devoted. In another place and time, Janson reflected, they would have rewarded extensive battlefield experience.

One of the women had been speaking to a jowly, heavyset man who wore an open blue blazer and a beeper clipped to his belt. A glint of badge metal from his inside coat pocket told Janson that he was an FAA inspector, no doubt taking his break where there was human scenery to be enjoyed. They broke off when Janson stepped forward.

"Your boarding card, please," the woman said, turning to him. She had a powdery tan that ended somewhere below her chin, and the kind of brassy hair that came from an applicator tip.

Janson flashed his ticket and the plastic card with which Pacifica rewarded its extremely frequent fliers.

"Welcome to the Pacifica Platinum Club, Mr. Janson," the woman twinkled.

"We'll let you know when your plane is about to board," the other attendant—chestnut bangs, eye shadow that matched the blue piping on her jacket—told him in a low, confiding voice. She gestured toward the entrance to the lounge area as if it were the pearly gates. "Meantime, enjoy our hospitality facilities and relax." An encouraging nod and a broad smile; Saint Peter's could not have held more promise.

Carved out between the structural girders and beams of an overloaded airport, venues like Pacifica's Platinum Club were where the modern airline tried to cater to the carriage trade. Small bowls were filled not with the salted peanuts purveyed to *les misérables* in coach but with the somewhat more expensive tree nuts: cashews, almonds, walnuts, pecans. At a granite-topped beverage station, there were crystal jugs sticky with peach nectar and fresh-squeezed orange juice. The carpeting was microfiber swank, the airline's signature blue-gray adorned with trellises of white and navy. On round tables interspersed among large armchairs were neatly folded copies of the *International Herald Tribune, USA Today*, the *Wall Street Journal*, and the *Financial Times*. A Bloomberg terminal flickered with meaningless numbers and images, shadow puppets of the global economy. Through louvered blinds, the tarmac was only just visible.

Janson flipped through the papers with little interest. When he turned to the *Journal's* "Market Watch," he found his eyes sliding down column inches of familiarly bellicose metaphors: bloodshed on Wall Street as a wave of profit takers launched an onslaught against the Dow. A sports column in *USA Today* was taken up with the collapse of the Raiders' offense in the face of the rampaging blitzes of the Vikings' linemen. Meanwhile, invisible speakers piped in a song by the pop diva *du jour,* from the soundtrack of a blockbuster movie about a legendary Second World War battle. An expense of blood and sweat had been honored by an expense of studio money and computer-graphics technology.

Janson settled heavily into one of the cloth-upholstered armchairs, his eyes drifting toward the dataport stations where brand managers and account executives plugged in their laptops and collected e-mail from clients, employers, prospects, underlings, and lovers, in an endless search for action items. Peeking from attaché cases were the spines of books purporting to offer marketing advice from the likes of Sun Tzu, the art of war repurposed for the packaged-goods industry. A sleek, self-satisfied, unthreatened folk, Janson mused of the managers and professionals who surrounded him. How these people loved peace, yet how they loved the imagery of war! For them, military regalia could safely be romanticized, the way animals of prey became adornments after the taxidermist's art.

There were moments when Janson almost felt that he, too, had been stuffed and mounted. Nearly every raptor was now on the endangered-species list, not least the bald eagle, and Janson recognized that he himself had once been a raptor—a force of aggression against forces of aggression. Janson had known ex-warriors who had become addicted to a diet of adrenaline and danger, and who, when their services were no longer required, had effectively turned themselves into toy soldiers. They spent their time stalking opponents in the Sierre Madre with paintball guns or, worse, pimping themselves out to unsavory firms with unsavory needs, usually in parts of the world where baksheesh was the law of the land. Janson's contempt for these people was profound. And yet he sometimes asked himself whether the highly specialized assistance he offered American businesses was not merely a respectable version of the same thing.

He was lonely, that was the truth of it, and his loneliness was never more acute than in the odd interstices of his overscheduled life—the time spent after checking in and before takeoff, the time spent waiting in overdesigned venues meant, simply, for waiting. At the end of his next flight, nobody was anticipating his arrival except another visored limo driver who would have misspelled his name on a white cardboard sign, and then another corporate client, an anxious division head of a Los Angeles–based light industrial firm. It was a tour of duty that took Janson from one corner office to another. There was no wife and no children, though once there had been a wife and at least hopes for a child, for Helene had been pregnant when she died. "To make God laugh, tell Him your plans," she used to quote her grandfather as saying, and the maxim had been borne out, horribly.

Janson eyed the amber bottles behind the bar, their crowded labels an alibi for the forgetfulness they held inside. He kept himself in fighting trim, trained obsessively, but even when he was in active deployment hc was never above a slug or two. Where was the harm?

"Paging Richard Alexander," a nasal voice called through the public announcement system. "Passenger Richard Alexander. Please report to any Pacifica counter."

It was the background noise of any airport, but it jolted Janson out of his reverie. Richard Alexander was an operational alias he had often used in bygone days. Reflexively, he craned his head around him. A minor coincidence, he thought, and then he realized that, simultaneously, his cell phone was purring, deep in his breast pocket. He inserted the earphone of the Nokia tri-band and pressed SND. "Yes?"

"Mr. Janson? Or should I say, Mr. Alexander?" A woman's voice, sounding strained, desperate.

"Who is this?" Janson spoke quietly. Stress numbed him, at least at first—made him calmer, not more agitated.

"Please, Mr. Janson. It's urgent that we meet *at once*." The vowels and consonants had the precision that was peculiar to those who were both foreign-born and well educated. And the ambient noise in the background was even more suggestive.

"Say more."

There was a pause. "When we meet."

Janson pressed END, terminating the call. He felt a prickling on the back of his neck. The coincidence of the page and the call, the specification that a meeting take place immediately: the putative supplicant was obviously in close proximity. The call's background acoustics had merely cinched his suspicions. Now his eyes darted from person to person, even as he tried to figure out who would seek him out this way.

Was it a trap, set by an old, unforgiving adversary? There were many who would feel avenged by his death; for a few, possibly, the thirst for vengeance would not be entirely unjustified. And yet the prospect seemed unlikely. He was not in the field; he was not spiriting a less-than-willing VKR "defector" from the Dardanelles through Athens to a waiting frigate, bypassing every legal channel of border control. He was in O'Hare Airport, for God's sake. Which may have been why this rendezvous was chosen. People tended to feel safe at an airport, moated by metal detectors and uniformed security guards. It would be a cunning act to take advantage of that illusion of security. And, in an airport that handled nearly 200,000 travelers each day, security was indeed an illusion.

Possibilities were considered and swiftly discarded. By the thick plate glass overlooking the tarmac, sitting in slats of sunlight, a blond woman was apparently studying a spreadsheet on her laptop; her cell phone was at her side, Janson verified, and unconnected to any earpiece. Another woman, closer to the entrance, was engaged in spirited conversation with a man whose wedding ring was visible only as a band of pale skin on an otherwise bronzed hand. Janson's eyes kept roaming until, seconds later, he saw her, the one who had just called.

Sitting with deceptive placidity in a dim corner of the lounge was an elegant, middle-aged woman holding a cell phone to her ear. Her hair was white, worn up, and she was attired in a navy Chanel suit with discreet mother-of-pearl buttons. Yes, she was the one: he was certain of it. What he could not be certain of were her intentions. Was she an assassin, or part of a kidnapping team? These were among a hundred possibilities that, however remote, he had to rule out. Standard tactical protocol, ingrained from years in the field, demanded it.

Janson sprang to his feet. He had to change his location: that rule was basic. *It's urgent that we meet at once,* the caller had said; if so, they would meet on his terms. Now he started to make his way out of the VIP lounge, grabbing a paper cup from a water cooler he passed. He approached the greeting counter with the paper cup held in front of him, as if it were full. Then he yawned, squeezing his eyes shut, and walked straight into the heavyset FAA inspector, who staggered back a few feet.

"I am so sorry," Janson blurted, looking mortified. "Oh, *Christ,* I didn't *spill* anything on you, did I?" Janson's hands moved rapidly over the man's blazer. "Did I get you wet? God, I'm really, really sorry."

"No harm done," he replied with a trace of impatience. "Just, you know, watch where you're going, OK? There's lots of people in this airport."

"It's one thing not to know what time zone you're in, but—*Jesus,* I just don't know what's wrong with me," Janson said, the very picture of a flustered and jet-lagged passenger. "I'm a wreck."

As Janson made his way out of the VIP lounge and down the pedestrian corridor that led toward Concourse B, his cell phone buzzed again, as he knew it would.

"I don't think you quite understand the urgency," the caller began.

"That's correct," Janson snapped. "I don't. Why don't you let me know what this is about?" In an angled stretch of the pedestrian corridor, he saw a recessed area, about three feet deep, and then the expected steel door to a room that was off-limits to travelers. UNAUTHORIZED PERSONNEL KEEP OUT was emblazoned on a plaque above it.

"I can't," the caller said after a beat. "Not over the phone, I'm afraid. But I'm in the airport and could meet you—"

"In that case, call me back in one minute," Janson interjected, ending the conversation. Now he hit the door's horizontal push bar with the heel of his hand and made his way inside. It turned out to be a narrow room that was lined with electrical panels; LCD displays measured outputs from the airport's heat and refrigeration plant, which was just to the east of the terminal. A rack of pegs held caps and windbreakers for outdoor work.

Three airline employees in navy–blue twill uniforms were seated around a small steel-and-Formica table, drinking coffee. He had obviously interrupted their conversation.

"What do you think you're doing?" one of them yelled at Janson as the door banged closed behind him. "You can't *be* here."

"This ain't the fucking john," another one said under his breath.

Janson smiled without warmth. "You're going to hate me, boys. But guess what?" He pulled out an FAA badge, the item he had lifted from the heavyset man in the lounge. "Another drug-abatement initiative. Random testing for a drug-free air-transport workforce—to quote the administrator's latest memorandum on the subject. Time to fill those cups. Sorry for the inconvenience, but that's why you make the big bucks, right?"

"This is *bullshit!*" the third man yowled in disgust. He was nearly bald, save for a graying fringe around the back, and he kept a short pencil behind an ear.

"Haul ass, guys," Janson barked. "We're following a whole new procedure this time. My team's assembled over at gate two in Concourse A. Don't make them wait. When they get impatient, sometimes they make mistakes with the samples, if you get my drift."

"This is *bullshit*," the bald man repeated.

"Want me to file a report saying that an Air Transport Association member protested and/or sought to evade the drug audit? Your test comes in positive, better start combing the want ads." Janson folded his arms on his chest. "Get the hell out of here, *now*."

"I'm going," the bald man grumbled, sounding less sure of himself. "I'm *there*." With expressions of exasperation and disgruntlement, all three men hastened out of the room, leaving clipboards and coffee cups behind. It would take them a good ten minutes before they reached Concourse A, Janson knew. He glanced at his watch, and counted the few remaining seconds until his cell phone buzzed; the caller had waited one minute exactly.

"There's a food court near the ticketing pavilion," Janson said. "I'll meet you there. The table on the far left, all the way to the back. See you in a few." He removed his jacket, put on a dark blue windbreaker and cap, and waited in the recessed area. Thirty seconds later, he saw the white-haired woman walking past.

"Hey, honey!" he called out as, in one continuous movement, he reached an arm around her waist, clamped a hand over her mouth, and hustled her into the now abandoned service room. There was, Janson had verified, nobody around to see the three-second maneuver; if there had been, his actions, coupled with his words, would have been taken for a romantic embrace.

The woman was startled, and rigid with fear, but she did not even try to scream, displaying a measure of professional composure that Janson found not the least reassuring. Once the door had closed behind them, Janson brusquely gestured her to take a seat at the Formica table. "Take a load off," he said.

The woman, looking incongruously elegant in the utilitarian space, sat down on one of the metal folding chairs. Janson remained standing.

"You're not exactly the way I'd pictured you," she said. "You don't *look* like a . . ." Conscious of his frankly hostile stare, she decided against finishing the sentence. "Mr. Janson, we really don't have time for this."

"I don't look like a *what?*" he said, biting off the words. "I don't know who the hell you think you are, but I'm not even going to list the infractions of protocol here. I'm not going to ask how you got my cell phone number or how you learned whatever you think you've learned. But by the time we're finished here, I'd better know everything I want to know." Even if she were a private citizen legitimately seeking his services, the public nature of the contact was completely inappropriate. And the use of a field legend of his, albeit a long-disused one, was a cardinal violation.

"You've made your *point,* Mr. Janson," she said. "My approach was, let's agree, ill advised. You'll have to forgive me—"

"I will? That's a presumption." He inhaled, detected a faint fragrance about her: Penhaligon's Jubilee. Their eyes met, and Janson's anger diminished somewhat when he saw her expression, mouth drawn with anxiety, gray-green eyes filled with grim determination.

"As I say, we have very little time."

"I have all the time in the world."

"Peter Novak doesn't."

Peter Novak.

The name delivered a jolt, as it was meant to. A legendary Hungarian financier and philanthropist, Novak had received a Nobel Peace Prize the previous year for his role in conflict resolution around the world. Novak was the founder and director of the Liberty Foundation, which was devoted to "directed democracy"—Novak's great passion— and had offices in regional capitals through Eastern Europe and other parts of the less developed world. But then Janson had reasons of his own to remember Peter Novak. And those reasons constituted a debt to the man so immense that Janson had occasionally experienced his gratitude as a burden.

"Who are you?" Janson demanded.

The woman's gray-green eyes bore into him. "My name is Márta Lang, and I work for Peter Novak. I could show you a business card, if you thought that would be helpful."

Janson shook his head slowly. Her business card would provide a meaningless title, identifying her as some sort of high-ranking employee of the Liberty Foundation. *I work for Peter Novak,* she had said, and simply from the way she spoke the words, Janson recognized her type. She was the factotum, the point person, the lieutenant; every great man had one. People like her preferred the shadows yet wielded great, if derivative, power. From her name and the barest trace of an accent, it was evident she was Hungarian, like her employer.

"What are you trying to tell me?" Janson said. His eyes narrowed.

"Only that he needs help. As you once did. In Baaqlina." Márta Lang pronounced the name of that dusty town as if it were a sentence, a paragraph, a chapter. For Janson, it was.

"I haven't forgotten," he said quietly.

"Then all you have to know right now is that Peter Novak requires your assistance."

She had spoken few words, but they were the right ones. Janson held her gaze for a long moment.

"Where to?"

"You can throw out your boarding card. Our jet is on the runway, cleared for immediate departure." She stood, her desperation somehow giving her strength and a sense of command. "We must go now. At the risk of repeating myself, *there's no time*."

"Let *me* risk repeating myself: Where to?"

"That, Mr. Janson, will be our question to you."

ROBERT LUDLUM'S
THE HADES FACTOR
A COVERT-ONE NOVEL

by ROBERT LUDLUM AND GAYLE LYNDS

COVERT-ONE

One of the leading suspense novelists of our day, Robert Ludlum has over 200 million copies of his bestselling books in print. Now Ludlum unleashes **Covert-One**, a bold new series of intrigue, espionage, and modern warfare, featuring three brave men who risk their lives to uncover the truth behind today's most deadly power plays . . .

ROBERT LUDLUM'S
THE HADES FACTOR

A baffling virus has claimed the lives of four people across the country—including Dr. Sophia Russell, a research scientist working to understand the disease. Bitter and broken-hearted over the death of his beautiful fiancée, Jon Smith is determined to uncover the cause of the virus that killed her—and prevent it from turning into a pandemic of epic proportions. He'll travel across the globe and into the darkest corridors of murder and greed, to find a killer who would sacrifice millions of lives for his own success . . .

"Ludlum pulls out all the stops and dazzles his readers."—*Chicago Tribune*

AVAILABLE WHEREVER BOOKS ARE SOLD FROM ST. MARTIN'S PAPERBACKS

Visit the Covert-One website: www.CovertOne.com

HADES 5/01

THE THRILLING
NEW YORK TIMES BESTSELLER

THE
PROMETHEUS
DECEPTION
ROBERT LUDLUM

After fifteen years as a brilliant master spy, Nick Bryson has disappeared into anonymity as a professor at an exclusive college in western Pennsylvania—until he's suddenly lured back into the game. Recruited by the CIA, he's been commissioned to track the moves of The Directorate. Once, the ultra-secret intelligence agency was Bryson's training ground. Now, it's a multinational terrorist conspiracy bent on global domination. But to eliminate the core of corruption means infiltrating a secret nexus of power called Prometheus that holds the terrifying clues to his past—and the even more terrifying possibilities of the future...

"His most ingenious novel yet."

—*The New Yorker*

"Explosive...*The Prometheus Deception* will not disappoint."

—*San Francisco Chronicle*

"A page-turner of nonstop action that should leave his fans begging for more."

—*New York Post*

ROBERT LUDLUM'S

The Cassandra Compact

A Covert-One Novel

ROBERT LUDLUM
AND PHILIP SHELBY

Covert-One operative Jon Smith and CIA undercover agent Randi Russell have unearthed a terrifying global conspiracy that threatens to unleash a plague of immeasurable proportions. A Serb terrorist has been dispatched from Russia to spirit hazardous vials of deadly bacteria into the United States. His mission: Deliver it to an unknown American government agent—a shadowy figure whose own motives for acquiring the bioweapon are made all the more unfathomable when both men are found murdered, and the strain is stolen. Now Smith and Russell must track it down, find the madman who possesses it, and stop him before he holds a defenseless world hostage with the power to render the human race extinct.

Visit the Covert-One website: www.CovertOne.com

TCC 05/02